Thomas the Poisoner

TALES FROM THE
READING DRAGON INN
BOOK 2

Tales from the Reading
Dragon Inn series

Book 1
The Lucky Cricket

Book 2
Thomas the Poisoner

Book 3
Triskaidekaphilia

Thomas the Poisoner

Tales from the Reading Dragon Inn
Book 2

Kelly R. Martin

Published by

Myth/**Logic** Press, West Virginia

Library of Congress Control Number: 2010906240

ISBN: 978-0-615-37113-9

Published by Myth/Logic Press,
27 Wilson Street,
Philippi, West Virginia 26416

Interior design and layout by Kelly R. Martin
www.mythlogicpress.com

Cover Illustration and design Copyright © Lance Red
www.reddaydream.com

Dedication

This work is dedicated to my dear friends Steve Ahrens and Virgil Boerio. Steve was always a grand dreamer with an exciting vision of the future as well as an appreciation for our past. Virgil was always a serious pragmatist and a curmudgeon who still had an optimism that the human race would eventually get it right. They were both friends and mentors to me, and they are deeply missed by all who knew them as I did.

Contents

Acknowledgments

First I would like to acknowledge my family: my parents Thomas and Linda, my older brother Tom, and my younger sisters Colleen and Patty. Thanks to them I was raised in a family of readers which started my love of books from an early age. I also want to thank my wife Merly Calizar Martin and my daughter Moira. They are my inspiration to make an attempt at writing a novel, and for me to take the risk in hopes of inspiring another generation.

I also want to thank my Grandmother Dorothy for being there for her many children, grandchildren, and great grandchildren. She's a cantankerous old donkey at times, with the stubbornness to never quit when she sets her mind on something She is one of the few people remaining in my life from the "greatest generation."

I want to give a loud, "Hello!" to all my various aunts, uncles, in-laws, nieces, nephews, cousins, etc. I come from a large extended clan with relations literally around the world. They've taught me many lessons in life, but mostly that I truly am just the holder of one perspective among many different points of view.

I want to thank my friends in the gaming crowd who put having fun and enjoying life ahead of getting into trouble. The old high school pen and paper party: Paul, Chad, Joe, Ken, Stacy, John, and Darron. The old college pen and paper party: Pat, Jeff, Sam, Kathy, Katrina, Fritz, Mike, and Eric.

I also want to thank my friends who have been there when I needed a hand in hard times as well as good times: Adrienne, Russ, Regina, Rick, Jane, Zenia, Fannie, Marissa, Allen, Jimmy, and Andy (bad Andy). Also I want to thank Hal for the oddball free legal consultations I occasionally pester him with during our weekly lunch breaks.

I would like to thank my many inspirations among the authors, game designers, animators, producers, teachers, artists, musicians, and directors. Unfortunately it is a Herculean task to even attempt to list them all. I do want to shout out to the web comic community in particular to thank them for bravely blazing a path in the self publishing field. Their hard work has opened the doors for other independent creators.

I want to thank my brother Tom for all of his helpful editing and proofing suggestions.

As an addition in the second edition release I want to thank Lance Red of www.reddaydream.com for his exceptional cover illustration. He's brought the world of the Lucky Cricket alive with his wonderful art.

Finally, I want to thank you, the reader, for showing an interest in this work.

Introduction

Let's be frank here. You probably don't know me yet (unless I already mentioned you on the acknowledgments page), and I likely don't know you. We are essentially two strangers crossing paths by chance. I live in my world, and you live in yours. Thus it is with most people in life.

However, this is a chance for you to share a vision of the world in my dreams. Yes quite literally many things I've written in this novel occurred in some form in my sleeping and waking dreams. These works are the culmination of the dreams of a twelve year old youth from many years ago who loved the worlds in books so much that he eventually wanted to write them.

This work is admittedly not very literary, but in essence it was never written with any pretense to be such. It was written to hopefully be enjoyable to read. This is likely much to the potential chagrin of my college rhetoric professors.

The plot developed naturally as an extension of the characters I envisioned. From my perspective no great plot drives us. We all act and react to the events of the world around us from the day we are born until the day we die. We make choices in our lives based on who we are as people, and based on the circumstances with which we find ourselves involved. This is what I know about life, so it tends to be how I write as well.

I will unabashedly admit that pen and paper gaming has influenced the themes of my works as well as numerous authors I've read over the years. However, they are still original works. Every word of them has been written by me, they are not based on the particular work of another, and I'm solely to blame for any flaws.

This work is also influenced by the themes in numerous works of manga and anime. I find that different cultural perspectives provide an interesting way to look at a particular society. There is nothing quite as enlightening as looking at your own culture through the eyes of another culture. I personally recommend you the reader try it sometime.

These works give you a chance to look at things through my personal culture. The culture I'm referring to in my case is the culture of a fantasy, science fiction, horror, thriller, drama, action, comedy, anime, comic, technology, and gaming (material and virtual) obsessed nerd. There I've said it. I'm a nerd, a fan boy, an otaku even. Wow, maybe this was just a twelve step program after all.

Finally I must admit I've actually been influenced by the great literary works of Homer and Shakespeare. I'll leave it to the arguments of the literary minds who may read this to try to figure out which works I'm referring to by this statement. Here's a hint for those with a penchant to analyze such things, a few of the character names used are admittedly based on anagrams of names from the classics. However, the characterizations themselves are originals.

What was the point I was trying to make again? Ah, let's just allow you to get into the book to discover for yourself. I hope you enjoy it.

Thomas the Poisoner

Chapter 1 Son of a Knight

Thomas the Poisoner was a mystery in the Kingdom of Ard. His work was well known throughout the entire alliance of kingdoms. That is to say the results of his work were well known. From high ranking aristocrat to low ranking peasant, if the agreed price was paid, then it was rumored every one of his targets for every contract accepted ended up dead. Those authorities who tried to find or capture Thomas the Poisoner soon discovered that he was as elusive as the departing night fleeing before the dawn. A mysterious man indeed thought many people who spoke of his rumored exploits.

One of the most mysterious aspects behind Thomas the Poisoner was that no one seemingly knew who he actually was. There was a name to be sure, but being so pointed a name it was obviously an assumed name. Not even a suspected client could say whether they had actually ever met him in person. Many times a suspected cohort was caught, only to be later found either innocent of suspicion, or dead before any serious interrogation could begin.

Some people speculated that Thomas the Poisoner was actually a cover for an entire shadowy organization of assassins. However, all serious inquiries through the criminal underworld of various nations where his work occurred failed to turn up any sign of this organization. The various thieves and assassin guilds all claimed to have no knowledge of who he was. Honestly speaking the numerous thieves guilds were too locally based to be so internationally involved.

It was also rumored that several of the various assassins guilds had tried quietly accepting a bounty to kill Thomas the Poisoner over the long years. Eventually all assassin guilds stopped accepting these bounties after a series of dead assassins and guild leaders every time a bounty against him was pursued. The point had been explicitly made throughout their ranks many years ago, and none of the remaining assassin guilds would ever dare accept such an offer now.

The other lesser mystery was that while many of the victims of Thomas the Poisoner were indeed killed by a verifiable use of poison, quite a few were rumored to have died by less conventional means. Those individuals who took special precautions against the use of poison were usually still found just as dead.

Some people speculated that Thomas the Poisoner only killed people who had committed a crime of deadly violence against an innocent. This was hard to confirm in most cases, but it was certainly fairly clear that quite a few of his targets were widely acknowledged as brutal and cruel by those who knew them.

This account is my tale of how I went from being Mikael Lidron, to someone who encountered Thomas the Poisoner. That encounter dramatically changed the course of my life. Perhaps changing the course of my life is not even a strong enough way to put it. Let me restate that encounter with him changed the very nature of my existence. To better explain what I eventually became; I have to start with a brief description of where I began.

As youngest son of Knight Commander Armand Lidron, I had little chance of inheriting any property of worth from my father. I had spend my youth learning martial skills and my letters until I was old enough to serve in the local militia. I learned these skills alongside my two eldest brothers Gregoric and Stanis who stood to inherit the minimal lands my father oversaw.

My third older brother Kalach was the most gifted of us, and he was accepted into service with the martial arm of the clergy of the god Palnor. My father pledged me into government service as a young man after my mandatory term of service with the militia was completed.

Such was the normal fate for a fourth son with healthy older brothers, and I did not begrudge my lot in life. I had gainful employment with the land governance agency for the Kingdom of Ard, a small residence, and I was able to occasionally hang around the fringes of court activity in the Capital of Ard. I figured myself to be lucky. I was also grateful because many fourth sons of barons did not receive the same opportunities which I had received.

When came the day destiny intervened in the course of my life. I did not know it at the time, but in retrospect I can now see the hand of destiny in action. I was passing along the river in the early evening on my way from my place of work in the Capital of Ard to my apartment in the merchant's quarter of the city. I noticed a short man with close cropped straight black hair and an exotic cast to his dark brown eyes fishing with a pole made of bamboo along the banks of the river.

The figure was dressed as a peasant might. Except he wore an odd conical woven bamboo hat. He looked directly back at me as the other city denizens passed by us. Some strange compulsion caused me to stop near him for a moment. He gave a gentle smile at me standing there, and waved me over to his side with a casual hand gesture.

The man raised the brim of his odd hat as he spoke, "You look like someone who skipped their lunch today. Do you like fish?"

I was startled at the unusually forthright direction of his remark, but I had to admit to myself that I had a busy day with little chance to eat.

I gave him a polite smile, "Yes, I do enjoy eating fish. I usually can not find it around here. All of the good fish have been taken from the river now, there are only the small fish left."

The man looked back at the river, "You will do then young knight. If our paths cross again you can call me Cricket. For what it's worth, I am sorry to know that you're going to die."

I froze in place, "Was that a threat?"

Cricket shook his head, "Merely my observation of the mortal condition. Take the time to enjoy some fish before you must meet your eventual end though."

With that he pulled a large fresh caught fish from his fishing creel cooling at the water's edge. He handed the still flopping fish to me.

Cricket smiled, "This one is quite tasty I imagine."

I took the fish, and asked, "What do I owe you?"

Cricket shrugged his shoulders, "It was of small cost to me. You may consider it a gift. If your knightly bearing will not allow for such, then you may pay back the favor by listening to the offer you will receive soon. You will understand my meaning when it happens. Consider it carefully, and make the choice which is suitable to your disposition."

I raised an eyebrow, "Listen to an offer, and make the choice I want?"

Cricket nodded, "I trust it will be the correct choice."

The next week I was in the scroll room in the basement of the Kingdom of Ard Land Governance Agency which we sometimes referred to as Kalga amongst ourselves to keep it shorter to say. My immediate superior Baron Dumfries came into the room a bit out of breath.

Baron Dumfries spoke with his typically booming voice, "Mikael, there you are my lad."

I gave him a slight smile, "Might I remind your lordship that I am twenty four now and no longer a young lad."

Baron Dumfries gave a brief chuckle, "It's all relative my lad. To me and your father you will always seem young. Speaking of relatives I have a bit of a quandary on my hands."

I paused a moment, "A quandary you say?"

Baron Dumfries nodded his head, "I'll need you to find two deeds in the files. The properties of Baron Marco and a Baron Glenmoor are what I need you to research. In particular they both have a property in dispute where they have lands which divide a portion of one of the King's forrest preserves. According to one of the Dukes at court they are bickering with each other about the boundary between those lands."

I held back my feeling of excitement, "Do you think they may require a survey sir?"

Baron Dumfries smiled, "Ah youth. Traveling around does appeal to the young of posterior. It's too early to know if a survey is needed, but I think if one is needed I would be willing to let you assemble the team to conduct it."

I gave him a broad grin, "I think I have the survey team I want in mind sir."

Baron Dumfries gave me a sly look, "Yes. I suppose you do. Now don't get ahead of yourself. Get the deeds first. Review them if you like so you are familiar with the situation, and then bring me your findings."

After reading the various documents, the source of the trouble was clear. A stream was the dividing boundary between the two properties, and as streams were wont to do it had likely wandered in its course over time, thus presumably leading to the current dispute between Baron Marco and Baron Glenmoor. Our modern method was to establish fixed positions based on less mobile markers than a fickle watercourse.

Thus, my team would need to go to an estate with a boundary in question, and resurvey the boundary while establishing more permanent magic boundary stone reference points. These stones were a great achievement in survey work. They established a location based on reference to positions in the firmament. Thus the ground or plant life could be changed or moved drastically, but they could still locate an exact position established earlier.

Later I stood in Baron Dumfries office explaining my findings while pointing at the enormous map on his wall, "So if I go out and resurvey the points between this anchor point and this anchor point, then we should be able to clear up this dispute."

Baron Dumfries smiled, "Well done lad. It seems you're right. Now don't get in a hurry yet. I'll need to relay this information back to the Duke who brought it to my attention, and send letters to each of the Barons so they will know you're on the way. We wouldn't want them misunderstanding the purpose of your presence there."

I became excited at the prospect of traveling with my preferred surveyor, "I'll put together a team, and head out in two days to see the Barons before conducting the survey."

Baron Dumfries shook his head, "Give it a week. I don't want any surprises. Let's avoid any accusations of being influenced by one side or another as well. Just conduct the survey and leave informing the barons of the results to me."

The next week I set out with Firanda Zarcha. She was one of our contracted magical surveyors from the mages guild. I had also hired a porter called Larwick from the porters guild. I particularly enjoyed working with Firanda since she was a young part human part elvish woman of about my age, and she had many interesting stories to tell of her magical studies. Firanda considered the survey contract work a bit dull in comparison, but it kept her in enough steady money to pay her sizable tuition at the Mages University.

Although meeting him for the first time, Larwick seemed like most porters I had ever met. He was both durable and dull. He was perhaps a bit more portly than some porters, but it seemed to fit him somehow. He rode an aging mare as he followed behind our horses, and led a cargo laden mule as we set out on our journey. The mule was packed with the survey gear along with our personal belongings required for travel.

Firanda had forgone her typical mages robes in favor of her more practical riding outfit. She looked more boyish in this outfit with burgundy pantaloons and shirt, but it suited her red hair and fiery personality well. I would never mistake Firanda for one of those fancy simpering women who strutted around the king's court.

Firanda was a brash and bold future adventurer in my estimation. As soon as she graduated from Mages University she would be dealing with untold perils on the edges of civilization. I envied her the freedom perhaps, and to be honest I dreaded her moving on to other things just a little bit. I hoped to make a good impression on her this time as our relationship up to this point had remained strictly a professional one.

With hard riding we could have made our destination in two days, but in favor of spending more time with Firanda, I opted to keep our pace more reasoned. We were not in a rush to complete this job.

So as we rode Firanda and I talked of the scenery, court politics, the weather, and our upcoming assignment. As we discussed the details of our assignment, Firanda got a concerned look on her face for a moment.

Firanda edged her horse closer to mine and lowered her voice, "I don't like it Mikael. Something does not quite seem right here. We usually discuss the survey work with the land owners in advance."

I gave her a light laugh, "Is that your adventurer's intuition at work?"

Firanda raised her eyebrow in a challenging manner, "It has nothing to do with intuition. It's irregular. It doesn't fit. We're on the King's business after all. Why would we need to skulk around?"

I gave her a little chuckle, "I never thought you the skittish type Firanda."

Firanda gave a little huff as she maneuvered her horse behind mine, "Just keep your sword close at hand. You be the meat shield, and I'll knock them down as they come."

I gave her a smile over my shoulder as I softly spoke, "I'll always protect you."

Firanda called forward, "What did you say?"

I loudly called back, "On protection duty as ordered."

We stopped for the next two nights of travel at the roadside inns located in small hamlets along the main roads. Firanda did join me for dinner at the inns both nights, but chose to retire to her room to study and sleep shortly thereafter. I was left to share a room with our porter Larwick who remained as expected a dull conversationalist who normally restricted himself to five word or less replies.

In a flight of fancy the second evening as we sat in our room I asked Larwick, "What do you think of the adventuring life?"

Larwick grunted, "Henchman work. Dangerous. Short life."

I raised an eyebrow, "What do you think is wrong with being a henchman? It's not much different than being a porter really. Both types follow people around and manage their possesions as they travel."

Larwick thought a moment, "Porters serve goodly folk. Henchmen now, that's fool's work."

I looked over at him curious about the distinction, "Why is it fool's work as you say?"

Larwick's expression let on he was thinking me foolish as well, "Adventurers of course."

I tried to follow his line of logic, "Why do you say adventurers? What's wrong with them?"

Larwick laughed, "They are not in their right minds."

I nodded, "I guess I can understand that perspective. Why do you think they do it then?"

Larwick's reply was both simple and striking, "We all have a role. The trick is finding it, and sticking with it."

I seriously considered his words as they were the wisest and longest thing I have ever heard him reply to an inquiry.

The next morning we set out again. Shortly after our midday break we came across the stream which divided the two barons' estates. A few miles up stream their lands would begin. We followed the small trail which paralleled the stream until we came to the edge of the king's preserve. Since the sun was still up we made camp. For the exact initial measurements the firmament would have to be visible in the night sky.

Firanda called over to me, "I have to study my charts to find the exact ones I'll need. Do you think you could be a dear and set up my tent first?"

I looked at her seated on the ground with that endearing expression she had when she focused on her reading.

Firanda glanced up at me with a shy expression, "Did you forget something?"

I wanted to say something charming, but my wits failed to work, "Nothing actually. I was just thinking I could cook us some early dinner after the tents are up."

Firanda replied with a faint smile, "That would be nice actually."

Firanda paged through her reference charts until she found the set which was valid for this time of the year. After setting up the tents, I fixed us a quick meal, and then Firanda retired to her tent to rest while Larwick took charge of caring for the horses. It would take us the better part of the evening to plot the survey course, so after finishing up the organization of the camp, Larwick and I retired to the other tent to rest as well.

Evening came and the stars began to show in the sky. Firanda lit the glass sphere on the top of her staff with a red flame. She referenced her charts again, then pulled out the magical apparatus which measured the movement and position of the firmament. She paced around for about an hour taking various readings as Larwick and I stood by ready to follow when it was time to move. After one last reference of her charts she retrieved the boundary stone from the mule with the assistance of Larwick and me.

We placed the stone on the spot she indicated, and watched her cast the spell which bound the stone in reference to the firmament. Now the stone could not be tampered with for if it was moved the writings on the stone would show both its correct location, and its current location. It was true that the course of the stream was a good thirty-four yards from the location of the stone. It had definitely changed its course, so one of the barons was likely correct in his complaint about lost lands. It remained to be seen whether the stream had also shifted at the far end of the forested preserve, and if so, then which way.

After Firanda had me write down the corrected figures for the boundary stone on a fresh deed draft, we packed up the supplies, and moved upstream on foot with Larwick leading the mule laden with the survey gear. As we walked through the darkened forest Firanda would periodically take a short reading to verify our course relative to the stone we left behind. The stream occasionally wandered closer to and further from our course, but it generally remained off to our right side. The side granted to Baron Glenmoor.

As we neared the middle of our trek through the preserve we came across something unexpected, but not totally surprising to my eyes. The stream was quite close, but it was clear that another channel had been dug and the original channel had been blocked with stones.

I looked over at Firanda as I spoke, "This was obviously deliberate work."

Firanda nodded to indicate that she understood the implications of this act. Baron Glenmoor was being deliberately cheated of his rightfully managed lands. I saw Firanda's eyes grow wide as she looked past my face and over my shoulder.

I turned around to see what looked like a leather clad huntsman with a bow over his shoulder and a saber in his hand. I backed up and drew my own sword, while giving Firanda a clear line of attack if anything should go wrong.

The huntsman spoke first, "What do we have here? Trespassers at the very least, and poachers most likely I think."

I continued to back enough so I could see Firanda out of the corner of my eye. Then I replied, "I am Mikael Lidron of the king's land governance agency. Interfere with our work at the peril of the king's justice."

The huntsman smirked as he spoke, "Ah good. He's the one I want. Stop her."

I sprung into a defensive posture at those words. I saw Firanda begin the casting of a spell to smite the huntsman into submission.

Thinking back on it I keep remembering it as if time itself had slowed to a crawl. I tried to call out as I witnessed a black clad figure step from out of the shadow of the tree next to Firanda. My mind was briefly uncomprehending as I saw him brutally shove his dagger into the base of her skull from behind. In my memory of it she slowly crumpled as she dropped, but I already felt from her empty expression that she was dead even before she hit the ground. Her fading staff dropped to the ground beside her body throwing wild shadows around.

My mind filled with madness and anger as I cried out, "No! You've killed her."

I charged the huntsman in front of me. He grinned and charged me in return. We exchanged a furious series of blows, me being driven in speed, but not to a lack of skill by my anger.

As we exchanged the first series of ringing blows, I noted the huntsman's skill with his weapon was high, higher than I expected. Unfortunately for him my skill was greater than he expected as well. My years of martial training as the son of a knight had not left me lacking.

Then the huntsman shouted, "No Ulric. He's mine!"

I realized then that in the heat of battle I had somehow forgotten about the man who had struck down Firanda. I glanced over to see him loose an arrow in my direction. I was shocked to see Larwick lurch forward from his position by our mule and intercept the arrow before it could strike me. I felt lucky for the moment that the arrow did not kill me, yet it had obviously injured Larwick severely as he stumbled in my direction and fell toward me. I realized I had made a critical mistake in being distracted at that point. I felt my opponent's saber bite into my side below my rib cage. I dropped on the ground in heavy pain.

I heard the huntsman speak again, "Cursed henchman! Why didn't you stay by your mule! Ulric, why did you shoot at him!? I told you Mikael Lidron was mine to fight alone."

The shadowy figure calmly spoke back, "I recommend you be careful with your tone Davel. I shot the fat bastard because he was reaching for something on the mule. Besides it looked like you needed the help to get your job done."

I presumed that one of them must have run Larwick through at that point. I heard the sound of a sword strike followed by a soft moan.

Davel spoke again, "Cursed pest. Now it will be your turn Mikael Lidron. Tell your father Armand hello for me when he joins you in the afterlife."

His boot struck me in the head, and I knew no more.

Chapter 2 The Dream

First there was pain, sharp and intense. Then there was a feeling of ease. I fought that feeling. The powerful rage I was feeling wouldn't leave. I realized that I did not want it to leave. I desired that mighty anger to fuel my being.

Slowly I became conscious of standing in swimming darkness; almost drowning in the thick air. The landscape around me was more monochrome inky black muffled in shadow. Nothing was familiar. I vaguely recalled being injured and falling unconscious as the source of my anger, but certainly I didn't know how I could be standing in this dark starless desert. I thought I saw a dark shade of a figure moving in the distance. I looked at the wavering figure, and felt like someone was calling me.

It wasn't the figure moving toward that horizon. Whatever was calling was beyond the figure. I looked around and saw a shaded figure standing beside me. It pointed toward the horizon in the direction of the other figure, and took a step in the direction the first figure was moving. I shrugged my shoulders.

I turned aside from this second somehow familiar shade. The nearby figure began moving toward the horizon following the path of the first briefly before looking back to see if I would follow. I still heard the call over the horizon in a direction I considered "north" for convenience and due to a lack of a better directional reference. However, my anger stopped me from joining it.

Then I realized it wasn't my anger which stopped me, but some kind of intuition. It was also a need to have righteous justice which muted the pull of that mysterious call. Over by some tall rocks halfway around to the "northeast" I saw a pulse of red light.

This red light blinked steadily on and off in the distance. I felt a rhythm to it like an unheard deep primal drum. It reminded me of the beating of a slow and steady heart. At this point I began to believe I must be asleep and dreaming. This place bore no resemblance to any reality as I knew it.

I had an intuition that toward the "northern" horizon the calling voice could possibly mean wakefulness and the return of the pain of my injuries. I also felt that the beating of the red light in the rocks might possibly lead to justice and a release from my righteous anger.

I walked toward that beacon. I looked behind me as I began and noticed the familiar female figure was following. As we traveled I could never tell how much time was passing. For the longest time it seemed like nothing changed and our progress was hard to determine in this nearly featureless landscape. I didn't feel hunger or thirst; just a continuing drive to reach the beacon.

After an unknown passage of time that left a vague impression of days or weeks in this timeless place; it appeared that we suddenly closed the gap with the rocks. It was a white tower perched atop a rocky cliff from which the beating red light came.

The construction resembled a lighthouse by the sea. I noticed a small number of dark figures moving around the base of the tower. I briefly wondered if they were also seeking justice for the wrongs they had endured. I followed a path slinking back and forth up the slope of the cliff. When I reached the top I entered the tower doorway without hesitation. Inside a set of stairs wound up toward the top of the tower. However, instead of heading up the winding stairs toward the beacon I had seen, we walked down another set of stairs leading deep into the foundations of the rocky cliff below the tower.

Ahead of me I eventually came up to the back of a shadowy figure also standing on the stairs. I peered past him, and saw more figures lined up waiting. I tried to gesture my concern about where this was to the figure, but it moved its shoulders in a shrug. Looking behind me up the stairs the now familiar female figure was standing behind me. Occasionally the line in front would move down a step, and then we would wait again.

For what seemed like weeks we waited without a change beyond moving further down the long flight of stairs over time. Even as my frustration built, I didn't know what else I could do. Eventually the stairs ended in what seemed like a stone corridor leading up to a simple wooden door.

One by one the figures ahead of me would enter the door, time would pass, and another figure would enter. No figure ever came back out of the door. The other figures waiting did not appear concerned that no one departed by the same door. I continued to wait until our turn came to enter the room beyond the door.

We entered and found the first source of light beyond the vague red glow I had seen for weeks. A white garbed figure glowed brightly, yet not blindingly in the room. This figure had the features of an elderly man. He pointed me to a chair, and sat on a similar one himself.

Next the man spoke to me, "I extend my greetings to you young man. My name is Thomas. This is an interview to determine your suitability. You may ask a couple of questions if you have some immediate concerns. However, I may or may not answer them. You will tell me the truth when you speak with me, so think carefully about what you want to say. Please tell me who you are and why you are here. You may speak now. "

I found myself able to speak for the first time in my dream, "I am Mikael Lidron. My companions and I were ambushed. The fiends killed Firanda Zarcha and I think Larwick. I need to find the men responsible and bring them to justice."

Thomas nodded, "Yes. That kind of thing does happen at times."

Thomas looked at the figure standing beside me, "How about you young lady? It is very unusual for someone to be joined in the interview process. Who are you and why are you here?"

My companion spoke, "I'm Firanda Zarcha. I came because I followed the one I love. I'm scared. So very scared, but I came."

Thomas gave a gentle smile, "That is very interesting, but you need not be frightened of this place."

Firanda Zarcha replied, "This is not what is supposed to happen. We don't belong here. We ignored her call."

Thomas replied, "You were a theologian perhaps, or trained in matters arcane?"

Firanda nodded, "A student combat mage."

Thomas asked, "You understand where it is you are?"

Firanda answered, "Yes. Well not exactly, but the general concept of where yes."

Thomas turned back to me, "Is this need for justice important for you?"

I answered him, "It is what has brought me . . . well here. Just where are we anyway?"

Thomas nodded, "We are in my interview room in my office as it were. Tell me what Firanda means to you."

I replied, "She shouldn't have died. It was senseless, she was collateral damage. It seems like I was the target of the attackers. Although I don't know why that would be."

Thomas nodded, "I think that is true. However, is there more truth to it as well? Truth you didn't admit even to yourself perhaps."

I thought about it a little more, "Firanda was special to me. I liked to work with her, so I made sure she was hired whenever my team needed the services of a mage. I liked her very much. I wanted to get to know her better. Now she is dead, and her shade is haunting my dream. It's all my fault because someone seeking my life is responsible."

Thomas nodded in a fatherly manner, "Yes. I understand how you youth are driven by your passions. I can sympathize with your plight. Now answer me, where were you killed?"

I thought this a strange question, "I'm not dead. I'm just dreaming this. However, Firanda was killed in the tract of land along the estates of Baron Marco and Baron Glenmoor."

Thomas smiled, "Ah, my mistake, but your answer is very interesting. Could you please tell me in which country do Baron Marco and Baron Glenmoor reside."

I thought this also a strange question, "The Kingdom of Ard of course. Haven't you heard of it?"

Thomas nodded his head again, "Yes, I have heard of it. This should work out well. Now a few follow up questions. Have you ever committed a crime?"

I thought back a bit, "I once poached a hare off of the adjoining estate to my father's when I was a child of about nine years. My brother Kalach helped me cook and eat it. No other crimes though."

Thomas smiled, "Very good. Firanda are you also innocent of any criminal activity?"

Firanda answered, "The Mages University of Ard won't accept criminals, and they use truth potions to verify it."

Thomas gently smiled, "The blood of innocent victims is so sad they say. If you are interested, then I will make both of you an offer for a job. You won't be able go back to your old ones I'm afraid."

I rose up from my chair, "What about justice for those people who slew Firanda?"

Thomas looked stern and serious, "That's very important in what we do. I think you may be able to help with finding them justice, and others besides if you take my offer. Well do you both accept?"

I proudly answered, "If I can bring those people to justice, then I will entertain your offer."

Firanda thought a moment, "What about 'her'? Won't she object to you disrupting 'her' plans for us?"

Thomas chuckled, "I've been granted her dispensation to work here. You need not worry about incurring her wrath."

Firanda sighed, "Then I will go where Mikael does."

Thomas smiled again, "That's what I like to hear. Just step through that open door on your right. Your dream will end soon Mikael, and you will be feeling better in no time."

I walked through the door he indicated. I followed the hallway until I found another door. I saw a small two tailed black leopard spotted cat standing before the door. I looked into its jade green eyes which besides the red beacon light were the first bits of color in this monochrome dream. The dream then became hazy as lost portions of dreams often do.

The next thing I remembered was opening the door and stepped into the room with Firanda. It was a large chamber filled with row upon row of white marble pedestals about three feet high. A large diamond floated a couple of inches above each pedestal on the right. A large ruby floated above each of the pedestals on the left. At the far end of the room a giant clear crystal was hovering above the floor while slowly rotating. The giant crystal pulsed with the same slow beat which had drawn me to the tower. I moved through the room and stood before it.

I became entranced by its comforting beat. I felt at home. I relaxed into a deeper dream and lost consciousness of the first one.

I awoke lying on a bed covered with white linen sheets. Sunlight streamed through the window off to my right. My body was stiff and sore, but not in the terrible pain I had anticipated I would awaken to. I tentatively flexed my muscles, and while they were definitely stiff and weak from disuse, they still worked. I tried raising my arms and they functioned as expected, then I noticed that something was strange. My hands didn't look right. Neither did my arms for that matter. They were different. My hands were more delicate than I recalled. My arms thinner and less defined. A gold ring with a small diamond rested on my right index finger.

I pulled back the covers over my body and noticed that my entire frame was leaner and paler than it should be. There was no hair on my arms and legs as well.

I began to think this might be another odd dream, and I pinched myself to see if I would awaken. The pinch hurt as I half expected, but I didn't awaken again. My body had strangely changed. I began to notice more subtle differences as well. The various faint scars earned from fighting matches with my brothers were gone. I pulled up the linen shift I had been dressed in and saw no wound or scar from the sword blow which had stuck me down.

I moved my legs over the edge of the bed and carefully sat up. I felt woozy and light headed with the attempt. A wave of pale blond hair slipped forward over my shoulders. My hair, yet it was not the proper brown color. I was feeling very confused when I heard the approach of soft footsteps from somewhere outside the door of my room. I sat there regaining my sense of balance as the foot steps continued their lengthy measured approach. They grew strangely louder over time, though still with a soft tone. Eventually they stopped outside the door of the room.

The latch was lifted and the door opened rather loudly to my ears to reveal an elfin woman with platinum blond hair wearing a pale green shift, green soft cloth slippers, and a pair of gold and diamond earrings. She smiled sweetly at me sitting there with a confused expression on my face.

She spoke with a honey sweet voice and an odd accent, "I see you are awake and still somewhat confused by the change."

I nodded my head in affirmation, "Yes. I don't understand what is happening here. What is going on?"

My confusion deepened as my very voice was truly no longer my own. Its quality was higher, and sweeter in comparison to the voice I'd had since puberty. Something very different and completely unexpected had happened.

She smiled at my concern, "I'm told this happens with many who are just entering into service with Master Thomas. It's a hard adjustment to make. Some can't cope at all, and are freed from service. You're doing fairly well given the scope of the change you've experienced. Let's just say for now that you are no longer the person that you once knew. That person is as good as gone."

I grasped the implications of this explanation, "If that's the case, then who would you say I am now?"

She approached and smiled even more, "You're the person who will right the injustice done to your former self. Then if you are willing to continue serving Master Thomas you will help right other injustices done to other people as well."

I thought back to the vaguely remembered dream from before. She had mentioned a Master Thomas, and I recalled a glowing figure who called himself Thomas had spoken with me in my dream.

I looked into the pale green eyes of this elfin woman before me, "Who is this Thomas? I vaguely remember a dream I had before awakening."

Her smiled lessened a bit, "Master Thomas is the one who has helped you. He is the owner and master of Thomas' Isle where we are currently. Don't worry that you haven't heard of it before. Thomas' Isle remains uncharted by your home country and most other countries as well."

I shook my head, "Why was he in my dream I wonder? I don't recall meeting him before."

Her smile turned mysterious, "Master Thomas comes to all first in their dream as you say. That so called dream is where those who search find him waiting. If your desire for justice is strong, then Master Thomas offers a chance to receive it in return for service."

I frowned a bit at the thought, "It sounds a bit like slavery to me."

She shook her head, "It's not slavery really. You perform your service to Master Thomas, and Master Thomas will help you obtain justice for the wrong done to you."

I thought about it, "What if I wanted to change my mind? I don't really think one can make a binding bargain in a dream."

She smiled broadly at my naiveté, "Oh this bargain is definitely binding. Tell me truthfully though. Do you want to pass up the opportunity to seek justice for yourself?"

I thought about it and felt that same righteous anger rising, "No. I think I do want to make sure justice is done. You're right of course. I believe I must have somehow come here for a reason of my choosing. It would be foolish of me to back away from that reason now."

She nodded her head and smiled sweetly again, "Such it is with all that Master Thomas selects to serve. They have a will and a drive to do so. It is in your own interest that you serve. You will quickly learn that Master Thomas simply makes it possible for each of us to help the others. In this way you should understand that ultimately it is Master Thomas who serves us all."

I gave a quick nod of affirmation, "I think I can understand a little of why this is happening now. I just am not ready to understand how this all works yet."

I then remembered that in all of my uncertainty I had forgotten to introduce myself, or learn the elf woman's name.

I extended a hand to her, "I am Mikael Lidron from the Kingdom of Ard."

She looked at my extended hand briefly before giving a little laugh before shaking it, "You may call me Lirae as that is what I am called now. You will need to learn that Mikael Lidron is no more as far as the world is concerned. A new identity will be provided by Master Thomas when the time is right. How about for now I simply call you Mica."

I replied, "Mica then."

Lirae gave me a shy smile as she continued, "I am relatively new on Thomas' Isle myself. I've only been working here for Master Thomas for four months. Before I came here I was in the field researching my problem. I recently was told by Master Thomas that more assistance was being sought to help with my situation. I suspect that you are the assistance Master Thomas meant."

I asked, "What kind of assistance do you need?"

Lirae replied with her smile fading and a hard glint showing in her eyes, "I need help stopping the elves that destroyed my family. No other race would be allowed to get close enough to their leader Reminas. He and his followers are the worst kind of extremists who are continually blaming all the other races for the decline of the elves in Letheron. Reminas had my family slaughtered because I dared to marry a human male and bear a child with him. He took those I loved from me, and I will see him and his cause destroyed for it. Only then will justice be done."

I looked into her eyes as they began to mist over, "I'm sorry to hear of your loss."

Lirae sat down on the bed next to me and leaned in close. I looked at her with a feeling of expectancy. She turned her head toward me, and I faced her watching as tears slid down her cheeks. Lirae pressed her forehead gently against my own, our eyes gazing into one another.

Lirae softly spoke, "This is how the elves of Letheron who are close greet each other. It is a sign of trust, and fellowship. You are going to help me defeat that bastard Reminas and his accomplices who destroyed my family."

I softly answered back, "I will help you as best I can."

Lirae drew back and stood up again, "I thank you for your help."

She nodded back, "You are a wise and kindly elf. Most are never ready to face this kind of challenge."

I was confused, and then shocked as a bit of the mystery of the strangeness of my form was revealed to me, "I'm an elf?"

Chapter 3 The Isle of Death

Lirae looked at me with a bit of seeming confusion and concern, "Yes you are obviously an elf. Why shouldn't you be?"

I started to laugh at my catching her off guard, "I certainly wasn't born an elf."

She appeared shocked in return, "That's surprising even to me. It seems Master Thomas was having some kind of joke at my expense perhaps. I never realized this kind of change would result. Master Thomas is getting better at this all the time I guess."

I still was quite confused about how this could have happened, but I remained willing to see what lay in store for me.

I looked her in the eyes, "I don't know what happened at all. I'm out of my element here."

Lirae spoke, "Well, we can think on this later. It has been a long time since your body had any food to eat. Do you think you can manage to walk? "

I swung my legs back and forth a little, "They seem to be working fine. I will give it a try."

I stood up and found that I was weaker, but also that my body was much lighter than I was accustomed to being. I took a couple of tentative steps at first. Everything seemed fine so I stretched my arms above my head, and then looked expectantly at Lirae.

She gave a faint smile, "I will lead you to the dining hall."

Lirae and I left the room. We traveled down the hallway of the structure where I had awoken. I observed that the walls were made of an odd form of bamboo interwoven in thin horizontal and vertical straps. These straps were lashed together and woven around vertical spacers of whole bamboo.

As we stepped out through the doorway into the bright sunlight I noticed a warm and humid air accompanied by an unusual scent. I looked out across a compound constructed of similar buildings. Beyond the compound was a stretch of white sand beach with a turquoise blue sea beyond. The smell was the salty smell of the ocean that I was seeing for the first time in my life.

Further along the shore the beach ended and a rocky cliff rose up above the ocean. I noticed a familiar seeming trail winding up the cliff face. On top of the cliff was a white stone tower shaped in a manner similar to the one from my dream. A dim white light periodically shone from the top of the tower. Pulsing like the slow beating of a heart. I must have unconsciously stopped walking as I stared at the tower in the distance.

Lirae spoke, "Are you coming along Mica?"

I looked back at her, "That's the tower. The one I entered in my dream, or at least much like the one in my dream. How can it be here?"

Lirae replied, "That's Master Thomas' home and offices. He is very busy there, so we only go up there when we are summoned. Occasionally though he comes down here to socialize with those of his servants in residence on Thomas' Isle."

I nodded my head, "What happens to unannounced visitors?"

Lirae smiled again, "They never find this island in the first place. The only ones who come and go here are those who serve Master Thomas, or those he has invited here."

I nodded again, "I understand we are remote, but what happens if some explorer were to leave the established sea lanes, and find this place."

Lirae frowned a little and started walking forward again, "I am not certain. I imagine that Master Thomas would instruct us to greet them according to his whim. If they were lost, then I imagine that they would be sent out on the correct course. If they were hostile, then I imagine that Balinac would be assigned to deal with them."

I was curious as I also walked forward to catch up with her, "Who's this Balinac person?"

Lirae frowned even deeper this time, "Balinac is not something you refer to as 'a who'. Balinac is . . . well, I guess best described as Master Thomas' cat."

I held my hands out about a foot apart with a bit of confusion, "They would be afraid of a cat?"

Lirae looked at me with a little smirk, and yet there was also a touch what I took as fear in her eyes, "Not a little cat, a great big cat."

While Lirae said this she raised her right hand as high as it would go over her head. Much higher than the head of any horse I had ever ridden.

I began to understand her look of fear, "Ah, I think I understand now. Is that also the reason no one visits Master Thomas at his tower without invitation?"

Lirae nodded her head in answer and picked up her pace. She glanced at the tower and then back at me where I attempted to catch up, "It is best we eat now, and leave such a line of questioning for another time."

The next two months for me went by in an intense passage of instruction and learning. I also became accustomed to the physical changes I had undergone. My new body was strange and awkward to me at first, but I underwent a regimen of physical exercise which helped me to become at home with my new form. I found my senses to be more acute than I was accustomed to them being. My sight and hearing were better, although my strength was somewhat less than I had known as a human. I especially found that my physical control and speed had greatly increased. With the couple months of practice I could move with much more grace than I ever had in my former life.

One of the other permanent residents on the island compound was a dwarf named Hardtack. I don't think it was his given name, but then again my current name of Mica was not the one I have been given at birth either. Hardtack was both the cook for the dining hall, and the martial combat instructor.

In these two months I had also undergone a regimen of weapons training under Hardtack's guidance. I thought I had learned much in the nearly twenty years of martial instruction I had received training along with my brothers and in the militia. However, in two months with the calm and knowledgeable instruction under Hardtack I began to understand just how little I really knew about the various martial forms used in the world.

My father had practiced the common sword and shield fighting popular in Ard for nearly fifty years having started as a young child himself. In contrast Hardtack had been learning and training people for over three hundred years by his estimation. He claimed to still be a novice in his mind because he had yet to master every form. In my best estimation even bare handed and unarmored Hardtack could defeat an armored and mounted knight.

Hardtack also kept a large assortment of various forms of armor and weapons on hand, and I witnessed his amazing proficiency with any one he chose to demonstrate. In order to train me in my new role he restricted my instruction to weapons favored by the elves of Letheron. After finding I was not likely to be an archer as proficient as a natural born elf anytime soon, he focused on training me in using an elfish saber. It was considered a bit of a heavy weapon by elfish standards, but it meshed closest with my long sword and shield background. Replacing my customary shield was a long elfish dagger. This new two weapon style was tricky, but I was coming along in a satisfactory manner.

Surprisingly I learned more about finesse and technique in two months from Hardtack than I had in my last five years of instruction in swordplay in the militia. From Hardtack's training I also came to realize something else. I had thought before that I was almost evenly matched against the huntsman Davel who had ambushed us. I was learning that I was wrong about how relative our skills were. It was my outrage that kept me going at Davel hard, but I could see now that he had been carefully biding his time for an opening to appear while providing none himself. I had been Davel's prey, and he had already known the ultimate result of a fight between us would be my defeat.

It began to occur to me as I learned the two weapon style from Hardtack that I would not be very likely to learn enough to close that gap in skill in a short amount of time. So it would take something more than simple force of arms to defeat Davel. It was going to take help from people with enough skill to bring about justice.

My physical conditioning took most of my daylight hours. This consisted of the time between the morning and midday meals being filled with martial training under Hardtack's wise methods. When Hardtack ceased my martial instruction to prepare the meals for the compound I ran or performed a physical regimen to improve my strength and dexterity. Our meal times were not just for eating. They were also a time for Lirae to instruct me in common elfish etiquette. My experience with court training in Ard made this part relatively easy to learn the differences.

I spent my evening hours in instruction under Lirae's guidance. I studied the elfish language, the geography, and the culture of the country Letheron under her tutelage. Letheron consisted primarily of a large temperate forest bounded by the lands of humans on one edge, the wild country on the other, and the sea on the third. They were decade after decade squeezed and reduced by the pressures of being between this immense and expanding cultural force and the hard place inhabited by the less savory and less civilized races.

There were conflicts surrounding them both externally and internally. Some people like Lirae advocated partial adoption and integration with the ways of the humans. Others like the followers of Reminas advocated bloody assault on any who suggested compromise which led away from their long established ancestral ways. Thus Lirae had lost her family in the resulting philosophical conflict turned bloody.

I had the geography and social context of Letheron down pretty well. However, I was not doing too well with learning to speak the language of Letheron without an accent. I kept at it as best I could, but it was very difficult for me. Lirae was patient with me, but I could tell that she was anxious to begin her quest for justice.

During this time, I met the few regulars who also lived on the island. Most of them worked in a capacity to support the island. They performed the tasks of farming, fishing, community management, or otherwise tending to the business of Master Thomas. The majority ate at the dining hall in a regular manner, and they represented an odd lot being comprised of an assortment of elves, dwarfs, humans, and a handful of the uncivilized races from the wild lands.

There was also a visit nearly every three weeks in those two months when a ship would come into the protected cove of the island. On those days most of the community would help unload supplies from the ship including several large crates which would be sent up to Master Thomas' lighthouse home. The crew of the ship looked like a very rough crowd used to rowdy behavior. However, on each of these visits they did not join us on the island. When we unloaded the cargo, they generally steered clear of us with a wary eye and a hint of fear in their manner.

Their captain was called Roberts and showed no fear in his demeanor however. He would disembark on the island to oversee our off loading and storage of the cargo in our small warehouse. He received payment, and a list of the next set of goods to be delivered along with the location of the warehouse on the mainland in which the next load of goods would be waiting. On his most recent visit the captain had escorted two passengers to the island, and two of the inhabitants of Thomas' Isle I had considered regulars, the gnome Cogstone and shortling Alvos, left as passengers on the ship when it departed again.

The new arrivals went up to Master Thomas' home when they had first arrived, and the ship was unloaded and sailing back out to sea by midday. After I had finished my afternoon run, I went to the bay for a short swim to cool off. As I swam, I noticed three people walking down the trail from the lighthouse. The two people who had disembarked from the ship earlier in the day and an older man dressed in white pantaloons, a white shirt, white jacket, wearing leather sandals, and a jaunty white hat. As it had neared dinner time, I swam for shore. I was drying off as they reached my section of the beach.

I noticed a large black leopard spotted cat of about thirty to forty pounds and nearly two foot high at the shoulder walking along beside the older man's right side as the other two men stayed on his left. I figured this must be Balinac, a large brute of a cat for certain, but Lirae had exaggerated his size and ferociousness quite a bit. The odd thing about this cat besides its very dark fur with black leopard spots and its jade green eyes was the curious fact that it possessed two tails swinging independently of each other.

I approached them as they neared, and Balinac gave out a lower and deeper growl than I would have thought possible. I stopped and the older man wearing white spoke.

He first looked at the cat and said, "Balinac, behave yourself. Mica here is one of my projects."

Balinac gave me an indifferent look, and the man in white spoke directly to me, "Hello Mica, I'm Thomas. You may not remember me well from when we first met."

I gave him a smile, "Hello Master Thomas. I was wondering if I would get a chance to meet you in person. It's hard to get to know someone well in a dream."

Thomas gave me a friendly smile and the other two men accompanying him exchanged a knowing glance with each other. I was curious about that glance, but I couldn't think of a way to politely question what it would mean in my present company.

Thomas spoke again, "Please come along with us to the dining hall then. I hear Hardtack is preparing a special dinner with his new supplies. I have the evening free for a change of pace, so I will spend at least part of it catching up with everyone in the community."

We set off in relative silence as we approached the dining hall. The two men walking to the left of Thomas were lost in thought it seemed. I chose to follow their example and joined them on the left side of Thomas leaving Balinac alone on his right. The dining hall was just starting to fill as we approached.

Everyone at the dining hall looked at Thomas with a smile, but they each also reserved a touch of a careful or fearful glance at Balinac. Thomas for his part exchanged greetings, nods, and handshakes with all of them and sat down at one of the tables as the rest of us moved to help Hardtack bring the food out from the kitchen.

As I got out of hearing distance of Thomas I spoke to one of the newcomers, "Hello, I am called Mica. Perhaps you would answer a question for me."

The man nodded back "The name is Jack now. Go ahead with your question."

I asked, "Why is everyone seemingly afraid of Balinac? He's a large beast of a cat for sure, but he can't scratch and bite that hard can he?"

Jack gave me a wicked grin. "Just don't get on Balinac's bad side is all I can warn you. I saw it happen once to an intruder on the island. The ship crews don't call this the Isle of Death for no reason."

I gave him a grin in return, "This is a trick, right. You're pulling a joke on me are you not? This place is called Thomas' Isle, not the Isle of Death."

Then Jack's look turned serious, "You're pretty new here so I'll let you in on a secret. The residents call this place Thomas' Isle and such it is. The crew of the ship the Mystic Dawn that comes here, they don't know it by that name. To them it is called the Isle of Death. That's because it has become known that to come here uninvited means you will never leave here alive. That's why they are all afraid to leave the ship when it comes ashore."

I shook my head, "If they are that scared of this place, then why do they sail here at all?"

Jack looked at me like I was a slow learner, "Money drives a man to face a lot of his fears. On one six week jaunt those sailors can earn as much money as they would make in a year serving on another ship. If they follow the simple rules and do the job, then they can quit early and with enough good pay to retire with a fair amount besides."

As we walked out from the kitchen with dinner serving plates laden with food in hand I asked, "Where does Master Thomas make that kind of money from?"

Jack looked at me and shook his head, "Master Thomas had a lot of connections in very high places. He provides certain services that can come at a premium price."

I looked at Jack, "What kind of services does he provide that make that kind of money?"

Jack laughed, "The same service most of us are here to receive, justice of course. Master Thomas provides justice. We are simply paying our bill in the form of return services rendered to others is all you understand. Others pay in gold or favors as best suits their abilities and means."

I nodded, "I think I understand, but how can Master Thomas know what action is justice?"

Jack nodded his head toward Thomas sitting at the table as we came out of the kitchen with our loaded platters, "Master Thomas is very careful, and some would say he is slow to act. He doesn't act in a hasty or rash manner. He bides his time, and makes sure he knows what is happening before he acts. He does his research, and uses it very effectively. He never takes an assignment just for the money. Also he only takes money as payment when it can be afforded by the client. Once he has agreed to perform a contract, he makes sure the job is done, completely, effectively, and neatly."

As Jack spoke I thought back to the many stories and tales heard and told in my childhood. One set of tales in particular were of an infamous assassin who had never been located, whose face was unknown, who always killed his mark, and who was rumored to never have killed an innocent.

As I approached the table I unconsciously blurted out, "Thomas the Poisoner!"

Master Thomas turned toward my unthinking outburst as the rest of the people in the dining hall became quiet. I felt their combined gazes locked onto me, and I felt embarrassment along with a touch of uncertainty. I set the platter on the table while trying to avoid everyone's gaze. Master Thomas then gently laughed and the others joined in as well. It was a light and humorous laughter. I was confused yet less embarrassed as the laughter died down.

Master Thomas then spoke with a smile on his face, "Yes, I see you have finally figured out that I am also known as Thomas the Poisoner. Most of the people in this room are also known as Thomas the Poisoner when acting as my proxy in business matters. You too will bear the name Thomas the Poisoner in time when you are pursuing the course of justice using my name as both weapon and shield. If it pleases you though you can just call me Thomas when on the island or Master Thomas like most here opt to do."

The general conversation started up again in the dining hall as we sat down to dinner. I noticed several people passing over coins to Hardtack as we ate our meal. As it had not been our custom to pay him for our meals before, I nudged Jack sitting beside me and asked him why people were paying Hardtack. Jack looked a bit embarrassed himself.

Jack said to me, "There's a betting pool as to when the new recruits will figure out what Master Thomas is called by the outside world. I couldn't participate this time since I was out working when you were recruited."

Hardtack had heard our conversation and made an addition, "Chatty Jack here also has a reputation for talking a lot. He's not allowed to bet anymore because new recruits usually figure it out after they talk with him too long. Of course it didn't hurt my guess since I knew when Chatty Jack here would be coming back from the outside. I gave Chatty Jack about nine hours from his return until you caught on."

Jack got a bit red faced and fired back, "Now you know my name is just Jack. Speaking of names how's your cake cooking coming along now Hardtack."

Jack mimed trying to gnaw a wood plank.

Hardtack kept his usual calm demeanor, "You know that is how a proper Dwarfish cake is made so it will keep well for travel or work. We dwarfs don't take to that light and spongy stuff them elves call cake. No offense intended Lirae."

Lirae smiled back at Hardtack, "None taken Hardtack. I figure that each person has their own tastes. Personally, I prefer the light and spongy cakes the elves of Letheron make."

Hardtack smiled in return, "Oh the taste is pretty enough, but it sits in a belly like a bunch of air. It needs more substance to be worth eating in this dwarf's humble opinion."

The dinner continued with genial conversation among the inhabitants of the island. I ate in relative silence, but occasionally glanced down the table to take a closer look at the man known throughout the alliance of kingdoms as Thomas the Poisoner. He looked to be in a fit physical condition, yet not imposing. His hair was white, and yet he didn't seem to be of extremely advanced age. His demeanor actually came across as fatherly in a way. He seemed to beam proudly over this strange assortment of his "children".

In a way I noticed for the first time that our odd collection of individuals from the human, elfish, dwarfish, and wild races were a kind of extended family. They were celebrating the return of two of their own, and the recent departure of another pair. Yet at the same time they were also the minions of one of the most infamous assassins ever spoken of in tales and legends. I still felt uncomfortable about the revelation I had received, but I was not in any distress regarding my own personal well being.

As we finished eating Thomas casually waved me over to his side. I approached him carefully to avoid stepping on the tails of Balinac waving about near his feet.

Thomas spoke softly to me as people began departing the dining hall, "I must tend to some farewells here before I return to my home. Please wait for me. I want you to walk with me at least part of the way back. It's finally time we had a bit of a longer talk together."

I waited by the door as Thomas spoke to a few of the people leaving the room. He patted Jack on the back as he departed, and gave a friendly handshake to his partner from their journey. Thomas then sought out Lirae, and had a brief quiet conversation with her out of my hearing. She seemed a bit dejected by his comments, but he kept his pleasant smile. As they approached the door where I stood I heard Thomas counseling her to remain patient, and that her turn would come in time. It seemed a strange thing for a human to be saying to an elf with such a long life span.

I thought Thomas would depart with me then, but he bade his farewells to the last people departing. Then he held up his hand in a gesture of patience, as he went into the kitchen. A couple of minutes later he came out with Hardtack following him. Thomas gestured for me to join them as they walked out into the night.

I realized that I had forgotten about Balinac when I suddenly saw the beast standing a few yards outside the doorway. The cat seemed larger and more threatening than before. Where in daylight it had seemed about two feet tall, in the approaching darkness it seemed to have gained a foot of height and total of seventy pounds. I quickly vacated my position on Thomas' right side and joined Hardtack on his left. Balinac seemed fiercer as well, and its two tails switched back and forth in the manner of a stalking cat as it paced to Thomas' side.

Thomas smiled at me yet his tone was serious as he spoke, "It's time I told you some more things you'll need to know. This conversation may be unpleasant to hear, but there is some good news in it as well. I can't explain everything to you. You'll have to accept as everyone else does that of necessity I keep my secrets closely guarded."

I nodded my head in acceptance, "That is an understatement Master Thomas."

Thomas continued, "I am, shall we say, the head of this . . . organization known collectively as Thomas the Poisoner. One of the secrets of this organization is that there is more than one of us performing the role of Thomas the Poisoner. You will work in teams when on the outside, and perform the mission provided with the assistance of, let us say, informants and other people who owe me favors."

I nodded my head again, "I have finally figured that part out based on what was said earlier this evening."

Thomas smiled, "It's not one of my deepest secrets by any means. What it does mean is that to maintain the mystique of Thomas the Poisoner two strike teams may not be operating in different areas at the same time. One of our many rules is that the work of Thomas the Poisoner must account for reasonable transit time between two locations to maintain the illusion that Thomas the Poisoner is a single yet gifted individual."

I chimed in with my next guess, "Is that why one team returns before the next team departs?"

Thomas spoke again, "You are correct of course. I told you he was a sharp one Hardtack. The teams are also composed of a senior member, and a junior member. The senior member executes the task and makes the appropriate tactical decisions, and the junior member assists as directed. Hopefully the junior member learns from the actions of the senior member and becomes proven as an effective resource in time."

I interrupted Thomas, "How long does this take?"

Thomas nodded, "Good question. You've got your eyes on your own prize don't you young Mica. I like that you understood from the beginning that there is a mutual association going on here. It can take as little as one year with a particularly challenging mission, or five to ten years with easier tasks assigned."

I stopped in my tracks, "Ten years? I'll have to wait up to ten years?"

Thomas waved me to continue following, "Yes that is one possible case. Which leads me to more bad news for you, and yet I have some good news as well."

I continued following and braced myself, "What could this be?"

Thomas held up his right hand with his fingers extended, "First I must explain some of our, let us say, restrictions."

Thomas curled in his thumb, "Rule one. We never deliberately take the life of an innocent."

I nodded at this comment and let out a sigh of relief at the same time, so this much of the tales told was true.

Thomas curled in his index finger, "Rule two. No matter how much time it takes, once we determine that our suggested target is guilty of intentionally harming an innocent we take the job, and ensure that justice is served. There is no backing out once a job is accepted. However, we do acknowledge that justice is often best served by many ways other than death. If another way of serving justice is better, then we never kill our target. Only in extreme circumstances do we actually bring about the demise of the target."

Thomas then closed his middle finger, "Rule three. We never inflict collateral damage. Only the intended target is dealt with. We are efficient, effective, and clean in the execution of our task. This is one of the reasons poison is used as the preferred method of death. It is carefully administered so as to only impact the intended target."

I noticed that we were heading away from the path leading to Thomas' house on the cliff and approaching the dock warehouse instead.

Thomas closed his ring finger, "Rule four. We don't work for money, political ideology, or revenge. We work to bring the guilty to justice. We especially don't interfere in the course of national politics unless it is very clearly to bring the guilty to justice."

After my time studying with Lirae I ventured a guess, "This rule four is standing in the way of Lirae's pursuit of justice isn't it?"

Thomas nodded his head, "The primary target she is interested in bringing to justice is, let us say, positioned in a manner to determine the course of the future for the nation of Letheron. Her mission requires a fine tuned use of delicacy, and unfortunately I am not in a position to apply a large number of information assets in that particular kingdom. This is good news for you however. Due to the difficulty of her task, if the two of you successfully accomplish her mission when it is time without significant repercussions to the political structure in Letheron, then your mission will be fast tracked to next on the list."

I smiled at the thought of being promoted to the next mission after Lirae's, "Thank you Master Thomas. I shall endeavor to be the best junior possible."

Thomas nodded his head again. I noticed his smile was gone as we approached the warehouse door.

Thomas closed his pinky finger turning his right hand into a fist, "Rule five. You may not even allow death to stop you. Now I have the bad news for you. It has already been two years and eleven months since . . ."

A sudden blur of motion from out of the darkness had me ducking and weaving to the side with my heightened elfish reflexes. I also saw Hardtack seemingly effortlessly pluck a strange looking knife out of what had a moment before seemed to be thin air in front of his nose. I looked to my right past Hardtack and saw Thomas crumpled on the ground with a large dark stain spreading on the front of his white shirt.

Chapter 4 The Assassin

I crouched in stunned shock for a moment as the normally calm Hardtack cried out, "Crap stick! Bleeding ninja! Get 'em!"

As I began to rise up I saw something mentioned and hinted at by the others. I had dismissed it until then as people pulling an elaborate joke on me. I could dismiss it no longer now. Balinac surged forward at Hardtack's cry. In two great bounds Balinac had reached the warehouse, and in a great leap landed onto the roof two stories above. With each of these bounds Balinac had surged in size until it was larger than the biggest horse I had ever seen in my life.

I stood there for a moment in confusion as Balinac disappeared from my line of sight over the roof line. I felt Hardtack slap me on the shoulder with his left hand while he still held onto the strange knife with his right.

Hardtack looked me in the eye, "Go after them Mica, make sure Balinac doesn't do severe damage to that ninja. I want to talk with him before he dies. I'll see to Thomas. Now go!"

I gave another quick glance at the crumpled form of Thomas on the ground. Then I sped off after the course Balinac took. I ran around the warehouse instead of trying to go over it. I spotted the point where Balinac must have entered the jungle canopy on the other side.

I increased my pace following the obvious signs of passage by the enormous beast through the jungle. It was very dark under the canopy by now, but my elfish vision adjusted to allow me to see heat emissions. I could see the faint tell tail signs of recent human passage, but only the disrupted foliage showed where Balinac followed in pursuit.

I then heard a terrible yowl that would have disrupted the very sleep of the dead. This was followed by a loud booming noise like a nearby thunderclap. My acute hearing felt abused, but it led me straight to where Balinac had a human covered from head to toe in black cloth pinned to the ground. Balinac appeared to be around eight foot tall at the shoulder now, and curiously gave off no heat patterns I could detect but instead remained the same temperature as the air. Balinac was batting at the human like a cat tormenting a mouse. I looked up and could see where the top portion of a tall palm tree had been torn off. The intruder had obviously attempted an inopportune choice of hiding locations.

As I approached the man to examine him Balinac emitted a deep low growl that vibrated my very body. I kept approaching making a shooing motion with my right hand as I came within range of the monstrous beast. Balinac swatted a paw in my direction with claws extended. I nimbly jumped over the paw and landed beside the great beast's head. I then sprung up and grabbed the large ear with my left hand and hung on as I reached out to swat Balinac on the nose with my right hand.

I called out loudly into its ear, "Behave yourself, and back off!"

Surprisingly I wasn't shredded to pieces on the spot. Balinac casually shook me off, backed up a couple of paces, and gracefully shrank back down to a more reasonable lion sized beast. In an attempt to preserve its dignity Balinac began to lick the blood from its claws as if that had been its plan all along.

I carefully approached the human who lay on the ground dressed in black. The cloth covering did a fair job of masking his heat pattern except for the exhalations of breath I could still see, and the places where the cloth had been torn by Balinac's claws. It appeared that his left arm might be broken as it was bent at an unnatural angle, and he seemed unconscious. Not trusting how things seemed much anymore, I approached him from above his head. I gave him a swift kick to the side of his head along his jaw. The man winced from the pain, and stopped trying to pretend to be unconscious.

He attempted to sweep my feet with his arms, but his injuries hampered his movements. I managed to avoid his uninjured arm while his injured arm obviously caused him duress. Next he attempted to spring away, only to notice that Balinac had quickly moved to interpose itself to block any retreat. His good right arm swept down to his lower calf, and I saw him grab another of those strange knives. He quickly swung it up in his hand with the point aimed toward his own throat.

I surged forward in an attempt to block his arm, and then flinched back as I witnessed another thrown knife intersect the one held in his hand. Both knives spun off into the darkness, and I stepped back into a defensive posture. I noticed Hardtack approaching while pulling a strangely tied length of rope with three weights tied to three separate ends from his belt.

The man in black gained his feet, and tried to leap up toward a nearby tree branch. Meanwhile Hardtack gave his strange contraption a seemingly gentle twirl over his head and casually launched it intercept the man in mid leap. I mentally reminded myself to learn to use some of these more exotic weapons from Hardtack someday as I watched the man collapse back to the ground tangled up in the ropes and weights.

Hardtack gave a wicked grin, "You did a good job keeping this one intact. They usually try to kill themselves rather than suffer the indignity of a capture. Strange bunch of assassins these ninja happen to be."

I watched as Hardtack casually approached the bound up fellow, and pulled another length of rope out to more securely tie him up. Hardtack carefully grabbed the limbs he wanted. While avoiding the struggles of the captive he bent and twisted the man's extremities until the fellow complied with every movement Hardtack directed.

Hardtack stood back up as he finished securing the ropes, and heaved a sigh, "Now comes the hard part. These fellows are as slippery as eels when they want. The only way to get most of their weapons is to take all of their clothes off. Which as you can see is pretty hard to do when you have them tied up so much. In the mean time he is going to be trying to either get out of his bindings, or to cause himself fatal harm. Isn't that right you . . ."

Hardtack uttered a strange set of words I had never heard before. The man's eyes widened in shock, and he seemed to stop struggling for a second. I saw a look I could best describe as proud fury in his eyes.

I looked at Hardtack and asked, "What did you say to him to cause that reaction?"

Hardtack laughed, "I called him a gutless coward too afraid to face a superior opponent. It's a deadly insult in his culture. Of course it is another act of deceit on his part, since he understands the trade tongue well enough or he wouldn't have gotten aboard Captain Roberts' ship. I highly doubt a skilled ninja like him would be baited or insulted by the words of any person. No more likely he's just shocked that I know so much about them. They like to think they are very secret after all. Ha!"

I noticed the look of proud fury disappear in the eyes of the ninja to be replaced by a look I could best describe as cold contemplation. He was balked at the moment, and obviously considering his alternatives. Certainly he feared to be made to reveal secrets of his craft under torture.

I thought about it as well, "What do we do with him now then?"

Hardtack thought a bit, "I guess I'll drag him by the ropes near his ankles, and you keep a close watch on his hands and head. If he twitches or looks like he might be trying to worry those ropes any give him another one of those solid kicks to his head."

I shook my head while keeping a close watch on the ninja, "You saw that one did you?"

Hardtack laughed, "I saw the whole thing, I figured you might need the back-up. Balinac can be a handful sometimes. Good job at controlling Balinac by the way. That beast has everyone but Master Thomas, me, and now apparently you scared witless generally speaking."

I glanced around, and didn't see Balinac nearby anymore, "Don't tell anyone, but I thought it might try to kill me when I grabbed its ear like that."

Hardtack looked back at me as he began walking forward with his prize in tow, "You don't know the half of it yet. That took a lot of guts, so it was a good job anyway, even if it was a very foolish move."

I looked at the rope handle Hardtack had made and noticed that it was carefully secured away from the front and back of the ninja's shoes. I thought this a curious manner in which to tie his feet off.

I spoke up as we walked, "Why did you tie his feet that way? It seems excessive. Wouldn't a single rope have been easier?"

Hardtack laughed, "These fellows keep knives in the front or back of their shoes sometimes. The blade is short and on a spring. It's good for kicking, or cutting ropes I guess. Thing is they never think to put knives in the sides of their shoes, so it is better to tie them that way."

I noticed the ninja roll his eyes and pound the back of his head on the ground in exaggerated frustration. Suspecting an attempt to access another of these hidden blades I gave him a quick kick on the other side of his jaw to match the first one. Then I thought I was forgetting something. It suddenly struck me.

I spoke in a hushed tone in elfish to Hardtack, "Do you understand the elfin language?"

Hardtack responded back in elfish with a very rough dwarfish accent, "I can understand it better that I can speak. Black clothing fellow will likely be not understanding about it though, so it is a good idea if you want to speak something he not understanding."

I thought carefully, "How is the owner of the island doing? Was his injury deadly or critical?"

Hardtack laughed and replied in his rough elfish, "Stronger than this young dragon here. You'll see."

The return trip to the compound took a bit of time, but it seemed that the ninja had decided that Hardtack was a formidable foe. As a result he seemingly chose to bide his time waiting for whatever chance he might have to seek his freedom or own death later. Hardtack dragged his package into the dining hall, and back through his kitchen. He then opened a trap door in the floor and dragged him down the stairs into his cool storage cellar.

It was a fair way down the stairs, and I could tell our uninvited guest was smarting from each of the stairs smacking the back of his head on the decent. We finally cleared down into the foundation stone, and entered a dwarf cut tunnel which ended in a solid metal door anchored to dwarf worked stone. The chamber beyond the door was stocked with perishable supplies kept cool by the room carved from the surrounding stone.

I looked at the room, and began clearing a spot for Hardtack to prop up our prisoner. Hardtack kept a close eye on him as I moved some potato sacks aside. Hardtack casually pulled him over to the spot I'd cleared and set him down with his back up against the wall.

Hardtack spoke to me in elfish again, "Bring a sharp knife from upstairs and one of my big pots and a big spoon. Carry the pot upside down when you come back."

I went upstairs fairly sure why Hardtack might want the knife, but at a complete loss as to why he needed a pot carried upside down and a spoon. I grabbed his largest pot along with a small sharp paring knife from the kitchen and brought them down.

Hardtack indicated that I should put the pot down on the floor next to the prisoner, and took the paring knife in his right hand and the spoon in his left. Hardtack sat down using the pot as a stool, and brought the knife up quickly against the prisoner's cloth covered throat.

I realized then that this must be pretty scary for the prisoner since he couldn't see in the darkness as Hardtack and I could. I noticed him shutting his eyes and bracing himself for the pain of the blade. Instead of cutting the prisoner, Hardtack deftly sliced a small hole through the black cloth then with the sharp portion of the blade outward cut a slice through his hood. Hardtack removed the hood to reveal his head and face. The man was obviously young with an exotic cast to his features. I figured he was perhaps as young as sixteen. His black hair was close cropped with a bound ponytail in the back.

Hardtack looked over at me and spoke in trade speak, "Not a local breed of human, though likely trained in ninja practices by a master from childhood. He was probably purchased as an infant, and raised in their assassin cult. It's a pity he had to be raised to kill from such a young age."

I thought back to my own martial childhood, "Not a pity perhaps. I don't bear any grudges for my father for teaching me to fight. It's sometimes necessary to fight to protect people."

Hardtack nodded his head, "True, we dwarfs are raised in a martial tradition as well, but these fellows learn to kill for politics. They don't kill to save people, they kill to promote ideology."

Hardtack carefully pawed over the removed hood and pulled out three unusual small metal implements.

I looked at him curiously and asked, "What would those be used for?"

Hardtack smiled, "Any dwarf worth his salt would recognize a lock pick when he saw one. It's pretty obvious that would be overlooked by an elf like you who never locks up their homes or belongings."

I understood Hardtack was reminding me to stay in my new persona as an elf. Next Hardtack began a similar cutting procedure on the high cloth shoes worn by the prisoner. After removal he demonstrated where a click of a toe released a short sharp razor along the front edge of the shoe. I could see how it might be perfect for cutting ropes when captured and left unattended or making a kick extra damaging.

Hardtack looked at me, "Now comes the tricky part. We have to take off the rest of these clothes and that sash to get the rest of these tools away from this ninja. We have to do it without loosening those ropes any too. So well roll him over on his belly first on top of his bound hands. He'll likely grab something tricky then, but I'll take care of it when we bring him back around."

Hardtack stood up, pulled the prisoner out flat, and turned him over on his belly.

Hardtack puzzled the problem a moment and asked, "Would you set your knees on his shoulder joints there. Just face his head, and use his buttocks like a seat cushion. If he wiggles just lean forward on your knees a bit, the pain should settle him down some."

After I got into the indicated position Hardtack gave his next direction, "Now that pot I had you bring down. I want you to place that over the feller's head."

I struggled with the job of getting the pot in position over his head, but eventually I got it in place. I was a bit confused about why I was doing this though.

I shrugged at Hardtack, "Now what?"

Hardtack picked up his large spoon, and gave the pot a sound strike on the rim. The pot reverberated like a small bell, and in the stone walled space the noise was quite overwhelming. It must have been much worse for the prisoner with his head inside the pot. He squirmed in obvious discomfort unlike the maneuvering he submitted to earlier.

Hardtack gave a broad smile, "If I tell you, or if he moves in a way you don't like, then give that pot a good hit again."

Hardtack then cut each pant leg of the prisoner's black clothes up along the back. He carefully worked around and underneath the ropes until the pant legs had been cut clear. As I glanced back I could see that our prisoner had several lacerations along his legs, but that despite a fair amount of blood being present, there were no deep or currently bleeding wounds.

Hardtack removed three sharpened coin sized disks of metal, and one more of those strange knives from the legs of the pants. He then had me lean forward until he could cut through the pant bottoms and sash worn by the prisoner. For the moment he left the loin cloth underneath in place.

The sash was a miniature arsenal with containers, pockets, and exotic looking items inside. Hardtack set it aside without closer inspection for the moment. Then he had me shift back to sitting on the prisoner's calves as he worked at cutting around the ropes to remove the back of the shirt.

I was confused to see that under his shirt the prisoner was already wearing a set of wrapped bandages. These bandages were wound from the bottom of his rib cage to the base of his armpits. It was helpful I guess because they had already staunched the bleeding from the raking claws of Balinac.

Hardtack stood up thoughtfully and considered this as well, "I don't recognize this as standard ninja equipment. The rest of the stuff is pretty common, but who bandages themselves before an injury? If I think back that looks more like how the . . . oh my."

Chapter 5 Revelations

I was curious about what had changed Hardtack's manner. He indicated I should stand up as he removed the pot from over the prisoner's head.

Then he asked me, "Go upstairs and bring me a lighted lantern. Get me my load stone knife holder as well. The one that keeps the knives on the wall, just leave the knives up there though."

I fetched the requested items, and brought them down the stairs to the cellar. I kept the lantern partially shuttered at first so as I approached Hardtack would have an opportunity to let his eyes adjust to the light. I entered the room and noticed Hardtack was carefully moving the ninja items out of reach onto a high shelf. He handled the sash with its secret containers with extra caution.

As I entered the room I gradually opened the shutter of the lantern as Hardtack took the load stone from my hand. Our eyes adjusted to normal vision quickly. I could see our prisoner with his exposed legs and back shivering as he lay on his front on the cool stone floor.

Hardtack stepped over to the prisoner and spoke, "Set that lantern down on the pot. All right, now let's get her turned over carefully."

I helped him turn the prisoner over, and noticed that he was shivering from the cool cellar stone, and yet very flush in his face. Then my mind caught up with what Hardtack had said, and I glanced down at the loincloth the prisoner was wearing. It was less full than I previously would have expected. The physical appearance caught up with Hardtack's last remark. The ninja assassin was a young woman, not a teenage boy as we had first assumed.

I noticed that she was flush due to the embarrassment of being forcibly stripped by two male collateral targets. Nothing in her training had prepared her for this kind of humiliation. I exchanged a serious glance with Hardtack who looked concerned.

He shook his head, "No sense in hesitating now. We have to make sure that all of the items are removed before we can safely deal with this one. Take that serving platter up there on the shelf with all of her gear. Put it up in the kitchen in the locking cabinet. Bring me back the key after you lock it. Don't touch any of it since there is no telling what may be trapped or poisoned. When you are done with that then please bring Lirae here. She will be better suited to deal with our guest when we are done.

I went upstairs again and put the items in the cabinet as indicated. I left the dining hall to see a small group of the island's inhabitants waiting patiently outside for news. I waved Jack over.

I spoke first, "Hardtack wants Lirae to come inside. Our prisoner is a ninja woman, and continuing the search for weapons is a bit delicate. How is Master Thomas?"

Jack frowned a bit, "I'll fetch Lirae for you. It's a bit underhanded to send a female ninja here. You'd think by now that they'd have learned to attempt taking Master Thomas' life is an automatic death sentence for the assassin and their group's leader. Unfortunately, it is one of our rules we enforce in order to guarantee our protection by having a ruthless reputation. I'll bring Lirae over as soon as I can."

With that Jack left and I returned to the kitchen to wait within hearing distance of both the cellar and outside. Down below I only heard the steady regular breathing of two people. Yet there was no other sound. Eventually I heard soft footsteps approaching from outside. Lirae entered the dining hall, and I waved her over to the kitchen. We walked down into the cellar side by side. I entered the room first followed by Lirae.

The assassin still looked embarrassed as I entered, and then showed a look of surprise followed by a look of gratitude upon seeing a female elf in my company. She clearly understood that we might eventually kill her, but that her dignity would not be further violated. Hardtack stepped over to her side and gently put his right hand on her throat while with his left hand he rapidly pressed a series of points on her head. The prisoner slumped unconscious before my eyes.

I looked at Hardtack and spoke with a slight tone of accusation, "If you could have done that before, then why did we go through that whole elaborate routine to remove the weapons."

Hardtack laughed at me, "It will only hold for about thirty minutes or so. The reason we did it the other way was for the psychological effect. It had to be clear that we were fully in control of the situation, and knowledgeable of any trick they may attempt. Let's finish by removing her bonds and disposing of the remains of her outer garments. They are a bloody mess anyway. Then we will give her enough clothes to satisfy modesty. First however let me take care of this."

Hardtack carefully grabbed a portion of her torn clothing, and using it as a cover for his hand gently removed a small object concealed in her hand. I looked at it with a deep suspicion.

I asked, "Is that small thing very dangerous?"

Hardtack nodded his head, "It is a magical trap. Most likely a suicide device, but who knows what enchantment it may carry. Explosions, poison gas, fire, deadly cold and more are all likely suspects. Hard to tell how it triggers, so pardon me while I make my way out of here and dispose of this somewhere safe."

I looked at Lirae and said, "I guess we should get started removing these ropes."

She looked at me with a smile, "Don't worry. I will protect her virtue, not that she can claim much in her line of work. She is a killer for hire after all."

I began cutting the bonds tied by Hardtack as it was beyond me to figure out how to quickly untie them. I then unwound the exotic weighted rope weapon Hardtack had used to entangle her. The remaining portion of her black top was removed as carefully as possible so as not to trigger any other possible traps. She lay there somewhat pitiful with the claw marks and broken arm with her upper attributes firmly strapped down by her bandages.

I heard a strange explosion sound in the distance outside, and sprang up to my feet. I contemplated going out to investigate, but realized the rest of the residents would have to manage any other problems at the moment. I was responsible for assuring that our prisoner remained intact.

A couple of minutes later Hardtack returned with a grin on his face. I nodded toward our prisoner lying on the ground. Then I noticed that he carried a basic set of female clothing with him.

He handed the clothes to Lirae, "All right, before we get this one dressed she is going to have to be stripped nude and checked. Lirae, I figure that you are pretty well versed with the ways a woman might conceal small objects. Mica and I will leave the room after I check using this first. You'll perform the examination, and get her dressed."

Hardtack moved the load stone in his hand over her body starting with her head and working his way carefully down to her feet. Everywhere he felt the load stone tug he made a closer examination. He found five more objects in her ponytail including the band holding it in place. The bandage wraps on her chest and her loin cloth also indicated items were present which he left for Lirae to find.

What I found amazing was that beneath the skin of her hands and the soles of her feet there were also four more needle like items. I presumed this was for the subtle introduction of poisons in intended targets. I left the room with Hardtack and we waited in the corridor outside with the door shut as Lirae finished the removal of her clothes, and the rest of the physical examination.

I asked Hardtack, "What was the noise I'd heard outside?"

He grinned again, "A wee bit of dwarf ingenuity at work. I cleared the people away and set that little trap on a hard stone. I then had a couple of the regulars help me move my small anvil over next to the stone. Next I built a quick fulcrum and lever out of a log section and another rock."

I gave him a confused look, "What was all of that for?"

He laughed, "So I could lever the anvil onto that trap from a distance of course. It worked like a charm since it looked like a combination frosty cold and poison gas attack. It must be one of their signature items I guess. Lucky for us it will help in tracking down which ninja clan sent them."

I looked at him still grinning, "Why are you smiling so much?"

He laughed again, "I'm just remembering a favorite old dwarf saying. Never underestimate the utility of a good anvil."

I gave a polite laugh in return, "I see, very humorous."

Hardtack gave me a skeptical look, "Been working on that elfish sarcasm I see."

Lirae indicated that she had removed three larger objects from concealment including a curious copper disk with writing on it. Then she redressed the prisoner in her new undergarments and opened the door. We assisted Lirae in putting some bandages on the ninja's wounds, and rigging a sling for her broken arm. Lirae and I dressed her in the new pantaloons and shirt while Hardtack carefully removed the rest of her gear from the room.

As Lirae and I waited in silence, I noticed a subtle shift in the breathing of the ninja. Glancing her way I could see that she was very convincing in pretending to still be asleep, but that it was not enough to convince the sensitive hearing of an elf in a quiet room. I glanced at Lirae and could see that she understood our prisoner was awake, unbound, and planning her next move.

I pretended to be distracted while looking at Lirae and spoke in elfish, "She is likely to try something soon. Watch for it."

I noticed that the prisoner had slipped open her eyes a crack and was judging the distance to the lantern sitting on the pot. I personally noted that she was a smart one since that was likely the most viable pair of makeshift weapons remaining in the room. As the ninja tried to snake out her good hand toward the lantern I quickly stepped forward and kicked her hand aside.

To prove the point as to who was in charge I quickly bent over and soundly tapped the bridge of her nose with my finger, and stepped back into my original position just as quickly. I was getting fairly used to having these rapid reflexes now.

I looked her in the eyes as I said loudly, "Behave yourself. If I'm not afraid of that monster beast that roams the Isle of Death, then what makes you think I'll be unwilling to put you in your place?"

Lirae looked at me strangely as I said that. I heard Hardtack returning up above and watched her closely as he entered the room. Hardtack noticed that her eyes were open now as she lay on the floor.

Then Hardtack spoke to the woman, "I know you speak the trade tongue. It was the language you used quite fluently when you sought to become a crew member on Captain Roberts' ship. Remain quiet if you will, but understand that your equipment has been found, including the stash you made to hold your seaman's clothes and extra gear. Also understand you are on an island unknown to most at least one hundred miles from any other nation. There is no where to flee to, and no reason to kill yourself. You will never be allowed to leave this island alive anyway. However, if you are patient you might just find there is a reason to cooperate with us."

He looked at us next, "Let's escort her up to the female's quarters on the eastern side."

The woman looked a bit uncertain and scared after this proclamation. She had obviously been expecting either success or failure on this mission. She probably accepted that she had at least managed to eliminate her primary target, but that she had failed in her attempts to escape. However, while she had expected torture leading to death as a possibility, she obviously had not expected limited freedom and the promise of a lifetime restriction to the island.

I walked out of the room first, followed by Lirae beside the assassin with a hand on her good elbow as Hardtack followed behind. We walked out of the dining hall and headed for the building which held the female's quarters. I guided us to the empty room beside Lirae's room. A comfortable bed with white linen sheets was inside. There were also a couple of chairs and a simple vanity.

I stood beside the door inside the room as Lirae led our now guest over to the far chair facing the door. Hardtack took the chair across from the woman as Lirae stood near the window. Following Lirae's lead I moved to block most of the doorway myself. I suddenly felt cool fur brushing up against my ankles and looked down to see a very normal cat sized Balinac brushing up against my legs.

Lirae could not avoid the look of what appeared to be combined shock and fear at seeing Balinac behaving in such a familiar manner with me. The woman looked at the cat in confusion, then a glance from Balinac in her direction gave her the moment of insight she needed. She too looked at the cat rubbing against my legs with a hint of fear in her expression.

The woman sitting in the chair silently and expectantly then turned pale with a look of astonishment. I felt a gentle hand press against my shoulder even though my sensitive elfish ears had not heard the sound of anyone approaching.

Thomas spoke as he stepped beside me, "It seems you've made friends with Balinac. An extremely rare feat, but I approve. It shows that I've made a good judgment in selecting you."

The woman ninja spoke for the first time in my presence, "You should be dead. That poisoned blade would kill anyone, there is no known antidote."

Thomas smiled in his fatherly manner as he addressed the woman, "Young lady, I beg to differ. If you were chasing after a common target what you say would be true. How could your clan be foolish enough to think that Thomas the Poisoner could be killed by a mere blade with an application of a not so rare poison really? You are talking about my stock and trade now. I'm insulted by the implication this makes against my sterling reputation. It's shoddy work after all."

She shook her head in disbelief, "The blade hit your heart. No one could survive my attacks."

Thomas pointed his finger at his chest, "Yet here I stand."

He pointed at me, "As does this fine elf here."

Then he pointed at Hardtack, "As well at that dwarf sitting there. As I said already it's shoddy work. Inexperienced, too young, too eager for the kill, no patience, just what kind of depths has your clan sunk to my lady. You ruined my good jacket and shirt as well. I'll have to order the delivery of another just like it."

The woman had the good graces to look ashamed by her failure as an assassin.

Thomas smiled at her again, "There now it's not all bad. You'll get to stay here on the island with us. I'm certain we can find a job here that you'd like to do. You are very brave after all. It's not everyone who is willing to walk into such an obvious trap."

The woman looked at him with a shocked expression again, "A trap?"

Thomas shook his head, "What are they not teaching young assassins these days? Of course this island is a trap. They don't call it the Isle of Death because it is a place someone can visit uninvited and return to where they originated. You know too much and can never leave here alive. Didn't your sensei teach you these things at all? Wasn't that your partner and sensei who tried to board my ship seeking a job as your fellow crew man? He's not very good if he hasn't realized he was bit old to play that part, perhaps."

The woman leaned forward in her seat, "My Sensei Hapusai was the best ninja master in Yokito. He was disgraced and banished as a ronin ninja because you poisoned his warlord and master Togusawa."

Tears of frustration and defeat were forming in her eyes. She looked around the room at our calm faces, and understood then the futility of her mission. On the Isle of Death Thomas the Poisoner was obviously fully in control.

Thomas gave her his smile again, "You're not to blame for having your sensei poorly prepare you for this mission. He simply only taught you to fight and use fancy toys. His failure was in not teaching you the basics. It comes from many years of study that your sensei in his haste to revenge Togusawa forgot to provide you. That was his mistake as well. In his haste for revenge he has only made you into a disposable weapon. You have to understand that a proper assassin is no simple weapon. They are a well rounded full being."

I noticed Thomas was looking at Lirae as he said this last part. It was clear that she caught some implication he was trying to impart to her as well as our guest.

Thomas lightened his tone and smiled in a fatherly manner, "Now cheer up some lass. What's done is done as they say. I will forgive you the loss of my shirt and jacket if you forgive yourself for the failures of your sensei. I recommend you perhaps start fresh tomorrow with learning some cooking with our cook Hardtack there. In spite of his misleading name he's rather talented at it."

The woman seemed to brighten up a small bit yet still slightly confused, "The dwarf is just your cook?"

Thomas nodded his head, "That's his job here, though he has a hobby of learning every fighting style ever used by humanoids. How many are you up to now Hardtack?"

Hardtack answered, "I know forty-eight different unarmed styles, twenty-three improvisational styles, and let's see. If my count hasn't gotten off I believe I have mastered three hundred fifty-six different weapon types and variant styles. Though I have quite a few I am still trying to master, and there are probably numerous styles I haven't even discovered yet."

The woman dropped her mouth wide open at hearing this. I was a bit surprised myself though I was careful not to show it. I knew Hardtack was very good, I just hadn't understood how well versed he was until now. It was becoming clear to her just what kind of lion's den this was in which her master had sent her off to die.

She hesitantly spoke up to Hardtack, "You're not the top assassin here, the number one killer?"

Hardtack laughed, "I haven't killed anyone in over two hundred and fifty years. I lost the stomach for it long ago. I've kept an interest in mastering combat though. Just to keep a hand in as it were I guess. But just as Master Thomas already said, my main job here is cook."

She looked over at Lirae next, "And are you an assassin here?"

Lirae smiled nicely at her, "I'm just a junior associate. My main work here is cultural and language instruction at the moment. I specialize in the elfish nations."

The woman looked next at me, "You must be the lead killer here then? What about you who move so fast and sure?"

I kept a stern face, "I'm a rank novice here at best. I'm just the most recent recruit to join. I've never killed anyone in my entire life."

She looked depressed again as she spoke, "I was thwarted by a mere novice without a single kill to his name?"

I noticed Thomas give me a slight nod and I replied to her softening my expression a little, "I did have a lot of help you understand."

Thomas chimed in at that moment, "If it makes you feel any better these pupils of mine are being instructed by arguably the most notorious assassin in the known kingdoms. I have exceedingly high standards of performance, thus even highly skilled individuals such as these are not fully up to my measure of excellence yet. If you must know I have consigned one hundred fifty six thousand five hundred forty-two spirits to their final resting place. This was all professionally done in the service of justice mind you. None of this sloppy business is tolerated on my watch under my name."

A look of disbelief formed on her face first. Then it dawned on her that Thomas was not joking or kidding in the least with his statement. He meant it as a cold hard fact. I understood it to be meant that way as well, but I had heard of the reputation of Thomas the Poisoner as legend since way back in my childhood.

It seemed to truly register that her sensei had literally used her to test if a trap was present. She was just a disposable weapon indeed. She obviously didn't stand a shadow of a chance if her sensei was remotely aware of Thomas' reputation. Since he didn't bother to tell her how dangerous it really was she probably assumed he was either a fool or a heartless bastard. I figured he was probably both.

Thomas turned for the door, then turned back to make another comment, "If it matters to you at all Lord Togusawa was a brutal hateful man. This so called Lord killed his own wife and newborn daughter in a fit of anger because she failed to bear him a son. I personally assassinated him because their immortal spirits cried out for justice. I'm sorry your sensei lost his job over the affair. That was never my intent. It should have been very clear to anyone who grasps my reputation that he couldn't have ever stopped me from succeeding in bringing justice for those two. However, I will not allow his meddling in my business while seeking his foolish revenge. It was over twenty two years ago, he should have simply left it alone."

Thomas pointed to Hardtack and then me, "Let us go and finish our earlier conversation. Lirae if you would kindly mind the needs of our guest for the evening."

Lirae nodded her head in reply. We walked out of the female's quarters in silence. I noticed that Balinac didn't seem to mind my walking near him on Master Thomas' right side anymore. I could see Lirae glance out the window with a look of concern in our direction as we departed.

Chapter 6 Good News, Bad News, Odd Tale

Thomas eventually spoke up as we got out of hearing range of the building, "Well played all. I think we're pretty far along in bringing her over. Give me five years with that girl and she will be quite a talented catch. Her sensei is quite good obviously, but it is a shame he didn't use her as the valuable asset she can become."

I looked at him in little bit of surprise, "You are complimenting her master now?"

Thomas smiled at me, "Of course I am. He is a clever strategic operator. He obviously never intended for her to be sent here alone. My trap sprung too quickly for him to adjust his plans is all. My trap separated the two of them leaving her without proper guidance. He must be pretty frustrated to have my standard procedures trip him up."

I asked, "What procedure is that?"

Thomas smiled, "A simple one really. I'm the owner of the ship which comes here, and Captain Roberts is one of us as it were. The crew is all hired from locals on the continent, and as a general rule they are all thoroughly vetted before being hired. However, I always have Captain Roberts leave one junior crew position unfilled. Every time one of the teams is followed back to port and makes to board the ship, if any other people ask for passage they are denied by saying the guest cabin is full. They are given a chance to volunteer for the one remaining crew position though. Honest passengers and cautious investigators almost always skip the offer to join the crew. The assassins though usually take the bait, breaking up any team they may be working with in the process. It is a simple procedure really, but regular procedures often defeat elaborate planning."

I replied, "That's very clever."

Thomas smiled, "Thank you. It works pretty well in most cases. It also gives me a chance to evaluate new talent or dispose of the ideologically driven as necessary. If given an alternative of multiple assassins looking for passage, then Captain Roberts will pick the youngest for his crew while telling the rest to look for a position on another ship. Those usually turn out to be the easiest to poison."

I gave him a confused look, "You want to poison the youngest? Why is that?"

Thomas gave me a thoughtful look, "I witnessed you participating in our poisoning session tonight. Think carefully about it. Not all poison is meant to kill, and some poison hurts, but it can cure as well. The important thing is to be careful about the dose. You should also know that not all poison is physical in nature."

As I listened to his explanation it occurred to me what he meant, "You're talking about words, poisoning people with words."

Thomas bowed, "It is my specialty. Although most people on the outside never realize until it is too late. I've slain many more people through the proper application of words than I've ever killed by lifting my hand. I've also cured some people of ideological blindness, and wanton hatred. Lirae is sort of a project of that nature. I will eventually grant her the pursuit of justice, but I will only do so after she stops searching for revenge as well."

I contemplated what he was saying, "Why not grant her revenge as well as justice?"

Thomas looked at me, "Is revenge what you seek, or is it to right the wrongful death through justice?"

I looked back at him, "Justice, but I think you know that already don't you? I don't seek anyone's wanton death."

Thomas smiled as he looked forward again, "That's why I like you so. You are more concerned that the right thing be done for those who are wronged than in seeking vengeance. Your parents and older brothers did well in bringing you up."

I looked at Thomas in a different light than before. I could see that he was likely a father figure to many here on his island. However to me he was more of a mentor. I already had a father who raised me, and I really didn't need another. I did need someone who could help me become more than I could ever have become before.

Thomas spoke up again, "It's a shame really that Hapusai planned and waited twenty two years training a child for vengeance that he rescued from his Lord's own rage."

I wondered at this reversal in the conversation, "What do you mean about our guest? Was she another child also hated by Lord Togusawa for some reason?"

Thomas looked thoughtful, "She is Lord Togusawa's outcast daughter of course. I knew it the moment I saw her slipping off the ship before it departed the island. She has her mother's countenance. Although I'm pretty sure she was never told so by Hapusai. It is very likely that Hapusai raised her as his own daughter in a way. I had thought her dead along with her mother until now, but obviously Hapusai failed to carry out his Lord's orders in disposing of her."

I began to feel a touch of pity for our guest for the first time. She was raised to kill for vengeance the man who killed her father for justice. The same father had ordered her death simply because she was not a male. It didn't make sense to me why people would do such things.

I spoke up again, "Do you feel you brought justice to her mother Thomas?"

Thomas smiled a sad wistful smile, "Most certainly. I know her spirit is at rest now. I talked to that so called Lord Togusawa, and I convinced him to drink down the poison I'd handed him. At the end he felt remorse for his actions, and he atoned for his wrong deeds. All are finally judged by the White Raven."

I felt uncomfortable at the mention of the name of the death goddess and tried to change the topic. I remembered we were walking to the warehouse for some unmentioned reason.

I spoke up, "Thomas what did you want to discuss early this evening before all the excitement. Something about bad news and rule number five."

Thomas seemed to come back to the present and held up his closed fist again, "Yes rule number five. You may not even allow death to stop you. Well let's go into the warehouse and I'll show you what that means."

We approached the warehouse door again. However, this time we safely entered without incident. Hardtack looked a bit grim as he lit the lantern hanging just inside the door. Thomas led me over to the larger side office for our warehouse. Just past the door inside I could see a table with three decayed bodies obviously dug up from once damp ground. Most of the flesh was removed and mainly just the skeletal remains and the more durable accouterments were intact.

I was obviously expected to examine each body, so I started by looking at the first. It was a shorter fellow perhaps; the bits of remaining gear suggested a man. I was a little confused about this first corpse it seemed like it should have been familiar for some reason yet I couldn't place why.

I turned to Thomas and asked, "Why are these here? Where did you get them from?"

Thomas looked at me with a cautious look in his eye, "After Hiram and Jack finished their last mission I sent them on a side journey to the Kingdom of Ard. They followed my description of your tale, and found the place where you mentioned you had been ambushed. A little bit of examination led them to the shallow unmarked graves there by the stream. At my request they brought back the remains you see before you."

Hearing this I quickly looked past the first set of remains to the second. Turning the skull I could see where a dagger had entered the back of the skull and into the brain. The staff next to the body with a crystal head confirmed my fears. These were Firanda Zarcha's remains. I looked back at the first set of remains and it sunk in that this must be Larwick.

Then I puzzled about the third set of remains. They had been the only two killed. Why was there a third body present? Perhaps someone else who was ambushed and buried there as well? A sinking feeling entered my gut as I realized that the third body had a nick on the lower rib and spine on the left side from a sword strike. I could also see a fracture on the skull where the head was struck in the temple. Finally I noticed the cut on the ribs where a saber must have been stabbed into the heart. This was most likely the fatal blow.

The sinking feeling continued to get worse as I looked at the gear and recognized the decaying remains of my sword sheath, my boots, and the belt buckle that my father had given me for my twentieth birthday. My decaying body lay on the table before my eyes. I took a step back, followed by another. I started to drop down onto the floor, and Hardtack was there to guide my fall.

Thomas spoke up at this point with a grim look on his face, "Rule five. Even death may not stop you. Death hasn't stopped you. You came to me seeking justice in the land of shadow, before the valley of death, and I judged the merit of your case. I have consigned one hundred fifty six thousand five hundred forty two spirits to their final resting place. Your spirit was one of the very few held back from its final destination for now. As are all the spirits which work for me."

I sat on the floor in shock, "I'm dead. I'm truly dead."

Thomas nodded and spoke, "Your original body is dead, and lies on the table before you. Your spirit is everlasting as far as I can tell, at least in this existence. I have been granted dispensation by the White Raven to suspend the passing on of a few spirits seeking justice. That dispensation was a singular event mind you, so don't take it lightly. I am very careful who I choose to work with me. I do however try to seek justice for as many of the other spirits passing on as I possibly can."

I tried to gain my composure back in light of this news. I couldn't fully grasp the meaning, but the dream where I first met Thomas was starting to strike me as no kind of dream at all. I relaxed as best I could, and stood up again with a hand from Hardtack.

I looked at Thomas, "Everyone else here on the Isle of Death is dead as well?"

Thomas shook his head, "Most have died at least once, and been provided new forms. However, a couple of special exceptions exist. Hardtack there has never died and is an old friend of mine. Balinac is as you may have surmised not a natural creature and is quite certainly immune to the very concept of death. Lord Togusawa's daughter is still alive as our guest. Pretty much everyone else on this Island has died at least once. Some have passed on multiple times."

I thought about what Thomas was telling me and tried to make it work in my brain. I looked him in the eye and thought about how he had taken the strike from the blade coated in deadly poison to his heart earlier this evening.

I asked the question suspecting the answer already but needing to hear it from his lips, "How about you Thomas? Are you alive or dead?"

Thomas gave a coy smile, "Someone had to negotiate the deal with the White Raven to make this all work. I was just back renewing my contract for my eighth lifetime this very evening in fact. So far the White Raven has been pleased with the quality of my work I would guess. Personally I can never really tell what those gods and goddess are thinking. They are well beyond my reckoning."

I thought about it, "So you have been killed eight times then?"

Thomas shook his head, "No, just the one time. Self administered poison you see. I wanted to check out what was happening on the other side. I somehow got an audience with the White Raven that first time, and she granted me the contract for my current job. The eight lifetimes are sort of like one hundred year contracts with an option for both of the parties to renew. Even though it is very legalistic over in the White Raven's kingdom, a smart bargainer can make a good deal at times."

I asked my next question, "You're saying you're eight hundred years old?"

Thomas laughed, "Hardly. I've only been around for about seven hundred and fifty years. Since I was close by anyway this evening I renewed my next lease early."

I shook my head, "You must be the oldest human around."

Thomas shook his head again, "This is getting beyond the scope of our original conversation now. To answer your final question for the evening I am not even the oldest human I've ever met. That record as it were would belong to a fisherman called Cricket who I believe has got me beat by at least one thousand years or so. Nice fellow and a fine mentor. The scary thing is he doesn't have a contract with any of the deities as far as I know. It means much less paperwork for him, lucky fellow. Although I'll give you a word of warning, if you ever meet him never push the Luck. It was quite likely the scariest experience of my life. Balinac still cowers in fear any time Cricket visits."

I thought he was joking about this last part. Then looking at Balinac I could see it its fur was raised on its hackles. The mere mention of the Luck and this Cricket person had set it on edge.

I asked one more question, "Why is Balinac so afraid of this person?"

Thomas waved me off, "I must return home as I have a lot of work to do and this evening has already gone on longer than originally planned. Ask Hardtack for the explanation."

I watched as Thomas left the room, and looked to Hardtack for an answer. He pointed to the door. We left the warehouse and headed toward the male's quarters.

We walked and Hardtack asked a question of his own, "Have you ever heard of the spirit shamans?"

I shook my head, and Hardtack continued, "Well they are kind of like the god priests in a way, but not really. Instead of gods they court the attention of natural spirits you see."

I nodded my head at the explanation, "A medium you mean."

Hardtack shook his head, "The same rough concept perhaps, but most Spirit Shamans generally interact with the natural world, not the spirits of the dead. A few rare ones like Thomas can see the spirits of the dead much clearer than the natural spirits. Most shamans have a totem spirit from the natural world at their command. Have you got all that?"

I nodded my head and added, "So Balinac is Thomas' spirit totem then?"

Hardtack smiled and nodded his head, "You catch on quick lad. Except Balinac is not a natural spirit if you understand me. It is definitely an unnatural spirit that the few remaining spirit masters would normally steer clear of since they are considered extremely dangerous."

I nodded my head, and began to have very healthy dose of respect for Thomas' seemingly limitless bravery.

I asked another question, "How rare is this?"

Hardtack shrugged his shoulders, "In three hundred and fifty some years I've met a few dozen spirit shamans in my life. Only two or three of those could work with dead spirits at all. Only one ever attempted to make an unnatural spirit his totem spirit."

I made an educated guess, "You mean Thomas then?"

Hardtack nodded the affirmative, "Yes, Thomas and Balinac."

I asked, "How about this fisherman Cricket you mentioned?"

Hardtack shrugged his shoulders, "He is unique. One of a kind I would say. No record exists to explain what happened to make him what he is. He might well be the oldest human in the entire world, possibly older than any currently living elf even. Vague hints and rumors about his presence go back for over a thousand years before Master Thomas' birth."

I was a bit confused, "So he's an immortal then?"

Hardtack shrugged his shoulders again, "It's hard to tell. He's generally very shy and extremely hard to locate. Even the stories about him tend to be minor footnotes in the stories of other famous people who claimed to have met him and had their lives changed."

As we approached the male's quarters I spoke up again, "I understand so this Cricket fellow is very mysterious and I presume a spirit shaman of some kind as well, correct?"

Hardtack carefully thought a moment about my question, "In some ways it might be more accurate to say that Cricket isn't a spirit shaman actually. It's probably more accurate to say that Cricket is the spirit shaman. It is believed by some that he is the very core from which the other spirit shamans draw their abilities."

Hardtack took a breath and continued, "The spirit shamans I've talked with say that no natural spirit will disobey him, not even the totem spirits of other spirit shamans. I think it's possible that he's somehow linked to every spirit shaman currently in this existence and maybe in those strange existences beyond. Don't mention I said this, but I think Cricket scares both Balinac and Thomas tremendously. Thomas glibly talks about his deal with the White Raven for those in his inner group. Understand I say this knowing that the goddess of death herself does not bother Thomas."

I held my breath as I heard this admission, "Why do you think they are so scared of this Cricket person?"

Hardtack whispered, "The Luck."

I was confused again, "I don't understand."

Hardtack continued, "It is . . . an unnatural presence never intended by the gods to exist here it is rumored. I saw it once and I nearly had my heart fail merely by being on this same island here with it."

I held on breathless, "What happened?"

Hardtack walked into my room and sat in one chair as I sat down in the other. He looked around nervously.

Hardtack continued as if he was afraid he might accidentally summon this strange power with his tale, "Well I told you how Balinac is Thomas' totem spirit. Well the way I hear it Cricket had warned him against trying such a thing. Thomas attempted it anyway knowing from his research that such things had been conjured and controlled in the past. After the summoning it turned out that Balinac in its nine foot tall full presence was terrorizing the island."

I nodded my head as he continued, "Thomas himself was safe, but everyone else was in dire peril of this rampage. Thomas gets a boat out safely with a message for Cricket asking him to help. When the next boat arrived this humble looking middle aged fisherman comes out carrying his fishing pole. It was the first time I had met the fellow, but he was dressed like a poor peasant. He walks up to Thomas' home, and I presume they had some kind of harsh words with each other because Thomas comes out later looking like he'd eaten something sour. This Cricket comes out looking as calm and dull as when he entered."

I interrupted his story briefly for a clarification, "Just how long ago was this?"

Hardtack apparently thought back a moment, "I would say approximately two hundred and fifty years. Getting back to what happened you know that mountain at the southern end of the island?"

I thought a moment and asked, "You mean that small volcano?"

Hardtack shook his head, "That's not a volcano. It's a mountain. Trust me on this I'm a dwarf and we know our stone. Anyway, on top of this mountain was where Balinac was resting between his periodic rampages. This Cricket goes walking over there with Thomas and me following behind even though I would have rather not been there at the time."

Hardtack began to get into the story making gestures to emphasize his words and action.

He continued, "Well, I was a pretty cocky fellow back then though so I stuck in with Thomas as we climbed the slopes. As we neared the top of this mountain Balinac comes charging out in his nine foot tall furry at this Cricket fellow. Cricket just stands there doing nothing and looking at Balinac like it is some kind of minor curiosity."

Hardtack mimed tilting his head to the side, "Well, Balinac is confused for a few seconds that this fisherman doesn't react negatively in his presence. Then letting go of one of his loud howls begins to launch himself at this poor peasant fisherman. I figure he's going to be swallowed in two bites, and that I would be next if I didn't stick close to Thomas."

I was enraptured and couldn't stop listening. I sat there looking at Hardtack sitting there in the chair and noticed that he seemed as excited telling the story now as if he was living it then. Hardtack wiped his brow on his sleeve as he began the final part of his story.

Hardtack talked with a slight tremor in his voice, "Then the most insane thing I have ever witnessed in my life happened. This short by human standards little fisherman just says in a calm mild voice, 'Luck release.' In the next split second there was no fisherman there anymore. Instead there was this gigantic orange and black striped furry leg stretching up into the sky."

Hardtack tilted his had back and continued, "I looked up and up until I began to grasp that I was standing relatively directly underneath an enormously giant tiger. This thing was at least ninety feet tall at the shoulder and around thee hundred feet long with seven sixty feet long tails whipping through the sky creating hurricane winds. The very trees were falling over in the wind, and just as I looked down and tried to find a place to cower in fear I saw Balinac collide with the leg of this titanic monstrosity."

I saw that Hardtack was hunkered down in his chair at this point as he gulped and continued, "Then the second most insane thing I'd ever seen in my life happened. This huge dragon sized tiger looks down at its leg where Balinac collided with it and growls. It then faster than thought sweeps its paw high into the sky and roars out 'Behave Yourself' in a voice that shakes the entire island."

Hardtack grins widely at the next part, "That paw then comes sweeping down faster than thought again out of the sky over our very heads and knocks Balinac and the entire top of the mountain we were standing on at least one mile away into the ocean."

I then saw Hardtack's grin disappear as he told the next part, "Then the most frightening thing I've ever seen in my life happened. This unnatural being bends its head down and in a menacing low voice says, 'Thomas I highly recommend you don t push me again. Deal with your own problems from here on out. Cricket is too nice for saving you again. It would serve you well to remember in the future that I am not even remotely nice.' Thomas was more shaken than I'd ever seen him before. Being there I could understand his sentiment."

Hardtack then sat back in his chair as he finished, "This horror then says 'Cricket release' and our humble little fisherman is standing there again as the thing dissipates like some kind of bad dream.

Hardtack began to grin again, "Then I hear the strangest statement I'd ever heard in my life. This little mild mannered fellow looks at us and sees our expressions. Then he says, 'I'm terribly sorry. Was the Luck rude again?' I burst out laughing on the spot from the sheer terror and craziness of it all."

I thought hard about this odd tale more fantastic than any I'd ever heard. I wouldn't have believed it in my previous life, but here I was reincarnated as an elf so I figured who was I to be the judge of how accurate it was.

I let Hardtack relax a bit and then asked another question, "So I take it Balinac returned?"

Hardtack laughed, "The next day small as a tabby, wet with sea water, and holding both tails between its legs. It doesn't like to remember that day I think, but it hasn't managed to forget it."

I asked, "So what is the Luck then? Is it Cricket's totem spirit?"

Hardtack shook his head, "None of the spirit shaman's I've spoken with ever felt that was the case. They each have a variation on a theory though. Mostly it relates to a forbidden and forgotten spell casting that combines a spirit shaman with a powerful unnatural beast."

Hardtack sat back in contemplation, "If it was ever practiced more than the one time in the past, then it is certainly not ever attempted now. The only example of it is the Luck and Cricket. No one is crazy enough to try that ever again. Frankly speaking that Cricket is a pleasant enough mild mannered fellow, but no one who has ever encountered the Luck wants to do so a second time. Beyond being imposing and threatening which I can attest to from first hand experience, the tales say it knows things that were not meant to ever be known in this existence"

Chapter 7 New Style

I sat there in my chair a while after Hardtack had departed for the evening. I thought it an interesting tale to say the least. However, I suspected that parts of the story had been left out or changed for some reason. Perhaps it was because Hardtack didn't know the whole story, and perhaps it was because he was told to change parts of the tale.

As I got up from my chair to begin preparing for bed I heard a strange quiet knock at my door. I opened it to see Balinac standing there in its normal cat size. I stepped back from the door and Balinac came into my room. Next it jumped up onto my bed and curled up on the sheets. I closed the door.

I thought this a strange behavior as Balinac was normally said to stick with Thomas pretty much all of the time, but I figured that it was possible that Thomas had sent it to me for some mysterious reason. I finished changing into my night clothes and lay down on the bed next to Balinac.

I did not expect that Balinac would stand up as I lay down, and walk over placing its head next to my ear.

Then I was surprised when Balinac softly spoke into my ear, "It serves my interest that most people think of me as some kind of ignorant beast. However, Thomas knows better even if the rest do not."

I quietly whispered back, "Then what are you?"

Balinac replied, "For now I am the guardian of this island and the island's primary inhabitant. However, I was not summoned by Thomas. I was provided to him by other powers."

I asked, "Why were you given to him?"

Balinac purred then replied, "I am uniquely able to simultaneously monitor his activities both here on your world, and at his home in the land of shadow. I would like you to know I was not the one chastised by the Luck as you heard in Hardtack's story. Thomas was among those being chastised. The mountain on the island is simply worn down by the weather. The Luck is the being who sent me here. Thomas unfortunately attempted to reject my presence overseeing his assigned task."

I was a bit confused, "I don't quite understand. What does the Luck want with Thomas?"

Balinac purred again, "The Luck wants Thomas to serve out his contract as agreed. This contract Thomas has with the White Raven was not put in place by him. It was negotiated by Cricket and the Luck with the White Raven to save Thomas from his own pursuits. It keeps Thomas occupied and out of the business of other powers being disturbed by the direction his pursuits were taking. I was added to the deal later to insure compliance after a few of these powers thought that Thomas was breaking faith with his contract. In simple terms I am an enforcer."

I then asked, "What does this have to do with me?"

Balinac nuzzled my ear and asked his own question, "Why is your human spirit in the body of an elf? Such a thing can normally only be accomplished by the power of a god or goddess. The powers are interested in how Thomas managed to pull off this same feat. It has ramifications well beyond your world."

I nodded and asked, "What is it that I am expected to do?"

Balinac lifted his head, "I haven't been told that yet. I expect that you should continue to work as Thomas directs. You will get your justice in time, and Thomas will presumably ask you to stay on after you do. Whether you do or not is your choice. You will be a free agent then, your debt for services rendered paid as far as Thomas' contract is concerned. However, some of the powers that be think that Thomas has bigger plans. These plans may include you."

Balinac walked away from my ear and I softly called out, "What is the Luck and Cricket?"

Balinac turned back, "Something that should never have happened. The Lucky Cricket is a single being with both a mortal's spirit and an immortal's spirit. You might say they are now the demigod of the spirit shamans on this world. Even though the spirit shamans do not worship the gods, they still must instinctively recognize the Lucky Cricket as something beyond them. They don't worship the Lucky Cricket as divine, but they all acknowledge him as The Spirit Shaman. Such a thing has never happened in the past, and some powers think it should never happen again in the future."

It occurred to me that Balinac was holding back, "Do you fear them as Hardtack says?"

Balinac switched its tails back and forth and it looked at me curiously, "I must acknowledge them as my superior. I do not willfully disobey our mutual agreement. Let me just say that my kind does not normally enjoy that feeling. My kind acknowledges rightful supremacy. Number Seven certainly has supremacy over Number Two, but the mortal spirit combined with the immortal spirit is just not accepted by the rest of my kind. It hasn't been successfully done before them, and my kind thinks it should not be done again if the other tailed spirits have any say in the matter."

Balinac jumped out of my bed and changed size until it was large enough to lift the latch on my door with its mouth. It entered the hall silently closing the door behind as it departed.

The next morning I awoke early and began my usual run around the island. I took a trip to the slopes of the southern mountain and looking around could not see a volcano caldera or on closer inspection any sign of action which changed the mountain by anything more than normal erosion. I ran back down the slopes. I then headed to the Dining Hall to have my breakfast and morning instruction with Lirae.

I found Lirae at our usual table with her elfish scrolls waiting for me. I sat down next to her and gave her a smile.

She looked back at me with a worried expression, "I saw you departing with Master Thomas last night. What did you talk about?"

I gave her a more reassuring smile, "Thomas let me know about what had happened to me."

She looked sad, "So you now know that you are one who has not passed on as intended. Most of us here are the same. It is a very sad thing which has happened to us."

I nodded, "I saw what was left of my body last night. It was an unreal feeling. I found it disturbing to contemplate."

She nodded her head, "I was thankfully spared that horror. My body was turned to ash along with my husband and daughter. They wanted it to look like humans had burned us in our home in order to cause hateful sentiment among the elves against the humans."

The two of us sat there in glum silence for a while, each wrapped up in the thoughts of our own earlier demise. I noticed a change in the dining hall this morning. Instead of one of the island regulars taking turns as a waiter, I noticed our new guest coming out of the kitchen carrying our breakfast with her good arm. Her other arm remained in a sling, and it was clear that it pained her still. She stopped by a couple of other tables first, and then she came by with our food.

Lirae smiled at her, "It is good to see you have accepted Master Thomas' advice to find something useful to do Yuki."

Yuki gave a slight upturn of her lips, "Your cook Hardtack said he would instruct me in combat when my wounds healed. As a condition of his training he said I was to become his kitchen helper."

I nodded at her and returned her faint smile in kind, "It will be good to have a fellow student in our instruction sessions."

Yuki looked at me and an odd expression crossed her face along with a touch of a flush. She politely bowed in my direction and rapidly moved off back to the kitchen.

I shook my head after Yuki left the room, "I don't think I'll understand that woman."

Lirae had a mischievous grin after my remark, "You may not understand it, but you should know that your elfish body is very handsome even by elfish standards. I know quite well that most humans tend to find even average looking elves to be physically attractive. If I had to guess, then I would say that our young charge there is conflicted between wanting to prove her martial prowess to you, and wanting to kiss you."

I looked at Lirae. Even though I felt like Lirae was more of an older sister to me, I could not deny that she was a very attractive female. Yuki on the other hand was exotic looking for a human, but much more like an intelligent yet shy boy in mannerism and composure. I must have had a skeptical look on my face.

Lirae continued, "Doubt it if your will, but if you don't handle her carefully she will likely develop a crush on you. She asked about you after you left last night.

I have a feeling that she's been isolated from the company of males except for her sensei her whole life and is quite naïve about relations."

I shook my head, "I guess that makes two of us. I've only ever worked with women. I've never . . . been intimate."

Lirae gave a brief light laugh, "Just how young were you when you joined us?"

I began to feel as if I were under a strange pressure, "I was recently turned twenty four, and there was someone with whom I was interested in becoming involved. I just didn't get the opportunity to make it work out before we were both killed."

Lirae looked sad again, "I'm sorry to hear that, and if I have hurt your feelings. I understand what it is like to lose someone close. How much worse it must be if you had not a chance to consummate a relationship together."

We ate our morning meal in silence skipping our usual lesson to deal with our thoughts. I thought about the interaction between Lirae and me over the past couple of months. While most of our time was spent as instructor and student, in terms of our personal interaction and my feelings she seemed much like an older sister to me.

Because of our conversation, I began to see Lirae in a different light. I began to realize that she didn't always look on me as a student or a younger brother even. I was slowly becoming the replacement for her lost child in her mind. I was someone for her to bring up in the elfish traditions while acknowledging my human heritage.

I then realized that my becoming an elf was perhaps something that Thomas was using on many levels. I was part of some larger plan perhaps, but in the short term I was a surrogate child to give Lirae a chance to be the mother she had desired to be. I thought it likely that Thomas was aware of this reaction, and counting on it to lessen her drive for revenge.

On realizing this I raised my respect for Thomas another notch. He was not just good at his job of killing people. It was becoming clear that he was a master at the subtle manipulation of those around him. He created bonds where none existed before. He created loyalty in newcomers like myself to those people already loyal to him, and by extension loyalty to himself. His assignments matched people best suited to work together and form bonds.

Thomas saw what weaknesses people had, and provided them a means of shoring up those weaknesses. I thought about how Yuki worked in that picture. I wasn't particularly compelled to like her, but at the same time I didn't find her objectionable either. Yuki was just a mystery to me at this point.

Then I thought about how I lost any chance with Firanda when she died. Firanda was brash and bold. She had a skilled mind and she would have become a future leader in her profession had she lived. In many ways Firanda was already the person I secretly wanted to become. I realized then that was a big reason why I had been interested in getting to know Firanda on a personal level.

Then it struck me that Lirae and I had missed the mark with Yuki. She didn't have a crush on me just because I was physically attractive as Lirae had suggested. I was to Yuki like Firanda was to me. The one we desire because they represent the person we secretly want to become.

I looked at Yuki as she left the kitchen carrying breakfast to another table. I caught her subtle glance in my direction. I gave a casual nod in return and noted her shyly look away from me with a slight flush on her cheeks again. I saw a lot that suddenly reminded me of my former self in that behavior. I was concerned about what this might mean for her. I didn't particularly relish the thought of breaking her heart.

I gained a subtle appreciation for Firanda as well. This must have been a taste of what it was like for her to work with me. Firanda had stuck it through with grace and wit without ever giving me any opening to broach the topic of a relationship outside of our work.

My internal perspective changed at that point. It took the situation being reversed before I could understand and appreciate the kindness Firanda had exhibited toward me. I realized now that she had spared my feelings without giving me any chance to hurt myself by acting like a fool and being rejected. It was a high benchmark she had set. It looked like I would need to follow her example, and possibly obtain some advice on how to manage the situation to keep it from getting out of control.

My morning combat session began after Hardtack had finished in the kitchen. We traveled out to the commons green of the community, and this time Hardtack had brought along a pair of exotically shaped wooden swords. They were not much different in form from a saber, but the handles were longer and suitable for a two handed grip. He also brought along a set of quilted and padded hauberks. To top it off he carried a set of full light helms with face guards backed by wire mesh.

Hardtack had also brought along an observer. Yuki was in tow as he approached with her good hand empty of any gear. Hardtack pointed her to wait on a section of lawn where she stood quietly watching us. We donned our hauberks, and I experimentally picked up and swung one of the wooden sparing weapons. The weapon's heft was a little off for one handed use, but when I switched to a two handed grip I noticed that it came into balance quite nicely.

I looked at Hardtack as he picked up his own wooden sword and grasped it while entering a wide braced couched stance with one foot to the side and rear and the other foot bracing up front and directly ahead.

I asked the question, "So we are learning something new today?"

Hardtack nodded as he began to limber up, "In honor of our new trainee we are going to be working with a style familiar in the part of the world where she was born. It is a style used by the knights of her lands. I don't have any of their armor in stock, but I do have some of their swords and practice swords."

I nodded in affirmation, "By your stance this is a charging style then?"

Hardtack smiled, "Good eye. Yes it does involve charging, but there is generally no slashing, no stabbing, and no hacking on meeting. This style is closer to the saber and is used with a drawing slicing cut from a blade normally as sharp as the sharpest of knives."

I looked at him curiously, "Their armor is not metal?"

Hardtack shook his head, "Light wood similar to the bamboo you see here. It is treated with a resin called lacquer and fastened with ties of the strongest silks."

I nodded, "I get the general idea. Shall we try some low speed runs until I get the basics of the form?"

Hardtack nodded affirmation and picked up his light helm. I placed mine on my head, and adopted my variation on the stance taken by Hardtack. I tried as best I could to emulate his sword position, and signaled ready with a sharp nod of my head. Hardtack returned the signal.

We stood there a moment until Hardtack bellowed out a sharp cry and slowly paced forward in a variation on a sword wielder's charge. I watched his footwork for a few paces, and begun my own charge emulating his method until I got the basic rhythm of it. Then I watched the positioning of his blade and moved mine to what I would consider an appropriate counter position. As we closed and clashed I struck his blade a sound blow edge to edge while avoiding his slow speed strike.

Hardtack held up one hand in a stopping gesture, and we removed out masks.

Hardtack spoke with a smile on his face, "That's pretty good with the footwork on the first run, but you have to realize that I have to adapt it a bit due to my stature. If you are going up against a human or elf sized opponent, then you won't want to be crouched so deeply at full speed.

Hardtack scowled a little bit next, "However, here is a word of caution. The real swords are very sharp like I said. It is considered bad form to bang them together edge on edge like that. It notches up the blades something fierce and ruins a quality weapon in no time. If you want to deflect the opponent's blade then your weapon's side to the opponent's weapon's side is used for that purpose. It keeps the edge intact that way. Don't present the side of your weapon to his edge though. These blades in the hands of a master have been known to cut through the opponent's steel."

We ran through a few more slow speed runs until I had a chance to witness most of the basic attack maneuvers. I began to see how the blade was used in a charging drawing strike. The opponents didn't run directly into each other, but instead would run just off to the side of each other as they attempted to slice the opposite number while moving past. It was essentially a dismounted variation on what I knew as a horseback sword charge.

I was feeling warmed up and called out normal speed to Hardtack. He nodded affirmation and we launched at each other with him giving out a sharp cry, and me in deadly soft footed silence. I felt his blade graze the side of my armor as my stroke missed. What surprised me was as we stopped I heard something I hadn't expected.

Yuki called out from her observation spot on the field, "Point Sensei Hardtack with a non-fatal strike to Sensei Mica."

I glanced over at Yuki and could see that she was deeply interested in what we were doing. Her guarded personal barrier was dropped as she became intellectually involved in our activities. It struck me this might be the first time she had ever witnessed combat training from the outside position of an observer or judge. It also occurred to me that she already understood the intricacies of this particular form.

I caught Hardtack's eye and he gave me a wink not visible from Yuki's position. This change in style had been done for her benefit more than mine. It was to present her with something familiar to help draw her out of her shell. Our recruitment was still happening without her even realizing what we were doing.

I also understood then that Thomas must have picked up on her first subtle hints of being drawn to me. He was placing me in her path as an object of desire. It was becoming clear that Thomas worked on many different levels, and that I was not going to be immune to his subtle manipulations.

We worked at this approach for about an hour with Hardtack graciously leaving me the occasional clean opening so I could learn how to complete a strike with this weapon style. Yuki began to unconsciously grin as she continued to call out the results of each attack run.

I understood now that combat in her culture must be a pretty formalized affair for this style to be effective in battle. I also understood that her training had certainly not emphasized the formalized aspects of combat either. She had demonstrated a lot of improvisational capability last night. I was also not a slouch at improvisational maneuvering thanks to a father who unfortunately had too much practical battle experience. I also had a bit of time learning from Hardtack who had mastered every dirty trick in the book, then wrote several more chapters to that book, and the whole follow up edition.

Now that I had the basics pretty well in hand I figured it was time to have some fun with mixing it up. I held up a hand to halt while removing my mask. Hardtack and I approached and I could see that Yuki looked a bit disappointed that we were stopping already.

Hardtack quietly asked, "What's up lad? You can't be tired out yet?"

I shook my head, "Let's give our guest a small sample of what the two of us look like when we work at full speed, no formal approach. Try not to kill me though."

Hardtack grinned wickedly, "Oh you won't die. You'll just feel like you want to when we are done."

I knew that in any real fight with Hardtack I would be dead within a minute if he wanted. I also knew that he could dole out any level of punishment short of death he deemed appropriate. I hoped today that he was under orders to help make me look good before he brought me down.

We began our running charge as usual, but before meeting I rapidly changed direction into a cross side approach while taking a hard slice at Hardtack's head. Hardtack countered with an almost casual backhanded slash at my legs. I easily jumped over his slash into a flip striking down while upside down in a stabbing motion at the top of his head. Hardtack had already somehow interposed his weapon to block the stab. I landed back to back with him and rapidly stabbed under my own arm only to be blocked again by his sword miraculously in position.

I chose to use my fine crafted speed and reflexes and began using my two handed blade like a rapier as I spun around to face Hardtack. It seemed like my transition caught him off guard as my tactic allowed me to get a couple of good jabs in as he suddenly closed distance with me. I felt a punch hit my padded lower abdomen and I leaped up and back in an attempt to get clear of his hand to hand expertise.

I noticed that Hardtack had somehow managed to obtain some kind of leather strap in his left hand without my seeing from where he had obtained it. He pressed me hard with a series of sword slashes alternating with slashes from his leather strap. I opted to enter a series of rapid backwards handsprings to avoid his strokes. I felt pretty proud of the distance I was making away from Hardtack until on the third spring something wrapped around my ankles and tripped me up.

As I collapsed on the ground I saw Hardtack had stopped and was laughing at me. I looked down and saw that my pants were tangled in my ankles, and that my belt was the object in Hardtack's left hand. As I lay there in my loincloth and hauberk I also realized that Yuki was bent over holding her stomach and laughing hard. I felt embarrassed at my exposure and gave Hardtack a foul look.

As I pulled my pants up and walked over to Hardtack to retrieve my belt I asked in my most disapproving tone, "Did you really have to go so far?"

Hardtack looked at me with a smile on his lips, but a serious look in his eyes, "Yes lad, I did. Look at her. She doesn't feel so bad about her failure anymore for the moment. She realizes that you are not perfect either now. Anyway, turn about is fair play. You got to see her in an embarrassing condition, now she has been able to see you the same way. Besides, your little demonstration was plenty enough to let her see that you could best her in any fair fight between the two of you. You learned in a single morning the basics of a style that takes some people many years to master. She will have certainly noticed that you went from unfamiliar to basically proficient in very short order."

I shrugged even as I put my belt on, and I grew less embarrassed, "I am already proficient with sword work. It was just a matter of picking up some new variations."

Hardtack shook his head, "Don't underestimate your skill lad, you picked up a lot today compared to most students I've had. Maybe even an admirer also."

I looked over at Yuki sitting on the grass and smiling at us still, "That's kind of what I'm afraid is happening."

Chapter 8 First Mission

The next two weeks went by with a change to the rhythm previously established. I still did my exercise sessions alone. However, Hardtack had been correct in that Yuki witnessing my failure had made me seem more approachable to her. Yuki began to initiate conversations with me during our brief rests in our combat practice sessions even though she could not join in with her broken arm still healing.

I continued my elfish studies with Lirae, but she also began to advise me on how to manage Yuki's personal interest in me. I noticed that after two weeks of growing familiarity with each other that Yuki would no longer hesitate in giving me a return smile. Following Lirae's advice I was able to keep Yuki focused on professional issues related to weapons handling and technique. I felt I was lucky that this level of interaction seemed to satisfy her interests and needs for the moment.

I sat down to my most recent morning session with Lirae. I noticed that Lirae didn't have her usual collection of scrolls related to etiquette with her. I could tell that something was bothering her, but waited for her to speak first.

Lirae gave me a hesitant smile, "I guess we need to talk about . . . personal matters again."

I glanced at the kitchen and could see that Yuki was not in the room, "Yuki matters?"

Lirae seemed a touch embarrassed, "Some of that and more I guess. Yuki approached me last night after our study session. She asked me directly whether you and I were lovers."

I flushed a little embarrassed as well, "I hope you told her something . . . convincing. Well that's not it. I guess I hope you told her the truth."

Lirae nodded, "I told her I was your instructor, but she asked if there was more between us. I told her I didn't know. I told her we are friends. I also told her that you were very young by elfish standards, and that I was more than old enough to be your mother."

I saw Lirae became a little misty eyed as she said the last part. What I had suspected had come to pass. I was already like her lost child in her heart, and here she was asking me to be that child. I saw Yuki coming out of the kitchen a couple of moments earlier. I could tell that she was also within hearing distance for the last part of Lirae's statement.

I made a fateful choice, "You are like a mother to me as well. I thank you for all the time and trouble you have spent on my behalf."

I reached over and patted Lirae on the shoulder. Lirae gave me a genuine smile through her forming tears. Out of the corner of my eye I saw that Yuki also formed a slight smile and a little twinkle was in her eye as well. Yuki went over to her destination with a bounce in her step from barely suppressed joy. It was likely that Yuki believed that any possible competition for my affection was not a concern for her any more.

Yuki approached our table with our morning meal and Lirae managed to put on a pleasant smile for her benefit. Yuki served us our food and received our usual thanks. Then she departed again for the kitchen. I shook my head regretfully.

Lirae asked, "Is something wrong?"

I smiled at her in return, "I'm glad we are friends, and I appreciate the care that you show me. It is just that this is not the best timing in the world as far as Yuki is concerned."

Lirae looked at me sadly, "The woman you desired? The woman whose death you still morn?"

My voice shook a little, "The one who was killed before my very eyes, and whose very life was placed in my care. The one for whom I am seeking justice."

Lirae looked at me with a little glint in her eyes, "I understand completely. Let me talk with Yuki tonight and provide her a little perspective."

That evening as I swam before dinner I saw Thomas coming down the trail from his tower on the cliff with Balinac at his side. I headed to the shore and met them on the beach. Balinac seemed indifferent compared to its earlier friendliness, but at least it wasn't hostile. I joined Thomas and walked by his left side.

Thomas spoke with his fatherly voice again, "It is good to see you again Mica. I'm coming down to dinner again this evening to gather with everyone. After dinner I want you to gather up our young guest, and we will all take a leisurely walk up to my home for a little discussion. After which you will escort her back to the female's quarters."

I asked, "Is something going on that I should know about in advance?"

Thomas nodded affirmative, "I am going to be sending you on a little mission. A certain Sensei needs to be discouraged from his current course of action."

I gave him a concerned look, "Do you plan to kill him?"

Thomas shook his head, "I don't plan to kill him. Well truthfully speaking I do have a back up plan to kill him, but that is not my desired outcome. To tell you the absolute truth I always have someone's possible death as a back up contingency if necessary. I would even arrange your death young Mica if I saw no better option to my desired course of action."

I looked hoping to see if he was joking. I didn't see any sign of it.

Thomas looked over at me, "Don't be shocked. Killing is a part of what I must do. It is a necessary function you understand. I don't take pleasure in it, and I do take steps to avoid it whenever possible."

I nodded back at him, "I understand it is a part of your job. Why do you need to deal with Hapusai? Why not just let him wait in frustration until he gives up?"

Thomas sadly shook his head, "The man trained his fallen Lord's daughter to be an instrument of a singular death for twenty two years. I don't think a few weeks of uncertainty have changed his mind about his goals. As a matter of fact if

Hapusai were being paid or ordered to do this job I would have had the departing team eliminate him as an object example to any others who might contemplate such a foolish activity."

I sensed his hesitancy, "Why do you not do so this time then if such is your policy?"

Thomas wistfully looked at the sky, "While I admire the man's loyalty to his former master, it is his capacity to empathize with the fate of a new born girl child which is rare in his culture. Unfortunately, I have heard from my sources that he has tried desperately to arrange passage on my ship again. When they denied him passage, and the other ships at port would not offer to follow Captain Robert's ship at any price he became quite desperate."

I looked a bit confused, "What did he do?"

Thomas looked sad, "The poor man broke down and cried in the street. It seems that he really does love our little Yuki like a daughter. I imagine he was quite stern with her as a child seeing how she has grown up, but it is clear now that he loves her dearly. Once again that is quite remarkable for his culture. They are generally not prone to such displays of emotion, or such close attachments to their female children. It's likely that their Master and Student relationship has a lot to do with it."

I thought back, "So he really didn't intend to send her against you then?"

Thomas shook his head, "Unlikely. They were probably simply following Jack and Hiram as their best lead to finding me. They simply failed to understand in time that this part of the journey is a trap for assassins like them. It is very likely that he is certain of it now. I'll need to convince Hapusai that his adopted daughter and he only live by the grace of his next decisions."

I hesitated, "You plan to kill them if he fails to comply?"

Thomas replied, "Like I said up front, I don't plan to kill anyone at this time. I will however use that contingency if my hand is forced."

We walked in silence for a while then as we approached the dining hall I had a curious question arise, "Why wouldn't any other ship in port follow Captain Robert's ship for any price?"

Thomas smiled, "You have to understand that it is a somewhat less than legitimate port I do business through. Surely even in Ard they have heard rumors about the Dread Pirate Roberts scourge of the southern sea."

I shook my head, "I should have figured that one out. Hasn't he been dead a while though? He would be at least eighty by now."

Thomas continued smiling, "Even more interesting yet he hasn't pirated a single ship in the nearly fifty years he has worked in my service. It's amazing how well a properly supported reputation can do its job. It certainly keeps any other ship captains very wary of pursuing him though. They don't want to become his next victim."

I asked the final question as we approached the door to the dining hall, "How should I follow your lead?"

Thomas smiled, "Look as if I have given you some bad news. It will prepare our guest nicely for our evening together."

I didn't have a problem making a displeased expression work. I began to feel sorry for the trials that Thomas was likely to put Yuki through tonight. As we entered the dining hall the island regulars greeted Thomas with smiles and Balinac with their usual hint of fearful looks. As Yuki came out of the kitchen she stopped and gave Thomas a fearful look of her own, and turned to reenter the kitchen.

Hardtack was coming out and gently grabbed Yuki's elbow. Hardtack turned her around in a somewhat stern fatherly manner, and he led her over to sit on the left of the head of the big table. I took a seat opposite her at the right of the head of the table.

Thomas circulated around the room greeting people, and the others gradually began going to the kitchen to bring out platters of food and sitting in their respective spots. Lirae sat at my side with a concerned look on her face which nicely complimented my displeased look.

Yuki kept her eyes focused on Thomas for a while as he cordially talked with the people around the room. Then she looked at Lirae and me with our obviously unpleasant expressions. I saw the beginning of what I believed to be genuine worry enter her expression.

Yuki looked carefully at Lirae and me, "What is wrong? Has the time for my execution been determined?"

I gave her a tenuous smile, "That's not quite the problem. Master Thomas has asked me to escort you to his home after dinner. Then Master Thomas wants me to escort you to your quarters when he has finished talking with you."

Balinac settled its large head on the table just to the right side of Yuki. She flinched in surprise and fear as it had approached silently from behind to do so. A quick low growl acted as a reminder to behave. Everyone at the table showed an obvious look of fear besides me who just kept my displeased expression in place.

Yuki looked nervous and on the verge of possible tears. I wasn't certain if my look or Balinac's presence was the greater contributor to her distress. Thomas approached and placed a hand gently on Balinac's neck.

Thomas spoke in his best fatherly tone, "Balinac please show a little respect for our guest. You've given her enough of a scare to last a lifetime already."

Balinac shrunk back down to his cat size, and moved over to curl up on the floor between Thomas and my feet. I don't think anyone in the room missed the significance of the gesture although several of them seemed very confused about what it might mean.

Thomas spoke to the assembled room, "We are here tonight to celebrate the arrival of our guest. I know that guests are rare for us, but I think this young lady might be a nice addition to our staff if our guest is allowed to continue on with us in a more permanent fashion."

A polite combined welcoming greeting came from the assembled group.

Thomas spoke with a touch of sadness, "However, I am afraid negotiations are not quite complete at this moment."

Yuki showed a worried look at that remark. She glanced at me and I nodded in a reassuring manner while maintaining my general look of displeasure.

Thomas continued, "Now I know several of you have grown fond of this nice young lady since her arrival, and I hope that my negotiations for her continued service are successful."

I noticed that Yuki began to blush about being the center of attention. She lowered her head a bit and looked down at her plate.

Thomas then finished up, "Let us enjoy this meal together then. Our ship shall be arriving in about one week if the weather remains calm. I will be sending our envoy to negotiate the severance of our new guest's prior contract when our ship arrives."

Yuki's head snapped up and looked at Thomas as he pointed at me during the last part of his speech. I changed my expression from displeased to glum as Yuki's eyes snapped to my face. I didn't fail to notice the fine work of Thomas' masterstroke. Yuki quickly understood the predicament placed before her. It was clear to Yuki now that her Sensei and the object of her desire would meet. What was unclear to everyone was whether both or neither of us would survive the encounter. I could almost tangibly feel her heart being strained by this conundrum.

The point that Thomas was holding my life in the balance as a possible alternative to reaching his desired outcome became much clearer to me. I hoped Thomas would be as convincing to Sensei Hapusai as he was to me at that moment.

 Chapter 8

Chapter 9 Tower in Moonlight

We sat through our meal in a bit of a grim mood. I understood the effect that Thomas was attempting to achieve, and it certainly seemed to be working on all of us. Thomas continued to play his fatherly role through the dinner. The rest of the room seemed to understand that it was now appropriate to take their cues from me.

I couldn't help but wonder at how well synchronized they all were with Thomas' intended approach. It seems that this wasn't the first time this method had been used to apply pressure on someone. They were both sympathetic and empathetic at a hidden command. It wasn't Yuki they were empathetic with however, it was me.

I could feel Yuki torn by the conundrum she was facing. At the same time I could see that she desired the same empathy I was receiving as well. In her eyes I was hurting and getting support from everyone else in the room. However, Lirae and I were her only beacons of support in the room. She could see I was facing my possible death sentence with the same courage and pluck she felt when she had faced her own. I could see it drawing her heart even closer to mine, while making her weak in her resolve.

Over her shoulder I saw Hardtack give me an approving nod and a wink. I had managed to pick up on Thomas' needs and play her feelings to a perfect pitch. She would be ready to be broken by Thomas soon. Then I was certain Thomas would find a way to break her Sensei Hapusai's will as well, or destroy him in the attempt.

Strange as it might seem I really didn't feel that endangered by what Thomas was proposing. While there was certainly a chance I would be killed, I thought it much more possible that I would survive the encounter even with the likely difference in combat skills between Yuki's master and myself. I wasn't being sent to fight. I was being sent as Thomas' envoy.

Yuki didn't eat any of her meal, instead spending most of her time watching her plate or stealing glances in my direction. I changed my expression from glum to worried and also picked through my meal as I glanced in her direction in return. I let her subtly know I was no longer thinking of my own situation, but of my concern for her pain. After a few minutes of this I could see that she was fighting back tears.

Thomas took this as his cue and left the table to begin chatting with the other island residents as they began to depart the hall. I stood up myself, and moved to the other side of the table. I looked at the slumped shoulders of Yuki and realized the part I needed to play. I placed both hands gently on her shoulders, and leaned over to place my lips by her ear.

With a touch of sadness and worry I said, "I will do my best to make this turn out right."

Yuki leaned her head back and rested it against my abdomen as she wiped away her tears. I let her stay that way a moment. Then patted her on the shoulders and moved to talk with Hardtack who was waving me over to his table.

Hardtack had me lean in close and whispered to me, "You're a quick study lad. I'm personally pretty bad at this emotional stuff, but you've done a good job here. Winning her over is going to be key to getting her Sensei to back down. What I've learned of him so far is that he's been a good fighting instructor, and a decent substitute father to her. I'd really hate to think he needed putting down like a rabid animal."

I nodded in affirmation and whispered back, "I'm interested in seeing where Thomas will take this next."

I was surprised to see Hardtack shudder at that statement, "Once was more than enough for me on this side of death. I don't envy you this next part lad."

Hardtack stood up then, "It looks like I will have to step in over there. Lirae may be overplaying her part, or off track a bit."

I looked and saw Lirae talking to Yuki. I listened close over the muted conversations in the room and caught the end of her remarks.

Lirae looked stricken as she said, "I've lost one child already. I don't intend to lose my adopted one over something this foolish."

I felt caught in a bit of a bind at that moment. Lirae was not following Thomas' lead at the moment. I watched as Lirae stormed out of the dining hall. I then saw Hardtack place his arm on the back of Yuki and lead her stumbling into the kitchen so she could recover a bit.

Thomas spoke beside me in a thoughtful voice, "Not quite according to plan, but I find genuine emotions help to move things along. Speaking of which, do you feel sorry for our young guest yet?"

I nodded my head a little, "She's in for much more tonight then?"

Thomas genuinely sounded regretful as he said, "This is just the appetizer to set her off her game a little. The terrifying part comes next. I got her worried about her Sensei and you first. Soon she will be crying in terror for herself."

I looked at him with a bit of shock, "Are you going to harm her then?"

Thomas tilted his head in contemplation, "Nothing physical if that's what you mean, but I am going to change her perception of reality for good. Most people find it devastating in the short term. Some few never recover. I think our young guest will rebound quite well in short order though. There is a core of good steel in that one. We will just have to work it to bring it out."

I departed the dining hall with Thomas, Balinac, and Hardtack in front of me and Yuki quietly walking at my side. It seemed that Yuki had calmed down some and was preparing herself mentally for her conversation with Thomas. I was genuinely tempted to reach out and hold her arm as her escort, but realized that the time was not right yet. Yuki was off balance at the moment as Thomas desired, and would need my support both physical and emotional as I walked her back later that evening.

I began to feel more sympathy for her as we walked to the beach and up the winding trail to Thomas' tower home. It was a delicate gambit that Thomas was using. He needed her spirit temporarily broken, but not so smashed that she gave up hope for her continued existence.

I had already understood that I was part of that gambit, but I hadn't realized until that walk how much I was also being made a victim of that approach as well. Thomas was cementing a relationship between Yuki and me. It would be the kind of relationship that was not ultimately of our choosing. I looked down at her beside me, and understood that I would grow to care for her personally by the end of what Thomas had planned.

It wouldn't be a romantic attraction on my part, but it would ultimately be a combination of guilt and duty that bound me into a strange affection for this young woman. These bonds would become much stronger than any mere attraction. They would be bonds of brotherhood. As the former son of a Knight, I knew what this would mean. I had seen the same bonds my entire life between my father and the men that had served with him through battle.

I tried to think about bracing myself for what might lie ahead. I looked up the cliff face and saw Thomas' tower up close. The white tower brightly glowed in the light of the full moon against the darkness of the night sky. I touched Yuki's arm, and pointed her toward the view in front of us.

Yuki looked at it, and then at me, "It's magical."

I nodded and replied to her, "Remember us looking up at it together. I think it will help you with what is to come."

Yuki gave me a brave smile, "I will do as you say."

The five of us had entered the base of the tower. It was lit by magic globes with a warm orange glow. A familiar looking set of stairs winding up to the beacon were there, but a corresponding set leading down were not present. Thomas pointed us to a set of comfortable chairs arranged two by two facing each other across a low table. Four delicate porcelain cups and a porcelain kettle of hot water already waited on the table.

Thomas sat on one side of the table with Hardtack taking the seat on his left. I held out the chair across from Thomas for Yuki, and then took the seat on her right across from Hardtack. Hardtack bowed from his chair, and began to ritually prepare the cups with a drink called tea. We sat in silence, but I understood this must have some kind of significant meaning in Yuki's culture.

Yuki didn't seem to relax, but she did seem to fall into a familiar pattern to her as the tea was prepared. She watched the preparation carefully. I realized that she was looking for the addition of a poison which she possibly suspected. Yuki still failed to understand the poison would be emotional, not physical. The poison wouldn't be in the tea, but in the words said.

We each took the cup presented by Hardtack. Thomas, Hardtack, and I did not hesitate to take a sip from our cups. Yuki held off a couple of seconds, and then realized that she was bound by the ritual to follow suit or risk offending her host. She took a sip, and seemed surprised that the tea was prepared to perfection with no hint of poison tasted.

Thomas nodded his head, "I hope the tea meets your approval Ms. Togusawa Nene. I must apologize to you for my earlier mistake."

Yuki shook her head, "My name is Nene, but I have no family name. I was found as an orphan and raised by Sensei Hapusai as his student. How did you know my real name though?"

Thomas shook his head, "That was the mistake I am talking about. I thought that Lord Togusawa had both your mother and you killed. I didn't realize until I did some further research that your Sensei Hapusai had disobeyed his lord and failed to carry out his orders to have you slain."

Yuki sat there in a bit of confusion, "Lord Togusawa was Sensei Hapusai's ruler, but you are wrong. His son died in childbirth, along with his wife. You killed Lord Togusawa for pay and politics. You shamed Sensei Hapusai into exile. You are telling lies to try to confuse me, but it won't work."

Thomas reduced his smile, and shook his head slowly, "I am telling you a truth you don't want to know. I never kill for politics. I could care less whether Lord Togusawa made political enemies or not. I only kill people for justice. Lord Togusawa killed his wife and your mother Akane because you were not born as a son. Lord Togusawa ordered you killed because you were a political embarrassment to him. Your mother's very spirit came to me seeking justice."

Yuki caught what she thought was the weak point in his argument, "What you say can not be true. The dead don't hire people to seek justice."

Yuki sat there barricaded in her position, prepared to weather any storm.

Thomas looked sad as he spoke, "I am truly sorry that you had to be made an orphan by my acts. However, if you will bear with me a moment, then you will find the truth you are looking to avoid."

Thomas stood then. Hardtack remained seated while nodding at me to follow Thomas. I lent a hand to Yuki to help her out of the chair. I saw as I turned that behind us was a set of stairs winding down into the foundations of the cliff. I felt a chill prickle go down my spine. This was the staircase from my dream. Thomas' office lay below, with untold other mysteries there as well.

Thomas led the way down the stairs with Balinac immediately behind him. I paced down the stairs lending Yuki my arm to give her support. Yuki clutched my arm firmly with her good arm and hand. I could feel even now that through her anger, confusion, and fear that she was drawing emotional support from my presence. I was her anchor now as Thomas had fully intended. He would send Yuki to the brink, and I would keep her from going over.

The stairs wound downward into the dimly lit interior of the island. Eventually we had even gone below the level of the shore outside with no end in sight. Yuki clearly realized that a massive amount of work must have been done to accomplish this task. I was relieved that there was no line of shadowy figures to wait behind this time.

After a long time spent descending the stairs we came to a straight corridor leading to a doorway. However, this time no physical door was present. A wavering wall of shifting shadows stood there instead.

Thomas turned to look at Yuki. He examined her face closely it seemed. I looked at her beside me as well, and could tell with my help that she had resolved herself for whatever she thought lay ahead.

Thomas gave a sad slight smile, "It is not too late to accept that I am telling you the truth. That you are the daughter of Lord Togusawa, and that your mother Akane's spirit came to me seeking his death for his murdering her and trying to kill you."

Yuki had gained courage from my presence, "I do not accept that such could be true. It can have no basis in reality. Sensei Hapusai would not betray his Lord. Lord Togusawa would never do such a horrible thing. Sensei Hapusai would never lie to me. Dead spirits do not hire the living to kill."

I could tell that her convictions were firm, and immutable in her estimation. For my part I was confident that Thomas had been truthful in his statement and was certainly prepared to prove it.

Thomas then dropped his smile, "Set your mind in stone if you will. Try to ignore the truth of my statements. I also invite you to step into my offices if you know you are correct. No harm will come to you there as long as you are under my protection. Don't disobey my advice on the other side though, or my protection may be withdrawn."

With that he stepped into the wall of shifting shadows and disappeared. Balinac moved to the side of the corridor. It became clear that it wasn't stepping through the curtain. I had already been on the other side though the memory of it was fuzzy. I didn't fear what I would discover. I looked at Yuki waiting for her decision.

Yuki looked me in the eyes, "Will you go with me?"

I nodded in affirmation, "I will stay at your side as long as we are there."

Hands clasped and arm in arm Yuki and I stepped through the wall of shifting shadows. We felt nothing on our skin, but as we reached the other side of the wall all color drained from the world. Thomas stood there now wearing a set of brightly glowing white robes lighting up this black walled monochrome world.

I looked at Yuki and saw that she was also dressed in dimly glowing robes as was I. Her broken arm was no longer in a sling. It seemed whole and intact to my estimation. Yuki looked at Thomas as she marveled at her arm, "What has happened? How did you do this?"

Thomas shook his head, "I have done nothing special here. You have merely stepped into my office. You spirit suffered no physical injury. So your arm is whole here."

Yuki was clearly confused while I had already caught on to what was happening. Our bodies hadn't left the base of Thomas' tower. We were here only in spirit form now.

ChapτeR 10 Plane of Shadow

A noise like the rumble of grinding boulders sounded behind us in the passage. Yuki and I were startled into looking behind us fearing some kind of collapse. Instead a monstrous shape filled the passage made of dark wisps of smoke like tendrils and shifting shadow.

Yuki collapsed into me and pressed me back into the wall. We may have been in spirit form, but her body felt as solid as her normal one would have. I realized the shape behind us was waiting, and the noise we had heard had been some kind of growl.

Thomas looked at the shape and spoke, "Balinac, would you please prepare the viewing area over the valley for our arrival?"

Relatively small shapes began to fall from the large form filling the hall. They became roughly cat shaped smoky balls of shadow which sped down the hall past our feet. They continued past the brightly glowing figure of Thomas. However, his illumination did not seem to reach or further detail the creatures. In a minute the large creature had obviously dwindled in size. In five more minutes the eventual end of the continuous stream of smoky tendril small shadow cats sped down the hall out of sight. One modestly medium sized of these strange cats remained behind and paced to Thomas' side.

As I peered to look closely at the illusive creature I could make out two switching tails. It was Balinac indeed, yet unlike anything I could imagine it to have been. Thomas waited a couple more minutes, and the remaining Balinac gave a gradual hiss.

Thomas waved us forward, and I held Yuki's arm again as we advanced. We walked down the hall and entered the familiar room where I had been interviewed by Thomas those months ago. We traveled through a different door than the one I had previously departed though.

The corridor continued for a while and another shimmering curtain of shadows was ahead. Thomas stepped through first and disappeared as before. I looked at Yuki who seemed more in wonder than in fear. Once again we walked through the portal together. We stood outside on a dusty plane with no visible stars above in the night sky. To the north I could feel the faint familiar pull that I had ignored on my first visit.

I noticed a shadowy circle of little shadow Balinac's surrounding us. They were acting strangely batting at unseen objects silently jumping and leaping. The circle closed around us some, and I noticed the small shadow Balinac's gradually merging to form larger versions of itself.

Yuki pulled me forward obviously feeling that call to the north much more strongly than I. I let her pull me even with Thomas, and he looked at me sharply so I halted. She tugged against my arm, and then tried to release her grip on me. With a nod from Thomas I held on strongly.

The three of us walked forward with me restraining an eager Yuki by my grip on her arm. The ring of smoky Balinac's became smaller as the individual beasts merged and became larger. They still continued their silent pantomime of batting and threatening a host of invisible attackers. I began to seriously expect a real unperceived danger lie past that circle of Balinac.

Yuki looked at me eagerly, "That voice calling me. I know it somehow. We must continue. I have to get there and meet them."

I nodded but didn't reply. Yuki simply had no clue where she was. I had a sinking suspicion as to where we were heading. After what seemed like an hour's travel I saw a great chasm in the ground before us. I continued to hold Yuki's progress in check with Thomas' pace. I could feel no hunger, thirst, or fatigue as we walked. Looking at Thomas it was obvious that his strength was being reduced somewhat by our journey. His glow while still quite bright was no longer as bright as it had been originally.

As we reached the edge of this great chasm Thomas held up his hand for a halt. The circle of Balinac's pulled closer and we looked down into the chasm from the edge. It was deep. The edges and bottom swarmed with vague shifting shadows. Down its length a beacon of brilliant light shone in very far distance. That beacon was the source of the call that we all felt.

Yuki looked around in excitement, "Where are we? Why are we stopping? I need to go there."

Yuki pointed at the glowing beacon down in the far distance in the shadow filled valley.

Thomas shook his head in clear denial, "It's time for the veil to be removed from before your eyes. It's time for you to acknowledge the truth of what has happened and what I represent."

Thomas stepped behind the both of us, and reached over our heads from behind. He made a motion like he was lifting an invisible bridal veil from over our faces. I pretty much knew what to expect already so I was braced for the impact. Yuki had no clue. The vision took her full force.

We stood in a veritable ocean of the spirits of the dead. They were inexorably drawn to our light, just as they were drawn to the beacon far away at the end of the chasm before us. Dead animals, dead creatures, dead humans, dead elves, anything and everything that could die was in spirit form around the protective circle of Balinac.

Thomas spoke in a booming and commanding voice, "Welcome to the very valley of death, you've passed through the land of shadow, and stand on its brink. The White Raven the goddess of the dead lies there beyond. If you doubt my word, then you only need to ask her to verify the truth of it. I warn you though the price will be eternal service to her cause."

Yuki looked out in frozen terror as Thomas spoke. When he finished Yuki collapsed on the ground screaming in the unending horror of this place. The screams and tears flowed freely from her form. The circle of dead pressed closer against the circle of Balinac protecting us. I was a bit shaken myself even though I had braced myself carefully for what I suspected would be there.

I looked down at Yuki seized by absolute terror. In turn pity and guilt seized my heart. I had known she would be broken. No unprepared mind could rationally accept this place at first glance. However, what I didn't know before was how bad it would be for me to watch it happen to her.

I reached down to pick Yuki up in my arms. Her screams began to cease and she shifted to sobbing uncontrollably. There was no defiance left in her; she was left bare to the harsh reality of this existence. There was also no longer any possible way for her to deny that what Thomas had told her was true.

I stood up cradling Yuki's form in my arms. She reached out clasping me tightly as she continued to cry. After a few more moments Yuki seemed to grow calmer.

With her eyes tightly shut she whispered to me with her voice trembling, "Thank you. I remembered the tower like you told me."

I looked over at Thomas and thought I saw a tear in his eye, and I know I felt them forming in mine. I realized then that Thomas wasn't heartless, but that certainly would not ever stop him from doing what he felt needed to be done in the cause of justice.

Thomas looked at the outer circle and spoke, "Balinac lead us out of here now if you please. It's time to go home."

The circle of ghostly shadow Balinac's merged into five very large ones. Two Balinac's crouched down beside Thomas and me so we could mount them. Two Balinac's furiously kept the area around us clear. One Balinac began clearing a path through the sea of dead spirits. We quickly raced across the land of shadow with one Balinac clearing a path ahead, and two more keeping the cleared path free as we rode furiously forward.

As a passenger I found the ride remarkably smooth even in the face of the incredible speed we were traveling. Eventually the sea of dead spirits thinned out to clusters, then just a few random spirits. The three leading shadow Balinac's merged up into one giant sized shadow Balinac. With our path clear our speed picked up to even greater levels.

I noticed that Yuki was no longer crying in my arms. She looked up at me with a look of fear and confusion still in her eyes.

Yuki spoke and her voice was weary, "What am I to do? How could I have known what we faced? How could I have been so wrong about the truth of things?"

I caressed her face, "You needed to have your eyes opened. I hope you can help me to open the eyes of Sensei Hapusai before it becomes too late for him."

Yuki glanced over fearfully at Thomas calmly riding beside us, "What is he?"

I thought carefully about my response, "He is Thomas the Poisoner. He serves justice by decree of the White Raven. He is beyond what any of us can fully imagine."

Yuki's face turned thoughtful as she looked up at me, "What are you?"

I braced myself and asked, "Are you certain you really want to know?"

Yuki hesitantly nodded and I gave her as much truth as she would be able to handle now, "I am a dead man, brought back to life as an elf through the intervention of Thomas. I have to bring my killer to justice, or else I will not be able to pass on to the other side in peace."

Yuki looked startled by my response at first. Then she grasped me closer.

Yuki then closed her eyes as she spoke, "I'm sorry for your death. I think I would have liked to meet you. I mean the person you were before you died."

I patted her shoulder and replied, "I thank you. I'm glad to have met you. I would also have liked to have met you under better circumstances than these."

Ahead of us I saw the familiar red slow heart beat glow of the beacon on top of Thomas' tower in the land of shadow. Having seen its source I understood now that this land of shadow was cast forth by the valley of death itself. It was a land of spirit not intended for physical form.

The Balinacs raced up the cliff face to the tower ignoring the winding trail. Once again I was amazed at how smooth the ride was and how easy it was to stay in place. A few spirits of the dead rambled around the base of the tower, but they seemed somehow oblivious to our presence. I figured that these were the seekers of justice too timid to continue on yet.

We dismounted the Balinacs and walked inside the door as the three remaining shadow Balinacs merged back into a single huge one. Thomas stood inside the center of the tower room and waved us to approach. He reached over the back of our heads and mimed the lowering of a bridal veil before our eyes.

Thomas smiled at us, "It is done now. You have been freed from the curse of my vision."

Yuki looked at him with a touch of fear and confusion, "What do you mean the curse of your vision."

Thomas shook his head, "I temporarily granted you the vision I have had of the world since I was born. I'm very sorry you had to endure it. I know I don't find it enjoyable, most especially at that place of all places."

I asked, "What about you Master Thomas? Will you not lower your own veil?"

Thomas briefly laughed with a slight bitter edge, "There is no veil for me. I will have to endure. Don't worry about me my young friends. I'm made of pretty tough stuff after all."

I set Yuki down as it seemed she had regained much of her composure. It was clear she was looking at Thomas with a new set of eyes. Her world had irrevocably changed, perhaps as much as mine had changed for me when I was killed. She knelt on the floor and bowed her head down to the ground.

Yuki spoke with a faint voice, "Forgive me my impertinence Lord. I knew not what I had done in implying you were dishonest with me. I was stubborn and willful. I beg your forgiveness for my intrusion on your island, and my horrible behaviors while your guest."

Thomas spoke in his most fatherly tone, "I forgive you your ignorance child. Now please stand up or I will become upset with you. I am not your Lord, though I do still want to extend you an offer as an employer."

Yuki stood up again and clasped my hand in hers. I could offer her no less comfort than what she needed at this moment.

Yuki kept her head bowed as she spoke up again, "I beg a boon of you Master Thomas."

Thomas spoke again in his fatherly tone, "What is it child? I can not guarantee any boon being granted, but I will consider carefully what you ask."

Yuki raised her head again, "Please don't send Sensei Mica to confront Sensei Hapusai. In a fair fight Sensei Mica is good, but Sensei Hapusai is much better. It is also very unlikely that Sensei Hapusai will fight fair."

Thomas stood in silence for a moment. I already knew that his preferred course of action had already been determined, and that her request would not change it.

Thomas asked a question as if he were seriously considering her request, "What would you have me do then child?"

I could see that she was torn, but that she had made a hard choice, "Send Sensei Hardtack in his place. He is the best fighter I have ever witnessed in action. He will make it quick and painless for Sensei Hapusai when they fight."

Thomas gave her a gentle smile, "You misunderstand my intent my dear child. I don't want to harm your Sensei Hapusai. He raised you like a father, saved your very life in fact, and it would be ungrateful of me to harm him. I would like you to help me convince him to give up his pursuit of me when the time comes. That is why I am sending Mica instead of Hardtack. He is well versed in court protocol you see and makes an ideal envoy to discuss an amiable resolution with Sensei Hapusai. If he agrees to a bargain with me, then I will be free to employ you without encumbrance."

I could see Yuki's face begin to shine as she realized the different nature of Thomas' intent. The darkness binding her heart was lifted. She gave my hand a joyful squeeze. Then she thought about her Sensei Hapusai's likely response to such an entreaty. A little cloud returned to her countenance.

Yuki spoke up again, "What if Sensei Hapusai doesn't believe Sensei Mica, and attacks Sensei Mica before he can convince Sensei Hapusai?"

Thomas had a thoughtful look on his face, "I hadn't considered that. Would you feel better if I sent Hardtack along to protect Mica until we can come to an agreement?"

Yuki's face brightened as she nodded enthusiastically.

I understood this was the result that Thomas had been searching for all along. Once again I had to admire his deft handling of people, myself included. It was clear to me that Thomas could easily become the power behind any throne he wanted to control. I had seen enough court politics in my day for me to understand his grasp of people and what motivated them was enormous.

Thomas pointed up the staircase, "The two of you can return by going up the stairs to the beacon room. I know it doesn't make sense yet, but trust me it works. I warn you that you will be tired when you arrive. Please escort Yuki to the female's quarters as I asked before Mica."

I asked Thomas, "Are you coming as well?"

Thomas shook his head, "I have a lot of work to catch up here. I will see you both in a few weeks."

Yuki and I climbed the tower stairs hand in hand until we reached the top. A large red crystal pulsed with red light like the slow beating of a heart as it turned hovering over the floor. One beat. Two beats. Three beats.

Chapter 11 Sea Journey

I awoke lying on a divan in the base of Thomas' tower. Across the room I could see another divan with Yuki's form laying on it still asleep. My body felt chill even in the warm air, and my muscles felt a bit stiff. I lay there a moment recovering, and looked out one of the high windows. The sun was up and I could tell the night had passed. I carefully sat up and stretched my limbs. It was better than my first return from the land of shadow.

I stood up, walked over to the door, and opened it to see the sun high in the sky above. Obviously we had been gone longer than it had seemed. I could see the normal activity happening at the compound below. I walked back over to Yuki's divan. I lifted her gently into my arms so as not to disturb her continued slumber. Her arm was back in its sling, but her color was good and her breathing was regular.

I began the somewhat arduous journey back down the winding trail. Yuki remained asleep in my arms. As I approached the compound the regular inhabitants gave me nods of approval. They understood my first mission had been a success. I saw Lirae come out of the dining hall. She looked in my direction, saw me carrying Yuki, and then ran over to join up with me.

Lirae smiled at me, "I take it that it went well."

I nodded and returned her smile, "Yuki here understands the way of things now I think."

Lirae nodded and her look turned serious, "I'm sorry about my outburst the last time we were together. I didn't mean to lose control like that."

I brushed up against her shoulder as we walked along, "I understand your concern. As my adopted mother you were worried about me."

I looked down at Yuki in my arms, "Yuki has never known what it means to have a mother in her life. She needs you even more than I. If you could find it in your heart to accept her I would be grateful."

Lirae looked me in eyes, "I will look after her as you ask. I may even begin to love her as my child in time as well."

Lirae looked down at Yuki sleeping in my arms, "She does look harmless now doesn't she. She seems just a lost young woman out of her depth, clinging on for life to her support."

I nodded as we approached the female's quarters, "I will need your support as well. Those of us who have seen need to stick together don't we?"

Lirae nodded her head in affirmation.

I looked up at the position of the sun, "I'm surprised so much time has passed already. It looks like it is lunch time."

Lirae shook her head, "It has been over four days since you left for the tower. Time does not pass there as it does here."

I looked a Lirae confused a moment, and then something struck me, "How long has it been since I was killed?"

Lirae looked at me carefully, "Thomas' best estimate is nearly three years."

I looked at her with a touch of panic, "My father. . ."

Lirae held up a hand, "Is still doing well. Thomas has placed someone on your father's estate to look after his well being, along with the well being of both of your elder brothers. Thomas' agents in Ard have the description of the men who attacked and killed you, and will notify Thomas if they are spotted in the region. They will be tracked, observed, and followed when Thomas' agents spot them. Otherwise they will be left unharmed."

I relaxed a bit with that news, "How about my brother Kalach?"

Lirae gave a slight grimace, "With his position in the church I think he will have to be considered safe enough. Thomas' reach is understandably somewhat short in those quarters."

I looked at Lirae as we stepped inside, "Thank you for that news. I had not realized how much time had gone since I had passed."

Lirae gave a small bitter smile, "None of us really do."

Lirae opened the door to Yuki's room as I carried Yuki over to her bed. Lirae pulled back the top sheet, and I gently placed Yuki down. Lirae pulled the sheet back up over her sleeping form. I walked to the door and waited for Lirae to join me.

I asked, "Would you wait with her for me? I will bring back some food for both of us in a little while."

Lirae nodded, "I will do as you ask."

The next two days before the arrival of Captain Robert's ship had passed fairly quickly. I waited on the docks next to an impressively armed Hardtack. He carried three swords worn in a sash around his waist. On his left side were two long swords of the exotic type I had practiced with him earlier. One of the two was sheathed in an elaborately decorated wooden and lacquered scabbard. The second was in a much more functional wooden scabbard and didn't bear any ornamentation. The third sword was a shorter one handed version matched to the longer more functional weapon he wore. Hardtack wore it on his right side for a left handed draw.

In addition Hardtack wore two balanced throwing axes and several obvious knives. I was unsure what other less obvious equipment he also kept on his person. It was going to be clear to anyone looking at him that he was all business. He had also brought along a small chest containing the gear that Yuki had brought with her to the island. This was to be returned to Sensei Hapusai as initial proof of our capabilities.

Personally, I was dressed in a somewhat elegant set of embroidered short robes and matching long pants. To finish the ensemble were a set of practical yet elegantly tooled short boots. I wore a nice yet functional saber and matched dagger for defense.

Hardtack and I talked amiably as Captain Robert's ship the Mystic Dawn unloaded the supplies for the island.

Hardtack shook his head, "I hate getting on these contraptions. These things are not properly built at all. Who would use wood for a boat when iron is much stronger?"

I shook my head in return, "Are you crazy? Don't you know that wood floats on water, but iron sinks to the bottom?"

Hardtack grinned at me mischievously, "That's what you'd think wouldn't you. When the dwarfs managed their iron-sides division they were the terrors of the sea you know."

I shook my head skeptically, "If such were the case why don't you see these iron ships around anywhere."

Hardtack looked at me with a conspiratorial wink, "They stopped making them because it took an enormous amount of iron to make one float. That and the dwarf crews began to get homesick when they left sight of land. We dwarfs don't trust the sea, it can be very treacherous. Give us trustworthy stone anytime instead of limitless water."

As we continued our conversation mainly for the benefit of the crew to grow accustomed to our presence I thought back over our instructions. Hardtack was our senior and would put together the operational plan, and make changes to the plan as necessary. I was the junior. As junior I would first have to follow his lead, second the plan he prepared, and third my own best judgment if the first two were not possible.

On the surface we would be traveling as an official and his bodyguard. This was mainly to keep any general interference at bay. It was not deemed likely to fool Sensei Hapusai if he lay in wait for us. In point of fact Hardtack was counting on it. After a search of the island after Yuki was captured he had found an object that she had dropped during her attempt to escape.

Hardtack determined it was a magical beacon of some sort, one of several she had on her person. He did not confirm the message it represented as it was likely context sensitive between Yuki and Hapusai. However, he speculated that it meant at the very least that their chosen target was dead since Yuki would have no reason to have believed otherwise at the point she had activated and discarded it. He also speculated that it likely also meant that Yuki was being pursued.

Hardtack had stated the thing probably had a very good range which would allow a person with the correct corresponding device to track it over a long distance. He hadn't briefed me on the details of how he planned to put this to use yet though.

The last couple of days also saw a change in the relationship between Lirae and Yuki. Lirae began to sympathize with her now that Yuki understood the nature of the inhabitants of the Isle of Death. Yuki hadn't died as we had, but she had become a companion of ours through shared experience in the Land of Shadow. I hoped that their relationship would continue to improve as Hardtack and I left the island.

In our absence Yuki was to take over running the dining hall. Lirae promised that she would help keep her from destroying any of Hardtack's cooking gear.

Last night after dinner Yuki had followed me out from the dining hall. She had seemed happy, and relatively unmarred by her traumatic experience. I knew that she would need more time to heal, both physically and emotionally. I thought that as Thomas had predicted she would come out stronger for the experience over time.

Without asking Yuki had approached me and clasped me in a one armed embrace. I had feared the worst, but I was relieved when she stepped back after a couple of moments. She stood up noticeably strong again, and simply thanked me for being there in her time of need.

Hardtack clasped his hand on my back, "Well lad. Are you ready to go yet? I think they are eager for us to board so they can be on their way."

I shook off my reverie, "Shall we board the vessel then?"

Hardtack grimaced, "Aye, we must indeed."

As we boarded the vessel the crew gave us a wary eye. As they prepared the ship to leave the dock I could hear the whispers among them. Captain Roberts came up the gangplank after us and began calling out orders as we tried to find a place to stand out of the way on deck. After he got his men started on their immediate tasks he came over and looked us both over.

Captain Roberts spoke to us, "Welcome to the Mystic Dawn. I'll have the men settle you into the guest cabin after we get underway. It has been a long time since you've left the island Harack. It must be pretty important for you to be leaving the Isle of Death."

I was confused by the name, yet Hardtack answered, "It is. We're going to save a life this time. That sometimes takes my delicate touch."

Captain Roberts grinned like he had heard some irony in the remark, "If you two will stand by the stairs of the poop deck we'll be underway momentarily. The men are always nervous when we visit the isle, and doubly so when we have passengers. It will do them good to see you out here for a while."

As Captain Roberts moved about the Mystic Dawn calling out orders, I noticed with my sharp hearing that the men near whispered the name Harack to each other. They usually added names like the Goblin Slayer, the Orc Doom, the Ogre Bane, or other similar appellations to the end as they said it.

I looked at Hardtack and quietly asked, "Let me guess. Harack is your real name, and it comes with a sizable reputation as well."

Hardtack nodded with a slightly grim grin, "You know how Captain Roberts has a reputation for sinking dozens of ships and killing hundreds of people?"

I briefly nodded for him to continue.

Hardtack lost all trace of a grin next and an unfamiliar grim visage remained as he spoke again, "Well I've done some things I wasn't proud of in my angry youthful years. One of which was pretty much single handed destroying what amounts to an entire nation of the wild races. Except that I didn't do it gracefully like Thomas could have by selectively culling their troublesome leaders. Instead I cut, chopped, hacked, and slew my way through thousands of them. I eventually drew the very attention of the White Raven herself with how busy I was making her minions."

I looked at him in a new light, "What happened then?"

Hardtack's visage grew less grim and his slight grin appeared, "Thomas paid me a visit and requested I retire on behalf of the White Raven. Let's just say it was an offer I wasn't given the choice of refusing. I hired on as his cook and weapons trainer. I haven't killed anyone in nearly two hundred and sixty years now."

I shook my head, "That's quite a change."

Hardtack's grin widened a bit more then, "Well I have injured quite a few since then, but I've gotten pretty good about not taking their lives. Unfortunately Captain Roberts understands that. I had to soundly trounce him in battle when he first came to us. He just would not concede that anyone might be better at rapier than himself. We've come to an understanding now."

As Hardtack said that I could see and hear Captain Roberts talking to his first mate in the hearing of a brace of his newest and currently boldest crewman. Captain Roberts was telling him how any sea dog that could take down Harack there would gain eternal fame, and the adoration of wenches everywhere for a lifetime. I looked at Hardtack and he gave me a subtle wink.

Hardtack whispered back, "It looks like Captain Roberts needs to break in a few of his more rowdy crew. Be prepared to not get much sleep for the next week and a half. He never did get over me beating him quite so hard I think. He likes to send his less seasoned boys at me so as to determine if he can spot any weaknesses as we fight."

I looked at Hardtack with a touch of shock as he continued, "The dumb ones will try to call me out on deck later after we lose sight of the Isle of Death. The slightly smarter ones will watch what happens, and figure out that ambushing us asleep is safer. The truly smart ones won't even take the bait and will leave us alone."

I whispered back, "What will you do then?"

Hardtack flushed a bit, "The hard part is I'm not allowed to rough them up too much. Captain Roberts needs them to crew the ship. If I put one out of commission, then he will gladly complain to Thomas about it. Let's just hope that no more than three or four of them decide to gang up on us at once. It's a bit tricky to keep them whole when they are rushing you in a haphazard fashion and start injuring each other in the attempt."

I though for a bit and asked, "What should I do about it?"

Hardtack just chuckled, "Stay clear like the dandy elf diplomat you appear to be. If one mistakes you for fair game, then just hold him off until Captain Roberts disciplines them. He's certainly not averse to leaving them in a less than working condition if they don't follow his commands."

As the sun set toward late afternoon it became clear that as Hardtack predicted the first of the challengers had worked himself up to the task of becoming famous. To look at the brute it seemed like he could have been the result of a cross between a large barbarian and one of the wild races forcibly taken and subjected to ungentlemanly congress by the hulking idiot.

The other crewmen were obviously somewhat intimidated by the size and strength of this monstrosity. I gave him less than a minute if Hardtack wanted him dead on the spot. I figured that Hardtack would give it a bit of a show to discourage the others from trying it.

I noticed that Captain Roberts had conspicuously left the deck for his cabin, and the first mate had needed something from the ship's hold. That seemed to be the signal for a few of the others to start baiting the brute into fighting the dwarf. They wanted to see some action, and the smarter ones wanted to gauge the abilities of the dwarf in question before committing themselves.

Overtly Hardtack had disposed of all his heavy weaponry in the passenger cabin earlier and only a couple of working knives were in view on his person. Following Hardtack's advice I kept my saber and dagger visible on my person as I watched. The show was about to begin.

The brute called out from over by the mainmast, "Hey little man. Your island is no longer in sight. You can not swim anywhere now. What are you going to do if I decide to throw you off this ship because I don't like your ugly face?"

Hardtack gave him a slight grin, and with obvious menace said to me loud enough for the others to hear, "Ah crap lad. We've got a talker here. He needs time and his friends backing him up to pick a fight with an unarmed elderly dwarf. Just stay back and let me talk to the stupid orc lover and explain how his orcish girlfriend will not pleasure him for challenging the Orc Doom. She will cry over his grave instead."

The large brute took a step forward from the mast and opened his mouth to hurl further insults. Several of the older and scar laden crew members grinned as they watched what happened next. They had likely seen or played this dance before sometime in the past, and were looking forward to the entertainment.

Hardtack launched himself up high and forward landing between the large brute's feet on his hands and the balls of his feet. Hardtack continued the motion into a roll between the brute's legs and twisted around facing the brute's back as the brute began howling in pain. I noticed then that Hardtack had pinned the brute's feet to the deck with two daggers.

I started to feel sorry for the idiot, but it was immediately clear that Hardtack just wanted his target stuck in place for his next move. Hardtack launched himself onto the back of the brute with yet another pair of daggers in hand. Hardtack drove them into the poor brute's shoulders and pulled himself up behind the head of his victim.

Next Hardtack wrapped his left arm around the brute's throat while he neatly and quickly sliced off the top of the victim's right ear. The brute collapsed to his knees with his feet still nailed to the deck. Hardtack hung there behind the fellow with his dagger poised in front of his victim's right eye.

Hardtack spoke in a clear and vicious voice, "I recommend you apologize real politely now, or I'll pluck out your eye next."

It was embarrassing to watch the brute blubber and cry as he said, "I'm real sorry. I didn't mean to offend. I was just joking. Please don't take my eye gracious sir. I've learned my lesson."

Hardtack dismounted the brute. Then he carefully plucked out his daggers from the brute's shoulders and feet so as to cause as little additional injury as possible. He turned in a slow circle as he menacingly glared at the gaping crew.

Hardtack spoke with low menace as he said, "As far as Captain Roberts hears from any of you this here idiot tripped and fell from the mast. If he hears differently from any of you, then I will know and pay you a special personal visit. Does anyone fail to understand my meaning?"

The watching crew nodded or shook their heads uncertain about how to correctly answer the question. They began to return to their duties as a few of them hurried their bleeding companion below decks for treatment. Seemingly with unintended timing Captain Roberts and his first mate returned to the deck. None of the crew seemed eager to rush forward to say anything to Captain Roberts, and he scrupulously failed to remark about the older crewmen who was scrubbing the blood off the deck.

Chapter 12 Mutineers

Later that evening Captain Roberts came to visit our cabin. He seemed a little displeased as he came inside.

Captain Roberts spoke to Hardtack, "I know you had to carve up that fool a bit to teach him a lesson, and I thank you for delivering it with relatively little mess."

Hardtack looked him in the eyes, "I sense a complaint coming somewhere."

Captain Roberts sighed then continued, "Did you have to scare the rest of the crew so badly in the process? Not a one of them has come forward to report to me what happened yet."

I chimed in with a remark, "Did you ask them what happened?"

Captain Roberts shook his head, "Of course I did not. What kind of Captain has to ask his crew what's happening on his ship? A Captain that has lost control and who is due to have a mutiny for certain. The crew has to volunteer that kind of information, and they won't do so if they are more in fear of Harack than me."

I shook my head as Hardtack answered, "Pretty simple really, just keep them in fear of both of us. It should be pretty entertaining that way. We could even bet on which ones will hold and which will break if you like."

Captain Roberts shook his head, "This isn't a battle or a bar brawl. This is a working ruffian crew. They have to be dangerous to be effective, but they also have to know who the top dog is before they will obey. If they see two top dogs, then they start dividing and taking sides. It's the very nature of this kind of beast."

I looked over at Hardtack, "What do you think about trying to back down a little?"

Hardtack scowled a bit, "Captain Roberts got his crew thinking of getting rowdy with me. I figure it is his job to rein them in again."

I looked back at Captain Roberts, "Which one of your unseasoned crew presents the most trouble by using the other people to do his dirty work?"

Captain Roberts gave me a cagey look, "I do not take what you mean."

I gave him a grin, "It should be simple really. Which one of your new crew talks other people into starting trouble? I saw several people instigating that brute to challenge Hardtack, which one of them is new?"

Captain Roberts cautiously answered, "Rod Darnis is the biggest instigator among the new crew. Why do you ask?"

I answered, "It seems like in a couple of days it may be time to deal with a potential mutineer who doesn't know his place."

Captain Roberts shook his head, "He hasn't advocated any mutiny on my ship yet."

I nodded, "I know. However, that type is always shooting their mouth off when their superiors are not present. Much of what he has said could probably be twisted to be considered mutiny in the right context. It's unlikely the new crew will think you way off base if you accuse him, and your seasoned crew should be used to your capricious whims by now."

Captain Roberts looked at me suspiciously, "How would an elf like you know so much about how a pirate crew operates?"

I laughed, "Try being raised around court politics sometimes. It's like piracy being done on a much larger scale is all."

Hardtack laughed along with me, "The lad is right. Give it a go. There's nothing like finding someone to blame for something to bring people back into fear of your orders again."

Captain Roberts had a sour look as he replied, "I'll try it your way this time. If it doesn't work though, then I may need your weapons to hold off a real full scale mutiny."

Hardtack spoke again, "They won't try it without backing from me, and any that asks will be dealt with severely by me. I also want it clear to your crew that the elf is not quite as skilled as me."

Captain Roberts shook his head, "Do you want them to try to kill him then?"

Hardtack shook his head, "Just make it clear that he doesn't know how to keep his foes alive yet."

Captain Roberts grimaced, "Aye, that should do the trick."

In the early hours before the dawn of the next day I heard the sound of a muffled footstep outside our cabin. A hushed whisper was exchanged, but I could not make out what was said. I looked down to see Hardtack laying in his hammock below me in sham slumber, and I knew he was prepared for what might happen.

I quietly slid out of my hammock and silently moved over beside the door. Without a sound I removed my saber from its sheath. The door to our cabin slowly opened a crack, and as the eye of the inquisitive crewman came into view I rapidly moved the point of my saber to within one half an inch of it. A look of startled shock and fear appeared on what I could see of the fellow's face.

I evenly asked in a quiet tone, "Did you want something?"

The fellow swallowed heavily and stammered, "M'mi my mistake, wra' wrong cabin."

Two sets of footsteps departed as I shut the door again. I looked over at Hardtack as he opened his eyes. I entered my hammock again.

Hardtack whispered, "Nicely done."

I nodded my head and whispered, "It was very likely that Rod Darnis was the other fellow prompting the one at the door to attack us with himself following behind. That fellow seems just smart enough to get someone to make the attempt, but not smart enough to figure out that it really isn't worth the attempt."

Hardtack softly replied, "I agree. It is a good way to get credit for the kill by sneak attacking his partner after we are dead. How did you know there was someone like him in the junior crew members?"

I smiled as I looked up at the ceiling, "There always is in any organization or group of a large enough size. I figure a ship this size has about three to four of them. Watching who goaded the brute yesterday as opposed to just cheering on the action pretty much confirmed my estimation. My only problem is in not knowing which of the crew were more junior or senior."

Hardtack questioned me although he already knew the answer, "Why would whether they were senior or junior make a difference?"

I replied, "I've seen a few of the older crew who have been carved up a little. This was obviously not the first time they had seen you in action, but a couple of them were happy to instigate knowing the result that was going to happen to someone else. Then a couple more people were instigating as well but they hadn't been carved up. I couldn't tell if they were the smarter ones who had already got other people to test you out, and then backed down themselves. Otherwise they were likely the kind of not really smart ones who didn't know you well. Thus they were willing to pile into your room while you slept with a friend or two going first to overwhelm you."

Hardtack had a note of approval in his voice, "Good observation, but how did you know the second fellow outside our room tonight was this Rod Darnis?"

I thoughtfully responded, "Captain Roberts already told me himself. Like he said before, he knows his crew well, and he has plenty of people willing to rat out someone like that before trouble can get too large. Captain Roberts doesn't seem the type to give up a crewman's name like that to us unless he wanted us to personally take care of his little problem."

Hardtack questioned me further, "Why doesn't Captain Roberts not just take care of it himself?"

I thought about it, "Oh, he knows the problem is there, but he is unwilling to cross a line of dealing with it before it is clear to the others that the problem is there as well. I think he's counting on us to make it clear to them."

Hardtack spoke with a warm tone, "You've got a good mind to figure all that out lad. It would do you well to understand that Captain Roberts is as sharp as that and more. He didn't earn his position by not being clever as a fox when needed. What do you suggest we do to fix both Captain Roberts problem and our own?"

I considered his request for a moment, "I think it may be time for a certain gossipy elfish diplomat to talk about the interrupted attempt at mutiny he witnessed in the wee hours of the morning."

Hardtack acted astonished, "You'd lie about it?"

I nodded my head, "Of course, is there any reason to not put my word against theirs. My word as an elfish diplomat against the word of a slandering, instigating, and untrustworthy sea dog, even a pirate jury would expect a pirate like him to lie about his involvement. Especially a pirate jury that has been a part of a crew with him for a stretch like we have on board at this moment anyway."

Even without looking I could tell that Hardtack was smiling, "I'm proud of you my lad. You'll do well on this mission I think."

few hours after dawn Hardtack and I paid a brief visit to Captain Roberts. I kept quiet as Hardtack asked him for a description of this Rod Darnis fellow. I heard him mention a squinty eyed, brown haired and young man with typical sailors clothes set off by a green bandanna worn about his neck. Only one of the instigators from yesterday's fight came close to matching the description given.

I then spent a lot of time on deck within hearing range of several of the crew mouthing off to Hardtack about the fellows I had seen sneaking about the ship armed in the hours of the early watch. I made it clear that they had bypassed Hardtack's and my cabin, and were lurking outside of the Captain's cabin with drawn knives when I spotted them.

I began to hear various muttering voices as Hardtack and I talked. I could make out that several people had seen Rod Darnis and his cohort Jim Smitty leave their hammocks in the hours of the early watch. The crew had originally presumed they were going to make a go at the dwarf. However, the talk had shifted around that it was possible they were trying to assassinate the Captain and blame the killer dwarf for the deed.

It wasn't long before a couple crewmen went below decks to warn Rod Darnis and Jim Smitty what was being said about them. I noticed also that a couple more managed to bring the word to Captain Roberts. He gave me a piercing look from his position by the wheel, but held off to watch what would unfold in the drama I was arranging.

Jim Smitty must have gotten the word first because he came up on deck looking at me and then at Captain Roberts in a kind of shock. It was certainly the fellow who had shown up at our door last night. I could not have arranged a more guilt ridden look on his face if I had worn it myself.

I pretended like I hadn't noticed his arrival, but I could certainly hear the remarks of the crew shift from being uncertain about my story to acknowledging it must be true once they saw him. Then I pretended that I had just spotted him, and very obviously pointed him out to Hardtack in front of the crew.

I deliberately spoke a little too loudly as I said, "He's one of the two." A few more people came on deck from below as the rumor spread through the ship. I saw that one had the same green bandanna that Rod Darnis wore in the description given by Captain Roberts. However, it was not the same fellow who had been wearing it yesterday. I saw the squinty eyed fellow from yesterday trying to blend in and hide among the crowd coming up from below.

Rod Darnis obviously knew I hadn't seen him from our cabin last night, and played a desperate gamble that I would accuse the wrong sailor in possession of his bandanna. He was a quick thinker, and I internally applauded his bravado. I stretched my hand out to point at him none the less.

I spoke in my too loud voice again, "That's the other one. I'd recognize that sinister figure anywhere."

Rod Darnis played it cool and looked around in confusion as if he were trying to figure out where I was pointing. Unfortunately for him his partner Jim Smitty was not playing along and stared directly at him with a dumbfounded and even guiltier look on his face.

There was a lot of general murmuring as Captain Roberts stepped forward from where he was talking with his first mate by the stern rail. His face was serious, but in control as he came down the stairs to the main deck. The men began to return to their tasks in silence.

Captain Roberts looked around with a sharp eye, and focused in on me. I gave him a particularly elaborate bow. Jim Smitty came forward toward the Captain as I noticed Rod Darnis in an internal debate whether slinking below decks or staying above was the better course of action. He started moving toward the hatch, and noticed the attempt had earned him a sharp glance from Captain Roberts.

I saw then Rod Darnis was going to be quick to choose to go on the verbal offensive now that he was caught out by the Captain's glare. Unfortunately for him his partner Jim Smitty had already approached the Captain and was speaking first.

Jim blubbered, "Rod and I didn't mean no harm Captain. We were just gonna teach a lesson too. Figured to catch em sleeping you know. Rough em up a bit is all."

Rod closed in quick, "Shut up you fool. It is all lies Captain Roberts. I wasn't sneaking around the deck with no weapon last night."

Jim continued to blubber, "I didn't mean no harm Captain. We were just trying to be famous is all."

Rod began to get angry at Jim, "Shut your lie telling mouth you idiot. I was not ever out of my hammock last night sir. Ask any of these men down asleep last night. They all saw me go to bed and there again in the morning."

The Captain called out to the crew, "Does any person here want to vouch his life on whether these two scurvy dogs stayed in their hammocks the entire night?"

The crew began shaking their heads or shrugging their shoulders.

Rod turned from Captain Roberts and cried out to the nearby crew, "I see how it is. Turn your back on a man in a hard spot beset by lie telling dogs. I'll see you all get yours in time. When my uncle hears of this the lot of you will pay."

Captain Roberts called out to the crew, "On pain of death if caught not telling the truth, did any man witness either of these two leave their bunks, and make their way to the decks last night."

The two members of the crew who had talked to Captain Roberts earlier raised their hands first. Then three more members raised their hands. Finally in a less than surprising move Jim Smitty raised his hand as well.

Rod Darnis opened his mouth to speak and stopped stunned as he found the tip of Captain Robert's rapier resting on his tongue. He looked down comically cross eyed at the blade and froze in place.

Captain Roberts quite convincingly said, "No more speaking from you unless I ask you a direct question Rod Darnis. It would do you well to understand that your uncle fears me and those I work for, not the other way around. You only made it on to my ship as a personal favor requested from your uncle. That favor no longer stands in force if you utter another word without permission."

Captain Roberts withdrew his rapier from Rod Darnis' mouth. Rod snapped his mouth shut as Captain Roberts placed his rapier back in his sheath.

Captain Roberts then called out to the surrounding crew, "On pain of death if caught not telling the truth, did any one here see these two armed last night near my cabin or the cabin of my guests?"

I raised my hand, "I did Captain Roberts."

Jim Smitty also raised his hand in self condemnation. My respect for his honesty raised a notch. He knew that for him it was the best policy when caught out. Rod Darnis silently fumed with his mouth clamped shut.

Surprisingly two other crewmen raised their hands as well. I saw that they were the two battle scarred senior crew members I had pegged as instigators yesterday. Then it struck me that Captain Roberts deliberately had instigators in among his crew that were in actuality trusted by him to spy on the others. They would be able to quickly ferret out any seemingly like minded individuals to be turned over to the Captain later.

Captain Roberts looked at him, "Rod Darnis you stand charged with attempted mutiny, attempted assassination of passengers granted safe conduct, and lying to your superior in the course of an inquiry. How do you plead?"

Rod looked at the Captain with defiance in his eye, "Not guilty of this travesty. If you harm me my uncle . . ."

Rod Darnis quickly shut his mouth as Captain Roberts grasped the handle of his rapier. Captain Roberts waved two of his crew over to Rod's sides.

Captain Roberts spoke out loudly so the whole crew could hear, "Search him for weapons and bind him securely to the mast in a sitting position. He is only to be allowed one ration of bread, and three rations of water per day until we reach Port Cirnore. On reaching Port Cirnore he will be turned over with the charges presented to the Captain's court. His wages for this voyage are considered forfeit, and will be evenly distributed among those of the crew who spoke up in honesty on this matter."

I saw that those crew members who had raised their hands at the appropriate times grinned in appreciation of their increased take on this trip. I also saw that it was a smart action on the part of Captain Roberts. It encouraged people to not hold back in the face of any future inquiries.

Rod Darnis meekly allowed himself to be led over to the mainmast. After a search a wicked looking knife was found in his possession. Two more sailors joined in helping to secure him in a seated position tied to the main mast facing the bow of the ship.

I could see that Hardtack was evaluating the work they did, and he nodded to me that it met his standards. Rod was securely fastened without being irrevocably

Thomas the Poisoner

so. They made it so he could be unsecured from the mainmast and led over to a chamber pot or the rail as necessary without slipping his other bonds.

Captain Roberts then spoke to the men near Rod, "Please gag his mouth for the moment. I would hate for him to let something slip which would force me to kill him before trial."

Then Captain Roberts looked at Jim Smitty standing before him shaking, "Jim Smitty you stand accused of bad judgment in listening to Rod Darnis and following his plot of mutiny. How do you plead?"

Jim Smitty stood up straight and concentrated on not shaking for his response, "I'm guilty as charged and more."

Captain Roberts nodded his head, "So be it. For the charge of mutinous action under the leadership of another I sentence you to five lashes of the cat o' nine tails and half rations until we reach Port Cirnore. However, in light of your honesty in this matter you too will share in the division of Rod Darnis' wages."

I could hear Rod Darnis screaming into his gag over the luck of honest idiots. I was personally impressed with Captain Roberts' good judgment. It was obvious he wouldn't over punish a mistake made in zealousness, or foolhardy decisions beyond what was necessary to prevent it from reoccurring. I could also see that he had secured the gratitude and loyalty of Jim Smitty for the future.

It seemed that Hardtack had a slight variation on this plan. He walked over to Captain Roberts and they had a brief hushed conversation. Captain Roberts gracefully surrendered to the request of his guest. Hardtack walked back over to me with a wicked grin on his face.

I gave him a raised eyebrow as a question, but he gestured to watch what he had planned next. Jim Smitty had a bit of a stupid grin about his unbelievable luck. The rest of the crew was whispering to each other about the results of the day's excitement as Captain Roberts sent a senior crewman to his cabin. The crewman returned with the cat o' nine tails. However, instead of bringing it to Captain Roberts' first officer to deal out the required punishment, he walked over to Hardtack and presented it to him.

Jim Smitty lost his silly grin in quick moment as it dawned on him who would be performing the flogging. Hardtack gave him and the rest of the crew the full force of his wicked grin. I could see most of the crew at large shuddering at the concept, and Jim Smitty nearly lost his legs from under him. Two crewmen moved up to secure him, but Hardtack waved them off as he approached.

Hardtack spoke with clear authority, "Jim you are going to take your punishment like a man. You will march up to the bow of this ship, and you will kneel before the rail. I will give you five strokes of the greatest agony you have ever experienced in your life. You may have wanted to endure fifty lashes by a lesser person than the five I will give you. However, I promise you this. None here will ever question your courage. You will be marked for life, and it will be with a badge of honor that no one can deny."

Jim Smitty steeled himself, and then I could see him change. His resolve obviously firmed up. He removed his shirt and bandanna. He carried them with him up to the railing on the bow in full view of the silent crew. He set them down upon the deck below his knees and grasped the rail tightly.

Hardtack stripped off his outer garments and handed them to me to hold. Then he removed his pants and shirt until he stood covered only in his loincloth. His body was covered neck to ankle in an interwoven mesh of countless scars. The sword strokes, dagger cuts, spear stabs, and arrow holes covered all of his visible flesh. Even the most harshly scarred of the crew could not even begin to compare with the sheer amount of injuries he had obviously undergone.

Taking a glance at Captain Roberts I could tell that even he was impressed by the amount of damage Hardtack had obviously endured through his life. Hardtack approached the bow and stood behind Jim Smitty. He leaned forward and whispered something in Jim's ear, and Jim tensed himself into position.

While I was familiar with the process of flogging for punishment, I had never witnessed it in person. I knew in general the person performing the flogging draws out the process making it mentally tortuous as well as physically so. That was not Hardtack's approach.

Crack, crack, crack, crack, crack came the sound of the cat o' nine tails almost faster than thought. A haze of blood hung suspended like a mist between Jim and Hardtack. Jim gave out a great tortured cry of pain, but held on to the rail and didn't collapse. The crew was suitably impressed by the speed of the event.

Then the haze of blood mist cleared and the miraculous became evident to them as well. Clearly carved in bleeding cuts on Jim Smitty's back was the rough cut image of a decapitated orc's head complete with crossed out eyes. Harack Orc Doom had placed his mark, and it was a badge of honor that none witnessing the event could deny.

I approached carrying Hardtack's gear as he turned to the assembled crew. He gave them his fiercest glare and called out across the ship.

Hardtack's voice boomed out, "I am Harack Goblin Slayer, Orc Doom, Ogre Bane. I have personally slain over twenty thousand of the wild races and many others besides in my time. I have been banished by the White Raven to the very Isle of Death as punishment for all the killing I have done. If anyone else seeks to gain honor at my expense, then they simply need to step up to the rail there."

I figured they would all slink away at the end of Hardtack's remarks. I was right about the majority of them. The two instigators who had called out Rod and Jim's activities last night surprised me though. As the others began to return to their work they came forward to Hardtack.

They bowed to Hardtack and the first one spoke, "We both agree that we like the style of your work, but we don't want to take anything away from Jim there. Is it possible you could carve something suitable on our arms though?"

Hardtack gave them both a grin, "Don't you both bear the signs of my work from a few years ago already?"

The second one nodded, "We're kind of jealous though. We didn't get anything with quite that level of artistic achievement in it. Do you think you could help us?"

Hardtack laughed, "That cat o' nine tails is terribly tricky to work anyway, would you settle for a bit of knife work instead."

They both nodded enthusiastically. Hardtack quickly set about cutting a sketch of a decapitated goblin head with crossed out eyes on each one's forearm. They left grinning together to show the rest of the crew.

After Hardtack got dressed more of the senior crew came over telling stories of the wounds Hardtack had inflicted on them over the years. They each wanted a knife carved sketch done on their arms, and each one received a decapitated goblin head. After the dozen or so senior crew members had a sketch done I noticed the brute from yesterday hobbling around nearby.

I waved him over to my side, "Are you feeling any better after your fall from the mast yesterday?"

He gave me a generous grin with a slight wince, "My name is Breagor. I have always been considered the biggest and the toughest of those around me, but I have quickly learned that doesn't mean much to the likes of him."

Breagor pointed at Hardtack as he said the last part. He seemed at a loss for how to ask for what he wanted, but seeing the others grinning over their new artwork it was easy to guess.

I waved to Hardtack to get his attention, "Do you think you could come up with something for Breagor here. He's a little shy about asking."

Hardtack came over and spoke quietly to him, "Sorry I got rough with you yesterday. I have to make a bit of an example of the first one who challenges me to let the others know what they are in for you see."

Breagor nodded his head enthusiastically, "I know. It hurts, but it's a good kind of hurt now you know. It's a hurt few can say they have suffered. Not many can say they fought Harack Ogre Bane and survived to tell of it. Of those living the few that have are among the crew aboard the Mystic Dawn. We will become legendary in our own way you see."

Hardtack gently smiled at him, "That's good. Now what can I carve for you. Would you like an ogre's head?"

Breagor nodded his head enthusiastically again, and Hardtack carved a quick sketch of the decapitated head of an ogre with crossed out eyes on his massive bicep. After Breagor departed and no more crew approached for a carving Hardtack gathered up his gear, and then looked over at me.

Hardtack looked me in the eyes, "Are you up for a sketch as well?"

I gave him a light laugh, "I'll come by my scars naturally thank you. They have more personal meaning that way."

Hardtack laughed in return, "I think that's one of the reasons Thomas likes you so much. You have an abundance of good sense."

Chapter 13 The Fear Watch

The crew seemed generally in a good mood as the day continued. The notable exception was Rod Darnis who seemed downcast, but not too worried the Captain's court would find him guilty, at least not of mutiny anyway. I figured that this uncle he threatened to involve must have been pretty connected in Port Cirnore. Undoubtedly this uncle could and likely would influence the court's decision on his behalf.

I figured that Captain Roberts also knew this fact, but that he was more concerned with having a pretext for legitimately removing this trouble maker from his ship than in seeing him severely punished. It obviously would not hurt Captain Roberts' position in Port Cirnore that this pretext was being provided by the envoy from the legendary Isle of Death.

Hardtack and I retired to our cabin after our midday meal to rest. As we lay in our Hammocks I considered our mission which lay ahead. Two days had gone by already and we had not figured out how to best approach Sensei Hapusai. It was up to Hardtack to take the lead as senior, but I was sensing a hesitation on his part. I didn't quite understand it, but I figured something was wrong.

I asked Hardtack, "Are you sleeping?"

Hardtack replied, "Just resting a bit. Do you need to talk about something?"

I put it bluntly to him, "Do you have a plan for how to manage Sensei Hapusai yet?"

Hardtack hesitated then spoke, "I don't have a clue. I could kill him in a moment's notice if necessary. However, I don't have any real idea how to convince a man who loves his daughter to surrender her to people he believes are murderous enemies."

I thought about his response a while, "Do you mind if I think about it a while? I think I could put together the beginnings of a plan with your help. I take it that the fancy sword you are carrying is very valuable, and meant to be a possible bribe?"

Hardtack answered, "That sword is the Murumasa blade. It's beyond very valuable. In the right hands it could be used as a means to control the actions of certain nations."

I asked, "Nations like the one Sensei Hapusai called home?"

Hardtack spoke, "Some swords have a history. This sword is history. It is said in the hands of its bearer they can claim divine right of rule."

I spoke again, "Impressive weapon. It can certainly not hurt our offer if presented right. I take it that it is likely this Sensei Hapusai is as honor bound as any knight?"

Hardtack adjusted my assessment, "They are not bound to the same kind of social rules as the knights you know. In many ways it is less about the external perception of their honor, than it is about their own feelings of honor. This Sensei

Hapusai would not have been part of the royal guard as it were. It's more like he was the leader of their special elite forces."

I replied, "They consider stealth assassination part of honorable elite forces action?"

Hardtack continued, "Most certainly. That kind of work doesn't bear the stigma of dishonor that is common in this part of the world you understand."

I thought about it a while, "I take it they have a knight class who do provide royal guard services then?"

Hardtack replied, "The Samurai are their knight class. Each warlord keeps several on hand as a personal guard. They are professional warriors, born and bred for warfare. The ones who failed to protect Lord Togusawa would have committed ritual suicide along with their commander to atone for their failure."

I smiled to myself, "I think I have an idea of how to approach Sensei Hapusai now. We were thinking of this wrong at first. Sensei Hapusai did not lose his honor because he failed to protect the life of his lord. It wasn't his job to do so, and he would have taken his own life if it had been."

Hardtack agreed, "I see your point, but what is his problem with Thomas then?"

I continued, "Sensei Hapusai was an elite offensive force commander, not a defensive force commander. Sensei Hapusai had already lost his honor because he disobeyed a direct command from his warlord to kill Yuki, even if he was the only one who knew he had done so. Sensei Hapusai must have figured it to be acceptable to lose this personal honor since he would have many chances to regain his honor with future service to his lord. When Thomas killed his lord, he lost his opportunity to regain that honor."

Hardtack listened to me thoughtfully then spoke, "It sounds about right there lad. How do we use this information to our benefit though?"

I pondered a moment, "We don't give him the Murumasa blade as a bribe. We endow him with the Murumasa blade as a responsibility. Divine mandate trumps lost personal honor any day I figure."

Hardtack laughed at my last remark, "You'd certainly be right on that count."

That evening Captain Roberts invited us to his cabin for dinner. We were joined by his first mate and a junior officer as well. The five of us sat at the small table and began eating with little ceremony. I noted that Captain Roberts and his officers seemed in a better mood than when we had first boarded his ship.

Captain Roberts took a break after we finished our main course, and served us from his private stash of rum. I sipped carefully at mine like a cultured elfish diplomat. Hardtack quaffed his down like a typical dwarf bar patron and held out his cup for more.

Captain Roberts spoke up, "I want to thank you both for your assistance with that problem of mine. His uncle is Leonides Darnis. Unfortunately for the crew of the Mystic Dawn, Leonides is in charge of collecting the tariffs from the ships doing business in Port Cirnore. I had arranged to get a break on tariffs for doing Leonides the favor of teaching Rod an honest trade. It did not take me long to see I was getting the worse end of the bargain in exchange."

I looked at Captain Roberts as I raised my glass, "You're most welcome."

Captain Roberts spoke, "I hadn't thought of charging him with mutiny. Even if I had, it would have caused all kind of trouble if the accusation had come only from me or my crew. The Captain's Court would have likely sided with Rod Darnis against me to cull favor with Leonides. However, a passenger under protection of safe passage and a duly punished accomplice speaking against Rod with the court will change matters a lot. I think Leonides will potentially lose enough face over the deal that he will gracefully just bribe us Captains to overlook the matter."

I spoke up a moment, "Perhaps you could also sell Leonides on the fact that you saved his nephew from being butchered by Harack Orc Doom? Presenting Leonides with Jim Smitty should be sufficient evidence of what happens to those who cross Harack."

Captain Roberts smiled, "A hidden threat veiled within a convincing argument. I like the way you think sir. However, Thomas doesn't like me or my crew advertising who our passengers are to outsiders."

I looked at Hardtack who nodded, and then I spoke to Captain Roberts again, "I think Thomas will make an exception in this case. Our task is going to require word of Harack's identity and arrival to circulate around the docks and ports a short while before he disembarks from the ship."

Captain Roberts looked at Hardtack and then me, "You want my crew to talk about what they witnessed on the ship this trip? You have an interesting strategy sir. I take it your business will be in Port Cirnore then?"

I shrugged my shoulders, "We need word of Harack's arrival to travel around Port Cirnore yes."

Captain Roberts gave me a keen look, "This wouldn't have something to do with that new crewman who skipped ship a few weeks back. The old man he was with was trying to find out where he had gone when we last docked in Port Cirnore. Word is the old man even tried to talk a couple of other Captains into following the Mystic Dawn before we left Port Cirnore last time. Of course none of those scurvy dogs were willing to lose their ship by crossing my path on the open seas."

I shrugged my shoulders again, and casually said, "This old fellow you mentioned does seem interesting. Could you describe him?"

Captain Roberts looked at me closely again, and then at Hardtack before he spoke, "The fellow was not a local. His features were exotic, in much the same way the crewman we took on board had exotic features if you understand my meaning. He was an older man dressed like a local sailor, but he was not someone that moved liked an old sailor."

I raised an eyebrow and asked, "How would you say he moved if not like a sailor?"

Captain Roberts looked directly at me, "He moved like you. He kept his step sure, his gaze wary, and his mind alert. He moved just like a trained killer moves."

I was curious that he picked me as his comparison, "Why like me and not Harack?"

Captain Roberts laughed out loud along with his two officers, "That's easy to see sir. You move like a graceful trained killer to one who knows the look. Harack there moves like a natural born engine of destruction. I'd rather face twenty of you than one of him ever again. No offense intended sir."

I smiled gracefully, "No offense taken. I fully understand the merit of Harack's ability."

Captain Roberts then looked to his two officers in the cabin, "Prepare the men for the fear watch tonight. I want the designated crew on deck, and everyone else sealed below decks."

The first mate affirmed his order as I raised an inquisitive eyebrow. Captain Roberts detected my unspoken query as Hardtack leaned back in his chair.

Captain Roberts looked at me, "Tonight in the early hours of morning we make the transition. I recommend those people who are unprepared to deal with their fears to remain below decks or in their cabins. I only allow my bravest and most experienced crew to stand the fear watch."

Hardtack spoke up, "I've seen the transition already, so if you don't mind I'll choose to get some rest instead. It will be good to have a voyage where I don't have to keep an eye open all night for a change."

I was intrigued by Captain Roberts' statement, "If you don't mind Captain Roberts, would you please summon me from my cabin when the fear watch is called to stand on deck?"

Captain Roberts gave a suspicious smile, "Are you certain sir? The transition is nothing that most people are prepared to experience. It is found to be disturbing for some, and terrifying for many."

I knew this was bait placed by Captain Roberts. He was preparing a test of my mettle. Consequently I was prepared to face the test with what dignity I could manage. Given my experiences so far I thought myself as equal as any of his crew for the challenge. I gave Captain Roberts a semi bored look to let him think I was unimpressed and unprepared.

I answered in return, "It sounds like it could be something of interest."

Captain Roberts smiled deeper as well as his two officers, "Very well sir. We shall summon you for the fear watch."

As Hardtack and I returned to our cabin after drinks I lay in my hammock unable to sleep. I looked down to see Hardtack still looking up at me. He had a slight grin on his face.

I asked, "So is there anything I need to be afraid of during this transition?"

Hardtack shook his head, "It might make your balance a little wobbly and your stomach a little uneasy, but there is no particular danger in it. I don't want to spoil Captain Roberts' fun, but ultimately I think the surprise is going to be on him and his crew."

I managed to get a few hours of sleep in before I heard someone approaching our cabin. Once more I slipped out of my hammock and quietly positioned myself by the door. I kept a hand near my dagger, but didn't draw it when I heard the knock outside. I immediately opened the door to see one of the senior crew members with a new Harack mark on his arm standing politely outside waiting for me. He looked a little startled that I had opened the door so soon.

He spoke to me quietly, "The Captain says you were to join the fear watch."

I nodded to the man and followed him onto the main deck. I saw that it was fairly dark out on deck with only the light of the stars showing in the firmament. The large lanterns were hung fore and aft with another small lantern hung near the wheel on the stern deck. Captain Roberts stood by the wheel reading his navigational charts and referring to his compass and sextant. It struck me that this was not that different from Firanda referencing her magical instruments and charts all those years ago on the night we were killed.

I approached the bottom of the stairs on the stern deck and looked up at Captain Roberts. After a couple of moments he noticed me.

Captain Roberts called out, "If you'd like the best view of the transition, then I recommend you stand up by the bow rail. However, I do not recommend you look down over the rail as we pass through."

I nodded at Captain Roberts and moved forward on the ship. I understood this was the first part of the challenge. I was to be the first to experience whatever this transition was.

As I passed the mainmast I could see Rod Darnis awake and without a gag. He was obviously nervous about being present for this transition, and he looked already fatigued by his first day of light water and food rations. The senior crew hands were the only other crew above decks. Each one had gotten a Harack mark on their arm earlier that very day. I could tell these were the only crew Captain Roberts trusted to obey his orders in the midst of this transition.

When I reached the bow and looked down into the waters below I realized the ship was currently more floating than sailing. I looked back over my shoulder and up. There were several men in the rigging waiting for Captain Roberts' orders, and the majority of the sails were furled as if in port or waiting a storm to pass. The mainsail was partially deployed giving us reduced forward motion at the moment.

Captain Roberts checked his instruments again, and called out for the men to wait for it. I looked forward as I waited along with his men. Around two hundred yards ahead of the ship a vibration rippled across the relatively calm surface of the sea. I felt the deep rumble in my chest more than hearing it in my ears as the ripple hit the ship.

Captain Roberts called out, "Deploy full mainsail. Keep it steady helm."

Suddenly at the source of the ripple a great curtain of darkness unfurled upward from the sea against the night like a flag caught in a strong breeze. I recognized this as being similar to the shifting curtain gateway in the base of Thomas' tower home. I grasped the reason why the Isle of Death was so difficult to locate now. Only by being at the correct place at the correct time could a ship discover the gateway through to the land of shadow.

If this was the surprise Captain Roberts had in store for me, then he would be disappointed. I had already encountered the land of shadow, and I was not going to be intimidated by its eerie landscape. The Mystic Dawn picked up forward speed with the sail, and as we closed the gap with the rippling curtain of shadow I heard the sound of rushing water across the intervening distance.

The sea water was pouring through the enormous shadow gate. It made sense to me since this was to be a physical transition not just a spiritual one. A rushing channel of ocean formed through the gate and Captain Roberts expertly directed his crew to guide the Mystic Dawn into the channel. Our forward speed picked up greatly as we got closer. Captain Roberts ordered the mainsail furled. Then he called over the noise of the rushing sea for the fear watch crew on deck and secured fast.

I looked back at the crew and saw them tie themselves securely to the ship as they came out of the rigging. Captain Roberts began to tie himself off to the wheel along with his first mate. I took this as my cue to tie myself similarly to the bow rail. I wondered why we were taking this precaution as it struck me.

When we traveled to the land of shadow in Thomas' tower we had gone down, deep into the foundations of the cliff. We had gone below the level of the sea and further down again until we reached the gate to the land of shadow. I stood fast as the front of the Mystic Dawn crossed the shadowy boundary. I looked down over the rail and saw a disorienting view of empty air below the front of the ship as it began to be tilted forward at a greater and greater angle. The rear of the ship must have cleared the resistance of the gate because we then plunged rapidly down on the crest of a wave toward the land of shadow far below us.

I held on to my stomach and kept my resolve intact. I then heard the terrified scream of Rod Darnis. His screams continued over and over as we plunged down riding this falling wave of water. As we reached bottom the rushing wave was focused into a channel that shot us forward very rapidly. Also a great spray of cold sea water came rushing over the bow to drench me. I realized now why Captain Roberts had insisted the best position was forward. I had fallen for his trap and been initiated. I resolved to keep my dignity as intact as possible.

I looked back and noticed the others untying themselves so I followed suit. I walked back toward the stern deck noting that Rod Darnis had lost the remnants of his meager meal for the day on the deck planks. The other crew were either in various states of excited rush or serious focus as they returned to their positions.

I looked up at Captain Roberts smiling down at me, and I said in my driest tone, "I found that very invigorating. Is there another like it as we depart?"

Captain Roberts smile reduced somewhat, "Only on the return trip. Would you be good enough to get the end of the large rope by the bow anchor? When our tow arrives you can toss it over the channel to them."

Being from an inland kingdom I was familiar with the concept of a portage system between two bodies of water. Of course the portage system in the Kingdom of Ard was only large enough for small barges. This was the first portage system I had seen that worked for a sea going vessel. The fact that it ported a ship across a portion of the land of shadow just made it rather incredible. I wondered what kind of system they would use for pulling the ship forward.

As I approached the bow again I heard a familiar yowl come from the distance. I looked from the channel to the direction of the sound and saw a large shadowy form bounding across the land. I could tell the rest of the crew was terrified of the approaching beast. Even Captain Roberts lost most of his smile, but he still held a small sneer for me. I casually tossed the rope to the huge shadow Balinac approaching the channel. A small shadow beast fell off from the first and in a tremendous leap launched itself at me.

The crew looked on in shock as I caught it in my arms and began to carry it back to the stern while scratching its shadowy smoky fur. I heard mutters of demon tamer, cursed one, and unholy as I approached the stairs to the stern deck and climbed them for the first time on the voyage. Captain Roberts gave me a wary eye as I approached, and I could see a hint of fear for the first time ever in his face.

Captain Roberts quietly spoke with a touch of disbelief and fear in his voice, "Even Harack does not casually approach that unnatural beast. It is only controlled by the will of Master Thomas. What are you? How can you do this?"

I looked at him casually, "It is nothing special really. Balinac and I have come to an agreement is all."

The humongous Balinac looked back at Captain Roberts and gave a long low growl that shook the ship. It then picked up the large bow rope in its mouth and began striding forward with the ship in tow.

I looked Captain Roberts carefully in the eye, "It might suit you well to remember that I can be much better as a friend than as something else. I think Balinac and I will take a nap for now. Please send someone around later so I can witness the next transition."

With that said I casually returned to my cabin. I noticed on the way that Rod Darnis had thankfully passed out from sheer terror. When I entered the cabin with the small Balinac in my arms I could see that Hardtack had a smile on his lips and silent laughter in his eyes.

Hardtack whispered with a touch of joy in his voice, "I guess you showed to be of stronger stuff than Captain Roberts understood."

I shrugged my shoulders, "I think we're even now for him getting me soaking wet at least."

Hardtack gave a quiet laugh, "That you did boy. That you did."

Chapter 14 Port Cirnore

I slept for a while in my hammock with the small shadow Balinac napping on top of my chest. Once more I awoke to the sound of someone approaching the cabin door. I moved Balinac aside and approached the door. I heard the tentative knock and opened the door to see one of the Harack marked crewmen standing there. I followed him to the deck and could see the gigantic Balinac still pulling the ship forward through the channel.

I moved to an advantageous viewing position at the bow and I could see that we were approaching a large pool or small round lake at the end of the channel. A slow moving small vortex was in the center of the lake. It looked maybe five feet across, and certainly no danger to a ship the size of the Mystic Dawn.

Down below the surface of the lake I could see a large red crystal slowly spinning in the water. It looked like the one on top of Thomas' tower except that no light came from inside it. I could see that it was the slow motion of the crystal below which generated the vortex on the surface.

As we reached the end of the channel the gigantic shadow Balinac released the tow rope. I began hauling the rope in and carefully coiling it up as the ship gradually drifted toward the center of the lake. I saw the gigantic shadow Balinac bound off into the distance until it was out of sight. As the ship reached the center of the lake it began to turn about in a slow lazy fashion caught in the motion of the vortex.

I felt a familiar pulse accompanied by a red glow from within the lake below us. One beat. Two beats. Three beats.

I awoke to the light of dawn breaking the horizon as I lay on the deck at the bow. I sat up and noticed the crew and even Captain Roberts himself all lay on the deck in slumber. It seemed my elfish form had slightly greater recuperative powers from the effects of the transition from the land of shadow.

Deciding to take advantage of this ability, I quickly and quietly moved from the bow to the stern of the ship. I stood propped against the stern rail. I watched as Captain Roberts and his crew began to awaken from the transition. Captain Roberts stood up and turned to see me standing at the stern rail.

Captain Roberts gave me a thin smile, "Welcome to the other side of the outbound transition. It's always refreshing to see the Mystic Dawn has made it through to see another sunrise. You've done well to manage the transition with such ease."

I returned his smile with a larger one, "It's not my first time going over, although going over by ship is quite a different experience. How long before we make Port Cirnore?"

Captain Roberts replied, "In about two days with favorable winds."

I replied, "That sounds good. I will head to the cabin to rest a while."

As I headed for the cabin I heard Captain Roberts call for the relief of the fear watch. I entered the cabin to find Hardtack already awake. I also saw that the more normal looking two tailed leopard spotted black Balinac lay in my hammock waiting for me.

Hardtack looked at me with an odd look as we entered, "It seems you've brought Balinac over with you. I wonder how Thomas will take it now that you've made off with his guardian. Not that there is much threat to the Island. Thomas and the other inhabitants can protect themselves more than adequately."

I shrugged my shoulders, "Do you think I could get Balinac to do anything it did not desire to do on its own?"

Hardtack gave me a close look, "I really don't know lad. Not anymore at least. That beast has never left the Island since it arrived. Here it is with you. I just don't know what to think."

I shrugged my shoulders again, "I don't know what to say. I didn't command it to come. It came on its own initiative, or maybe on Thomas' orders."

Hardtack shrugged his shoulders as well, "Well I'm going to head out to the deck. I think its time to enjoy what sunshine we have today. A rain storm is coming soon."

I looked at him with a raised eyebrow, "How can you tell that? The sky was fairly clear when I was on deck."

Hardtack stretched a bit and laughed, "When you have had as many injuries as me, then you too will be able to know when a rain storm is approaching. Sometime after midday I would guess."

I replied, "Are you going to tell Captain Roberts?"

Hardtack laughed and shrugged, "Depends on whether Captain Roberts will play nice today. If he does not, then he can figure it out when he sees the dark clouds coming."

Hardtack left the cabin. I moved over to the higher hammock and picked up Balinac so I could enter it. I placed Balinac on my chest and tried to rest. Balinac opened its eyes.

A light purr came from Balinac before it quietly spoke, "I came on my own, although Thomas may realize I am here as well as there. Little escapes his notice over time."

I was curious about its statement, "You say here and there? Does that mean you are still on the Isle of Death too?"

Balinac purred, "Such I was charged to do by the Luck. However, I am not limited to a single location. My mass is variable as you may have noticed. I can divide my form or combine it. I grow larger as I am combined, and smaller as I divide. I rarely divide on the Prime though. It is much more challenging."

I understood the gist of it, "So you grow larger here by borrowing from yourself in the Land of Shadow. Doesn't it grow confusing keeping track of all of your different selves?"

Balinac answered, "No more than it grows confusing for you to move all of your limbs in different yet coordinated motion. It is just natural for me. Multiple forms on the Prime are a bit like juggling though. It takes a bit more concentration."

I thought about it for a while, "Are there other places?"

Balinac looked at me and yawned, "What do you mean other places?"

I replied, "Places other that the Land of Shadow and what you call the Prime?"

Balinac spoke, "Yes. There are many other places. Places where the gods and goddesses keep their dominion. Places ruled by demons and devils. Places where other powers maintain sway. Some places are small, some are large, and some are infinite."

I asked the question that was leading up to my conclusion, "Are you in those other places as well?"

Balinac shook its head, "I am only in the Land of Shadow and the Prime."

I asked, "Is that why you have two tails?"

Balinac nodded, "My manifestations have two tails since I exist as one being in two places."

I followed up with the question I had been seeking an answer for all along, "Does that mean a seven tailed manifestation is a single being in seven places?"

Balinac purred, "That's why I like you so much. You are very clever for a no tail. Yes, the Luck as it is known on the Prime is a big player in the information broker business. Its work on the Prime has been limited by its condition, but it has full sway on six other existences to barter and trade information."

I pondered, "So that is why I heard that the Luck knows things that were not meant to be known. Yet it sent you to watch Thomas. That's because it can't manifest in the Land of Shadow."

Balinac purred, "The form from the prime can travel to the Land of Shadow, but it can not stay there indefinitely. It doesn't belong there, so it needs my help to watch Thomas' activities there."

I then began to think about something different now that my curiosity was satisfied on that point. I wondered what caused Balinac to perform this juggling trick of splitting on the Prime. For some reason I trusted Balinac as if it were my friend.

Balinac purred, "You're thinking. I can see it in your eyes. You can ask your question. I will answer as best I am able."

I went ahead and voiced my concerns, "Why did you come along with me? What has really drawn you to watch over me?"

Balinac shrugged its shoulders, "I don't know what compelled me to come, but compelled I was. I have a suspicion that Thomas has done something to both of us. Something I have heard that the Lucky Cricket could do, but that until you came had never been done by another."

I looked at him with a raised eyebrow, "What do you think he has done?"

Balinac looked back at me, "I think Thomas has bound us together with a link. It has long been thought that the Lucky Cricket does this with spirit shamans and certain others. It is not a bond of control exactly, but it does cause people to cooperate with each other who might normally not think to do so."

I thought back to my second experience in the Land of Shadow, "How do you feel about Yuki now?"

Balinac thought about it, "Now that you mention it the compulsion is similar. I feel you both need my help and protection when there is risk involved. That is where he might have completed the process, but I suspect he started the process when he brought the three of us together at the warehouse."

I thought about it and then shook my head, "I think it goes back even earlier. Do you remember when we first met on the beach at the bay? You growled as we approached each other."

Balinac spoke, "I did that to warn Thomas of an intruder. Yuki had passed by there earlier. Even though her visible trail was gone with the tide, I could still sense the essence of her presence."

I put it together, "I recall then that Thomas said 'behave yourself' to you then. For some reason I selected those same words when I spoke to you in the jungle, while you held Yuki pinned to the ground. I think there was some power behind that phrase which was triggered and caused those bonds between the three of us to begin to form."

Balinac slowly shook its head, "It might be the power of the Lucky Cricket. It used the same words when it linked Thomas and me. Thomas may have figured out the way to trigger these links."

I nodded, "I believe it was through excitement, fear, and other kinds of extreme emotional response. Thomas is very good at evoking these things in people. They act as the basis for his formula and assist the power he is using in its working. The question remains though, why is Thomas doing this?"

I rested in the cabin for most of the day. Hardtack and I joined Captain Roberts for dinner again that evening. Balinac remained in the cabin content to rest. The dinner conversation was genial and stayed in safe areas of conversation. It seemed a truce was in place between Captain Roberts and Hardtack, which was going to help make the rest of the trip more peaceful.

While I had been resting earlier that day Captain Roberts had told the crew that they would be given a short liberty and a portion of their wages as spending money. Captain Roberts would also deal with the matter of Rod Darnis and the charges before the Captain's court.

Captain Roberts had also conducted a briefing with his officers, and they directed the senior crew to talk about what Harack had done as a passenger this trip. At the same time they were directed to not mention my presence at all. Their obedience to Captain Roberts along with memory of my carrying the small shadow Balinac was enough to convince them to comply.

I kept the fact that Balinac remained on the ship quiet for the moment. I knew it would only stir up fear among the crew for them to see what they knew as the

Death from the Isle of Death. Hardtack didn't seem prone to raise the issue with Captain Roberts.

It was still gently raining on the deck when we returned to our cabin. The storm was calm enough that we were able to maintain full sail along our course, although the rain certainly made things somewhat dreary. Hardtack figured the rain was likely to precede us to Port Cirnore.

We sat in a couple of chairs in our cabin by the small table. It was time to plan our next moves. I had been thinking about our discussions from the prior day and thought I had the basis of a plan. The presence of Balinac suggested some possible opportunities that were not present before.

Hardtack asked first, "So have you come up with something lad?"

I nodded my head, "I think so, but first I need to confirm something about resources available to us. Does Thomas have a couple of safe houses in Port Cirnore?"

Hardtack nodded, "There are several we can use. Some just for traveling teams, some for gathering information, and some for private discussions in more public seeming surroundings."

I nodded, "Is there one that Thomas can afford to have compromised by Sensei Hapusai? I'm hoping for one preferably that lends itself to seeming like a public place."

Hardtack nodded, "There is the inn on the far side of town away from the docks. It's called the Puking Dragon. Sensei Hapusai has already seen Hiram and Jack use that location, so it is considered compromised as far as he is concerned."

I was sidetracked by the name of the inn, "You don't mean the Drinking Dragon do you? It has a sign of a dragon with its head in a bucket. There was an inn like that in the Kingdom of Ard near the capital gates. It was infamous for attracting all of the adventurers."

Hardtack grinned a little, "It's a bit obvious, but each of our inn safe houses uses the same image for the sign. The names change but the sign remains the same. We encourage adventurers to meet and exchange stories at those inns. It keeps a couple of travelers from sticking out too much in that kind of outlandish crowd. It's a good way to pick up local gossip and rumors too. We even sometimes encourage other groups to use them like a safe house such as the local thieves' guilds. Always a place of safety in a storm we say. Of course they don't quite realize that Thomas owns the franchise as it were. It also helps to fund our business arm too. Those inns make a healthy profit really."

I listened politely, and then tried to get back on subject, "This place sounds ideal. If it is like the one in the capital of the Kingdom of Ard then it had a nice sized public dining room as well as some private meeting rooms. Lots of bodies around should reduce the chance for armed conflict hopefully."

Hardtack nodded, "I see where you are going. Keep him feeling safe enough to follow us to the inn. Then approach him open handed. It should give us a chance to speak with him without being attacked."

I shook my head, "That's it mostly but it's you that he'll be following hopefully. He'll hear the rumors of your arrival, detect that beacon you are carrying, and go to where you have gone. With your reputation it is unlikely he will attack outright, but with you carrying Yuki's beacon he will be hopefully unwilling to avoid coming to check you out."

Hardtack nodded, "I see how that might work, but what about you then?"

I smiled, "I'll leave after you, but take a more direct route to the inn. I'll get a private room and meet you inside after you talk to our friend and tell him we mean no harm. Take some time working your way near the taverns and bars by the docks and markets so the sailors already on land can point you out to any interested listeners. You'll leave an easy path for Sensei Hapusai to follow if he isn't waiting for us, and give me time to set up."

Hardtack smiled, "It sounds good, but what if he gets curious about me being alone and goes after you instead? It's pretty likely that he has realized we work in teams, and he is smart enough that he may be looking for the hidden member more than the obvious one."

I pointed at Balinac apparently sleeping on my hammock, "I think Balinac will be up to the task of keeping me alive in case that happens. I will carry the chest with the rest of Yuki's things to set up my sales pitch. You haven't left any of the magical or explosive things in here have you?"

Hardtack shook his head, "That was too dangerous to play around with so I destroyed all of it. The only things left in there are weapons and tools that don't kill you unexpectedly. At least they won't without a wielder. Thomas has appropriated all of the poisons though. He likes to study them to see if any new variants are in use."

I thought about it some more, "Can you play dumb muscle if necessary?"

Hardtack smiled stupidly, "Almost as good as I can cook."

Hardtack lost his grin, "You'll have to remember that Sensei Hapusai has been in position in Port Cirnore for a good length of time. Time he can have gotten some information and time he can have hired some muscle of his own."

I nodded, "I realize that is a possibility. That's why I'm hoping to get him out of Port Cirnore to conclude our deal. We will want all the leverage to be on our side of the table."

I looked over at Balinac, "Can you get a message to Thomas if we need it?"

Hardtack looked at me strangely then gaped a bit when Balinac nodded its head, "That beast can understand what you are saying?"

Balinac spoke back, "You're not the only one who can play dumb Harack."

Hardtack stared at Balinac in surprise, "Crap on a stick! All these years and you could understand everything people have been saying. Why didn't you speak up before now?"

Balinac looked at him with disdain, "Did any of you other than Thomas and Mica here ever bother to try?"

Hardtack looked a bit constipated then, "How long has Thomas known this?"

Thomas the Poisoner

Balinac purred, "Since the first day I came to him. We spoke then before he threw me out. I had to call the Luck to straighten things out. I just hate going to it for help."

Hardtack looked at me, "You knew about this as well?"

I shrugged my shoulders, "It was a confidential kind of thing. No offense intended, but Balinac likes people to not know about just how intelligent it is."

Hardtack looked back at Balinac, "Just how smart are you?"

Balinac returned Hardtack's look, "You are very good with your four limbs and twenty digits. Try multiplying that by more than one hundred sometime. The ability to do that and the intelligence to pull it off successfully are in my command."

Hardtack thought about it a while and shook his head, "Four hundred limbs and one intelligence, amazing. Does that mean you are still on the Isle of Death too?"

Balinac nodded, "Now you know why I don't like to talk. It is nothing but questions after someone knows that."

We made some more rough plans the next day, but a lot would ultimately depend upon how Sensei Hapusai decided to move. Hardtack would be the overt threat of certain doom for Sensei Hapusai if he did not cease his pursuit of vengeance. I would be the promise of hope held out to him. We would present him with a choice, but I didn't plan on letting him actually choose anything other than what I wanted.

Hardtack gave me directions on how to reach the Puking Dragon Inn. So once he and the sailors had departed the ship I would have to make my way there on my own. Hardtack also told me the pass phrase to tell the innkeeper to get me use of the reserved back meeting room, and he provided me with the twenty gold needed to rent it.

Toward the late afternoon the Mystic Dawn entered the bay which was surrounded by Port Cirnore. I had expected a run down shanty city to be the kind of locale which harbored and dealt with pirate crews. What I saw instead was a busy port town prosperous and clearly well kept. Many docks surrounded the bay, and the Mystic Dawn was led through the harbor and into a suitable berth by the pilot ship.

I was pleased to see that Breagor was assigned as one of Rod Darnis' guards along with one of the other senior crew members. Jim Smitty joined the small company that would go present Rod Darnis to the Captain's court for the filing of the charges. Jim went without his shirt proudly displaying the healing severed orc's head scar he had received from Harack. After they were safely away Captain Roberts released everyone other than the watch for shore leave.

Hardtack and I stayed on deck making small talk for several minutes till we figured that word had started to spread about his actions on the trip. He was dressed to kill, and would likely scare any common attackers away from him just by a glance. Hardtack set off from the ship making his way through the port toward the first set of taverns and bars. I already saw several people looking and cautiously pointing at him until he left my sight.

I was preparing to return to the cabin myself when I saw a puffed up looking officious man moving down the dock with a pair of guards in tow. I presumed this to be Leonides Darnis, and looking at Captain Roberts' sour expression on the stern deck confirmed my impression.

Captain Roberts met him at the top of the gang plank, "Greetings Leonides. I take it word has traveled fast about your nephew's misdeeds."

Leonides grew puffed up and red with anger as he glared at Captain Roberts, "This is an outrage! I will not only cancel our deal, I will see you banned from this port permanently."

Captain Roberts gave him a sharp glare in return, "I could have keel hauled that lad for his attempt to incite mutiny on my ship. Not only that but he attempted to do harm to passengers I have sworn safe passage to as well."

Leonides blew his breath out in a scoffing remark, "Ruffians and murderers more like. I've heard some of the rumors already circulating around the docks."

I figured this was my cue to join the discussion, "My dear sir, are you impugning that I am some kind of ruffian or murderer?"

I stepped forward using my training in haughty elfish airs to its fullest. I could see Leonides was caught off guard by the obvious expense of my clothes as well as my noble demeanor.

Leonides struggled to regain his manners, "Your lordship I beg your pardon, but this man is implying that my very nephew attempted to commit a heinous crime. You can understand that reflects poorly on my family and my own character. Such a lie will not be tolerated."

I soothed his ego, "Perhaps we can discuss this in my cabin in private. There is no need for your guards. Your safety is assured in my presence. Is that not right Captain Roberts?"

Captain Roberts played along with my game, "Yes your lordship. Shall I have some rum brought to you?"

I waved him off, "No thank you Captain Roberts. Hopefully we shall not be long."

We left Leonides' guards waiting on deck as I led Leonides to the cabin. I sat in the chair facing the hammocks while pointing to the chair across from me.

Leonides sat down, "Thank you your lordship. Now, about these charges placed against my nephew. It is obvious to me that Captain Roberts just wants to break the deal we made."

Leonides looked over his shoulder at the hammock and noticed Balinac sitting there with both tails twitching.

I drew his attention back to me, "I understand. A deal is a thing to be honored. Did this deal include your nephew attempting to incite mutiny?"

Leonides looked at me again, "Of course it did not. My nephew has proven to be somewhat lazy and unreliable. However, I wouldn't think it possible he would attempt something criminal."

I glanced over at Balinac who had subtly put on a bit more size, "I understand it is hard to believe, but I have to say that I don't personally appreciate assassins waiting outside my door in the middle of the night."

As I spoke Leonides had glanced over his shoulder at the subtly larger Balinac and then looked at me in confusion.

Leonides spoke while looking at Balinac again, "That's a very unusual cat."

His mind caught up with what I was saying then, "What assassins?"

I brought his attention back to me, "Your nephew and his accomplice who confessed to his involvement. They were standing outside my very door with drawn daggers in hands. Intending to assault my very well being I would guess."

Leonides began to get angry with me, "You must be part of this scam. You are no Lord. I'll see that Captain Roberts and his entire crew are tossed out of this port."

A low growl came from Balinac disrupting his train of thought. He looked over and could clearly tell that Balinac had grown larger.

I spoke calmly to him, "That won't suit my employer at all. You are correct that I am not a Lord, but I am an envoy for a very important man. It will not please him if you take unjust action against Captain Roberts. You nephew did just as I told you. He came to my cabin in the dead of night seeking to do me and my bodyguard harm."

Leonides was starting to bluster, "We'll you'll find that around here I am also a very important man. I don't think your employer can threaten me any. I don't care what kind of brigand or pirate he is. Yes, I know that Captain Roberts is a pirate. More than half the ships that dock here are pirates. I'm not intimidated by them I tell you."

I kept a calm face in front of his bluster, "Master Thomas will be so disappointed if I don't find a way to settle this."

I saw the hint of greed enter Leonides' eye as he spoke, "Well perhaps a slight increase in tariffs to make up for the humiliation done to my family name will be amenable."

I shook my head, "On the contrary we expect that you will maintain the lower tariffs Captain Roberts negotiated with you. You will likely need to make a similar deal with the Captain's currently in port if you want to save your nephew's neck."

Leonides shifted back to anger again, "That's outrageous blackmail. I won't stand for it."

I put a calm yet sad tone in my voice, "Master Thomas would be so disappointed I'm afraid. Are you sure you won't agree to my terms?"

Leonides hedged his bet, "I don't know who this Master Thomas you speak of is, but if he thinks he can threaten me with blackmail then he doesn't understand the strength of character behind the Darnis name."

I stuck with my calm tone, but added a touch of carefree menace, "I think you have heard of my Master Thomas. Perhaps his other name would be more familiar?"

Leonides cautiously challenged me, "What name would that be?"

I shook my head, "My employer requires the utmost discretion you understand. If word of this gets out there could be consequences."

Leonides called my apparent bluff, "Who is your master?"

I lowered my voice conspiratorially, "Thomas the Poisoner is the one I serve."

I kept my face disinterested as I witnessed all color drain from Leonides' face. It was clear that reputation was valuable after all. Balinac gave a deep low growl, and Leonides flinched as he looked in that direction. Then he stood up sharply and backed to the far corner of the room in fear as he looked at Balinac filling the entire hammock now.

I looked at him standing there shivering in fear, "I hope we have come to an understanding. I don't expect you to lose too much profit on this deal. You just need to collect the actual taxes you are required to collect from the Captains serving at court, and cut your share of the skimmed overcharge profits by half. Everybody wins, and I think you will be able to save your nephew's neck in the process. Don't you find that an agreeable solution?"

Leonides looked at me with a desperate plea in his eyes, "I'll do it. Just let me leave here alive."

I looked at him calmly as I strode over to Balinac in the hammock and petted its cool fur, "I'm glad we have a deal, but I must inform you I always intended to let you leave here unharmed. I gave you my word, and I fully intend to keep it. Let us hope this is the end of the matter then."

I opened the door and Leonides practically fled from the room. Even though he was pale faced he signaled his guards to follow and left the Mystic Dawn without a word to Captain Roberts. I came out on deck a few minutes later.

Captain Roberts looked at me with a hint of confusion, "That went well I hope. He looked more than a little bit scared as he left."

I looked at Captain Roberts and spoke, "He will abide by your bargain, and extend a similar bargain to the other Captains sitting on the court to get his nephew free of the charges. Please give them the word to accept it as a good deal in exchange for their cooperation. If you will excuse me I need to gather my things."

Chapter 15 The Puking Dragon Inn

I asked one of Captain Roberts' crew for a length of medium rope. I returned to my cabin and tied together a shoulder sling for the small chest which contained Yuki's gear. I picked up the chest, and adjusted my weapons to make sure they were both in easy reach. Then I picked up the cat sized Balinac and carried it in my left arm leaving my right hand free to draw my saber.

When I left the cabin I met Captain Roberts standing on the deck. He was apparently looking for further instructions.

I spoke first, "It has been a pleasure traveling with you Captain Roberts. Stay on your normal schedule, and if our business is concluded soon then we will leave with you on your return voyage. If there is a delay, then we will await your return."

Captain Roberts replied with a slight grin, "I shall be here for two days at least between shore leave and dealing with the Captain's court. The Mystic Dawn shall leave in three days at the longest."

Captain Roberts then looked down at Balinac held in my left arm, "I can see why Leonides was in such a hurry to agree with you now. I think you can be very convincing when you want to be."

I modestly waved him off, "Master Thomas is the convincing one. I just am judicious in how to use his reputation to best effect."

Captain Roberts nodded in agreement, "It is true his name can open certain doors. However, remember it can also bring untold trouble as well. It is best used sparingly."

I reached out my hand to Captain Roberts, "I also wish to thank you for putting up with the trouble we've made for you on this trip."

Captain Roberts smiled as he shook my hand, "You are a smooth devil aren't you. Gracious in victory, and calm in the face of danger. I can understand why Master Thomas picked you for this job. I offer my thanks for the help you've given me as well, and I'll pray to the goddess for your success."

I traveled along the docks until I found the central street through town. My sensitive ears caught bits and pieces of conversations about the renowned Harack Goblin Slayer, Orc Doom, and Ogre Bane being in town. I was pleased to see my tactic for drawing the attention of Sensei Hapusai was working even if the final result was still unclear. I traveled up the main street and left the area of the docks. The conversations and people on the streets tapered off to a reduced amount. Twilight was nearly upon me.

I saw the first youth go running off toward a side alley obviously bearing a message of my presence to someone. It was maybe a person acting as a lookout for thieves searching for a mark. The other distinct possibly was Hapusai Sensei had hired someone to find the hidden partner.

Casually looking around did not lead me to discover anyone clearly following me. I figured that just meant someone very good was following me, or several people were working together on lookout. I let a slight grin appear on my lips. It would make pursuers think they might have been spotted, and anyone else would likely ignore it. I figured when you might not be as good as your competitor, it was wise policy to make them think you were better.

I saw another youth running off to bear a message somewhere ahead of me. I casually rested my right hand on my saber to discourage regular rogues from attempting to surprise ambush me. After a few minutes I had not spotted any obvious observers, yet a third youth was running up the street directly ahead of me to a large building complex.

I looked ahead and saw the city gates a little ways past the building, and recognized the sign of a dragon with its head in a bucket hanging by the building. I had reached the Puking Dragon Inn. There was a sizable stables complex on the right side of the street, and a large courtyard beyond a low stone fence on the left side. Several people sat at tables around the courtyard enjoying drinks or food in the pleasant summer weather.

The structure of the inn itself was large and rambling. It varied between three and four stories tall, and several other structures were on the property as well. It was built solidly of stone on the lower floor, and aged wood on the upper floors. In spite of the warm weather several chimneys had smoke pouring into the sky above the building.

I could see that the people outside had various accouterments common to those living the adventuring lifestyle. They had bags, bedrolls, chests, staffs, swords, and armors both light and heavy among them. Several races and cultures were represented including some individuals from the wild races. I clearly understood why Thomas favored these kinds of locales for his safe houses. I didn't stick out at all as an elf carrying a small chest and a cat.

My sensitive hearing caught a few of the people outside scoffing things like new guy or amateur to each other. It was clear I wasn't considered quite one of them yet, but that I was accepted as someone who might be talked into buying drinks while they explained the proper way to adventure.

One comment as I approached the door caught my ear.

I heard someone behind me quietly say to a companion, "He looks like a trained killer, he might be the one."

I remembered back to Captain Roberts' comment of a similar nature. I knew for the future I would need to learn how to mask the presence of my martial training to fit in with certain groups. It was working in my favor for now, but I was quickly discovering that being inflexible would force people into certain expectations about behavior.

I also quickly surmised that Sensei Hapusai was already at my intended destination. Perhaps he had even been waiting here for the next arrival of the

Mystic Dawn. I could see where losing confidentiality of a safe house quickly turned it into a liability in normal circumstances.

I also saw this could possibly work to my advantage. The question which remained was whether Sensei Hapusai was looking to randomly kill someone, or was he looking for information to help him decide his next course of action. I was counting on the later for my idea to work, but I could well be wrong in my estimation of Sensei Hapusai as a person.

I continued into the main room of the inn with confidence. I was a touch stunned by what I saw inside. There was a counter near what was obviously a doorway to a kitchen. An innkeeper waited at the counter looking largely intimidating yet generally genial at the moment. On the wall next to the main entry door several bounty posters had been hung to give anyone inside a quick reference for anyone walking in or out. Over near the large yet unlit fireplace was a section of wall hung with parchments offering employment of various dangerous varieties.

There were tables all over the large room, long tables with benches, round tables with chairs, booths with high walls and curtains, and curtained alcoves with room for larger groups. The irregular shape of the room also provided several corners for small tables where people could keep their backs to a wall. These seemed to be among the most popular tables as every one of them was filled with a lurking and suspicious seeming person.

The noise was incredible as various groups of adventurers ate, drank, talked, and looked around the room at everyone. I was plainly in the midst of scrutiny as people weighed my value and abilities. It was quickly clear to me that I was simply one part of a larger crowd of people who were also getting their apparent worth measured by the others. I also took a long gaze around the room before making my way to the innkeepers' counter.

A large sign was hung over the innkeeper's counter which read: Welcome to the Puking Dragon. A smaller and longer sign below it read: Brawling, killing, and/ or robbing on these premises not welcome. Surviving offenders will be stripped naked and tossed outside the city gates.

I leaned in toward the innkeeper so he could hear me over the noise, "Hello good sir. I was told that you could provide a private room for the isle. I'm expecting some guests to come by soon."

I produced the purse with the twenty gold coins. The innkeeper held the purse below the level of the counter. He then opened it took a look inside, after a quick count he nodded his head.

The innkeeper leaned in close and spoke softly, "The fee is correct. You may want to know that a few of your guests have been waiting a couple of weeks for your arrival I think. They keep asking about visitors from there. Shall I let them back right away, or give you time to set up."

I replied with a smile, "If you could hold them ten minutes, or at least five if they are in a hurry it would be well. Don't forget to collect your finder's fee from them."

The innkeeper smiled broadly, "Oh they have already paid me half in advance, and will need to pay the other half before they are given the spare key to the room. Will you need a clean up crew in a while?"

I shook my head, "I will let you know, but this should just be a discussion I hope. Harack should be coming along soon, do you know him?"

The innkeeper smiled and nodded his head, "Brought out the heavy weapons this time hey. You must really be planning to impress. I'll keep the buckets and mops handy just in case."

I spoke again, "Have someone lead me to the room, and then bring a small cup of honey mead."

The innkeeper waved a young serving maid over and instructed her to lead me to the special room and to fetch me a cup of mead. The young woman was pleasant looking enough, but she was obviously new to this business. She looked back over her shoulder as we went to the hall leading to the kitchen.

She smiled a moment and said, "I have to fetch the key from the cook. Just wait here a moment. I suppose this is guild business then? That's a curious looking kitty cat you have there."

I smiled back but remained silent while she entered the kitchen, and shortly returned with a cup of mead in one hand and a key ring in the other. She passed me again and went down the opposite direction passing several doors until she came to one set in a heavy frame and made from heavy wood. She unlocked the door and handed me the entire ring of keys. On the inside was a comfortably appointed room with tile floors, stone walls, sturdy wooden dining furniture, and no windows.

As I entered the room I could see that it also had a bar for the inside of the door if desired. I presumed it was possible that one of the floor tiles could be lifted to reveal a passage to a subterranean exit of some sort. Since I wasn't briefed on this feature I didn't presume to be able to work it. The young serving woman placed my cup on the table, and departed the room. I closed and locked the door behind her, but I didn't bar it. The noise from the main room reduced greatly.

I thought it likely that one or more of the staff had been compromised, and the mead cup was potentially dosed with something unpleasant or deadly. I looked at Balinac as I set it and then the small chest I carried on the table.

I asked Balinac, "I don't suppose that poison affects your current form any?"

Balinac shook its head, "Nothing natural from the Prime will affect me adversely. Certain magic types can be unpleasant though."

I pointed at the cup, "Would you be so kind as to drink that up then. Leave just a little residue in the bottom though."

As Balinac began to drink my cup of mead, I opened the small chest and brought out the kunai knife that Yuki had attempted to use in suicide when captured. I coated the end of the blade with the sticky residue of honey mead from the cup. I then set the chest on the floor under the table.

Balinac looked up at me, "I didn't taste anything strange about that drink. If it was poisoned it was a very expensive one."

I was relieved, "At least the staff has likely not been too directly compromised then. Would you mind resting on the floor near my feet?"

Balinac left the table and curled up in front of my feet under the table. It blended in to the shadows in the dimly lit room until I couldn't see it down there any more.

Balinac spoke up quietly, "Three people are coming down the hall. Heavy tread, all muscle it seems like."

I frowned a little, "Hired hands, and not the person we need to speak with it seems. It is time to force the issue."

I could hear them finally just outside the door over the background noise from the main room. I brought the point of the kunai knife to just under my jaw and pointed at my throat. I awaited the sound of the key in the door and made a disappointed face.

The door burst open and three hired muscle started to enter the room until they saw me apparently prepared to kill myself. I looked the first one in the eye and gave him my best petulant glare.

I spoke with a weary tone, "Sensei Hapusai finds out nothing if I die. I will kill myself if you three don't immediately leave and send him in alone. This blade is poisoned with the blood of a tyrinax and will kill me instantly and painlessly."

Chapter 16 Sensei Hapusai

The first one looked at me in shock, "We don't know any Sensei Hapusai. We're just following the orders we were given."

I looked at him with a sharper glare if possible, "The old man who hired you silly fool. Hurry up about it or you will not be paid for your failure."

The three of them hurried out of the room leaving the door open. I kept waiting for a couple more minutes. Then I saw a meek looking short old man in a peasant's outfit cautiously peek his head around the door frame. It was obvious from his exotic features that he came from a similar part of the world as Yuki.

I smiled at this old man but carefully kept Yuki's kunai in place, "Sensei Hapusai please enter the room and close the door behind you. I only wish to have a conversation with you, but this threat of arms does not become you."

He spoke with unaccented trade tongue, "I don't know this Sensei Hapusai you are talking about young elf. I've just come by to see what all the noise is about."

I shook my head, "I have failed then. Togusawa Nene will be so disappointed in me."

I shifted my blade and started a motion as if I were going to slice my own throat. I watched his eyes go wide in shock at the mention of her name, and he moved forward into the room almost in a panic.

His eyes began to mist up with tears as he cried out, "Stop young elf. Don't do it. I am Sensei Hapusai. I will listen to what you have to say."

I looked at him closely as I held my hand in place, "Very well. Close the door but leave it unlocked. Please have a seat and mind my cat under the table."

He glanced cautiously under the table as he took the seat opposite from me. I knew that Balinac was now nearly impossible for my sharp elfish vision to see. It was likely not detectable by him.

I slowly moved the kunai knife away from my throat. The old man sitting across from me looked at it carefully as I set it down on the table between us. I smiled my best elfish court smile at him.

I spoke, "I take it that you are Sensei Hapusai and I want to say it is a pleasure to meet you. If you don't mind I want to set some ground rules for this meeting. First, I have no plan or ability to injure or harm you Sensei Hapusai. Second, any harm which comes to me will bring about great displeasure in my employer. Third, a very angry and murderous dwarf is making his way here through any impediments you may have set in his path. His name is Harack Ogre Bane and he will slaughter a path through this entire town to get here if necessary. I hope you haven't hired anyone foolish enough to try to forcibly stop him."

The old man spoke up, "I've heard his reputation. The orders I gave were to slow him down, not to engage him in a fight. He will be delayed, but not harmed."

I smiled again, "Very good then. Are there any conditions to the beginning of negotiation you would like to set?"

The old man spoke up, "What negotiations are these? The release of my student you have taken prisoner? Do you plan to exact vengeance on me for her slaying Thomas the Poisoner?"

I shook my head, "You don't understand the situation yet Sensei Hapusai, and it may not ever be completely explained to you. Your decisions now will affect your fate as well as the fate of your adopted daughter, the child of your Lord Togusawa."

The old man spoke again, "How did you know whose child she is? Even she did not know that fact, and no torture could have revealed it."

I smiled again, "While your daughter Nene did unfortunately suffer a broken arm while being dislodged from a tree where she was hiding, she is otherwise in good health. No torture has been performed on her. No potions have been administered to break her will."

Sensei Hapusai looked anxious as he spoke, "If she has not been harmed beyond her capture, then just what do you want from me?"

I gave him a serious look, "If you want to check your tracker, then I will allow it. I would like to know where Harack is at as well since he is bringing something precious here."

I could tell that Sensei Hapusai was on edge as he brought out a small magical device. It had glowing figures on it in a foreign script. Then he made a short mental calculation.

He smiled, "They should be here soon. How did you know I had such a thing?"

I shook my head, "I have some bad news and some good news for you. Harack is traveling alone. Nene has not come with him although she is quite safe for now. There will be no rescue attempt possible, and this situation will not be resolved as soon as you think. The other bad news from your perspective is that Yuki's message beacon was premature. She was mistaken about killing her target. Thomas is quite well in fact."

He looked at me suspiciously, "This is a trap then, you are delaying me until your murderous dwarf can arrive to kill me."

I shook my head, "That is the good news. Thomas figures since no harm was done there was no reason to take drastic action. He wishes to employ Nene in his service. He feels responsible for making her an orphan when he killed her father to find justice for her mother. He is grateful that you have looked after her all these years, and that you had enough strength of will to disobey a wrongful lord who would have another man slaughter his own infant child."

Sensei Hapusai looked confused yet wary, "You were sent to ask my permission to hire Nene?"

I nodded my head, "Exactly right Sensei. Thomas is a stickler for protocol after all. He wouldn't feel right hiring her without her adopted father's blessing. Nene already has the beginnings to become an excellent assassin, and Thomas feels that a change in emphasis from the martial to the social can do wonders for the quality of her work, and most especially for her as a person."

Sensei Hapusai remained wary, "You need me out of the way then to convert her to your cause. My death has been planned then. The killer is you not the dwarf."

Sensei Hapusai looked at the knife on the table and I took a guess as I spoke, "It is Nene's kunai. Unfortunately she originally sought suicide rather than capture. It is certainly the price of being an assassin as we both know. However, we had the Luck on our side and prevented anything serious from happening."

Sensei Hapusai raised his head sharply, "What do you mean by you had the Luck on your side?"

I became serious in my appearance, "You have heard of the Lucky Cricket then? How extraordinary and rare. Most people these days think him just a myth."

Sensei Hapusai became cautiously suspicious, "You've done your research well young elf. You are right that not many know of the Lucky Cricket Hap Sing. Hap Sing is also known as the legendary fisherman, the Spirit Shaman, and the bearer of the curse of the seven tailed beast."

I looked back at him calmly, "The seven tailed tiger to be more exact."

Sensei Hapusai looked at me with a measure of respect and curiosity in his eye, "Why do you know of such forbidden lore? Only the highest of spirit shamans know of such things, and those who work in the inner circles of secret knowledge. What does this have to do with our discussion today?"

I raised my hand slowly for a moment, "In time if you will. I have some items to return to you first. There is a small chest under the table which I will bring up and slowly open. There are no surprises or traps. However, I will open it or let you open it if you wish."

At Sensei Hapusai's nod I brought the chest out from under the table giving Balinac a gentle rub while reaching down below. I slowly placed the chest on the table next to the kunai knife. He waved for me to open the chest. I did so slowly so as to reveal Yuki's gear inside. After a quick glance inside he nodded.

Sensei Hapusai looked at me carefully now, "So at least one part of your story is proven true. It is only through capture or death that Nene would have surrendered all of these items. My eye says you are telling the truth about her being alive, but my heart says there is more for you to reveal."

I nodded, "What more can you tell?"

Sensei Hapusai continued, "You have handled Nene's belongings with care. You knew which kunai she would have used to attempt her own life. I can see the mark of an interposing blade on the kunai which prevented her from doing so."

Sensei Hapusai looked into the small chest again, "All of the dangerous and magical devices have been removed from this set of belongings along with all of the poisons. The basic weapons are all that remain."

I nodded, "Removed to help insure everyone's safety."

He looked me in the eye, "Was it your blade that kept her from suicide?"

I shook my head, "I was making the attempt when Harack's thrown kunai intercepted Nene's. You must forgive me Sensei Hapusai as I am still just a novice."

Sensei Hapusai looked up at me, "You are hardly a novice young elf, even if you are not yet a master. I can see skill at work behind your ability, and there has been great care put into your training. You are probably deadly fast on your feet, but I suspect your mind is even quicker."

I ducked my head down, "You embarrass me with your estimation Sensei Hapusai."

I could see Sensei Hapusai took some time in thought before speaking again, "The dwarf Harack is a slayer. Reputedly he is a nation killer and possibly the most deadly opponent one could ever face in single combat. He also has mostly disappeared over two hundred years ago."

I nodded my affirmation, "Harack Ogre Bane has retired from killing. Now he occasionally takes on one or two apprentices."

Sensei Hapusai was calculating in his mind, "The killing machine teaching future generations to be perfect killers as well. Harack is training you? Yes, I can see it in your eyes, and Harack will train Nene if I agree as well."

Sensei Hapusai looked me in the eyes, "Thomas did send you to come here, but you are the junior member of the team he sent."

I nodded, "I was not sent to kill you if that is what you mean. Nene even begged Thomas not to do so for fear you would kill me outright."

Sensei Hapusai nodded, "You are a skilled negotiator for certain, but I still am unclear what advantage comes to me for ceasing my quest for vengeance."

I could tell by the sudden silence in the main room of the inn that Hardtack had likely arrived and shocked the patrons into silence with his intimidating presence.

I spoke up to cover the change in ambient noise, "I think I will be able to amply demonstrate that for your satisfaction in a moment."

Sensei Hapusai looked at his tracker and his body language showed that he had visibly surrendered, "Your killer is outside. I have fallen for your trap now and must hope that my demise is not what you are seeking all along. You have successfully intrigued me into listening to the rest of your case."

I called out loudly, "Come in please Harack. Sensei Hapusai is looking to make your acquaintance."

Hardtack casually strolled into the room with a broad grin on his face, "I knew you could talk a little sense into Nene's Sensei my boy."

Hardtack stuck out his hand casually toward Sensei Hapusai, "I'm real glad to meet you sir. You've done quite a fine job in training Nene. I'm looking forward to starting her accelerated training as soon as she is ready."

Sensei Hapusai looked surprised, "You are not quite the brutal killer I was expecting."

Hardtack laughed, "Sorry to say that was in my misbegotten youth. I'm reformed now and haven't killed anyone in nearly two hundred and sixty years. I just keep my hand in learning new forms and styles out of habit mostly. Take on the occasional promising student like the lad there. You know how it is right."

Sensei Hapusai looked at Hardtack with a touch of disbelief, then his glance came back over to me, "Slaying his way through town you said. I can see that I've been masterfully played here. I take it that you are prepared for the next part of your plan now."

I nodded and spoke up, "Shut and bar the door Harack. Nothing funny here but now that our delivery has arrived I think you will be impressed."

Hardtack stepped back over to my side and slowly reached for the Murumasa blade. I could see Sensei Hapusai master his will as he prepared for any contingency. Hardtack pulled the blade and sheath from his sash and laid it across both of his hands as he reached out to set it on the table in front of Sensei Hapusai.

Sensei Hapusai frowned slightly, "Is this meant as some kind of payment or bribe?"

I kept a serious face as I shook my head, "That blade is not for you. Examine it if you will."

Sensei Hapusai stood up and carefully drew the blade from its sheath. He peered down its length, and then grasped it in what I recognized as a killing grip and suddenly swung it for my head. I held steady as Hardtack casually and properly interposed his short blade to deflect and block its motion without damaging either blade.

Sensei Hapusai withdrew the blade and looked at it very carefully again as he considered my solid serious appearance and Hardtack's casual use of his own blade in my defense.

Sensei Hapusai bowed before us, "I am most sorry for my rudeness. A test had to be made on my terms to determine your character. Sensei Harack you are most assuredly a superior master to myself and I completely acknowledge the fact. I never saw your blade clear its sheath before you had intercepted my stroke. No one I have ever met could best you."

Hardtack returned his bow, "I have been practicing for nearly three hundred and fifty years. I have a slightly unfair edge on many."

Sensei Hapusai then looked at me, "You claim to be the junior, but you are as confident and poised as any senior I have ever encountered. You stood before my stroke without fear, and fully prepared to die. That shows great confidence in the skills of your Sensei, but it shows even greater conviction in your skills in convincing me."

I shook my head, "I was just shocked and slow perhaps. You give me too much credit."

Sensei Hapusai shook his head, "You could have dodged my stroke I would guess. You could have even flinched in front of my stroke. You met it with your eyes open and your nerves steady. You did see your Sensei's blade clear its sheath even if I could not. You knew your protection was coming. That takes nerves like steel. Not many could stand before such a threat like you have."

Sensei Hapusai shook his head, "Neither of you are slaughters or killers. I unfortunately stand before men of honor displaying my own shame. I apologize once more and beg your forgiveness."

I spoke up, "Consider it given for there is nothing to forgive. This is a meeting before dangerous individuals, and rough spots are to be expected. I take it you have a full understanding now that we intend no harm to you or Nene."

Sensei Hapusai nodded, "I acknowledge that either one of you could have slain my daughter had it been your wish. Sensei Harack could have easily slain me had I brought you to harm. What would you have done if I had attacked you instead of talking with you though?"

I shook my head, "It is meaningless to speculate on that point right now. It is a good thing that issue is in the past."

Sensei Hapusai looked at me then, "What does this blade mean? It seems like I should be familiar with it, but I don't recognize the markings or the craftsmanship. It appears very old, yet well kept anyway."

I casually pointed at Hardtack, "It is something that has come into his possession over the years. It needs to be returned to its proper owner, yet Hardtack has other obligations and can not take the time to find them. We were hoping to find the right person to take the responsibility to find its proper owner. Perhaps you have heard of the Murumasa blade?"

I could see a visible change come over Sensei Hapusai. The stuff of legend was in his hand. This was the sword he understood which could win control of a kingdom. His hand began to slightly tremble and he carefully placed the sword back in its sheath. He laid the Murumasa blade gently on the table.

Sensei Hapusai looked at us with a sense of wonder then awe, "Why me? What have I done to earn this? I used it like a common sword. I couldn't be worthy to bear it in my hands."

I looked at him with a genuine smile, "I could not find a better man for the job than someone who did what was right rather than just satisfy their own honor. You saved Nene from Lord Togusawa's order of death. You sacrificed your personal honor for the life of a mere child. I don't think there is a better choice of person anywhere to bear the burden of finding its proper owner."

Sensei Hapusai looked up at me with a different set of eyes, "I think I can see what has happened now. Nene has fallen in love with you hasn't she?"

I nodded my head carefully in consideration, "It started as a simple crush on her part, but it is changing and growing instead into a love of brotherhood."

Sensei Hapusai thought about it, "You are sparing my life to make her happy?"

I shook my head, "Thomas is sparing your life to make her happy. I am just his instrument in this matter, though I am glad I have become successful."

Sensei Hapusai looked at me carefully, "This wasn't Thomas' plan or your Sensei's plan. You planned and executed it to perfection."

I ducked my head again, "You embarrass me once more Sensei Hapusai. It was clear to me that threatening your cooperation would have never worked. I needed you to understand that Thomas does not kill needlessly. Thomas only kills for justice."

I lifted my head and looked him in the eyes, "However, an injustice was also done when you lost your honor for doing the right thing. I am the one who is sending you on the quest to find the rightful bearer of the Murumasa blade. You can restore your lost honor, and justice will be fulfilled."

I figured it was time to put the deal sealer in place. I tapped the floor under my foot as I stood up to face Sensei Hapusai and perform a bow to him. He returned my bow then looked down at Balinac walking out from under the table and the concealing shadows. As Balinac jumped up into my arms Sensei Hapusai stared at it in confusion.

He casually looked at it and a nervous look entered his eye, "From where did that cat come? It seems a most curious breed."

I smiled and spoke, "I mentioned that my cat was under the table."

A second identical Balinac jumped up into Hardtack's arms. Hardtack took it in stride and held it gently. A third Balinac came out from under the table and stood in the rear of the room. The three Balinac's were twitching their six respective tails.

Sensei Hapusai looked at me with the color draining from his face, "This doesn't make sense. I looked under that table and nothing was there."

I answered his question he had asked earlier, "My insurance policy was there. Remember you asked what I would have done if you had entered attacking. Balinac there would have solved my problem quickly and messily. I am very glad we were able to come to an agreement for Nene's sake."

Faster than the blink of an eye the Balinac from the back of the room jumped forward and stood enlarged face to face with Sensei Hapusai. A low growl came from all three of Balinac at once. Sensei Hapusai stood firm but slightly shaken.

Sensei Hapusai looked past the Balinac in front of him and into my eyes, "Do you understand what this thing is?"

I calmly spoke, "That is Balinac the two tailed beast assigned by the Lucky Cricket to Thomas as his guardian and the guardian of those who work for him. I hope you understand the ramifications of what this means in regards to our deal."

Sensei Hapusai nodded, "If Thomas wanted me dead then I would have been so without ever knowing it had happened. You are a very clever person young elf. I once more have to bow before another kind of superior Master. I clearly see why Thomas has placed his trust in you. What shall I call you if we ever meet again?"

I smiled at him once more, "You may call me Mica. It is the name your daughter Nene uses for me. I want you to know that I love her like my shield brother as well. I will always protect her from harm to the best of my ability."

Sensei Hapusai bowed after the third Balinac retreated and shrunk again in the back of the room, "I could not ask for better protection than you will provide my daughter Mica. I also could not provide better instruction to my daughter than you will give Harack. I consign Nene to your care. I also set her free to enter employment with your Master Thomas, and I will write her a scroll detailing that you have dealt with me fairly and with good intent. I will also inform her that my honor has been restored by the task you have given me to accomplish."

I watched as Sensei Hapusai pulled a small scroll from his garments along with a quill and ink. He wrote a message in his native language which I could not read, but felt would adequately explain things to her. Sensei Hapusai then sealed the scroll with wax and an insignia stamp. I accepted the scroll for Yuki with a bow. I carefully placed it in an inner pocket of my shirt.

I reached out my hand to Sensei Hapusai. He in turn reached out to provide a surprisingly warm handshake.

Sensei Hapusai looked me in the eye with what I felt was a genuine smile for the first time, "I thank you Mica for looking after my daughter. I also thank you for going out of your way to find me a clear path to leave her in good conscience. I will depart now."

Sensei Hapusai collected up the Murumasa blade and the small chest of Yuki's gear. Hardtack unbarred the door and opened it for him to exit. I sat back down and relaxed with Balinac on my lap. I could still hear the murmurs from the main room of the inn as Sensei Hapusai departed our presence.

I sat back rather satisfied that I had successfully encouraged Sensei Hapusai to move on to other pursuits than vengeance over the death of an ignoble man. I looked at Hardtack and gave a slight grin.

Chapter 17 Rest and Relaxation

I sat back in the chair and breathed a sigh of relief. I was feeling the tension become noticeable now that Sensei Hapusai had left.

I spoke up, "It was a bit touch and go there. I had to be careful not to reveal my trump card too soon, but to keep him interested in both my hints of threats and hints of secrets to learn."

Hardtack looked at me, "How did you keep him from grabbing you or killing you outright?"

I smiled, "I held Yuki's kunai to my own throat covered in mead to look like poison. I threatened to kill myself if he wouldn't agree to talk with me alone."

Hardtack looked at me with pride, "Good opening bluff, but he should have seen through it"

I grinned, "He did, and he even came in with crocodile tears in his eyes too."

Hardtack nodded, "He's a crafty old ninja to be sure. He was full of compliments and apologies too. Trying to manipulate you as hard as you were trying to manipulate him I would guess."

My smile lessened, "Do you think so?"

Hardtack nodded, "Most certainly. He got the information he needed to determine his vengeance was completely out of reach. Like most ninja he is a very practical man. Do what you can, leave the rest up to fate kind of thinking. You probably had him convinced that he needed to rethink his actions long before I got here."

I was serious now, "What makes you say that?"

Hardtack grinned, "He knew that it was to be a battle of wits, bluff, and counter bluff the moment you sent his bully boys packing without laying a finger on them. We thoughtless killer types don't play the game that way. We maim and kill as our system of threat and bluff. You saw me at work on the ship using it after all. The fact that you wanted a discussion instead of a fight probably left him very interested, and trapped by his own curiosity. It was a brilliant plan."

I smiled again, "I hate to say it, but I was improvising that part. I didn't originally expect him to be waiting here for my arrival. I was lucky to spot his messengers running alerts of my position to the inn."

I thought about the change in plans a bit, "Why did it take you so long to get here anyway? Sensei Hapusai mentioned a delay arranged, but seemed confident you were not slaughtering anyone."

Hardtack laughed, "Sensei Hapusai won that round over you for sure. I think he caught on to your ruse about my fierceness, and sent a bunch of toughs looking to get knife art like the Mystic Dawn crew in my direction. It kept me busy for way too long dealing with the requests."

I shook my head and laughed, "We just handed that crafty old fox the blade to win a kingdom."

Hardtack shrugged his shoulders, "I don't think you did any wrong there. I do think he is a man of honor, and that he will take your quest seriously. I think he was mostly concerned with the type of people who would be caring for his daughter. You did a good job of satisfying him there. You showed him a fierceness, bravery, loyalty, and intelligence which is a rare combination my lad. Mostly you showed your core of good sense in handling a situation outside of your full control."

I was curious about something which happened earlier, "Hardtack could you read the message he sent Yuki?"

Hardtack nodded with a subtle smile, "It was a personal message between a father and a daughter, but it conveyed what we wanted it to as well. It lets her know that accepting employment and other things like trusting us are acceptable. If you noted the seal he used, then you should know the orientation is likely very important. A few degrees one direction likely means the message isn't to be trusted. A few degrees in another direction means the message is valid. It is impossible to know which orientation means what between them, but I suspect Yuki's reaction to the message will let us know once it is delivered."

I sensed that Hardtack was holding back on me somehow, but that it would be futile trying to learn more from him now. I also thought about the fact that we were doing pretty good in terms of finishing our mission objective with two days left in a thriving port community to relax and enjoy ourselves. I looked over at Hardtack and thought I caught a mischievous gleam in his eye.

I spoke up, "The Mystic Dawn is in port another two days at least. What do you plan to do with your time in Port Cirnore?"

Hardtack had a sly grin cross his face, "I think it may be time to do some bare handed practice tonight. Adventurers always have so many new moves they've learned. I might see something new here, especially if there are any monks in the crowd."

I gave him my dry smile again, "That sounds like great fun."

Hardtack shook his head, "I understand that's not quite your taste in entertainment. You should know that some of those lady adventurers are like cats in season if you catch my meaning. They'll leave a handsome elf like yourself all scratched up, but it will be great fun in the process. At least so I've been told."

I shook my head, "I don't think so. I've never been comfortable with that kind of behavior. I would like to talk with a couple of the magus here though. I always find their stories fascinating."

Hardtack shrugged his shoulders, "Good luck with that. Those types are always closed mouthed about their work to outsiders. It's easier to get a thief telling secrets about their trade."

The other two extra Balinac returned to the shadows under the table leaving just the Balinac in my arms. Hardtack and I came out of the back room and returned to the main room together. Once again there was silence as all attention in the room focused on Hardtack's presence.

I returned the ring of keys to the innkeeper who smiled at me. The innkeeper returned my pouch with only one gold piece removed. I quickly grasped that the fee for the room was just a single coin, but that the amount of gold kept in the pouch was a secret between the Isle of Death and the Inn. The number changed with each use of the room and thus was kept by the holder of the pouch and the innkeeper's memory.

Hardtack looked at me, "The word is out my lad. It doesn't look like I'll be getting any fun tonight. Let us just grab a table there in the middle and have a couple of drinks."

Hardtack looked at the room at large with a wicked smile, "Since none of you seem to be ignorant about who I am, I think you can go back to your drinks. I won't be killing anyone tonight for your entertainment. Though if any monks or fighters are present I wouldn't mind a discussion about any nifty combat moves you know."

A group of mixed dwarfs and humans waved Hardtack over to one of the long tables. A somewhat elderly looking bearded gentleman in blue robes sitting at a table by the unlit fireplace nodded in my direction as I remained by the counter. I asked the innkeeper to send a serving girl over, and approached his table.

I gave him a warm smile, "Did you want to speak with me?"

The elderly gentleman smiled in return, "I did indeed. Would you join me sir?"

I nodded my agreement, "I would be honored to sir. My companion is going to be in a rowdy discussion for half the night. I was looking forward to a more sedate and reasoned one."

The noise in the room gradually grew back to its previous levels although several people still looked at Hardtack and me frequently. I shrugged my shoulders as I took a seat. It seemed that my Hardtack rumor had caught up with us in a major way. I should have figured that adventurers would be on top of such things quickly.

I sat down and noticed the elderly gentleman was of mixed elfish and human heritage. I figured he must have been fairly advanced in age indeed. He kept a pleasant look on his face as I took a seat.

I held out my hand, "You can call me Mica."

The elderly gentleman extended his hand to me as well, "I am known as Glorandel the Blue Sage in these parts. I couldn't help but notice that you were conducting private business with our mysterious recent visitor and the legendary Harack the Slayer."

I nodded my head in confirmation, "My employer requires discretion about the nature of his business you understand."

Glorandel nodded and continued on, "I take it that in my observations of the three of you that everything was concluded in a satisfactory manner for all parties."

I smiled, "We did reach a mutual accord with one another."

Glorandel spoke, "The Murumasa blade was a part of that accord then?"

I looked at him carefully, "You are a remarkably well informed individual."

Glorandel smiled broadly, "I am a sage after all. It is our business to be well informed about objects and people with legendary status. For example since Harack the Slayer originally disappeared two hundred and fifty seven years ago he has only been reliably spotted around eight times. Five of those times in Port Cirnore at the Puking Dragon Inn, and three of those times in the last fifty two years."

I smiled broadly as well, "It does seem you have done a lot of research then."

Glorandel nodded, "The elderly gentleman who sent those hired thugs to visit you, then came to see you himself is Hapusai Ran. Supposedly a disgraced ronin ninja and at one time considered the premier ninja master in Yokito the capital of Ran Li. It has been said in certain circles that for the last twenty some years he has wandered on a mysterious quest with his student to find his Lord's killer. Yet today he departs with the sword that could set him up as the ruler of Ran Li and any of three other kingdoms if he desired. A sword I noticed was in the possession of Harack the Slayer earlier this evening."

My smile decreased a bit, and I was feeling saved by the arrival of the serving woman. I ordered a loaf of fresh bread and a glass of wine. Glorandel ordered a burgundy.

Glorandel's smile remained genial as he began talking again, "Then there is the matter of the arrival of the ship the Mystic Dawn in the late afternoon. Of course this is the very ship which Captain Westly Roberts, also known as the infamous Dread Pirate Roberts, commands. The curious thing there is although the Dread Pirate Roberts has a bloodthirsty and ruthless reputation in general, no one can reliably credit him with any actual acts of piracy in over fifty years. He is also remarkably well kept in all that time since he should be well over eighty five years of age by now."

I nodded at him, "While this is fascinating information, I am a bit confused about what does this has to do with me."

Glorandel nodded and continued, "I'll get there soon my fellow. What I found curious is my sources told me that Harack entered the port as a passenger from that very same vessel. He was preceded by several of the crew bearing stories of his dramatic actions on their journey from whatever undisclosed port they picked him up. Mind you this is a notoriously tight mouthed crew normally."

I took a sip of my drink and a bite of bread before I responded, "You don't say."

Glorandel took a sip of his brandy in exchange, "Furthermore a bound person was escorted from the ship. It turned out to be one Rod Darnis well known riffraff from Port Cirnore with advantageous social connections. Namely the overly self important Leonides Darnis his uncle and the minor noble in charge of customs enforcement for Port Cirnore."

I was beginning to get the hang of this challenge now, "My dear sir your knowledge is like a tome of great length."

Glorandel took another sip of brandy, "The fascinating part was that this Rod Darnis was charged with conspiracy to mutiny before the Captain's court. I personally find it hard to countenance that a dullard like him would have the courage to stand against Captain Roberts. Most interesting was what happened next though. An upset Leonides Darnis shows up and has for some reason, most likely money I presume as that is his primary motivator in all things, conjured up enough courage to confront Captain Roberts."

I set down my glass after another sip of wine, "What happened next?"

Glorandel smiled, "Well you came on deck and Captain Roberts deferred to you to speak with Leonides about the matter. The two of you disappeared from sight into a cabin, and when Leonides came back out he looked like he was about to faint from fear. Leonides collects his guards and rapidly leaves the deck of the Mystic Dawn without even a glance toward Captain Roberts. Later after you left the ship bound for the famous adventurer's hangout the Puking Dragon, Leonides is seen in conference with each of the other Captains currently in port who comprise the Captain's Court. The charges of mutiny are dropped against his nephew Rod Darnis who was released from custody, but Leonides looked none too pleased about the outcome."

I looked at Glorandel with a raised eyebrow, "You learned all of this while being here by the fireplace since I arrived? It seems like a lot of current knowledge for a Sage. Don't you specialize in ancient knowledge?"

Glorandel nodded his head, "Of course I do that as well. Take for example that strange creature of feline form you hold in your lap. To the uneducated eye it may appear to be some kind of relatively common magical aberration which bears two tails. To a Sage like me it appears to be a Prime manifestation of the two tailed beast Balinac. This two tailed beast Balinac is of relatively immense power and intelligence when compared to most common Prime denizens. These multi tailed beasts as they are called by those who are Spirit Shamans are generally unique examples of multi-planer beings. The more tails the more planes of existence they concurrently access you see."

I nodded my head, "You are an absolute font of knowledge. Are you not afraid that the others in the room might accidentally hear something you don't intend for them to know?"

Glorandel shook his head, "Oh that might be a concern for others, but I've put up a minor magical barrier that allows sound in to us, but doesn't allow our conversation to be heard by others. It's is one of my earlier pieces of spell research. I find it very valuable for a sage who desires privacy while remaining in public. The regular patrons here are quite used to not being able to hear what I say. My spell also has a component similar to a god priest's sanctuary spell. Most people grow disinterested in hearing or listening to what I am saying unless they are within the barrier itself."

I smiled again, "A brilliant bit of work, but what if someone was to interrupt your spell."

Glorandel grinned, "None have ever found it worth their while to try a second time. A counter spell is also interwoven with the first spell. If someone attempts to disrupt my original spell their ears become filled with the gentle sounds of me reciting the entire Cycle of the Qualanti. It's a tragic ancient tale of the lost elfish nations during the time of the Great War over two thousand years ago. It's very beautiful especially as I recite it in the original elfish tongue. Occasionally a new adventuring spell caster is tricked by the others here into attempting to disrupt or bypass my spell. They seem to find it funny for some reason. I like to think that I am providing them an education myself. I believe certainly on one level if not on many."

By this point I had noticed three youths cued up near the main door of the inn looking in our direction, "Pardon me Glorandel, but it seems more of your messengers have arrived."

Glorandel looked embarrassed, "I'm sorry they are told to wait if I am with company. They would only interrupt if something of note was learned. If you don't mind would you give me a moment of privacy?"

I rose from the chair with my empty glass. I looked around the room to see Hardtack still at the long table listening to the description of an encounter with an Ogre from one of the dwarfs at his table. Looking back I saw that the first youth who was waiting at the door now stood next to Glorandel. True to Glorandel's word I not only could not hear what was being said, I also had to actively fight to keep from losing interest in their conversation. Glorandel was obviously very talented at what he did.

I stopped fighting the effect of the spell, and looked back over at Hardtack again. Hardtack was complementing the dwarf's solution to his Ogre problem, and then Hardtack began suggesting alternate ways to manage a similar issue in the future. I could see that the entire table was listening intently to Hardtack's advice with nodding heads and broad smiles.

I realized I could use a break, so I went outside and looked for a privy. Several adventurers watched me with a new level of respect from when I had first entered. The privies were lined up near the city wall, with multiple ones available for use. I entered one and set Balinac down while I relieved myself.

Balinac spoke, "The first message was that Sensei Hapusai has booked passage on a ship heading for a major port where he can make his return journey to Ran Li. The second message was that the search of the elvish ancestry registries requested failed to locate any elves of your generation named Mica. As we were leaving I also made out that the third messenger had not managed to return with any desired information."

I nodded my head, "Glorandel is checking up on me, and it's bothering him that he can not figure out who I am. He is narrowing in on what I am very quickly, but that doesn't mean anything to his type if they can't place the who as well. If you don't mind I am going to continue this game a bit. It is about to get fun."

Balinac jumped back into my arms, "I would advise you to be careful with Glorandel. I can easily believe that he is quite capable of causing large problems if provoked. Those who are not spirit shamans who know as much as he indicated about tailed beasts are not individuals to be casually annoyed."

I thought about the information Balinac had for a bit, "Is his spell somehow flawed? How did you hear his conversations with the messengers?"

Balinac smiled, "Glorandel is a right about one thing. Tailed beasts are very intelligent. I knew better than to tangle with his spell as I've already heard the Cycle of the Qualanti more than once. I simply watched his lips moving."

I was a bit surprised, "You can understand what people say that way?"

Balinac purred, "Even across a very noisy room. I was following twelve separate conversations. It is one of those large intelligence activities to follow that many conversations at once. It's a valuable skill to watch lips to understand what is said. Even you could learn it over time."

I returned to the inside and saw Glorandel waving me over to his table again. I noticed fresh drinks were already waiting as I sat down.

I gave him a smile and spoke, "Sorry a call of nature precipitated my departure. I heard that Hapusai Ran managed to book passage on his way back to Ran Li on my way back inside though."

Glorandel looked a bit surprised, "Did you really? It seems you are well informed of current happenings as well."

I saw him glance down at Balinac suspiciously and I asked him, "Did your messengers have similar news?"

Glorandel returned his attention to me, "Why yes they did in fact Lord Mica. At least such was the title used by Captain Roberts. It is not a particularly common appellation for an elf though. Most of the remaining nearby elfish nations are formed using a Republic model. Several non-elfish nations of a feudal nature do occasionally have elfish nobility though."

I shook my head, "I'm sorry the use is deceiving. I am merely a representative of a business, and have been trained in manners and etiquette which might accidentally lead to an inaccurate conclusion like the one made by Captain Roberts."

Glorandel made a move for what he thought was the kill, "What is it like working for Thomas the Poisoner, arguably the most notorious assassin in history. Also notably never accurately described and if you follow the stories about him back far enough he must be approximately somewhere in the range of five hundred or more years old. I would speculate that more than a bit of elf blood is in him don't you think?"

I calmly shrugged my shoulders, "As I mentioned before I am not at liberty to discuss my employer's business dealings. However, I would be fascinated to hear what you can tell of this Thomas the Poisoner. He's an elfish assassin you say? That sounds exceeding rare as most elves cherish life."

Glorandel's eyes followed the motion of my hand picking up my refilled wine cup. I lowered it down to a level which would allow Balinac to drink from it. As Balinac lapped it up Glorandel raised an eyebrow.

I smiled at him, "My pet is thirsty, and wine tends to run through me. I wouldn't want to depart our conversation for another call of nature. Please continue though."

Chapter 18 Psychological Warfare

I noticed that Hardtack was heading outside along with the whole table of others to perform some demonstrations of martial technique. It was for this moment that Glorandel had been waiting to turn up the heat of his interrogation. It was clear that he knew a whole lot about history, and what transpired within his area of control. However, it was also pretty clear that he didn't know exactly who I was or what I knew.

Since Balinac had consumed the potentially altered wine, and since I showed a continuing interest without hostility I left the opening for him to begin his next level of assault. It would be less about him proving what he knew, which likely had gaps he did not want to reveal, and more about him coaxing out what I knew. Every piece of information gained from either of us at this point would be from a cautious battle of wits.

Glorandel grinned, "The tales tell of a mysterious assassin who only killed the wicked. The reality is that the Mystic Dawn comes into Port Cirnore every three weeks to obtain enough supplies to support a fair sized community. Perhaps even an island community. This community can not be far from here as the Mystic Dawn makes the journey in a reasonable amount of time even in foul weather."

I shook my head, "Why a community? Wouldn't it be simpler to just spread people out in inns like this one? Someone could even let the local thieves' guild use the facility for a safe house and blend in with their presence. Why one could even be talking to a mage in a place like this and not realize that a smart man like that could be the head of such a guild. He wouldn't need the skills of a thief after all, just the brains to run the operation effectively, secretly, and safely."

Glorandel laughed, "You knew it already. I've underestimated you as it seems our departing ninja has also underestimated you. I applaud your information organization. They have managed to remain hidden from my view in the very heart of my power."

I bowed slightly before Glorandel, "Nothing of the sort. I'm just an astute observer of people and situations."

Glorandel smiled, "I can believe that as well, but as you've already noted my power base might be compromised. I'll take that as friendly advice that it's time to do some routine house cleaning soon. I already know that the passengers carried by Captain Roberts use this inn and five other locations as safe houses in Port Cirnore. It's nothing fancy mind you; it's just that I'm being paid by an unidentifiable outside benefactor to maintain security at those locations after my people discovered the first two."

I added my other speculation, "Let me also guess that being a fence for stolen goods from the pirates and selling information between various parties is the more profitable side of your business."

Glorandel shook his head and laughed now, "Are not even my accounts sacred to your employer? Like I said before you've got one good intelligence gathering organization. We do keep our hand in some traditional thievery, but it's mostly pick pocketing the drunk sailors for their pay and the occasional scam of outsiders. I know to keep my boys clear of the adventuring parties though. They like to chop first and talk later. Of course we charge all of their visiting Rogues dearly for a temporary guild membership. Keeps them in line and lets us place the blame for any robberies firmly on their shoulders if they don't comply. We've got a no robbery clause in our agreement with the city leaders. They don't like banged up citizens or visitors."

I smiled, "I take it that running a profitable business keeps you in research money for your sage hobby."

Glorandel smiled back, "Ha, you finally have gotten one wrong for a change. Being a sage is still my main occupation. I just head up the local thieves guild as a means to get other people to do my footwork. My information trade business actually comes in handy to support my sage occupation. It bugs me to death that I can't get any good information about the operation of Thomas the Poisoner beyond hearing about someone dying months or weeks after he has already taken credit for the job. Your boss is certainly one crafty operator."

I nodded, "You are right that my employer is very good at his business. I think he could still learn a few things from this Thomas the Poisoner you mentioned. It sounds like he is a very effective person."

Glorandel smiled, "You know and I know that Thomas the Poisoner is an organization not an individual. Just like I've seen that the Captain Roberts running the Mystic Dawn is the fifth one to do so since they've been using Port Cirnore as a base. The organization just passes the title and the reputation along if a Captain Roberts fails or is killed or retires. It is quite clever really, but I am not the only one to already come to that conclusion."

I looked surprised, "That does sound clever. I was under the impression that this Thomas the Poisoner from legend has really only been around for about fifty years or so. I thought he had just planted stories in libraries all around making it look like he has been going on for longer than that."

Glorandel shook his head, "I've lived nearly five hundred years lad. Stories of Thomas the Poisoner have been circulating since before my childhood. I even adventured with your friend Harack there when he was a youth for about six months. I'm always impressed with the change he has made in himself since that time. Back then he used to scare me in the worst way. He can still manage the look when he wants, but I can tell his heart is not entangled in his former madness anymore."

I looked at Glorandel, "His former madness?"

Glorandel looked back at me, "It's true you are too young to know the Harack the Slayer from back then. It really is better that no one can truly experience that Harack the Slayer anymore. He's a reformed berserker lad, and it is a tricky thing to do that. Racial animosity toward all the goblin kin you see. It drives him blood mad and turns him into a very nasty engine of death. He was the most unskilled yet brutal killer I've ever witnessed in action. He would ignore all wounds, any pain to destroy his enemy. Hands, fists, elbows, rocks, broken weapons, any anything else you could pick up and beat something to death with were his tools of choice. Not a lick of finesse, but a natural born killer none the less."

I kept my gaze steady and unaffected by what he said, "It seems he is quite a different person now."

Glorandel nodded, "A miraculous transformation, if a lengthy one. One day he simply vanished. No one ever heard rumor of him again for years, decades even. Then one day about one hundred years ago I caught a rumor of him being spotted in Port Cirnore. The physical description matched, but the behavior made me think it obviously couldn't have been the Harack I had known. Reportedly he was polite, he was cheerful, and he was looking to buy some weapons which require a great amount of finesse to use properly."

I nodded, "That does sound like the dwarf who I met here tonight."

Glorandel nodded his head, "Yes it does. I came to Port Cirnore and set up my sage business here. The trail grew cold as far as Harack was concerned, but business picked up in the information selling trade. I stayed and set up a kind of shop in the Puking Dragon Inn here. The adventurers kept me in research funds, and the thieves' guild soon asked for a cut to keep my business in operation at one of their approved facilities. I offered to help them improve their overall efficiency for a cut of their proceeds instead. They took me up on the offer on a trial basis and liked the results. In a mere fifty years I moved up form being a potential mark to the leader of the guild."

I smiled, "That sounds like quite an accomplishment."

Glorandel shook his head, "It was trivial really. In actuality my privacy spell took a lot more effort to develop and refine as a matter of fact. Business is easy, even the business of thievery compared to the practice of magic. It seems to me that you would likely be qualified to study the magic arts. You have a keen intellect young Mica."

I nodded my head again, "I'm sure my mother would be happy to hear you say that as well."

Glorandel surprised me as he spoke next, "The Kingdom of Ard I believe. Yes. That colloquialism is commonly used there, and the hint of accent you have matches that region of the known alliance kingdoms. It seems you've spent a lot of time there in the past. Not a common location for a full blooded elf to reside, but it certainly isn't unheard of for them to have an embassy there. You are most likely the child of a diplomat, thus you have a background in court etiquette. Yet since you come from another country you are not a Lord."

I pretended that his conclusion was fully accurate, "Your powers of reasoning are quite remarkable. I don't know how you got so much information from so little detail."

Glorandel began to show off a bit more, "It started with your choice of Saber and dagger. Not unheard of among the elves, but notably missing the bow popular with the elfish people who are martially trained. You also obviously had exposure to the trade tongue early since it only had a very small amount of elfish accent to it, and is accented and contains phases common in Ard. Given that mixed elf humans like me are more common in Ard than pure elves like yourself I estimated that you were not a native. Since you know a high degree of refinement you must have had some exposure to their court. So I surmised that left few options open after that point is all."

I nodded, "Your powers of observation are quite good. I did spend most of my life in the Kingdom of Ard."

Glorandel started another of his now infamous digressions, "Did you know that when I became guild master I tried to buy this very bucket dragon inn."

I shook my head, "No I didn't realize that."

Glorandel nodded, "It is true. I tried to find the owner and traced it down to a business in another city. That business was partially owned by another business in Ard which owned two more of the bucket dragon inns."

I asked the question, "Why did you call them the bucket dragon inns?"

Glorandel laughed, "That's what the adventurers call them privately. It's well known among seasoned adventurers that the bucket dragon inns are the place to go. Information is traded; they cater to adventurer interests and needs. Privately speaking quite a few of them act as safe houses for several local thieves guilds. The funny thing is there is one in the Capital of the Kingdom of Ard called the Swimming Dragon Inn I think."

I nodded, "I think you mean the Drinking Dragon Inn"

Glorandel nodded, "That's the one. I kept following this chain of companies and it turned out they all owned each other and they all own various parts of the bucket dragon inns. The money these inns make, and they are all at least moderately profitable as far as I can tell, well this money swirls around in an incestuous circle. Then eventually it disappears as it flows to somewhere mysterious."

I smiled again, "That is quite fascinating."

Glorandel stalled a second as he looked at me and continued, "I have come to learn that due to their almost ubiquitous nature, and common acceptance among adventurers they are likely one of the largest single business ventures in the known world. Their exposure is enormous. Everyone in adventuring has heard of them. A lot of information crosses those doors you know."

I gave him a wicked smile, "You don't say."

Glorandel looked at me again in slight confusion and then he stopped cold. His look was suddenly thoughtful and appraising. Then he gently struck his forehead with his open right palm.

Glorandel looked at me again, "You know already don't you. It's been in front of my face for nearly four hundred years and I didn't figure it out. I've researched them extensively and I didn't figure it out. The bucket dragon inns are all owned by one person aren't they? Not just one person, but a single organization that has been in operation for over six hundred years. Thomas the Poisoner owns them, every single one in every single major city or adventuring hot spot throughout most of the known world. His information resources available at his command would be enormous."

I continued to smile, "That is a fascinating conclusion."

Glorandel considered the implications further, "Most major thieves' guilds use them for meetings. Adventurers take assignments posted on their message boards, and pursue their wanted posters. Sometimes those bounties are put up by unknown private parties and paid by the innkeepers. I've been working under the roof of this organization for nearly one hundred years and didn't know who ultimately owned it. This thing is more massive than most governments."

I smiled some more, "Go on, you are almost there."

Glorandel looked at me, "What does that make you?"

I reached over and patted him on the shoulder, "Your new regional manager."

Glorandel looked at me in awe, "The ninja Hapusai Ran? What was your bargain with him?"

I smiled broadly, "He's starting our new expansion franchise in Ran Li."

Glorandel shook his head, "I'm beginning to realize that I am a little fish swimming with the sharks. What about Harack then?"

I laughed, "He's the lead cook for figuring out recipes that adventurers like in the bucket dragon inns. He only learns new weapons and fighting styles as a hobby now. He's been the head chef for almost two hundred and sixty years now. It has helped with his anger issues a lot. Well, I'm glad we've had this chance to talk. I'll be through here again fairly soon. I'm looking forward to any information you can provide me on the current situation in Letheron when I return. More franchises to open and the elves over there are notoriously troublesome I hear. I'm glad we've had this time to talk."

Chapter 19 The Isle of Death Revisited

The rest of our time spent in Port Cirnore was generally unremarkable. That isn't to say nothing happened, but what did happen was of a surprisingly ordinary nature. I spoke with a couple of other young elves while at the Puking Dragon Inn and neither of them made any comments about my accent or manners being out of place. Hardtack made several friends among the fighting folk having most of his meals and drinks purchased by the visiting adventurers in exchange for his input on various maneuvers he discussed or demonstrated.

Hardtack was right on one point. The magus staying at the Puking Dragon Inn usually took one look at my saber and Balinac before they politely rejected my offers for conversation. It seemed that the word was out that I kept very dangerous company, and they were not going to take the chance of being accidentally associated with me.

Glorandel the Blue Sage kept his usual spot near the fireplace in the evenings, but didn't invite me over again. I noticed a fairly continual stream of messages being delivered to him. I simply decided to let Balinac tell me if anything critical to my interests was being relayed.

After two days I was strangely relieved to be back on board the Mystic Dawn as it prepared to depart Port Cirnore. At high tide the guide boat led us back out of the harbor, and as the crew was satisfactorily in good spirits we didn't have any difficulties there either. I slept in my hammock above Hardtack in the passenger cabin as we made the transition during the fear watch on the return voyage. During the passage through shadow Balinac had left my presence. I think it presumed me to be safe at that point.

On the final day of the voyage as Thomas' Isle came into view I began to feel like I was coming home again. The sight of the familiar shore was refreshing somehow, and the lighthouse on the cliff was a welcome sight. I saw several of the regulars from the community waiting near the dock as the ship gradually approached. Hardtack was grinning as the gangplank was lowered down.

I smiled in return, "It's good to be home."

Hardtack nodded, "Yes it is indeed. It was a good trip. Thomas should be pleased with the results. I can't wait to check out my purchases either. I took some time shopping while you were otherwise busy in town. I got some items for the kitchen, including some new spices I want to try out. I also picked up a couple of really nicely crafted weapons as well. It's going to take a bit of time learning their proper use I think. Some of the boys at the Puking Dragon were kind enough to demonstrate the basics for me."

I noticed Lirae waiting near the small warehouse as Hardtack and I walked down the dock. She was smiling in an enchanting manner. I could see that our good mood had translated down ahead of us. Lirae approached as we reached the end of the dock.

Lirae spoke, "It is good to see you return Mica. It's good to see you as well Hardtack."

Hardtack spoke up, "It was an easy trip for me. The lad here did most of the hard work. You might consider listening to his ideas when your turn comes Lirae."

Lirae grinned back, "That's the good news from my end Mica. Thomas said that if your mission with Sensei Hapusai was a success then he would be sending my team out after the current team returns."

I placed my arm around her shoulders as we began to walk down the beach, "That is good news indeed. We should begin some preliminary planning tomorrow after I talk with Thomas today about my completed mission. A couple of thoughts about ways we could approach your mission in Letheron have been bouncing around my head for the last week, and I hope you will like what I'm thinking."

Lirae looked at me with a touch of surprise, "You've had time to think about my mission?"

I nodded, "After we successfully completed my mission a couple of ideas about how to address your problem became clear to me. I'll talk with you about it tomorrow if I get Thomas' blessing."

Lirae nodded, "I'll be glad to speak with you then."

I dropped my arm from her shoulders and held her hand instead as we continued down the beach. I asked how things were on the island, and learned that Yuki had done a passable job as a cook, but that she could use some instruction from a professional. Hardtack offered to take her under his wing both as his cooking student in addition to his martial one.

Eventually we reached the trail leading up the cliff to Thomas' home. Lirae headed back to the community as Hardtack and I continued up the cliff. Hardtack was practically beaming as we reached the base of the tower and he knocked on the door. A few moments later Thomas answered with Balinac curled about his legs. We entered and I saw the familiar setting of the table with comfortable chairs and a waiting kettle and cups.

Hardtack once again took the job of the tea server, and prepared the tea for us. I drank from my cup and found myself beginning to appreciate the hot beverage even with the warm weather.

Thomas put his cup down and spoke with a gradual smile, "I would normally spend a bit of time finding out how your mission went, but fortunately for us Balinac decided to accompany you on the trip and updated me with most of the pertinent information. I must say that I am impressed with your positive attitude Mica. It's good you were making so many useful suggestions as to how to approach the mission."

I nodded my head, "I have been trained under some good tutors on how to manage etiquette and calm under pressure. It's a useful tool I find at times."

Thomas nodded his head, "It is indeed. I am quite pleased that Sensei Hapusai took the bait and accepted that mission you assigned him. Not many would have taken that approach, but it shows that honey is sometimes more successful than vinegar in the course of diplomacy."

I smiled back, "I find that giving someone a chance to redeem themselves goes a long way to securing their loyalty."

Thomas' smile reduced a little, "I am a bit concerned that my name is being linked to the Mystic Dawn in Port Cirnore. That rumor could prove troublesome in the future."

I took my rebuke in good stride, "As you told me before, your name can act as sword and shield. I may be a bit rusty in their use, but I will endeavor to improve my performance in the future. The judicious use the one time did expedite a bit of problems being faced by Captain Roberts in removing a troublesome member from his crew."

Thomas nodded, "I understand the effect quite well. The problem is politicians and nobles unfortunately soon forget their fear, and sometimes make silly errors which eventually cost them their lives. I may need to reinforce that fear periodically now to prevent that from happening."

I nodded, "I understand, and I will be more careful in the future."

Thomas continued this time looking at Hardtack, "Then there is the growing problem with your friend Glorandel. He is becoming too inquisitive into matters not of his direct concern of late I think."

Hardtack laughed, "Glorandel always has been a nosy bugger. It's just a part of his nature you know. He is pretty harmless though. The lad here has a good idea with directly recruiting him to be an information source. Glorandel is well placed in Port Cirnore business dealings after all. Just hire him outright and give him a few things to research to keep him busy. He would be as happy as a hog in slop. Believe it or not he does understand when to be discrete."

I added to Hardtack's remarks, "I think the trick will be to simply make him feel invested in the process. Perhaps letting him sink some of his personal wealth into non-majority ownership of the local Bucket Dragon Inn will give him a sense of belonging."

Thomas looked at me, "Bucket Dragon Inn you say. I see the local adventurers have been talking to you. Your idea does have some merit young Mica. It is always better to recruit a potential problem if possible than it is to deal with them another way. Could you work up a plan for my approval?"

I nodded, "I think it's not too hard really. Just give Glorandel a cut of the profits from the local inn equivalent to his investment share. Hand him a few tasks on the side, and eventually he could take over my position as regional manager."

Thomas raised an eyebrow, "Regional manager? I wasn't aware that such a position existed, or that it had been assigned to you."

I smiled, "I did make that up to satisfy Glorandel, but there is merit in his vision of the Bucket Dragon Inns becoming an information conduit for your use under his organizational skills. Like Glorandel did for the thieves guild in Port Cirnore before, just use him on a trial basis for a couple of years, and see if you like the results he generates."

Thomas nodded, "I will take it under advisement. It looks like you also have a couple of other new ideas as well."

I nodded my head, "After sending Sensei Hapusai off to Ran Li with the Murumasa blade and a mission to find the new ruler for Ran Li I spoke with Glorandel. I told Glorandel that Sensei Hapusai would be opening a Bucket Dragon Inn franchise there. It was pure fabrication of course, but it got me thinking about Lirae's mission and your problem with getting operatives on the ground in Letheron."

ur conversation continued into the early afternoon with me laying out bits and pieces of a preliminary plan for evaluation. Thomas authorized the suggestions with which he agreed. Amazingly I found that where he didn't agree wasn't because he thought I was wrong, but instead it was where he saw an opportunity for improving the plan I was devising.

I was told that I would be given strategic control over the overall mission planning, but that Lirae as the senior partner would maintain tactical control of any situations which occurred while we were in the field. I happily nodded my assent at that situation. I didn't want Lirae to feel like I had taken over her mission, just that I was helping her to realize it.

Hardtack and I left Thomas' tower in high spirits. Thomas didn't accompany us back to the compound this time, although a somewhat reserved Balinac did. As we entered the dining hall for a late lunch we were greeted by a jubilant Yuki. She gave me a broad smile. She practically skipped over to me and embraced me in a brief hug.

Yuki spoke with a happy lilt to her voice, "Lirae told me that you have been successful in convincing Sensei Hapusai to cease his vengeance against Master Thomas."

I gave her a broad smile in return, "I think you will find even more than that in this scroll your father gave me."

I handed Yuki the scroll Hapusai had written, and watched her expression as she observed the seal upon it. I saw her smile broaden even more as she recognized the seal and the orientation of it on the scroll. I could tell her smile was genuine since it showed in her eyes as well.

Yuki broke the seal and read the message inside with an initial look of confusion breaking way to a barely constrained energy. She grabbed me by the arms, and pulled me close for an unexpected kiss on my right cheek. Over her shoulder I could see Lirae standing in the kitchen entry slyly smiling. I really wanted to ask Hardtack what that message said in private now.

Yuki stepped back and spoke with excitement, "Sensei Hapusai writes that you have provided him a way to restore his lost honor. I did not expect such wonderful news from him. I was at best hoping to hear that you had convinced him that his cause was an already lost one. Sensei Hapusai also writes that I am to take the employment offer from Thomas. He places my further learning in the hands of Sensei Hardtack, and my protection in your hands Sensei Mica."

I smiled and gently clasped her arm, "I am glad that this is good news for you."

Hardtack spoke up then, "Now how about a sample of your cooking. We're hungry from our journey. From this point on you are no longer a cook's assistant and server. You are to become an apprentice cook and we only have a couple of months at best to get you up to speed."

Yuki smiled, "Are you going somewhere Sensei Hardtack?"

Hardtack grinned at her as he led her to the kitchen, "I wouldn't want to spoil the surprise."

Lirae came over to my table with a bowl of soup in hand. I noticed a clear broth with something like thin pale worms inside. I raised an eyebrow at Lirae.

Lirae laughed, "It is called noodle soup or Ramen in Yuki's native language. It really doesn't taste as bad as it looks. You should try some."

I took a sip of the broth from my spoon and recognized it as a chicken based stock. I tentatively tasted one of the pale worm noodles, and was relieved to discover that noodles were not a type of worm after all. I took another spoonful and looked at Lirae.

Lirae nodded, "Yuki says this Ramen was a staple of her diet for years. It seems to be pretty much what she has learned to cook under Sensei Hapusai. It's not too bad, but it gets a bit repetitive after several weeks. Since you've been away I've taught her how to bake bread and some basic sweets, but it seems like a lot of the domestic side of life was skipped in her upbringing."

I looked at Lirae and smiled, "I hope you have gotten on well with Yuki."

Lirae nodded, "The two of us have come to an agreement with each other."

I smiled broader, "That is good. I spoke with Thomas about my ideas for your mission, and he has given me some refinements and improvements to my basic plan. It involves a change in approach though."

Lirae looked at me cautiously, "What kind of change?"

I grinned a little, "I've come to realize that I'll never be fully able to pass as an elf from Letheron. I know a lot about the country now thanks to you, but I will never be considered a native by the locals. My accent and basic mannerisms will prevent that from happening."

Lirae looked at me with concern, "Go on."

I kept a faint smile, "That means I'll never be trusted enough to infiltrate Reminas' organization. My accent will make them suspicious, and if they check my background story would not hold up. This got me thinking that another way might work better. We don't even try to infiltrate Reminas' organization."

Lirae looked at me with a serious expression now, "Would you have me not succeed in my mission?"

I shook my head, "Not at all. It's just that destroying them from the inside seems too difficult with the kinds of resources we have available. Instead we let them destroy themselves from the inside. What we will do is present ourselves as outsiders who represent what they detest the most."

Lirae looked confused, "What is that?"

I smiled wickedly then, "Elves who have integrated with humans and others with a great deal of success and yet still maintain our racial identity. We will become the model for it working across Letheron."

Lirae began to smile, "Let them be consumed by their own hatreds then?"

I nodded, "We will draw them out and expose them for the hate filled destroyers that they are."

Lirae shook her head, "It is against the rules. Thomas never kills for politics."

I shook my head, "That's the neat part. We won't be killing anyone except as absolutely necessary for self preservation. They will be the ones attempting to kill us for politics, and it will hopefully bring them down."

Lirae looked confused, "Thomas does not involve himself in politics though. How could he approve this plan?"

I smiled at her again, "That's the presumption that Thomas wants people to make. The truth of it is that Thomas is actually deeply involved in the politics of many nations. He just does not kill for politics. That was the point I had to discover to make this work."

Lirae then looked concerned again, "What about Reminas? How are we to kill him then?"

I looked at her with a serious look, "We don't. Like you observed we don't kill for politics. You have two options here. We either kill Reminas and let him stand as a martyr for his ideals, or we expose his ideals to destroy them and let him live the rest of his life in their ruins. Where does the course of justice lie?"

Lirae was clearly displeased but answered, "The greater good lies in stopping his ideals from taking permanent root, and not in killing the person behind them."

I looked at her with a faint smile as I clasped her hand, "I'm glad you can set aside your personal gratification for the bigger picture. Reminas will eventually die, just not by our hand. The important thing is that you will kill his dream and hurt him worse than any blade ever could. That is what he tried to do to you and your family. He tried to kill your dream. Now we will kill his dream by making your dream a reality. I can't think of a better way to obtain justice for you and those you've lost."

Lirae placed her head on my shoulder as slowly forming tears came to her eyes, "You are right my son. I've forgotten what my dream meant to me in my lust for vengeance. I will help you plan the approach you need to make destroying what Reminas stands for a reality."

Chapter 20 Plans and Surprises

Two months had gone by in a relative blur. Our plans were gradually set in motion awaiting our input by messages delivered through a crude postal system set up via the Mystic Dawn. The first stage primarily involved the complex system of cross owned companies started and ultimately owned by Thomas. The first step was to have several of these companies form a new entity with one Mica Lichan listed as the primary owner and president. I decided on the name the Isle Company for this new entity.

The second step was to officially hire Glorandel the Blue Sage as a consultant on current events and legal matters in Letheron. Thus the Isle Company had its first outside employee. With each trip of the Mystic Dawn extensive reports on the situation in Letheron and new and proposed laws were provided. Luck was with us in that while Letheron had tightened their borders with their human neighbors they had not locked them down yet. It was still possible to apply for business visas with a good chance to obtain them.

The third step was officially applying for those business visas. As the Isle Company was newly incorporated in the Kingdom of Ard, but listed under the primary ownership of an elf it wasn't too difficult to get approval for the advance team. The advance team consisted of one Lirae Quintalas as the second official employee of the Isle Company and vice president in charge of new development. The balance of the advance team consisted of two subcontracted elves which were native to Letheron which we had hired as experts in avoiding the legal tangles of the Letheron business community.

I had stood on the dock watching the Mystic Dawn depart with Lirae on board as her mission "A" team. She was first heading to Port Cirnore, and then eventually to Letheron to begin the site selection process for our new business venture as her two subcontractors had lined up several likely candidate locations. Our passports from the Kingdom of Ard had recently arrived with the Mystic Dawn complete with visa documentation for Letheron. After the team currently out on Thomas' mission returned I would make my way from the Isle of Death with the Lirae mission "B" team.

The Lirae mission "B" team as I had called it would be initially comprised of Yuki and me. I picked the "A" to stand for the Advance team, and "B" to stand for the Bait team. Lirae would go in first to make everything look like a legitimate business venture comprised of elfish ownership. The Bait team would eventually go in to rile up the followers of Reminas after our legal bases were covered and more importantly the politicians of Letheron were invested in obtaining the money our business would bring to their community.

The last two months had also been spent in the evening strategy sessions I had conducted with Lirae to flesh out the first two stages of my plan, and to outline the longer term goals. Thomas had entrusted me with a significant amount of resources for this mission, and I was going to do my best to make it a success.

My daytime routine on the Isle had also changed a bit. Yuki was learning various elfish recipes described by Lirae under Hardtack's direction in addition to some common dwarfish and human favorites. I was one of their primary test subjects during the meal times. Their early attempts were a touch questionable, but after two months the results were quite passable. Yuki even began experimenting on her own under Hardtack's guidance to create some fusions between elfish cuisine and Ran Li traditional dishes. This generally entailed the addition of noodles or steamed rice to common elfish staples along with some new spices with which Hardtack was experimenting.

Yuki and I also trained martially together under Hardtack. I was being taught to refine my saber and dagger technique. Yuki on the other hand was going in a different direction. Hardtack was emphasizing improvised weapons from kitchen utensils. In the last couple of months she had focused in on an unexpectedly balanced carving knife and a large skillet as her primary weapon combination. In the last couple of weeks she began to seriously challenge my saber and dagger skills when we sparred.

The final trick Yuki was learning had to do with Hardtack firing blunted arrows in her direction. This was a variation on something I remembered from my sword and shield training days. Back then I had learned to pretty much duck behind my shield or interlock shields with a company of soldiers in the face of a concentrated archery attack. Yuki on the other hand was learning to deflect or block individual arrows with her skillet.

When I questioned the effectiveness of such a technique against non-blunted arrows Hardtack had me lift the skillet in question and hold it out from my body. I was surprised to discover the large skillet weighed nearly as much as a small shield. Hardtack shot an armor piercing arrow at it as I held it out. The only result was that it vibrated the skillet significantly in my hand as it struck, but it did not even put a scratch on the skillet surface as the arrow broke into multiple splinters.

I was subsequently informed by Hardtack that the skillet wasn't common iron or even steel. It was made of dwarf forged armor grade steel and would resist damage from the force of a ballista even. Additionally it had various artisan grade enchantments on it to preserve its incredible durability. It also doubled as a cudgel if necessary in addition to being a fine skillet in its own right. I complimented Hardtack on his choice of cookware.

I had not informed Yuki yet about the fact that I had negotiated her inclusion on our mission. It had taken Balinac describing the full contents of the scroll message from Sensei Hapusai privately to Thomas to get him to agree. I still was not party to the full details of the message as everyone who had read it insisted it contained personal information between a father and a daughter when questioned.

I approached where Yuki and Hardtack were training on the practice green and watched them for a while. I could see that Hardtack was perhaps as drawn to his newest student as Sensei Hapusai had been. His smile was infectious, and it was obvious to me that Hardtack sometimes treated Yuki more like a favored granddaughter than as an assassin in training. Yuki also showed promise in learning weapons more so than cooking it was clear. She kept a focus in her training that was similar to the focus I had kept as the son of a knight.

Hardtack raised his hand to signal a break, "That's good Yuki. I see that Mica has returned from the dock. Have we gotten our latest cooking supplies yet?"

I nodded to Hardtack, "The new supplies are waiting in the warehouse."

Yuki bowed to Hardtack and then ran up in front of me, "I heard that Lirae left on the ship today. Does that mean you will be going soon as well?"

I nodded with a smile, "I will likely be going in a few more weeks."

I brought out my passport from Ard to show her, "See there is my passport paper just like the one Lirae is using on this journey already."

Yuki looked at the passport, "Lichan is a strange name. It is very similar to pig in my language you know."

I looked surprised, "I was wondering why Hardtack suggested that name. It seems his sense of humor is still intact."

A sad look began to show on her face, "Will you be gone for a long time when you go?"

I nodded, "This mission is a difficult one it is true. It can possibly take a long time to complete."

I could clearly see that she was unhappy with the prospect. I brought out the other passport that had been sent along on the Mystic Dawn.

Yuki looked at it in my hand, "Does this mean Sensei Hardtack will be leaving with you as well?"

I held it out for her inspection, "Take a look."

Yuki looked confused then stunned, "Why is there my name on this passport? What does this Yuki Lichan mean?"

I smiled mischievously, "We will be traveling together as husband and wife for this mission."

Yuki looked me in the eyes briefly as a bright red blush came to her face. Then she looked down. I noticed a slight quiver in her form for a moment before she looked up in my eyes again.

Her voice quavered as she spoke, "You are teasing me? I was told I could never leave this island again."

I began to blush a little too, "I'm sorry to say that was a bit of a bluff at the time. Now that you work for Thomas you are considered an employee like Hardtack and me. I convinced Thomas that your skills were needed on this mission, and Hardtack has been training you to fit your new position."

I could see a look of hope enter her eyes, "I am going to Letheron then. That is why I have been learning to cook elfish food."

I nodded as I replied, "I have been working up a plan for this mission, and your acting as my wife is a key component to our success. Tonight after dinner I will start filling you in on your role in this mission."

Yuki nodded her head and broadly smiled, "I'm looking forward to it."

Yuki and I sat together in the dining hall after dinner. I explained the basic concept of Lirae's mission, and the reason I would need to have a human woman to be my wife to cause outrage from Reminas and his followers. Yuki listened intently to the basic outline of my plan, but for some reason seemed somehow a little less enthusiastic than she had been that afternoon at the concept.

I spoke after the briefing, "Do you have any questions or comments about the mission ahead of us?"

Yuki looked carefully at me it seemed as she spoke, "So the staff of the top assassin in the world is going to peacefully overthrow an extreme political faction without violence?"

I shook my head, "I do anticipate that violence will happen, but our plan is to be clearly seen not initiating any violence ourselves. We are to provoke the extremists with our philosophical differences, and take the high road in the public eye. I'm hoping in light of their violent past that Reminas will take it as a challenge to drive us out or to kill us off. I don't plan to make it easy for them to do."

Yuki changed her line of thought, "Whose idea was it that I should act as your wife?"

I smiled, "Mine of course. Lirae agreed with it after I had received Thomas' permission for your help. It would not work as effectively if the leader of this new business was not practicing as he preached. There will be visible interracial acceptance and cooperation with room for individual racial identity in our group. Look at this very island as an example. At least eight different racial backgrounds are represented here; humans, dwarfs, elves, kobolds, goblins, orcs, and one ogre even live and cooperate here. Let's see that's only seven. Of course, I forgot our gnomish accountant Olivia who has been helping me with the financial plans for this mission. She's a funny person. She keeps insisting the new business has to turn a consistent profit in ten years."

As I spoke I noticed that Yuki's mood seemed to improve some. I didn't notice exactly when the change occurred at first, then it struck me that it must have happened when I had mentioned it was my idea that we be together as husband and wife. I began to wonder again just what Sensei Hapusai had written in his personal message to her.

I changed the topic a little, "Yuki I was wondering something. I watched as your adopted father Sensei Hapusai wrote that message to you, but I realized that I am woefully unlearned in your native language. As we travel together could you teach some of it to me? I think it will help convince others we are a married couple."

Yuki flushed a little at my request, "I would be pleased to help you establish our assumed identities together. Perhaps you could instruct me on the elfish language as well. I may even think of another idea. If I do think of something else can I tell you later?"

I was pleased with her apparently renewed interest and enthusiasm for the mission, "Of course you can Yuki. Well that is pretty much it for the initial briefing. We will work out some more details over time, and I'm interested in your suggestions if you think of something which may improve our plans."

I went to my room in the male's quarters that evening feeling that my plans were working nicely. I was going to begin the second phase of the mission soon when Yuki and I reached Port Cirnore. I made a mental note that since I had discussed cooperation among the races that perhaps it was also the time that I sought out some of the residents of the island who were from the wild races for some insights as well. The better armed I was with information, the more likely I could make the mission successful.

I read for a while from the newest batch of intelligence on Letheron we had received from Glorandel from the Mystic Dawn post today. This batch had a lot of information about the border conflicts with the wild lands and was of particular interest for the second phase of our mission. I planned an early day tomorrow so I turned down the lamp in my room after changing into my night clothes which in the warm isle weather consisted of a thin cotton sleeveless shirt and basic cotton knee length pants.

I lay awake on my bed thinking about my schedule for tomorrow when I heard a stealthy approach in the hallway outside. It wasn't surprising to hear such on a compound full of trained assassins, but I didn't expect to see the latch on my door being lifted either.

I closed my eyes and pretended to be sleeping as I heard the door open and a stealthy approach being made to my bed. I didn't feel physically threatened, but I was nervous what I might see if I opened my eyes. A warm thinly clad form slipped into my bed beside me. After a couple of minutes a small hand gently grasped my own, and slowly moved my arm around her firm waist as I pretended to sleep.

I knew I was emotionally feeling embarrassed and shocked, but at the same time the physical feeling of her being beside me was not at all unpleasant. I understood what Yuki meant now about practicing our established identities as husband and wife. It would not work for us to be seen as physically uncomfortable with each other. I continued to pretend sleep even as I gradually moved to spoon Yuki beside me in my bed. It was socially easier for us this way. As if we were two other people actually married and used to being with each other.

I could feel her nervous taut belly under my hand. I could tell that Yuki was excited that her bold approach was successful. I would pretend sleep, and she would of necessity be allowed to become even more familiar with me.

I thought about it a bit more. Maybe it wasn't just a necessity after all. I realized I desired this type of comfort as well. Yuki was attractive in an exotic way, in addition to being smart, capable, and shy. Yet as evidenced by her actions tonight she could also be bold and decisive. Yuki hadn't discussed her plan with me. She simply executed it with success.

It occurred to me then that I could love Yuki. Not just as a shield brother, but as a friend and a mate. Then I wondered what Lirae might have told her about my preferences in romantic attraction. Tonight I had to admit that Yuki was on the mark for what attracted my desire. I moved my head close to hers and smelled her clean hair. She pressed gently back against me in response. I began to feel that dangerous territory lay ahead so I spoke up.

I whispered in her ear, "Yuki we can be close, but at this time we can't be overly intimate. There are too many risks to the mission if something were to happen you understand."

I heard her whispered reply, "Can we be together just like this?"

I gently caressed her belly as I answered, "This is fine. In fact it is more than fine, it is very pleasant. Let's try to get some sleep now."

It took us a long while but I eventually fell asleep spooning Yuki in front of me. I think she may have fallen asleep shortly after I did.

Chapter 21 Good Advice

I awoke before the first light of morning. Yuki was still in my bed beside me, but I could tell that she was also awake from her breathing. I placed my hand on her closest shoulder and gave it a gentle caress to let her know I was awake as well.

Yuki gave a slight sigh and spoke quietly, "I need to get back to my room in the female's quarters before anyone else is awake to see me. The morning breakfast preparation starts soon, and I need to get dressed for it."

I gave her shoulder a light squeeze as I softly replied, "I understand."

Yuki rolled to face me. She placed a light kiss on my lips. I put my arm around her back to keep her in place a moment longer and responded in kind. Our kiss began to get longer and a touch more passionate, then Yuki slowly drew back.

I could see the smile on her lips as she whispered, "Soon Mica. I must go for now".

After Yuki had left my room I lay in bed wide awake wondering where my acceptance of her bold advances would eventually lead us. I was mature enough to understand that many potential problems could lie ahead. Unfortunately I had to acknowledge to myself that I was also inexperienced enough that I didn't know how to avoid any of those problems.

I stopped hesitating for the moment and got up out of my bed. I changed into my exercise clothes and went on my early run about the isle. I chose to run up the slope of the southern mountain as that was the most difficult terrain that was passable without resorting to climbing.

I pushed myself hard, and I could feel my head starting to clear as the force of exercise drove my doubts away. I realized that Yuki and I had already started on a course of action initiated by her, and accepted by me. There would be a danger in going too fast down this way ahead of us. I realized that the two of us would have to establish some mutual boundaries and guidelines pretty soon to keep this path from becoming treacherous for either of us.

Strangely I realized that I wanted Lirae to advise me with this. I felt that there was still some remaining tension between Lirae and Yuki, but that Lirae would have the most experience with what Yuki and I were facing as Lirae had been married in her previous life. I then thought about Hardtack as a possible source of confidence for my problem.

Then it struck me that Hardtack was pretty much a lifelong confirmed bachelor who now tended to treat Yuki like an adopted granddaughter. I had a mental vision of Hardtack on the rampage for my head about what Yuki and I were doing. I felt that he might not be the best choice to begin with after all.

As I came back down the slope of the southern mountain I picked up some cautious speed. I could see a figure approaching the dining hall in the distance and recognized that it was Jack. It occurred to me that Jack was pretty approachable and might just have some insight into how woman behave. Then it also occurred to me that if I told Jack anything the entire isle might know what was going on between Yuki and I before noon. Once more visions of an angry Hardtack came to mind.

I surrendered to the fact I was temporarily stumped by my quandary. I wanted to move forward, but to be cautious and smart about it at the same time. I figured that dwelling on it further at the moment would not be of much use. I finished my run back to my quarters, and got cleaned up before breakfast.

I entered the dining hall and saw Talgash, one of the resident kobolds on the Isle of Death, sitting at one of the small tables in the corner. Prior to this Talgash and I had been casually introduced, but we really had not spent any time talking with each other. I remembered my decision from last night to seek some input on our mission from our resident wild races representatives. I approached his table and gave him a casual nod.

I gave a light smile, "Could I join you for breakfast?"

Talgash wrinkled his dog like nose as if smelling something then said, "Do sit. Friend good for meal."

I wondered slightly if he meant it was good to have company or whether it was good to dine on a friend. I took his invitation at face value and sat down. Another of the island residents on service duty for the day came by for my order. I choose a light traditional elfish breakfast. My job as taste tester still continued even if I found myself strangely not too hungry.

Talgash looked at me, "Talk friend. Advice Talgash can give."

I spoke up, "I am going to be near the borderlands of Letheron soon, and was looking to discover what I could about your people in the area."

Talgash made a spitting noise, "Many clans. Other races bully them. They seek help if like my old clan."

I nodded my head, "I see. How could I offer to help them?"

Talgash gave me what I figured to be a smile even if it looked more threatening than friendly, "Give sign of parley. Sign used between clans and kobold friends."

Talgash carefully demonstrated the gesture which was comprised of first placing the right hand on the left shoulder, then the left hand on the right shoulder. The second phase was initiated when the other party replicated the gesture. If the parley was agreed to then both parties at the same time moved their right hand to their right ear, and then their left hand to their left ear. He cautioned me to not follow the gesture by dropping my right hand to my right waist then my left hand to my left waist as that indicated I would be seeking a member of their clan for mating purposes.

As Talgash practiced the gesture with me several times to make sure I had gotten it correct I noticed that instead of the server who had taken my order Yuki came out of the kitchen with my breakfast. Once more Talgash made the curious gesture of wrinkling his nose as she approached. Yuki gave me a smile, and brushed my hand as she set down my plate. She lingered a few moments looking at me before she returned to the kitchen.

Talgash gave his hideous smile again, "New one female marked you with scent. This one could smell you with female scent when you came. New one breeding heat is begun. There are pups soon?"

I felt taken aback by Talgash's perceptive nose, "There should be no pups soon Talgash."

Talgash snorted, "Hurry quick young one. Another will quickly stake claim to fine mate like that female. Call out you choice female before another do."

I asked a question to change the topic from Yuki and me, "You have had pups before?"

Talgash nodded, "Over forty pups from eight mates. Clan was strong and stronger. Then orc bastards killed us. Now I am here. This one killed orc chieftain killed by my hand. May filthy bastard rot forever in abyss."

I was a bit surprised, "You don't like the orcs?"

Talgash shook his head, "Goblins, orcs, all wild races treat clans badly. Clans are small and weak. Clans are easy prey for bastards unless we grow to be many."

I asked, "What happens when you grow to be many?"

Talgash gave his hideous grin again, "Clan with many feasts on bastards that harmed clan."

I nodded with respect, "Will your people parley with elves and humans?"

Talgash spoke, "If sign given clan will listen. Elf or human must speak true. You need to offer advantage to clan. Clans are clever and not accept bad deal. Clans understand there many clans of human and elf. Clans know one can not speak for all clans. Clans expect you and you clan to be true. They will not blame you for those not you clan. Mark you clan with color or smell so they know you clan. Then clans know which clans true. Clans know there are false clans."

I nodded to Talgash, "Will a clan recognize a flag or a banner?"

Talgash nodded, "Clans can do. Smell is better. False clans not fake smell. You flag you enemy can steal. Try to make you clan seem not true."

I thought I understood the basis of what Talgash was saying. If I entered parley and successfully made an agreement with a kobold clan, it would be up to me to identify those of my own clan who were a part of that agreement. Any breaking of the agreement would lose shared trust and likely damage or break the agreement. The kobold clan would not oblige other clans to hold the agreement, and would not expect others not of my clan to hold the agreement either.

I knew it would be in my best interest to not too broadly identify anyone as my clan if I did not trust them implicitly. The most trusted way for the kobolds was to have all of my clan members have their scent identified so the kobolds would only hold the agreement with those of the correct scents. The drawback was that this approach was going to have to be established with each individual kobold clan where an agreement was sought. The clans did not recognize a central authority. The advantage was that the actions of any central Letheron authority would not be recognized as impacting my clan's private agreements.

I ate my breakfast as Talgash finished his own meal. When he was done he expectantly waited for me to finish in silence. Since my breakfast was light it did not take me long.

Talgash spoke, "Each clan will want differently. Strong clan may not bargain, but will still accept peaceful parley. If parley agreed, all must allowed leave peaceful. Weak clan may want payment, protection, territory, or peace. Offer hurt those that hurt clan will make friends. Get know where goblin, orc, or others are that way. Caution strong clan may have deal to tell goblin, orc, or others where you are."

It dawned on me that Talgash had demonstrated parley request process with three distinct parts. The first part seemed to indicate a lack of hostility, the second part the request for discussion, and the third unused part a desire for a mate which was obviously an important consideration in kobold society. This led me to my next line of thought.

I demonstrated just the second part of the process where the hands are brought up to the ears to Talgash, "What happens if this is the only gesture given?"

Talgash grinned, "You smart to ask Talgash. Means you clan want to talk. Not mean you clan kobold friend. No parley given or recognized. Clan may or may not listen. No protection of parley granted. Killing may happen anytime by clan. Agreement may happen. All agreement temporary as advantage is known. No trust given."

I demonstrated just the first part to Talgash and he smiled, "You kobold friend. You don't seek parley. May grant you free passage through clan territory, or turn you back where you entered clan territory. Clan with honor will not killing unless you kill."

I smiled at Talgash, "Thank you for your advice my friend. If you can think of anything else that is useful."

Talgash gave his hideous grin again, "Take you new one as you female. Make female you mate even if there no pups yet. Call you out you territory. Do not shame you female with cowardice."

A short while later I waited on the practice field for the arrival of Yuki and Hardtack. I was seriously considering all of the advice given me by Talgash. I knew that some preparations would need to be made first. I smiled at the two of them as they approached from the dining hall.

I waved them over and placed a hand on Yuki's shoulder and lightly squeezed as I spoke, "I have to skip practice this morning to make some arrangements. I'll need to get a message to Thomas, but I think I should be able to see you both at lunch. If Thomas agrees with my plan, then I will let you both in on what I'm doing."

Hardtack gave me a wink, "Keeping secrets from me lad? Well as long as you don't keep me in suspense too long. I'll expect you to be present for afternoon practice after your planning session."

I nodded at Hardtack and gave Yuki's shoulder another light squeeze. As Hardtack turned away I gave Yuki a wink and I could see her a little uncertain but still happy. I left the practice field and began a rapid walk to the beach and toward the trail leading to Thomas' home. Before I reached the base of the cliff I saw Balinac bounding down the cliff side toward me. I gave Balinac a wave as it met me at the beginning of the path.

I looked at Balinac, "I would like to speak to Thomas with a request. Is it possible?"

Balinac replied, "Thomas is out at the moment, but I can relay a message to him. I take it that this has something to do with Yuki's scent all over you today."

I shook my head, "Talgash and you have amazing noses after all. I ran this morning and cleaned up after, and you can smell her on me still?"

Balinac huffed, "You may be surprised how long the scent of a female will stay with someone when your nose is sensitive enough. Yuki must have spent several hours in direct contact with you for this much scent transfer to happen. I can even tell that only prolonged close proximity and no mating has happened yet."

I flushed a bit red at this observation, "Well it seems I must hurry some before word gets out. Would you ask Thomas whether I can move into more private quarters suitable for two people?"

Balinac nodded, "This is tricky. There is a variable time rate difference between here and there you understand. Give me your entire message and I will relate it to Thomas as he becomes available. Then I will relay his entire response when he replies."

I nodded and began, "Master Thomas, I have found that Yuki and I have become attached with mutual affection. I don't know where this will eventually lead for certain, but I feel we will need to openly explore this relationship without disturbing the rest of the Isle's residents in the process. I am requesting assignment to more private quarters suitable to accommodate a couple. I feel that with the proper precautions this will enhance the chance of a successful resolution to Lirae's mission. To speak frankly though the reason I am making this request is because Yuki and I both desire this chance to develop a relationship together."

Balinac began walking down the beach and I followed. I marveled at Balinac's ability to perform so many different actions across such incomprehensible separations of self. I looked down at Balinac and it looked back up at me as we walked.

Balinac spoke, "It shouldn't be too long. Thomas has been in his interview a while already and should be available relatively soon."

I asked a question that had been bothering me for a while, "What did Sensei Hapusai write to Yuki that changed her attitude? Yuki has been much more, well I must say, she has been somehow much more attractive to me lately."

Balinac purred, "I will not tell you everything I read as it was very personal between a daughter and her father. However, since you have come to this juncture I will say this much, Hapusai Sensei was highly impressed with you. His message to Yuki relayed his approval of you as a choice of future husband quite clearly to her. It almost approached an order that Yuki do her best to secure your desire and cooperation."

I shook my head, "I feel the truth of what you say, but how did Yuki know what to do to change her behavior and mannerisms to ones that would draw my interest?"

Balinac jumped into my arms, "I would speculate that it is very likely that Yuki swallowed her discomfort and pleaded with Lirae for advice on how to approach you. I think Yuki pleaded with Lirae's motherly instincts toward you that it was time for you to leave the nest and find a mate. It must have been hard for Lirae to accept so Yuki must have been very convincing about her desire."

I was a bit confused, "Why do you say that?"

Balinac rubbed its head against my upper arm, "It is simple. They are two women who love you. Lirae is likely experiencing a mix of mostly motherly and friendly love feelings. Yuki feels an attraction for a suitably strong mate for breeding and social position."

I caught the fine distinction in Balinac's comment, "Why do you say mostly for Lirae?"

Balinac responded, "You have to understand that even though Lirae had married and bore a child, in terms of emotional maturity for an elf I would estimate she was closer to someone you would consider a young teenager at the age she was killed. Lirae may have had more years than you, but not by many, and you were of much greater emotional maturity when you died. Lirae's act of marrying a human was likely done out of a mix of love, infatuation, and rebellion against an ideal with which she could not identify. I do not doubt that Lirae loved her child very much and that you helped fill that gap. However, I also think Lirae finds you physically attractive as well though".

I was surprised by Balinac's answer, "I didn't realize."

Balinac purred, "Lirae likely does not likely want you to realize this fact. At this time I would believe Lirae is not ready to surrender her feelings of love for her lost husband, so she did not express her attraction to you. Now Lirae has likely accepted that Yuki is able to love you without the reservations Lirae has in her conflicted heart. Lirae has placed your interests before her own like many mothers would with their child."

I shook my head, "I wonder now if I am making the right choice."

Balinac huffed again, "Personally I don't think you have a choice. Those two women who love you have come to an agreement. Lirae gets to mother you and be your friend. Yuki gets to be your lover and likely your eventual wife. Yuki got the advice she needed from Lirae to become both more feminine and attractive to your desires for assertive confident women. Lirae was given distance so she would not have to witness what Yuki was planning as Yuki moved in for the kill if you will pardon the expression. My advice to you is to just sit back and enjoy the ride as best you can. It is bound to be bumpy for a while, but it should settle down smoothly in the end."

I shrugged my shoulders, "Women will continue to mystify me I guess. Well my choices for the moment are limited. However, I think it's time I become a bit more assertive."

Balinac huffed, "Beware of following a kobold's advice about females. Female kobolds are much more understanding of male proclivities. They don't expect or desire lifetime attachments. They only expect a suitable mate to produce lots of strong pups in their next litter. They generally can reproduce by three years of age, and frequently don't live past twenty five. They mature much faster than many humanoids, but they need to breed a lot to survive in a harsh world as a species. They can gestate a litter of three to five pups in only five months, and if with a strong mate produce two litters in as little as a year."

I was a bit confused by this information, "While this is fascinating I don't quite understand the relevance."

Balinac huffed again, "The point is kobolds don't have the luxury of time, they work very fast when it comes to selecting mates and breeding. They never know if they will live to try again if they wait. Other species have different expectations as many don't need to reproduce as fast as possible to survive. For example elves have long life spans and limited periods of fertility. In adult males this expresses itself as a general disinterest in reproductive activities though bonding activities are still frequent. In elfish females it is usually an inability to conceive except at certain points in their lives. Since they have the luxury of time they are generally much more careful with selecting whom they choose to bond and reproduce."

I nodded, "So human and elf pairings are at times frustrating because humans are comparably closer to kobolds in their reproductive capabilities."

Balinac purred, "Actually they are still fairly reproductively compatible surprisingly enough. For being essentially different species there is still a fair chance of a viable offspring between the two. What elves sometimes find frightening is that elf and human pairings are more likely to produce more offspring over a shorter period of time than even a pairing between two elves. Thus they culturally fear being bred out of existence as a distinct species. I take it that your plan is counting on this fear in your enemies to work. However, I would caution you that you could end up making fewer allies than you think if not handled correctly."

I nodded, "I know my role is to present options for integration and acceptance to the elves which are willing to countenance such. I also have to seen as reasonable in my approach to cooperation without threatening cultural identity. At the same time we also have to represent that social integration that elves culturally feel threatened by to draw out Reminas and his followers. It is a delicate tightrope, and I hope my moderation is clearly seen as a better option when compared against his extremism."

I noticed that I was unconsciously until that point walking toward the warehouse near the dock. I realized I would need to pick out some suitable furnishings and accouterments if Thomas granted my request and allowed me to move into private quarters. Balinac jumped to the ground as we approached and enlarged to about one hundred fifty pounds and nearly four feet at the shoulder.

I was not prepared to hear Thomas' voice come from Balinac's mouth, "Ahoy Mica. I have received your request. I will grant you bungalow number three along the beach for your needs. I do hope you are considering that many more than young Miss Togusawa and you could be impacted by this decision. This choice has several long term and very far reaching implications which likely have not occurred to you yet. I expect you to do the right thing. I will defer to your personal judgment on this matter, and I hope my trust is not misplaced. This is Thomas signing off."

Chapter 22 Preparations

Balinac shrank back down to its cat size. Then it jumped back into my arms as we entered the warehouse. I approached the warehouse front office and saw there was an orc working there. I recalled his name was strangely known as Puck. While Puck's tusks were still all intact he was notably missing his front upper and lower teeth. This gave him an unfortunate light whistling lisp when he spoke.

I waved at him as I entered and he grinned and showed his missing teeth, "What brings you here today Mr. Mica?"

I spoke with a smile, "I have been assigned bungalow number three by Thomas for my use. I'll need suitable furnishings for two people. I think I will need a large bed, a bureau with a mirror, some chairs and a table if you have them. Of course I will need some suitable linens and utensils for light dining."

Puck nodded, "We have several items which will fit that item list. However, if you don't mind a bit of advice, I suggest that after the basic furnishings you let Miss Yuki pick out the linens and such. You know how females like to select the surroundings for their lairs."

I shook my head with less surprise than expected, "I suppose that orcs have better noses than they let on about?"

Puck laughed with a punctuating whistle at the end, "Nothing that fancy young lad. You should realize us orcs are nocturnal in nature. I was walking around enjoying the night when I saw Miss Yuki slipping out of the male's quarters wearing her night clothes just before dawn. It didn't take much imagination to understand where she had just spent the night. Talgash was also walking around after breakfast today all excited about the prospect of new pups on the island. Kobolds certainly love to spend time with their children teaching the next generation how to survive you know. They consider teaching their youth about hunting, mating, and eating in that order is very important to their species. It is very likely that he misses the presence of their young since he came here."

I shook my head, "I should have asked him to keep quiet."

Puck laughed again, "It wouldn't have worked. Kobolds have never been the picture of discretion generally speaking. When one kobold knows something soon all their clan knows it. On this island we are all considered Talgash's clan."

I looked at Puck and raised an eyebrow, "How about orcs?"

Puck laughed with a touch of wariness, "We male orcs consider children a menace personally. The next generation is always looking to supplant the current generation which also supplanted the prior generation. Children are both a necessity and a threat in orc tribal culture. Too few children and there are not enough shock troops for battles. Too many children and they get ideas about forcibly taking charge. It is always a careful balance with the orc tribes. It's one of the reasons we fight so much with each other and other races. The orcs in charge are always trying to keep the balance between the old and new intact."

I asked a question, "What happens when an orc tribe loses a leader in combat?"

Puck looked at me with an appraising glance, "Generally chaos is the result as most seasoned adventurers know. Orc tribes rely on dominance by leaders to maintain organization. When an orc leader is slain the first priority is the destruction of the slayer if an outsider. The one who can destroy a chieftain slayer is in good position to become chieftain himself. Unfortunately for most orcs they haven't quite understood that serious adventurers are going to kill off the best and most promising of the next generation that way."

I asked what I figured was the logical follow-up question, "What happens with the orc that is smart enough to not pursue adventurers?"

Puck nodded at my assessment, "That orc is in a good position to take over the tribe as his competition dies off. Realistically speaking a tribe is better off when they get a smart leader like that. The orc tribe of that nature is more likely to realistically evaluate opponents and select a better course of action. The most successful tribes are the ones who know when a potential fight is a losing proposition."

I looked at Puck with an appraising glance, "I take it you were such a leader once?"

Puck nodded and laughed yet looked embarrassed, "I was until I got killed by my own idiot nephew in an ambush. After my death my nephew claimed to the tribe that he fought me in an open duel for leadership. What really happened was he gathered a force of malcontents and outnumbered my guard. They killed me by the use of a combination of brute force and a bad alliance he had made with untrustworthy outcast ogre-magi. My nephew was driving my tribe to ruin by overextending them beyond their capabilities after he took over. For the good of my tribe I came back from my own death and killed him before my tribe could be destroyed by his idiocy in following the suggestions of the ogre-magi. My former tribe is struggling still, but they are being led wisely by my grandson as they rebuild what my nephew lost."

I summed up what I learned, "So an outside attack can eventually unify and strengthen an orc tribe, but an outsider offering assistance to an ambitious orc can destroy a tribe."

Puck looked shamed as he answered, "Such is the foolishness my people are prone to indulge in I am afraid. They are forever ambitious and often not thinking about the good of all. Sadly the truly worthy leaders among the orc tribes seem to dwindle year after year. It is much of the reason there is friction between them and other peoples even where none need exist."

I asked the bold question next to distract him from his painful past, "What happened with your front teeth?"

Puck laughed again, "I went to see the island dentist."

I must have looked puzzled, "The isle has a dentist?"

Puck nodded, "All the wild races here are aware of the dentist as I named him. He's also the cook and serves to remind all that we are integrated in one purpose even if some new arrivals don't always want to be."

I spoke, "You mean Hardtack."

Puck smiled again, "I got a bit upset with the presence of a dwarf on the isle when I first came here. Our kind does not always get along well you understand. Little did I know I was challenging the Orc Doom when I stepped onto the field with him. He broke out my teeth, and he left me unconscious yet basically unharmed with one punch. I felt very lucky to survive when I eventually learned whom I had foolishly challenged. It gave me a new perspective on brotherly harmony. Sometimes you have to knock someone in the head for them to see the value of it. It could have been worse."

I had to ask, "How so?"

Puck grinned wide, "Rumor has it that back in his slayer days the dentist knocked the head clean off a hill giant. If you have ever met a hill giant then you would understand the impressiveness of the feat."

By this time we had looked around the meager selection that the warehouse held in terms of furnishings. There were plenty of items made from local materials on hand, but not much in the way of the style of furnishings I was accustomed to in the Kingdom of Ard. I made due with selecting a basic bed for two, a simple wicker dresser, and a dull tin wall mirror. I was told the extra tables and chairs were kept by the dining hall in the dry storage room.

Puck looked at me, "Where do I deliver those items then?"

I spoke, "Thomas mentioned bungalow number three as my new quarters."

Puck nodded, "That is the third bungalow up the edge of the beach from the warehouse here, the middle bungalow in the beach row. It has a good view and was unoccupied for a long while."

I asked, "What happened to the prior resident?"

Puck shrugged, "It has been a long while, way before my time really. I've only been here eleven years after all."

I asked the personal question then, "Do you ever go off the island on missions anymore?"

Puck shook his head, "Once I left my grandson in charge of my former tribe I left the fate of the orc tribes to the younger generations. Such is the way of my people. Every change of hands should not need to be violent. Hopefully my people will learn to be more accommodating as a people before the other races decide we are too much of a threat. I have done what I can do for my people now. I am considered too old to lead anymore."

I could not begin to guess his age, "How old are you now if you don't mind my asking?"

Puck laughed with a touch of sadness, "I'm an over the hill forty four now. I had a son at fifteen, a grandson at twenty nine, and tribal leadership from thirty to thirty three. I think my grandson has learned a caution I did not always keep, and wisely leads my people from a young age. It is to be hoped he continues to make them prosperous. I live out my retirement now here on the island learning a new way of thinking. I may just be the most educated orc around you know. I can read now unlike most of my kind. I have learned much from discussing the ways of others. I have learned the mistakes the orcs make by not passing along learning and knowledge to the younger generations instead favoring hatreds and conflicts."

I thought about a notable omission in our discussion as I helped Puck load the furniture onto a hand cart. We had talked much about the males of his tribe, but I had not heard anything about the females.

I looked at Puck as we left the warehouse with each of us on a handle of the cart, "You haven't spoken of your spouse. What happened to her?"

Puck looked embarrassed again, "You speak of what I consider another shame of my people. We don't love or marry our females. We treat them as breeding stock and slaves. Our tribes are made weaker because of it. They are capable and smart, but held back from realizing their potential. It is tradition and custom, and we are trapped in the mind set given to us by our ancestors. I see how you elves have more than doubled the strength of your numbers by treating your females as equals. Many humans are catching up as well. Lucky for us the dwarfs do not reproduce as fast as the humans or we would really be in trouble."

I thought about something I'd heard as a rumor in my youth, "What about the dwarf females? I have not heard of them being seen much in the world."

Puck gave me a mischievous smile, "With good cause I hear. Rumor has it that the female dwarfs rule their kingdoms. They are the thinkers, and the brains behind the dwarfish power base. The dwarf males are the workers and brawn guided by the brains of their females. It is a backwards world for an orc, but we must still respect their prowess even in light of their dwindling numbers. The gods were kind to them in many ways, but cruel in one."

I thought about it, "Why cruel?"

Puck shook his head, "It is said their females are homely even by dwarf standards. That is one of the reasons they have so few young. The dwarf males would rather be drinking and fighting than mating. It is also rumored they are sterile in regard to every other race. So their numbers decline. Who knows what will happen with them in time? The kobolds may win against all of us some day by sheer breeding prowess."

I chuckled along with Puck. We eventually reached my new bungalow as Balinac jumped from the cart and began walking up the beach toward Thomas' lighthouse. Puck helped me unload the furniture and set it up in the bungalow. The bed required some assembly but we managed in short order. I borrowed the cart and headed for the dining hall next.

I went past the training field and noticed that Hardtack and Yuki had departed already. I began to realize that it was later than I thought and they must be starting with lunch preparations. I left the hand cart outside the dining hall and went over to the dry storage area. In the back of the room I noticed several tables and chairs stacked so I selected four chairs and a small round table to carry out. I loaded them into the cart without seeing anyone look out from the kitchen at the noise I had to make in removing them. The sounds of cooking from the kitchen must have masked my presence.

I then went to the male's quarters and put my meager belongings on the cart as well. It mainly consisted of several styles of clothes and the weapons which Hardtack had provided me. Once I reached the bungalow again I was getting tired and rested a bit before unpacking the cart.

After unpacking the cart I noticed that while the bungalow had been maintained over the years it hadn't been cleaned recently. I would need some sponges, a broom and a bucket for water to begin. I returned back to the warehouse to return the cart and obtain some cleaning supplies. Puck even managed to find some scented cleaning soap that smelled faintly of a conifer forest.

I dropped the cleaning supplies off at the bungalow and moved on to the dining hall as the lunch hour was beginning. I entered the hall and took a seat by one of the windows to enjoy the light breeze. My sensitive hearing could detect whispered mentions of my name and Yuki's name as I sat down. I was beginning to understand what Thomas meant when he said there would be a larger impact from our decision than I had realized. I noticed one of the resident goblins Quizak come in to the hall, and once he spotted me he came over to my table to sit.

Quizak gave me a wicked seeming smile, "Word is you are looking for an understanding of the wild races. You are going to Letheron soon and setting up a business near the border. I would guess you are trying to make trouble among the elves which killed Lirae and her family."

I nodded and smiled back, "That is essentially true. I'm looking to understand how I can reduce conflict along the Letheron border to put pressure on the extremist elf views."

Quizak grinned, "While I am an exception I will warn you to not trust your average goblin. In general as a people goblins live for betrayal and cruelty. They will make bargains and deals with you. However, they will also strike you down regardless of any deal if they think they can succeed. Only through being in a position of unassailable power can you bring the goblins under a semblance of control."

I nodded, "What do you recommend then?"

Quizak laughed wickedly, "Drive them off if you must. Let them flee your approach. Do not bargain with them, and do not trust them. You are better off making deals with the kobolds as they will generally keep their word when given. Also understand that the hobgoblins are the worst of the lot. They will lie, cheat, steal, rob, and kill and think they are the better person for it."

I looked at Quizak, "How about you then?"

Quizak gave a bitter laugh, "Some of us individuals exist who do not fit in with the goblin culture. We are identified by our trusting nature, or honorable thinking. It doesn't take too long before even a cautious goblin like that makes a slip in behavior and the others kill them as an aberration to the cause."

I furled my brow, "What cause is that?"

Quizak shook his head, "The cause of mischief, wickedness, and reveling in misfortune brought upon another. If a goblin is seen not partaking in the cause, then they are likely to become a victim of it."

I shook my head, "That seems like a miserable life to lead."

Quizak nodded, "It certainly was. I much prefer the life of a farmer here on Thomas' Isle. While not everyone is kind, no one has ever been cruel to me here."

I asked next question, "How did you end up here? Did the goblins get you in the end?"

Quizak shook his head, "No it is a funny thing there. I had successfully escaped from the goblin community when I figured out they would eventually discover my aberration. I was living peaceably alone as a hermit when an adventuring party came upon me. They captured me as I never fought them or tried to escape. I only surrendered when they approached. They brought me back to their village where they proceeded to turn me over to the jailer claiming I had committed various heinous acts before they captured me. Eventually I was executed simply for the crime of being a goblin."

I shook my head as well, "That is a shame then. Did you kill them when you were given the chance?"

Quizak laughed, "Are you kidding me? They would have just slaughtered me a second time. No unfortunately I acted like any goblin would have when faced with a superior foe. I gained the confidence of a minion of a dragon and let them know that group of adventurers was seeking to slay the dragon for its treasure hoard."

I nodded, "So the dragon had them killed for you then."

Quizak laughed, "It most certainly did. I heard the last three of them were eaten by the dragon personally. Do you want to know the irony behind it though?"

I raised an eyebrow, "What is that?"

Quizak gave a hearty laugh, "I had told the truth. They really were planning to kill the dragon to get its treasure hoard. They expected to somehow be able to sneak up on it sleeping and unaware. The fools didn't understand that dragons are almost never caught by surprise and unprepared."

I laughed, "That was very clever of you."

Quizak laughed, "I like to think so. Justice was served in that they were treated in much the same way they had treated me. The only difference was that they actually were planning death and mayhem while I have never harmed a sentient being in my life."

I raised an eyebrow, "Never a sentient being. What about killing other kinds of beings?"

Quizak laughed, "I must admit I enjoy a good chicken or pig properly prepared. I am a bit of a food fanatic. Lucky for me we have a fine selection of cooks here since I am not much of one myself. I raise most of the island's local livestock though. Unfortunately I've got a black thumb when it comes to plants. It seems your new mate is coming with some of her latest creation today."

Chapter 23 Engagement

I turned to see the Yuki come out from the kitchen with two bowls of a new soup dish that she had prepared. It clearly had more of the noodles she liked, but she had also included some seafood in addition to a new mix of spices. I smiled as she approached and she smiled in return. I also noted that the whispers of our names and muted conversations in the dining hall had been replaced with normal conversations as she entered from the kitchen. I understood then that all sense of discretion had thankfully not been lost on the island yet.

Yuki set the bowls down in front of Quizak and me, and then spoke, "Here is my latest creation. Sensei Hardtack said to warn you that those little dried peppers you see in the dish are very spicy and should not be eaten directly if unprepared. I hope it has a suitable flavor."

I smiled at Yuki, "It should be delicious. Do you have any cool wine to go with it?"

Yuki nodded enthusiastically, "Another delivery came on the Mystic Dawn yesterday. There is some rice wine known as Sake in my home country. I will go fetch a glass for you."

I noticed that Quizak had already started on his soup as Yuki departed for the kitchen. He seemed to take a bit of relish in tasting the soup with each spoonful as he swallowed.

I spoke, "I didn't realize anyone else was sampling the experimental cuisine."

Quizak paused between spoonfuls, "If you had ever tried goblin cooking you'd appreciate how good things are here. Even on the worst days the food here tastes better than the best goblin food. Most goblins tend to either burn or under cook every dish they make. They aren't big on seasoning things either, or generally caring much whether the food is fresh even."

I nodded at Quizak's comments as I sampled the broth of the soup along with some noodles. There was a definitively salty and fishy flavor to the broth, and the noodles held a touch of heat from the addition of the peppers. Overall it was quite tasty and I ate it with the same relish that Quizak was showing.

Yuki returned from the kitchen carrying a pair of small ceramic cups and a ceramic flask. Yuki set the cups down on the table, and poured a clear beverage from the flask into the cups. I took it to mean that the small size of the cups used was an indicator of the relative potency of the rice wine.

I smiled at her, "The soup is very good. It is a definite choice for our use if we can get the ingredients."

Yuki placed her left arm along my shoulders, "It is very easy to do as long as we can get seafood and the peppers. The noodles are standard as is the broth I use. I can also control the spicy quality by the number of peppers and the length of time it is cooked. If given a half day to simmer that soup should knock someone out of their shoes."

I looked at her with surprise, "Are those peppers that strong?"

Yuki nodded, "They were added last and have only been in the soup for about ten minutes. Try a small bite but be careful."

I saw that Quizak had ignored the suggestion and taken a spoonful with an entire pepper in it. He munched away on it and seemed generally unaffected. I picked a pepper out of the soup with my spoon and took a tentative nibble on the end of the pepper. It was a bit hot at first, but the longer it was in my mouth the hotter the piece of pepper became. I swallowed it down and drank carefully the rice wine I had been provided.

Quizak was in a bit of distress as he continued to chew the whole pepper he had eaten. Suddenly he reached to grab his cup of rice wine and drank it down in a single gulp. He then looked at Yuki with a pleading expression.

Quizak spoke, "Do you think you could bring me a cool glass of goat's milk. It seems that pepper was quite a bit hotter than I imagined it could be."

I continued to eat my soup by working around the peppers as Yuki went to get some goat's milk for Quizak. Quizak strangely smiled at me as he fanned his head.

I spoke, "So do you find it still as good as you thought before?"

Quizak nodded enthusiastically, "It's better. I like food that is interesting. This is definitely interesting. It just needs to be handled with proper caution next time."

I also noticed that each time Yuki left the dining hall for the kitchen there were quiet conversations among the people at the other tables discussing our relationship, and that each time she had returned the conversations had changed to topics like the weather or maintenance of the isle. As much as the people considered Jack a gossip here on the Isle I began to understand he was just the less discrete among all the gossips present.

Yuki returned to the dining hall again with the goat's milk for Quizak who gratefully drank it down in one long pull. He then continued to spoon down his soup peppers and all. However, I noticed that he did not chew the peppers themselves anymore choosing instead to swallow them whole. Yuki gave my shoulders a squeeze before she left again for the kitchen.

I looked at Quizak as he lifted his soup bowl to get the last drops of soup from the bottom. I had been working on my own soup still cautiously avoiding the peppers inside.

I paused between spoonfuls and asked Quizak, "I'm surprised that you are not supplying advice on relationships like many of the others have."

Quizak shrugged his shoulders, "The only advice I can give is don't get involved. Of course that is based on my very limited personal exposure to goblin females who are just as wicked and cruel as the males. You'll have to forgive me but I've spent my whole life avoiding any intimacy with members of my species, and not too many other species are volunteering to bond with goblins if you catch my meaning."

I nodded, "I hadn't thought of that. I'm sorry I brought it up if it is painful for you."

Quizak shrugged his shoulders again, "Don't judge Yuki by my experiences. If I had a chance to bond with a female who could cook like that then I would likely change my mind pretty quickly. Then again I would probably bond with a female orc if they could cook like that. I'm not very picky about appearance; it's the person behind that appearance which matters most to me."

I nodded as I finished my own soup, "That seems like a wise policy. It has been good to talk with you Quizak. I thank you for the advice."

I headed into the kitchen to see Yuki and Hardtack. They were making the last preparations for the late arrivals to lunch when I entered. Both looked up surprised to see me.

I spoke to them, "I am going to be at the beach after lunch. If you would both come over when finished with the kitchen then we can have a discussion."

Yuki gave me a smile, "Does this have to do with your morning project?"

I nodded my head, "Yes that is part of it. I have to put some final touches on first, but I'm almost done with it."

Hardtack smiled at me, "Are you going to be ready to practice this afternoon then? I'm going to need you to make up for missing the morning session."

I gave Hardtack a smile, "I hate to say it but I might be missing the afternoon session today as well."

Hardtack gave me a sharp look, "It must be pretty important to be missing a whole day of practice."

I nodded, "I think it is pretty important. I've been working fairly hard this morning too. I think I've gotten as much exercise as practice today so far. I'll let you two get back to work and head out to finish my own project."

I spent the next hour sweeping and cleaning the bungalow number three as best I could in the time given. While a bit of sand had crept in over the years, the place was actually not in too bad of a condition. The conifer scented soap helped to make it seem fresher when I was done.

I had placed the table and chairs on the covered front porch and taken a seat for a couple of minutes when I saw Yuki and Hardtack walk onto the beach near the warehouse. I stood and waved to attract their attention. As I watched their approach I caught what I assumed was a knowing look in Hardtack's expression. Yuki on the other hand seemed surprised to see me standing there.

Hardtack kept a neutral expression as he spoke, "Been working on one of Wright's old bungalows have you?"

I smiled back, "I've been fixing this bungalow up some yes. Who is this Wright you mentioned though?"

Hardtack waved his hand to encompass the scope of the compound, "He was the original architect and builder of this place. When Thomas moved here and started having people move in they were in his way at the tower. So he brought Wright here. Wright designed and constructed the compound for him. It's one of his early works focused on using native materials as much as possible to build working structures."

I nodded, "That is interesting. I was wondering though about the dining hall. It seems to have a different construction than the other buildings."

Hardtack nodded, "That was because I built that structure. You obviously need a dwarf to do the necessary mining work for a cellar like that. I did keep with the native materials theme, but I also applied some dwarfish engineering sensibilities to the construction as well. You'll find my kitchen is much more fire resistant than the original that Wright built."

I was curious, "How do you know that?"

Hardtack laughed, "That's easy. His original kitchen burned down when a novice dwarf cook was working there. Mine has stood up fine ever since I built it. Even after a couple more fires happened the kitchen and dining hall are still standing fine."

We all laughed as I pointed Hardtack and Yuki to a seat at the table on the porch. I sat on Yuki's left while Hardtack sat on her right. Yuki seemed to understand there was some significance to the arrangement. Hardtack also seemed to be ahead of me. I surmised that he had heard the rumors going around by now. However, he was willing to let me start the conversation.

I cleared my throat, "I've asked permission, and I have been granted this bungalow as my new residence on the isle. Now Hardtack I am asking your permission as Yuki's Sensei and Sensei Hapusai's successor in her care and training. I am seeking to make Yuki my wife if she will have me as her husband."

Hardtack sat in silence for a moment, and then responded with a gentle smile, "I can only follow Sensei Hapusai's wishes in this matter. Both of us were present when Sensei Hapusai committed Yuki's training to me. However, it was to you Mica that Sensei Hapusai committed Yuki's care and protection. Sensei Hapusai's permission has already been granted for you to seek her hand in marriage."

As we had said this I could tell that Yuki was practically bursting with excitement and emotion. I could see tears of happiness welling in the corners of her eyes. Her smile was wide as I looked at her directly. I left my chair and kneeled down in front of her as she stood.

I looked up into her smiling face as tears started to fall, "Yuki, you are known as Nene to some, but you will always be Yuki in my heart. I seek your hand in marriage. Do you accept me?"

Yuki wrapped her arms around me with my face pressed against her belly. Then she pulled me back up to my feet to kiss me passionately on the lips. I wrapped my arms around her back and we stood there for a couple of minutes in a passionate embrace. I heard Hardtack cough after a couple more minutes. We stepped apart holding each others hands.

Hardtack mused, "Well it's your turn to give an answer miss Yuki. Don't leave the boy waiting all day."

Yuki giggled, "I do Mica. I will be your wife."

Hardtack spoke, "As the Sensei for both of you I have witnessed and approved this engagement. I hope the White Raven will bless your union. When your mission is over and you all return I'm certain Lirae will be pleased to officiate at your wedding."

I held Yuki's hands still as I looked at Hardtack, "Why would Lirae be the one to officiate at the wedding? I would have thought Thomas would choose to do so."

Hardtack shook his head, "The only priestess of the White Raven on Thomas' Isle is Lirae. Thomas is the White Raven's servant, but Lirae is the only one trained to perform services in her name."

I looked at him with a touch of surprise, "I guess I never realized that she was a priestess of the White Raven. Lirae never mentioned it."

Hardtack laughed, "Well it's not like the White Raven demands formal routine services from her priests and priestesses. They generally only administer the funerary rights and occasionally the odd ceremony among her followers."

I hugged Yuki who was looking on with a touch of uncertainty, "I don't know that I'd really considered myself a follower of the White Raven."

Hardtack shook his head, "Make no mistake, you were one of her followers the moment you strayed from the path and came to Thomas' home on the plane of shadows. You would have never felt the call of the beacon if you weren't recognized as one of hers."

I smiled and hugged Yuki close, "Well be that as it may. We have some more chores ahead of us in setting up the house here. Yuki would you like to pick out some linen and other items for the bungalow?"

Yuki smiled and looked up at me, "That sounds wonderful. Let me take a look inside first so I know what our house will need."

Hardtack called out as we stepped inside, "Remember we still have to work on dinner preparation in three hours. I'll expect to see you both then."

Chapter 24 The Price of Failure

From my experience with my mother and the penchants of the women around the court in the Kingdom of Ard I had presumed that Yuki would spend a lot of time at the warehouse choosing between options and placing orders to be sent out with the next arrival of the Mystic Dawn. I was pleased that she very practically picked out the necessities, and only ordered a couple of sensible items to supplement what the warehouse didn't have in stock. We didn't even need a cart to move the load as her selections were easily managed between the two of us.

After dropping off the goods from the warehouse at the bungalow we walked over to the women's quarters and picked up Yuki's clothes. Once again I was surprised by how basic her choice of belongings was. It was mainly just some simple and practical clothing and women's garments with only a couple of simple yet elegant decorative accouterments for style. It did not take us long to get back to the bungalow and put everything away. As we finished making the bed together I looked across it at her.

Yuki looked out the window toward the beach at the position of the sun in the sky before she spoke, "We have some time left yet. Would you like to practice?"

I looked at my dagger and saber hanging from a peg near the bed, and then answered, "I didn't think to get any weapons assigned to you."

Yuki smiled mischievously as she spoke, "I was thinking of some indoor grappling."

I looked around the relatively small space inside the bungalow, "I don't know if we will have enough room. Wouldn't it be better outside?"

Yuki came around my side of the bed and gently pushed me down upon it while she climbed on top of me.

I slightly trembled under her close presence, "Oh, that kind of grappling."

I pulled her close. The rest was . . . well let me just say something private between two people in love.

In the next three weeks we got into a slightly altered routine. Our time training and honing our skills continued as normal during the day, but Yuki and I were practicing being a couple in the evenings after dinner. It was very enjoyable for us at first, but I began to get the feeling that a certain frustration was there as well. I was feeling a desire to get on with the execution of our mission. Yuki on the other hand seemed content to have my undivided attention in the evenings.

The other problem was that the people on the island seemed to have no problem with giving us advice about our relationship and upcoming wedding. The males generally spoke to me about how lucky I was to have found a mate. The women began to huddle around Yuki in her free time with all kinds of advice about her behavior. As I had seen previously there were many different modes of thought about what relationships required to be a success.

I discussed this with Yuki on the evening before we expected the return of the Mystic Dawn, "It is so . . . I don't know, hard to live up to everyone's expectations about us."

Yuki nodded, "I am feeling the same thing. It is like everyone is an expert on relationships, but none of them seems to even notice the opposite gender on this island themselves. If I have to listen to another lecture about how I should be a better fiancé then I might just have to stab someone."

I smiled, "You shouldn't worry about it. You are doing a fine job Yuki. I have no complaints."

Yuki gave me a kiss on the cheek, "You are kind to say so Mica. The only ones who have not tried to give us advice so far are Thomas whom we haven't seen in weeks, and Hardtack who seems to have already washed his hands of meddling in our personal lives."

I gave her a kiss on the lips, and then spoke, "Let's just promise to talk through any problems which come up. I don't think anyone here really knows what is actually best because none of them have ever been in quite the same situation as us. Sure some were married before, or had kids, but that was always before they joined a group of assassins as a professional career choice."

Yuki looked at me, "What does that have to do with their having a relationship?"

I kissed her on the lips again, "It's like being an adventurer in many ways. There is a lot of uncertainty. Death is always a possibility. The chance of loss is pretty high."

Yuki hugged me back, "Let's not dwell on that. It will just cause us to potentially hesitate when we can't afford to do so."

I nodded, "I agree. We know the risk is there. However we just can not worry about what might happen. There are too many possibilities to plan for everything that could happen. In the long run I think it is better to plan loosely and think on your feet as necessary."

Yuki smiled, "Speaking of feet do you think you could rub mine for a while. Standing in that kitchen is making them ache sometimes."

I gave her a grin, "Is there anything else that needs to be rubbed?"

Yuki placed her feet in my lap, "Start there for now while I think about it."

I awoke in the middle of the night from a large cold nose pressed against my ear. Balinac stood beside our bed looking at me then moved its head toward the door. I motioned Balinac to head outside, and then carefully woke Yuki beside me.

She looked at me groggily, "I was having a nice dream."

I pointed out the window to Balinac standing on the beach waiting for me, "I have been summoned. I should be back soon."

Yuki nodded and curled up in my spot in our bed as I got up and went outside to Balinac. We paced down the beach away from the cliff and passed the dock. As we approached the edge of the jungle I looked at Balinac.

I quietly asked, "Where are we going?"

Balinac almost silently replied using a strange voice, "To have a touch of privacy. Too many eyes have been curious about you lately here."

We ended up climbing the slope of the southern mountain until we got to the clearing on its side. We were far enough from the jungle that no one could casually hear our conversation.

Balinac spoke then, "I have a message to relay from Thomas. He wanted you to hear it personally and alone. I would consider this information private until you hear otherwise."

I nodded my head, "I understand. I shall not share this information or the fact that I got it before anyone else."

Balinac changed size and Thomas' voice issued from its mouth, "Ahoy Mica. I am sending you this message through Balinac. There has been news from the current mission team. Their primary assignment has been completed. However, there has not been a completely clean execution of their task. I regret to say it, but the junior team member Alvos had been captured and had to commit suicide to avoid torture. This was not due to any procedural error on the part of the team, but the associates of the target seem to have been particularly zealous in their pursuit of those responsible. The senior team member Cogstone has managed to send a message along, but he can not make it to the normal pickup point in Port Cirnore as he is still being actively pursued. With the arrival of the Mystic Dawn I am sending you ahead to Port Cirnore along with Yuki and Balinac. You will initiate the next portion of Lirae's mission. After your plans are in motion for Lirae's mission just Balinac and you will arrange to locate Cogstone. When you locate him you are to provide him a safe and discrete means of return. I trust you will maintain secrecy about this matter in the meantime. Word of mission failures prematurely leaking out can be harmful to the morale of your teammates and the reputation of our trade. This is Thomas signing off."

I looked at Balinac, "Let me guess. Rule three no collateral damage."

Balinac shrank back to its cat size, "That would seem to be the problem here. The collateral personnel have obviously been riled by the completion of the primary task and possess resources of an unanticipated nature."

I nodded, "No killing of innocents and no massive body counts of minions I fully understand. How about discouraging pursuit though?"

Balinac jumped up into my arms and shrugged its shoulders, "Not really a trademark for a Thomas style mission. The general rule is to accomplish the task without being detected."

I thought about it a moment, "It seems that being detected has already happened. The trick now is getting Cogstone to disappear from before their eyes. I would guess that they want him alive, or for him to lead them back to his point of origin. Presumably they have access to skills and possibly magic that makes avoiding their pursuit difficult. Let me ask a question of you Balinac."

Balinac purred, "Go ahead. I will answer as best as I can."

I stroked its fur as I asked, "How flexible is your assignment to guard Thomas?"

Balinac continued to purr, "As long as I perform my duties as assigned by The Luck I am free to operate in a manner which suits me."

I asked the necessary question, "Are you bound by the same rules as Thomas?"

Balinac stopped purring, "You are getting clever now. I am not restricted in the same ways that Thomas and those who work for him are restricted. I can not be made to die to eliminate pursuit. I can only be requested to act in furtherance of his goals, not compelled. My own conscience is my guide. That being said I generally do not harm primes needlessly."

I caught an interesting bit of information in the explanation, "What do you mean by being made to die?"

Balinac placed a paw on my hand touching the diamond ring on my right index finger, "Your jewelry there. Did you never question the reason for its existence?"

I looked down at the ring in surprise having completely forgotten about it since I first awoke on the Isle. It occurred to me then that some magic had to be at work for me to forget the presence of a piece of jewelry on my person all these months.

I petted Balinac's cool fur, "It is obviously magical now that you mention it. What purpose does it serve?"

Balinac purred again, "It is the magic loadstone which binds your spirit to the body which you now have. Remove the ring and your spirit returns to Thomas. Your current body on the other hand dies. No divine casting by a priest can compel your spirit to return to that form. Your very existence is within the control of Thomas until your debt of service is paid. After that you are given discretion over how to spend the remainder of your life."

I thought about it for a while more, "So has the spirit of Alvos returned to Thomas already then?"

Balinac nodded, "If Alvos' spirit has not yet returned it is most assuredly on its way back to Thomas' tower on the plane of shadow. Remember there is still a differential time flow there."

It then struck me that almost everyone on the island had a piece of jewelry with either a diamond or a ruby on it. Lirae had diamond earrings I now recalled and so did Jack and Hiram. The residents who always stayed on the island all had ruby earrings, ruby bracelets, or ruby rings on their persons. Only Thomas, Hardtack, and now Yuki had no obvious jewelry on their persons.

I looked at Balinac and spoke with a touch of concern in my voice, "I think I understand why Thomas was reluctant to let Yuki leave. Thomas can not recall her spirit at will can he?"

Balinac nodded, "You understand now why I was required by Thomas to accompany you. Thomas made it a condition of my request to him about allowing Yuki to go with you. I have accepted the responsibility for Yuki's protection and safety while she is off the Isle. If I fail at that task and Yuki is captured by a foe, then I am responsible for her termination."

I slipped back under the thin sheet and cuddled close to Yuki after I returned to the Bungalow. She stirred barely still sleeping as I hugged her and gently rubbed her head. Her breathing indicated she was drifting back into a deeper slumber as I lay awake worried about the position in which I would be placing her.

Then I remembered our conversation about risks earlier that day. We could not be what we needed to be while living in fear of the worst which might happen. I could only plan to the best of my ability, and be flexible about dealing with changes in our situation. I could no more leave Yuki behind to protect her than she could keep me from going.

I also understood that Balinac found it challenging to be divided too much and too long on the prime. It had to keep a presence on the Isle. It had to stay with me, and it now had to protect Yuki. Thomas likely wanted Balinac challenged, and possibly distracted from something he was attempting to do. Yuki and I were his pretext to do so. Thomas would be sending us into danger, and obliging Balinac to split again to keep track of the two of us in separate locations.

I did not understand what master plan Thomas was attempting to execute. I did understand that many beings more powerful than Thomas were concerned with what he was potentially trying to accomplish. I was bound to work for Thomas, yet I also understood that my conscience and mind were still my own. I recalled the orders which Balinac had relayed and realized that there was enough room for some personal interpretation. I finally fell asleep thinking it was time to make a slight alteration to Thomas' plans.

Chapter 25 Fitting Inn

Yuki and I rowed the small boat in through the surf toward the shore as the Mystic Dawn continued sailing up the coast. Balinac stood in its cat sized form in the bow as we rode the gentle breakers toward a small stream emptying into the sea. We were a day's sail further south of Port Cirnore. I had arranged for an extra boat to be placed aboard the Mystic Dawn when we left the Isle, and requested that Captain Roberts find an alternate location to launch us ashore out of sight from the Port Cirnore region.

On my last visit I had unfortunately become a person of interest to the community in Port Cirnore. This time I only wanted a single person to eventually know of my presence for the time being. So Captain Roberts had been provided our shopping list, and sent on to acquire the items we needed as if this were a standard trip for provisions.

As we reached the shore by the stream Balinac jumped off the boat to the land as Yuki and I moved in the oars. I kept one oar as a rudder in the rear as Yuki tossed the lead rope to Balinac. Balinac changed size to that of a medium jungle cat and picked up the rope in its mouth. As Balinac ran along the shore it pulled our boat upstream. I steered the boat to maintain the center of the narrow channel.

After a few miles we came to the first set of shallow rapids. We were forced to land the boat and hide it under cover on the southern bank. Since it was possible that we might return this way I made sure to mark the position of the boat and its surroundings carefully in my mind. Balinac reformed back into its cat size and began to lead us toward our destination.

I looked at Yuki walking beside me as we moved forward. She was dressed in practical peasant trousers and a homespun long sleeved shirt instead of the sleeveless light cotton shirt and short pants she favored on the Isle. She also carried a backpack with her clothing and gear in addition to some basic food ingredients. Finally Yuki wore a cook's work belt with several cooking knives sheathed on it and her dwarf armor skillet hanging from a hook on her left side.

In opposition I wore a long tunic with short pants. I had a light set of shoes, and as was usual for me I wore my saber and fighting dagger. I carried a haversack with my basic gear and a rucksack with my additional clothes. I also had several signed and sealed notes with me which would be good for producing money and other resources from any Bucket Dragon Inn we visited.

A few more miles of walking south away from Port Cirnore through the light forest and we eventually crossed a trail made by sapient beings. We moved onto the trail and continued to follow the trail until the forest thinned more and the trail merged with a lane. We could see signs of cultivation and habitation in the distance so I picked up Balinac. Balinac situated one of its tails inside my tunic between the laces. It hopefully appeared to others like I was carrying a mostly normal dark cat instead of an abnormal one.

We eventually saw sapient inhabitants about the fields and around their dwellings. They gave us a wary eye and kept their distance from us as we walked down the lane. None seemed overly eager to greet strangers, so we kept moving at a fair pace on our way. Where the lane actually joined up with regular road we stopped and had a bit of a rest sitting in the shade under a tree.

I heard the sound of a hand cart being pulled in the distance. I asked Yuki to prepare a suitable traveling meal for three. Yuki got out some traveler's pocket bread, and used some water from a flask to moisten a portion of dried meat. She used a cleverly stacked spice tin to season the meat with a touch of ground dried peppers and salted garlic.

I eventually saw a hand cart top the rise of a nearby hill being pulled by an older human farmer piled high with early season vegetables from a local field. I waited for him to close the distance with us while Yuki and I began working on portions of our pocket bread and meat sandwiches. The man looked at us sitting in the shade under the tree, and he slowed his pace a bit as he approached.

I extended a friendly wave to him, "Hello, we are travelers not from these parts. Could you tell us the best way to reach Misty Green from here?"

The older man gave a tentative smile as he approached, "I can lead you there if you don't mind going at a slower pace. That's where I'm taking my harvest. From the way you are dressed up and where you are sitting I take it you are adventurers."

I nodded my head, "Why yes we are on a bit of an adventure. Would you care to share some of our lunch while we tell you about it some?"

The older man nodded and parked his cart beside the road before he walked nearby and spoke, "My name's Clem. It is awfully brave of you to be sitting under that tree."

I extended the third portion of pocket bread with meat toward Clem, "Really? Is dangerous somehow?"

Clem came closer to take the offered sandwich, "Not the tree itself. It is just an oak. However that tree is at a crossroad so it is used for hanging villains. Tales tell of haunted spirits who bedevil travelers who stay near there after dark. Thank you kindly for the sandwich."

Clem retreated some to sit in the shade provided by his cart as I spoke, "Ah then it is a good thing we plan to reach Misty Green before then. Is it much further down the road?"

I noticed Clem carefully watch us eat and enjoy our meals before he tried a bite of his. He took a cautious chew of the sandwich. I could see that he was enjoying the flavor of the seasoned meat. He ate the rest of his meal with more relish. I saw him watch us finish then reach into his cart looking away from us. Yuki moved to grab one of her knives but I waved her hand back down.

Clem turned back and carefully tossed a pair of tomatoes one at each of us as he sat back down to finish his sandwich. Yuki and I both caught them with ease and began to eat them ourselves without waiting for him to eat as well. After we finished I stood up and Yuki packed her gear.

I spoke to Clem, "Those were some good tomatoes. Thank you kindly for sharing."

Clem smiled back, "I figure as you are well armed if you'd wanted to harm me you'd have done so by now. Most adventurers don't have the patience to enjoy or prepare good food."

I nodded, "It is true that my wife and I are not your typical adventurers. We are actually starting a business soon. I am currently scouting out the competition to learn where they are doing things right, and where we can make an improvement on how they do business."

Clem smiled as he got a hold of his cart again and began walking down the road, "What kind of business are you going to start?"

I looked at Clem and pulled out my sheaf of hastily written plans I had put together on the Mystic Dawn over the past few days, "It is all here my good man."

Clem looked at the sheaf of parchment with a bit of interest in his eye, "Is it some adventurer's map to a fabulous treasure?"

I began to wax enthusiastically like a petitioner before the court of the king, "Oh it should help to make me rich once I pay back my investors, but it is no common adventurer's map. It is my business plan. I am going to open up a series of inns."

Clem started to become a bit confused, "An inn you say?"

I nodded with a happy grin, "Of course you see. It is much safer to have adventurers tramping around finding hidden treasures for themselves. What do adventurers really need though?"

Clem was falling into the prepared script I was leading him into, "An inn?"

I laughed, "Exactly, you are a wise man Clem. They need an inn."

Clem looked a bit confused again, "But Misty Green already has the Looking Dragon Inn."

I nodded, "You are very smart indeed. That is where I am going to scout out the competition."

Clem shook his head, "They are already very successful. I don't think you will find it easy to draw business from them."

I nodded, "How right you are my good man. That's why I'm setting up my first inn in Letheron where the competition is practically non-existent. I already have my advance agent's scouting out suitable properties for purchase."

Clem shook his head, "Where's this Letheron you speak about?"

I smiled, "It is a distant kingdom of elves next to Galidor."

Clem shook his head again, "I hear those elves are none too friendly to humans anymore. Yourself being an exception of course sir."

I smiled, "Right you are again. They are stuck up prigs for the most part. I plan to show them how humans like my lovely wife here can help them out with their problems though."

Yuki gave Clem a winning smile, "Is my husband smart or what?"

Clem shook his head again, "How are you going to help them out?"

I smiled wickedly, "I plan to do that by attracting adventurers of course. We build an inn and the adventurers will come to spend their money there. Then we ask the adventurers to help the elves, and the adventurers will make more money which they spend at my inn."

I spent the balance of the day explaining to Clem my elaborate plot to build an inn inside Letheron. I soon found that through careful observation that it took about twenty minutes before Clem stopped actually listening to what I was saying, and just started filling in the gaps in my sales pitch with the occasional appropriate noise.

I was nice enough to take turns with Clem in pulling the hand cart as we traveled. It was surprisingly hard work, but we were able to keep up a good pace by alternating. My real reason for letting Clem know my plans was I wanted to practice not seeming strange, mysterious, or dangerous. I simply attempted to portray the personalities of the most pedantic and boring petitioners before the court in the Kingdom of Ard I could recall.

By the time we reached Misty Green Clem was clearly convinced that it was a pair of enthusiastic entrepreneurs he had spent the afternoon traveling with instead of a pair of assassins. I knew that word would spread pretty quickly in a small community like Misty Green that we were generally harmless except to someone trying not to be bored to death.

I quickly spotted the Looking Dragon Inn by the edge of the community. It had a set of stables across the street and a high fence surrounding it. The building was smaller in keeping with the size of the community and as we entered the fence gate it was pretty clear the inn had much less in the way of adventurers visiting, and more locals stopping by to share some drinks.

Inside the layout was basically similar if on a somewhat smaller scale. There was still a wall full of job posts near the main fireplace, and wanted posters up near the door. Several tables had lurking and furtive figures sitting at them, but most of the patrons seemed to be affluent locals taking a late afternoon break.

Yuki and I walked right up to the innkeeper at the counter, "Excuse us my good fellow. Would you happen to have a private room still available for a weeks stay?"

The innkeeper smiled back at me and nodded, "That we do sir. A couple of choices are available. Do you require a room with two beds or a double sized one?"

I smiled at him in return, "A double sized bed for my wife and I would be fine."

The innkeeper nodded, "We have a couple more choices. One room comes with a vanity and a large tub for washing off after a dusty day. The other room is on the second floor, but it doesn't have the tub or vanity."

Yuki looked at me while subtly rubbing against my leg with her own, "We haven't washed since we began the trip Mica."

I noticed the innkeeper's eyebrows perk up at the mention of my name, "Mr. Mica that room will cost fourteen pieces of gold for a week."

I looked him in the eyes as Yuki surveyed the other patrons while wearing a somewhat petulant expression, "Is it possible to get the Isle discount?"

The innkeeper's eyes narrowed a bit as he said, "Let me show you the room before you make a final decision."

The innkeeper waved one of the serving girls over to cover the counter while he led us to a hall next to the far side of the fireplace. He took a ring of keys from his pocket, and opened the first room for our examination. We stepped inside while he followed after and locked the door.

I turned to face him with one of my sealed Isle notes in hand, "I think this is what you will need."

The innkeeper took the note and closely examined the seal of a lighthouse tower on it before breaking it open. I could see the message inside directed him to render all reasonable assistance to the bearer.

I saw him smile at me as he looked up, "Will you been needing money, food, and some equipment then?"

I nodded, "Eventually all three most likely, but for now this room and some food should be fine. Some spending change to make it look like we are paying for our room and board would be good as well. We're traveling light and left fairly rapidly without a lot of on hand funds."

The innkeeper nodded, "There was a message delivered here for the Isle a couple of weeks ago. Unfortunately, it had already been opened when it arrived, although the courier claims he didn't know how it happened. I will bring by the note later this evening for your perusal, but it essentially was a request for help signed "C". Nothing specific about the nature of the request was mentioned."

He handed me some coins from his purse, "Give me this when you get back to the counter. Is there anything else you'll be wanting for your stay here?"

I nodded, "Yes, actually. We are traveling as a competing businessman and wife looking to get into the inn keeping business. We'll want to snoop around your open inn operations and kitchen a bit while we are here. You'll see me taking notes and such. Make it seem like I've bribed you to pry around your operation if anyone asks. I won't need to see any secret happenings though. I'll also need a courier to ride to Port Cirnore tomorrow with a message delivery. Can that be arranged?"

The innkeeper nodded, "There is a daily courier from here to there. Just have your message ready early, and he will deliver it to the post in Port Cirnore."

I looked at him carefully, "You recognized my name when my wife mentioned it. Is there anything I should know about that?"

The innkeeper smiled, "You're a sharp one I see. A sage in Port Cirnore has circulated your name and description around to all of the local inns. It seems he's interested in your location or any information which can be gathered about your person. He is paying pretty well too."

I smiled, "Very good then. Does he have one of his messengers waiting in the common room?"

The innkeeper smiled, "Indeed he does. For some reason he doesn't fully trust the innkeepers at the Dragons to give him an accurate report sighting. His messengers are likely told to follow you as best they can."

I nodded, "I won't need a courier then. Point the messenger over to my room later when it is convenient, say sometime after most of the regular crowd leaves for the evening."

The innkeeper nodded, "Let's head back out and conclude our exchange. Will you be mingling or dining in private this evening."

I looked at Yuki first then answered, "I think mingling this evening. We will need to lay down our cover story some I think."

Chapter 26 Regional Manager

A couple of days went by as we waited in the Looking Dragon Inn. Our first evening there I had a conversation with the lookout stationed there by Glorandel the Blue Sage. He agreed to send a message along to Glorandel to the effect that I desired a private meeting with him in Misty Green. The last two days mainly consisted of me taking various measurements of the structure and discussing with the local customers what they liked and didn't like about that particular inn.

Yuki on the other hand ingratiated herself quite effectively with the cooking staff by demonstrating the making and cooking of noodles. The cooks liked that the noodles could be made when business was slow and stored for long periods of time if dried correctly. The cooks really liked that the noodles were quick to cook, and could be served in large quantities fairly rapidly. In those two days Yuki was in the kitchen teaching some more tricks with seasoning dishes which she had learned from Hardtack. She had also learned how to make several of the local specialties by then as well.

I made it a point to have the noodle dishes with every meal. It wasn't long before one of the lurking adventurers tried one of the noodle dishes and liked it. Soon almost all of the adventurers were giving it a try. Several of them even requested the recipe from the kitchen staff. The locals not to be left out were soon trying the noodles and finding they enjoyed the food as well.

The innkeeper came by my table later on the second evening where I was making notes about my observations, "Do you mind if we have a little talk?"

I pointed to the other chair, "Please have a seat."

The innkeeper smiled, "I don't want to sound like I am making a complaint, but business has been doing pretty good since you arrived."

I smiled at him in return, "I am glad to hear it."

The innkeeper then came to the point, "You aren't planning on setting up another inn nearby are you?"

I shook my head, "We will be starting with putting together an inn somewhere in Letheron. You shouldn't have to worry about any direct competition with us anytime soon."

The innkeeper nodded his head, "That's good news for the Looking Dragon. However, I was kind of wondering something?"

I nodded and smiled, "Yes, go ahead good sir."

He lowered his voice some, "Well when the Isle occasionally comes through they usually end up taking some of our profits. Not that I'm complaining mind you, but even with the assistance we've given you so far your wife's ideas have actually ended up increasing our profits. This will happen even more so in the long term I suspect."

I smiled, "Thank you for the complement good sir. I'm really quite fond of her abilities myself as well. Was there something else?"

The innkeeper nodded, "My name is William Crusher and I was wondering if when you get your new inn off the ground whether you could use a good innkeeper to manage it."

I extended my hand to him and we shook, "I'm Mica Lichan and I would be pleased to hire you as the innkeeper in our new location. You understand there might be some difficulties with the new operation."

William nodded his head, "I'm a reformed adventurer myself, but I can handle a spot of roughness when needed. I understand there will likely be some friction there, but frankly speaking it is a touch dull here sir."

I wrote some notes about our decision, "Very well then William. As soon as your replacement is arranged and trained by you here I will arrange for your reassignment to my new facility. The construction should be ready to start by then and I am interested in ways you think things might be improved compared with the current layouts in use."

Toward the third day in the late afternoon Glorandel finally arrived. He seemed surprised by the hustle and bustle at the normally sedate inn. Word had gotten around to the locals and many people were there now to drink and try this new noodle food. He had forgone his robes for a bright blue shirt and deep blue pantaloons. To top it off he carried a long ash staff topped with a blue crystal and wore a jaunty brown hat.

I sat at a small table by the main fireplace. I waited for Glorandel's eyes to adjust to the dim interior before I waved him over to my table. I watched him approach with a look of wonder in his eye. He sat at my table and smiled at me.

I spoke first, "It is good you were able to make it. We have a lot to discuss about the tasks ahead. I have an offer for you and I want you to consider it carefully."

Glorandel nodded, "I've noticed through my sources that you've been pretty busy from where ever it is you work from normally. You've arranged for new companies to be formed, documents to be issued, and certain people have even begun to work their way through the legal system in Letheron to arrange permits and work labor visas. I must say it seems that when you move you move on a very large scale when someone knows what activities to watch."

I nodded in agreement, "Do you think you can use your privacy spell?"

Glorandel shook his head, "I could do it, but it tends to make the natives a bit skittish when I first cast it. They are used to me in Port Cirnore and don't mind my activities. However, here in Misty Green I am a bit less known."

I nodded my understanding, "Perhaps the privacy of my room would be better. We should free up this table for the influx of diners anyway. I'll let my wife know first."

I walked back to the kitchen and saw Yuki helping the cooks prepare for the evening meal, "Yuki! I will be in a meeting in our room. Please bring by some of your special Ramen in a while."

Yuki nodded that she understood my request. I led Glorandel to my room and locked the door. He carefully looked around first and selected to stand in the corner between the small end table beside two chairs. His fingers traced gracefully complex motions through the air as he recited a complex series of arcane phrases which faded from my mind shortly after they were heard.

Glorandel sat down in the one chair as I took the other. I saw him glance toward the large bed where a pair of eyes could be seen looking out from the darkness beneath. Balinac was in position to hear what was being said and report upon it.

I spoke first again, "Yes my friend Balinac is here with us, and my wife Yuki will be joining us later with some light dinner. Let us start with my offer to you. I do not need an answer right away, but I would like one in a few days. First I would like to offer you a job."

Glorandel nodded, "Straight and to the point I see. However, if you recall I am already working in your employ at the moment."

I nodded, "Certainly as contract labor on a single assignment which was submitted by you so I could sample your work product on a trial basis. Your work is solid, and I want you to join us as a full time permanent position."

Glorandel shook his head, "I already have a full time position as a sage and a sideline as the head of the Port Cirnore thieves' guild. I don't have the ability to take on a new job."

I nodded, "This wouldn't entail you quitting your old job. Instead think of it as you being promoted to a more senior position with additional responsibilities. You'll delegate most of the other work much in the same way you already have at a lower level. I want you for your big picture organizational skills."

Glorandel sat back with a smile, "Why do I get the impression you are going to be making an offer I will find very difficult to resist?"

I smiled at him, "Because you are a very intelligent man. I am offering you a senior regional manager position over the start of a ground level creation of a new chain of adventurer focused luxury accommodations. Think of the Bucket Dragon Inns expanded to cater to a richer class of adventuring personnel. Not only do they provide adventurers with information leading to extreme danger, but they also provide a place to spend that large fortune in rewards and treasure."

Glorandel looked at me skeptically, "How do you do this?"

I grinned back, "We go beyond being a simple location to sleep and eat. We provide luxury accommodations suitable for traveling rich merchants and nobility. We attract the intelligent adventurers who appreciate the finer things in life. The Reading Dragon Inns will provide better food, convenient locations to sell their miscellaneous booty, a place to repair or replace their equipment, and a place to find discriminating entertainment."

Glorandel looked at me in a strange manner, "The Reading Dragon Inns you say?"

I nodded, "Of course I am looking for a literate and intelligent class of adventurer. Let the ruffians enjoy the cheap thrills to be found at the Bucket Dragon Inns. If you want serious recuperation while enjoying luxury, then the Reading Dragon Inn chain is where the serious and rich adventurers will be at."

Glorandel nodded, "I see where you are going with this. There will be a brisk trade in information sales going on as well?"

I nodded, "In a few years of operations it is believed that several nations will begin to rely on us as discrete diplomatic meeting points."

Glorandel's eyes got a bit narrower, "How discrete?"

I whispered, "It is hoped that eventually even the wild races will participate in using us as means of opening diplomatic contact between them and their enemies."

Glorandel's eyes got bigger as he let out a low whistle, "You don't think small scale when you operate do you. Let's just say I'm intrigued by your concept. What is your plan for me?"

I smiled, "Frankly speaking I need a skilled regional manager who can help me get this whole operation off the ground. I need someone with your information organization skills to sort through the communication chatter of the operation, and find the pertinent information very quickly. We need to move faster than our potential competitors when they start catching on to this new trend in our line of business.

Glorandel looked at me behind a neutral expression, "If I were to refuse your offer, then what happens?"

I shrugged my shoulders, "You miss out on the opportunity to be in on something very big from the ground up. You've already noted how influential the Bucket Dragon Inns are already. This is the next step in the process."

Glorandel nodded, "I understand the sales pitch. Now what is the threat?"

I formed a neutral expression, "You have the opportunity to compete with us if you choose, or you can go back to Port Cirnore and live your life as a big person in a relatively small pond. Understand though that our resource pool is very large already. Competing with us would be very expensive and time consuming. However, let me sweeten the pot some. Even though we have a head start, our resources are not unlimited. I can go as far as offer you a chance to invest in our endeavor for less than a controlling share mind you, and then you get to have more direct input on how the operation is run as well as a share of the profits."

Glorandel shook his head, "It sounds like a lot of work to go through to create a series of safe houses for your organization. Is this some kind of diversion?"

I smiled again, "It is hardly a diversion. Each Reading Dragon Inn franchise has to turn and keep making a reasonable profit within ten years. It may sound like a long start up period, but there is significant investment cost involved for each location. A large amount of local work forces will be involved in the operation and maintenance of each franchise. Additionally each franchise will allow for facilities and spaces for lease to independent operators."

Glorandel anticipated my next statement, "You are suggesting thieves' guilds, armories, merchants, and other enterprises?"

I smiled and nodded, "Exactly! You have read my mind. Add facilities to support friendly priests and priestesses as well as libraries of interest to Wizards and even Sages. It will be a model of cultural integration if we pull it off, and hopefully very successful in time."

Glorandel nodded, "Your first location is to be Letheron then. Not a lot of competition, but you will face a lot of stiff resistance from Reminas' faction there when they figure out just what you are going to attempt to accomplish."

I reduced my smile, "Your reports indicated as much. I am also looking for insights on ways to, let us say, reduce the power of his opposition. Letheron is a key starting point for us. It is the basis for our eventual expansion."

Glorandel sat back and contemplated, "I can see that a lot of work would need to get done. Laborers need to be hired, architects lined up, and merchants and suppliers brought on board. Yet I find it interesting that one Mica Lichan who didn't even exist one year ago is the power behind this plan. You are playing a deeper game here. The Reading Dragon Inns may well be a legitimate business venture, but there is a reason you are starting with Letheron."

I sat back with a neutral expression, "It has less competition from our own brother franchise chain, and more importantly they have a hotly contested border which could use some adventurers to make some strategic inroads against the wild races."

Glorandel put his hand to his chin, "You're underestimating the amount of radical support that Reminas will likely bring to bear. His supporters are not fans of anyone who is not an elf. You'll be challenging his power base directly and they will respond to block your efforts. There has to be a better place to start an integrated business model than a hostile environment like Letheron presents."

I shook my head, "That's why it is the best place. It is the test bed for a worst case scenario. If we can make a success there, then we can make the Reading Dragon Inn concept work anywhere we would want to set up."

Glorandel dropped his hand, "You haven't read my reports, I am pretty sure that they may even resort to violence given that their opposition to outside influence is so strong. Sure there are plenty of moderates in Letheron, but not enough."

I smiled a wicked grin, "I've read your reports quite thoroughly. I'm pretty sure I can make it a success in the long run."

Glorandel got a cautious look, "I don't like when you get that look on your face. It means I've overlooked something. Let me think. Your employer is the top assassin in the known kingdoms. You're not afraid of conflict with a very connected power in Letheron. Instead you are setting yourself up for this very conflict with your approach. I don't understand why you would do so."

We heard a knock on the door. I got up to let Yuki in to the room as she carried a tray with two bowls of her spicy Ramen. She set them down on the small table between the two chairs and then gave me a hug and a kiss before departing the room. As I sat back down I could tell that Glorandel was furiously processing this new information.

Glorandel spoke, "If you don't mind my asking, who was that exotic human woman who brought what looks to be a traditional Ran Li Ramen style dish into our room."

I laughed, "That is the new executive chef for the Reading Dragon Inn franchises. She is also my wife Yuki Lichan. Try her spicy Ramen it is quite good. It is also one of the many featured dishes that the Reading Dragon Inns will provide."

Glorandel took a spoonful of his Ramen carefully avoiding the peppers without need for warning. He took a sip as I also ate from my soup. I could clearly see that he was thinking furiously as he at his soup with relish.

Glorandel looked at me, "Your wife you say? It's interesting that it is very likely that she is Hapusai Ran's apprentice, although I believe he called her Nene. Did you realize that a woman named Yuki Nene was a famous Spirit Shaman, what they call a Greater Destiny Chi Master in Ran Li, over two thousand years ago? It was said Yuki Nene even knew the Lucky Cricket before he was adopted as the unofficial demigod of the spirit shamans. I'm sure the name couldn't be pure coincidence. The soup is very good by the way."

I nodded, "Thank you for saying so. I will pass your complements on to Yuki."

Glorandel shook his head, "Lichan is a minor derivation of the Ran Li term for pig. It is a highly unlikely last name in that culture, but would certainly pass in this one without comment."

I began to get a touch uncomfortable with this line of questioning, "You may safely assume our identities are solid."

Glorandel nodded, "I'm sure they are the best identities which money can buy. However, sometimes money can not hide all the truth to a careful examiner."

I gave him a wan smile as I ate my soup. He closed his eyes as if he was drawing upon a concentrated thought.

I saw him smile, "I got it wrong. Yuki or Nene as Hapusai Ran called her was not just his apprentice. She is his daughter. Her proper name is Hapusai Nene."

I nodded in appreciation, "You are very good to figure that out that she was raised as his adopted daughter without having seen them interacting together."

Glorandel smiled with a knowing look, "Oh your wife Hapusai Nene is not his adopted daughter. When I imagined them side by side I could see the tell tale marks of a common family resemblance. Your wife Yuki Lichan is most certainly his real daughter."

I was taken a bit by surprised by this revelation, "That's an interesting conjecture you have there Glorandel."

Glorandel shook his head, "You didn't know did you. Which likely means Yuki doesn't know either. Why would Hapusai Ran not tell his own daughter that he was her father?"

I began to suspect that Glorandel was right, but that Yuki's mother was still Togusawa Akane. The nature of Sensei Hapusai's shame and the source of his lord's anger became clear. Sensei Hapusai had made his lord a cuckold in his own manor. As a minor member of nobility I could understand how upsetting that could be to someone concerned with the proper linage of their heirs. Looking at Glorandel I could see him working around the edges of the same problem.

I spoke up, "Her mother was Togusawa Akane."

Glorandel put the rest of it together very quickly after that, "The wife of one Lord Togusawa Akira who died in childbirth along with her son. However, she only had one child. Ah I see it wasn't a son after all. It was the daughter of Akane and Ran, which Lord Togusawa immediately recognized at not being his child. To save face he must have ordered his wife and daughter killed."

I finished for him, "Sensei Hapusai Ran rescued his daughter from the death order of his lord. He was the one ordered to slay her by Lord Togusawa. Sensei Hapusai fled Ran Li and raised his daughter elsewhere."

Glorandel nodded his head, "As a ninja assassin no less I would speculate. She is a literal sinister princess assassin actually. Will wonders never cease to happen? That is a very interesting family you have married into Mica Lichan. The blood of rulers is there, and yet you remain a mystery to me. Much like your notoriously hard to locate employer."

I decided to change the topic, "So what do you think about the job offer I am presenting. Your work is impressive as always."

Glorandel shrugged his shoulders, "It would normally seem like an ideal investment of my money and time."

I sensed his hesitancy, "What is your issue then?"

Glorandel smiled at me with his own wicked smile, "I don't like being kept out of the loop about the full set of objectives of a project I am working. I don't need to know everything about your mysterious organization, but I do need to understand everything you are attempting to achieve before I decide to sign on to a task of this magnitude."

I decided to play a cagey approach, "What is at issue here that you don't understand?"

Glorandel sat back again, "You are deliberately trying to rile up Reminas and his followers. However, you still claim you want to make a legitimate business operation here. Since I speculate that it is unusual for two assassins to be so involved with a legitimate business venture, your goal must be to kill Reminas after drawing him away from his support so he becomes an easier target. It won't work though. Reminas is an old crafty bastard like me. He values his life too much to become an easy target, but even more he values his political stance too much. If he gets killed, then he becomes a martyr to his cause, and your business will likely fail."

I smiled, "What if I told you our goal is not to kill Reminas."

Glorandel shook his head, "Then what you are doing is so complex I can not make sense of it. Trust me when I say that such plans have a built in tendency to fall apart."

I nodded, "I understand your concern. Our business goal is to make a long term profit with this venture and its eventual expansions. My employer's, let us say, personal goal is to kill the dream of Reminas, and to free the citizens of Letheron from his clutches."

Glorandel looked a touch surprised as he thought about the ramifications, "You are implying a cultural revolution through peaceful commerce. Your organization does think on a big scale. It is just bold enough that it could just work. I don't know that such a thing has ever been tried before."

I nodded, "You now have access to information which can destroy our goals if it reaches the wrong ears. You understand we don't intend to let that information get into the wrong hands."

Glorandel nodded, "Your warning is noted and my discretion is assured. If your mysterious employer is who I think he is, then there is no way I would consider crossing him. Even if this were not so I would still keep this conversation and its resulting conclusions private as this is a business negotiation between the two of us. I can conclusively say I will accept that regional manager position to start. I will begin with helping you organize the basic forces you need to put your business together."

I smiled and shook his hand, "I am glad you are aboard with us."

Glorandel smiled, "You always spin an interesting tale my lad. I'd like to see what working more directly with you is like. How long does that window for becoming an investment partner stay open?"

I thought about it a moment, "I can give you at least one month. I could possibly allow two months, but after that I am going to have to have my other investors lined up to move forward with my timetable."

Glorandel nodded again, "That will give me enough time to look into the status of my resources, and possibly liquidate some unused assets. Oh by the way, I've brought you something that you may want to read. My employees intercepted it from a courier waiting for the Mystic Dawn. It seems some free-lancers and a couple of new individuals in Port Cirnore were very intent on tracking it down to its destination. When I heard you were looking for me, I made sure it fell into my hands to deliver to you."

Chapter 27 Journey to Grimvale

I became a little concerned, "Did they follow the message here with you? It would be bad if they caught on to me already."

Glorandel shook his head, "My people are good, and they shook them off the trail before delivering it to me. They also kept any pursuers off my back trail here. Although it seems you made it here without my people spotting you before your arrival. You are an illusive target when you choose to be."

I accepted his compliment, "Let me see what it says."

I opened the message sealed with the tower insignia marked wax. It read simply "Need help. Need exit. Follow the pilgrim's trail. C." I frowned at the note a moment trying to puzzle out how it would help me find Cogstone while confusing any pursuers.

Glorandel watched me carefully, "That does not look like good news. I hate to give you more bad news then. However, my man out in the main room of the inn signaled me when I entered and indicated that two potentially hostile bounty hunters and some unknown people were also in residence at the inn here. They may not have made you yet, but it might not take long for them to do so."

I shrugged, "I am traveling as a future innkeeper looking to start a business, and trying out some new cooking at various inns to determine reception of my new products."

Glorandel nodded, "Your team impresses me as being very clever. Tell as much of the truth as possible without revealing your real goals. It probably is working quite well actually. That explains the sizable crowd of locals here. If the rest of the dishes are as good as the Ramen it might be drawing a sizable crowd."

I smiled, "Yuki's cooking is doing a bit of good yes. It certainly helps my cover along with this."

I pulled out my notes and the rough business plan I had penned together for the new venture. I handed them over to Glorandel to peruse.

Glorandel took a tentative look though my documents, "I see you have been thinking about this quite extensively. There is a lot more than just a sales pitch here. Multiple stages of product sample testing along with a word of mouth advertising campaign. You keep a focus on fusion cuisine with elfish and Ran Li influences. I'm very impressed with the various angles you have considered in putting a business like this together. You're even hiring skilled staff such as the innkeeper here so as to reduce training, and to produce skilled employee input from the beginning. I'm beginning to feel like I'm cheating you a bit here. A lot of my ground work has been initiated already."

I smiled at him, "I'm glad you understand I am very serious about this endeavor. Please keep those documents. I already have the basis memorized. If you can find any improvements on what I have put down for stage two, then feel free to implement them. I would rather those documents not reach the hands of any competitors in the Inn business. However, if other curious parties try to obtain them, then it is fully understood that problems occur if they become lost."

Glorandel nodded, "I will make sure to leave them suitably unprotected in my room after my review. After a solid read through I will not need the written documents to recall their content in full."

I smiled, "I presumed as much given what you are able to recall about individuals and history from memory. Well I think I have a bit more work to do this evening before I retire. I leave it to you to line up the necessary resources for our second stage while I complete the first stage. Don't hesitate to ask for help if any of those persons of interest decide to give you trouble."

Glorandel smiled wickedly this time, "If they attempt to interfere with me or my associates they won't live long to regret it."

After Glorandel left the room Balinac came out from under the bed. It looked at me shaking its head when I opened my mouth to speak. Balinac grew in size until it was about equivalent to my own mass.

Balinac surprised me as it spoke with what I recognized as my own voice with a distracted tone, "I need to remember to send that message to the isle."

I showed Balinac the message from Cogstone as it shrank down to cat size again. It nodded its head after it had seen what was written. Then it took the parchment in its mouth and ate it. I wrote a new message on a parchment as Balinac watched. I decided the following would be the most suitable for anyone seeking to intercept it. "Mission a success. Minions are involved. Beware intruders. M." I sealed the outside of the message with an unmarked blob of white sealing wax. I addressed the message to Ulric care of the Drinking Dragon Inn in the capital of the Kingdom of Ard.

I picked up Balinac and tucked one of its tails under my arm out of view. I then left the room and spoke to William Crusher about where to find the post in Misty Green.

As we walked through town Balinac whispered to me, "I could still feel Glorandel's spell at work. It is very possible he will be able to hear what happens in your room until the spell lapses now. So don't speak to me directly there anymore. I would rather he didn't understand my full set of capabilities."

I nodded slightly and whispered, "Understood. I also make two people from the Dragon main room watching our progress through town."

Balinac whispered back, "They are the hired muscle. Likely the bounty hunters mentioned by Glorandel. There is also a third very stealthy one following them. The third one is likely the one who worked for C's target. I recommend we get back to the relative safety of the inn before dark. They might get ideas otherwise."

I continued until I could see the office for the post ahead. I went inside and paid the clerk for secured delivery of my message. On the way back to the Looking Dragon I noticed that one of the bounty hunters had stopped following us and waited near the office of the post.

I whispered to Balinac, "One remaining behind to watch the courier depart tomorrow I would guess."

Balinac whispered back, "Why did you address your message to an Ulric in Ard? Is it some kind for distraction?"

I chucked under my breath, "They seem insistent on finding the assassin organization responsible. I gave them my best lead to one. Ulric was the name of the assassin who killed my friend Firanda. I figured it was time his life became a little difficult."

Balinac whispered, "Your boss will not be happy that you are working that goal before you finish your current objectives."

I whispered back, "Then he doesn't need to know. Besides it is the best way I can figure to get some of the heat away from C while we locate him. We'll have to give them what they think they are looking for before they become satisfied. We're not allowed to put them down, but nothing in the rules says we can't arrange for a misunderstanding between two groups which are opposing our goals."

Balinac whispered again, "I caution you to not play too loose with those rules. Your boss is not the one who set them."

I was curious, "Who did then?"

Balinac purred as it whispered, "My boss and the raven. The second one is also the answer to the message from C if you haven't figured it out yet."

I caught on to what Balinac was suggesting and whispered, "How many locations in the area?"

Balinac responded, "Six within four days of normal travel from here. At best those locations only create a stalemate. They don't have unlimited capabilities to withstand a determined assault at those locations."

I nodded in response as we approached the Looking Dragon Inn.

We spent five days traveling. In that time we visited the local inns and two select temples. We had finally drawn near the town of Grimvale where the third temple of our journey was situated. I could see from a distance as we approached the town that this particular temple was built and fortified like a small keep as was most of the rest of the town fortified and surrounded by a thick stone wall. Of even greater interest to us was that what looked like an entire battalion of armored knights patrolled, guarded, or performed martial drills around the community.

We had been subtly followed so far since Misty Green, but pretended up to this point that we were ignorant of our persistent pursuers. Yuki mentioned their presence on the first day of travel. Since I had been instructed by Thomas to not involve her operationally in Cogstone's rescue, I merely told her that the company was unwelcome but not unexpected. I didn't like the fact that our pursuers seemed fully confident in their abilities.

Grimvale was in the region bordering the free lands around Port Cirnore and the country of Tirna. It had been the sight of numerous border skirmishes between the two countries. As such the populace here was used to being in a state of military readiness. This could work to both our advantage and disadvantage depending on how well situated our enemies had become if Cogstone was to be found here.

Suddenly Balinac made a quiet growling hiss as I carried it. It looked up at me expectantly after I stopped. I took a good look around and could see that we were in full view of the town gates ahead. Yuki carefully observed our back trail, but shrugged to indicate she hadn't seen anything obviously threatening close to us. I took a step forward, but Balinac hissed again.

I looked at Yuki and spoke, "We need to wait a bit. Balinac probably senses something we can not."

Yuki laughed at that, "I'm not about to question its judgment. If it can catch a ninja in full retreat no telling what else it can detect."

Balinac then closed its eyes and seemed to sleep. I noticed that the guards by the gate were curious or suspicious of us stopping about five hundred yards from their position. One went inside the gate for the moment to likely get instructions or reinforcements.

I looked over at Yuki, "It seems we are going to have to come up with a plausible reason for not approaching their town yet. I don't think it is a good idea to continue until Balinac gives an all clear signal."

Yuki smiled at me, "Just seem friendly and a bit confused about where we are right now. It might be time to pull out some of your parchment and read from it some."

I handed Balinac to Yuki who took it with a bit of trepidation. Then I pulled some of my business plans from my haversack. I began referencing my documentation as I saw a guard in a plumed helmet and two others come out from the gate. They cautiously approached our position with hands close to their weapons.

I looked up at them as they approached and called out first, "Hello good men. Is this the high road to Letheron?"

The man with the plumed helmet stepped forward of his companions about ten yards away, "Halt and identify yourselves."

I looked at him with a bit of confusion, "I have to say that we are already halted and have been for a few minutes while you approached. I am Mica Lichan, and this is my wife Yuki Lichan."

The lead guard spoke again very loudly this time, "What is your business in Grimvale?"

I guessed the markings on the uniform of the lead guard meant that he was a Sergeant in rank, "Well Captain our business is not in Grimvale. It will eventually be in Letheron if you care to visit. We are planning to build the most wonderful inn there."

The Sergeant seemed confused in return by my remark, "I'm not a Captain. I am a Sergeant. I work for a living instead of telling others what to do. Now why have you come to Grimvale?"

I noticed that the expressions of the two guards behind the Sergeant seemed to make a lie of his remark about working for a living.

I shook my head with a confused look again, "That's what I would like to know."

The Sergeant seemed a bit more confused, "If you don't know why you are here, then why have you approached our town?"

One of the young subordinate guards behind the Sergeant spoke, "Sergeant I would have to say that they didn't approach the town. Is that not why we came all the way out here?"

I nodded in agreement, "Exactly my point. Your town was not supposed to be here. This is why we did not approach it."

The Sergeant steeled his jaw and raised his voice again, "Look here you. Our town has been in this valley for over two hundred years. I don't need your worthless opinion about where it belongs. This is where it has been and where it will remain."

Yuki chimed in to save me, "What my husband is trying to say in his lovable if somewhat strange manner is that we have become unexpectedly lost, and did not expect to find your nice town along our course."

The Sergeant seemed to get even more irritated at me, "Why didn't you just say you are lost?"

I gave him a weak smile, "Well a couple days back we asked for directions to Letheron from a man we met on the road. He told us that this was the way to go. Unfortunately we have spotted him a couple of times traveling the same path as us since then."

The Sergeant looked at me with confusion again, "Why would you say unfortunately?

I slowly pointed at the town past the Sergeant and put a sheepish look on my face, "I was afraid he might be a bandit and that this might be his bandit camp."

The Sergeant got an incredulous look on his face while both of the men behind him chuckled.

Yuki smiled at the Sergeant, "I tried to tell him that no bandit camp would be so organized or well defended, but he still had his doubts."

The Sergeant shook his head, "Well we are not bandits. We are a border town in an often disputed valley. Things can get tense around here at times, so we have to be careful about strangers."

I noticed that Balinac opened his eyes while in Yuki's arms. Balinac nodded its head slightly which I took as permission to continue.

I smiled then, "Well if you are not a town of bandits, then we will be seeking accommodation for the evening, maybe for even a couple of days. I'm sorry to say that fellow following us has me all concerned. I have hardly slept at night knowing that he was out there somewhere. Would there happen to be a temple in town by any chance?"

The Sergeant nodded and pointed, "There is a temple to the war god in town. It is the one that looks like a keep. You'll have to stop by customs inside the gate and provide your travel papers."

I looked confused again, "We will?"

The Sergeant nodded as we moved forward toward the gate bracketed by the two junior guards, "Of course you will. This is the last border town before Tirna. You will need to declare your belongings and be searched to show you are not carrying contraband."

I nodded as if I was beginning to understand, "Ah that is good to know. What is considered contraband then?"

The Sergeant smiled, "Intelligence regarding the military disposition of the free lands, unusually powerful magic items, large amounts of currency, and other stuff like that."

I acted hesitant for a moment, "I am carrying several bank notes from my business investors. We are starting an Inn in Letheron soon. We plan to cater to the elves there and other high end clients."

The Sergeant gave me a friendly smile as we went through the gates, "A bit of advice for you. Those people in Tirna are none to friendly with Letheron at the moment, and the people in the country of Galidor bordering Letheron and on the other side of Tirna are even less so. If I were in your shoes, then as an elf I wouldn't go around advertising your plans to go there too loudly as you travel through their countries."

I gulped in nervousness, "Your advice is well heeded Captain. What do you suggest then?"

The Sergeant and his men led us into the customs house, "If I were in your shoes I would suggest you make for Port Cirnore and hire passage on a ship to Letheron. You are less likely to run into trouble that way."

Chapter 28 Challenges

After we cleared the customs house without losing anything more than an entry tax we made our way toward the inn closest to the gate. It had been touch and go for a bit over Yuki's moderately enchanted skillet. I finally challenged them to prove how a dwarf made skillet necessary for my future business venture could conceivably be dangerous to the security of Grimvale. When placed in that context they seemed suitably challenged and embarrassed by the concept and settled on charging us an extra exotic goods tax instead.

Surprisingly the inn was not a Bucket Dragon Inn, but I recalled that Balinac had told me back in Misty Green that Grimvale did not attract adventurers so there was not a franchise here. Given Grimvale's general tendency to seize magical items of a possibly dangerous nature I could understand the sentiment of the adventurers.

I found it very curious to note that the contracted wizard who surveyed our gear completely passed over the gold and diamond ring I wore without any reaction. That meant in my estimation that the ring was either very subtly enchanted, extremely powerful, or possibly both. From what I had learned of magic from Firanda before we died my understanding was that permanent masking enchantments of that capability were extremely rare and very difficult to cast.

With the lack of a Bucket Dragon Inn in Grimvale I had settled for heading to the nearby inn. Upon entry I could see it was mostly deserted in the common room area. There was no friendly fireplace, and no lurking adventurers in the corners. No wanted posters were hung by the door, and no advertisements for adventuring work were posted on the wall. From my prior life I quickly recognized the closest parallel to the kind of facility this represented. It was a civilian version of a military barracks.

I raised my eyebrow at Yuki and she shrugged her shoulders. Given how lifeless this place was I doubted we could learn anything useful for our business other than examples of what not to do. I approached the counter and looked at the innkeeper who looked back at me. I could see from his sour expression that he was a middle aged man who likely had little good to say to anyone.

I gave him my best smile and tried to make a good impression, "Excuse me my good man. My wife and I are looking for a room for a couple of nights."

The innkeeper pointed to a small rectangular box at the far edge of his counter, "The line forms there. Take a number from the box and wait."

As I got closer I noticed that the box contained a neatly stacked row of tiles inside, each presumably with a number painted upon it. I pulled the one out closest to me and noticed that it was the number four. I stood there holding Balinac with Yuki standing beside me. The innkeeper looked at me and I looked back at him. I noticed from this angle that there was a hook hanging on the wall with a tile hanging from it with the number three on it behind the innkeeper.

I smiled at the innkeeper and raised my tile, "I am number four. Does that make us next?"

He glowered back at us, "One number per person."

Yuki pulled the tile with the number five on it from the box, "I have the number five now."

The innkeeper shifted his gaze to her, "Wait your turn in line."

I began to understand how the game was going to go with this fellow now so I returned his glaring gaze with a smile, "I have the number four now."

The innkeeper glared at me, "Give me a moment."

I saw a slight sneer curl his lip as he turned to pull the number from the hook on the wall behind him down. He turned to place it somewhere under his counter. He then came out with another tile with the number four on it and hung it on the plaque behind him. I made a noise as if I were stepping to stand in front of his position at the counter.

He started out speaking sharply while he turned and faded as he said, "You have to wait until I call your number . . ."

He glared at me still standing in position in front of the box. I waggled my number in the air beside my head.

I saw his slight sneer again as he called out, "Number Four."

I stepped into position in front of him at the counter still displaying the number on my tile, "I have the number four."

He looked at me with a sour look and a glint in his eye, "I can see that. Do you think I am stupid?"

I shook my head, "No I don't"

He pointed at the box at the end of the counter again, "Put that tile back in the rear of the box then. Make it right side up and number forward as well."

I placed the tile in the box as he instructed and resumed my position in front of him. The routine seemed very familiar from my martial training in my youth. It was obvious that the innkeeper was likely retired from the local military, and had spent a lot of time training recruits. The problem I was facing was that he was also a bit of a sadist and poorly adapted to life in the civilian sector.

What he didn't understand was that I had been through all this kind of treatment during my training as a soldier and was immune to the effects now. I understood that the game was being played by his rules, and that he would deliberately find fault with anything said and done by us where ever possible. One glance at Yuki and I felt that she did not understand this game yet. I would have to provide the example and hope that she followed along.

As he stood glaring at me I kept my silence. He looked at me sharply playing the waiting game as I passively looked back at him with no expression on my face.

He finally broke first, "Speak up. What do you want?"

I nodded, "My wife and I need a private room for a couple of nights."

He glared at me and then at Yuki before he spoke with another glare, "I've got no private rooms for you and your whore. You'll take a common room and like it.

There is no philandering going on in my barracks. She'll have to stay in the female's common room."

While Yuki was normally shy and reserved I could tell that he had just insulted her deeply from her sharp intake of breath. Below the line of the counter and the sight of the innkeeper I held my right hand palm out toward Yuki indicating I wanted her to keep the peace here.

I played my next gambit already suspecting the response I would get, "Ah I see. We seem to have come to the wrong place. We will seek other accommodations then. Good day to you."

As we approached the door he called out, "You'll be sleeping with the wolves outside the walls then. This is the only place in town allowed to house outsiders. They arrest vagrants in the streets after curfew in Grimvale as well. By the way little whore it is a crime to steal in this town as well. I want my number tile back."

Yuki gave him a polite smile and spoke through clenched teeth, "You'll find it in the box already."

As we walked out into the street I looked at Yuki with a sheepish grin, "I'm sorry about that my dear. I should have figured this was an almost purely military outpost. They sometimes have a certain rough edge when it comes to dealing with newcomers. Let's make our way to the temple and see if we can leave the town before nightfall."

Yuki smiled back, "Don't worry. I've learned to dismiss any insults like those as immaterial to the mission. It sometimes helps to be trained as I was you know. Besides I put the tile back in the box backwards and upside down in the wrong position when he was distracted with you."

I laughed, "Very good. I couldn't be more proud of you."

I really had wanted a chance to speak with Balinac about what had disturbed it before, but I found that we were being obviously watched by locals as we walked down the streets of town. We even had an unofficial escort in the form of three "off duty" soldiers shadowing our path since we left the inn.

It became clear that we needed to get clear of Grimvale soon since they were not likely to give us a moment's bit of privacy while we remained in their territory. In the worst case scenario they might even consider it fair game to accuse us of crime and incarcerate us without just cause.

I was impressed as we approached the gate of the temple keep. There were several guards present, some of which were on the parapet even in the warm weather. Others stood in the full sun wearing their armor and weapons. They cautiously watched our approach as we strode up to their post. One guard raised his hand and called out for us to halt.

This routine was becoming a bit familiar, but I knew we would have to submit to it to get our answers. A guard bearing a mace and a shield with the emblem of a clenched fist holding a lighting bolt came out of a shaded enclosure by the gate and stepped forward to speak to us.

I saw that he had a serious expression as he spoke, "What brings you to the gates of the Temple of Cordane."

I bowed before the guard, "We seek admittance to speak with one of your clergy."

I guard smiled, "You do? That is well and good since I am a member of the clergy here. Do you seek the granting of a blessing of the great Cordane before battle?"

I rose from my bow, "We seek final rights to be said for one of our dead comrades."

I saw that his smile diminished as he replied, "Oh. You'll want to speak with one of hers. Surrender your weapons to the care of the guards here. I will summon an escort."

Yuki and I passed our weapons to the temple guards for safe keeping as a young page went off toward the temple keep. They didn't argue about her keeping her skillet and seemed to be a bit better mannered than the town guards had been.

I quickly caught on that these were clerical forces and not military ones at work here. Undoubtedly each one of them felt that they knew enough divine magic to handle a pair of unarmed travelers such as ourselves if we got out of hand. We stood to the inside of the gate in the shade of the wall until we saw a pale skinned middle aged woman wearing a dark habit and short cropped black hair approaching us. I saw that as she approached she gave Yuki and me a careful look which ended in a wink. I winked back at her as she strode past us to address the gate guards.

She spoke in a no nonsense tone that suggested that no disagreement would be entertained, "These two are in the care of my mistress now. You can provide them their weapons back. We will vouch for their conduct while they remain in Grimvale."

I saw that the guard clergy of Cordane nodded their heads in agreement. As they passed our weapons back to us the town guard which had been trailing us seemed a little surprised by this turn of events. The woman in the dark habit saw the direction of my gaze, and looked at me briefly. I nodded slightly in silent reply.

She then strode out into the street and spoke to everyone within hearing of the gate, "These two have been granted sanctuary by the White Raven as long as they remain in Grimvale. Suffer her displeasure at your own risk. Know that anyone who violates that sanctuary is to be denied final rights by us."

I saw that the "off duty" town guard who had been not so subtly following us all blanched at this proclamation. They likely found it of personal interest to report what they now knew to their superiors. I had high hopes that we had managed to come to the right place.

The woman wearing the habit came back to stand before Yuki and I. I bowed before her while Yuki performed a curtsy.

She gave us a pleasant smile, "Word of your search has traveled ahead of your arrival from our sister chapters. What you seek is here. Follow me to the vaults and we will find you both a cell for your stay."

We followed the woman to the side of the keep like temple and approached what looked like a small stone building with a metal door. She opened the building and the inside was also cool stone. A set of stairs descended below the ground. After we traveled several yards down the stairs ended in a series of long passages with intersecting cross passages.

The walls of the passages were lined with stone shelves which had skeletal forms lying upon them. We had entered a dark mausoleum occasionally lit by distantly spaced torches burning in sconces on the walls. We traversed the main passage for several yards until we came to a metal door.

The woman pulled out a small ring of keys from a hidden pocket in her habit. She quickly located the correct one and unlocked the door. After we were all through she closed the door and locked it from our side again. Then she motioned us to stand near the wall. A repetitive chant came from her lips and worked it way past our minds. I noticed that Balinac had shut its eyes and a slight quiver moved through its form while the chant was performed. I saw the woman nod at us after she finished her divine casting.

She smiled again at us, "My name is Deaconess Resla. I am sure the Raven Mistress Istane will want to speak with you over dinner in an hour. Your friend Cogstone awaits your arrival ahead."

I smiled in return, "I am Mica Lichan and this is my wife Yuki Lichan. We are glad to hear that Cogstone has made it into your care. What was that casting about?"

Resla shrugged her shoulders, "We live in interesting times it seems. Your friend Cogstone came here with a whole lot of interested parties seeking to find him. Unfortunately some of these parties have been outsiders. That casting guarantees they can not broach our sanctuary."

I noticed that Balinac had perked up its ears as I spoke, "Outsiders as in people not from Grimvale?"

Resla shook her head but smiled, "No, not that kind of outsiders. This is the kind of outsiders that don't yet properly understand they should not have broken the rules of the White Raven."

My interest was piqued, "Which rules are those?"

Resla looked me in the eye as she said the next part, "They did not understand they incur her wrath when they avoided their mortal fate. They think they have cheated the White Raven of her due. They will hopefully find out just how wrong they were to make an enemy of her."

I was nervous but went on with my next question, "There is no exception to this rule?"

Resla smiled at me, "Of course there are occasional exceptions made, but it requires the White Raven's personal blessing. However, as one who has traveled her lands and seen the palace of the White Raven you understand that already don't you."

I nodded, "Yes I do. How could you tell though?"

Resla's smile grew even bigger as we started walking down the corridor, "As a loyal servant of the White Raven I can easily spot those rare few which have been marked by her favor. I have seen seven in my lifetime now. This is the first time since I joined the order that four have ever been at this temple at the same time."

I smiled back at her infectious smile, "Why do you find this so amusing then?"

Resla voice was almost infectiously happy, "If all goes well, then soon I will be treading the halls of my goddess with several recalcitrant souls in tow. I'm sure she will be pleased with my efforts."

Yuki looked at her with a serious expression, "You are happy to die then?"

Resla shook her head, "I'm not happy to die. I am happy to die serving the White Raven. There is a big distinction there."

Chapter 29 Raven Mistress

I kept pace beside Yuki as we walked down the corridor after Resla. This hall was still dimly lit, but it seemed to be of newer construction. It did not have the crypt shelves along the walls or any cross corridors. Before long we came upon another doorway.

As Resla pulled her key ring from her hidden pocket again I asked the question, "You say there are four here who have the favor of the White Raven?"

Resla laughed as she opened the next door, "I see two before me now. Both of you bear the look of people who have seen the palace of my goddess. Not many can say that who still live. Your friend Cogstone also bears that look. The final one is of course Raven Mistress Istane who had to travel to an audience with the White Raven before she was granted the title of Raven Mistress."

We stepped into the chamber beyond the door and Resla shut us into darkness. We heard the door lock and a brief phrase was spoken. The room was dimly lit by the symbol of the raven held in Resla's hand. Resla held her hand aloft and lit the space. At the far side was a set of stairs leading upward following the rounded wall until it reached the ceiling.

I asked Resla, "So do you know what it is we do?"

Resla shrugged, "I know that many of our donations come from a mysterious set of benefactors. I know that whenever the tower or the isle is mentioned that we are encouraged to provide assistance. I know that those who bear the favor of the White Raven are rare indeed. Many serve her throughout their lives without gaining such favor. I also know that those who inquire too closely into the business of the White Raven are summoned to her side."

As we started up the stairs I smiled, "You mean they are killed?"

Resla smiled and laughed, "That's one way they are summoned yes."

After a few yards of travel up the stairs we climbed up into a circular room with a high narrow window admitting sunlight. There was a barred door on the room and more stairs winding up what I now recognized as one of the four corner towers of the temple keep building. Several modest furnishings adorned the room including austere chairs and a simple yet functional desk. A young man sat at the desk looking at Resla and us as we entered. The young man wore a simple dark homespun robe and also had close cropped hair.

The expression of the young man seemed a bit surprised, "Oh my. Our visitors are here already? Please have a seat here while I ready your cells upstairs. We were not expecting you for a couple more days at least."

As the young man ran upstairs I pointed Yuki to a chair while Resla sat down on one herself. I sat beside Yuki and looked at Resla closely. I could see that she was smiling on her lips, but that there was no smile in her eyes. This was someone used to consoling the grieving, and not someone who was frivolously happy. The cheerfulness was a front, and she was deeply concerned about what was happening.

I looked in Resla's eyes, and she smiled broadly until I spoke, "You look happy, but you are not. Would you care to speak of it?"

Resla's smile reduced a little then settled into a pursed grimace, "You're right I'm not happy at all. Some necromancer bastard recently had the gall to try raising the dead corpses in my mausoleum. A mausoleum dedicated to the White Raven most importantly. It is an abomination of the highest order. We blocked their casting, but that takes a real bastard to even attempt it. They have no respect for our goddess, and they shall be made to pay for their foolish insolence."

I nodded, "I understand that is not welcomed. Is there more to it?"

A voice came down the stairs toward us, "It happened after I had arrived here. They were likely trying to kill me."

I looked toward the stairs and saw Cogstone silently walking down them. He was cheerful enough, but I could tell that there was a worried look in his eye. In turn he looked surprised to see that Yuki was sitting beside me. Then I saw a look of shock on his face as he recognized Balinac in my arms.

Cogstone shook his head with a touch of fear in his eyes, "How is it that the Isle's guardian has come along with you?"

Resla looked at both of us in a strange manner as Cogstone finished descending the stairs as I stood still carrying Balinac. I reached out my hand to shake Cogstone's, and he took it gingerly. Then Yuki pulled him into a friendly embrace.

Cogstone looked at her carefully, "I did not realize you were to be part of the mission."

Yuki replied, "I did not realize it either until now. My husband has been keeping some things from me."

Cogstone smiled, "Your husband you say? I guess I have been gone too long already. I need to speak to Olivia to find out what I've missed in my absence."

I gave a sheepish smile, "I was under instructions to not involve her. That is also the reason that Balinac is on hand to guard her person."

Cogstone nodded knowingly, "I can understand that Balinac might be convinced to come for Yuki's protection, but unfortunately by bringing her here you have involved her. We're trapped here surrounded by their forces. They are too weak to besiege us while we are in this sanctuary, yet they can keep us from escaping. It's a stalemate until one side or the other brings more forces to bear."

Resla looked a bit angered now, "This has more than a single necromancer and a few of his summoned followers behind it. Raven Mistress Istane suspected as much. Only an insane necromancer would be so bold as to attempt such a thing without serious assistance."

Balinac hissed once quietly in my arms and closed its eyes. The gaze of all three of the people in the room settled on me. I shrugged my shoulders.

Cogstone spoke first, "What is happening here? Balinac has never behaved that way before to my knowledge."

I tried to ease the tension in the room, "I think it means Balinac is busy."

Resla looked at me with a strange expression, "How can a sleeping cat be busy?"

With that a loud bell sound rang in the tower. I saw Resla's face blanch.

I spoke, "That bell means something bad is happening doesn't it?"

Resla looked at me with a new fear showing in her eyes, "That can't be possible. It is the signal used for a breach through our wards from the land of shadow. Such a thing has never happened in all my years of service, never in the history of our chapter."

I waved her over next to Yuki who was holding her dagger and skillet already. Cogstone had a staff on hand as well as a grim look in his eyes. We saw a point of darkness form in the air near the stairs to the tower foundation. It rapidly expanded to a one foot hole. A dark shadowy arm reached through the aperture.

Suddenly another arm pushed through spreading the opening even further. Silently the boundaries between the plane of the tower and the plane of shadow were being pushed aside by whatever being was forcing the gateway. A great shadowy horned head pushed through next. I felt a cat's paw gently prick my forearm. Balinac had its eyes open and gave me a wink while it lightly nodded at the shadowy abomination trying to force its way into the room.

As the thing managed to get its shoulders through the widening opening I launched Balinac at it with a high arching underhand toss. Balinac landed on the back of the shadowy creature's neck. As it reached to bat away this minor menace, Balinac suddenly changed size tall enough to reach the high ceiling. A quick bite later and Balinac had severed the shadowy head from its body. The head and the body quickly dissipated like a light fog and the aperture slowly shrank in size until it was no longer visible.

I smiled as Balinac shrank back down and jumped back into my arms purring, "I don't think they are likely to try entering here that way again anytime soon."

Resla looked at me with a numb smile on her face but uncertainty in her eyes, "Your cat is one impressive guardian. It is not a normal cat is it."

I shook my head, "Balinac is very unique. I would dare say there is not another one like it anywhere.

A voice from the stairway upstairs spoke, "Except when it is in more than one place."

I looked at the elderly woman in black robes standing on the stairs. I had heard her approach but waited for her to announce her presence.

Cogstone looked at her and bowed, "Raven Mistress Istane, I apologize once more for the disturbance I have brought to your temple."

I bowed and Yuki curtsied, "Raven Mistress Istane, I am Mica Lichan from the Isle and this is my wife Yuki Lichan."

Raven Mistress Istane looked at us with a neutral expression, "Ah I see, even more visitors from the Isle. You have even brought the terror from the Isle along. An unprecedented occurrence I believe. Even the White Raven finds it difficult to strike a bargain with the Balinac. I sense that many powers are at work here."

I nodded, "It is true that much is involved in our presence here."

Resla looked at Raven Mistress Istane with a pleading look, "What do you mean by saying the cat can bargain with the White Raven?"

Raven Mistress Istane raised an eyebrow, "You recognized each of these people as having seen the palace of the White Raven yes?"

Resla nodded at the Mistress Istane, "Yes it is visible in their eyes if you know how to look."

Raven Mistress Istane spoke again with a touch of amusement, "Then what do you see when you look at what you have mistakenly dismissed as a cat?"

Resla looked into Balinac's eyes for several moments, "Nothing. I can not see anything."

Raven Mistress Istane nodded, "That is exactly my point. You know Resla that you can see the spirits of living creatures, but that cat has nothing you can see."

Resla looked up at me, "It is some kind of spiritless abomination?"

I shook my head, "I think Raven Mistress Istane is implying the opposite from what I know of it."

Resla stepped back and took a broader look at Balinac in my arms, "I can see it now. It is an illusion, a trick. The spirit is all that is there. The physical form doesn't exist at all. You tricked me. It isn't real."

Raven Mistress Istane shook her head, "You are right and wrong. It has a spirit but no fixed physical form. It creates form from thought. You are in the presence of a rarity beyond rarities. That is what the spirit shamans call a tailed beast. This particular one is Balinac the tailed beast of the prime and the shadow. A being which has existed since before the beginning of the worlds it is said by some."

Resla looked at her with a touch of confusion, "What do those heretics know of the divine? How could anything exist before the beginning of the worlds? All living creatures are subject to the laws of the White Raven."

Raven Mistress Istane nodded her head, "You don't know but you are starting to ask the right questions. Don't be too quick to discard knowledge just because it did not originate within our faith. The deathless are not limited by the same restrictions as the rest of us. Their thoughts create form. Their thoughts created the planes and the gods and goddesses. At least such is the belief of the spirit shamans."

Resla looked concerned, "What do you believe Raven Mistress Istane?"

Raven Mistress Istane shook her head, "I can tell you what I know. The White Raven guides the spirits of the mortals to their final destinations. However, new spirits are always being born in the worlds. Who is to say that there is not a mechanism by which spirits travel back to the worlds to take new physical forms after they have rested? Who is to say that the spirits have not always existed even before the gods? Such is what the spirits shamans believe. I can only say I have never heard different from the White Raven herself as she has always remained silent on the subject."

Resla looked at Balinac again, "Does it know what we are saying? Can it understand us?"

I kept a neutral expression as I spoke, "I really couldn't say."

Resla nodded at my evasion. However, I caught a glint in Raven Mistress Istane's eye at my comment as well as Cogstone's expression seemed a bit amused.

Raven Mistress Istane nodded in our direction, "Let us go upstairs to my dining room while your cells are being prepared. I apologize for our lack of comforts here. We don't normally entertain guests. It is usually the priests of Cordane who have company. Our ascetic is a bit plainer."

Cogstone answered for our group as we started up the stairs, "Your hospitality has been much appreciated. We will make certain your expenditures on our behalf are properly compensated."

As Resla walked beside Istane my sensitive hearing listened to them whispering to each other.

Istane whispered first, "You should have noticed the elf said he could not say whether the Balinac could understand. He did not say that he was without knowledge. You must understand the tailed beasts are powers. Not necessarily as strong as the gods and goddesses, but not as limited either."

Resla whispered in reply, "What do you mean?"

Istane whispered back, "Do you not yet understand that the roles of the gods and goddesses were chosen for them. Not by mortals, but by the spirits. The spirits are the ones who choose. Individually they may be weaker than the gods and goddesses, but together they are very mighty indeed. Without them the gods and goddesses would cease to exist."

Resla seemed awed as she whispered back, "What does that make Balinac?"

Istane gave her a slight smile, "One of the unaligned great spirits. They pick their allies at will, but they do not serve the gods and goddesses."

Resla replied, "Who do they serve then?"

Istane shrugged her shoulders, "They serve their own interests. Sometimes it is a good thing such as when their interests coincide with the interests of our goddess. Yet at other times our goddess simply has to let them have their way since she ultimately has no power over them."

Resla questioned, "Why doesn't she have power over them?"

Istane whispered back, "The goddess only has power over death, fate, and winter. These beings can not die as the very concept is alien to them. They are as you observed beings only of spirit. Yet they also have the power of making, so thus they also have form. However, it could not be properly said they have life. The can make themselves at will, although it is rumored that they generally chose a particular form on the prime. Since the prime is a creation of the gods and goddesses they seem to have some limitations here."

Resla whispered back, "What about that thing that tried to enter the temple from the plane of shadow? Was it destroyed?"

Istane shook her head, "It was a shade. They are essentially a magical reflection of a spirit. They have incomplete form and are thus potentially very dangerous.

Lucky for us the Balinac finds them particularly simple to destroy. A powerful being of spirit like that has no problem canceling a mere reflection of a spirit."

We reached the top of the stairs having bypassed the second floor and making it to the third floor of the tower. The top of the tower seemed to be divided into three spaces. One was a fairly large dining area, and the other two areas were likely the office and quarters for Raven Mistress Istane. We were directed to seats at the table where simple fare of baked bread and warmed potato soup were set out for our arrival.

I placed Balinac on the floor and it moved next to my feet between Yuki and me. Cogstone steered clear of it as most of the Isle's residents tended to do. We sat down at the table at Istane's direction. She stood at the head of the table while the group of us bowed our heads. After a brief thanks given to the White Raven for another day of life, she then uttered a complex series of phrases which faded quickly from our minds.

Istane nodded and sat at the head of the table, "The room is warded and protected from any magical viewing now. I think it is time we told Resla the rest of what she needs to know."

I nodded to Istane, "Why don't you begin Raven Mistress Istane? We will fill in any details where necessary."

Istane nodded, "You can start by not using Raven Mistress as an address to me in private. We are all servants of the White Raven here. With one exception that is of course. Let us be a bit more informal."

I nodded, "Very well Istane if you will let me. I was sent from the Isle to start up a new Inn in Letheron. As a side mission I was sent to locate Cogstone in order to extricate him from the difficulties he has encountered on his mission."

Cogstone chimed in at that point, "My mission seemed to be going well at first. The mission seemed to be going in as much of a routine manner as they ever get, but as we got closer to completion sudden unexpected complications arose. We stirred up one ugly hornets nest hidden in with the flowers if you get my meaning. We struck down the queen hornet, but that just made the rest of them madder. They stung Alvos before we could get clear."

Resla shook her head, "Now I didn't follow what that was about at all."

Istane nodded, "It was a good example of what you are going to get from the four of them directly. It is their very craft and trade after all. They excel at speaking around the issues, using metaphor and implication instead of straight speech. For their type it tends to be their natural language and habit."

Istane pointed at me first, "Talk about what you do."

I smiled my best sales smile, "I am future innkeeper who is going to set up an establishment of high end adventurer's inn's starting in Letheron."

Istane held up her hand, and then pointed at Cogstone, "What is your profession?"

Cogstone smiled as he spoke, "I am a traveling wizard and story teller miss. I create delightful illusions to entertain the good folks where ever I travel."

Istane held up her hand, and then pointed at Yuki, "Do you love your husband?"

Yuki smiled, "I love him very much."

Resla shook her head again, "My truth detection spell didn't indicate any lies being told."

Istane nodded her head, "That is why Thomas the Poisoner is the best assassin in the world. His minions are hand picked from the best available. They each told you the essential truth of themselves and their actions, but each one also told a lie at the same time. They used the lie of omission. No amount of torture or threat of death can get them to tell you what they don't want you to know."

Istane pointed at me again, "That one there is plotting to overthrow a powerful leader in Letheron through peaceful commerce."

Istane pointed at Cogstone, "That one there recently assassinated the top priest of the demon god Mortis on the continent. He even made it all the way here afterward against incredible odds through his use of arcane skill although not without the loss of his comrade."

Istane pointed at Yuki, "That one there loves the elf, but they are not properly married. Not yet at least. I will soon fix that problem. I would also wager she has been trained as a ninja assassin."

Istane called out to the room, "You can come out from where you are hiding under the table Balinac. Please have a seat at the table like a sentient being."

With that Balinac came out from under the table and grew in size. This time however something I didn't expect or predict happened. Balinac shifted form to that of a tall black skinned black haired elf wearing a long black leopard print dress. I maintained my neutral smile through the process, but I was going to need to have a talk with Balinac later. Cogstone on the other hand had his jaw drop open. Yuki looked to me for guidance and seemed to manage witnessing the change pretty well.

Balinac took a seat looking none too pleased as she spoke, "I am going to have a little discussion with your goddess later about the meaning of the term discretion."

Chapter 30 Wedding

Fogstone spoke barely ahead of Resla, "It talks?"

Resla spoke just after him, "It can understand us?"

Yuki instead looked at me after the other two spoke, "How much did you know already?"

I just smiled in a good natured fashion, "Well this soup looks pretty good."

Balinac looked at Istane with an odd expression, "I think you may be visiting your queen pretty soon."

Istane nodded, "You are perceptive. The White Raven has directed me to go on the assault against the forces of Mortis which have been arrayed against you in the area. I am to use as many of these followers of the god Cordane as necessary to do the job. Once the followers of the god Cordane are set on a path of warfare I think the local forces of Mortis are not going to understand what has hit them."

Resla looked at her, "You can't be serious. You mean to spend all of those lives for these three?"

Istane looked at her, "I don't just mean to do it Resla. I must do it. What I may want means nothing do you understand? The White Raven herself has given the order, and I am not afraid to die at her bidding."

Resla spoke up, "I will stand in your place. Let me go to battle for the White Raven."

Istane shook her head, "It has been decided already. You are to become my replacement after I am gone. Don't be so quick to die Resla. Your time will come when the White Raven calls for you."

I looked at Balinac and gave her a nod.

Balinac looked back at me, "What do you want now?"

I raised and eyebrow, "Do you think you could relay a message?"

Balinac looked up at the ceiling, then back down at the table. Then a slight twitch shook her being as she closed her eyes. Balinac shook her head as her eyes opened again. I heard a familiar voice speaking through Balinac's mouth.

Thomas spoke, "Ahoy Mica. This is a direct connection this time. Damnably tricky this is. The White Raven is helping some by synchronizing the time phase between the plane of shadow and the prime. I must say though that it is rather rude to keep using a being as complex and intelligent at Balinac as a mere communication system."

I spoke to Balinac, "Ahoy Thomas. Could you relay a message to the White Raven for us?"

Thomas laughed, "Why she is right here at the moment. It seems we have upset her a bit by mistake. It turns out that one of our clients was looking to have assassinated a high priest of Mortis. It is a damnably pesky inconvenience mind you. How could I have known a minion of Mortis was our target? It raises all kinds of divine vengeance issues. This is of course why we avoid political assassinations.

However, as I explained to the White Raven here if Mortis insists on hiding his high priests among the general population of areas populated by the followers of other gods, then we simply can not be held responsible for their accidental assassinations. If his priest had been working from a properly designated temple, then none of this mix up would have happened."

Of course I understood that if one of Mortis' priests were in the open at a temple in this part of the world, every paladin on the continent would have been seeking his head. Once again I was struck by how Thomas avoided the politics while at the same time playing them quite adroitly. He managed to please the White Raven while at the same time giving her the ability to plausibly deny involvement.

I spoke to Balinac again, "Thomas I need to request a favor of the White Raven. I understand if she denies it in her wisdom. However, in good conscience I must ask."

A different voice issued from Balinac's throat at that point. It was both utterly beautiful and terrifying at the same time, "What is your request half mortal?"

I smiled at Balinac as I spoke, "Your divine radiance. Must you send Istane and the followers of Cordane to their ends now?"

The divine voice spoke through Balinac and echoed throughout the chamber, "I have decreed that Istane's time has almost come. None can change her fate now."

I nodded, "I see my divine queen. Would you consider allowing Istane to access more of your blessings in her final hours to perform her last tasks in the glory of your name?"

The divine voice spoke again, "I know why Thomas has chosen you as one of his. I will grant what you ask since it suits my needs. Istane I will grant you unlimited access to my powers for three hours on the prime starting in three hours. This shall devour your remaining life force, but your spirit will come to me in glory. Make sure the followers of Thomas make it back home without impediment or harm. You may strike down any follower of Mortis who dares to interfere with your final assignment. You Istane shall be my reaper. Teach them that I am still the true goddess of death."

Istane nodded and spoke, "I shall do as you bid my goddess. I thank you for this honor. I also have a boon to ask of you my goddess."

The divine voice called out through the air, "You may ask your boon, and I will consider it."

Istane looked at Yuki and me as she spoke, "I have performed many funerals in my service to you my queen. I ask that you allow me to perform a wedding for two of Thomas' chosen who are in love before I must go."

There was a pause before the voice answered through Balinac, "Thomas has given his permission, so I will grant mine as well. The spirits of Mikael Lidron and Hapusai Nene shall be joined by you."

Balinac closed her eyes and shivered slightly before opening them again, "That was singularly unpleasant."

I began to eat my soup as Cogstone asked, "Why is that?"

Balinac spoke again with a grimace, "Just be glad you don't have to translate from deific to common in real time. That takes quite a bit of thought to digest divine speech into a mortal tongue. Deities tend to get upset when you get their intent wrong."

I understood now Thomas' comment I had heard what seemed like months before about not being able to grasp what the White Raven was thinking. He had meant it literally. In the end analysis Thomas was likely just as dependent on a translator for divine thought as we had been.

Yuki followed my example and began to eat her food as well. Cogstone ate a little of his bread while Resla and Istane seemed to have lost most of their appetites. Yuki and I finished our meals quickly and quietly while the rest seemed absorbed by their respective thoughts.

Istane watched the two of us curiously, "You two don't seem nervous. I would assume most soon to be married couples would be."

I gave Istane a slight grin, "Being killed once before has given me some perspective. I try not to sweat about those things which are out of my control."

Istane looked at me curiously, "That would explain the White Raven referring to you as half mortal. You've not seen her palace while alive then?"

I shook my head, "I was alive. It was just my second life. I was born a human the first time."

Istane looked at Yuki, "Your name is Nene then?"

Yuki nodded, "Such was the name given to me by my father. However, in my heart I shall be Mica's Yuki."

I looked at Istane, "If you are ready, then I think we need to hold a wedding and make some plans for reaching the isle."

I then looked at Balinac, "Could I ask for another favor?"

Balinac looked at me with a slight grin, "That depends on what you ask."

I gave her a large smile, "Would you consent to be our bride's maid for the service?"

Balinac laughed like a light bell, "I suppose I could serve in that capacity as long as I hold this form."

I looked at Cogstone and he replied before I asked, "I'll stand up for you in Hardtack's absence. He isn't going to like it though."

Istane stood up and we all followed along with her down to the main floor of the tower again. We reached the barred door and Resla unlocked and removed the bar from across the opening. After walking down a short hall we entered the central chapel area of the temple keep. A priest of Cordane wearing vestments hurried over to greet us.

The priest looked at Istane and cautiously asked, "Revered Raven Mistress what brings you to our temple today? I was not told of any funeral rights to be held."

The priest then looked past Istane and Resla and spotted the black skinned Balinac standing toward the rear of the party. His eyes widened in surprise as Istane answered his query.

Istane spoke a slightly imperious tone, "I will be performing a wedding ceremony today instead."

The priest looked worried, "That is highly irregular. The White Raven generally does not have wedding rituals."

Istane looked at the priest sharply, "My goddess might consider your attitude insulting. I advise you to speak with your superior before you judge whether I can follow the commandments of the White Raven."

The priest straightened up, "Yes, you are right. I shall do so. Please have a seat."

The priest passed through a door behind the altar. He was gone for a few minutes. When he returned a tall cleric wearing a helm and carrying a mace and shield was also in his presence. The cleric knelt down in front of Istane and bowed before her.

The priest lowered his head as well as the cleric spoke, "We have been informed by an emissary of the mighty god Cordane to grant your requests as much as possible as your final hours approach. What is it that you require of us?"

Istane smiled, "First Falstar I want you to officially recognize Resla as my successor here. After I pass she shall assume my position by the will of the White Raven. Second I will need this temple briefly to officiate a wedding between the elf and the human. They wish to be married and the White Raven has already granted her blessing. Third after the wedding in a couple more hours those four and I shall be departing Grimvale. The local forces loyal to the demon god Mortis shall be arrayed against our departure including his foul undead. I need you to prepare the city for defense against assault in the remaining time before our departure. They may have already infiltrated the city, so beware of invaders from within. Any forces of Mortis who assault Grimvale are yours to manage. However, we shall be riding out hard and will likely be leading most of them away from here. Once they are clear of Grimvale and no longer a threat to the community my goddess bids that you consider leaving them to their own devices as many of them are highly dangerous."

Falstar raised his head, "We beg you to let us form an escort for you."

Istane shook her head, "This one is a bit personal my boys. Mortis has upset the White Raven, and his forces are going to pay the price in spirits and blood. Many of his unholy creations shall fall in the final hours given to me."

Falstar looked both shocked and impressed, "You have been granted the blessings of your goddess?"

Istane nodded, "I shall wield her full powers briefly on the field before my end."

Falstar gave a wicked smile, "You are granted the power of an Avatar! It shall be a sight to behold then. Mortis himself will never dare do the same since he does not trust his minions. We shall do as you ask Raven Mistress."

I took Yuki's hand in my own and we approached the altar together. Istane had moved to stand facing the nearly empty temple in front of the altar as Balinac stood behind Yuki and Cogstone stood behind me. I gazed down into Yuki's eyes as we faced each other in front of Istane. Resla, the priest and Falstar all sat down in the front row of seats.

Istane began the ceremony, "We few have come to witness a great rarity today. A marriage performed on the eve of battle and death. A marriage performed between two people from different races and cultures. A marriage blessed by the White Raven the very goddess of death. Who better than the White Raven to recognize such a marriage? The White Raven who understands that all spirits are finally shown to be equal before her in death. Marriage is a joining of two beings. Under the White Raven marriage is also a linking of two spirits that lasts beyond the passage to death. Two eternal spirits stand here looking to be joined."

Istane looked at Cogstone, "As the representative for the groom do you have the symbol of the bonds of matrimony."

Cogstone pulled out a white gold band affixed with a bright emerald from his pouch and handed it to me.

Istane looked at Balinac, "As the representative for the bride do you have the symbol of the bonds of matrimony."

Balinac opened her hand and a dark metal ring was inside her palm. She handed the ring to Yuki.

Istane looked at me, "Do you Mikael Lidron take Hapusai Nene to be your wife under the eyes of the White Raven."

I looked Yuki in the eyes as I said, "I do."

I placed the gold band upon the ring finger of her left hand. Surprisingly it fit as if it had been made for her. I suspected it was a magical ring.

Istane looked at Yuki, "Do you Hapusai Nene take Mikael Lidron to be your husband under the eyes of the White Raven."

Yuki smiled at me as she said, "I do."

Yuki placed the dark metal band upon the ring finger of my left hand. A slight tingle was felt on my skin and the metal felt slightly cool on my finger.

Istane looked up toward the ceiling, "Let it be known that where two individual people stood before, there now stands one couple. They are held in the bonds of matrimony, and their spirits are now joined under the gaze of the White Raven. They have received her blessings. By the power of the White Raven they shall go forth from this point forward as Mica and Yuki. For such they have become in their eyes, and in the eyes of the White Raven. You both may now kiss."

I embraced Yuki in a warm hug and kissed her passionately for several long moments in front of our witnesses. When we separated Falstar approached with the priest of Cordane behind as Resla moved to the side of Istane who was smiling almost as much as we were.

Falstar spoke first to us and then the assembled group, "I want to be the first to congratulate the new couple. Now is also the time for the preparations to join battle. I call down the blessings of Cordane upon this marriage. I also call down his blessing upon those who are soon to engage the enemy. The enemy shall find your weapons deadly and your wills indomitable."

Falstar and the priest of Cordane began a synchronized chant which buoyed up my spirit and refreshed my body. The rest of the group except Balinac also seemed to be affected by the chant. Balinac merely seemed indifferent. I presumed that the inability to experience this kind of fulfillment was part of the inherent penalty for not having a living body.

Falstar spoke again, "The blessing has been granted. Let us plan until you must depart. I beg you to at least consider allowing us to provide an honor guard to the city gates. That should discourage any infiltrated forces from attacking you before you depart."

Istane nodded at Falstar, "An escort to the gate will be appreciated. Send word out to prepare the defenses of Grimvale."

Chapter 31 Avatar of the White Raven

As we walked from the temple of Cordane to the front gate of Grimvale the sun sank lower into the west. Surrounding us as we went was an honor guard of twenty armed clerics of Cordane. We had spent nearly two hours in planning the diversion for our eventual escape. Cogstone was prepared with some impressive illusions for the living minions of Mortis we might encounter, and Istane was prepared to deal with any undead or summoned minions which may join the fight.

Balinac had revealed to us that before entering Grimvale she had chased off or destroyed several shadows which had been lingering on the nearby portions of the plane of shadows. Balinac had also marshaled most of herself nearby in the plane of shadows to make her upcoming tasks easier.

As exciting as events were leading up to the time of our departure, I still found myself thinking about what master plan Thomas was possibly executing. I did not doubt for a moment that Thomas had deliberately sent Cogstone and Alvos after the high priest of the cult of Mortis. There was no doubt in my mind that there were also plenty of innocent spirits of those killed by the high priest who called out for justice.

However, Thomas certainly would have also been aware of the political ramifications. I suspected that he had engineered our rescue mission of Cogstone so that for several hours Balinac would be very busy keeping us alive and unable to respond to her mission of watching Thomas for the other powers. Thomas had the added benefit that the White Raven would be focused on her Avatar Istane as we escaped in that time as well.

As we reached the inner gate of Grimvale I gave Yuki a long hug and a kiss. I then nodded at Balinac in her dark skinned elf form and moved with Yuki into the growing shade at the base of the wall away from the hearing range of our retinue. Balinac looked at me with a questioning look as she followed us.

I gave her a raised eyebrow, "Is Thomas adequately guarded? I would not want to hear that we had been protected only to lose him."

Balinac shrugged her shoulders, "That is a subjective measure. It is highly unlikely that any outside influence could harm him in the period I am working elsewhere. His personal defenses are quite adequate even without my help. However, I take your other meaning. Thomas has provided himself the time he needs for his plan. Now I can only hope that the results of what he is doing do not come to the attention of the wrong beings."

I nodded back at Balinac, "Let us hope that he is good at covering up what he plans to attempt then."

Balinac, "Thomas is very good at keeping any secrets. I still have not figured out how he managed what he has with us."

Yuki looked concerned, "What has he done?"

I hugged Yuki again, "Thomas has somehow managed to link Balinac and I at a spiritual level. This began when you first arrived on the isle and was finished when I got Balinac to stop standing on you. Other powers are known to have this ability, but it is unlikely that they wanted Thomas to discover it."

Yuki looked at Balinac, "Is this true for you as well? Do you feel a link with Mica?"

Balinac nodded, "I feel an affinity for both Mica and you to speak the truth. It is not a natural occurrence for my kind. Then again by the estimations of many my kind is anything but natural. We only have superficially similar motives or capabilities. Each one of us is very unique as individuals."

I looked at Balinac, "Will you inform your boss of what is happening?"

Balinac nodded, "It has already been done."

I nodded, "That is good. Is it possible that they will provide support to us here?"

Balinac shrugged her shoulders, "It is unlikely they can help us immediately. However, it is possible they will be able to bring some support in eventually. Let me remind you that such actions come with a price to be paid."

I grimaced, "As long as the price is not too high we will do what needs to be done."

I looked back over at Istane who was leaning against her staff with a bowed head encircled by her honor guard of clerics of the god Cordane. Cogstone standing a ways behind her caught my eye and nodded. We would be ready soon. Cogstone came over with his retinue of four volunteer clerics. It hadn't been a problem finding enough volunteers among the followers of Cordane, but there had to be a number of the volunteers cut in order to meet our criteria. The group of the eight of us entered the guard house at the gate and closed the door.

A few minutes later I watched as a Cogstone, a Yuki, a female elf Balinac, and a Mica joined up with the Raven Mistress Istane. Istane raised her head from prayer, and looked at the people who had joined her side. She then gave a glance and a slight nod at four apparent clerics still standing in the guard house. The Raven Mistress Istane headed out the main gate of the city with the four brave clerics with covering illusions cast by Cogstone.

Meanwhile the members of the Isle team left the guard house and mingled in with the cleric honor guard in front of the main gate. The honor guard then dispersed to various sections of the wall surrounding the city. The Isle team rejoined each other as a portion of the honor guard sent to the western postern gate. As we reached the gate we could see a fair amount of the citizenry of Grimvale was heading up onto the walls around the city.

The citizens were all looking south along the main road, and even across the distance a loud booming sound like thunder could be heard. The Raven Mistress Istane and the disguised clerics of Cordane had engaged whatever followers of Mortis challenged her departure. A bright flash went up into the southern sky as the setting sun lowered beyond the horizon. That was the agreed upon signal.

The four of us approached the gate guard who had been informed to only allow one group of four clerics of Cordane to exit the gate for the next three hours. We nodded and raised our shields, and the gate guard opened the gate for us to slip through the wall. Under the wall with the dimming twilight shading our presence Cogstone then cast another spell making our group invisible to anyone except ourselves.

Balinac changed shape back to a giant black leopard. Yuki, Cogstone, and I all climbed onto Balinac's back. Balinac then set off west at a furious pace yet still managed a smooth ride for her passengers. Even though the breeze of our passage was fiercely stinging my eyes Balinac moved with an astounding silence and light step. As we were invisible to anyone else looking in our direction, I presumed we looked like little more than a stiff breeze stirring the fields.

Balinac then called back to us, "Hold on tight everyone. We've been spotted."

At first I didn't see what Balinac was referring to as nothing was radiating heat in the deepening darkness around us. Balinac changed course suddenly, and I saw a figure I initially took for a scarecrow in the field. It turned to face us and I could see its faintly glowing eyes as it opened its pale skinned mouth and emitted a sharply piercing cry.

Cogstone called out from the rear position on Balinac, "It's an undead of some kind. My invisibility is not much use against them. It works on the mind, not on the actual vision."

I called back, "Is the same true for all of your illusion spells?"

Cogstone called out again, "Yes. That's one of the reasons I was having a hard time slipping them in the first place. I can't fool moderately intelligent undead at all."

I saw a point of bright light from the southeast of us. I understood what must be happening soon and smiled.

I spoke again, "It looks like the time has come. Balinac if you will."

Balinac veered her path southward and Yuki, Cogstone and I looked off to our left. We saw a bright pillar of white light shoot into the darkening sky. The undead creature endeavoring to catch us flinched away and hissed ceasing its pursuit for the moment. The Raven Mistress Istane had breathed her last. The Avatar of the White Raven was on the field of battle.

The pillar of light diminished, and a general glow remained over at the battle site. Balinac took this as a sign to increase her speed. The wind blew into our faces from the speed of our travel while we hung onto the back of Balinac. Several bright flashes of light came from the battle as we sped south. I presumed this to mean that the Avatar of the White Raven was prevailing against the minions of Mortis.

Before a half hour had passed we came upon a light track of forest. Balinac slowed her pace somewhat to maneuver between the trees without rapid changes in direction. The battle was a few miles behind us now. We were moving slowly enough now to be heard while talking quietly.

I asked Cogstone, "Did that thing continue to follow?"

Cogstone answered, "It seemed stunned by that pillar of light. I didn't see it move toward us any time up to the point I lost sight of it."

I spoke to Yuki, "How are you doing my love?"

I could hear the exhilaration in her voice as her arms around my waist briefly tightened, "It's too bad we couldn't join the battle. I would have liked to see it from a closer perspective."

I rubbed Balinac's shoulder blades, "How about it Balinac? Did we leave a big trail for them to follow?"

Balinac gave a low growl, "I left no physical trail behind. However, I can't do too much about the scent you three make. If they have noses then they can follow us. If they can feel magic then they will be able to follow as well. If they can transition between planes then they may even be able to get ahead of us. With beings of this level of power there is not much certainty of safety before reaching safe haven."

I spoke again, "Will we be safe on the island?"

Balinac laughed, "As safe as anywhere you could be. It would take a major power to find that place. I hold the key and only those I choose can enter. It would take something more powerful than me to gain access against my will. The island only touches the shadow and the prime. No other planar path leads to it. It is a unique place."

I thought for a moment and asked, "Couldn't someone just sail there?"

Balinac laughed again, "Not from this world's oceans. The island exists on a different world entirely. It's in what planar beings refer to as a pocket dimension."

I asked again, "Are there any other life forms on that other world?"

Balinac spoke, "Nothing bigger or more dangerous than a cow on the land. Some impressively big whales in the water, but they are generally peaceable. It's quite a nice island Thomas has there."

After a bit more thought I put together an earlier conversation I had with Balinac. It had mentioned that it was assigned to watch Thomas there by the Luck. Someone had granted Thomas use of the island, and I suspected that the Lucky Cricket was involved with that as well.

I asked Balinac again, "Where did this world come from? Who uses the rest of it outside the island?"

Balinac turned her head to look back at me with her left eye, "Sometimes you are too perceptive. The world is called Shangri La in the tongue of Ran Li. In the common tongue it is referred to as Fishing Hole."

I spoke my guess, "So it was created by the Lucky Cricket. He is the one who leases the Island to Thomas."

Balinac nodded her head, "The Lucky Cricket is the creator of Fishing Hole. It is his personal retreat."

I nodded, "Is this power of creation why the Lucky Cricket is considered a demigod then?"

Balinac cleared the forest and moved ahead through more farm fields, "That is part of the formula. Immortality is another part. The path forward to full godhood from his current point really only requires significant quantities of followers. The Lucky Cricket has not actively courted followers or worshipers so those followers he does have seem to be generally limited to spirit shamans. Seeing as they don't like worshiping higher beings, and he doesn't seem to be interested in achieving a broader group it is likely he will remain a demigod indefinitely."

As if dreading where my conversation might take us next Balinac began speeding up again through the fields. The rush of wind made it hard to talk softly. I wondered how the Avatar of the White Raven had fared in her objectives. I glanced back behind me. I could see Cogstone wore a contemplative look. It was clear that even though Cogstone was a more senior member under Thomas I had managed to comprehend a greater picture in the scheme of events in less time.

Cogstone nodded at my look in his direction. I knew he wanted to talk, but that he was uncomfortable speaking around a broader audience. I didn't know exactly how much of Thomas' man Cogstone really was. It was my surmise that as a senior he was trusted by Thomas. It would be important for me to make sure I didn't shake Cogstone's confidence in my ability to follow the directions given by Thomas.

Chapter 32 Ambush

We traveled in a fairly straight route at high speed for several hours. Balinac did not need to follow the roads as even the most tortuous terrain presented her with little difficulty. The only things Balinac avoided were sizable communities and sheer cliffs. I thought that Yuki sitting in front of me may have lightly slept a couple of times during our journey, but Cogstone and I stayed pretty much wide awake if relatively silent.

I heard an unexpected snarl come from Balinac. Balinac stopped and held position. I recognized a crossroads in the near distance. It was the place by the hangman's tree where we had eaten lunch the day we had first left the Mystic Dawn. Off to each of our sides two overly large wolves paced through the fields. However it was the man sized bat which hung upside down near the hangman's noose which concerned me most.

The wolves stood up on their hind legs and stretched up to about seven feet in height as they howled. I knew that we would not likely get a chance to run so we dismounted to create a small perimeter. I was cautious about the wolves, but kept my primary focus on the large bat hanging from the tree. The bat dropped from the branch and with a flip landed as a man wearing a dark cloak.

The cloaked figure spoke in a menacing tone, "Impressive were leopard you have in your employ. It is quite large and fierce. No doubt it could menace one of my werewolf minions very effectively. Two however, that should be too much of a challenge for it."

I looked into the reddened eyes of the figure ahead of me noting that it did not radiate any heat into the darkness. It was a vampire I figured. If the legends I had heard were true then it was intelligent, swift, and highly resistant to most forms of weapons. I was also sure that it was on the kill on sight list for the White Raven. Intelligent undead were especially abhorrent to the goddess of death.

I positioned myself to face the vampire, "I would like to learn the name of the man who faces us."

The figure laughed, "A cocky young elf you are. I would kill you on the spot if I hadn't been ordered to capture you alive and unharmed. The human beside you looks quite tasty though. I don't think they will mind if I have a little bite."

The vampire showed its fangs and glared in an attempt to affix me with fear as it spoke, "I will take you to the dungeons of my keep, and torture you for days until you tell us what we want to know."

I laughed, "I don't think you are in a position to bargain for your existence in any way. I figure a sizable reward will come our way for destroying you."

I patted Balinac on the back as I nodded for Yuki to do the same. A small kitten came away in my hand as Balinac transformed into her female elf form. I noticed that Yuki also held a kitten Balinac.

The vampire seemed confused as it threatened, "Your petty illusions will not distract me gnome. Your path ends here for killing the chosen servant of our master."

Cogstone tapped his staff on the ground as he spoke, "Illumination!" A fairly bright light lit the space around us. Everything except the three forms of Balinac which were instead inexplicably shadowed.

The vampire took a hesitant half step back, "You can not escape me with petty tricks. I can see through your illusions."

I bent over to set my Balinac kitten down as I pointed to the werewolf off to the right, "Balinac please make an example of that one for us."

The little kitten Balinac ran forward in a blur, and then bounded up toward the werewolf which also moved forward almost casually to snap at the little Balinac. It bit the Balinac kitten and swallowed it down with a wicked grin.

The vampire spoke up as it took a step forward, "See your tricks are useless. You can not hope to defeat them."

I nodded at the elf Balinac standing to my right. She grinned as the werewolf to the right began clutching its chest in spasms of terrible pain. It got a somehow sad look in its eyes and dropped to the ground apparently dead. The vampire before me looked taken back by the event it had witnessed, while the other werewolf to the left howled although whether in fear or anger I couldn't tell.

I called over to my left as I pointed to the body on my right, "I suggest you find somewhere else to be. My business is with the man in front of me. You don't need to get killed like your friend there."

We could see that the body of the werewolf on the right transformed into the body of a dead man. The werewolf on the left looked at the vampire and snarled.

It spoke with a rough voice, "You said we were fighting humanoids Petri. You made no mention of demonic powers. You have cost our clan one of our brethren. Our deal is broken."

The werewolf transformed back into a large wolf and rapidly ran away from the conflict. The vampire seemed to be considering its next options. It likely understood that it had underestimated our force. I watched for its next move.

Petri threatened us again, "Don't think I needed those fools to kill you all. I merely needed their help to capture you alive. If I can't take you alive, then dead it shall be then."

The vampire Petri lunged forward quickly. It was quicker than I would have thought possible for it. It just as quickly dodged backward to avoid the kitchen knife thrown at its chest by Yuki. It lunged forward again only to be met with my menacing saber before its eyes. Once more it dodged back out of reach.

Petri then cagily circled around wide to attempt rushing Cogstone. A fan of blue flames shooting from Cogstone's fingers and left its cape singed yet it had managed to avoid the brunt of the attack. It circled wide around to Balinac's side seemingly most uncertain at how to approach the unusual being. I saw my chance.

I looked at it, "You seem at a loss for how to proceed. I suggest you look behind you at the body of your fallen hireling to understand what is about to happen."

The vampire Petri scoffed, "I'll not be fooled by your simple trick."

It missed hearing or seeing the shadowy and silent Balinac growing from a miniscule kitten into an identical dark skinned shadowy female elf behind it. The Balinac beside me smiled as the Balinac behind Petri snaked her arm across its throat. The vampire twisted and pulled heaving with tremendous strength to no avail against Balinac. The Balinac beside me walked to stand in front of the struggling Petri.

Both Balinacs smiled as they spoke in unison, "The White Raven rewards quite well for wayward spirits such as yours. I don't think you are going to like what she has in mind for you though. Don't expect your master Mortis to care much either - spirit bind!"

The body of the vampire turned to dust and the figure of Balinac which had been holding it had disappeared as well. The remaining Balinac came back over to our group.

Balinac smiled at us as well, "Do you want me to do something about the other werewolf who is still watching us from a distance?"

I smiled back, "There is no bounty on werewolves is there?"

Balinac shook her head, "Not from the White Raven. They are simply cursed, not the corrupted spirits of the undead."

I looked at the kitten Balinac in Yuki's arms, "Would you be so kind as to make sure he doesn't follow us as we depart then."

The kitten Balinac jumped from Yuki's arms and went running off in the direction the other werewolf departed. Yuki went forward to retrieve her thrown kitchen knife as Balinac transformed back into a horse sized two tailed cat. Cogstone looked at me.

I saw a wry smile on Cogstone's face as he said, "You get a lot done for someone who doesn't do much on his own."

I shrugged my shoulders, "What can I say. I'm a babe in the woods. I need a lot of help. I'm not up to working solo like you are yet."

Cogstone laughed, "None of us work solo. We all depend upon our support mechanism. If you had not come to retrieve me then I would not have been able to make it this far. You just have a very different style than I'm used to seeing in our trade. It takes a lot of nerve to face down opponents like that, even when you are confident in your abilities and the abilities of those around you. It also takes a generous heart if questionable judgment to let an opponent go who could come back to pursue you in the future."

I smiled, "I like to think that someone like that might realize how lucky they were to not be killed when they could have been."

The three of us mounted on Balinac again. Balinac used a somewhat more sedate pace until we reached the point where we had concealed our longboat after the shallow rapids of the inlet we had moved up from the sea. I could tell that

Yuki was somewhat tired by our long evening as we pulled the boat to the water. Cogstone, Yuki and a smaller sized Balinac jumped in as I pushed off from the shore and took up the steering position.

Yuki leaned against me and dozed as Cogstone took up the oars and slowly rowed us downstream. Looking to the side I noticed a second kitten sized Balinac pacing us along the shore. I looked at Balinac sitting in the bow.

I spoke softly, "Balinac were we followed?"

Balinac came back to the stern and curled up on Yuki's lap, "I made sure that I paced the werewolf back to his clan. He ran quite quickly when he initially saw me coming his way. If killing his clan member didn't convince him of the seriousness of his situation then his witnessing the capture of the vampire's spirit convinced him that I was best avoided."

I nodded, "What happened to the vampire's spirit you captured then?"

Balinac purred, "Delivered to the White Raven who was still very angry with Mortis. Too many times Mortis' corrupted undead minions escape her grasp. She was very pleased with my efforts. I've earned a future minor favor from a god today. Not a bad thing to have when needed."

I was a little surprised, "You require the favor of a god?"

Balinac laughed a little, "Not usually. However, when you do need one it is better than not having one."

Cogstone asked a question as he rowed, "Balinac why is it that you are so active now. You've been on the isle since before my arrival one hundred and twenty eight years ago but never shown any tendencies to be anything other than Thomas' spirit guardian. Sure you were unusual with your presence on both the plane of shadow and the prime. It seemed you were mainly just a vicious and clever beast."

Balinac looked at Cogstone with a penetrating gaze, "Cogstone what you and most of the others from the island fail to understand is that you all are Thomas' beasts. I am not his beast. I am his keeper. The White Raven is his current patron. The one I work for though is another power. It is a different power. Not unlike me, but on a higher order."

Cogstone looked concerned, "What do you mean we are his beasts?"

Balinac laughed, "You all come when called. You all do as you are told. It all seems very reasonable to you, but you don't understand you have no choice. Thomas has you by your very spirits in a literal sense."

Cogstone looked shaken, "You mean we have no choice?"

Balinac nodded, "You have a choice, obey or cease to be in this life. Each one of you is clinging on to this life desperately. You have goals to achieve, and are willing to bargain your spirits to achieve them as long as the payment is not too onerous. Thomas is very good at making it seem like a good deal. He provides plenty of down time on a tropical retreat, a feeling of worth and accomplishment, and something to do which focuses your mind. You are all well trained and stable killers."

Cogstone looked at me and nodded in my direction, "What makes him different then? Why do you all of a sudden change how you have been behaving for all of these years?"

Balinac twitched her tails and purred, "Mica is the first one in my time with Thomas who questioned the deal they were being given before they accepted it. Mica went in with open eyes and didn't judge everything he saw by what others have said about it. Mica cares to understand why Thomas does what he does, and how things are working behind the scenes. Frankly speaking Mica interests me in ways that most mortals have not interested me in several millennium. I believe that is what also interests Thomas."

Cogstone looked at me still, "What do you say to that Mica?"

I smiled, "I have a goal like everyone else. I'm willing to help other people achieve what they need to get their help for my goal. I also want to know with whom I'm doing business. I am going to achieve my goal my way. My rules and my conscience are my guides. Thomas' rules are close enough to what I need that I can work within his restrictions. My life is my own however. No one has ever owned me as property. I work with Thomas as our goals coincide at the moment. I don't work for him. If I must die to establish that fact, then so be it."

Cogstone smiled, "I don't think you have to worry about it from me. I'm just doing my job after all these years. Balinac is right that I don't question why I'm doing it. I don't think I really ever have. I have just been glad to have this time. Things are changing though. Even I can tell that much. There are larger forces at work. Speaking of which Balinac what is this power you mentioned was your employer?"

Balinac purred, "You should meet him soon. I believe he is coming to meet us by the shore. He is known as the Lucky Cricket."

Chapter 33 The Lucky Cricket

ogstone blanched a bit, "We are meeting someone you called a demigod? You certainly travel in with a strange crowd Balinac."

Balinac seemed unaffected, "You have no clue how strange. As one of the few great spirits remaining not many of us can be said to have been seen in person by mortals. It is a rarity many gods have not experienced to be in the presence of two of us at once. We tend to be solitary and of very different dispositions. The Luck can be a singularly unpleasant individual when it chooses. Cricket is pretty nice when you get to know him though."

I looked serious as I spoke, "It looks like the sun is rising soon. We are also drawing near the sea. I can hear the waves."

Cogstone looked confused, "I thought you said it was a single person, not two."

The Balinac on shore ran up and jumped over the water onto the boat. The second Balinac curled up on my lap.

Both Balinacs said in unison, "It can be a bit confusing for you mortals. I understand you are not used to thinking of disparate physical beings having one mind. In the case of the Lucky Cricket it is a single being sharing two spirits. A troubling thought even to one such as me."

Cogstone looked at Balinac with concern again, "Just how many of you are there?"

I grinned at the question, "I think you might need to ask how much of Balinac there is. The answer to how many is one as Balinac is unique."

The Balinac on my lap answered, "Mica is correct. There is only one of me. I simply have the ability to divide and shape my physical form as needed. If I had to put an estimate on my total physical mass at the moment then I would say approximately forty two tons or so. That is a deceptive measure as it doesn't take into account my abilities though. It is also a variable based on my current needs."

Cogstone began thinking, "How about this Lucky Cricket you mentioned?"

The shadowy female elf Balinac behind Cogstone whispered into his ear, "You should ask him that. I wouldn't even begin to speculate on a unique being of that nature."

Cogstone shuddered, "You would make one great assassin. Not many can sneak up on me like that, especially from nowhere on a boat out on the water."

The Balinac in my lap spoke, "It is a trivial task for me really. I simply used your shadow with the rising sun to transport more of myself from the plane of shadow. It gets tricky where there is only light and no shadows or darkness though. I have to cast a shadow first, and then transport myself. It tends to give away my approach."

Cogstone shook his head, "I've learned more about you in one day than I knew in the previous one hundred and twenty eight years. I just thought you a peculiar and dangerous being. It seems you are very much more."

I nodded, "Aren't we all."

Cogstone shook his head, "I think I've finally reached the point where I'm getting done with the killing side of this business. It's hard to bring myself to do it any more, and it's harder yet to watch a comrade die even if it is not permanent. I think I'd like to exercise my options of freedom. Perhaps I will ask if I can help Olivia with the business management side of things. Maybe even learn what's going on beyond my job assignments. Do you think Thomas will let me change what I am doing?"

I nodded, "I think Thomas is not going to squander you as a resource. If you want to do something different, then there are plenty of spirits looking to join the assassin side of the business. In fact I could use a corporate manager for the Isle Company on Lirae's mission. The risk is low, and the only killing is from the long hours. Are you interested?"

Cogstone nodded, "I think I am."

Balinac purred, "I am sure Thomas will accept your offer. I'll put a good word in for you. He won't likely refuse me a reasonable request."

We finally broke clear of the trees near the pebble strewn shore as the stream joined the sea. The sun was just up over the horizon, and I could see a small rowboat out on the waves in the distance. It carried a single passenger who wore a simple homespun shirt and a strange hat shaped like a broad shallow cone and woven from apparently long dried grass stems. I could see the passenger held a fishing pole up in the air as it sat calmly in the boat on the gently tossing waves.

I noticed that even though Yuki had kept her eyes closed through our conversation that she was still awake while resting. She was the picture of innocence, and a very intelligent ally and spouse as well. Since the fisherman seemed occupied at the moment I guided the longboat to the pebbled shore. I gently touched Yuki's shoulder, and she opened her eyes as the keel ground against the small stones.

Yuki sat up as Cogstone and I stepped out of the boat. We pulled it above the tide line. I began to prepare a small camp fire near the forest. I noticed that the two Balinac cats had walked into the shadow of the female elf Balinac and subsequently disappeared. I rubbed the dark metal wedding band on my left hand with my thumb. I suspected now that Balinac had subtly guaranteed she would always know my location by placing a part of the physical matter under her control on my finger in the form of Yuki's wedding band.

I tapped the ring once sharply with my right index finger. Balinac turned partially toward me and winked once in my direction before turning back toward the sea. As Yuki, Cogstone and I gathered wood and kindling for our fire I looked over at Cogstone.

I smiled as I spoke, "I forgot to thank you for the wedding band you provided for Yuki. In the heat of events I hope we didn't put you out. If you need me to replace it I can make some kind of arrangement to give it back to you."

Cogstone waved his hand at me and smiled, "Think nothing of it. I have a few more just like it. Magical jewelry is a bit of a hobby of mine. I like to collect and make various pieces. It is one of the things Thomas has me do in my non-mission time."

I held up the ring on my right finger, "This is one of your pieces then?"

Cogstone nodded, "Thomas likes the diamond and ruby pieces I make."

I asked in a thoughtful tone, "Did you enchant them then"

Cogstone laughed, "Not the pieces I make for Thomas. I make them as enchantment grade pieces, but the actual enchantment on them is well beyond my abilities. I have never been able to figure out how those spirit link enchantments he uses work. There is nary a glimmer of magic to them. That emerald ring worn by Yuki radiates more power. As an expert enchanter I can tell you that those low magic enchantment rings are a masterwork of the art. They are easily missed by a magic inspection, but very subtly effective regardless. They can only be removed after death or released by Thomas you know. Once removed the spirit bind holding our spirits to our bodies dissolves and can not be reestablished by outside forces. That is definitely masterwork grade enchanting. Not powerful, but very unique and effective for their purpose."

I nodded as I lit our small camp fire, "That is very interesting. What about the ring you gave Yuki?"

Cogstone smiled while holding up his left hand to show a similar ring on his index finger, "One of my favorite enchantments. I wear one like it myself. It is also a fairly subtle enchantment in its effect. There is nothing flashy or showy with her ring. No dramatic effects or key phrases required. It does however improve the luck of its wearer. Which one of us couldn't use a little more luck."

Balinac called over to us, "I think you are about to find out."

I saw that the figure on the small boat was rowing in toward the shore. He handled the boat confidently and expertly as he approached the breakers. Then he shifted position and used one of his oars like a rudder as he rode a small wave crest on to the pebbled shore. He deftly stepped from his boat and pulled it up beside our longboat. Finally he reached into the boat and pulled out a wet wicker basket.

As he approached our campfire I got a good look at him. He was of exotic appearance with black hair and tanned skin. His eyes had a cast similar to Yuki's. His face was clean shaven. His age appeared to be indeterminate. Surprisingly he was shorter than even Yuki, although he was still taller than Cogstone.

Balinac performed a formal bow as he reached us. The rest of us followed suit. The Lucky Cricket returned an even deeper bow and it appeared that he was somewhat embarrassed by the formality.

Cricket held out his wicker basket and asked, "Would you all like some fish? I have some nice ones I have just caught."

I pointed to a place before the fire, "Please have a seat everyone. Some fish sounds quite tasty. Would you mind preparing the catch for our guest Yuki?"

I saw Cricket raise an eyebrow at her name as Yuki responded, "I would be honored to Mica. If I might have the fish you have collected good sir."

Cricket passed the basket over to Yuki who got out her cooking supplies. She began to deftly prepare the fish for frying over the fire. As the rest of us took a seat except for Balinac I saw that Cricket had briefly closed his eyes. He opened them again and took a close look at all of us. I saw that he spent a fair amount of time examining Balinac in particular.

I smiled and spoke, "Does something concern you Hap Sing?"

A look of surprise crossed Cricket's features, "That is a very old name. One I have not heard used for me in centuries. It seems that you are well informed about who I am since the name Hap Sing has never been known much on this continent. If you don't mind I would prefer to be called Cricket though. It is much more comfortable for me now."

I shrugged and smiled, "Of course Cricket. I've run into a sage who specializes in obscure knowledge and a former ninja Master from Ran Li who remembers the old tales. It didn't take long to put a lot of information together."

Cricket nodded and looked in Balinac's direction, "I also presume that Balinac has been more than a little informative as well. That is very uncharacteristic for her as she is normally quite the loner and prone to keep her own counsel. By the way my dear, I think this new elfin form is quite striking. You should certainly use it more when among the mortals."

Balinac uncharacteristically ducked her head as if in embarrassment, "Thank you Lucky Cricket."

Cricket looked back at me, "You on the other hand young man are a host of unnatural contradictions. I'm afraid it wouldn't do to let any deities see what you have become anytime soon. Thomas has been tinkering again. I'm afraid quite extensively in your case, if in a lesser manner with these other three."

Balinac's head rose up sharply, "I've done the job we agreed to. I've watched and reported every move of Thomas."

Cricket calmly raised a hand, "I'm sure you have done your best. That is between you and the Luck however. You must understand that I am simply commenting on what I can plainly see. I'm fairly sure that if word of Mica's condition gets out to any deities soon, then Thomas is going to be in very deep trouble. I'm not sure that my protection will mean much. Now let us change the subject for a bit. I find that serious discussions before lunch tend to spoil my appetite. I am curious about your name Miss Yuki. Is that from your family line?"

Yuki seemed embarrassed to be the subject of discussion, "I am Yuki Lichan just recently married to Mica Lichan. I was born with the name Nene though. My father's family name is Hapusai."

Cricket nodded with a smile, "Do you know where the name Yuki Nene originated from then?"

Yuki blushed at the attention, "There are old legends of a famous spirit shaman, what the people of Ran Li call a Greater Destiny Chi Master called Yuki Nene. The legends say she tamed a great demon, what my people call an Oni, with her striking beauty and spiritual powers."

Cricket laughed, "It seems time has changed the nature of truth perhaps. While it is true that I knew Yuki Nene as a tall exotic blond haired beauty, I hope that no one is foolish enough to confuse me with an Oni. In the first case I obviously don't have any horns. In the second case I hope that no one thinks I am that ugly."

The rest of us save Balinac laughed at his comment. I noted that Cricket came across as reported by everyone so far. He was as an affable person. However, I also sensed a deeper current within him. I could tell he was thinking. I could see he was cautious. I could also understand that he wanted people to perceive him in a certain way. He wanted people to see him as harmless and inconsequential. I could also feel that of any one of us sitting by the fire there he was likely the most consequential person short of a god I would ever meet. I saw in some ways a lot of myself in him, and it made me very curious.

Yuki put the fish onto her dwarfish skillet over the fire to cook. I noticed that Cogstone was looking at Cricket extensively as if memorizing his features and mode of dress. Then I realized that as a master of illusions he was likely doing just that. Here was fodder for his cover as a traveling story teller before his very eyes.

I asked Cogstone, "What are you thinking Cogstone? You've been pretty quiet so far."

Cogstone laughed, "Pardon my observation, but I'm thinking that if this fellow is a demigod then I need to learn some of his tricks at misdirection and disguise. For the life of me except when he talks he looks and seems every bit like an ordinary fisherman."

Cricket chucked a little in return, "I have never claimed to be any kind of demigod or other deity. That is an appellation misapplied by others. As for seeming like a fisherman, I would have to say I have been fishing pretty regularly since I was about six years old. I'm much more of a fisherman than anything else I've ever been in my whole life."

We ate our meal of fresh pan fried fish in relative silence. I noticed an unusual hunger that the fish seemed to satisfy quite well. It had been expertly prepared by Yuki, but the fish itself was the very essence of freshness as well. I realized that in the excitement of the run for the coast we had not taken a real break in hours.

I was somewhat surprised to see Balinac eating as well. It was the first time I could recall her eating anything she hadn't been asked to make disappear. She was somehow becoming less unusual and alien in nature. I was not sure if it was due to my becoming accustomed to her presence, or if she was adapting quickly to a more elf like form. Maybe she just liked the fish and her actually partaking in an action normal to people made the difference.

As Yuki cleaned up her cooking gear the rest of us sat around the fire in contemplation. I looked at Cogstone and he looked at me in return. I gave him a small nod which he returned. Then he stood up and stretched. Balinac stood up as well.

Balinac smiled and said, "I must see to it that Cogstone makes it back to Thomas' Isle now. Please let the Luck know I am sorry to miss his presence this time. If you don't mind Cogstone and I will borrow the longboat. We'll leave it on the Isle for you."

Yuki hugged Cogstone and then Balinac, "Be safe you two. When shall you return Balinac?"

Balinac ducked her head, "If the Lucky Cricket will see you safely to the shores of Letheron, then I shall meet up with you there."

Cricket nodded his head, "I will bring them there. The Luck will still not be pleased by what Thomas has done though. It is best you not be seen by the Luck anytime soon. I will try to mollify it as best I can. I understand you have done all that was within your ability."

We watched as Cogstone rowed the longboat a few yards from shore as Balinac steered. They then stopped and after a moment a small gateway of shadow opened before the longboat. A slight rush of water occurred and the boat slid through the gate. After their passage the gate disappeared.

Chapter 34 The Unnatural

Cricket looked at Yuki and me, "There are some things you should know Mica. Things I have seen in you that others may not recognize. I am, let me say, uniquely able to understand what has happened in your case."

Yuki sat down next to the fire and said, "What is wrong with my husband?"

Cricket looked at Yuki and gave a faint smile, "Daughter do you not understand what you could become yet? Why you have found yourself drawn to this man?"

Yuki frowned, "I am drawn to Mica because I love him."

Cricket nodded, "While that is true what you don't understand is that you love him because his spirit calls out to you. It is a beacon among other things."

I said, "Why do you call her daughter?"

Cricket smiled, "It is an affectation of mine. I consider all of the potential Greater Destiny Chi Masters as my children. That is very likely why Thomas didn't have her executed for violating his island without permission. Thomas knows how much I value them, and he would easily recognize someone with the potential on sight. However, in her case it goes even deeper."

Yuki trembled slightly, "What do you mean?"

Cricket continued to smile, "You probably don't know it. It is very likely that on your mother's side of the family you are a distant descendant of the original Yuki Nene. You have a royal lineage and a powerful one as well. With the right instruction you could become a powerful Greater Destiny Chi Master."

I felt an important insight was to be learned, "This Yuki Nene was very important to you Cricket?"

Cricket blushed, "We were lovers for a time. Nene helped me to make the adjustment in fully accepting the Luck as part of who I was. She was a very powerful Greater Destiny Chi Master in her later years, nearly as powerful as my own father who may have been the most powerful Greater Destiny Chi Master ever."

Yuki bowed her head, "How can you tell this just from looking at me? Are you really a deity?"

Cricket shook his head, "Nothing so complex my dear. As a Greater Destiny Chi Master I can easily see the resonance of Yuki Nene's spirit in your own. It is carried in all of her descendants, and all of her descendents have to potential to unlock their power with the right guidance."

I asked, "How does Yuki unlock her power?"

Cricket smiled, "There are a couple of traditional ways. One is through years of meditation and study under a master at a monastery dedicated to the form. I personally never recommend that route because they tend to treat every individual as a uniform part. The other traditional way is to spend even more years in quiet hermitage interacting with the spirit world. This is the approach I took. It takes a long time to work; it was at least fifty years before I could do anything significant with my abilities. However, it has the advantage in that new and unique abilities can be discovered instead of just learning what everyone else has done before."

I grinned, "How about the non-traditional way?"

Cricket looked serious, "I don't recommend this in most cases. The non-traditional way is to be in the presence of the Luck. The Luck can unfortunately be very impatient at times. It tends to unlock abilities before the maturity to understand or use them properly can be learned. This can be a bit traumatic to the individual who is unprepared for the experience."

I asked, "Why is it so traumatic?"

Cricket blushed again, "Well the Luck tends to be somewhat rude at the best of times. It can really hurt a person's feelings when it is in a foul mood. Even some deities find it worthwhile to avoid it when it is worked up. Frankly speaking it scares the crap out of most mortals too, even when it is not in full manifestation."

I shook my head, "How does the Luck manage to upset deities?"

Cricket got a slight grin, "The Luck doesn't have a problem reminding the deities that the spirits came first, and without the spirits they would cease to exist. In the case of some specific deities it knows quite a bit more about them and their operations than they are willing to let any competing deities know about. As I understand it sometimes the interactions of the deities are like kids at a youth academy. All gossip and rumors with hurt feelings. It is also like a big popularity contest. The more spirits under their influence, the more popular they become and the more important they feel. The Luck knows many ways to tip the balance of that popularity through the information is has and the influence it wields."

I got a flash of insight, "Is Thomas doing some of the same things by changing the balance of influence among the deities?"

Cricket shrugged, "That is what several of the deities think. That is why I have been vouching for him, and putting him under the patronage of the White Raven who steers clear of most of the divine politics except where Mortis is concerned. This latest escapade has riled up Mortis and the White Raven pretty well, but in the end it will likely come out in her favor. Mortis simply makes too many enemies even of his occasional allies to easily take over her position. The White Raven is very conscientious about the dispensation of spirits after they pass, while the other deities fear Mortis would interfere with them reaching their final destinations. It basically is a matter of trust. The White Raven is generally trusted if not well liked, while Mortis is generally neither trusted nor liked."

I looked at Yuki while she digested what she had heard. I understood that Cricket had steered her away from the subject of my condition. I was a problem. A problem of a nature that Cricket didn't want anyone else to learn about. I suspected that even Balinac was unknowing about the full extent of my condition. I knew that I certainly wanted to learn.

Cricket stood up and smothered the campfire with dirt. Then he doused the dirt with sea water. Yuki and I stood up and followed him over to his small boat. It would be a bit of a tight fit, but the three of us would make it inside. Cricket shoved off from the shore. Then he pointed at a paddle.

Cricket asked, "If you don't mind taking the one side I will handle the other. Two people make it easier to cross the breakers."

I paddled along until we were clear of the waves rolling into the shore. Yuki sat in the bow watching us as Cricket and I matched strokes with each other.

I looked over at Cricket and asked, "Where are we headed?"

Cricket smiled, "I said I would take you to Letheron. Better sooner than later yes?"

I nodded knowingly, "We are going to use a shadow gate then?"

Cricket shook his head, "Never had an affinity for shadow myself. I need help to cross over to those lands. It's part of the problem with being part of the seven tailed beast. I'm limited to manifesting where either the Luck or I have control. That's part of why we had to make a deal with Balinac. She's the only tailed beast with a presence in the land of shadow, or at least the only one with which the Luck is willing to bargain. Thomas himself is a shadowine, one of the shadow people. His kind has a natural affinity for the land of shadow as their race originated there. Many of them become servants of the White Raven just as Thomas did."

I was surprised, "You mean he is not human?"

Cricket shook his head, "No. I don't think he ever claims to be either. However, the shadowine were considered humans at one point in their very distant past. It is just that most people have never heard of the shadowine. Those that have are filled with unreasonable suspicion and distrust. They are generally a mysterious people who tend to keep to themselves. Thomas is one of the rare individuals of their kind who also has an affinity for spiritual manipulation. I regret that if I had met him but one hundred years before I had, then I could have properly trained him as a Greater Destiny Chi Master. As it was by the time I met him he was already far down the path he has traveled. Thomas has learned some things from me anyway, but I'm afraid that he has learned some things I never intended and that all of it has not been put to good use."

I noticed that we had made a decent pace at paddling and the shore was receding. I also saw that the rocking of the waves was putting the already tired Yuki into a light doze where she curled up in the bow of the boat. I could tell that Cricket had mastered the art of misdirection as well. He had told me much I didn't know about my situation. However, at the same time he had kept me from learning much about him personally.

I saw him close his eyes briefly again while whispering a faint phrase. I recognized it as resembling a softly sung nursery tune. I could tell then that Yuki had transformed from a light doze to a deep sleep.

I smiled at Cricket, "That was an interesting melody. Was it from your own country?"

Thomas the Poisoner

Cricket smiled, "It was a nursery song from my youth. My mother used to sing it to me when I was a small child. It also acts as a sleep spell so we can transition to the next phase of our journey."

I nodded, "Why did it not affect me?"

Cricket smiled, "It has affected you. It has affected me. It even put Yuki to sleep."

I shrugged, "I don't feel any different."

Cricket smiled, "Not yet. However, I recommend you look around some."

I could see that we had made a transition outside of sight of land somehow. The sky was bright blue with fluffy white clouds, and the sun had somehow risen to its zenith. The sea below us was a brilliant turquoise color with gently rolling waves.

I looked around in wonder, "Where are we?"

Cricket still smiled, "We are in the dreaming. This is my special place in the dreaming. I like to come here to fish. The fish here are quite exciting, but not nourishing except to the spirit."

I questioned Cricket, "I am asleep then?"

Cricket shook his head, "Not in the sense you understand. Your mind is aware, it is conscious of what it comprehends. Your wife is a mortal though and can only perceive this place through the filter of half remembered dreams. At least until she learns to harness her Greater Destiny Chi Master abilities."

I nodded, "Why haven't I fallen asleep like her then?"

Cricket shook his head, "That is partially why I have brought you to this place Mica. It allows me to show you some things you have not understood about what has really happened to you. Let me reveal piece by piece some of what I can see through my second sight when I view the world."

I nodded, "Let me first tell you something. I understand that there has been a change made to me. I am not the same person as when I was born. However, I'm not sure I would change anything that has happened to me though. I am ready."

Cricket smiled, "It is good you feel this way. I don't think I've ever seen a destiny as entangled as yours has been, and trust me, the Luck is a master at changing destiny."

I was serious, "So what has Thomas done to me besides making me an elf?"

Cricket shook his head, "It may seem like Thomas' work at first, but there is more to what has happened here than the work of Thomas. Let's walk through where you began to where you are now so we can both get a better idea of what is happening. First I will let you see what a relatively normal spirit looks like."

I saw a pale aura of green glow form around Yuki where she lay asleep in the bow. Then I noticed a short trail of green ribbon like glow stretch from Yuki to a phantom bird's egg cradled in her lap.

I looked at Cricket, "What is that egg I see?"

Cricket smiled, "It is the egg of the phantom raven spirit guardian. When her powers awaken then the egg will hatch. Those who have the raven spirit are uniformly the descendants Yuki Nene. It is how I recognized her, but let it remain our secret for now. Next I will reveal the connections which make Yuki unusual."

I watched as a white ribbon stretched between Yuki and me. Then a second black ribbon stretched between Yuki and the wedding band on my finger. I also saw a red ribbon stretch between Yuki and me.

I looked at Cricket, "I understand the link between Yuki and me, I also suspected the link between Yuki, Balinac and me, but why would Yuki and I be linked twice."

Cricket shook his head, "There is one more to go."

I watched as a green ribbon stretched between Yuki and me.

Cricket said, "There are three distinct spirit linkages there. I have let you see them as colored to help you understand the differentiation between them. The green one is the link Yuki and you formed together. The black one is the link between Yuki and Balinac as represented by the ring made of Balinac you wear. I should let you know to not worry. Balinac can not see or understand anything which is happening here in the dreaming. The white ribbon represents the bond forged between the two of you by the White Raven when you married. The red ribbon represents the bond forged between you both by the god Cordane when you both married. While it is unusual to see so much divine interest in the destiny of a couple, it is not a dangerous thing which has happened."

Then I saw several fine gray threads spread out from Yuki and disappear from my sight. I wondered what those could be.

Cricket nodded, "That is the fine detail level which most spirit shamans can not see to. Those are the links normally made between two people who share bonds of love or friendship. For me I generally filter them out unless I am looking for a particular association. For example that one there is to her father. This other one is to her mentor. It looks like Harack which is somewhat interesting to me."

I said, "Hardtack is teaching her how to cook."

Cricket smiled, "It's good that he has dropped his old habits."

I added, "He is also teaching us both to fight."

Cricket shrugged, "Ah baby steps I guess. It takes baby steps. Let me clear your slate for a moment and show you what something considered very unnatural looks like in terms of spirit vision."

The aura, ribbons, and threads disappeared from around Yuki. Then I noticed an orange aura with bestial features surround Cricket. Seven aura tails swung about through the space behind him.

Cricket grinned, "This is what the suppressed aura of the Luck looks like to another spirit shaman. Brace yourself for this next part."

I sat steady as the aura exploded out until it resembled as Hardtack had once described a ninety foot tall tiger over three hundred feet long with seven sixty feet long tails swinging through the sky.

Cricket said, "Then an example of the links the Luck makes to other people."

Thousands of ribbons of every conceivable color began to unfurl from the aura of the Luck. They were quickly joined by thousands and thousands more. Soon the number of ribbons was inconceivable even in estimation. Every direction I looked was filled with them.

Cricket said, "Each of these links equals a change in someone's destiny by the Luck. Most of them are to Spirit Shamans as the Luck has learned how to make such links automatically when their powers manifest. What they know, the Luck can access as it desires. It has had to do so ever since it became bound to me on the prime material plane due to it being spirit linked to my spirit by my father."

The slate became cleared again as I was faced with a vision of a simple fisherman sitting in his boat. A look of concern was on his face.

Cricket looked at me, "Are you prepared to witness what I can see around you? I must warn you to not speak some parts of what you learn here to any others. Those who understand what it means will not accept it, and those who think they can control it to their own ends are wrong."

I saw a dark blue glow spread from my form. It was very large compared to Yuki, but no where near as large as the aura of the Luck had been. Then a black shadow with two tails enveloped me about one half the size the Luck had been, but the blue glow remained bright at its dark center. Then I saw a dim yellow glow also shown in my being along with a bright red glow.

Cricket looked sad, "Thomas' resurrections normally have two auras. The first is implanted aura of your spirit as represented by the dark blue glow surrounding you. The second is the supplanted residual aura of the spirit which belonged to the original holder of your body as represented by the light yellow glow. This he has the permission of the White Raven to do in the pursuit of her goals."

I looked at the black aura and at the red one with confusion, "Why does Balinac's spirit reside within me? What does this red spirit mean? Why is my own spirit so large?"

Chapter 35 The Wonderful Luck

Cricket shook his head, "I don't know all the answers as to how he has done this. I don't even know if it was Thomas who did all of this. I suspect he tried something different with you, and that an unexpected result occurred. First there were two people killed about the same time with their spirits set free at the same location. Instead of bringing back one spirit in a new form Thomas likely tried making the stronger one dominant while combining the weaker of the two. I would surmise he used an elfin form as their bodies tend to be more durable under spiritual manipulation."

I thought about it, "Firanda. I remember that she was the spirit waiting for me when I died. Larwick was the one which had traveled on ahead. She followed me to Thomas' tower and was interviewed by him at the same time that I was."

Cricket nodded, "That seems very possible, but Thomas is not the type to force a spirit against its will. There must have been a bond between you for her to have followed and to agree to join you."

I nodded, "I liked Firanda very much. Well frankly speaking I loved her, but I was uncertain about her feelings for me."

Cricket smiled, "She loved you for certain. No spirit without a deep connection would have followed you against the call of the White Raven otherwise. It is unlikely they would have otherwise agreed to what Thomas has done either."

I guessed, "Thomas combined two compatible spirits to see what would occur."

Cricket nodded, "It is possible he didn't understand there were problems which would happen from such an attempt."

I asked, "Why and how did he combine me with Balinac then?"

Cricket shook his head, "I don't think he did it at all, or even intended it to happen. As far as Thomas understands he likely just thinks a link has been made between Balinac and you. If I had to hazard a guess, then I would say that you were the possibly the one who captured Balinac's spirit on the prime material. Thomas' spirit combining experiment has granted you some unusual and very unwelcome results if any other tailed beast or deity discovers what has happened."

I sat back a moment, "Why doesn't Thomas understand what has happened?"

Cricket shrugged, "He doesn't have the capability I would guess. He is extremely smart. I would say he is smarter than me by far. However, he doesn't have the level of spiritual acuity I possess. Likely the most he can see is this."

A bright blue glow surrounded my form. A black ribbon stretched from me off into space along with a white, red, and green ribbon stretching between me and the sleeping Yuki. Occasional glimpses of a faint red glow could be seen at times. There was also a fine golden chain leading off from the ring on my right hand, and a fine black silken cord leading off from the ring on my left hand.

I shook my head, "They have me bound pretty tightly then."

Cricket looked at both rings, "It would seem so, but this much I can do without causing harm to you."

Cricket reached out to touch both rings. They gently slid off my fingers into his hands. He breathed on them both clutched together in his palms, and then handed them back to me.

I looked at him with a puzzled expression, "What now?"

Cricket nodded, "You can put them on again. They will continue to work as their makers intended, at least until you don't want them to do so anymore. You can now remove them at will without any harm. If they are taken off then neither Thomas nor Balinac can recall your spirit to their control. You are now essentially a free man. What will you do with yourself?"

I smiled, "I will continue to pay my obligations. I still owe Thomas for his help and Balinac too for that matter. I now find myself indebted to you as well Hap Sing. How would you have me pay?"

Cricket nodded, "I am a simple man. There isn't much I need. You can consider it a gift freely given and without much cost really. If you do feel indebted and feel an obligation then I would ask that you help look after my children when you find them. The Chi Masters are special to me."

I nodded, "I think that can be arranged. I can certainly provide them shelter in my new inn when I get it built."

Cricket nodded, "It would be appreciated. I will warn you though that Letheron is linked in many places to the Fey Realm, the realm of the high elves as they like to call themselves. There are places there where your elfish body will cross the boundary, but the Balinac will not be able to follow you as it is usually limited to manifestations on the prime and shadow. You may have enemies which figure this out and take advantage of it."

I smiled at Cricket, "Your advice is appreciated. Does that explain why Balinac could not take this course through the dreaming?"

Cricket shook his head, "All the great spirits can come to the dreaming. This is where they are from after all be they tailed beast or no. The Luck simply told the Balinac that our conversation was to be private. She obliged us of course."

I grinned, "The number of tails thing again?"

Cricket shrugged, "The tails are symbolic really. It is the power they represent that speaks mostly between the tailed beasts. However, in this case it is more of a favors owed and markers cashed in thing. The Luck has quite a large business going across the planes servicing spirits, gods, and others with information. If they don't pay when the bill comes due, well I'm afraid the Luck makes sure the information it sold loses value quickly."

I nodded, "What deal has the Luck made for Balinac's help then?"

Cricket gave a slight grin, "I'm sure you would have to ask the Luck yourself. It doesn't make me privy to that kind of information. I would caution you that the Luck sometimes charges up front for the information, and at other times it collects later. With it there is almost always a price to be paid. It is much like with Thomas really, at least in how it thinks. When I bring the Luck forward please prepare for a lot of yelling and meaningless threats and insults. That is how it establishes dominance in its bargaining position before entering a deal. I recommend a tough approach to counter bargaining with it. You will gain respect from it if nothing else. It also may try to use the power of its aura to intimidate. You are likely going to be immune if anyone semi-mortal is going to be immune, the mess Thomas has made with you will likely give you that much help."

I smiled, "I think I understand. A lot of bark, but not much bite until the bill needs to be paid. Sounds like some dukes I've seen arguing before the king's court. I'm ready as I will ever be."

Cricket nodded and spoke the phrase, "Luck Appear!"

I could see Cricket still sitting in the boat, but instead of the kind gentle fisherman sitting next to me there was a feral aspect to his demeanor. I could see the orange glow of the aura of the Luck emanating from it. Its eyes were bestial in nature, and its expression twisted to one of displeasure. It glared at me fiercely.

The Luck bellowed out, "What kind of rat ass crazy kind of mess is this? No one told me that rotten spawn of the bitch would be here. What a bony chicken slut that whore was."

The Luck then looked at me as its rant continued, "You let not just one, but two gods link you to that bitch? Then let Balinac jump in for some fun as well? You must be the biggest idiot I've had the displeasure of meeting in two thousand years you ignorant bumpkin . . . ouch!"

The Luck was sitting there cross eyed with a bloody nose where I had struck it hard and fast with the back of my hand.

I smiled back at it and calmly said, "Behave you. I want to hear an apology and some better manners from you for the rest of our conversation."

The Luck's aura grew bright as it roared back, "What kind of crazy ass bastard are you . . . Ouch! Stop hitting me please. I'm sorry for offending you kind sir."

I could see by the large smile it wore that the Luck wasn't actually hurt by what I had done, but that I had managed to amuse it.

I calmly spoke again, "Are we agreed on the rules for this conversation now?"

The Luck smiled back and laughed with blood trickling down its nose, "We certainly are my friend. I've been trying to provoke someone into taking a punch at Cricket for over two thousand years now. You're the first mortal who has ever had the balls to try while I was present."

I smiled back, "You find this amusing?"

The Luck laughed, "I most certainly do. I also owe you one for the favor. I've wanted to take a swing at Cricket for a long time, but it kind of looses meaning if I have to do it myself. It is much funnier when he has to realize that someone will gladly punch him out. I think you and I will be pretty good friends."

I nodded, "I'm glad to hear it. I have some information you might want, and some questions for you."

The Luck smiled, "Certainly we can do some business then. I'll give you some free questions for the service already rendered and some more free questions if your information is any good. I'll even let you know when I start charging. I don't let most people know that in advance. Consider it my friend discount. Start with what you know first, that way I can figure out the value of the whole lot and when you start owing me. Before you begin I already have what Balinac knows on file. So it had better be original stuff."

I nodded and began by filling the Luck in with the rough details of my life which would have been outside of its level of interest leading up my death and reincarnation on Thomas' Isle. I also let it know what Cricket had speculated about my current state, and what he had done to my rings.

The Luck nodded, "Interesting. Most of it was certainly below the level of information my prime contacts could have easily received, and I will also note where Balinac was lax in reporting. That will come against her final bill. I would also like you to keep an eye on that Glorandel the Blue Sage when you can. Mortals with that level of knowledge beyond them soon find themselves in serious danger. It is a good thing that you have hired him. It might be time in a few years to retire him altogether, a nice quiet retreat on Thomas' Isle perhaps. I'm sure Harack would like the company of an old acquaintance."

I nodded, "If you don't mind my observation I think that Thomas is also slipping any restrictions you might have placed upon him. This last operation was clearly designed to curry favor with the White Raven and to hide his actions from her and you."

The Luck shrugged its shoulders, "Of course it was. No extra credit for that observation, I knew that all along. I don't mind though. I was never intending to get in the way of Thomas' actions. I was only trying to get him to be more careful about them. He has learned his lessons well. Nothing outside of our little club is aware that Thomas is moving forward with his plans. That he does so carefully and secretly is all that concerns me. Thomas is a pet project of mine, and I want it to be a success."

I shrugged my shoulders, "Since I didn't ask I won't consider that payment against my tally then."

The Luck nodded, "Wise move. I like you even better already. You know when to keep your nose out of certain things. It would really do you no good to learn what I speculate is going on there. So if that is all you have for me then I think I can provide quite a bit of insight you would find informative or interesting. What would you like to know?"

I smiled, "I may not know the right question. I leave it up to you to let me know what would be in my personal best interest to know. Please tell me when knowing more begins to tally up costs."

The Luck smiled, "I like you a lot my boy. You make some pretty smart moves for a semi-mortal. I can definitely see why Thomas has picked you as one of his projects. The reason is first that your natural destiny is very strong. You resisted the call of death, and only one in a billion spirits manages that feat without divine assistance. The second reason is that you have focus and drive. I think the extra spirit of that girl Firanda might be part of that. She strikes me as someone who was a touch more driven and ambitious than you were in your first life. For a gutter born half-elf she had managed to come far in life, and was seeking to go further when she met you. Both of you had strong destinies, and as such you found yourselves drawn together."

I nodded, "I haven't heard anything I have not already figured out for myself. I hope you are not considering this as part of my repayment."

The Luck shook its head, "You are a savvy bargainer. No this is just setting up the situation. So you have these strong destinies combined in two individuals who find themselves strangely drawn together. Attraction may have been the excuse they used, but I would like to think of it as destiny. As Cricket likes to say strong destinies attract other strong destinies. Thus you ran into someone with a strong destiny who wanted you dead for personal reasons beyond your knowledge."

I spoke, "Which is pretty much what I just related to you."

The Luck nodded, "The question remains for you as to who put Davel up to it."

I shrugged, "Why would he have needed someone to convince him to kill us?"

The Luck smiled, "They laid a trap for you. Baron Dumfries pointed you into that trap, knowingly or not. Either he is a party to the action or a dupe of someone else. My information suggests he was a dupe of another player in this little personal drama of yours. Someone has a grudge against your family. My odds are on your father being the source of their ire, and that you and your brothers are the means through which they mean to punish him before they end him."

I nodded, "I suspect something like that myself. My father has had many years to make enemies through his actions and associations. My brothers and I were never generally disliked enough for anyone to want us personally dead. Why is what you have told me of any value then?"

The Luck smiled, "Because I have a lot more experience and information than you will ever have the ability to access. I am confirming your suspicions as being highly probable, if not definitely true for certain yet. I am also able to apply resources on scene if you so request, but I will warn you in advance that is an action which will come with a price. You don't have to decide now. Just let Balinac know when you are ready for my assistance if you are interested. I will put some resources on it which may give you a necessary advantage to achieve the success you desire. I will warn you that I need time to work though. I can not provide instant aid upon demand. I am not a deity, so I don't have their mass of available resources on call. I also don't make personal visits unless there is something valuable to be learned. What I have seen in you today qualifies to make this trip worth the effort this time."

I smiled at the Luck, "Have I run out my free allotment then?"

The Luck shook its head, "Not yet but it is running low. I can give you several valuable bits of information which would finish out the deal, but it is hard to choose which one might be the most useful to you. I am a good predictor of future outcomes, but I don't have an ability to see the future. I'm just really good at figuring the odds of something happening a particular way. Do you mind taking a more valuable bit of information which comes with a reasonable price instead?"

I shrugged, "That depends on the price. What are your terms?"

The Luck smiled, "Very smart again. I know something interesting about someone. I simply ask that if you meet them and interact with them, then simply let Balinac know what you learn or suspect about them. I expect complete candor in your report with no suspicion or speculation withheld. I prefer to filter through the observations in their raw form."

I thought for a moment, "You want me to become one of your agents then?"

The Luck nodded, "On a trial basis in this case at least. It lets us get to know about each other a little bit more, at least in a business sense. I also predict there will come a time when Thomas and you will reach a parting of the ways. Not that it is any news to you. When your obligations to him are done I will very likely have other work which may interest you without offending your personal sensibilities."

I was interested in its observation, "Why do you say that Thomas and I will come to a parting of the ways?"

The Luck smiled, "Personally you are just not his type of employee. However, you are my type of employee. I frankly think Thomas is trying to bribe me with you. I am seriously considering taking him up on the offer."

I nodded, "What type of employee is that?"

The Luck smiled, "Smart, curious, a good judge of character, and a person with a level head in a crisis. The curious part is what doesn't fit Thomas' usual employee profile. Most of his choices are more the types to follow orders creatively perhaps, but not with a lot of questions. So do we have a deal on this information I am willing to provide in exchange for some observations."

I looked over at Yuki sleeping in the bow of the boat and considered Cricket's statement about her heritage as a Chi Master. I thought about his statement that the Luck could unlock that power if it chooses to do so.

The Luck looked at me, "That is a separate deal you are considering. We can come to it in a moment since the price to be paid ultimately will be hers not yours."

I nodded, "Very well. What is the information you have? Who do you want me to watch and report upon?"

The Luck smiled and clasped an arm across my back, "You are probably not going to like this. However, this knowledge may well serve you in the upcoming days. Lirae is not what she seems or pretends to be."

I was a bit confused, "I don't understand. Are you saying she somehow lied to Thomas? I thought he was very good at determining which spirits are of use in his goals."

The Luck nodded, "Yes and no. Lirae likely told a very true story to Thomas, it is just very likely that a critical detail was omitted."

I nodded, "What detail would that be?"

The Luck smiled, "Lirae was not the one killed by Reminas' orders. It was most likely a different elf who was slain."

I shook my head, "Why would she do such a thing? What gain is there from taking another spirit's place?"

The Luck nodded, "Good question. I have my suspicions, but that is part of what I want you to confirm if possible. I also suspect that your arrival as Thomas' employee has altered her mission in ways she didn't suspect."

I nodded, "What does that make Lirae then?"

The Luck smiled, "Lirae is an imposter at the very least. She is most likely a spy for another power, and not a low level servant of the White Raven as she claims. If I had to place a bet this early I would put good odds that some deity somewhere doesn't like where Reminas is taking Letheron and put her in place to do something about it. The White Raven was likely bribed to submit her spirit to Thomas, and you should not think that deities are beyond such behavior. All it would take is another deity promising some assistance against Mortis for the White Raven to sell her favorite toy down the river."

I thought about it a moment, "Thomas knows doesn't he?"

The Luck nodded, "It is very likely he does since very little slips past him. He also knows very well how this game is played, and understands the part he is playing for his patron. Frankly he is making a smart move by pretending to turn a blind eye to it. It allows him to make another deity obligated for his services provided. Thomas can see a bargain in the making as well as anyone."

I smiled, "Why does it interest you then?"

The Luck frowned, "I like to know what powers are messing around with my pet projects. It is information of much value, especially if it is information the power wants kept secret. Revealed secrets collect a high price from the right buyer at the right time. Protected secrets can also collect a high price from the interested party. If I can get more solid information, then I have another marker I can use."

I nodded, "How did you know this?"

The Luck leaned back with an odd expression, "Well Balinac had her suspicions. I would almost call it female intuition. However, seeing you confirmed it for me. I don't think the power involved counted on Lirae becoming attached to you."

The Luck waved a hand and a faint gossamer silken thread appeared attached to me and trailing off toward the horizon. The Luck leaned in close and sniffed at the thread.

The Luck smiled as it spoke, "That is definitely a power at work. If I had to guess right now, then I would say one of the elfish deities. The responsible power likely finds it difficult to take an open stance against Reminas. Which means another power is backing Reminas' position. Thus they have resorted to subterfuge and assassination. This is unusual behavior for their kind, but not completely unheard of behavior. They were smart enough to pick the best as well. Thomas has a reputation for being a master at his craft even in divine circles. He has certainly sent enough spirits along their way to them."

I leaned back, "I told Lirae that I wouldn't help her assassinate Reminas. I would only expose his foul deeds and help destroy his dream of controlling the future of Letheron."

The Luck leaned forward again, "Interesting. I was wondering what the Balinac had left out in her reports. Thomas agreed to this?"

I nodded, "Thomas suggested some improvements to my initial plan, but put me in charge of the strategic planning while Lirae remains in charge of the on scene tactics."

I smiled, "Was that information worth anything to you?"

The Luck nodded, "Most definitely. It goes against Thomas' usual approach, but at the same time it will lead Cricket to like working with you better. Cricket is notoriously squeamish about killing anyone. He is quite the pacifist actually. It is limiting sometimes, but I like the challenge it presents with getting what I require. Often it is too easy to kill in attempting to achieve a goal. Sometimes killing is exactly the wrong thing to do. You are wise enough to see that killing Reminas only makes him a martyr to his cause. Exposing him for a murderous hypocrite, that is going to hurt him much more, and harm his cause greatly in the eyes of the moderate elfin community. I will consider granting another modest answer to you in exchange, but after this the tally will add up again."

I spoke the question which had been on the fringe of my consciousness since Cricket's revelation to me, "Why did Balinac merge herself with me?"

The Luck got a cagey look in its eyes, "What makes you think that? Didn't Cricket tell you that it was something to do with what Thomas had done with you?"

I nodded, "I believe him. However, unlike Cricket I am not naïve enough to think that something like that happens to a tailed beast against their choosing. Balinac chose to merge with me just like you chose to merge with Cricket."

The Luck leaned back, "Didn't you hear about the great spell cast by Hap Yang? The spell cast by Hap Yang which entrapped me in Cricket as an infant?"

I nodded, "That is the story I heard, but I certainly don't hear you confirming that version of events. This leads me to conclude that something different happened, something which no one but you and maybe only the other tailed beasts likely know about. Something doesn't match up."

The Luck smiled, "What would that be?"

I smiled, "How could a mortal perform a severe act like that without your immortal consent?"

The Luck nodded, "You are right. They couldn't do so."

I nodded, "I figured as much. Hap Yang didn't trap you then?"

The Luck smiled, "Is that the answer you are looking for? I will consider it payment for the balance and you will not get your answer on Balinac."

I shook my head, "I think my guess about you is close enough for my needs."

The Luck nodded, "In terms of Balinac she wants to become something like me. Not restricted from direct action on the prime per say, but combined with a mortal spirit. Let me just say that certain advantages are gained. Thomas' tinkering with spirit manipulation gave her many opportunities to pick a select host. I would think she wanted someone brave enough to stand up to her. Someone brave enough to stand up to me even. She found you. She tested you, and as I have seen for myself today you have passed."

I smiled, "What advantages are gained? Where does this lead?"

The Luck sat back and grinned, "Last free answers for today. The bill begins after these. Let me just say that one advantage is an interest in things again. After countless millennium of existence this is very valuable to a tailed beast. There is an element of actual risk which brings excitement, a chance for failures to have consequences which personally matter, and an opportunity to learn from failures as well as successes. Our kind underestimates the value of such things not being mortal. Having a mortal aspect teaches us well. As to where this leads I really don't know for certain. That is part of the fun of it. It certainly concerns many powers greatly. I like keeping them off balance too. I wouldn't be surprised if the other tailed beasts catch on in a few more millennium. You'll likely see our mortal avatars manifested in the prime more frequently in the future."

I nodded, "So that is why Balinac agreed to work for you?"

The Luck smiled, "Of course. I let her know the secret of how and why I did it in exchange for a few centuries of select tasking of a non-objectionable nature. It was just up to her to select the subject and make the deal with them."

I was concerned, "I made a deal with Balinac?"

The Luck smiled, "Of course you did. It is likely that you just don't recall it. You made the deal in Thomas' tower, before Thomas placed you in that elfin body. Making the transfer from free spirit to mortal form likely lost the memory of the deal in the process. It is much like the deal Thomas and you made with Firanda to combine your spirits together. Nothing happens on the spirit level of this nature without permission or divine intervention. Divine intervention didn't happen in your case. That means everyone agreed to it even if their personalities can not always remember it afterward. Remember this is going to cost you, but you kept asking."

I nodded, "Understood. So I take it that Cricket agreed to the deal as an infant then?"

The Luck smiled, "You are correct even if you think it wrong or cruel. On a spiritual level certain infants are very aware actually. Cricket as an infant was very spiritually aware of what a good offer it was getting. He just didn't understand it on a mortal level yet. Don't worry he may be slow, but he is catching on after all. Of course I hope you understand that confidentiality is desired on my part and Balinac's part regarding these deals."

I nodded, "As to your price I have my offer for payment. You can make a connection to me if you like. I will grant it. I will also permit you to discuss making a deal with my wife Yuki. I think you will find that of sufficient value to pay my current debt."

The Luck grinned widely, "I think that will cover most of it. I will ask one other payment from you as well. Cricket's nose seems to have stopped bleeding. Could you strike it one more time for me?"

I quickly struck the Luck in the face before it could move. Its nose started bleeding again as it smiled at me.

The Luck nodded its head, "I hope this hurts quite a bit now. I really don't understand how you mortals process pain sensations so I can't tell for sure. I've already unlocked the powers of your wife Yuki, but I'll leave it to Cricket to actually open the door for her if she asks. He is much better at those things than I am after all. I've also linked to you. What you learn from now on I will know as well. You won't need Balinac to relay messages for me anymore. I have a direct conduit. You may consider your bill to me is paid up at the moment, but please consider buying my services in the future if you need them. I still think you may owe Cricket some though. He isn't going to be happy about his nose."

The Luck leaned far back until it was almost falling over backward then spoke the phrase, "Cricket return!"

Cricket fell over into the bottom of his boat and clutched his nose in pain with a moan. He looked up at me with a surprised look.

I looked at him with an expression of embarrassment as I helped him back up onto the bench, "I'm sorry about that Hap Sing. It took a couple of sharp blows to get the Luck to get serious about business. Then it asked me to leave you with another strike before it departed. It seemed to think it was funny for some reason. You might want to know that it says it can't feel pain while in your body by the way."

Cricket touched his nose gingerly, and then held his palm against the end of his nose for a moment. I noticed a soft glow spread from his hand and the bleeding stopped. He splashed some water on his face and wiped the blood off.

Cricket then looked at Yuki and myself, "It seems you got off lightly then. Did you learn what you needed to know? The Luck seems to have seen fit to link with you. Not unexpected really, and not of any permanent harm. If you need in the future I can undo it when you want. However, for now it will let me keep tabs on your progress, and will certainly protect you from any harm being dealt to you from Thomas. It seems a change has occurred with your wife Yuki as well. She is not linked, but the egg shell on her spirit guardian is cracked."

I nodded, "The Luck indicated that it unlocked the door, but that it would leave it to you to open it. It didn't talk with Yuki or demand any concessions from me about her. It also said my current bill is paid up."

Cricket smiled, "That is good then. I take it you had a satisfactory discussion with it then?"

I nodded, "We both gained from it I believe."

Cricket smiled, "You don't need to tell me anything it didn't ask you to relay. Don't worry about my nose either. No permanent harm done. I am glad to see that you put the Luck in a good mood. I'll let it handle its side of the business while I handle mine. Now I should deliver you to your destination and look after my daughter."

Chapter 36 The Shores of Letheron

Cricket and I picked up the oars once more and began rowing. We sat in relative silence for a long while as the boat moved through the water. The waves eventually grew larger I could see that the sky became less blue. A high layer of grey clouds moved into view and below them I could see the faint sign of forested shoreline. In the bow of the small boat Yuki opened her eyes and looked at Cricket and I.

Yuki spoke, "I had an odd dream. There were ribbons spreading through the sky of many colors. I heard voices talking but I could not understand them. Both of your voices were there, and a third voice I didn't recognize. I was briefly scared of some danger, and then I was comfortable for some reason. Something has changed."

I nodded, "I had a meeting with the Luck. We have learned some things, and your heritage as a Chi Master has been unlocked by its presence. It remains to you to decide whether you want to explore that heritage or leave it dormant. Cricket here has offered to help if you wish to learn more."

Yuki was a bit muted as she spoke, "What will this mean for me?"

Cricket answered, "It will mean you could have access to abilities which are considered rare among people. It will take a long time to realize the full scope of these abilities. Training will help you learn faster, but ultimately may limit your abilities more. Self discovery will take many more years, yet it will allow you to unlock your full potential in time. Leaving your abilities untouched and unused will not harm you. You will pass the potential along to any children you bear though, as your mother has for you."

Yuki nodded, "I would know all that I am capable of in time. Where should I start?"

Cricket reached down and touched her gently on top of her head, "It is done. Your spirit guardian has hatched. In time you will learn to control it, and through it control your environment in the prime and spiritual realms. You spirit guardian is an extension of your own spirit not an independent being. It may behave strangely and in ways you don't predict at times. It will help you to know that your spirit and your mind are not always in agreement about the best course of action. Learning to reconcile the two will teach you how to unlock your abilities."

Yuki raised her head, "I can't feel my spirit guardian. How will I know it is there?"

Cricket smiled, "Not to worry. You are trying to perceive the physical; it is what your body already knows. Your guardian is spiritual. Try relaxing while closing your eyes and envisioning a baby raven chick. Then think about viewing the world through its eyes. Don't worry if it doesn't work right away. It takes some people a long while to figure this part out."

Yuki closed her eyes briefly then opened them again, "I can see it. It is perched on Mica's shoulder. Mica is glowing brightly. There is a strange shape to your aura Cricket. It resembles a tiger with many tails. The legends were true weren't they? What are these faint luminous lines I see between Mica and me? I see another one between you Cricket and me."

Cricket nodded, "You are doing very well. A natural talent like your namesake was said to be. Don't push yourself too hard. Looking into the spirit realm for too long can be taxing. I will let you know this much. The lines you see are the spiritual bonds between you and the people who are important to you. With time you will be able to perceive bonds between other people. You have done very well to do this much upon the awakening of your power. I will know when you are in trouble due to the bond between us. I will help as much as possible if you call upon me through that bond, but I do not have the relatively unlimited resources of a god at my disposal. A better bet will be to call upon the bond between Mica and you for it will ultimately be a much stronger bond. It was set in place by both of you, and strengthened by two gods and one other power."

Yuki nodded, "I think I understand. Thank you Cricket for what you have done."

Cricket smiled, "It would have eventually happened naturally had you desired it my daughter. All I did was to show you where to begin. I personally recommend you discover what you are capable of from here on out on your own. Each Chi Master is unique and special. Don't try too hard though. Let it come naturally to you. If you must, then spend some time relaxing each day and letting what you have learned become part of you. Personally I prefer fishing, but some other activity may help for you."

Yuki thought for a moment, "Would cooking work?"

Cricket shrugged, "Possibly. Do you enjoy it? Does it calm your center?"

Yuki nodded, "I find it fun and interesting."

Cricket nodded, "That may be the best place for you to start then. Remember to let it come naturally. Trying to force it can be counter productive."

I pointed toward the shore, "Let's put in there at that small cove. There is not much of a beach, but it looks like we can move up the slope to the forest easily enough from there."

Cricket and I rowed toward the shore. This portion of the coast looked uninhabited, but I remembered that Lirae had spoken of many small elfish communities being indistinguishable from natural surroundings at a distance. I didn't see any signs that we were watched during our approach. The breakers were rougher than near Port Cirnore or Thomas' Isle, but I realized both of those were relatively sheltered bays. This small cove was more exposed, and the clash or the waves against the surrounding rocks was sending up impressive plumes of spray.

Cricket guided us expertly along the course until the keel of his small boat ground against the stony shoreline. Yuki and I stepped out of the boat and grabbed our gear. Cricket nodded at us again and smiled.

Cricket called out over the noise of the surf, "I hope the Luck is with you. Goodbye for now my daughter. Look after her as you promised young Mica. As well as any others you meet. They may not always be easy to get along with, but my mark upon you should convince them of your sincerity."

Yuki reached over to hug Cricket, "I thank you once more honored sire. You shall be as a second father to me as well as my Sensei."

I bowed to Cricket, "I thank you as well Sensei Cricket. If you need me to ask the Luck for anything, then you can just let me know."

Cricket returned my bow, "I thank you for the offer. I have gotten used to its secrets by now though. As long as it helps those I find in need I will let it do what it must."

I helped Cricket push the boat from the shore back into the water. He deftly turned it around and began rowing powerfully against the incoming surf. I stood with my arm around Yuki's shoulders watching him depart. It did not take him long to clear the outer breakers, and we watched for a while as his boat eventually became a small spot out on the water.

Then his boat was gone in a shimmer of sun upon the waves. One moment there in the far distance, the next returned to the dreaming. I sensed other presences watching us from the line of trees above as we looked out over the water. I hugged Yuki and gave her a passionate kiss. Looking into her eyes I could feel that she knew we were being observed as well.

I stopped kissing her for a moment, "Alone at last. Some honeymoon isn't it?"

Yuki pressed her lips gently against mine in another kiss, and then she spoke, "Come let us find the port and the customs station so we can report our arrival. It wouldn't do to have anyone think we were some kind of smugglers now. We can finish this once we have some reasonable accommodations in town."

Yuki and I picked up our gear and began walking hand in hand to the edge of the forest. We kept the sea in sight as we headed southeasterly between the shoreline and forest. Neither of us moved in a suspicious manner, and Yuki was particularly good at ignoring the presence of our hidden observers. I found myself looking for their positions from time to time.

However, they were good at avoiding exposing themselves. I could tell they were nearby, but I couldn't pinpoint their locations as we moved. I then saw a ground squirrel watching me intently from a tree branch, and a circling hawk above. I figured that we were facing at least two arcane practitioners using familiars to observe our actions.

I looked up at the hawk circling us overhead as I spoke to Yuki, "My dear that hawk is quite marvelous. I've never seen their kind in Ard. Have you?"

Yuki shook her head, "That banded ground squirrel and brown fox are quite unusual as well. Such creatures usually don't follow people so intently. Perhaps they are hungry. Do you have any more of that fish we had for breakfast?"

I shook my head, "I'm sorry dear. It was too delicious. I didn't think to save any for our guests."

As we continued down the coast above the shore I eventually detected the stealthy approach of three people. Two of them stayed under cover of the tree line beside us while the third stepped out in front of us carrying a bow with a knocked but not drawn arrow.

Yuki and I stopped, and I spoke in the elfish tongue with a smile, "Greetings to our escort. We are heading for the port to go through customs. I am Mica Lichan and this is my wife Yuki Lichan. I apologize but her elfish tongue is somewhat limited. Would you mind speaking in the common tongue so she can understand our conversation?"

The elf in front of us spoke in the common tongue, "I am Ranger Trimiel. It is my duty to patrol this portion of Letheron's borders for intruders. Why have you come to Letheron without permission?"

I smiled back at Trimiel, "I am sorry we couldn't arrange to arrive at an official customs point, but our transportation was provided by a busy friend whom we were imposing upon. I felt it best to not press our friendship by having him row us all the way down to the port when we could as easily walk instead. My wife and I do have our travel visas issued from the Letheron embassy in Ard. We are here on a business venture."

Trimiel replaced his arrow in his quiver and approached us, "Let me see this visa document."

Yuki and I produced our travel papers and business visa to Trimiel for inspection as I said, "I hope this satisfies your curiosity."

Trimiel took the documents and looked over them for a moment before returning them, "They seem to verify your account, but I am not an official customs agent. You will still need to go to the town of Findor to get official permission to enter Letheron. I will escort you there."

Trimiel gave an obscure hand sign then moved to stand beside me as he spoke again, "If we make good speed we can reach Findor by early afternoon. Are elves from Ard up for running?"

I looked at Yuki, "Are you game my dear?"

Yuki spoke, "I will let you know when I need a rest."

Trimiel set a brisk miles eating pace. Even though Yuki was shorter than both of us she held our pace without complaint. After a couple of hours of running I could see a ridge line stretching into the sky ahead of us. The trees went up the steep slopes and the ridge extended out into the water. I realized it must be the outer part of a natural breakwater for a bay. Trimiel raised his hand for a halt. Trimiel obviously noted that while Yuki and I were breathing deeply we had not tired from our long run.

Trimiel pointed toward the ridge, "Beyond that slope is Findor. It seems the people of Ard have a hearty constitution. Not many merchants in my experience could maintain the pace of a Ranger for so long."

I smiled back while Yuki nodded and spoke, "We thank you for the consideration. That slope will be difficult to attempt without a brief rest."

Trimiel shook his head, "Somehow I doubt you will find this climb much trouble. Rare are the humans who could maintain my pace with such ease. I find it hard to believe you are just merchants."

I nodded, "We are not. We are traveling business people prepared for the trials of the journey. Out business is establishing a new location in Letheron with the approval of the governing counsel. We are the main project coordinators for our company. Our advance team has already secured the appropriate permissions, approvals, permits, and property for our first location."

Trimiel smiled, "If you don't mind my asking out of personal curiosity what kind of business is it?"

I smiled back, "A traveler's rest. We are establishing a safe haven inn with accommodations for food, sleep, and opportunities to purchase items useful to other travelers."

Trimiel shook his head, "You will find that there are not many travelers through Letheron anymore, and all of the major communities have housing accommodations for official visitors."

I nodded, "That is why a business opportunity exists here unique to Letheron. I plan to provide luxurious accommodations for casual travelers in a location without such accommodation readily available. I think in a few years of operation it will do quite a brisk business."

Trimiel got a neutral expression on his face, "I don't think you will find such business here. The country of Letheron is finding itself pressed on all sides, and even now the debate of whether to close its borders to outsiders spreads among our people."

I smiled again, "I hope to convince them that the well being of Letheron is not going to be established by shutting out the rest of the world. The future Reading Dragon Inn shall hopefully attract a particular clientele up near the border to the wild lands."

Trimiel thought a moment then a sly grin came on to his face, "You plan to court adventurers don't you. Don't deny it. I can see it in your eyes. Ready adventure, supplies provided, information traded, and safe accommodations on a hostile border."

I nodded, "It should do well as long as your borders are not completely sealed. It may even help relieve the pressure on your northern border in a few years if enough warlords and chieftains fall."

Trimiel looked at us closely, "You're adventurers yourselves. The high stamina shows it. You both are probably very good with your weapons too."

I nodded, "I won't bother denying our capabilities. I am no slouch with a saber, and my dear Yuki is a clever hand with her cooking knives. However, Yuki is also a very good cook, and the head chef for the new inn. If you don't mind we can break for lunch while Yuki prepares some of her flat bread pockets for us. Do you prefer yours with meat or without?"

Trimiel thought a moment, "What kind of meat?"

Yuki began moving through her haversack, "I have domestic foul with me, and a bit of domestic sheep left."

Trimiel smiled, "I'll try some of the sheep. It has been many years since I've had some. We don't raise it in Letheron."

I smiled, "So you've been outside of Letheron before?"

Trimiel watched closely as Yuki prepared our meal, "I used to be an adventurer myself. Then came day when the call went out for elves loyal to Letheron to return to the homeland to protect it from invaders. I've spent twenty years patrolling the borders since. The last ten have been along the relatively quiet sea shore due to my 'questionable sympathy' for humans. I probably don't need to warn you that some extreme factions in Letheron would find that an elf being married to a human to be a distasteful situation."

I lost my smile, "I have heard rumors of such. I prefer to judge people based on their own merits, not on what others say about their race. I grew up in a community in Ard where humans were the majority, and found myself generally accepted among them. I have also found that problem individuals are everywhere and in every race. The best you can do is stand up against their prejudices and show them for the mistaken beings that they are."

Yuki handed out the pocket flat breads to both Trimiel and me. I started into mine with relish as Yuki ate hers with more reserve. Trimiel watched both of us for a moment, and then sampled his. In a few moments he found himself eating as quickly as I was.

Yuki ducked her head with apology as she finished and spoke, "I hope they were acceptable. The ingredients were not as fresh as I prefer. I am also running low on some of my seasonings."

Trimiel responded, "I haven't had sheep as tasty in many years. If this is not up to your standards, then I can't wait to sample something from your kitchen. This inn you mention interests me. I think that when you have it running you will already have at least one patron in line for your kitchen."

Trimiel took a piece of dried meat from his pouch and tossed it over near the tree line. A brown fox came out of the tree line to grab the meat and rushed back under cover. Trimiel looked on with a touch of amusement.

I asked, "A familiar? You are a wizard then?"

Trimiel shook his head, "No, just a ranger. Tut-tut has just been my companion since she was born. I look after her, and she warns me of anything strange nearby."

I looked a bit surprised, "I almost forgot little Balinac dear. She might be very hungry by now."

I surreptitiously tapped my wedding ring as I raised my hand to call out, "Balinac. Please come get some dinner little puss."

A small black kitten Balinac came running out from the forest toward Yuki and curled itself around her legs in a figure eight pattern. Yuki brought out a piece of fish from breakfast and placed it down for Balinac.

I looked at her suspiciously, "I had thought we were out."

Thomas the Poisoner

Yuki smiled, "We were. Only the little bit left for Balinac was all I saved. You know how much she likes her fish."

I reached down and Balinac arched her back into my hand as she daintily ate her fish. Trimiel had a look of concern as he watched the two tailed Balinac eat her meal.

I smiled at him as he spoke, "From where did that cat come? Such a creature is not native to Letheron. I didn't even know it was there and neither did Tut-tut."

Yuki picked Balinac up as she finished licking her lips, "She's a very stealthy hunter, and fast for a little puss too. She likes my fish breakfasts best though."

Yuki poured a portion of water into the palm of her hand for Balinac to drink. Balinac lapped away at it. Yuki then set Balinac down. She finished packing up her cooking gear and looked at me.

I nodded, "Ready to complete the journey to Findor my dear?"

Yuki smiled, "Of course I am now. Keep up if you can."

Yuki took off at a sprint. I gave Yuki a ten pace lead and took off after her. Trimiel was a touch surprised yet launched off at the same time as me. After we had gone one hundred yards a small black blur went hurtling past us. Then Balinac passed Yuki with ease as well and disappeared into the brush well ahead of us.

Trimiel kept pace along side of me for the first half hour. Then the slope began to increase and he started to breathe heavily.

I nodded at him, "We will wait for you at the top before descending the other side of the rim."

I opened up my pace and began outstripping Trimiel with ease. I soon caught up with Yuki who began running hard alongside of me now. We were seriously racing and Yuki was giving as good a chase as I was. The slope increased and I leaned forward sharply picking up speed instead of slowing down. Yuki maintained her hard pace but found that she wasn't able to keep up. My advantage in stride length was coming to the fore going up slope.

I realized that Balinac was casually pacing along with me as we neared the top. I pushed even harder and thought of all the times I had run up the slope at Thomas' Isle. I had been training for this mission I realized, and this speed was likely going to be needed for real soon. I looked at Balinac, and felt that she understood my feelings as well. There was anticipation, along with a touch of fear in my mind. Not fear for myself, but a fear at failing in my objective.

I slowed my pace a little as I closed on the top. I began to bring it back until I was no longer at a sprint. I could hear Yuki a ways behind me now, moving quickly yet with ease. Further off I could hear the labored breathing of Trimiel. He was keeping his pace, but unable to increase it further. I was just walking fast as I reached the top and Findor came into view below.

I could see a forested town with docks reaching out into a large sheltered bay. It was covering a much larger area than Port Cirnore, but at the same time it was more disperse, and less concentrated. It was a community in the manner of the elves, built in harmony with the natural environment around it. I gently paced back and forth holding Balinac as Yuki came running up to my side.

Yuki smiled as she breathed deeply, "Unfair advantage. You have longer legs."

I nodded, "I have also been running the mountain while you have been cooking."

Yuki nodded, "Observation acknowledged my dear. I need to improve on my slope work."

I shrugged, "I still bet that you could out climb me any day. A different focus is what I was indicating. You will always excel in certain areas, and I will in others. It doesn't make one of us better than the other."

I looked down the slope where Trimiel was gamely trying to reach us. He was obviously tired, but still proud enough to do his best. I saw him looking up the slope at us with a look of relief at seeing us waiting for him. Yuki and I began performing some cool down stretching as we awaited his arrival.

I greeted him as he joined us, "Well met Trimiel. I'm sorry about running so hard. I have been running slopes for the last year or so. It gives me a slight terrain advantage. I'm sure that I couldn't out pace you in a forest though."

Trimiel laughed, "Don't flatter me. I'm the fastest runner in my whole squad and you left me like I was standing still. Additionally you did it while carrying all of your gear. The Ranger patrol would be lucky to have someone like you in their midst I think."

I laughed, "Don't overestimate me too much. You haven't seen how poorly I perform with a bow yet. There is a reason I stick with using a saber."

Trimiel gave me an appraising look, "I thought for a moment that the two of you would leave me behind and disappear on me. I would have been in a touch of trouble if that had happened."

I shook my head, "It never crossed my mind. We are here on legitimate business so there is no reason to avoid any authorities here."

Trimiel looked at me still, "I think you are telling the truth. You could have avoided my patrol in the first place if that had been your intent I think. Let me tell you that your unusual choice of landing points is likely to cause trouble with the customs officials in Findor. I know a couple of reliable people in customs who will listen to my evaluation of your character at least."

I shrugged, "We may have avoided Tut-tut and the squirrel in your patrol, but I don't think we could have avoided the hawk that spotted us first, no matter how fast we could run."

Trimiel thought for a bit, "Sharp eye there. How did you know it wasn't just a hawk out hunting for a meal?"

I smiled, "Not a great time of the day for it. Most of their game would be resting, not traveling around. They are more likely to hunt at dusk or dawn unless their prey was flushed during mid morning."

Trimiel spoke, "If we had been hostile, what would you have done then?"

I frowned, "I would have defended my wife, and I believe she would have defended me."

Yuki nodded at this statement as well, "I don't recommend testing us in that way."

Trimiel reacted to our statement as it was intended. I could see he treated it as a statement of fact, not a threat. He could obviously tell we were confident in our capabilities.

Trimiel leaned in close and whispered in my ear, "Where did the human in the boat go? He simply disappeared after rowing off a ways. It was like he had never been there in the first place."

I smiled and whispered back, "I really don't know for certain. I suspect that the only place you will see him again is in your dreams. People tend to find him there if they want to find him at all. I personally recommend you don't mention him to anyone else. They are likely to disbelieve you anyway."

Trimiel nodded and whispered, "Understood. For my own personal curiosity would you tell me what his name was? You said he was a friend of yours."

I smiled and whispered my reply, "He is most commonly known as the Lucky Cricket, though I believe he prefers to be called just Cricket. If you do some research then I am sure you can find out more about him. You might even find him in your dreams if you look hard enough. You can also tell the forces with bows trained on us that we have our travel papers and are going peaceably into town where they can examine us at their leisure. Would they like us to turn in our weapons?"

Trimiel leaned back and made a hand gesture followed by a nod. Twelve elfish archers appeared from cover carrying bows down the slope toward Findor. They seemed relaxed and nonthreatening.

Trimiel looked at me, "I am placing my reputation in your hands now Mica. I have given you my recommendation. I hope this isn't a mistake on my part, but I think you have been honest and fair dealing with me. I wish you good luck."

I looked back and extended my hand to him in a handshake, "May the Luck look favorably on you as well. If you ever need it then look for that fisherman in your dreams. You never know where he may show up."

Chapter 37 Findor's Shaman

Yuki and I were escorted by Trimiel and two bow carrying patrol members down the slope into Findor. The community was unusual in my experience in that the buildings were incorporated into their natural surroundings. Nothing was placed in rigid rows or lines. I could detect that some efficiency was lost perhaps, but that a lot of ascetic value was gained by the exchange.

As we walked along the trails we were looked at by passers by as a polite curiosity. It may have been Yuki's unusual appearance, or my own different manner which caused this. I suspected the fact that we had an armed escort also likely had something to do with the looks though. We approached a structure near the docks which clearly had some human influence to the design. I recognized a customs building when I saw it.

There was a fairly brisk business happening at the docks as two cargo vessels were being unloaded. It looked like the cargo being off loaded was inspected directly on the docks by a set of uniformed inspectors. Yuki and I were lead inside the customs building where I saw that a couple of sailors were being interviewed while at desks by uniformed customs employees. There was a counter near the door where a bored looking female elf with short dark brown hair sat looking out at the sky. She perked up some when Trimiel walked into view with us.

The female elf spoke in the elfin tongue with a slight grin, "Caught a couple of loose travelers finally Trimiel? Why are you bringing them here? Don't you usually take them to the stockade first? I think you just wanted to get close to me again."

Trimiel hesitantly smiled and also replied in elfish, "I don't think so this time Lionette. They have travel papers and what look like proper visas from our embassy in Ard. They are here on business and had to stop short of port as they had sought transportation with a fisherman who was heading back home before dark. They asked for escort to the port and have come to present themselves to customs."

Lionette frowned slightly, "It is highly unusual. Passengers are supposed to arrive at the docks."

I spoke up with a friendly smile, "I extend our greetings to you Miss Lionette. As you can see we have arrived at the docks, just by a slightly different route. It has always been our intention to arrive legitimately at your fine country."

Lionette shook her head with a mildly quirky grin, "Trimiel why did you bring me such a handsome elf? Are you losing interest in me already?"

Trimiel's seemed a bit surprised, "No of course not. These two are married anyway so I doubt that he is seeking your personal attentions."

Lionette had a brief look of surprise on her face, and then gave Trimiel a sharp look, "Are you implying my attentions are not worth seeking?"

Trimiel gave a weak smile, "I'm sorry Lionette, but I have to get back to my patrol. Could you kindly process these two while I return?"

As Trimiel made a hasty retreat back out the door Lionette turned her attention to us, "Well if you will kindly ignore my little game let's get to business. You guards can go back to your patrol area as well. I'm sure they won't cause any difficulties while they are in town. You two can follow me to the interview room."

Lionette waved another elf over to take the station at the front counter. She then led us over to a door that went down a set of stairs into a lit underground hallway with several doors along its length. She opened one of the doors where we could see a room with four chairs, a table, and a broad shelf against one wall under a barred window near the ceiling. I noticed that the door could be barred from outside the room. Other than the furnishings it resembled a cell.

Lionette pointed to the bench under the window, "Place all of your belongings other than your worn clothing on the shelf here. They will be inspected shortly. Please have a seat while I bring in the inspectors. I will return to conduct your interview after the inspectors have examined your belongings."

Yuki and I placed our gear on the bench. I also unbuckled my sword, removed my pouches, and emptied my pockets. Yuki followed my example and then we took our seats. We waited a couple of minutes and I realized that we had unconsciously joined hands together as we sat next to each other. I looked at Yuki and raised my eyebrow.

I spoke in a low voice, "Alone at last. It has been a while."

Yuki nodded, "Yes it has, but this might not be the place for it."

I shrugged, "Who will know?"

Yuki looked at our sparse surroundings, "It is hardly romantic."

I leaned over and gave her a long kiss. Yuki was a little stiff at first, and then grew more passionate in a couple of moments. I felt a gentle paw bat my leg and glanced down to see Balinac shake its head. I gently drew apart from Yuki and looked down at Balinac. Balinac jumped up into Yuki's lap and curled up with only one tail visible.

As we resumed sitting while holding hands for another couple of minutes I could hear quiet walking out in the hall. A few minutes later I heard the approach of two sets of footsteps. The door opened to reveal an elf dressed in an inspector's uniform carrying a tally board, and another elf wearing elaborate yet elegant gray robes.

The inspector set his tally board on the table and as we watched he opened up each of our gear containers and carefully removed all of the items within. He placed each item carefully on the bench as if any one of them could potentially be dangerous. He also unsheathed my saber, my dagger, and Yuki's cooking knives. Then finally picked up our travel documents, took one of the seats across from us, and began inspecting them.

The elf wearing the robes addressed us in elfish, "Greetings. I am Yastalus the resident government mage of Findor. I am going to ask you both to tell me which items you own have enchantments on them, what the nature of the enchantment may be, and who gave you these items. I will also ask for the explanation for the alchemical ingredients which appear here as well. Know first that few things are outright forbidden entry unless dark magic was involved in their creation. There are, however, tariffs on most magical items possessed by individuals."

I nodded and replied in elfish, "Greetings. I am Mica Lichan and this is my wife Yuki Lichan. As you can see from the money we brought I have come prepared to pay the necessary tariffs. I believe the saber and dagger there while being of high quality are also enchanted to hold their fine edge. They were provided to me by my martial instructor as a gift. The skillet you see there is forged from dwarf grade armor plate and is enchanted for durability. It was provided to my wife from her chef instructor also as a gift."

I raised my hands and nodded at Yuki to do so as well, "The rings we wear on our left hands are our wedding bands. The enchantment regarding Yuki's ring is supposed to bring luck. My ring on my left hand is enchanted to prevent removal, and the ring on my right hand is also enchanted to prevent removal. They have no other effect to my knowledge."

I lowered my hands and held Yuki's hand again as she lowered hers as well, "As far as the cooking ingredients you will have to ask my wife about those in the common tongue as her elfish is unfortunately not very good yet, and I am regrettably ignorant about most of them."

Yastalus nodded and spoke in the common tongue, "I apologize for my oversight. Could you please explain your cooking spices to me Mrs. Lichan?"

As Yuki explained her cooking spices to Yastalus I watched the inspector examining our papers. He had moved past the travel and visa documents rather quickly, but was lingering on the many notes of mark. The inspector noticed me watching him and turned to look at me directly.

The inspector asked, "What is written on these parchments? None of it is in the elfish dialect of Letheron."

I smiled and noted, "Those are notes of mark held by the Isle Corporation which is our employer. They represent commodities which can be traded for goods or services of value."

Yastalus moved his attention from Yuki's spices to the documents, "Let me take a look."

Yastalus reviewed several of the notes of mark and a frown appeared upon his face. He looked at me and shook his head.

I gave Yastalus a smile, "Is something wrong?"

Yastalus nodded, "There is no value assigned to these notes of mark. Each of them is open ended, and restricted to execution by your wife or you."

I nodded, "Yes that is true. We left them open ended due to cost uncertainty in our planning phase. The accountants at the Isle Corporation keep track of how much liquid value the Isle Corporation can use for this project and limits the maximum execution amount accordingly. They also require detailed receipts for items and services provided to justify the cost expenditures. There are a number of investors to which the Isle Corporation must answer."

Thomas the Poisoner

Yastalus nodded then looked at the inspector, "Let that be a lesson for you Nedulainus. The next time you think wizardry is unnecessarily complex just talk to a businessman. They can make any simple concept harder to understand and execute."

Nedulainus looked back at him, "What do you mean sir?"

Yastalus pointed at the papers on the table, "Those simple pieces of parchment are money. Open ended amounts of money that can only be spent by these two through an exchange with another local company for resources held by their company. It also makes charging a correct tariff next to impossible since no fixed valuation has been assigned until they are used. I'm afraid we're going to be seeing more of this happening in the future unless our government legislates accordingly."

Nedulainus shrugged his shoulders, "Not much we can do about it then. Does it really matter? Would it really be any different than if a Wizard summoned a pile of gold coins after they arrived in Letheron? When they buy the goods locally they will pay the appropriate purchase taxes, and it will still stimulate the local economy. As long as they don't cheat the local companies I don't see any problem."

Yastalus smiled, "Perhaps you're correct Nedulainus. It really isn't our problem. Value them as standard parchment scrolls and let me test the enchanted items. Then let's move on to the next ship coming in to port."

Yastalus stood back and cast a brief spell which caused a glow to form around several of our items. My saber, dagger, and the ring on my right hand had a faint glow. Yuki's ring of luck and cooking pan both had a moderate glow.

Yastalus raised an eyebrow when looking at us, "This was not quite what I expected. You may have been cheated by someone Mr. Lichan since that wedding band you wear is not enchanted after all. You wife's wedding band has a higher level of enchantment than I would have expected however. I will need to examine it to determine its proper value. Her magic pan also has a serious enchantment on it. I will need to look at it closer as well."

Yastalus stood next to Yuki who removed her ring and handed it to him. Yastalus pulled out a jeweler's eye loop from a pouch and examined the ring closely. He then held the ring out in his open hand while his expression turned a bit incredulous.

Yastalus looked at us with surprise, "Do you know what this is?"

I smiled, "I was told this was a ring which brings luck to the bearer, and it was used during our wedding."

Yastalus nodded, "Yes you are correct this ring brings luck. It has a much more powerful enchantment than most examples of this variety. However, it is also a very rare example of a work crafted by Crystalgear Nimblehands."

I raised an eyebrow, "You don't say. What would that mean?"

Yastalus grinned with excitement, "Each of his rings of luck are considered masterpieces of that form of enchantment by those who practice the art. There hasn't been a new work of his discovered since his death over one hundred years ago. Less than a dozen of them were ever recorded to have been made, and each of those has a known owner. Such an item couldn't be valued as it is considered priceless and thought non reproducible until now. Where did you obtain such a rarity?"

I smiled, "It was provided to us as a wedding gift by a friend."

Yastalus looked a bit longer at the ring in his palm before handing it back to Yuki. As Yuki put the ring back on her left ring finger Yastalus glanced again at the ring on my right hand. Once more his expression turned a bit incredulous.

I smiled, "Would you like to examine this one as well? As I mentioned before it is enchanted to prevent removal."

Yastalus nodded and I held out my hand for his inspection. He tentatively looked at the ring with the eye loop and gently tugged on it while observing the reaction. Then he pulled out a crystal and gazed at the ring briefly. He put the crystal and eye loop away and pulled out a set of spectacles with various lenses which he shifted and moved as he looked at it closely. A look of complete puzzlement showed on his face as he took the glasses off and looked at me.

I asked, "Is something wrong again?"

Yastalus gave a faint grin, "I've just witnessed something I would have considered an impossibility I think. Your ring resembles very closely the craftsmanship of a work by Crystalgear. Except for one thing that is. The enchantment is not one he was ever known to use. It is also known that Crystalgear never made rings for other enchanters. This enchantment is also something I've never read about. You have to understand that enchanted items and especially enchanted jewelry are a specialty of mine. This is unlike any enchantment I have ever seen."

I grew curious, "How so?"

Yastalus shook his head, "It radiates arcane energy as a minor enchantment. Most likely the arcane energy is producing the effect which prevents it from being removed from a living user. However, this ring is empowered using primal energy of an enormous quantity."

I was unimpressed, "Is there a problem with that?"

Yastalus shook his head, "Yes, no. I just can't tell. In all of my studies I have never heard of an item being empowered with raw primal energy. Enchantment is an arcane craft if you understand. Primal energy on the other hand is simply released as I understand it. It usually has either a destructive or restorative effect on the material form if you understand. No caster I am aware of can create a lasting enchantment using primal energy, not even one of the spirit shamans. This defies every rule of enchantment I have ever learned."

I nodded, "You seem pretty well informed about what spirit shamans can or can not do. I had heard they were relatively private about their abilities."

Yastalus nodded back, "Well normally they are yes, but since I work with a spirit shaman here we sometimes exchange information out of professional curiosity. Since enchantment is a specialty of mine I have discussed it at length with her."

Yastalus took a glance at the wedding band on my left hand provided by Balinac which had not shown up as enchanted under his spell. His eyes narrowed with suspicion. Yastalus fumbled into his pouch and pulled out his jewelers loop again.

Yastalus looked at me and asked, "Would you mind showing me that odd ring you are wearing?"

I smiled, "Not at all. We are at your disposal."

Yastalus looked at it with the jewelers loop and a more puzzled look appeared on his face. He then pulled out the crystal again and gazed through it. His eyebrows moved up again. Once more he pulled out his spectacles with various lenses and moved through them in a detailed and methodical order. He flinched back at one point blinking his eyes furiously, and switched lenses once more. After several minutes of examination he seemed to be satisfied that he had discovered something and began to look away from my hand and follow an invisible line over toward Yuki.

I suspected that he had found a way to view the connection to Balinac and I didn't want him using those spectacles in a manner that would cause more questions than we could answer. I gave a nod and a wave to Balinac who jumped onto the table and started batting away at the papers sitting there. Yastalus took off his spectacles with an exasperated sigh.

I heard Yastalus mutter, "Lost it, quite a tricky enchantment indeed."

I questioned him, "So what do you think?"

Yastalus sighed, "I would dearly like to study it under proper laboratory conditions. I thought the other work was highly unusual and unique. It seems this ring defies all expectations about what an enchanted item can be. It is made from a material I do not recognize. No obvious craftsman marks or typical signs of tool markings can be seen. The surface is completely unmarred even at an extreme level of detail. I would surmise the substance is inordinately durable and because of such I couldn't begin to guess what process was used to shape it so perfectly. That is an enigma in itself. It also has more raw primal power invested into it than any major enchantment I've ever seen. In the primal spectra of energy it is literally off any charts I have ever used. I would have to design a whole new apparatus to even begin to evaluate its level of power."

I nodded, "So what do you think the fee will be for the item."

Yastalus looked surprised, "Fee?"

I nodded, "This is a customs inspection, so I am assuming there is a fee to enter with such a thing."

Yastalus took a brief look at his surroundings then returned to focus on me, "Ah, yes. I seem to have gotten off track. Let me check out your skillet first, and then I will discuss this with our expert on primal power."

Yastalus looked over the skillet briefly and breathed a sigh of relief, "Ah good. Something I understand at least. It is an odd application perhaps, and certainly an unnecessary extravagance but a known enchantment."

I smiled, "So just the enchantment of durability I mentioned?"

Yastalus nodded, "A powerful one, but yes a durability enchantment. Only a dwarf smith would consider doing such a labor on a mere cooking implement. This was made with adamantine ore, and enchanted to resist damage and arcane power. I dare say it was reformed from what was once the shield of a mighty king given the expense of such an item."

I hesitated a moment and spoke, "How expensive would you say?"

Yastalus shrugged, "Given the quality of craftsmanship, materials, and enchantment I dare say you could purchase both of the ships in the harbor and their entire cargo for the price of this item. It was a gift you say?"

Yuki smiled, "It was a gift from my cooking instructor. He called it my graduation present."

Yastalus shook his head, "I'd have to say he was the most generous elf about whom I'd ever heard."

I smiled, "I'm sure Hardtack would be happy to hear you say it, but he's a dwarf actually."

Yastalus looked stunned again, "A dwarf gave away an item this precious?"

Yuki smiled, "Hardtack ordered it for me special he said. He already has a complete set just like it himself. He swears they are the best cooking gear available."

Yastalus shook his head again, "Let me guess. He was a former adventurer and struck it rich plundering some dragon hoard or some such. Really those people have no understanding of the value of the wealth they spend. Well this is outside of my ability to adjudicate. Nothing here seems like it is forbidden materials, but I am at a loss to valuate all of these items properly. I'll call in the Mistress Lionette and she can discuss it with you. Let's present her with our findings Nedulainus."

Yastalus and Nedulainus left the room together. Yuki looked at me, shrugged, and smiled at me. I stood up and began to pack up our gear except the items which were under discussion. I left the dwarf armor pan, my saber, my dagger and our rings out in full view. Balinac jumped off the table and batted at my legs. I ducked my head under the table where Balinac came close to my ear.

Balinac whispered in a faint version of Yuki's voice, "Lionette is the spirit shaman the wizard mentioned. You will not want her to inspect us both with her second sight without preparing her first. It could cause an incident or even potentially cause her to go into shock. Some spirit shamans are disturbed when they view beings like us unknowingly."

I picked Balinac up and spoke, "I got you Balinac."

I rose up from under the table. Next I stood behind Yuki rubbing the back of her neck with one hand while holding Balinac in the other arm.

I bent over to kiss Yuki's ear and whispered, "Greet her nicely when she comes in as she's one of the Lucky Cricket's. You'll need to keep her distracted from using her second sight on me if you can. I suggest getting a look at her spirit companion and using that as your opening."

After about a half hour of waiting we again heard the approach of footsteps outside the door. I stood near the window looking outside with my back to the door. Yuki sat in a chair positioned to be the first thing in view when the door opened. There was a brief hushed conversation outside the room and Yuki closed her eyes for a moment. When they opened again there was a raven like aspect to them.

As Lionette opened the door and as she saw Yuki sitting there Yuki spoke, "That is an interesting mountain cat you have following you."

Lionette seemed to freeze in place for a moment, "What did you just say?"

Yuki spoke quietly, "The Greater Destiny Chi Masters have a saying, greater destinies attract. Don't you agree?"

Lionette stood frozen for a moment more before she spoke, "Pardon me for a short bit. I have something to take care of first."

After Lionette closed the door and retreated I could hear another door opening and a hurried and hushed conversation. I caught the words, "Stop scrying right now!" It was said with harsh emphasis in elfish along with an added, "Aleadon curse you! Get out I said!" A few footsteps could be heard heading up the stairs. I then heard what sounded like Yastalus' voice raising a quiet objection, which was quickly countermanded by Lionette's voice.

Then from the hallway outside our door I heard Lionette make a comment, "Contact Trimiel on the crystal and then leave. I need to have a private consultation with him. No, I don't think they are dangerous."

Yastalus spoke louder, "What about the items I told you about. The one is a very powerful artifact grade ring of unknown primal magic. The other ring is of a scale that the primal magic readings are completely off the charts. Aleadon be blessed! Their cooking pot alone could buy this entire town."

Lionette spoke with frustration, "Let me correct myself then. I think they are potentially extremely dangerous. So dangerous that I don't think they could possibly present a threat."

Yastalus huffed, "What do you mean?"

Lionette spoke as if to someone stupid, "I think that if they wanted this entire town raised to the ground and left as ash they would have done so already regardless of what we attempted to stop them. Do you think provoking them any is going to help us?"

I heard Yastalus leaving as Lionette muttered in the common tongue outside the door, "I hope the Lucky Cricket is with me on this one."

I grinned at Yuki as she returned my smile. We had almost properly prepared Lionette. I figured it would only take a little more convincing to have her let us go without keeping any untoward information regarding our passing.

I looked at Yuki and nodded. Yuki sprang into action. She made a strange gesture with her right hand and the external bar on the room door silently released. Without a sound Yuki opened the door and crept out into the hall. Balinac and I moved forward to the open doorway to better hear what was happening. I watched

Yuki glide down the hall and trigger a latch on a secret doorway at the other end. She stepped silently into the room as Balinac and I advanced quietly to stand outside the secret door.

Lionette's voice came from inside the room speaking elfish, "This is very important Trimiel. Tell me everything that happened from the point your patrol first spotted them. No don't come back here. Just tell me now through the crystal. I'm fine, nothing has happened. Don't worry about it. We are just clearing up a point about how they got here. A boat you say? One moment it was open water, the next moment a boat drifted out of a shimmer of sun on the waves. Yes, it was likely a magical transportation. No, I don't know. Maybe it was fixed to that location to avoid collisions with other objects. They didn't mention a third person, but I haven't asked them yet. Didn't get out of the boat? Did you get a close look at him? I understand. Just skip forward to the journey here. How was their demeanor? Confident, yes, that matches. Calm matches too. Did they seem dangerous to you? No everything is fine you don't need to return. Friendly you say. Well that verifies what I wanted to know from you. Something else you say?"

I could hear Lionette's voice quaver next, "What was that name? Were you sure? You're positive they said the Lucky Cricket? They said you might meet him in your dreams? Oh crap, what am I going to do now?"

Lionette's voice became strong, "You are under no circumstances to return here today unless I summon you. In fact you are to forget about ever meeting them. On my authority as the local chief representative of the central government is all you need to know. Because I'm telling you that you are to consider this as no longer a matter of concern for Findor's local forces."

Lionette's voice broke slightly, "Please, Trimiel trust me on this one. I will make sure that Findor is kept safe. As you noted they have been friendly. Trust me. I just know that we should be able to keep them that way by staying out of their path is all. No we most certainly do not want to cause any alarm. I promise I will explain this to you when I can. It just might take a long while. I haven't figured it all out myself. I'm releasing the connection now. Thank you Trimiel."

There was a sigh from Lionette then she gave a slight yelp and I heard a bumping noise inside the room. A sudden inhale of breath was heard along with a slow exhale.

I then heard Yuki speaking softly in the common tongue "Is everything fine Miss Lionette?"

Lionette's voice was quivering, "You startled me is all. How did you get here so quietly? What did you hear?"

Yuki backed up until I could see her in the doorway as she answered, "I don't speak your language very well yet, but I am hoping to improve. I'm glad you and Trimiel are friends though. He seems like a very nice person."

Lionette's voice became stronger, "He said you arrived by a small boat. You arrived on a boat that came across from somewhere else and disappeared to somewhere else when it departed. According to Trimiel that somewhere was not the Fey Realm."

Yuki smiled, "According to Cricket it was the dreaming we crossed. You've heard of the dreaming I believe."

Lionette responded, "I have traveled there. Though I wasn't aware anyone could cross over to it with their physical form. Then again it doesn't surprise me given your power. I find this somewhat confusing though. I understand you say you came here across the dreaming. However, I can see many unusual connections made to your spirit. The connection made to all of us by the Lucky Cricket, and the connection presumably to your husband I can understand. There are several other ties I can not understand though. Your aura is so bright as well. I've never seen another of our kind as bright as you. I never thought to meet such a potent spirit shaman. Your spirit companion is very unusual as well. Is it the same as the legendary . . . oh great spirits. You are a descendant of the Yuki Nene? No not just that, you are also a disciple of the White Raven. I can see it now, oh great spirits, what has come to our lands."

I stepped into the room and Lionette's eyes grew wide with fear. She dropped slowly onto the ground and sat with her back to the wall. I noticed tears forming in her eyes.

Lionette began to cry softly, "I'm sorry. I didn't think it would cause any harm. I didn't know it was wrong to reveal our secrets to the magus. Yastalus has been a friend for most of my life. Please spare the life of Yastalus great being, and be satisfied with my own. He didn't mean any harm by his curiosity."

I walked over to stand in front of her and crouched down to look her directly in the eye as I spoke, "I think you have probably jumped to an incorrect conclusion about why we are here. I don't have any plans to kill anyone during my stay in Letheron. I am merely here to set up an inn you understand."

Lionette showed a glimmer of hope, "You didn't come here to kill me?"

I smiled gently, "I don't think Cricket would like that very much. I promised him I would look after his children."

Lionette seemed in a dream like state, "Cricket's children?"

I nodded, "The Greater Destiny Chi Masters or spirit shamans as they are known here. The Lucky Cricket considers all of them his children. He has done me some favors, so I have promised to help protect his children where I can."

Lionette looked over at Yuki as well, "Your wife is one of his children too then?"

Yuki smiled, "Of course I am. I also respect the White Raven for her service to the great cycle."

I reached out a hand to help Lionette back to her feet, "I have also made a bargain with a favored servant of the White Raven among others. Don't worry about us being some kind of crude death cultists."

Lionette took my hand cautiously and allowed me to help her stand upright again. I stepped back beside Yuki who had stepped forward. I placed my arm around her. Lionette tilted her head slightly sideways.

Lionette spoke, "You seem so normal and usual until viewed with the second sight. Your spirit is the most powerful thing I have ever witnessed."

I gave her a hesitant smile, "Thank you I think. You might want to cease using it for a while. I'm told it can be a strain for spirit shamans."

Lionette gave a nervous laugh, "Oh, yes. Of course it is. How silly of me really."

I smiled at her again, "I was wondering if you could help us out here. We seem to be in a touch of a tight spot. We are not supposed to be so obvious about our passage you understand. I didn't expect to meet anyone here who would recognize what we are."

Lionette gave a tenuous smile, "I really can't say that I have any idea what you are. I take it that you are not a spirit shaman then?"

I smiled, "You are correct. I'm more of a problem solver than a spirit shaman."

Lionette nodded her head, "I understand, and I am not to know the nature of the problem you are here to solve or interfere in any way."

I nodded, "I think you understand my quandary. I don't want to ask you to shirk your duties, but if you could accept us at surface value as it were it would be appreciated. Usually, we can pass without much trouble. I wasn't expecting your friend Yastalus to be so diligent or observant."

Lionette nodded her head, "I think I see your problem. You are here with a purpose. A purpose as disguised as your power. One filled with danger and supported by enormous powers."

I smiled, "That is as close as you need to speculate. Would it help for you to discuss it with one of these powers?"

Lionette looked stunned, "You can summon the Lucky Cricket here?"

I shook my head, "He is quite busy I would imagine. I also tend to be an independent operator if you understand my meaning. I am not one of his children, although my wife Yuki most certainly is."

Lionette shook her head, "What power do you mean then?"

I smiled, "I suggest you stick with your normal vision for the moment. Balinac I think Lionette is sufficiently prepared."

Balinac came walking into the room twitching her two tails. Lionette kept looking at me for a moment, and then followed my gaze down to Balinac. Then she looked over at Yuki who nodded.

Lionette looked at me blankly and then asked, "Where is this power you mentioned? All I see is your pet."

Balinac changed size to approximately five hundred pounds and coughed out, "All I see is a relatively dim witted elf way out of her depth. The Lucky Cricket turns out some real winners at times."

I cuffed Balinac playfully on the ear, "Be nice Balinac. Lionette please meet Balinac."

I saw Lionette close her eyes and I moved in front of her quickly yet gently covering them before she could open them again, "I am giving you a friendly warning Lionette. Make sure you are well prepared before you do that."

Lionette nodded her head and said, "I am ready to witness it."

I stepped beside Lionette and removed my hand from over her eyes. She cautiously opened her eyes and looked at the presence of the Balinac briefly before her eyes rolled up into her head and she passed out unconscious. I caught her before she dropped and gently lowered her down to the floor.

Balinac laughed, "Like I said. She is a real winner there Lucky Cricket."

I gave Balinac a quick glance, "Give her a break. You know tailed beasts scare the living daylight out of people."

Balinac nodded, "You warned her as well. This one seems to be always pushing boundaries she isn't prepared to cross. That is a very bad habit to get into. Someone should break her of it before it gets her seriously hurt."

I looked at Yuki, "Can you revive her to consciousness?"

Yuki nodded, "A couple of my spices should be able to do the trick."

I looked at Balinac, "Let's get her back to the interview room and wake her up again."

Balinac shrugged as she shrank back down to cat size, "She's small enough for the two of you to handle. I'm going to keep an eye out. They won't be giving us privacy here forever you know. I'll bet that Trimiel is heading back here at full speed, and that Yastalus is bound to check in on her soon as well."

Yuki and I moved Lionette cautiously to one of the interview chairs at the table in our original interview room. I closed the door to the secret room, and the door to our room while Yuki mixed some water with a small concoction of peppers and other spices. Yuki put a dollop of the concoction on the end of her finger, and waved it under the nose of Lionette. Lionette's eyes fluttered open and she sneezed violently. Then she groggily lifted her head and looked at us.

I smiled back at her, "I'm sorry about that. I warned you it was risky to use the second sight if not properly prepared."

Lionette shook her head, "It's my entire fault really."

I asked her, "Are you all right now?"

Lionette shook her head, "I don't know if I will ever be all right. I saw the powerful darkness and then I fell asleep. I found that I had gone to the dreaming. I was sitting on a small fishing boat with a short human man. The boat was drifting gently on the waves of a beautiful turquoise sea. Blue sky with towering white clouds passed over our heads. The man looked at me and smiled. Then he said to me, 'trust them my child'. I asked him why and he spoke again, 'they are there to make a better future for your people, a future for both my children like you, and the elves like you.' Then I woke to find myself sitting here. I've never had an image of the dreaming seem so clear and real."

I smiled, "That's the nature of the Lucky Cricket."

Lionette's face blanched, "The Lucky Cricket?"

I nodded with a smile, "That was him you saw on the boat. The same boat he crossed the dreaming with to bring us here. I think he likely summoned your spirit to him so he could explain in a way you will accept."

Lionette flushed, "I think that being with you was correct. I am way out of my depth here. I don't know what to do."

I smiled, "Might I suggest making up a suitable cover story and stamping our travel papers with approval to enter Letheron. As you may have guessed we can depart under our own power any time we desire, but I would rather keep this a legitimate visit. My employers are sticklers about not making waves or drawing unnecessary attention."

Lionette nodded, "What do you need me to do?"

I gave her a warm look, "How about we come up with something that you can easily follow along with?"

Chapter 38 Party

A few minutes later as Lionette was writing on and filling out our travel forms with the appropriate information Balinac appeared under the table at my feet and rubbed against my legs. I reached down to pet her with my right hand as I reached next to me with my left hand to hold Yuki's hand.

I began speaking with Lionette using our agreed upon cover story as I heard footsteps coming down the stairs, "I'm glad you could expedite this sensitive matter Miss Lionette. It wouldn't do to have too many locals aware of my undercover assignment in Ard."

Lionette gave a started look at me and then realized it was her turn to perpetuate our cover story, "Certainly Lord Lichan. I should have recognized the signet ring used by the council's hidden servants earlier. I apologize for any error in my understanding of the situation. Of course any duties and tariffs will be waved on your personal goods."

I smiled as I spoke, "Thank you my dear woman. It can be quite tedious to file the expense reports explaining why the government is paying itself money. Now I'm off to my new assignment to create the border station which will be using contracted labor to combat the incursions from the wild lands. I plan to make a good go of it, but I hope you understand I can't explain it any more before it comes to fruition. The very walls have ears you know."

I heard the departure of several sets of quiet elfin footsteps back upstairs and out of range of my hearing. I smiled as I understood that our interlopers had received an earful they didn't anticipate and quickly thought better of learning more.

I nodded at Lionette who spoke, "You could hear them outside the door?"

I smiled, "Quite well actually."

Lionette gave me a hesitant smile, "Would you mind if I asked you a favor?"

I nodded, "Please do Miss Lionette."

Lionette looked shyly down at my feet, "Who or what is that being?"

I picked up Balinac and began rubbing her between her ears, "This is Balinac. You might consider her, well let me see. How about saying a power? Would that be meaningful to you?"

Lionette shook her head, "There are many powers in the universe. I don't understand the nature of that one."

Yuki smiled, "Perhaps I could explain it better. My people have been known to call these powers the tailed beasts. They are among the most powerful of the greater spirits."

Lionette thought a moment and then blanched, "The Numbers. You're talking about the Numbers. That thing, it is Number Two is it not."

Balinac spoke up, "I don't care for that name much. The other Numbers only use it when they want to demean me. I much prefer Balinac if you don't mind."

Lionette began shaking uncontrollably, "That is a being of untold legend whispered of among the spirit shamans and the elves. It existed before the worlds, before the gods, before time it is rumored."

Balinac spoke with a bored tone, "One of the deathless, yeah, yeah, blah, blah. I always dread dealing with the elves and their ridiculously long historical memories. Please get over it sweetness. Yes, I'm an immortal being older than any of the gods you've ever heard of and the ones which came before them. I'm older than even this plane of existence or the other planes. I'm the original creator of the plane of shadow, and it is home to the passing spirits on their way to the next phase of the great cycle. I'm known as a Number those rare few remaining original inhabitants of the dreaming. Coincidentally, for your information some of the current gods haven't even met me. Several other gods drastically fear my presence. Yet here I am holding an audience with you."

I lightly tweaked Balinac's ear and admonished her, "Hush Balinac and behave yourself. You are scaring the poor woman witless again."

Lionette looked at Yuki's calm demeanor, "How can it not drive you mad with fear."

Yuki shrugged, "She was a bit intimidating at first, but now I know she is just a sweet pussycat."

Balinac looked up at me, "Why do I put up with this?"

I smiled, "You like her fish remember."

Balinac nodded, "You're right. Your wife does make a decent fish. Now as for you Lionette, I am letting you know that none of this conversation is repeated by you. It could be very damaging to my reputation. I don't want to listen to the Numbers calling me Twosie or Twotie pie you understand. In fact promise me you will pretend this never happened. This means you as well Number Seven. I know you are listening. No leaks on this."

Lionette looked even paler than before, "Number Seven is listening?"

Balinac laughed, "Are you kidding me? He has a direct pipeline to your spirit you silly elf. Just who do you think attached that spirit ribbon to you when your powers manifested."

Lionette seemed confused, "I thought it was the Lucky Cricket, the being which is also known as The Spirit Shaman."

I gave her a hesitant smile, "It is somewhat complicated from what I understand, but the Greater Spirit Seven Tailed Tiger is the Luck part of the Lucky Cricket. The man you met in the dreaming is the Cricket part of the Lucky Cricket. I think Balinac is quite right that it is observing the spirit shamans at all times, and I think it will keep its discretion in this matter."

Lionette shook her head, "You are so well informed. I've researched the past of my kind for hundreds of years, and yet you've shown me more than I've learned in a lifetime in a mere two hours."

I shrugged, "I guess I'm just lucky that way."

Lionette looked at me, "How did you do it? How did you get so far in your brief lifetime?"

I gave her a sad smile, "I suffered tremendous loss and pain. I even lost my own life. I don't recommend anyone else try it."

Lionette looked at me with a touch of fear, "You died?"

I nodded, "Once. It wasn't pleasant. Not many can come back the way I have."

Lionette looked closer, "Are you an undead?"

I shook my head, "I am a living breathing elf like you, although probably very young by your standards."

Lionette leaned back, "How young?"

I smiled, "I was twenty four when I died. A few years passed before I was alive again."

Lionette looked at me with pity, "You died as a child."

I shrugged, "I was a young man in my culture, but too early yes."

Lionette nodded, "Something seemed slightly off from the beginning. You are not like the elves here in Letheron."

I nodded, "I was not born here. I was not originally born an elf, although I was reborn as one."

Lionette nodded, "That explains the White Raven then. The goddess of death sent you back."

I smiled, "One of her chosen followers did with her permission yes. That is why I owe her a debt."

Lionette steadied herself, "I suppose you have also died Yuki?"

Yuki shook her head, "No. I have seen her palace, but it was in life. I served the White Raven for many years without knowing it. Now I serve her with my eyes opened. You should remember she is a part of the cycle of nature established by the gods and not fear her presence so. Remember the goddess of winter is necessary for the goddess of spring to create that which the elves love so much."

Lionette looked up with her color returning somewhat, "You mean life."

Yuki nodded, "Yes."

Lionette gave a sad smile while a tear dropped from her eye, "Thank you. I sometimes forget that is so very important to us."

I stood up from the chair with Balinac in my arms. Yuki stood along side me. Lionette looked up at Balinac with more tears forming in her eyes. I could sense the critical unspoken question on her mind.

Lionette asked, "Is it true Number Two, the most horrible legend told about you?"

Balinac preened herself and looked at Lionette, "Say it already."

Lionette asked, "It is also quietly rumored that you are also called the Godkiller. Is it true?"

Balinac looked at her carefully, "Nothing material lasts forever. Not even the gods. Only spirits are immortal and exist outside of time within the dreaming. Yes, the gods can die. Yes, I am the only Greater Spirit that can kill them at will and they all know it even if most of them never willingly admit it. Some of them unreasonably fear my presence because of it. The plane of shadow is the domain I created. Death is the part of the process of material existence which I also agreed to create. I did not exempt even the gods from it. The White Raven herself is standing on the ashes of the god that existed in her position before her whose spirit I took when it was time. When her spirit requires renewal I shall take it as well just as I have done for each of the elder gods in turn. Does this knowledge make you any happier?"

Lionette shook her head, "No it does not. It does make me wiser though."

Balinac nodded, "Good then. I would hope that you were not wasting my time just so you could be miserable. If you want to take some advice, go to the dreaming and look for Cricket when you are ready. Tell him you are ready to conceive a child. I'm sure that he will bless it, and through having the child you may find a measure of happiness. This too is part of the process created by the Numbers."

Lionette raised her head, "Which number?"

Balinac chuckled, "Number One of course. The others always claim he has a one track mind."

I asked the question I was almost afraid to ask, "Which plane did the greater spirit one tail create?"

Balinac laughed, "It's so obvious even you should get it."

I smiled and laughed, "The prime material. Number One is the first prime number of course. That is why the prime is the center of life and rebirth in material existence."

Balinac nodded, "That's also why only the prime numbered greater spirits can manifest here without help."

I smiled, "Is that really true?"

Balinac nodded, "Ask Seven if you don't believe me. Of course his rates for an answer to that one might be quite high. Fundamental knowledge of existence doesn't come cheap from him."

I nodded, "I can believe it. The last time I talked with him an answer cost me a promise to protect the spirit shamans when and where I encounter them."

Lionette looked up at me, "Is that the truth? You promised the Lucky Cricket to protect us?"

I smiled, "Yes, where it is within my ability to do so. I am only one elf after all."

Yuki had picked up her belongings from the shelf and passed my belongings over to me. I arranged my gear comfortably and walked over to the door of the room with Yuki at my side. I looked over at Lionette sitting at the table in silent contemplation.

I pointed to the door, "Is it fine if we leave now, or would you prefer to accompany us back upstairs so everyone can see that you are still in good health?"

Lionette's attention seemed to snap back to the room, and she looked out the window, "It is getting late outside. Where will you go stay tonight?"

Yuki smiled, "It wouldn't be the first time we slept on the road would it Mica darling."

I shrugged, "I think the weather will be fair tonight. Sleeping under the forest canopy seems like an acceptable idea."

Lionette stood and looked Yuki in the eyes, "You could stay at my place for the evening. I think that having a couple of guests over tonight would help relieve some of the mystery surrounding your appearance. I would like it very much if you stayed."

I had a flash of insight and nodded, "I think we should accept her offer my dear. I get the feeling that Lionette and you have some things to talk about in private."

Yuki jumped to the same conclusion I had, "You've never spoken with another Chi Master have you?"

Lionette nodded her head, "You are correct. I am the only one in my generation born with the power in Letheron that I know. There are some elder elves in the Fey Realm which possess the talent, but they are reclusive and seldom accept invitations or guests. Most modern citizens of Letheron don't even understand what a spirit shaman is unless they have an extensive education. It's one of the reasons I discuss it with Yastalus as he is curious, educated, and non-judgmental about my abilities."

We walked out of our room and up the stairs to the main floor of the custom's office. Lionette did a fair job of keeping a calm appearance while giving us directions to a market where food could be purchased as we walked to the door. I noticed several of the other workers were distracted from their duties while watching us closely as we passed through. Yastalus in particular was looking closely at Lionette for a sign that she might be under any kind of threat or duress.

Yuki and I were doing a good job of appearing happy and calm about our situation. As an observer of people I wouldn't have suspected Yuki of being anything other than what we pretended to be, a pair of enthusiastic and competent entrepreneurs. I enjoyed the looks of confusion as Lionette more publicly mentioned how to find her home where we would be staying that evening.

As we walked outside to the market I knew the rumors would be spreading fast and furious that afternoon, but it would hopefully work to our favor. We were exciting and new, but at the same time it was not suspected by anyone except Yastalus that we were potentially very dangerous individuals. Lucky for us Yastalus seemed confident enough in Lionette as his superior to follow her lead.

Yuki looked over at me as we entered the market, "You seem to be lost in thought my dear. Is there anything you need?"

I nodded, "I was thinking perhaps we could put your talents to use this evening. In addition to our traveling supplies I suggest we get enough ingredients to prepare one of your special meals. I think a cookout is in order to put to test whether the elves here will appreciate your original culinary designs. I'll even help with the meal preparation and pot cleaning if you need. I'm not much of a cook, but I can still peal a tuber when required."

Yuki grinned, "That sounds like a wonderful idea. We could even get Lionette a set of outdoor cooking gear if they have a selection available here. It is the least we could do for her assistance today. How many guests should we expect?"

I thought about it, "At least twenty of her friends will find a pretext to stop by once the rumors come around about our presence. Then once they taste your food and the word gets out we can probably expect another forty or more to invite themselves over. I would guess about enough for eighty should be right for a safety margin. I doubt any leftovers will go to waste."

By the time we had gone through town buying our supplies and the necessary equipment to put on a decent sized cookout the majority of the afternoon had passed. We had hired three youths as porters and had two handcarts to carry all of our purchases. One mason we had hired showed up with the flagstones we had ordered and assisted me with the construction of a simple yet functional dry fit outdoor oven and grill in Lionette's yard near the pathway.

While I worked on that project Yuki directed the youths like a professional innkeeper in setting up several tables and chairs we had rented. Various elves walked by to watch our efforts as the makings of a simple yet elegant outdoor kitchen and dining area were created by our small team. I paid our helpers and invited them and their families over for dinner that evening.

Yuki was beginning the serious preparations for the meal as I chopped, and pealed various foods at her direction. I noticed that Lionette had finally arrived at her home with an incredulous look on her face.

I smiled back at her, "Yuki and I are not used to your customs in Letheron yet, but it is not uncustomary for certain traveling members of the Isle Corporation to provide a sample of the cuisine being offered at their facilities as they travel through various communities. You need not worry as the oven and grill is of temporary construction and will be taken down tomorrow by the mason we hired. The tables and chairs are only rented and will be picked up by their owner tomorrow as well."

Lionette looked at all the food being prepared and the many tables in her yard, "This is much more than we can eat."

Yuki shook her head, "I expect it should be just enough. Mica has already taken the liberty of inviting the mason, the market workers, and three porters and their families to come sample our hospitality. We also figure you might want to go invite some guests of your own since you are hosting this affair."

I nodded, "I suggest you invite Yastalus, Trimiel, and a few of your more curious neighbors watching us at the very least. You may want to get ready after you make the invitations. Yuki should be ready fairly soon."

Yuki looked up at the sky, "It should be served in two hours. It would be sooner, but I like the effect gained when dining outdoors from dusk to twilight. I also find the anticipation adds a bit of savor to the meal."

Lionette looked a little shocked yet pleased, "You didn't have to go through all this effort. I had already invited Yastalus and Trimiel over tonight. I didn't expect you to have to work so much."

I smiled, "Lionette you have to realize this is for our benefit as well. We do have to advertise our new product, and I find that word of mouth is a powerful tool in our business. So I suggest you find about sixty of your closest and hungriest friends and coworkers, and invite them over to sample a small portion of what the future Reading Dragon Inn will have to offer for discriminating diners."

Four hours later I looked over at Yuki grinning as the desert trays were being passed out among the tables by our volunteer youth serving staff. The local community had turned out in force tonight as word of mouth had spread quickly about our endeavor. Lucky for us many of them had also brought along traditional local dishes to be served along with Yuki's new cuisine so there was enough food for everyone.

At least two hundred elves had shown up so far, but they were gracious about taking smaller servings so that all could at least sample Yuki's cooking. Many had brought tables and chairs from their homes, and the affair had spread into the yards of Lionette's adjoining neighbors who seemed pleased to share in the benefits of the attention.

Every local official had managed to receive an invitation, and I noticed that most of the local customs office employees we had seen were present as well. Also present were Trimiel and his patrol members who were off duty for the evening. They had brought five barrels of the favored elfish wine from the region. The local officials had hired several musical performers and had made eloquent speeches to the crowd between courses.

I hugged Yuki with one arm around her shoulders, "You've done a wonderful job my dear. I think the word of mouth about the Reading Dragon Inn will begin to pick up pretty well in the coming months as we begin our construction. We'll need to set up the kitchen facilities as soon as feasible so you can keep the construction workers motivated with your food."

Yuki nodded, "I think the food is a key ingredient to the success tonight, but it certainly isn't everything. It really is meaningless without the people. They came here looking to find something new and different, yet not too different. Change will always come slowly for you elves. However, it is encouraging that we have found some willing to try something new on our first attempt."

I hugged her again, "Don't sell your achievement short. You prepared a delicious meal tonight. It would have been hard for anyone to turn away from it."

Yuki smiled up at me, "How about you? I never knew you were that handy as a kitchen assistant. Why haven't you done more of that when we were back at home?"

I frowned, "Don't remind me. It was a skill I had hoped to forget. Back when I was still living with my parents and in the militia after I was given kitchen patrol as a form of punishment. Actually it wasn't nearly so bad this time though, it was almost fun."

Yuki nodded, "Wanting to do it instead of being forced to do it makes a big difference doesn't it?"

I looked at her slightly surprised, "I guess you're right about that. How did you know?"

Yuki grinned, "There were plenty of what I felt were unpleasant duties given to me by my father when I was training as well. When I realized it wasn't the duty which was unpleasant but my attitude about performing it, then my training became much easier for me."

I hugged her another time, "You're a very wise woman my dear wife."

Shortly after that Yuki and I were greeted and introduced to various members of the community as the business which had provided the catering services for the affair. We received many complements on Yuki's cooking, and quite a few people who wanted to hire us for future events. I spent the next hour giving the short pitch of my sales speech for the Reading Dragon Inn to various small groups of the people present. This version of the pitch focused on the luxurious nature of our future Inn contrasting with the rugged nature of the wild lands near the border.

Several of the elves who heard the speech seemed somewhat disappointed we would not be setting up a local operation yet. However, I noticed that among the younger elves there was a certain sparkle in their eyes at the mention of being near the wild lands. The lure of excitement and possible danger still held interest in those who were not yet settled into their lives.

I noticed as the evening wound down that Trimiel approached with two of his squad members to be introduced, "This is Mica who spotted our scouts so quickly this morning. You guys could learn something from this elf. He's sharp of eye, subtle of step, and unfortunately even faster than me."

The ranger on Trimiel's left spoke up, "I couldn't believe that you out raced the captain here. He is known for his endurance and tenacity among our squad. Unfortunately for him he is not so lucky with love."

Trimiel elbowed his squad member lightly in the ribs, "Please mind your manners. Our host tonight would be dismayed by your idle gossip."

The ranger on Trimiel's left spoke, "I guess that makes her the first elf you haven't been able to catch and him the second."

Trimiel looked embarrassed by the remark as he replied, "I think you two have had more than enough wine for the evening then if you are treating me this poorly."

The ranger on Trimiel's left plead with him, "Come on Captain. This is our first liberty time in a month. Let us have some fun."

I broke into their conversation, "Perhaps a little contest then. I hear that Letheron's rangers are among the best trackers in the world. I was wondering which of you would be the first to find my cat Balinac. She seems to have wandered off this evening and I would be indebted to you for locating her. You'll recognize her immediately as she is black with leopard spots. It's her two tails which make her distinctive though.

Trimiel looked at me sharply, "Two tails you say? I seem to have missed that detail this morning. Such a creature is very rare I would imagine."

I nodded, "Balinac is pretty unique and smart as well. She wouldn't get lost on me, but she might be mistaken by someone else as a lost pet."

The ranger on Trimiel's left spoke, "I think my ground squirrel Chichiri is the right one for this job."

The ranger on Trimiel's right responded, "Nonsense Captain, my hawk Windler shall spot it first, just like he did the boat this morning."

As both rangers walked off debating the merits of their pets Trimiel looked at me with a touch of gratitude as he spoke, "They are good men, but sometimes a handful when they have too much wine. I give you my thanks for distracting them. Where did your cat get off to anyway?"

I walked over by the outdoor grill oven where Balinac was calmly eating a fish Yuki had provided and pointed down at her, "Right where I left her. I figured it would take your men some time to consider starting at the beginning. Sometimes the obvious doesn't occur to people when they are distracted."

Trimiel gave me another sharp look, "You are trying to tell me something?"

I nodded, "Yes that you need to consider your timing."

Trimiel looked down at Balinac, "She does have two tails. Why did I miss that fact before? What do you mean about my timing?"

I smiled, "Are you easily distracted too? What was the conversation about a moment ago?"

Trimiel looked at me with a cautious look, "My personal life you mean."

I nodded, "I'm not prying in your personal business mind you. I just find that paying attention to timing is a key to making certain things work though."

Trimiel looked over at Lionette where she was talking to Yastalus and a group of her guests, "I don't know. Some people are stuck between various choices, and unable to choose it seems."

I gave him a pat on the back, "You don't seem to be one of those people."

Trimiel looked back at me, "Neither do you as a matter of fact. You might just be one of the most spontaneous people I've ever met, or one of the most thoughtful. I'm not sure which."

I looked at him with a smile, "Some people are not able to choose for fear of choosing wrong. I think our host this evening is normally one of those people. I know because I used to be like her at one time in my life. Then I decided to give away that fear since it was no longer useful to me, it was only going to get me killed."

Trimiel looked at me with a measure of camaraderie in his expression, "What happened to help you change?"

I looked Trimiel in the eye, "I lost the one I loved through my inaction at a key point. It drove me mad at the time and made me incautious in the heat of my anguish. I learned a valuable lesson from it though. I learned to hesitate at the wrong time is to potentially loose everything you care about."

Trimiel looked at me, "She chose someone else then?"

I shook my head, "She was killed by an assassin before my eyes. I didn't even get the chance to work up the courage to tell her I loved her and find out how she felt about me. Tomorrow isn't guaranteed to any of us Trimiel. Find your courage to express your thoughts and feelings before it is too late is my advice."

Trimiel looked over at Yuki talking with a couple of guests, "Your wife loves you and you love her correct?"

I nodded, "Yuki and me both love each other it is true. I found my courage and determined not to let the cultural, national, or societal fears of a relationship like ours dictate my life. I became resolved after my first mistake to not repeat it. I just hope that you can learn from my experience and save yourself from facing the same lesson."

Trimiel shrugged, "It doesn't help in my case I think. There is still that indecision on her part between him and me."

I looked over at Lionette and Yastalus speaking together, "They are friends certainly, even long time friends no doubt. However, Yastalus does not love her in the way you do. His magic is his first love. It often is for magus you understand."

Trimiel seemed deflated, "They are so close though. They work together. He does what she tells him to do without question."

I put an arm around his shoulders, "Is that the fear talking?"

Trimiel looked at me again, "Yes, damn it. You know that it is."

I smiled, "Yet when she begged you to stay away you returned to town anyway. You brought your men to watch me to make sure she really is safe. You've noticed that Yastalus is watching over Lionette like your ranger's hawk and scrupulously avoiding my wife and me. You sense his fear and uncertainty, but are confused by Lionette's relative calm. Yastalus has told you something he was told to ignore hasn't he?"

Trimiel seemed a bit startled, "I keep forgetting how sharp you really are. This is about distraction isn't it? The issue isn't Lionette, Yastalus and me. It is about keeping your real objectives while in Letheron hidden. Did you threaten Lionette? Did you threaten Yastalus?"

I shook my head, "I'm afraid you have me wrong on that score. Yastalus and Lionette needlessly frightened themselves. I simply reassured Lionette that Yuki and I were worthy of her trust."

Trimiel shook his head as he spoke, "I don't buy it. I know there is no secret force run by the counsel. The only decisions they make anymore are to retreat further every year. They wouldn't take aggressive action against a kingdom as far away as Ard. Lionette told a lie and I don't understand why she would do such a thing without good reason. Fear for her life, or the life of our people might make her do it."

I smiled, "Yastalus overheard that as well then? It seems we didn't keep our conversation quiet enough."

Trimiel looked at me, "I know it is not true. I can't let you threaten her or the rest of us. I am sworn to protect Letheron."

I nodded, "I am sworn to protect the spirit shamans. It seems we have something in common then."

Trimiel looked at me with confusion, "How did you know Lionette is a spirit shaman?"

I smiled, "My wife Yuki is one as well."

I observed that most of the guests around us had departed during our conversation as the hour was drawing late. Trimiel seemed out of his depth for a moment, and then something seemed to click in his mind. He looked up at me with a thoughtful expression and didn't seem to grasp where I was taking him anymore.

Trimiel smiled, "You're seemingly right. This isn't a threat, but I'm at a loss to understand what it is, unless, it keeps coming back to distraction. If you are here distracting me, and have already distracted my men then where is your wife?"

Trimiel looked around in a brief panic. He then turned his gaze to where Lionette was standing talking to Yastalus and Yuki. Trimiel seemed a bit stunned.

Trimiel looked at me, "How did she get over there without my noticing?"

I spoke to Trimiel in a calm and friendly voice, "Yuki walked over there normally is all. We all tend to dismiss the normal."

Trimiel nodded, "The two of you are anything but normal. I'm a trained observer yet I missed what has happened here. When did your wife pick up your cat . . ."

Trimiel's gaze had shifted back to the grill where he noticed the apparently snoozing Balinac laying near the warm surface. Then he looked at Yuki holding Balinac while standing next to Lionette. His gaze shifted back to me and the Balinac held in my arms. He looked back at Yuki leaning over to whisper in Lionette's ear and I could see a bead of sweat forming on his brow. He finally realized that the other elves had all departed to their homes and just the five of us remained amid the end of the party.

Trimiel's voice trembled, "You are deadly with a saber."

I smiled, "I am talented according to my weapons master."

Trimiel looked over at Yuki next to Lionette and Yastalus again, "Yuki is also deadly with a blade I take it? All her blades are here though."

I nodded, "Yuki is deadly with her bare hands if she desires."

Trimiel looked over at Yastalus as he said the next part, "Yastalus said you have items imbued with power beyond his knowledge. What he called primal power. He said it is power which comes from the spirit world."

I spoke, "I won't deny his observation in the matter. He has recognized the potential there that other wizards of a lesser nature would normally overlook without second thought."

Trimiel looked back at me, "You said go back to the beginning, and you even mentioned that deception and distraction were in use."

I nodded, "I did say that but you are not there yet. You are still trying to pick up the trail in the middle without understanding where it began."

Trimiel looked at the Balinac by the fire place, "You said it began there. How did all these cats that look alike get here without my noticing them?"

I gave him a mild grin, "Might I suggest that you may have had too much wine tonight and your observation skills are a little blunted by it."

Trimiel nodded, "I did have some wine but this is something else. That creature came from nowhere today. None of our animals could detect it until it appeared. It can't be natural. What is it I can't remember? Old tales and childhood legends come to mind. What did Lionette tell me? She was very intent about learning who dropped you off in the boat. You said he was the Lucky Cricket. That means something to her, and I don't know why. Everything changed when I mentioned that name to her."

I nodded in a friendly manner, "You've gotten back to the beginning now. Just piece it all together. It should be easier now that you know where to start."

Trimiel muttered, "You're saying the fisherman is the key. Why does that ring a bell? The Lucky Cricket can be found in my dreams you said. The dreaming is the source of primal power according to Lionette. The dreaming is the realm of the Numbers according to the ancient legends. How did those old stories and legends go? The Numbers are beings of vast powers and abilities. They each have a different form, but can be known by their number of tails. It is told that Number Two is also known as the Godkiller, the creator of mortality for all beings even the divine or demonic. Thus the Godkiller has two tails . . ."

Trimiel looked at Balinac and I saw his knees weaken, and Trimiel looked at me with true fear in his eyes as he whispered, "It is impossible to save her . . ."

I nodded, "If it had been our intent to cause harm there would be nothing you or even any of your very gods could do to stop it. Do you understand why we can be trusted now?"

Trimiel looked at me, "What do you want me to do to save her?"

I smiled, "Like I told you at the beginning of our conversation. It's about timing. Right now it's time to lose your fear of what might happen and tell Lionette how you truly feel about her. I'll see to it that Yastalus is distracted trying to figure out why we should be trust worthy while you let Lionette know how you feel in private."

Trimiel looked slightly relieved yet uncertain, "You just want me to propose to Lionette?"

I shook my head, "That is up to you. I want you to stop fearing what might happen if you let your feelings be known. I can not tell whether her response will be positive or negative, but such things are better not left unsaid lest the lost opportunity be regretted later. If you ask my opinion the timing will never be better to discuss it with her than now."

Trimiel walked over to speak with Lionette while Yuki walked over to me with Yastalus following her. I could see that while Trimiel seemed relieved that our intent was not harmful Yastalus would likely be a bit harder to sell. Yastalus seemed confident in his abilities to detect a problem even if he was uncertain with how to deal with it properly. Frankly, I didn't blame him. I didn't imagine that officials in Ard would be any more positive regarding our presence.

Yastalus stepped in front of me and shook his head, "I see that even more strangeness is present this evening. It seems your cat has had some very fast growing kittens. I don't suppose that you would be willing to part with one of them?"

I shook my head, "I don't think I could talk Balinac into that arrangement. She is very independent minded after all. Please have a seat with us. We've had a long day, and I wouldn't mind a bit of relaxation."

Yastalus took a seat with us, "Thank you for the hospitality. Your food was quite delicious tonight. As was the wine brought by Trimiel's squad. I do wonder if your cat is both as intelligent and magical I now surmise. Pardon my frankness but I did a bit of background research through our government this afternoon. My discrete inquires did not turn up any knowledge of a secret group run by the counsel. However, there is nothing surprising there as I did not expect to find any admission of such."

I laughed, "You'll have to pardon my poor jest I'm afraid. Lionette had some personal business to discuss with us, and I was aware that there were eavesdroppers outside of the door. I asked her to help me give them an unexpected earful to discourage continued listening."

Yastalus took my admission in stride, "I see. I thank you for clearing up that point. I must admit that my various inquires did show numerous legal arrangements being conducted and proxies being established by the Isle Corporation. It seems that a lot of money was being spent to effectuate the purchase of a somewhat undesirable piece of property. It is not undesirable in terms of condition, but because of its location near the border of the wild lands."

I nodded with a smile, "Yes. That would be the site of our new inn."

Yastalus smiled back at me, "All the paperwork submitted claims as much. There are also a large amount of labor visas being issued to various foreign craftsmen. I could also see that a large number of domestic architects and labor being sought for the project as well."

I spoke, "I find that I prefer to hire experts for certain functions. Many of the imported workers are dwarves skilled at stone masonry and mining. I plan to have them quarry any stone needed for the location, while the elves will be in charge of design and ascetics of the inn and its surrounding structures."

Yastalus nodded, "It has been very expensive for the Isle Corporation to import labor in this way. The labor visas for outsiders are not easy to obtain. It seems this project has been in the planning for a good length of time. Some might say an extraordinary length of time in fact for a simple inn."

I smiled, "I never claimed it would be a simple inn. I want it to be a masterpiece inn. I hope to create the kind of inn that will draw the envy of my rivals in the business. I hope to expand it into a whole resort with lots of opportunities for entertainment and civilized enjoyment within its structure."

Yastalus spoke in a conspiratorial tone, "I also found out that you are the primary owner of the Isle Corporation and its president, and that Yuki is the vice president in charge of culinary design. It seems strange that two people such as you would be cooking for a barbecue at Lionette's home."

Yuki smiled, "Cooking is also a hobby for me. I enjoy it both as pastime in addition to being excited by the potentials in new foodstuffs. It was fun sampling the local cuisine to see how people interpret what can be done with food."

Yastalus nodded, "It is also a convenient demonstration that helps people accept you for what you want to appear to be. Unfortunately, I also know that you are both potentially very dangerous. I could see that Trimiel was very nervous in your presence. I might even think that you had been threatening him."

I spoke with a serious expression on my face, "That's strange because Trimiel had asked whether we had threatened you and Lionette since you seemed nervous. When I assured him that was not the case he seemed to feel better about it."

Yastalus shook his head, "I can see where he might have made that observation mistakenly. I have been dwelling on your presence ever since you arrived, and it may have affected my normal mannerisms. You are both not our typical visitors if you understand. We mainly see sailors who want a brief land side liberty, and the occasional ex-patriot returning to the homeland as tensions increase between Letheron and our neighbors."

I nodded, "I can understand your concern. We have encountered people suspicious of our intentions before. It is one of the reasons we have chosen to establish Letheron as the first location of our inn chain. If we can make a success of it here, then any other desirable location should go much smoother. Letheron is a test of whether my concept for an inn can work in a broader arena. I hope to make it a proof of concept of sorts."

Yastalus spoke with a touch of concern, "Then why do you come here with humans, dwarves, and many other races which the current counsel seems to frown upon. You are only raising your chance of failure by not making this a wholly elfish project."

Yuki put her arm around my shoulders, "If we have to make this a wholly elfish project to succeed then we have already failed."

Yastalus got a thoughtful look, "That explains something which puzzled me. When I put a discrete query out about the strange items in your possession through some contacts in the wizard community most of the replies I have received so far have dismissed my listed observations as impossible or flawed. One unexpected reply simply asked for more information, and whether I had examined your cat."

I shrugged, "I don't know what more information we could provide."

Yastalus smiled, "You may not understand what is surprising about this. I made no mention of any cat in my query. I only mentioned the two rings with primal power sources."

I raised a querulous eyebrow, "Might I inquire about the source of the reply?"

Yastalus nodded, "It was a source to whom I had not sent a message, but who had replied anyway. Most curious to me is that he is a rather notorious half-elf mage who styles himself as a sage."

I smiled, "You mean Glorandel the Blue Sage then. Why do you say he styles himself as a sage?"

Yastalus raised an eyebrow, "You know of him? As a wizard and enchanter you have to understand that in our community it is rare for someone to brazenly apply the term sage to themselves. It implies a great deal of knowledge, learning, and wisdom. While I am an expert in my knowledge of enchantments and items that have been enchanted, my level of knowledge about it still does not reach the level of sage craft. There is still much I have not learned as is evidenced by my surprise at the items you carry."

Yuki queried, "How does this apply to Glorandel then?"

Yastalus shrugged, "While he undoubtedly has an enormous store of historical, political, and social knowledge about important movers and shakers in world events past and present, his magical knowledge is usually somewhat limited to things pretty much common knowledge in our field. Other than his oft cursed privacy spell he hasn't contributed anything remarkable to the store of magical knowledge, and he won't disclose the secrets behind that one. Glorandel is really more of an information broker than a sage. The question this raises is why would Glorandel be interested in a simple businessman and his somewhat remarkable cat?"

I chuckled a bit, "I have a piece of information that might answer that question for you. Glorandel works for me on a contractual basis. I'm courting him to become an investor in my business venture as well. He is probably doing some additional background investigation on me to make sure the investment is a sound one."

Yastalus sat back with a contemplative look, "I hadn't thought of that one. Why would he ask about your cats then?"

I smiled, "It is a good way to determine whether it is me who is being discussed. I'm the only one with a two tailed cat like that he knows."

Yastalus looked around, "Where did your cats go to anyway? I only see the one in your arms now."

I nodded, "They probably went off to rest. Glorandel recognized her immediately you know. Even knew her name right away. I think you should give him more credit for his Sage craft."

Yastalus looked at Balinac with a careful eye, "Glorandel knew the name of a magical familiar? That seems like a trivial detail even for his knowledge. He usually restricts himself to major movers."

Balinac looked back at Yastalus and spoke, "Are you implying I am not a major mover then? Perhaps you should think twice. Even Trimiel realized who I was given enough clues."

Yastalus sat in a moment of contemplative silence as I stroked Balinac and said, "Of course you are a major mover. You are just on a bit of vacation with us."

Yastalus looked at the three of us, "Your cat is more intelligent than I imagined. It can speak flawlessly in elfin."

Balinac replied, "Thank you but it is trivial compared to speaking and translating the various deific tongues. That can be actually challenging."

Yastalus looked surprised, "You've had a need to speak deific?"

Balinac nodded, "On occasion when a deity needs to be spoken with it helps to communicate in their native tongue."

Yastalus looked around again, "The other cats are all you are they not? You're a shape changer. No, I don't think that is the right term. You are a poly being aren't you?"

Balinac shrugged, "If you mean I only have one consciousness then I think your understanding of the term is close enough."

Yastalus looked at my wedding ring again, "Mica has a ring that controls you doesn't he. That's why it is so powerful. It is a cross dimensional summoning band isn't it. It wasn't crafted by normal means."

Balinac jumped up on the table while looking directly at Yastalus, "It doesn't control me. It is me, and allows me to quickly move a portion of my mass to Mica when I desire."

Yastalus looked confused, "Your mass?"

Balinac replied, "Is a variable amount shifted between my two planes of material existence."

Yastalus took a shuddering breath, "You exist concurrently on two planes?"

Balinac shook her head, "Technically three planes if you count my non-material source."

Yastalus looked over at me, "Do you understand what this means. At most any wizard can exist materially on one plane and project their consciousness into another plane. None can exist materially simultaneously on multiple planes except the gods, and even they reportedly must limit how often and how long they do so."

Balinac spoke in an unimpressed tone, "I can open a gate for you if you want to see me standing there on the other side. I warn you though I am not quite so small on the plane of shadow."

Yastalus shook his head, "There is no need to open a gate. You can perform such a ritual though?"

Balinac nodded, "I do so many times a day at will actually. I can even create permanent ones between the shadow and the prime if I so choose. Would you like to have one in your home?"

Yastalus shook his head again, "I do not think I want a planar gate to the Shadow in my home. It is kind of you to offer though. Might I ask what third plane of existence you are connected to though?"

Balinac shrugged, "It is not really a plane of existence in the sense you wizards understand such things. It is more the place of non-existence from which everything else came."

Yastalus looked surprised, "You mean the dreaming? That is the source of primal power according to Lionette. Even the gods stay away from the dreaming. Only the spirit shamans dare to visit it. It is rumored that the Numbers dwell there and that they don't care for visitors."

Balinac jumped down off the table and shifted form into a beautiful raven haired elf, "I think you have finally figured it out."

Yastalus looked startled, "You are a shape shifter after all."

Balinac shrugged, "What is shape to one who can control matter through thought alone?"

Yastalus blanched, "You're a Number, a Number in the flesh. It is said that you are one of the primal forces of existence. You are supposed to be apart from the world. Why would you be here now?"

Balinac placed her arm over Yuki's on my shoulders, "Because Mica here requested my help. I do like him and his wife Yuki very much after all."

I spoke with a light tone, "Don't tease him too much Balinac. She is here acting as our guardian only. You need not worry about her hurting anyone who doesn't seek to harm us."

Yastalus regained some color, "I understand now what Lionette meant by so dangerous that you were safe. You're Balinac, also called Number Two then."

Balinac smiled, "I prefer Balinac and appreciate that you refrained from using that other name."

Yastalus hesitated, "Other name . . . Oh yes. I wouldn't think of using such a poorly conceived appellation for you. You may consider me convinced about your sincerity. I fully understand why you are not a threat to our community now. Might I humbly inquire what brings such an august being as you to our little part of the prime?"

Balinac smiled back as she hugged Yuki and I close from behind, "I like to think of it as protecting my investment. Now if you will pardon me I think that Trimiel is done talking with Lionette about their mutual feelings for each other. I am also leading Trimiel's men back this way. I would appreciate it Yastalus if you would maintain your discretion about my presence. There are certainly beings in existence which would cause great harm to you and your village in trying to locate me. I would hate to have something like that on my conscience."

Yastalus nodded, "I understand. You are traveling incognito."

Balinac seemingly melted into the darkness and disappeared as we saw Lionette and Trimiel leaving her house side by side. As they approached two Balinac's came running toward our table, one from the north portion of the village, and one from the south portion of the village. The Balinacs jumped up into Yuki's lap and my lap respectively as we saw Trimiel's two squad members come chasing after them.

The squad members came fast and reached the table looking down in surprise at seeing two cats in our laps. Trimiel came up with Lionette behind him and looked at the situation as well. Yastalus just silently shook his head.

Trimiel laughed, "They seem to have led you both on a merry chase."

The one elf expelled, "It was a hard chase for sure. I understand what kept us so busy now. There are two of the things. They are stealthy as anything we've ever encountered. First we would see it north of the village, then south, then north again. We finally split up to try to confirm the location of them. Even when we started chasing them they moved from cover to cover faster than his hawk could keep up."

The second elf looked at me with chagrin, "That was as cruel trick you played. We missed the end of the party trying to find those creatures. I have even sobered up after all that running."

Trimiel spoke, "It serves you right I guess. Now help us get the remains of this party cleaned up some before we leave. We are due back on patrol the day after tomorrow."

Chapter 39 Planning

alinac, Yuki, and I departed Findor the next day. Yuki had a private discussion with Lionette in the morning while they prepared breakfast. I had gone out for a run before dawn and returned in time to pack our belongings and eat breakfast. Our host Lionette had seemed more at ease with our presence and in general with the situation between Trimiel and Yastalus although I didn't pry into the outcome of their private discussion.

I looked at Yuki as we walked down the trail out of Findor together, "That seems to have gone well. Perhaps it was even better than if we had attempted one of the land border crossings. I think we should arrange for some of our more questionable labor to be examined at customs here. Giving them documentation showing employment by the Isle Corporation should help expedite the process."

Yuki nodded, "That sounds good for the short term my dear, but what about our northern border point near the Reading Dragon? As the critical border point for our business it will take some careful handling to make sure that the right beings are allowed to cross to do business with us while creating a minimal disruption to Letheron in general."

I looked at her, "You are right of course. I hope we can recruit either Lionette or Yastalus to head up the border station in the north. If not we will have to do some work making sure the employees there are satisfied with our clientele."

Yuki nodded, "I expected as much. I've already mentioned the concept to Lionette this morning. She seems hesitant to relocate, but I suspect that things may work out better between Trimiel and her if there is more physical distance between her and Yastalus."

I smiled, "That's very innovative of you Yuki. I'm glad you took the initiative on that one. We would have to see to it that Trimiel is relocated as well if that is the optimal scenario. It would make it easier to have some direct government contacts nearby whom we could trust to keep us notified of significant changes in border control procedures. I would also like to keep a relatively reliable point of contact in Findor so we can expedite the clearance of any goods which are shipped into Letheron. I do think we should make sure to stay away from any contraband items being shipped in by us or our employees though. I would hate to put our contacts in any kind of compromising position."

Yuki looked at me with a somewhat strange expression, "Speaking of distance between people, when are we due to meet up with Lirae?"

I looked at her with a slight grin and reached over to hold her hand, "Lirae is not someone you should worry about with me. I'm more of an adopted son to her."

Yuki nodded, "I know. You have to understand that mother-in-laws are generally considered a pain for any new bride though. I'm afraid to say it, but we haven't always seen eye to eye about you."

I gave Yuki's hand a squeeze, "We should have at least a week of travel until we reach our new site, and Lirae will not expect us for two to three weeks yet. At the moment she is keeping the money flowing in the capital Letheros making sure the proper permits and visas are provided for our business. I can arrange for perhaps two weeks of our camping honeymoon in relative privacy my dear, and then it will be back to work for us."

Yuki looked pensive, "Working with Lirae?"

I nodded, "Of course. She still has tactical control over our situation after all. It would be hard for us to work apart from her for too long. Remember I am just covering the planning. The execution of our plan is still up to Lirae."

wo weeks of leisurely and relatively uneventful travel later Yuki, Balinac and I finally arrived at our future construction site. I was pleased to see that the local workers hired had begun with setting up the work camp for the first set of imported laborers on the project. This consisted of a temporary simple lumber and canvas bunkhouse to provide beds as well as a small indoor recreation area for the imported workers.

I also saw that a camp wagon kitchen had also been acquired to provide meals to the imported laborers. Even though the first imported labor was not due to start arriving for at least one week I was impressed with the initiative taken by the locally hired labor manager.

The location of our property was a good one for our purposes. Along the road ahead at the far end of the valley from the point we entered was the narrow choke point which demarcated the transition between this portion of Letheron and the wild lands on the other side. There was a minimal border station consisting of a well fortified structure alongside the road at that point, but more notably there was a series of very tall trees lining the road with platforms above the road creating a clear fire position onto the road surface. While that point would not hold against a dedicated siege assault for any significant length of time, it would certainly be able to put second thoughts into any group of typical wild lands strike and flee raiders.

A fair haired elf watched us approach the work camp and whistled out a bird call to the nearby workers. Several of them stopped working to look in our direction. A well dressed elf with short blond hair stepped out of the bunkhouse and casually ran over to approach our position. He waved at us in a friendly gesture, and stopped in front of me. I looked at him for a moment, and remembered my etiquette training. I leaned in until my forehead lightly touched his.

His smile lit up his face as we parted, "My name is Phini Intos. It is good to finally see you arrive. We were told to expect you soon Master Mica and Mistress Yuki. Mistress Lirae told me that you should be arriving any week now."

I smiled back in return, "It is good to meet you as well Phini Intos. You'll have to excuse our absence for these past weeks, but I have been in transit from our company offices. I take it that you are the work site captain hired by Mistress Lirae."

Phini nodded, "I have been hired from Letheros to supervise the construction of the work camp and the local elf labor force you have contracted. I have a working knowledge of the land in this region, and can take you on a tour of the property when you are ready."

I replied, "That sounds like a good plan. Perhaps you could introduce us to the workers here first, and a break for lunch afterward will be in order before I tour the property. You'll have to forgive my lack of knowledge regarding construction. I am more of a general project manager you understand. Several architects have been retained by the Isle Company to help with the design and ascetic of the property."

Phini led us over to the work crew and called them over for introductions by the kitchen wagon. I maintained a genial manner as each of them was introduced to Yuki and I. I carefully observed their reactions as they interacted with Yuki. Most of them seemed relatively unimpressed or disinterested by her in general. Two of them showed an awkward discomfort in her presence. Another two showed her a touch of outright disregard for her presence. In particular I marked the names and faces of the three that reacted with a hastily concealed negative expression when, as Yuki and I had planned, I moved to hold her hand after the introductions were finished.

I thought the locals comprising the work group were generally nice but included several misinformed elves. I had figured in advance that several Reminas sympathizers would be among my earliest labor sources. I even considered that one or more might be direct Reminas spies recruited out of the local employees. I wasn't sure yet which ones worked for Reminas directly. Any or all of them could be considered suspicious at this point. I couldn't help but give a smile.

I could see that my plan was working already. Reminas' faction was looking to dissuade us from beginning this project. His associates had planted future trouble makers among our work forces, just like with Captain Robert's ship the Mystic Dawn I was sure that Lirae had carefully chosen Phini as a construction captain who was sympathetic to our basic philosophy if in the dark on our real goals.

Yuki and I sat through an early lunch with the crew and found that the cook hired to feed the work crew was quite adept at preparing the locally favored recipes. I reminded myself to inquire if he would like a more permanent position in our inn after we had completed construction.

After our lunch Phini showed Yuki, Balinac and I the major features of the property we had purchased. The primary feature which interested me was the fact that our property extended to the road, could support some future gardens between the road and the relatively large if not extremely tall hill. It wouldn't make an ideal location for a typical Ard style keep as the slopes were not steep enough, but I was assured that due to the location near the edge of the valley the hill had a relatively light cover of topsoil over fairly solid stone. The property also lacked an obvious fresh water source, but the other side of the valley across the road from our property had a stream.

The valley as a whole was primarily covered in a loose collection of tall older trees and a fair amount of younger saplings which had likely sprung up after a fire had at one point in the past cleared the middle level trees and brush. Small signs of the fire could be seen still, but it looked like at least a dozen years had passed since the event. Lirae had chosen a site well to meet our needs.

I came down the hill again with Phini looking toward me with an expectant expression. Yuki carried Balinac who seemed to be napping in her arms. I looked around the site in anticipation of what the completed project might look like when we had finished.

I spoke to Phini before we approached the work camp, "Do we have any foresters present in your work crew?"

Phini paused, "Do you intend to cut down some trees for your building and gardens?"

I looked back at him, "Certainly not my good elf. I may have been raised in Ard, but I have more respect for Letheron than to callously destroy her heritage. I do intend to relocate many of the saplings to a more ascetic location and to make room for our ground structures. The main trees on the hill shall be the focal point for our Reading Dragon Inn. The architects will consider how to best incorporate their use in the structure. We can however see that the non-structural smaller and younger trees are relocated to a more suitable growing location for the time being. This is not going to be a rush job. No damage shall be done to anything growing here without very careful consideration of need first."

Phini blew out an unintentionally held breath, "I am glad to hear it. This valley was hit hard several years ago by fire. The locals may have objected to any wholesale cutting of the new growth or the old giants. I'm glad to understand that this won't be a point of friction with the local inhabitants."

I shrugged, "There will likely always be points of contention between us and the people living here already. I don't think we need to add any unnecessary new ones through poor management of the land."

Phini had a serious look on his face, "You have noticed already have you?"

I nodded, "Certain people on the crew have made their dislike of my choice of spouse clear through their expressions."

Phini ducked his head, "It may put us a little behind schedule to find replacements for them, but I will see that they are dismissed."

I raised a hand and looked at him, "On the contrary my good elf, before we dismiss anyone from the work crew you assembled I want your assessment on their work ethic and the quality of their performance."

Phini raised his head, "Master Mica?"

I smiled, "If I fired everyone who might dislike me or my spouse I would never get any work done. What matters to me is whether they can work with us around their dislike. As long as they put in a good days work, and don't cause any issues among the other work crew, I really don't care what their personal opinions of me are."

Phini smiled back and replied, "I have only started work one week ago with them so my evaluation would be premature at this time. However, they each came with good references, and have no record of poor behavior in the local community. There are no drunkards, or slackers in the lot of them."

I nodded, "Very well then. Please report any signs of poor performance to me personally while I am staying on the job site, but I will leave it to you to direct their individual labors and assignments as you know them best. I suggest completing the work camp in time for the arrival of the imported labor. The second task shall be the construction of a longer term kitchen and dining area near the road side of the property. Focus on relocating any smaller trees and saplings in the way of a suitable location. When the architects and planners arrive we will become more directed in our actions."

Phini nodded, "I will direct the men as you have ordered. Do you also want quarters set up for you and your wife?"

I smiled, "Yes, eventually that will be required, but the kitchen and dining room will be first, and then followed by a suitable bathing facility. We can make due with our travel tent until that task is done. The weather should remain fair enough until then."

Two weeks later we had completed the construction of the temporary work camp and moved enough of the trees and saplings to create room for a more permanent kitchen and dining facility near the roadway. Most of the small trees and saplings in that area had been moved by Phini's work crew and planted near the southern edge of the property. They were spaced in the beginning of a sixteen foot wide lane leading west around the hill to turn gradually north along the base to the side of the hill furthest from the road.

The elfish architect Samus and the elfish engineer Jarkon had arrived and the last three days had been spent by us reviewing the property, taking measurements, and making preliminary decisions where the structures would be placed on the property. The initial kitchen and restaurant would be the basis of our future dining establishment, and would be constructed in the local style. There would be a cold cellar constructed below the building first using the dwarf labor force when it arrived. Yuki's initial location would be the restaurant, and she would oversee all of the food production for our full work crew there when it was completed.

We also planned for a path leading from the road past our restaurant to a partial ring around the base of the hill. Along the lower slopes of the hill on the south, east, and north sides a series of shops would be set up with a retail space on the main floor, and a residential space on the second floor. We looked to accommodate six shops in this fashion so that the buildings could be fairly sizable without crowding each other.

On the west side of the hill where the lane led furthest from the road would be the carriage house and stables. Several trees would need to be relocated to accommodate the various structures there, but each of the major trees could still be incorporated into the design at that point. Facilities for a full service smithy and a wheelwright would also be provided, in addition to a cooper for constructing kegs, barrels, and other food storage containers.

The major feature of the property was to be the Reading Dragon Inn complex. The construction on the Inn would begin after the smithy and stables were constructed so that we could do a lot of our material production and tool maintenance using those facilities. The inn proper would sit on the top of the hill and incorporate the seven major trees there as features in its architecture. It would include elfin style housing among the branches of the trees in addition to a ground level common room, library, tavern, offices, meeting rooms, human style rooms, and a kitchen. Instead of being one large structure it would be based on radial spokes off the common room kitchen structure on the east side of the hill.

The space on the top of the hill not occupied by structures would be a combination small park and ornamental gardens. The area of land between the restaurant by the road and the base of the hill would be a set of working elfin style gardens. In between the trees would be orderly planting of various consumable vegetables in the portions bordering the northern section of our path to the hill. South of the path between the path and the lane to the stables would be our vineyards. I knew that we were going to need to get into the wine business if we were to ever be taken seriously in the production of elfin cuisine.

Finally, the western end of the property extended down to a slightly marshy low point, then eventually rose to a fair way up the valley wall. The marshy area we desired to convert to a rice paddy if the soil and weather permitted us to grow that crop. The area between the marshy area and the stables would grow a rotating combination of wheat, barley, hops, oats, and hay. Short of raising any farm animals we would be nearly self sufficient in terms of basic foodstuff production. We lacked sufficient meadow lands for grazing any significant herds of herbivores.

The far western side of our property would be where Yuki and I would have a home while we were in residence. It would also be the official Letheron headquarters for the Isle Corporation and a lookout point over our facility. It was also going to be built as the safe house for Thomas' employees. It would resemble a moderately sized human chateau on the outside, but it would eventually be fortified like a dwarf kingdom in the secure areas built into the stone of the valley wall underneath the structure.

For the moment we were going to have the dwarf work crew quarry any stone needed for the site from that location. We picked the least obtrusive point available to set up the mine, and with a dear price had already gained the necessary permits to mine or quarry any stone necessary for structural support and decoration of our facility. It wouldn't be a human style surface quarry, and our permits did not allow us to produce any metal ores or gems.

I had already arranged to provide a source for disposing of the waste tailing left over from our quarry operation so that we didn't produce an undesired slag pile on our site. The Isle Corporation would be helping to fund a road reconstruction effort in that portion of Letheron. Our waste stone would be crushed to gravel and used to repair the condition of any roads requesting it within a several mile radius. We would start by putting labor on improving the main road leading up to our facility from the border, and eventually spread out from there.

However, before that quarry was put into operation our dwarf engineers would be directed to plan for a series of cold storage rooms under the hill. Additionally they would design and build a suitable set of luxury accommodations to suit dwarfs and other subsurface dwellers beneath the hill. Suitable ventilation and lighting would be provided for this effort, but no underground smithy, smelter or forge would be built. I knew that the smell of a dwarf work production operation might be offensive to any guests.

As I had negotiated this general vision with Samus and Jarkon they had initially objected to the concept of integrating their familiar elfin design elements with elements of human and dwarf architecture. The underground storerooms they agreed to, but the dwarf style underground housing in particular disturbed their sensibilities. They complained of it potentially disturbing the great trees on the hill.

I had finally resorted to acting disappointed in their lack of architectural vision. I simply informed them that I would hate to need to rely on the dwarf engineers for the entire design of the project. I told them that if they couldn't produce the design which met my requirements, then I would be forced to pay them for their time so far and look for design resources elsewhere. They backed off on their complaints and agreed to creating the design for the elf and human portions of the structures, and creating the interface to that design where the dwarf engineers could take over on designing the cold storage and subterranean rooms.

The arrival of the dwarf engineers Irli and Taprock produced interesting results. The dwarf engineers themselves were professionals used to working with various races, and willing to travel to provide their services. They knew their business well, and were often hired by dukes, barons, and other nobility in Ard for their projects. However, they didn't come at a cheap price. This particular set of engineers and their work crew my research determined was capable, flexible, and innovative in their approach. They were not considered the best in the business by dwarf standards, but their crew had a reputation for being thick skinned and not prone to arguments or fights when verbally provoked.

I greeted Irli and Taprock on their arrival and got them settled down. I walked over the high level concept we had for the facility, and their contribution to it. They seemed agreeable to the overall approach, but began making suggestions for improvements in the design of the storage area in addition to the dwarf rooms. They suggested reversing the positions of the coach house and stables placing the coach house closest to the base of the hill. They explained that way deliveries could be made straight from the coach house to a tunnel into the hill leading to the lower storage rooms.

Next they recommended the forge and coopers buildings should be placed behind the stables and built of relatively low stone construction to prevent any fires from jumping to other structures on the property by mistake. The stone carved from the restaurant basement storage area could be the start of that material along with the stone carved from the initial tunnels under the hill. They agreed that any other stone required could be carved out from the quarry I wanted at the far western end of the property.

They then suggested that a double lift system be developed. One lift designed to bring goods up from the storage room areas to the top of the hill, while the other lift acted as a counter balance and would take passengers down to the dwarf living areas. They suggested that all of these areas be constructed level with the base of the hill with only the lift and an adjoining interior staircase leading to the top. It seemed that they concurred with the elf architect and engineer that putting the dwarf dwellings too high in the hill might interfere with the great trees on top of the hill.

They also pointed out that shortlings preferred surface entrance windowed burrows, and that they could design a series of them at the bottom of the hill on one side or another, but that they would like to consult with the elf architect to make sure it would not interfere with elements of their design. They said that creating a cold storage room below the restaurant would not be a problem, but they thought I had neglected to provide proper water distribution to the overall location.

When I discussed the nearby stream across the road on the other side of the valley, they both shrugged and noted that many an estate failed to prosper when water rights were not properly reserved. They noted that my proposed garden designs would call for a lot of water to support especially with so many water thirsty trees nearby. They suggested a dwarf designed underground aqueduct and water distribution system which could be put in place at a high cost, but which would provide potable water taken from the underground water source creating the marshy area at the west of the property. It would be even more reliable in dry weather than the surface stream on the other side of the valley.

Finally they suggested a dwarf designed water feature which would pump water from the aqueduct reservoir to the top of the hill using concealed pipes following the passage cut for the lift and stairs. The water could then be used for the kitchen, a smaller hilltop reservoir, a fountain or two, and a trickling rill flowing down the hill next to the path which would feed into a subtle irrigation system for the gardens. The water could also be sent to the restaurant kitchen. They would leave it to the elf architect to design the ornamental visible parts of the system, but would make it work as we desired.

When I told them that the estimated price for the upgrade was going to require approval from the company accountants they nodded in a knowledgeable way asking whether our accountant was a gnome. When I told them yes they got glum expressions on their faces and offered to cut down on some of the unnecessary features. Up until this point the dwarf engineers seemed reasonable and easy to work alongside.

The lead engineer Irli then asked, "Now that we have the rough concept together can I ask you a question about the job organization?"

I nodded, "Please go ahead if you have any concerns."

Irli frowned, "It's about your site boss Phini."

I smiled, "Is there a problem with him?"

Irli still frowned, "He's a personable enough fellow for an elf, just as you are sir. You'll need to understand though that the dwarf work crew will object to taking direction from him."

I sat back, "I was under the impression that your work crews were able to get along with other races. It is one of the main reasons your company was subcontracted for this job."

Irli looked over at his partner Taprock who spoke, "It is just that I took a look at what he's done so far, and its pretty clear that while he may make a good motivator for the elves on your crew, his knowledge of engineering isn't worth a hill of beans if you take my meaning. As soon as he makes a mistake in directing one of our crew they will lose respect for him, and it will be nothing but gripes from them about working with amateurs after that. Elves they can handle, but amateurs make them pretty irritable."

I nodded, "I see your quandary. What do you both suggest then?"

Taprock spoke, "For a reasonable fee you could retain me as the dwarf crew site boss answering to you directly as project head. I would also recommend you retain an on site elvish engineer to make sure the labor efforts of their portion of the task are not as ramshackle as this temporary camp they have built. If you don't mind me saying, I could collapse this entire bunkhouse structure with two well placed blows of a hand axe. It simply isn't reinforced properly. That tent you have been using for your personal housing is better constructed that this. That Phini may know quite a bit about landscape management, but he knows jack little about professional building, and neither does any of these other elf crew of locals from the look of their work."

I nodded, "I will take your recommendation under advisement. However, I am already having a professional elf building crew come for the construction. Phini and his crew are hired for site preparation and assistance with the menial labor tasks during construction."

Irli smiled, "I'm glad to hear it. Our crews are known to walk away from amateur run jobs. It isn't worth the damage to their building reputation. A bad job now would show poor results for getting accepted for any work offered by someone else in the future."

I looked around the bunkhouse, "Would you kindly point out which structural weak points you could hit with an axe to bring this structure down?"

Taprock indicated the two points to me. I examined them closely, but as a non-engineer I couldn't see what flaw had caught their attention in the design.

I asked the next question, "Would an average builder even pay attention to such a flaw?"

Irli thought a moment, "I don't think that most amateur builders would notice it. Any real professional would upon examination though. It wouldn't pass even a human inspector who knew his business."

I nodded, "Could such a design flaw be deliberately put into a building?"

They both looked at me with a surprised expression and Irli spoke, "It would be easy actually. Good buildings are harder to make than poorly done ones. Doing wrong things is easy. Finding things done wrong is what is hard, and the mark of a professional."

I smiled, "Would you like a job as my construction inspector?"

Irli shook his head, "It wouldn't pass muster with me doing construction and inspecting my own work. The local authorities wouldn't accept it."

I nodded, "I know. You won't be the official inspector. You will be my personal one."

Irli smiled, "Well if you put it that way I guess I wouldn't object to drawing an inspectors pay on the job in addition to an engineers pay."

I shook my head, "Taprock will be the engineer. I want you as my full time inspector when the construction begins if that is possible."

Irli nodded, "It's possible sure. We can retain my brother Taprock here as the site engineer. He's got the brains for it. It is going to double your overhead costs for us though."

I nodded, "I think it will be worth it to detect any sabotage which might happen on the main construction effort."

Irli grinned, "Sabotage you say? This could get interesting then, of course my crew will need hazard pay if such is the case."

I smiled, "Your company can negotiate that rate with my accountants, but unless any hazards actually show up, I will instead look into insuring your men against injury or loss instead. I think it's time to have our cleric come onto the job site."

Irli looked at me, "A cleric you say?"

I nodded, "Our executive vice president in charge of business affairs is also a cleric. It will be a good idea to have her nearby in case her other talents are needed. I would appreciate it if you keep her cleric avocation to yourself. I would hate for any potential saboteur to try hurting her as she is a close friend."

Taprock looked at me, "That's an interesting business manager. Is she an elf as well then?"

I nodded, "Why, yes, she is. Although my wife Yuki is human, and she is the vice president in charge of culinary design."

Irli spoke, "Any dwarfs working for your company? I mean in addition to the elves, human, and gnome."

I smiled, "I'm sitting with two of them now."

Irli was startled a second, "I guess you are right. I hadn't thought of it that way seeing as Taprock and I both own our own company."

I nodded, "Now when can I expect to see your initial drawn concept designs and rough order of cost bid. I'd like to see it itemized by construction, quarry work, and water distribution system, along with a breakdown of materials expenses as well as labor and overhead costs by job position."

Irli smiled, "My brother and I should have your concept designs completed within the week. The final plans will require coordination with your elvish architect and engineer to make sure we are on the same page with how things fit together. As far as that financial stuff, just have your gnome accountant talk to our gnome accountant. Soon as they are done haggling each other to death we can sign the construction contract and get started on the real work."

I nodded, "That sounds good. Please don't mention the design flaw in this bunkhouse to any one else yet."

Taprock spoke, "Planning to use it as a test for their people?"

I smiled, "Something like that, I also want to find out which one either did it wrong or turned this structure into a potential trap."

Irli shrugged, "It's a wood framed canvas building. If it came down on people here it wouldn't likely kill anyone. Just bruise them up a bit."

I nodded, "How about with a foot or more of snow on the roof?"

Irli looked contemplative, "It might well come down on its own then. That much weight might cause serious damage. Who ever did this is cleverer than we had thought then. It's a long term trap then, not just a flaw in design. It wouldn't take much to put it to rights though, let us fix it before you put up any workers in here."

I nodded, "Most certainly. I just want our elvish engineer to inspect it before you change anything. I would like to see what he says."

Taprock looked at me cautiously, "Don't trust us and want a second opinion?"

I shook my head, "No, I trust you both. I just want an explanation as to why he spent three days with me in this building going over plans without him noticing it or mentioning it to me if he did notice it."

Irli nodded, "Understood. We appreciate your trust. It is a rare thing in this world at times. Now that we have mentioned your design elements do you mind if we make a business recommendation for you?"

I nodded, "I am certainly not an expert in all things, so I am open to suggestions if you have some."

Irli smiled, "That's good then. I hate working with know it all types. You've got room on this property to link your main structure and your restaurant with a service tunnel if you like. It will make running water over there easier and the transfer of goods from storage easier as well. We can also put in a customer entrance at the coach house which parallels the service entrance without too much trouble. That way your fancy customers can go right from their coach through the passage to the lift. It wouldn't take much to fancy up the stonework in the customer entrance to make it nice and all."

Taprock spoke at that point, "We noticed that you are having a coopers shop behind the stables for barrels and kegs and such, but that you are only planning a winery. If you are going to attract more than elves to your facility, might we also recommend outfitting an area of your subsurface facility as a brewery and a distillery as well as storage and a winery. The room is there, and it will allow the production of a variety of beverages to appeal to your customers. Such things tend to be expensive to ship past border points due to the tariffs involved in those items. If your local sales are light, you can sell your excess to other places for their use under your label."

I smiled, "Those both sound like reasonable options, list them as such in your bid if you will then."

Chapter 40 Plotting

Late that evening I discussed the findings of Irli and Taprock with Yuki. She listened intently and smiled when I mentioned the structural flaw in the worker's temporary quarters. I leaned back on our double cot and looked at her delighted expression.

I looked at her with a little grin as well, "This pleases you?"

Yuki gave a light laugh, "Of course it does my dear. It means that things are proceeding according to your plan already. One or more of the sympathizers of Reminas' philosophy has made a move. It also means that the elvish engineer Jarkon is either compromised or too stupid to do his job right."

I shook my head, "There is another likely excuse here. I am tending to believe he noticed the mistake, and did not want to call it out as it would make the local eleven laborers look bad. They probably did not realize that it was a deliberate error just as Irli and Taprock didn't realize it. Neither Samus or Jarkon was on site before the worker's quarters structure was completed after all."

Yuki shrugged, "Either way it is not going to lead us to identify the culprit unless they deliberately try to spring the trap when the dwarf work crew arrives."

I shrugged, "I mainly want to test Samus and Jarkon to see if they are more loyal to their employer or their culture. I can always get a different set of engineers if these two won't work out. However, I would like to not have anyone springing traps or raising up the heat before we have a secured location built for defense. Our work forces are a bit vulnerable now."

Yuki smiled, "Thus the cold cellars first then."

I gave her hand a squeeze, "Then the tunnel to the construction under the hill. I want all of the overt work completed by the legitimate crews before we bring the specialists in for the extra features. The extra work should be easy to conceal during the finishing phase of construction. It will look like a simple continuation of our quarry operations to improve the roads in the area."

Yuki leaned back as well, "How is it going with having either Lionette or Yastalus assigned to this border post?"

I shrugged, "No luck so far. I think Lirae is having problems in getting traction with convincing the government agencies to do anything that radical. I think the request is going to have to come from one of them. We have to be careful to not push too hard for it because we don't want Reminas' faction to view them as compromised in performing their duties. I don't doubt that they wield much more political influence than we do at this time. It is only by remaining above board and playing by the rules that we will be able to make eventual inroads into his power. He has to be the first one seen as overtly violating them."

Yuki placed her hand on my chest, "What will you do then?"

I smiled, "I'll have a little meeting with our engineers tomorrow. I also want to hear from Phini which of our crew was responsible for the design and construction of the structure. I'm beginning to suspect that he is not as useful as Lirae thought when she hired him."

Yuki placed her hand other hand on her forehead, "It's a good idea to question him. I would consider doing it first before the elvish engineers. Based on the comments of the dwarf engineers I suspect that it's possible that he's another kind of professional."

I caught on quickly to her implication, "You're thinking a paid saboteur for Reminas' group? You think he is someone who is not a believer, and thus prone to reveal their sentiments."

Yuki shrugged, "I don't think he is necessarily the saboteur. I do think it possible he is a professional spy. His position gives him an opportunity to know a lot of what is going on here in addition to free movement over the facility. It is unclear just whose spy he may be though. I would not count out factions other than Reminas' followers being interested in our activity."

I thought a bit about the concept, "It could be the regular government, competing businesses, or even a rival faction to Reminas' group. Any of these might have good cause to investigate our actions. I still would not count out Reminas as a possible employer, but I think your estimation of spy is likely correct. Do you know if he can listen in on our conversations here Balinac?"

Balinac spoke from where she was curled up by my feet, "I am monitoring his position at the moment. He is at his home and not using any overt magical means of monitoring you. However, I am not adept at detecting magical emanations of that nature. It is certainly possible he could be using a subtle magical device which allows him to focus on and monitor nearby individuals. There is also the possibility that divine means of monitoring are occurring without my knowledge. I am shielded from such interference, but I am not certain if that protection extends to you both as well."

I mulled over this condition for a while, "We really could use Glorandel and his privacy spell at this point. I guess we will have to treat any of our conversations in the last two weeks as potentially compromised. I can't recall anything that would be too damaging being said in that time. It would be good if we could set up an alternate meeting place. Are you certain your responses can not be monitored Balinac?"

Balinac purred, "I know that we greater spirits generate a lot of magical and divine interference with our auras. It is part of the side effect of being a Number and a greater spirit. However, we generally have no direct control over how that interference impacts such things. Thus I am certain of nothing, but fairly sure that I create a minor scrying exclusion zone where I am present. It would take a pretty strong power to overcome that effect. Reminas and his forces would not be able to achieve such without divine backing or a very accomplished arcane caster."

I lay back on the cot next to Yuki, "I was afraid of that. The Luck speculated that a power might be backing Reminas, or at least his position. We need to set up a more secure location to talk somehow."

Balinac batted my foot, "You should have passed that information along earlier. It would have made me pay closer attention for signs of such. Of course it is pretty simple to guarantee a position where only friendly powers can listen in on us."

Yuki rubbed her bare toes on Balinac's back, "Good thinking kitty. Just gate us over to the plane of shadow. Nothing you don't want listening to us can observe you there correct?"

Balinac arched her back into Yuki's foot, "You are very correct. The White Raven can listen to what you say, as well as Cordane if he chooses to because of the connections they have with the both of you. So can the Lucky Cricket of course. Is there anything else the Luck told you Mica which might be relevant to discuss now?"

I gently slapped my forehead, "I didn't think about it because it is really the whole point behind why we are here. The Luck said that it seems that another power might be backing Lirae. It didn't reveal which power, but it might well have been holding back or uncertain about it. It said she had placed a spirit ribbon on me which indicated a subtle power behind it."

Balinac suddenly stood up and jumped off the cot, "Another power behind this mission? This does not seem like such a good idea anymore. Thomas does not work for beings he does not know about. Either he knows what this being is, and is making deals with it, or else we are caught in a subtle warfare such as played by the great powers. Please wait one moment while I check with the Luck and transport myself to Lirae's position."

I looked over at Yuki who smiled back at me as I spoke, "I'm afraid that we may have gotten in deeper than we realized."

Yuki hugged and kissed me with a smile, "One step at a time my love. Nothing is fully under your control. Do you still feel this mission has the right goals?"

I thought about it, "I would not have agreed to do it if that was not the case."

Yuki kissed me again, "Then don't worry about what may be happening behind the scenes so much. Concentrate on what you can manage, and hope the Luck is on your side. Remember it is up to Lirae to implement the tactical portion of the mission. Your job is to make sure the setting is what it should be for her to do her job."

Balinac looked over at the two of us on the cot together, "I am waiting to see the Luck, and there is no sign of Lirae in Letheros. I am expanding my search area in case she is traveling somewhere. One moment please."

Yuki looked at me, "How can Balinac search all of Letheros so quickly?"

Balinac jumped back on the cot and lay down at Yuki's feet, "It is called shadow sight. I can look from any shadow in an area. Given enough time I can cover a lot of ground. This isn't good though. There is not any sign of Lirae on her way here. She is no longer in Letheron on the prime. That means she is likely in the Fey Realm portion of Letheron."

I asked the obvious question, "Could she be dead?"

Balinac shook her head, "I would have been able to see that on the plane of shadow. Her spirit would have released and been on its way to Thomas' tower."

Yuki asked, "Could her spirit have been captured by someone?"

I thought back to the room in Thomas' tower full of white marble pedestals with large diamonds or rubies floating over them, "I think that is a definite possibility. I take it that with the right abilities or tools such a thing could be done."

Balinac nodded, "It is true. Divine beings or the Numbers could certainly capture and detain a spirit. Other powers might be able to if they know the tricks involved. However, I didn't see any signs of struggle in her quarters in Letheros. I would give better odds that she is fine, but handling some business in the Fey Realm."

The beginnings of a suspicion formed in my mind and I asked, "Could you tell me which powers are associated with the Fey Realm in particular, Balinac?"

Balinac rubbed up against Yuki's feet, "All of the elvish deities of course. Even Litha still has connections there. Most of the other fey deities as well, so those beings worshiped by sprites, fairies and so forth."

I nodded, "Are there any Numbers associated with both the Fey Realm and the Prime?"

Balinac's eyes narrowed, "That would be Number Three of course. I should have realized earlier. It is no wonder the Luck is dodging me about this issue. If Number Three is getting involved with Thomas, then something is happening to change the playing field. Number Three and the Luck have a tenuous relationship at best. Number Three and myself are generally not close either, it disagreed with the length of the mortal spans I wanted to assign to the elves. It gave the elves a shortcut method to extend their existence on the prime."

Yuki asked, "What shortcut method was that?"

Balinac switched its tails rapidly, "It allows them to transition to the Fey Realm at several locations. The Fey Realm was designed by Number Three to stop the clock for their spiritual decay while they are there. It also blocks my interference since I could not normally travel there without assistance from a power which has access to the Fey Realm."

I asked, "What would happen to the balance of higher powers if the elves moved from the prime and settled more permanently in the Fey Realm?"

Balinac shook its head, "It would please some of the elvish deities certainly as they would get more direct influence over their worshipers. It would offend other deities because they would also want similar concessions for their followers. I would not agree to change those rules again, and it would draw several powers into various sides of the conflict."

I nodded, "So it seems that for the moment Number Three is likely working to prevent this from happening, because it doesn't want to draw the issue into contention once more, and possibly lose the advantage in long lives the elves maintain. Balinac please tell me which Number would benefit from a conflict of this level, the kind of conflict which causes chaos and allows various rules to come into debate."

Balinac licked Yuki's toe, "There are two different Numbers which would be ideally positioned at this point to seek an advantage for their position under those conditions. They are the Number Thirteen and the Number Seven."

I nodded, "Is it possible those two are working together?"

Balinac shook its head, "It is very unlikely. They have been in bitter discord with each other for over three thousand years."

I smiled, "Which one of them is more likely to make a bargain with Number Three?"

Balinac licked Yuki's toe again, "Either one would do so if it were to their advantage. The better question is which one would Number Three trust to keep their bargain. From my own experience I would trust the Luck many times more than Number Thirteen. I can not guarantee that Number Three would agree with that sentiment especially since I have joined ranks with the Luck's alliance."

I placed my finger to my lips, "What if the Luck is not directly in negotiations with Number Three? What if the Luck taught Thomas how to get in touch with it?"

Balinac shrugged, "I would have caught onto it. I keep a pretty close eye on Thomas' actions on the Prime and the Plane of Shadow."

I nodded, "How about when you were distracted with keeping Yuki and me alive, and if they met instead in the dreaming?"

Balinac paced back and forth, "I would suspect that someone was going around behind my back and might get upset about it."

I smiled, "Would you really be all that upset?"

Balinac rubbed up against my feet, "Not that upset after all. The disagreement I had with Number Three was a very long time ago after all, since before the race of elves or the Fey Realm existed. I don't retain any grudge after this much time, but I think I still intimidate Number Three to a degree. It might still also find doing business with me distasteful for what I initiated all those thousands of years ago."

I grinned a bit, "What could you have done that was distasteful?"

Balinac jumped up onto my chest and lay on Yuki's hand there, "I showed the twiline queen Litha how to corrupt the some of the elves so that they would fight over rightful position in the Fey Realm. More elf spirits moved through the cycle then and I was satisfied the final results were close enough for my original purposes. I don't think Number Three appreciated the fact that I put my own shortcut into her plans."

Yuki looked at Balinac with an expression of shock, "You started the wars between the elves and the twiline?"

Balinac shook her head, "I did no such thing. I simply provided a key piece of information on how some spirits respond to certain actions to the deity Litha when she inquired. A little application of a special shadow material of my creation would temporarily darken their spirits. I carefully regulate how much of this shadow material Litha can obtain at one time. She never gains enough to have a clear advantage, and never loses so many she is out of the game. In essence the Fey Realm has ceased being an eternal safe haven for living elves. Only elf spirits can dwell there in safety. This is why the twiline are also called the twilight elves. I would have preferred the name shadowed elves, but the goddess Litha did not care to give me credit for my generous help. Over generations she has also darkened their skin and removed their hair through divine means now, but it is the darkness of spirit that denotes a true twilight elf, not the color of their skin. There remain plenty of light skinned, long haired shadowed elves if the truth were to be known, although they are not properly called twiline."

Yuki lay back, "I thought the wars of Ran Li were hard and vicious at times. I failed to understand how these conflicts have always existed over time. Is there any way you could patch things up with Number Three? It does seem like her agenda is more in tune with your goal at the moment."

Balinac lay her head down on my chest, "I don't think Number Three wants to open up contact with me. It has been many thousands of years since we last met."

I tilted my head up to look at Balinac stretched out on my chest, "I have a sneaky suspicion that isn't the case. I think you just didn't realize it. Has the Luck or Cricket ever met Lirae?"

Balinac looked me in the eyes, "What do you know?"

I looked at Yuki, "I'm sorry I didn't bring this up earlier, but I didn't know how to tell you this. It seems that the Luck has told Balinac how to combine with a mortal spirit in a mortal form. It said that we had agreed to do so after I died and was waiting in Thomas' tower in the Plane of Shadow."

Yuki clasped my hand, "I know already. The White Raven pretty much confirmed it back in Grimvale. Your aura also gives it away to anyone who knows how to look."

Balinac purred, "I thought the Luck might have revealed it to you. I never intended it to be a secret from you, but unfortunately spirits do poorly at remembering things which happen to them in the Plane of Shadow. I thought it best that you figure it out on your own."

I nodded, "I don't mind. How could I since you are a part of me now? Had Thomas somehow distracted you when Lirae was reborn?"

Balinac nodded, "She was not processed like the rest of you had been. It also seems her spirit crystal does not remain at Thomas' tower in the Plane of Shadow anymore."

I smiled, "That was why Thomas needed you distracted with Cogstone and protecting us. He needed the time to transfer the crystal to Number Three, just as he promised to transfer my crystal to you when my task is done."

I held up my hand with my dark wedding band, "Except you have already taken steps to guarantee that Thomas doesn't have control over us."

I took off both of my rings and handed them to Yuki, "Because it seems that the Cricket has chosen to free me from both connections if I so desire."

Balinac seemed surprised, "You frightened me for a moment. I thought you had just killed your body by loosing your spirit. It seems I have underestimated the Cricket. I forget that he is learning much from the Luck, yet still has his own personality, just as you retain your own."

I took my rings back from Yuki and placed them on my hands again, "For now I will keep them in place since I still owe Thomas a debt as well as you Balinac. I will also keep your wedding band in place as it was a gift from you in addition to the symbol of my commitment to Yuki."

Balinac purred, "It also allows me to come to you anywhere you are. The trick I can perform is that anywhere part of my mass is the rest can easily follow."

I smiled, "Even to the Fey Realm?"

Balinac purred while nodding, "Most certainly. The Luck was telling me the truth when it said that true material connections would have advantages as well as the disadvantages it suffers."

I asked, "What disadvantages?"

Balinac placed her head down on my chest again, "Feelings for one. They are difficult to manage for Greater Spirits. It also causes changes in personality in the Greater Spirits over the centuries. I have observed that the mortal spirit personality in the body tends to change the Greater Spirit. I was very careful to pick a spirit I could agree with when I merged. Number Nine was not so wise when it first discovered this trick. Number Seven watched its mistake, and more carefully selected his host based on his desired traits. Thomas came up with a combination in you that was most suitable for my desires."

I nodded, "Thank you for your confidence."

Yuki petted Balinac as she spoke, "I take it that Lirae is the being with whom Number Three has decided to merge. Thomas has likely arranged for a connection to be made in his tower to the Fey Realm. Number Three has given him a space to perform his forbidden research there in exchange for helping Number Seven and getting the secret to merging with a physical form. Balinac serves as the trusted auditor who has to remain administratively clear of the action while the Luck has arranged for you to receive to ability to make a plausible denial for Thomas' behavior if he is caught in the act."

Balinac purred, "That is why I like you so my Mica and Yuki. Both of you can keep up with the devious plots of even the Numbers. There are some gods who have troubles following this much."

I spoke, "Let's keep focusing on our mundane task here for now. Getting this place up and functional is still important. We'll keep trying to locate Lirae through her Letheros contacts. If it's true she is bound to Number Three, then she can probably extricate herself from any minor trouble. If we don't manage to re-establish contact with her in two weeks, then we consider our options for traveling to the Fey Realm to find her."

Balinac looked as if she was going to speak, but suddenly went limp on my chest. Yuki looked at me with a raised eyebrow. I shrugged my shoulders in return and reached down to stroke Balinac's form gently. She was still cool to my touch, but seemingly lifeless at the moment.

I looked at Yuki, "I don't know what's going on. I don't feel any threat, but it seems like Balinac's consciousness has left us for the moment. Let's give her some time, but what seems to be happening from the spiritual perspective."

Yuki closed her eyes briefly and then looked at Balinac's kitten form and at me, "Your aura is still fully blended with Balinac, but the cat form here no longer has an aura or spirit connection to it. I am only linked to your ring at the moment. Something is causing her to focus extremely elsewhere I imagine. This worries me some."

I touched my dark wedding ring to the body of the cat spread limp on my chest. The form evaporated into shadowy mist. I stood up along with Yuki and drew my saber as she grabbed her kitchen knife and magic skillet.

I felt an unusual sensation, "Let's step outside to get some more room. I think we have company coming in a moment."

Yuki and I saw two figures step from the shadows of nearby trees as we left the tent. We took up a quick defensive posture, but I noticed Yuki drop her guard immediately. I saw what appeared to be two pale skinned humans with several ritual tattoos along with stylized piercing in their ears, lips, noses, and eyebrows. Yuki sheathed her kitchen knife and gently touched my arm.

I looked at them, "Allies?"

Yuki nodded, "They are servants of the White Raven. Let's hear them out."

The one closest to me bowed then spoke, "The White Raven has learned of an impending attack on you. It seems possible an unknown power has engaged both the greater spirit Number Two and Number Seven in the dreaming. They appear to have withdrawn from the planes of material existence save for their avatars. In cooperation with their alliance agreement the White Raven has sent us to escort you to a safe position until the attack is over."

I looked over at Yuki who raised an eyebrow in return, "I see. Do you have any more information than this?"

The figure closest to me shook his head, "We were rapidly dispatched with minimal preparation. We were instructed to offer you sanctuary under the White Raven until some clarity as to the events happening outside of her knowledge can be obtained."

I sheathed my saber, "Can we have a couple of minutes to gather our things before we depart?"

The second figure shook its head, "I am blocking an attempt by unknown parties to gate to this vicinity even now. I am sorry, but we must depart immediately as my efforts will not last long."

Yuki spoke, "What about the local denizens here? They should be warned."

The first one spoke as it waved to a shadow gate which materialized before us, "They will most likely follow you after we go through the gate. It is best to meet them on ground the White Raven has already prepared."

I grabbed Yuki's hand as we stepped through the darkness of the gate together.

Chapter 41 Shadow into the Fey Realm

I was a bit surprised to find that we were in the main room of Thomas' tower on the plane of shadow. The gate closed behind us as the second shadowine minion of the White Raven stepped through after us. In front of us was an elaborate throne upon which sat a twelve foot tall white robed female figure with pale skin, dark hair, and icy blue eyes. Thomas knelt on one knee with bowed head before the throne, and Yuki and I quickly followed suit kneeling where we had first entered.

Both shadowine began an elaborate ritual casting for several minutes. They appeared worn and tired at the end, but the White Raven nodded at them and waved them to her side when they completed it.

A strange voice echoed through the air as the White Raven spoke in the divine tongue. A moment later my mind perceived a translated interpretation of the language.

The message roughly came out in my mind as, "I am the White Raven, goddess of dead spirits, goddess of winter. I have held to our alliance once more avatar of the greater spirit Number Two. Grant me eternal reign as the goddess of death, and such shall be the length of the alliance. Bind in place the demon Mortis such that he never prospers, and my cooperation will remain yours. I grant you continued use of my favored servant Thomas."

Thomas spoke up, "Pardon my interruption White Raven, but I am under the impression the avatars of the Numbers are not like those of divine beings. They remain semi-mortal, and thus the connection is somewhat one sided. While it is likely the Number being addressed can hear you, the local avatar can not properly answer in their absence."

The White Raven spoke again with the subsequent delayed mental translation, "The ritual is complete. The alliance remains intact. I have served my role as agreed in this contingency. I will return now to my palace. Avatar of Number Two I request you to look after my disciple as agreed. You are bound by me together as one until such time as all such bonds fade. Dear Thomas, I offer my gratitude once more for drawing out the forces of Mortis for my destruction. I will continue to overlook what you have done and the other bargains you have made."

The figure of the White Raven and her throne dissipated into nothingness. The two shadowine minions looked at us with empty expressions. Thomas rose from his kneeling position and shook his head briefly. Yuki and I stood as well.

Thomas looked at us and spoke, "I hope that went as well as I thought. It is hard to fully trust this kind of translation magic. Too many concepts can get lost. For example I wasn't certain if the Queen was asking you to renew your alliance, reminding you of the terms of the alliance, or simply expressing her wishes to never lose her position. It is very difficult to know when Balinac is not on hand to give its interpretation. At least she seems to have arranged for your protection and was pleased with the results of her latest conflict with Mortis."

I looked briefly at Yuki, and then spoke to Thomas, "Do you know what is happening?"

Thomas shook his head, "Not exactly, but I am pretty sure I know someone who does. It is possible that Balinac's direct involvement in thwarting Mortis' minions has raised some issues among the other Numbers. However, I have no idea how such things are normally resolved among beings of that nature, but it seems most likely to be the case that Balinac and the Luck have been called to answer for what happened. It would explain their evident disappearance from the material planes."

I shook my head, "They are not the only ones to disappear. I have lost contact with Lirae as well."

Thomas had begun to walk down the staircase to his laboratory, and then looked back at me, "Is that so?"

I nodded, "Balinac could not locate her on the prime."

Thomas smiled, "I think I understand why Balinac seemed so distracted moments before she vanished. You have been tasking her pretty hard."

Yuki and I followed Thomas down the stairs, "I wasn't aware it could be done."

Thomas laughed, "It is something I've learned about the greater spirits which have assumed avatar states over the centuries. They gain new abilities, and yet they lose some things as well. For example the Luck lost its ability to physically manifest on the prime. Now it can still spiritually manifest there, but it only has the physical form of Cricket. Balinac alternately has apparently lost some of her ability to multi task across the planer boundaries. The more she acts in multiple forms on the prime, the greater her distraction here in the plane of shadow. The opposite is also true. As you have likely guessed I have used that small flaw to my advantage."

Yuki had a little frown as she spoke, "Is she in danger?"

Thomas chuckled, "Not from anything physical. You should understand that normally her physical form is simply a convenience for interaction with physical beings. The Numbers are greater spirits after all. Within the dreaming is ultimately where their true selves reside. As Cricket once told me, all else is projection and perception. It is one of the reasons they find the semi-mortal avatar state so attractive."

I spoke, "When will we be able to return? I'd like to get back to my assignment soon."

Thomas shrugged his shoulders as we continued further down the stairs, "I really could not say my dear Mica. With the disappearance of Balinac all shadow gates created by her have ceased to function to or from the plane of shadow. It seems they are intimately tied to her presence here. Only a divine being or another Number can move a material object to or from the plane of shadow at the moment. I imagine quite a few arcane practitioners throughout the planes are quite baffled right now. To the best of my considerable knowledge on the subject such a thing has never happened since Balinac created the plane of shadow you understand. Only spirits can transition back and forth at the moment. I am sure this is a kind of fail safe mechanism in the nature of this plane which was designed by Balinac. It goes along with Balinac making an agreement with each god or goddess of death to exercise certain contingencies during its unplanned absence. Lucky for you she thought to make sure you were provided sanctuary here. I'm under the impression that something was hot on your trail after Balinac's disappearance."

I grew worried, "What will happen with our mission in our absence?"

Thomas smiled, "I'll release you from any responsibility for any resulting failures. Acts of the gods and such can be decidedly hard to counter after all. Even I have had to start over again occasionally when faced with enough divine resistance. It's nothing to be ashamed of to admit when you are out of your depth after all. It even happens to the gods sometimes. What else can mere mortal beings expect in a situation of this nature? However, I will let you know that I have already initiated my own contingency planning. Even though we must remain on the plane of shadow as guests of the White Raven, I still have the means to coordinate events elsewhere without making a material translation."

I looked at him in surprise as we reached the bottom of the stairs, "You do?"

Thomas gave me a wink, "Don't you think that after seven hundred years of this I have not come up with my own way of doing things that doesn't require waiting on some power to get off their behind to help me? There is a reason the White Raven considers me one of her favored minions. I am not an overly dependent or obedient one. According to Balinac I amuse her to no end with my ability to eventually circumvent any level of restrictions placed on me. How do you think I managed to get your spirit into that body by the way?"

I shrugged as we entered his interview room, "I have not the faintest clue. It seems even the numbers are confused by it."

Thomas nodded, "They are spiritually smart, much more so than me no doubt. However, they are lacking in divine and arcane wisdom. There are concepts which come naturally to many advanced material beings or even gods, and yet sometimes slip past the comprehension of the Numbers. Conversely on the opposite side of this equation, some concepts which are considered rudimentary to greater spirits are equally as bemusing to most material intelligences. That is one of the reasons the Numbers find having a semi-mortal avatar so advantageous. It gives them insights into the material, arcane, and divine aspects of existence they would not otherwise be able to grasp. They tend to learn very quickly as well."

I smiled as we entered his laboratory, "Where does that put you then?"

Thomas flipped a switch on the wall and his laboratory was lit from several glowing spheres along the ceiling, "Ideally positioned to discuss such matters with one of the first such avatars some six hundred or so years ago. I may not be as intelligent as any of these higher beings, but I can be quite creative in ways they could never anticipate."

I looked at the bizarre apparatus which dominated the central portion of the room, "What does this do?"

Thomas smiled, "It's part of one of my secret projects. You've directly experienced the result of its operation. This is the spirit injector which harnessed your dead spirit and bound it into a spirit jar. In your case I made a special mix of three spirits as an experiment on behalf of Number Two's request to merge with an acceptable avatar. Quite a few experiments were attempted, but this was the first time I could find not just two compatible and willing spirits but three willing to make the transition. I must say the result in you was most impressive, if somewhat unanticipated."

Yuki raised an eyebrow, "Why was it unanticipated?"

Thomas laughed, "Well I fully expected the elf spirit would be the dominant one in the combination as it seemed at my examination to be the most potent one. I hardly expected the human spirit to be the dominant portion of the set. Even the half-elf seemed a more likely outcome. Unfortunately, I had already prepared an elf body for the resulting combination. I do apologize for the mix up there. It really upset Lirae at first that I had somehow gotten that part wrong, but she accepted the result with grace."

I spoke, "Did you know that Balinac would choose me as her avatar?"

Thomas shook his head, "Not before I got started, but given the exemplary result of the mix which was created it certainly was not a surprise when I noticed it after the fact. Frankly speaking greater destinies as potent as Cricket before he joined with the Luck are extremely rare you understand. It took me quite a few centuries of study and experimentation to get this far."

Thomas pressed a panel on the wall and another entryway opened to a different chamber, "Careful entering here Mica. You are likely to find it somewhat disorienting at the very least, but I apologize for the necessity."

I stepped through the entryway and felt drained and weak. A buzzing noise sounded in my head and I began to feel a touch of nausea.

Yuki called out to Thomas ahead of us, "What is wrong with him?"

Thomas gave a little frown, "His spirit is being suppressed at the moment. I have a very sophisticated spiritual damper operating in this room. As a living being you won't feel anything, but beings such as Mica and me with our borrowed material forms are not made to enjoy this experience. If you take a look with your second sight you might find it enlightening, but don't take too long. We need to move on through here."

Yuki gasped, "Your aura is almost normal now. It is just around you. No spirit ribbons or other spirits can be detected. I can not see the aura of Balinac anymore."

I gasped, "It feels pretty horrible, is there a point to it?"

Thomas nodded, "Of course there is. It is a secure chamber. To the best of my knowledge we are safe from observation from any divine, arcane, or spirit bond monitoring now. In the big picture you temporarily no longer exist as far as any potential external observers are concerned. It is how I protect my trade secrets from the many other parties interested in my work. Let's move on to my other laboratory now."

Thomas walked to the opposite side of the room neglecting to explain any of the various apparatus we could see inside our current location. He pressed another wall panel. A wall section opened to reveal a magical gate which opened into a wood walled chamber. Thomas stood to the side as he waved us through.

Yuki and I stepped through into a wooden antechamber of some kind. The relief from the pressure was immediate. As my head cleared I noted that the room seemed more grown than crafted. I could hear a pair of light footsteps approaching from outside the only door. Behind us the magical gateway was gone and Thomas was nowhere to be seen.

Yuki looked at me, "Mica dear, while you appear back to normal it also appears that we are no longer on the plane of shadow."

I placed my arm gently across her shoulders, "If Thomas was telling the truth only a divine power or another number can open a gate there at the moment. I suspect that we might find out which in a moment."

A pair of armed and armored elves opened the door. Yuki and I stepped out onto a broad ledge which was attached to the trunk of a gigantic tree. I could not see the ground beneath us or the sky above us due to the density of the canopy of enormous leaves of the tree. The two elves flanked us on either side and led us to a broad staircase leading up to the higher branches and the platforms above our heads. Yuki and I climbed the stairs with our escorts just a step behind us. As we reached the top we could see a broad platform with two shaded figures seated at a small table and chairs which appeared to have grown from the platform on the far side near the edge. Two more empty chairs were at the table. Our escorts stopped at the head of the stairs and stood guard with placid faces.

As we approached the table I saw that one of the figures seated there was Lirae dressed in an elegant yet simple green gown. The other figure was a vaguely familiar white haired male elf dressed in casual yet finely crafted white clothing. The male elf stood as we approached and gestured toward the empty chairs.

I nodded as Yuki and I sat, "Many thanks. Who may I ask are our hosts today?"

Lirae opened her mouth to speak, but was interrupted by a gesture of the male elf who spoke instead, "You should recognize me even in this guise Mica."

I nodded, "The timber of your voice has confirmed my suspicions Thomas. So it seems that the numbers and the gods are no longer the only ones who can operate on multiple planes at the same time."

Thomas shook his head, "Not quite the same time actually. Due to time phase differences between the apparent versus actual reference time the passing of time can really not ever be called the same between the planes. However, your point is made that my consciousness does exist in multiple planes even if in different time phases. It is a difficult trick I am learning to perfect even now. Currently I can maintain three distinct intelligent spirit phases in separate planes or quite a few distinct intelligent spirit phases in a single plane. It is a little trick I managed to learn from observing Balinac over the years. I have revealed my capability to you now. I no longer need Balinac to believe I am only operating in one form at a time.

She has already figured out that I can transition between several material forms, and she has learned to follow my spirit transitions quite effectively after our first few years together."

I nodded again, "I think I grasp the essential concept even if understanding how you achieve it eludes me. I'm also curious to discover Lirae sitting here with you."

Yuki squeezed my hand and looked at Lirae as she spoke, "Lirae, it seems your spiritual aura is as potent as Mica's. Although the aura projected by Thomas seems a bit subdued in comparison to what I have seen previously. So I take it you are also the material avatar of a Number as well then?"

Lirae looked over at the elf, "Thomas you guaranteed me secrecy. You were not to reveal the nature of my avatar to anyone."

Thomas casually shrugged his shoulders, "It is your own fault my dear Lirae. I distinctly remember that I warned you that the children of the Luck would be unlikely to be fooled if they examined you with their second sight. You should have focused more on learning to dampen your aura as the Lucky Cricket does. I informed you it would be necessary to maintain your secret."

I spoke again looking at Lirae, "You need not blame Thomas. It was Balinac who led us to the conclusion that you were likely the avatar for a Number. Yuki has just finally confirmed our suspicion that a Number is involved in your being. Our presence in the Fey Realm now in addition to the nature of the mission you desire has led to the conclusion that you are the avatar of Number Three."

Lirae slammed a palm down on the table in front of her, "Curse that Number Two. Why does it still continue to interfere with my people and my plans? Isn't it enough that it caused the eons of strife in the Fey Realm already? Must it interfere with every plan I make?"

Thomas reached over to touch Lirae's hand momentarily as he spoke, "I don't think you need to worry about that at this immediate juncture. Balinac seems to have been recalled to the dreaming at the moment. Meanwhile Mica and Yuki here have been progressing quite satisfactorily at putting some stresses on Reminas' plans themselves."

Lirae looked over at me with a slight blush, "I apologize for my outburst. I sometimes find this form difficult. These emotional reactions have been more problematic than I first understood would be the case."

Thomas gave a gentle smile, "I did recommend you leave another greater destiny mortal spirit as the dominant personality you will recall. Inhabiting a mortal shell with only a lesser spirit is bound to have problems just as Number Nine discovered all those thousands of years ago. I also speculate that it may be drawing too much of your focus perhaps?"

Lirae gave a faint smile also, "Don't worry I am gradually learning to adapt. I don't like the idea of another spirit directing the actions of my avatar on the prime. I will endure these inconvenient emotions as best possible until I learn to master them. As you stated Thomas this form certainly contains its own advantages. My rapport with the elvish people of the Fey Realm has definitely improved. I find it much easier to influence their course of action from this more direct perspective."

Yuki looked at her quizzically, "Why is it easier as an Avatar than as a manifestation of a Number?"

Lirae gave a faint laugh, "As you may have noticed most mortals react poorly to meeting any Number which has manifested as a spiritual projection into material existence. At the very least it tends to frighten most of them silly. Only occasionally does it act as a good way to prevent direct violence. I find that unreasoning fear rarely leads to loyalty or long term cooperation. In this area of existence the gods certainly have us mere Numbers out matched. The gods can use fear and awe in varying proportions to easily command respect. However, my situation is somewhat unique compared to the other numbers. My normal form like the one here on the Fey Realm is not generally conducive to comprehensive communication and understanding with mortal beings."

Yuki raised an eyebrow, "So you are saying the Numbers are choosing to adopt avatars to gain the respect of mortals?"

Lirae raised her own eyebrow, "Of course not. The respect of mortal spirits is ultimately not the issue. The gods are welcome to it since dealing with mortal beings is their primary responsibility after all. The point is that with respect comes a measure of communication which can be used to obtain cooperation. The gods have continually tried to use their control of material beings to change the original rules set in place by all the spirits of the dreaming. Their position in existence has been growing stronger over the long swaths of time since their creation while ours diminishes. Several of the Numbers have mostly independently decided to take action on our own to place checks on this activity."

I spoke with a smile at Thomas, "It is interesting that you are now the common thread between at least three of the Numbers. Are there any more which have used your services?"

Thomas' smile faded, "Not at the moment, and really it has been only Balinac and Lirae who have fully availed themselves of my services. The Luck managed what it desired on its own long before I was born after all. I simply learned from my early association with the Cricket how much of its process worked is all. I refined that process to make it more adaptable to my needs and the individual desires of the potential customer is all."

Thomas looked over at Lirae as he continued, "I also gave you full disclosure of the uncertainty involved with custom hosts. As the Luck once told me each Number is uniquely enabled and certain estimations have to be made with the process. You must admit Lirae that the advantages you have now far outweigh the minor inconveniences."

Lirae nodded, "More subtle direct action is an advantage worth the cost. I just wish that I didn't have to rely on the discretion of the others. I would hate to find myself in the same pot as Number Two and Number Seven as the fire gets started. Additionally Number Seven is notoriously mercenary with information management. I don't know how many concessions I'll have to make to guarantee its silence."

Thomas smiled, "I don't think you have to worry. They would both find themselves in the so called pot much quicker than you. You are wise to restrict your primary manipulation to within your own stronghold as it were. Not too many other powers can interfere with you while you reside within the Fey Realm after all. Most of the Fey deities would never dream of causing you trouble save the one."

Lirae frowned, "Speaking of her, I still wonder how Litha managed to conscript Reminas to her side."

I raised my own eyebrows, "Reminas works for Litha?"

Lirae nodded, "In a way he does, so yes, that statement is true enough. My years of watching him and his followers have shown me the sign of Litha's preferred methods all over their actions. However, Reminas likely doesn't realize Litha is the goddess pulling the spirit threads attached to him. I have not wanted to admit it, but she has played a longer and more successful game against the residents of the Fey Realm than I am comfortable accepting.

I nodded, "If she manages to convince more elves to move permanently to the Fey Realm, then what happens?"

Lirae looked at me sharply, "A further weakening of the position of the elves on the prime, and an argument for their complete removal can be put forth as one possible outcome. The elves were never intended by me to remain only in the Fey Realm. The Fey Realm was designed to be a periodic respite from the travails of living on the prime. The Fey Realm is a place to purify the spirit so they could endure the long ages of other shorter lived mortals."

I speculated, "So the goddess Litha and her twiline are behind the unrest in the wild lands then?"

Lirae shook her head, "I thought as much many centuries ago, but in that time Litha was just a much an eventual victim of the conflict then as she was an initial benefactor. I think this time she is more patiently watching it happen and looking to take what advantage she can where the opportunity presents itself. Such an opportunity seems to be available with Reminas' isolationist agenda. I am afraid that Reminas' movement if seemingly successful will spread to other portions of the prime as well. That is why I am determined to nip it in the bud now before it has a chance to grow into something uncontrollable."

Thomas spoke, "Which is why it is wise of you to come to me for assistance with this matter. I can provide the means and mechanism by which you forestall Litha and her plans. I think it is a bargain since it is all for the reasonable price of a little space and privacy in the Fey Realm for me to conduct my continuing research."

Lirae added, "As long as you abide with the agreement that no living spirits are altered, then our deal stands intact."

Thomas smiled, "Of course that remains the case, just as it is with the White Raven in the land of shadow. I do have my trusted auditor to satisfy after all."

Lirae smirked, "Number Two might be trusted by some, but ultimately with my help it is not as effective as the others had hoped it would be."

The shadowy dark haired elvish form of Balinac rose from the shadow behind Lirae, and spoke, "I don't know about that Number Three. I'm effective and trustworthy enough to find out about Thomas' place here as well."

Lirae turned her head with a look of shock, "How dare you come here Number Two."

Balinac took a step closer to the table, "My dear Number Three, if you wanted to keep me out of the very heart of the Fey Realm, then you certainly should not have brought my avatar here."

The two elvish guards near the stairs drew their swords and began to run toward the table. Balinac placed a hand casually on Lirae's shoulder and leaned in close to her ear as they approached. A silent communication seemed to pass between them. Lirae had a look of both anger and frustration on her face. Lirae raised a hand and motioned the guards to return to their posts at the top of the staircase. They ceased their charge and cautiously returned to their posts. Lirae looked up at Balinac with a glare as Lirae gently pushed Balinac's hand from her shoulder.

I looked at Balinac with a raised eyebrow, "Balinac please be nice. We are guests in Lirae's company."

Balinac looked down calmly, "Lirae knows that her actions in regard to Thomas have managed to put me in a potentially tenuous position with the other Numbers. Fortunately for her, I was summarily recalled to the dreaming to account for my involvement against the minions of Mortis on the prime. My supposedly poor performance in monitoring Thomas' research activities were also called into question. I successfully explained that I was arranging the appropriate oversight of his activities outside of the plane of shadow, and that I only intervened with Mortis' minions that were interfering in performing that assigned task. With the help of the Luck it was eventually settled that I would arrange to watch and report on Thomas' other research as well. You were planning on letting me continue with my assigned duties were you not Lirae?"

Lirae looked back up at Balinac, "Was any mention made of my avatar or my involvement with Thomas?"

Balinac smiled, "The Luck and I were suitably vague about the exact nature of Thomas' activities and associations. As you are well aware Lirae, most of the other Numbers are uncertain on many of the concepts of material activities. No mention was made yet of your involvement or your plans to thwart the manipulations of Litha. The Luck and I will both keep it that way unless you become uncooperative in helping me perform my assigned duties."

Lirae seemed to be fuming, "I accept your initial terms for review. However, I will have to investigate what has become known, and I must insist that you

Thomas the Poisoner

not wander freely where Thomas is not active in the Fey Realm. Thomas' area of operation shall be cleanly delineated in order to satisfy everyone's best interests. Otherwise we can solidify the particulars in the usual manner."

Balinac leaned down close to Lirae again, "Also on a side note I would look beyond the twiline goddess Litha as the source of your problems if I were you. Number Thirteen seemed highly inquisitive as to what Thomas has been doing lately. It was not easy to forestall its questioning as it was the Number which raised the complaint against Number Seven and I once more. You should know as well as I that it uses more than one avatar on its various planes. If I were in your position right now, I would examine very carefully any handmaiden twiline with the ear of Litha if you find the opportunity."

Lirae turned around and looked at Balinac with a shocked expression, "You know this for certain?"

Balinac shook her head, "Of course I do not. Number Thirteen is as usual very cautious about not revealing such things to those of us it considers its rivals. However, as you well know the Luck can figure the probabilities for things like this out very easily. The Luck has been watching the probability patterns left by Thirteen's activities for many thousands of years now. The Luck has come to the conclusion that Thirteen already has multiple physical semi-mortal avatars in various planes in play at this point. The rest of us Numbers remain behind it in this aspect Lirae. You may want to consider this information carefully, and possibly consider discussing this with the Luck in the usual manner."

Lirae shuddered briefly, "I will contemplate what you have said. I don't like the idea of working with the Luck. The cost is not always obvious at first, and if the other Numbers sense collusion, then I will be drawn into the fire along with you both."

Balinac moved over behind Thomas next, "Thomas, you have been learning certain things too quickly for my taste. I will watch you both here and in the land of shadow now. How many other forms are you operating at this moment Thomas?"

Thomas smiled calmly, "Just the two you can presently see. I was not trying to cause trouble you understand. I am just working on the next step of my research."

Balinac shrugged, "I could kill these forms, but what real harm would it possibly do. You would simply inhabit another set wouldn't you?"

Thomas gave a faint frown, "I do wish you wouldn't. These forms are dreadfully expensive to make you know. The experience of losing one is generally rather disorienting and potentially painful as well."

Yuki slapped her hand down on the table with a large grin, "I knew I killed you that night. I saw a solid hit with that kunai knife before I fled."

Thomas looked at her with a slightly perplexed expression, "I hadn't figured you would learn about that part just yet. As Balinac well knows killing my current physical form is ultimately a useless endeavor. My spirit no longer fully resides in any of my forms. I have already set up a means of quickly getting a new body when I need one. I don't even generally use a physical form in the plane of shadow anymore. I find it tends to distract from my work there. However, as these Numbers could likely tell you, for certain tasks physical forms do have their advantages."

I looked at Thomas then, "So you were telling the truth that you have only died once. That time you took poison to meet with the White Raven."

Thomas nodded, "I have indeed technically been dead since that time. However the distinction to make is that I have never been what others consider one of the undead. That is the important consideration as far as the White Raven is concerned as the undead have spirits which have become corrupted. I still serve her in my own way, and so she allows me some latitude to pursue my interests within reason."

I looked at him closely, "The study of the nature of spiritual existence is your interest then?"

Thomas looked back at me just as closely, "As either Balinac or the Luck could tell you. I have learned much that the White Raven finds interesting or amusing. I have done that which has not been done before me. I am something of an enigma to both the gods and the Numbers, so both keep me around to see what they can learn from me. As long as what I learn is useful to them that is."

Lirae looked at Thomas with a mask like expression, "You are working for many different sides on the same problem? Why did you not tell me this at first?"

Thomas shrugged, "You merely requested a physical form from me. You did not think to ask what I might learn from the process of providing you one. Each request I satisfy brings me closer to learning how it works."

Yuki looked at him with a touch of uncertainty, "How what works?"

Thomas gave a chill smile in return, "Existence of course. The unified theory of existence is my primary subject of study. I am attempting to work on reconciling the material nature of existence with the spiritual one. I'm certainly not the only being working on this concept, and so I have to be cautious of leaking too many secrets lest a competitor get a jump on my research. It amuses the White Raven to let me work at it because long ago most of the gods came to the conclusion that such an endeavor could not succeed. However, she has taken a renewed interest in it because the Luck thinks my research is capable of producing promising results."

Yuki's expression turned a bit incredulous, "Such a thing is mad to attempt. Mortals were never meant for such knowledge."

I spoke with a faint smile, "Yet Master Thomas is not quite mortal are you?"

Thomas smiled back at me, "I ceased being mortal in the common sense of the word when I died. I am not properly considered an immortal, but much like Mica here I am likely best categorized as a semi-immortal. At least until the White Raven ceases to be amused by my activities and sends me along through the next stage of existence."

Balinac spoke with distinct menace as she placed two hands on Thomas' shoulders, "Next time seek my permission before you expand your operation to other locations. You can make deals with which ever powers the White Raven will allow, but don't think that my role of auditor will cease because of it. Also don't think the White Raven can stop me if your spirit is recalled by the Numbers. Stay within your set boundaries, and there will be no problems."

Thomas kept smiling, "Of course my dear Balinac. Lirae here can swear that I have kept within only researching life initiation processes while in the Fey Realm."

Lirae nodded, "Mainly forced growth cloning. Essentially nothing beyond what arcane practitioners have already accomplished in earlier centuries, although the process is somewhat different I surmise as arcane energies were not involved."

I spoke, "I think Thomas understands his position Balinac. You can have Lirae's permission to monitor after you work out the details. In the meanwhile Thomas will refrain from any new activities until your oversight is in place."

Balinac shrugged as she walked around the table to place her arms around Yuki and me, "It shouldn't be too much trouble. I will just need to sub-contract it out to a local resource. I can use a reliable verifying third party to seal the deal after all."

Lirae looked at the three of us nervously, "What do you mean?"

Balinac hugged Yuki and me close for a moment and purred, "I think that Lirae here will enter an agreement to monitor Thomas here on the Fey Realm. She did offer to lease him the space after all. It is only fair that I'm not the one obligated to monitor him someplace I can not easily manifest. Consider it the part of the cost for my continued silence on your involvement in certain matters of my knowledge. Let's formalize this in the usual place and manner then so that the conditions and terms are clear for all three of us. Thomas you shall get an amended set of rules to learn before proceeding down any new lines of research here."

Balinac changed form into a kitten which jumped up to lay on Yuki's lap as both she and Lirae went silent with closed eyes. They sat in relative stillness for an indeterminate amount of time before Lirae opened her eyes and shook her head with a regretful expression.

I smiled my most charming smile, "I hope nothing is wrong."

Lirae faintly started to cry, "I've become complicit. If anything goes wrong I'm going to be blamed as well."

Yuki gave her a moderately unsympathetic look, "You became complicit when you involved yourself with mortal affairs. I don't think feeling sorry for your self about being involved now will do any good. Look on the bright side of the situation; they haven't been in more trouble than they could handle yet."

Lirae shook her head as she wiped her tears, "The Luck maneuvered me. I thought I was free from its plans, but it has maneuvered me just where it wanted me. It left me little option except to join it or to join the opposite side."

I gave her a sympathetic look, "I'm glad you chose this side."

Lirae began crying again, "What real choice did I have? The other side is backing Litha who is trying to destroy my creation. The other remaining unaligned Numbers will not stand against these two factions as individuals. The best they will do is to continue pretending the creation of factions has not really happened. I was happy once with being in the unaligned, and now I can't ever be part of the unaligned again."

I calmly said, "At least this way you have friends."

Balinac shrugged its kitten shoulders as she spoke in a high pitched voice, "Don't worry so much about it Number Three. I don't deny that it is uncomfortable to contemplate at first, but it really isn't that bad after learning how to cover your tracks. Most of the others are not prone to pry deeply into matters they would prefer to ignore."

Lirae dropped her head, "Quiet Twosie. Your words are little comfort to me."

Balinac grumbled a little bit as she spoke, "There is no need to be rude. You are still in control of your area of influence. You only need to back us up during any gathering of the powers, otherwise the conditions of your membership are those already agreed. It is not as onerous as you believe to cooperate, and you will be able to ask assistance where needed."

Lirae raised her head again, "You will assist with defeating the mechanization's of Litha?"

Balinac slowly nodded, "As much as possible while maintaining the illusion of not working together. You must understand I can not violate my primary purpose to help even the Luck of course, just as we will never ask you to violate your purpose. I will take no greater spirit before its allotted time or harm a spirit in any way. Not even to help our alliance."

Lirae nodded slowly, "Your condition is understood. The Luck however could do more perhaps?"

Balinac shrugged, "The Luck will not even take a life directly. However, he does have a very good ability to manipulate the course of events as you well know by now. He has certainly enlisted assistance in achieving what he could not do alone in the past. I expect that he has done so in this case as well."

Lirae narrowed her eyes, "Like enlisting your aid in recruiting me using Thomas' knowledge and capabilities as bait to entrap me?"

Balinac huffed, "If you think that is what happened, then who am I to change your opinion. I also spent many centuries attempting to avoid entanglement in the affairs of the Luck. Ultimately I found it more sensible to go along than to hold onto an archaic principle which was violated thousands of years ago anyway."

I spoke up with a touch of curiosity, "Which principle was that?"

Lirae looked at me, "The general consensus of the Numbers has been that we would remain as unique individuals separate from the actions of material existence beyond assisting with its initial creation. You should understand that the creation of the elder gods by the other spirits did not meet our approval. When the other spirits came to the Numbers for assistance, we each agreed to help create a portion of material existence as best suits our individual dispositions with the understanding that they would abandon living in the dreaming forever. I created the life process as exemplified by the Fey Realm, and had to also tap into the greater chaos to empower it. Even now you sit in the heart of my physical embrace in the Great World Tree which combines the Fey Realm with the greater chaos to promote the existence of life on the prime material prime."

Yuki looked at our surroundings and then at Lirae with awe, "We are on the Great World Tree and you call this place your home?"

Lirae shook her head gradually, "You fail to understand the full extent of what I am. I am the Great World Tree the very root, bough, and branch of the source for all material life. Now I have become unwillingly entangled in the plans of the designer of death for all material things, as well as the most nefarious information conduit for both the material and spiritual existences. It should be easy to understand my displeasure with this situation."

I nodded my head, "I appreciate your candor Lirae. I do think we can still work together to achieve our mutual goals. At the very least I want to continue with my plan to put a stop to Reminas' ambitions."

Lirae glanced at Thomas and then returned her gaze to me, "That would be appreciated. I will also endeavor to help you with your plans as I am able."

Chapter 42 Reading Dragon Inn

I looked up from the reports on my desk over at the towel wrapped form of Yuki entering our bedroom from the adjacent bath. The predawn light was starting to filter through the curtains, and I felt a familiar comfortable desire stirring in my heart. Yuki came over to give me a hug as I sat in my chair.

Yuki whispered in my ear, "You seem distracted for how early it is my love."

I smiled back, "The sight of you always distracts me my dear."

Yuki squeezed me once more, and pulled back, "No time now. You have that important negotiation today. You need to have your mind focused. I need to get down to the restaurant to supervise the breakfast."

I reached back to put my arm around her waist, "They know how to cook already. They can get started without you I'm certain."

Yuki kissed me on the lips, and then stepped away, "The chef's job is in the kitchen supervising the troops. If you need some exercise to clear your head, I suggest a quick run to the border post to facilitate the arrival of our out of town guests."

I shrugged, "I'm pretty sure that Yastalus has it well in hand by now."

Yuki waggled her finger at me as she dropped her towel to the floor and began getting her clothes from the closet, "I know you trust him with good reason, but for forms sake since this is the first time you are hosting these meetings, it would be best if you were there to greet the out of country guests."

I watched the sensuous vision of Yuki getting dressed as I sighed, "I think it better if I take the closed coach over. The locals might get a touch nervous if they saw our guests."

After Yuki left for the restaurant to supervise the production of breakfast I bathed as well. I thought back over the two years which had elapsed since we had started construction of the Reading Dragon Inn complex. The actual construction of the inn had gone smoothly with the assistance of the dwarf and elf work crews. A couple of minor attempts at sabotage had occurred, but the dwarf engineers had done their job well in addition to spotting any potential problem and fixing them before any harm could happen to the workers.

The workers on the other hand had been occasionally problematic. Several elves had to be replaced on the project for attempting to instigate fights with the dwarf builders. True to their reputation Irli and Taprock's crew had remained thick skinned and not responded unprofessionally to any provocation set before them. At the end of their work on the facility I paid each of them a handsome bonus for maintaining their professional demeanor.

We were actually nearing of first full year of being open for business. The signs of recent construction were gone, and the planting in the vineyard and elvish gardens were coming along nicely with the irrigation system supporting them. Yuki's restaurant was doing very good business with the locals within a day's travel of the location. The word was also getting out among the more choosy travelers from Letheros thanks to the work Lirae had performed in marketing the Reading Dragon to the adventure prone elves of the capital.

The human style chateau on the western slope above the Inn complex had just been finished last month. Yuki and I were enjoying the relative peace and privacy it afforded us when we were not handling the Inn's business or making preparations for Lirae's mission. With the help of several itinerant adventurers hired over the past year we had managed to put a dent in the most aggressive and hostile wild lands leadership close to the borders of Letheron.

However, on my own with occasional protection from Balinac where needed I had also made some allies among the leaders of several tribes of Kobolds within the wild lands. In exchange for their information regarding the locations and dispensation of the more aggressive groups of other wild lands dwellers, they were afforded a measure of protection from any adventurer assaults on their territory. This was fairly easy to arrange as I made sure that the kinds of adventurers who would be interested in easy targets like kobolds were not generally able to afford the services of the Reading Dragon Inn.

The only drawback I found so far in these alliances was that early on I had been seen by one of the shamans of the kobold tribes. The shaman had taken one look at me with his second sight and fainted dead away. Before he had recovered his tribe was very upset and prepared to attack me for casting a curse upon him. Lucky for me the shaman had revived soon and proclaimed to his tribe that he received a vision from the Spirit Shaman that I was the Shinigami, the bringer of death incarnate.

Yuki had later informed me that Shinigami was the Ran Li term for a chosen spirit hunter of the White Raven. She found it curious that the term from Ran Li had somehow managed to be known to the wild lands culture on this continent. I assumed that the Lucky Cricket was the likely culprit for the linguistic choice used by the shaman. The practical effect was that after that time any kobold tribe within multiple days of travel with a shaman tended to treat me with a combination of awe and fear when I met with them. Fortunately the word about who I was spread quickly among the kobold tribes, and negotiating with them became much easier.

Unfortunately a certain reputation was starting to leak out from the kobold tribes over the past year and a half as well. While none of them had tied my identity as Mica Lichan president of the Isle Corporation and owner of the Reading Dragon Inn to the term Shinigami, there was a growing rumor on both sides of the border of a being of power disguised as a pale haired elf making pacts and alliances with the kobold tribes.

These events had eventually led us to this day. I could remember years back bragging to Glorandel that I would be using the Reading Dragon Inns as a neutral location where secret diplomatic discussions between hostile nations could occur. As I stepped from my bath I felt a bit of nervous anticipation. I had not expected such a thing to begin quite so soon. The envoy representing the moderate leadership in Letheron and his staff had arrived at the Reading Dragon Inn two days ago on a what was overtly a personal vacation to our facility.

In reality the elvish envoy was coming to discuss an armistice with the representative of the combined kobold tribal leaders and leader of the largest Orc tribe from the wild lands. While an official treaty would not happen anytime soon, this was certainly the first step in significantly reducing tensions along the northern border of Letheron. However, first I would have to convince the Orc leader that such a meeting would be in his best interest.

I finished dressing and stepped into the shadowed corner of our bedroom in the chateau, and out of the shadowed recess by the wardrobe in Glorandel's room in the human quarters of the Reading Dragon Inn. I silently walked up behind Glorandel where he sat at his table reading a scroll. Glorandel became startled and looked around in my direction as my shadow passed into his line of sight.

Glorandel looked at me with a frown, "It is more polite to enter someone's room by knocking at the door and requesting permission to enter than by using mysterious means and sneaking up on them silently."

I smiled at him, "I apologize for the oversight. I just wanted to let you know that I would be heading down to the carriage house at the second bell, and I will be expecting your company on my trip."

Glorandel nodded his head, "I will join you and your wife at breakfast first I hope. I'm interested to discuss the latest batch of news with you, and I already have the initial background information you requested."

I nodded, "It is good then Glorandel. I'm glad you could join us here for this."

Glorandel looked back at me as I stepped toward the shadow again, "Any comments on the rumors of this Shinigami being I have been hearing about recently?"

I spoke as I faded back into the shadows, "Today should be fairly informative."

I stepped out of the shadows in the cool storage basement of the restaurant. I heard the sound of a busy kitchen coming from the stairs leading above as they had just recently opened for breakfast service. In addition to building and operating the Reading Dragon Inn for the past two years I had also been learning several new tricks. The shadow walk ability was very useful for quickly moving about a known or visible location.

The other tricks were a bit more involved, and I had continued receiving even more advanced and focused assassin training from Thomas himself on a weekly basis since our meeting in Letheron. It was one of the terms Balinac had levied on Thomas in exchange for Balinac's complicity in concealing certain of Thomas' behaviors. This training was arranged through meetings on the Fey Realm using the magical gates facilitated by Lirae.

We had learned in the past two years that extended use of multiple direct presences on the prime began to take a toll in concentration and mental fatigue from Balinac over time, and in response she had reduced her time spent here in Letheron in order to concentrate on her Thomas monitoring duties.

In mitigation of the loss of a regular presence of Balinac as a protector neither Yuki nor I were simply the journeymen assassins we had been two years ago. We both were expanding our martial and mystical capabilities. Yuki had been learning to access the primal spirit abilities of the shamans, and I was learning the shadow assassin traits of the shadowine.

Finally, my spiritual combination with Balinac granted me abilities unknown to any natural elf, and beyond even the shadow tainted twiline. I learned from my meetings with Balinac how to manipulate the very nature of matter using primal spiritual energy mixed with shadow. Many of these were techniques that even Thomas or any other shadowine did not yet know. Unfortunately my reliability with these techniques was not absolute, and the range was still limited to items within my melee reach. Practically speaking I could temporarily alter the essential nature of my weapons or even my own flesh using a combination of shadow and primal energy.

I walked up the stairs to the kitchen and greeted the staff. They all nodded smiling at my presence and returned the greetings as I walked through the kitchen. Yuki met me at the door to the restaurant dining area and gave me a quick kiss.

Yuki spoke, "Good luck today darling. I'll keep you in my thoughts. Don't take too many risks."

I smiled, "I am hopeful for a successful resolution."

I walked out into the restaurant and noticed that the elvish envoy Eliasan and his staff were already seated for breakfast and enjoying their meals. I walked over to their table and gave them my best winning smile. Eliasan smiled back at me, and waved me to an open seat.

I spoke first as I sat, "I hope you are all enjoying your stay with us. I am going to be gone for a day, but is there anything I can arrange to provide for your comfort before I depart."

Eliasan glanced around the restaurant, "I am very pleased with your service and accommodations. I think we are fine barring the arrangements already discussed. I hope your business goes well today."

A waiter brought over my usual breakfast of fresh fruit and bread as I replied, "If you find you need anything prior to my return, don't hesitate to make your request to the staff here. They all pride themselves on the quality of service they deliver."

Eliasan nodded as he looked at the remainder of his breakfast, "I have no complaints, and many complements. This is some of the best fruit this side of the Fey Realm. I really must learn what supplier you use."

I smiled, "Most of our food supply is grown locally using local producers or our own lands, but I have a few connections for receiving special items of a more exotic nature. You'll pardon me if I don't reveal my suppliers since I would rather prefer to keep my trade secrets."

Eliasan nodded as I finished up my meal, "Yes, it is understood that certain secrets must be maintained. I look forward to your return then."

After my breakfast I made my way back to the main portion of the inn. I greeted Will Crusher at the reception desk and bade him to inform the staff to make the covered carriage ready for departure at second bell.

I went to the library to relax and read for a while. I selected a tome on elvish gardening practices to read for about an hour before Glorandel arrived with a sheaf of papers in hand.

Glorandel smiled as he entered, "It seems pretty hard to catch up with you these days."

I looked at him with a smile as well, "It is busy business running an inn. I try to relax and enjoy what free time comes my way."

Glorandel sat down and cast his privacy spell, "Lets get down to business since our time is short. Here is the information I have gathered from Letheron. It does not seem that Reminas' organization is aware of the impending meetings here. They are moving quietly, but not rapidly. I would expect some potential trouble after the envoy returns to Letheros if your plan goes well. In terms of that research, here is the information on the orc chieftain Jarlak you were looking to obtain. It seems his clan is not overly aggressive, but they are opportunistic to capitalize on the mistakes made by other races and other orc clans. By most accounts this chieftain is young, moderately intelligent, and exceptionally crafty for an orc, but also apparently still prone to their typical hatreds and distrusts. I'm sorry but the information is pretty skimpy, and primarily made up of second hand observations as this clan seems a particularly loyal and close knit group."

I nodded, "The kobolds have indicated that Jarlak's clan is not usually aggressive against them, but frequently uses them for information on their competitors just like we do. Many of the successful kobold tribes in the nearby wild lands have alliances with his tribe. It is through these alliances that this meeting is being arranged. However, first I must go to them to show my trust before they will trust what I have to say."

Glorandel looked at me sideways, "I hope you are bringing plenty of support. It is very likely that if they see you as weak they will attack you instead of listening to you. It is not uncommon among the orc clans to do so."

I smiled, "That is a risk I must take. I very much want to convince them to come to the table to talk about a cessation of hostilities between the elves of Letheron and his tribe at the very least. I'm not expecting friendship, but a beginning would be nice."

Glorandel shrugged, "I would like to be there to see how you convince them. If it were anyone else I wouldn't give very high odds for the attempt."

I stood up and patted Glorandel on the shoulder, "I'm glad to see that you are interested. I am planning to bring you along as my second."

Glorandel paled slightly, "Your second?"

I grinned, "If I am to duel an entire orc tribe at once, then a second will certainly be required."

Glorandel paled a bit more, "I keep forgetting about your upbringing in Ard. It is such a formal society in some ways. You know I never did track down any elves with your name born there."

I looked at him seriously, "That is odd. What ever did you find then?"

Glorandel regained a touch of color in his face, "It's very interesting. I found the son of a human knight named Mikael Lidron who went missing over five years ago. He would have been approximately the equivalent of your age if he had been an elf. The rumors were that he ran off to have an illicit affair with a half elf mage of his acquaintance named Firanda Zarcha who had almost enough credits to graduate from the Mages Academy of Ard, yet seemingly uncharacteristically abandoned her lifelong pursuit of the mystic arts for this man."

I gave him a friendly smile, "You don't say. That is very interesting."

Glorandel nodded, "I have also noted over our two years of acquaintance that you always use a variant on that phrase and deliver that winning smile when my statements about you hit too close to the mark for your comfort. Does it interest you to know that about two years ago three empty shallow graves were anonymously reported to the authorities on the property of one Baron Glenmoor? These graves were very near the adjoining property of one Baron Marco."

Glorandel waited for my response but I remained silent so he continued, "It seems you can change your habits quite quickly then when you are aware of them. I will provide a few more bits of information then. It seems this Mikael Lidron worked for the land management agency in Ard before he disappeared. This Firanda Zarcha was also contracted to work for them on occasion. The Barons Glenmoor and Marco even commented on someone apparently messing around with a boundary stream between their properties right near the empty graves. The funny thing was no record was made at the land management agency of any team being sent out to deal with this issue. There was also no record of Firanda Zarcha being contracted at that time by the land management agency at the Wizards Guild. I finally thought to have someone check with the porter's guild. It seems quite a few porters remembered one of their missing fellows who was hired by this Mikael Lidron. With enough coin they were willing to divulge that an official request from the court had forced them to destroy any records of that transaction."

I nodded, "Some of these events are known to me. The resulting official intervention to conceal these events was not."

Glorandel shook his head, "Shinigami indeed, one dead yet not undead. I begin to understand how this Thomas the Poisoner operation has kept going all these centuries. I also begin to comprehend how this Thomas the Poisoner may actually be alive after all these years."

I kept a grim visage, "I really can not comment on such matters."

Glorandel gave a slight smile, "It seems I have finally caught up to you. I suppose this means my life is in danger."

I shrugged, "Every life is always in danger. It is up to some of us to do something about it."

Glorandel looked at me closely, "By choosing who dies?"

I shook my head, "No, by deciding who to help live. The right person at the right time and place can work miracles. Harack was one of those people. As you have seen with your own eyes he worked terrible miracles of death in his time. Those are not the kinds of miracles I am attempting to work. Our methods may have some similarities, but I think you will find the effect to be quite different."

Glorandel stood up and looked at me, "Answer me this if you can. Are you truly Mikael Lidron?"

I looked at him with a faint smile, "Mikael Lidron is a part of what I once was. I would even say an important part. However, my death then has pretty much changed who I am now. I am not Mikael Lidron anymore."

Glorandel looked away from me, "Who are you now?"

I gave a light laugh, "For the moment I am Mica Lichan. In the future I don't really know what I will become. Life is a journey. I've met some strange fellows on the path yourself included. I've also found my love and my purpose. I don't regret dying, or risking what I must to make a better world. Shall we depart?"

Glorandel looked at me again, "Let me ask one more question under my privacy spell before we go. If who you are is Mica Lichan, then what are you now?"

I looked at Glorandel with a fierce expression, "The Shinigami as the Lucky Cricket has dubbed me. I am the one who holds the power of death and life in his hands."

I stepped out of the protection of the privacy spell cast by Glorandel and began walking to the guest elevator. Glorandel hesitated a moment and followed me. We rode the elevator down to the dwarf rooms below the hill, and followed the ornately carved guest passage to the carriage house. The covered coach and driver were waiting for our arrival. I told the driver to take us to the border station.

As we traveled down the lane I saw Yuki step out of the service entrance of the restaurant and wave in our direction. I returned her wave as we traveled up the road toward the border station at the head of the valley. We were stopped at the newly fortified checkpoint and inspection station as Yastalus came out of the building and joined us inside the carriage.

I spoke out to the driver, "Take us to milestone eight in the wild lands"

The driver called back, "Which one is that again sir?"

I replied, "The one near the cliff. We will be walking past that point, and the allied Kobolds there will protect the area from intruders approaching the carriage."

I returned my head inside the carriage and spoke to Yastalus and Glorandel, "Welcome Yastalus. Might I introduce you finally to Glorandel the Blue Sage. Glorandel this is Yastalus the local government mage for this checkpoint."

Glorandel smiled broadly, "Hello fellow practitioner of the arcane arts."

Yastalus had a pinched expression, "Your reputation precedes you Glorandel the Blue Sage."

Glorandel nodded, "As does yours Yastalus Leafbreeze. I believe you were in the top fifteen in your class at the enchanter's college if my memory serves me.

You recently wrote a most interesting if highly controversial work regarding the potential of enchanting items with primal power sources. While many of your colleagues have dismissed your observations as unlikely, I noted that you used the totems and tokens of shamanistic practitioners as working examples of such enchantments."

Yastalus perked up a bit, "Well it is kind of you to say so. It is really hard to get recognition in the enchantment area these days. Everyone either produces highly derivative products based on tried and true practices, or attempts either highly unlikely or impractical combinations to get noticed."

Glorandel nodded, "Is that why you chose to work as a simple customs inspector then? I was always curious about that choice given your outstanding college performance."

Yastalus smiled a bit, "Being a customs inspector does give me an opportunity to observe many kinds of enchanted items up close for certain. It is amazing what purposes some people will put enchantment to at times. Do you realize that Mister Mica's wife Yuki has a dwarf made adamantine cooking pot which could pay for the entire Reading Dragon Inn complex? It is such an extravagance. However, to make it even more outrageous is that a nearly indestructible material has masterwork grade durability enchantments cast on it as well. Even the hottest dragon fire couldn't harm that item now. It is a work fit for a dwarf king, and yet a chef at an inn has it as her common cooking equipment."

Glorandel shook his head and Yastalus' face grew a touch pensive as he responded, "You don't believe my observation?"

Glorandel smiled again, "I'm sorry that was not it. I was just thinking it strange that was how Harack the Slayer decided to spend the wealth of a defeated goblin kin nation. He never did have much of a care for money. He is one of the more unusual dwarves I've ever adventured alongside in my youth."

Yastalus looked strangely at him, "Why does the name you mention sound familiar? I really don't have too much experience with many dwarves."

Glorandel smiled broader, "It was a time before you were born young elf. Harack the Slayer, also known as the goblin bane, orc doom, and ogre slayer traveled the wild lands of the north wiping out the wild races literally by the thousands. I joined him briefly on one of his crusades as a young idealistic mage. Frankly speaking the sheer carnage and butchery of watching Harack in action two hundred and seventy-five years ago turned my stomach. I lost the taste for any killing, and settled into learning about people, places, and history instead. You made a wise choice in avoiding the career of a combat mage Yastalus. There isn't much reward compared to the risk."

Yastalus blanched a bit, "I think I recall the rumors of such a dwarf told as a threat to human children who didn't behave I believe. Are you saying he's a real person, and that you've met him?"

Glorandel smirked, "Not only met him, but traveled in his company for six months in my younger years. I shouldn't think it so hard to believe he's real. I saw him just about two years ago in Port Cirnore in the company of Young Mica here after all."

Yastalus looked over at me, "Is what he is saying true?"

I gave a faint smile, "It is true that Harack is one of the people who taught me much of what I know about martial technique, and he is certainly the most diversely skilled weapons master I have ever met. The real surprise for most is that he is also the one who taught Yuki how to cook as well as improve her fighting technique."

Yastalus smiled, "Well it seems you have more than one hidden side to your stories my good elves. So what mission brings us out into the wild lands this day?"

I gave Yastalus a brief smile, "I have to meet with an orc chieftain and convince him to discuss an armistice with Letheron."

Yastalus blanched again, "You have been authorized by the government to act on its behalf?"

I shook my head, "Of course not. As you well know I am not even a citizen of Letheron after all. That is why they have secretly sent an envoy to stay at the Reading Dragon Inn. I have simply contracted with the government to provide the meeting location, and to make the appropriate travel arrangements."

Yastalus looked out the window, "So this Orc chieftain has agreed to come meet the government envoy?"

I frowned a bit, "Not quite yet. I have to convince him of my guarantee of his safety first. I don't expect him to be quite so quick to understand my reasoning as you Yastalus."

Yastalus muttered, "So dangerous you must be safe."

Glorandel queried, "I sense a story I haven't heard here. What do you mean by that comment?"

Yastalus gave a shake of his head, and then reconsidered his response by handing an odd prism crystal held in a brass handle to Glorandel.

Glorandel looked at it briefly, "Interesting device. Does it carry an enchantment of your own design?"

Yastalus nodded, "Something I invented and now find myself too frightened to use as I originally intended."

Glorandel handled it gingerly, "Is it dangerous?"

Yastalus shook his head, "Not in and of itself. It is a meter for registering primal energy. It is very broad spectrum yet finely graduated. Theoretically it should measure the full spectrum of primal energies as I understand it."

Glorandel looked at it quizzically, "You haven't tested it yet?"

Yastalus shook his head again, "I have actually tested it quite extensively. You can read people's spirits with it. The spirits of living beings radiate primal energy in certain spectra. They come in varying wavelengths of energy comparable to colors in the visual spectra. It seems that the so called second sight of spirit shamans is also able to view these spectra. There is also a varying power level involved. I created a variable scale based on my best estimations of spiritual or primal power output. I am at twenty on that scale. My friend Lionette approaches ninety on the scale. I imagine you are likely a twenty as most adventuring types seem to register that high while average people register around a ten or fifteen."

Glorandel nodded, "I think I understand. What is your problem then?"

Yastalus sighed, "Conceptually speaking an artifact grade item with these energies would register somewhere in the two hundred to five hundred range of such a scale."

Glorandel smiled, "I think I see what you are saying. So how does it work?"

Yastalus gave a slight grin, "Well I am the baseline used, so use the command prism calibrate while pointing that end at me, and look for the reading to appear along the side in elvish script along with a color code."

Glorandel did as instructed, "Prism calibrate. Let's see the number is twenty like you said and the color is a light blue."

Yastalus gave a little chuckle, "At least it works for another arcane caster. It seems non-arcane casters or normal people can not use it at all. Now tell it prism clear, and then point it at yourself and say prism reading."

Glorandel did as instructed again, "Prism clear. Prism reading. It seems my reading is fifty six and my color is deep blue."

Yastalus nodded taking interest, "That is interesting. You are the highest reading I have gotten from a non-spirit shaman then. They always seem to register greater primal power than most others I have tested it on so far."

Glorandel smiled, "Higher even than yourself it seems."

Yastalus shrugged, "It is not a measure of knowledge or ability after all. It is just the primal power in a spirit or item when used this way."

Glorandel looked up at him, "What is the highest reading you have gotten so far?"

Yastalus looked sheepish, "I got a reading I secretly took from Mica's wife at three hundred and eighty. The color was deep green with traces of black."

Glorandel looked surprised, "Wow that seems pretty high. You are saying she has an artifact grade human spirit. How remarkable. So you are also saying the colors can be mixed?"

Yastalus nodded, "In some unique cases it seems to be possible. Now Mr. Mica would you kindly take off your wedding band and allow Glorandel to measure it."

I handed my wedding ring to Glorandel with a faint smile, "Here you go."

Yastalus spoke again, "I suggest you reset it on me first before taking a reading."

Glorandel nodded, "You read twenty-one this time."

Yastalus smiled, "There seems to be a couple of points of variance in the scale, possibly introduced by outside factors, which is why I built in the calibration function. Now try measuring that ring for me please. I am curious about the result."

Glorandel did as asked and whistled, "Well I'll be either this thing is way off, or that ring is beyond artifact grade in primal power. It just gave a reading of seven hundred forty two. The color is dead black. What does that mean?"

Yastalus shook his head, "That is something I was afraid might happen. The reading is accurate enough. The scale theoretically goes up to one thousand as that is the speculated measure of the potential primal power output of a deity. Of course since I don't have a deity to test it out on I may never validate that number. I didn't conceive of my scale potentially being off when measuring other kinds of things."

I looked at Yastalus and said, "Are you sure you want to do what you are thinking about now?"

Yastalus swallowed and nodded his head, "Return the ring to Mica. Reset the crystal on me again, and then please take a measurement of Mica."

Glorandel did as requested and then looked puzzled, "Its not working anymore all it gave was colors, but it was mostly black, quite a bit of blue, a small amount of red, and a trace of yellow. I don't understand this device. What is going on here?"

Yastalus shook his head, "The device isn't broken. Mica there has four spirit essences combined. This combination is granting him a primal power resource pool significantly greater than what is available even to the gods. I don't know how something like him happened, and I don't think I want to ever find out. He is literally so potentially dangerous he has to be safe."

Glorandel shook his head, "I don't understand the logic behind your reasoning."

I interrupted their conversation, "What Yastalus is getting at is the point of a conversation we had a couple of years ago. If I truly desired you to be dead, then there would be nothing even a god could do to stop it from happening."

Glorandel shook his head, "That's ridiculous as it's well known that divine beings and their most favored mortal followers can return dead people back to life."

Yastalus interrupted, "That may well be the case normally, but Mica here is certainly aware of the exception to that rule."

Glorandel looked quizzically at Yastalus, "What exception?"

Yastalus gave a faint grin, "It really isn't too surprising you don't know of it. It involves the ancient lore of the elves dwelling in the Fey Realm. It's not like a half human half elf mage like you would normally be allowed to access such lore. No offense intended of course, I'm just stating the reality of the situation. As Mica mentioned to me two years ago, your studies let you recognize the name of Mica's companion as Balinac. Probably even recognize it as one of the beings referred to as the Numbers even."

Glorandel looked a bit smug, "Of course I recognized that almost immediately."

Yastalus stopped smiling, "The elves of the Fey Realm have age long histories and memories. They have another name for that particular Number. That name is the Godkiller."

Glorandel scoffed a bit, "That's pure rumor and gossip. There is no truth in the legend of a god killer. The elder gods were trapped in the far realms during a rebellion of the new gods. All of the religions agree on that point."

Yastalus shook his head, "I am quite sure that all of the religions do agree on that point. It is the truth, at least as far as they are willing to admit to the uninitiated. The problem is that none of them will ever give credence to the Godkiller, and yet its avatar sits right there beside you. That crystal proves that he has sufficient power to balk the will of even a god in matters of death and life."

Glorandel looked at me with dropped jaw, "The Shinigami . . ."

Yastalus nodded, "Not a shinigami mind you. Those beings while frightening enough work for the White Raven. Much like the Lucky Cricket is called The Spirit Shaman by those who are spirit shamans; Mica here is recognized by them as The Shinigami. This is the ancient elvish term for the being otherwise known as the Godkiller in the common tongue. It is speculated the term existed even prior to the ancient elvish language and was adopted into it."

I entered the conversation, "In the language of Ran Li shinigami means spirit hunter. They make no mention of a godkiller in their interpretation of the phrase."

Glorandel seemed to gather himself, "That is easy enough to understand. Their language has remained little changed over a very long time. It is only in the last two thousand years that the worship of gods and goddesses has become prevalent on that continent. When the term first came in to use there it was unlikely the interpretation of godkiller would have made sense in their culture of the time."

I gave a relaxed smile, "Well it is just a term after all. I can tell you both that I haven't killed any gods or even slain any demons. I don't think we need to worry about such today. I'm just going to convince an orc chieftain that listening and coming to a discussion is a better path forward for his people than fighting."

Yastalus looked across at me, "I really am not suited to fighting. I tended to focus on the more pacifistic of the arcane arts in my studies and work."

Glorandel shrugged, "I don't worry too much about even a sizable orc tribe. I find that a few choice elemental spells tends to get them running away quick enough."

I smiled, "There is no need to worry Yastalus. Glorandel also knows a number of effective barrier spells I'm sure. I will have him cast several on you and the driver where we leave the carriage. You'll be staying with the carriage while Glorandel and I go to meet the orc delegation. After I convince their chieftain Jarlak of my trustworthiness we will return to Letheron and you will only be requested to expedite our crossing the border with no hassles as you have done before."

Chapter 43 Negotiation Tactics

I walked alongside Glorandel following the kobold scout who was guiding us to the caverns where we would meet with the orc Chieftain Jarlak. Glorandel had cast several protection barrier type spells on the carriage and people we left at the eight mile marker. Then the kobold scout team had arrived at the location shortly after at the scheduled time.

I noticed the early summer weather was pleasant in this part of the wild lands. It reminded me of my youth in Ard somehow. I looked over at Glorandel who glanced at me in return.

Glorandel spoke, "You don't seem too nervous. I don't know if it is a good sign or a bad one. Even Harack would get, well not nervous exactly. Probably more worked up before a fight is a better way to put it."

I shrugged, "It is a good day to die if that is what must happen."

Glorandel laughed, "Now you're trying to make me nervous. It won't work. I've been in much more hairy spots in the past and managed to get back out of them all in one piece."

I looked over at him casually, "Contingency spells?"

Glorandel chucked, "Like you wouldn't believe. It is probably why Yastalus got such a high reading on me with that gadget of his. I've got so many self triggering spells on me that I pity even a dragon which might mistake me for a snack. Not that I'm a bad hand with my selected casting either mind you. You don't survive long as a combat mage unless you learn to be quicker and stronger than the opposing side's counter mage assaults."

I smiled, "It is good to know I won't have to keep a spare eye out for your protection then. I don't anticipate you will need to do more than balk any attacker briefly if it does come to a need to defend yourself. I'll ask that you withhold any lethal casting unless you believe it absolutely necessary to preserve yourself."

Glorandel shrugged, "I was a full service combat mage in my time. If the team I'm serving wants a defense boost, then I stick with defense. I'm not some silly young adventurer who feels the need to have credit for all the kills. I will however most likely execute my get out of trouble options if things get too risky. Nothing personal, but I suspect you can look after yourself well enough."

I nodded, "Very good then. I think we have an adequate understanding of my expectations here. I'll need your observations on the personalities and politics in play mostly. I have no doubt I will be busy managing several aspects of the negotiation, and I don't trust that I won't accidentally overlook an important event or phrase. That is mainly my reason for bringing you along today. I'm also looking for your long term analysis of the potential outcomes of today's events."

Glorandel nodded, "I think I understand what you are asking. I will tell you that I am more used to dealing with the civilized races in these kinds of exchanges, even if it is mostly the less civilized members of those races. I can not guarantee which way the orcs might jump if pressed a certain way. Their personalities are too unpredictable without extensive observation. If you appear too weak, then they may attack where they see an opportunity. If you appear to be strong, then they may attack because they see a challenge or a threat."

I nodded, "If you appear to be impossibly strong?"

Glorandel chuckled, "I've yet to see an orc consider any elf opponent as impossible to defeat. It just isn't in their cultural mind set. At best they may consider the attempt difficult and prone to failure due to the situation. That usually does not stop the attempt. My best advice is to appear strong enough to defend yourself adequately, yet not so ambitious or cocky that they think you might be looking down on them. That is almost a certain way to start a fight."

I looked at the kobold scout walking ahead of us, "I have unfortunately appeared impossibly strong to the kobolds already, and I am sure that the reputation of the Shinigami has reached Chieftain Jarlak's ears. I think from what you have said he already considers me a threat, but that he is more cautious than a typical orc leader. My guess is that he will choose to gauge me in a way that proves either the kobolds are foolish cowards who exaggerate my strength, or that I am a threat to be eliminated. The remaining window of strong enough, but not a threat is a very narrow one indeed. That is why I am going to warn you that I am likely going to push them extremely hard so they understand that I am too dangerous to not be safe."

Glorandel looked at me with an appraising eye, "Just how do you plan to do such a thing without making an enemy of the orcs in this region for a lifetime? They carry their grudges very seriously, almost as seriously as a dwarf."

I shrugged, "I think the details will have to be played by ear, but I have a few ideas already."

Glorandel nodded, "I will watch and observe then. I will also keep my teleport contingencies ready. I am glad I set one for the Reading Dragon Inn this morning."

I glanced over at him again, "I would appreciate it if you could help protect Yastalus if things go badly."

Glorandel laughed again, "Don't take his apparent cowardice too seriously. While he may not be a combat mage in training, it is no slouch magician who can come out in the top five of that class in the enchanter's college."

I looked at Glorandel in surprise, "I thought you said he was in the top fifteen?"

Glorandel shrugged, "Yastalus was actually number two in his class. I was waiting to see if he would correct me when I said top fifteen. His reputation for being humble about his accomplishments is accurate. He was even apprenticed under the famous gnome enchanter and magic weaver Crystalgear Nimblehands at the enchanter's college. This Crystalgear had a reputation for being a genius in the field for his potency and the artistry of his works. You could see the influence in the prism device Yastalus designed and demonstrated for me today. He was hoping for complements from us I think, and that work would deserve those kinds of compliments from someone in his field if anyone took him seriously enough."

I looked at the kobold ahead of us, "Why didn't you compliment him then?"

Glorandel sighed, "It would have been empty praise in his ears. It is pretty clear Yastalus does not hold me or mages like me in any particular high esteem. I'm not an artist in his field who seriously knows anything about his craft after all. I'm just some common combat mage with pretensions of being a sage in his estimation. The only reason he wanted to see me cast the protection spells was to determine if I had anything unique up my sleeve. I could see he was disappointed I only used the same old standards."

I glanced over at the new kobold group merging from the tree line on our right, "Why did you cast the same old standards then?"

Glorandel laughed, "They are considered standards for a reason. They work well, and they are relatively tried and true. Not every spell needs to be a masterpiece new creation after all. There is nothing functionally wrong with using what is comfortable and works when appropriate. It is just like when he was fascinated about your wife's pot, not because he thought the enchantment was anything special I would guess, but the waste of highly valuable materials for such a common purpose was beyond his experience. It likely even offended his sensibility regarding the purpose of enchantment. However, it conversely excited his mind to think that enchantment might be applied in such an unconventional manner."

I smiled at him, "What do you think about it?"

Glorandel laughed, "An obvious waste as cooking implement of course, but a damn fine way to disguise a nearly indestructible magic resistant small shield for someone using an improvisational combat style. Knowing Harack he's certainly trained her how to use it quite effectively."

I nodded as I watched the eight new kobolds form an escort around us, "So you recognized what it really was while the expert enchanter missed it."

Glorandel shrugged, "I have about three hundred more years of practical experience on Yastalus. He's still a bit stuck on form dictating function. That is one of the limitations of people at the top of the class sometimes. They have a tendency to get into a rigid mind set about how they were taught to do things. Crystalgear likely drilled them mercilessly about the esthetics of the art as much as the function of the work. A practical combat mage has little time to learn to do things fancy, but has to learn what works well quickly or they don't ever live to be my age."

I nodded, "Where were you in your class then?"

Glorandel chuckled, "I was in the bottom half of a class of five hundred at a human mage college at that. Frankly speaking I got into being trained as a combat mage in school because all the young women of that time were hotly interested in fire mages as being the dangerous and interesting types. Enchanters were mostly considered too uptight and boring to get much interest from women in my youth."

I watched as our kobold escort led us into a concealed cavern entrance, "So Yastalus was considered socially boring for his career choice then?"

Glorandel shook his head, "Don't be fooled into thinking that, it was a different time and place when he attended enchanter's college. At that time a bit of a resurgence of female interest in enchanters was happening. Several prominent enchanters such as Crystalgear were on the scene making new changes in enchantment artistry, and working with expensive jewelry is a draw for some women. Yastalus was likely as drawn to his field by female conquest prospects as I was in my day. By the time he attended the enchanter's college the combat mages were considered hacks that couldn't learn complex magic requiring significant investments in time and resources."

I looked over at Glorandel, "Was that about the time you created your privacy spell?"

Glorandel's laughter echoed through the cavern passage as we walked, "I keep underestimating your sharpness. Yes, I did it at first because I saw a need. Then I made it needlessly complex and involved just to prove that combat mages like me were not untalented hacks. Then to make it worse for them I made it simple and cheap to cast, and never revealed the secrets behind it to anyone."

I smiled, "A one way extra-dimensional semi-barrier combined with a divinely enchanted sanctuary item. It is actually three separate primary spells triggered by a keyword. The final spell is an audio illusion which recites the Cycle of Qualanti set on a trigger in a demi-planar pocket which activates anytime someone attempts to breach the semi-barrier with a nullification magic. Did I figure it out?"

Glorandel shook his head, "You are way too sharp for your own good. I've had arch mages puzzling for nearly a century about what spell was involved, and you've figured out the primary elements in less than two years without being a mage yourself. There was of course a lot of refinement involved to get the desired effect, but yes you've got the gist of it."

I grinned, "Thank you for the complement. It also has a weakness that people can read your lips to figure out what you are saying."

Glorandel looked at me with surprise, "What was that?"

I nodded, "If someone has the skill to understand speech from watching the movements of your mouth, they can understand what you are saying."

Glorandel looked at me seriously, "The sanctuary spell should prevent that from happening."

I shook my head, "It just forces the watcher to concentrate harder. As long as they are not intending you physical harm, the sanctuary spell is not very effective. It doesn't make you invisible after all. Perhaps incorporating an illusion spell to make it look like your lips are saying something different? A true artist would make it seem like you were reciting the Cycle of Qualanti for consistency."

Glorandel shook his head as we entered a larger cavern with many orcs and a small group of kobolds inside. Then he whispered to me, "There goes another fifty years of research to make that appear seamless."

A kobold wearing bright face paint and bones through his nose and ears stepped forth in front of the assembled group of orcs, "I am Mak chosen speaker of tribe Kald. The Shinigami is summoned as requested. Our bargain is met, and our tribute paid."

A fierce looking orc stepped forth, "That remains to be seen. I see only elf kind, not bringers of death. I am amazed they have not started running before our mighty warriors already. They seem more simple fools than a threat. It is tribe Kald and their speaker Mak who is shown a bigger fool for fearing them."

Mak calmly stood his ground, "We do not fear The Shinigami. There is no need to fear death. It comes to all eventually. We are wise enough to recognize death when we see it. The bigger fools you are if you fail to understand what is before you, and if you fail to listen to its words as the allied kobold tribes have wisely done."

The orc grunted, "You'll find your death today at my hands little bug if you are challenging me."

Several other orcs began hooting out in a loud primal noise. Suddenly a large grizzly bear appeared in front of the belligerent orc who blinked in surprise and yelped in a high pitched tone as he stepped back. The other orcs' hooting changed to laughter as the orc stepped back shamefaced. Mak clearly wore a smirk of victory on his muzzle as the laughter of the orcs quieted. The bear then turned in my direction and visibly diminished in size. It crouched down on its knees and bowed its head at my feet.

Each of the kobolds in the chamber also knelt on their knees and bowed their heads in my direction save Mak who remained standing as he faced the orc crowd without fear. Then Mak turned and knelt before me as well.

Mak spoke from bent knee, "The Shinigami will you spare tribe Kald this day from your ultimate judgment."

I nodded at Mak as I spoke, "I do not plan to kill any of tribe Kald this day shaman Mak speaker of tribe Kald, representative of the allied kobold tribes. I have only come to speak here today, and none shall be killed by my hand here today unless their own action draws forth my ire."

An elderly orc came forward from the back of the cavern. He carried a long staff and a footman's flail at his side. He wore leather robes and the other orcs cleared out of his path. A sneer crossed his features, and I could immediately tell this was an influential member of the orc clan.

The elderly orc spoke, "One Eye, god of the mighty orcs does not recognize one of her lackey minions here. The icy queen of birds is pitiful in the sight of One Eye, a mere servant in his endless home which is filled rank after rank with only the greatest orcs who have proudly fought to establish our rightful rule of the lands we see."

The orcs began their hooting again in religious fervor. I let my eye wander around the assembled orcs until I spotted the relatively young one who had not joined in with the general excited jubilation. I caught his eye as I noticed him studying Glorandel and I intently watching our every reaction.

As the noise died down I called out in his direction, "What do you say to this Chieftain Jarlak? It is to you as leader of your clan I have come to speak. I have not come to engage in a religious discussion with your priest."

The young orc chieftain Jarlak responded as the cavern went silent, "I think you are a steely nerved bastard. I also think you brought Glorandel the Blue Flame an orc foe and former companion of Harack orc doom to fry us all alive if we fail to listen to you or give you any trouble."

I nodded, "Your intelligence is very good. Are there any other statements you want to tell me about before we begin?"

The exit from the cavern was blocked by three female orcs wearing leather robes carrying flails as Jarlak spoke, "I selected this cavern wisely as our meeting place since it is filled with a mineral which disrupts arcane magic. Those minions of One Eye behind you are not limited by that though. I also have a couple of questions I would like you to answer. Why is a mere innkeeper trying to bargain with our clan? More importantly for you is maybe how do you figure you are getting out of here alive?"

I looked over at Glorandel who had a slight grin, "Are you covered or do you need a hand?"

Glorandel smiled, "I'm quite fine lad. It seems his intelligence was not nearly as good as he thinks. I would guess it was definitely an uninformed inside source."

I took a half step back into Glorandel's shadow and shadow stepped to the position right behind Jarlak, "I am afraid Glorandel is correct. He's here as my second. As Mak already said I'm the truly dangerous one here."

Jarlak tensed a moment in a hint of brief panic rapidly concealed as he realized his precarious position. "Ah, the kobolds were not as full of dung as I suspected. You most certainly are one of her Shinigami."

I saw the elderly orc priest preparing to cast a spell as I spoke loudly, "I suggest that before you once more mistake your situation you carefully consider consulting a minion of One Eye."

The elderly orc priest hesitated, "I am the voice of One Eye here."

I nodded and spoke more slowly, "Yes. You are the voice of One Eye here. Did you bother to consult a higher authority over you before you do something very stupid?"

The elderly orc priest glowered, "I don't answer to one of her minions."

I looked over at Jarlak who had cautiously not moved an inch since I appeared behind him, "Is he slow or something. Would you please explain it to him in your own tongue as what I am saying is not sinking in quickly enough?"

Jarlak relaxed a bit, "What do you want me to relay? I will translate accordingly."

I nodded, "He should ask permission from the being as close to One Eye as he can reach in the beyond. Make it very clear that he is about to cause a disruption with The Shinigami, not a Shinigami. Do you understand the difference?"

Jarlak shrugged, "The difference in unclear in our tongue. We do not use articles."

I sighed, "Does the name Godkiller translate into your tongue?"

Jarlak nodded and spoke in a rough guttural series of phrases accompanied by gestures to the elderly orc priest. The elderly orc priest jabbered back at him for a while, and the other orcs began to shift nervously on their feet as the conversation moved back and forth between them in a more heated manner.

The elderly orc priest eventually acquiesced to his young chieftain, and drew a summoning circle on the ground and began a long ritual casting with the assistance of the other three orc priestesses. The head priest then looked over at Jarlak and spoke in common again.

The elderly orc priest glared in our direction, "There will be a price paid in blood for such a thing. Are you certain I should complete the ritual?"

Jarlak nodded and formally replied, "As Chieftain of the clan of Bloodspear I command it Priest Urgnot of clan Bloodspear. I must understand what I am dealing with before I can lead our clan wisely. I will not take rash action on your whim."

The Priest Urgnot and the three orc priestesses completed the ritual. A puff of sulfurous smoke entered the circle and a small brown imp could be seen looking over at the priest. The orcs in the cavern pressed themselves unconsciously further back from the circle to the edges of the cavern walls. A conversation in the diabolic language of demons occurred between Priest Urgnot and the imp briefly. The term Shinigami was used as Priest Urgnot pointed in my direction. I was surprised to learn it was the same in the diabolic tongue.

I was even more surprised that as the imp turned to look at me its eyes widened comically, and it opened its mouth wide in a piercing shriek. A black oily substance seemed to be shot from somewhere out of its lower section on the ground beneath it as it disappeared leaving behind a foul stench and another cloud of smoke.

The Priest Urgnot seemed highly confused at this point, while the rest of the orcs in the room seemed quicker to grasp the gut reaction of the imp. Except for Jarlak and the orc priestesses the orcs began slowly pressing themselves as far as possible away from me now. In contradiction to the reactions of the rest of the orcs, Jarlak seemed to relax even more standing before me.

A few moments later a bright light appeared within the summoning circle. A column of flame shot forth as a gigantic orcish demon rose from the base of the circle. Every orc in the chamber each bowed down in quivering prostration before the figure as it rose to a height of nine feet.

The demon's booming voice echoed through the caverns, "What could you nuisance pests have done to send one of my minions into a fit of incomprehensible babbling?"

I called out where I remained standing behind the prostrated Jarlak, "I hope you will please let these people know that I am growing tired of their insistence in treating me like some common enemy. If I don't get some requisite respect here soon, then I will have to take it."

The demon turned rapidly and crouched as if ready to spring in my direction. Its eyes narrowed as it looked at me, and then it chuckled, "Foolish Shinigami. I am a herald of Mortis himself, god of all the orcs and mightiest of all the gods. How dare you disrupt my business by threatening our people? A never ending rain of blood shall fall on your queen's palace for this insult."

I brushed my wedding band and a kitten Balinac stepped forth from my shadow. I then released my aura and a visible wave of force rippled through the air from my form hurling the orc demon from the summoning circle and pinning it against the wall. It howled in agony and the assembled orcs moaned in fear as I slowly step by step approached where it was immobilized.

I gave it a wicked grin, "I keep telling these fools 'The Shinigami'. Tell old One Eye that unless he wants to be dragged here to explain it himself all of these orcs had better come to understand just what that really means. No untruths now or you will be destroyed utterly by my hand, your spirit forever entrapped in the far realms."

The orc demon's face contorted painfully as it croaked out, "Fools this is the avatar of the Godkiller. It is also known as the Shinigami in the demonic tongue."

I nodded, "Please continue."

The demon continued in a pained tone, "The gods consider it the greatest abomination in existence. It dwells in the center of madness, and its kind hold the keys to the far realm of endless chaos. It destroyed the elder gods when the new gods rebelled and sought its help."

I smiled, "That's good. Don't neglect the prediction which is told regarding the Shinigami. You know the one I mean."

The demon cried out, "It is prophesied that in the unknown future the Shinigami will even come to end the existence of Mortis mightiest of the gods. Do not hasten that day by your foolish actions."

I nodded, "Please let One Eye know that I expect no retaliation against these orcs for this exchange, otherwise I will be displeased."

The demon spoke in a humble voice as I relaxed some of the pressure of my aura, "I give these orcs to you. Treat them as you see fit. Destroy them if you desire. They no longer belong to Mortis. Consider them a gift The Shinigami."

I smiled, "Let me send you on your way back to One Eye then."

I focused my aura and opened a shadow gate behind the orc demon as I shoved his spirit out of his material body with my left hand. I rapidly drew my saber and sliced the connection between the demonic body and spirit with my saber. I then closed the shadow gate as the spiritless and now lifeless demonic form collapsed on the floor with a loud thud in the surrounding silence.

I gave my winning smile as I sheathed my saber and looked around the room at the prostrated orcs and kobolds and gaping Glorandel, "Now is anyone still confused about the meaning of The Shinigami?"

Balinac walked up to me, "Pushing that thing's spirit out into the plane of shadow here is going to take it relatively speaking months to return to Mortis you know."

I picked Balinac up and gave her a quick pet, "I missed you too dear. How are things?"

Balinac purred, "Doing well you know. Just behind the ear please."

I scratched her ear, "Would you kindly expedite the return of that spirit to its plane of origin and give its master my thanks for his kind gift my dear?"

Balinac shrugged, "I'm sure The Spirit Shaman can find an applicable means to do so. It is going to cost again you know."

I smiled, "We can meet in the usual place. I was looking forward to some of that fish anyway."

A great racking sob came from the prostrated former Priest Urgnot, "What have we done? Madness has come. The end of the world is upon us. We are godless, alone and abandoned by the mighty One Eye. Cast into the arms of this unholy abomination like a sacrifice."

I noticed many of the orcs prostrated on the floor began trembling at his words. I needed to fix this situation before it deteriorated too much to control. I noticed the three orc former priestesses had managed to somehow keep their composure as had Jarlak and the Kobolds. I walked over to the female orcs first.

I restrained my aura again and a palpable relaxing of the tense anxiety seemed to permeate the room. I knelt down and touched each prostrated female orc gently on their heads. They tentatively raised their heads to look into my eyes and gently smiling face.

I spoke to them, "Sisters, please see to your father. Don't lose your heart, I will find a way for you to see divine grace again."

I stood and walked over to where Jarlak lay on the floor as the female orcs moved over to comfort the Urgnot. I looked down at him and touched his head gently as well. He looked up at me with a calculating expression on his face.

I spoke to him loud enough for the entire cavern to hear, "I am leaving for a while. I expect that Glorandel and these kobolds will be in good health and good spirits when I return. Then I will talk with your clan about my request."

I walked over to where the female orcs were clustered around their father Urgnot. His breathing was labored and he seemed in pain. I could feel that his spirit was almost done with his mortal shell. The shock of events had been too much for him.

I put Balinac down and spoke to her, "Balinac please open the tunnel of light. It is his time, and I would see that his journey is quick and painless. Is the White Raven ready?"

Balinac expanded to lion sized as she opened the gate, "The White Raven awaits your arrival, and thanks you for the gift. I will watch things here until your return."

I looked at the three female orcs, "Follow me sisters, and bring your father. He has served clan Bloodspear well, and his reward waits for his arrival."

I walked through the shadow gate into the dark tunnel with the brightly shining light at the end. The three orc females carried the body of their father between them as they followed.

Chapter 44 Beginnings of Peace

I learned it was approximately two hours later in the cavern when I stepped through the shadow gate in return with the three orc priestesses following me. The mood in the cavern seemed pensive and depressed. The orcs were obviously worried that they had grossly misunderstood their situation.

Each of the priestesses was now dressed in a fine black silken chemise with the white outline of a raven on the front and back. Each of the orcs looking in their direction seemed impressed by the radiance which came from them. I imagined by orcish standards they appeared like pure holy beauties. I simply had to recognize they were the nicest looking orcs I'd ever seen, but that really wasn't saying much as I still wasn't too drawn to the greenish skin and pearly tusks.

The middle orc priestess stepped forward to speak as I stepped aside, "I have seen a miracle today. Our clan was dropped down low as our god abandoned us. We doubted our future. My father Priest Urgnot himself grieved so deeply for our loss that the pain of it cost him his life."

A muttering went through the assembled orcs as she continued, "I myself personally felt the abandonment of One Eye, and I knew the powers he had previously granted were stripped from me. Yet, I also understood that One Eye himself fears The Shinigami. The One Eye is a coward at heart and he is an unfit god to lead us. Mortis is nothing to us anymore."

The crowd of orcs gasped at her brazen use of their former god's actual name and the condemnation for their former god coming from the priestess. Once more they shifted about nervously. However, I noticed that Jarlak was instead focused on my neutral expression.

The priestess continued over the noise, "I am here to tell you of the miracle I have seen. It is the miracle of our downfall, and it is also the miracle of our rise. The Shinigami brought us before the goddess of death, the goddess of winter, the White Raven. The Shinigami faced the goddess of death, and the White Raven faced The Shinigami knowing that it held her own future death in his deathless hand. The White Raven was unafraid, and accepted what must eventually come to even the gods."

I noticed a change in the orcs as a glimmer of hope began to spread through the cavern as she continued, "The White Raven is our example. Our deaths are foreordained by the gods we serve, and we need not fear them. For all of you who choose to serve the White Raven as I and my sisters have chosen to serve need not fear their own deaths anymore. The White Raven has guaranteed us service with her in the beyond. She has taken in the spirit of my father Urgnot, abandoned by the coward Mortis, and given it a place of proud service in her realm."

The orcs began to stand up straighter and prouder than before. I noticed that Jarlak had a slight grin now as he understood the shifting fortunes of fate had not yet abandoned his tribe, but simply closed off one path while opening another.

The orc priestess finished, "I am Dulga no more. Never will I answer to that name of fear and slavery again. I have been reborn as Munin Snowraven priestess of the White Raven."

The orc priestess on Munin's right spoke, "I am Elga no more. Never will I answer to that name of fear and slavery again. I have been reborn as Hekla Snowraven priestess of the White Raven."

The orc priestess on Munin's left spoke, "I am Fulga no more. Never will I answer to that name of fear and slavery again. I have been reborn as Jekla Snowraven priestess of the White Raven. All who reject a fear of death and who join us in the worship of the White Raven shall become known as part of clan Snowraven."

Jarlak looked me directly in the eye as he stepped in front of the assembled orcs, "I am of clan Bloodspear no more. Never will I answer to that name of fear and slavery again. I have rejected a fear of death, and enter into the service of the White Raven as Jarlak Snowraven leader of clan Snowraven."

I nodded to acknowledge Jarlak and he returned my nod as an equal. We both understood I could kill him at will, and yet there was no need to fear it happening. One by one each of the orcs stepped in front of me declaring their worship of the White Raven and their rejection of a fear of death. They all took on the name clan Snowraven, and proved themselves as tightly knit and as loyal to each other as Glorandel's reports had suggested.

The kobold shaman Mak stepped forward beside his bear spirit companion after the last orc had made his pledge, "Now you know why we kobolds do not fear The Shinigami. Will you listen to its request clan Snowraven?"

Jarlak looked across his gathered orcs who each nodded as they met his gaze, "We of clan Snowraven are of one purpose. We will listen to what The Shinigami has to say, and make our decision as best suits the needs of the clan."

I moved over beside Glorandel again as Balinac shrank back down to the size of a cat and jumped into my arms, "I have this to say to clan Snowraven. I have worked with the elves in nearby Letheron searching for less conflict between them and their neighbors. I have made alliances with the kobolds here in what the elves call the wild lands. Through the kobolds I have learned of which clans were foolish and which clans were wise. I have hired adventurers to hinder the foolish clans. I have watched which clans were wise enough to see an opportunity where others only seek violence. I have seen clan Snowraven expand and grow through wise action without unnecessary violence and wrongful assault. I now extend an invitation to clan Snowraven to enter a discussion with the moderate representatives of Letheron. I place no terms on this discussion beyond that it remain a peaceful one on both sides, and both sides listen to what the other side is saying. I have a carriage awaiting the representatives from the allied kobold tribes and from clan Snowraven if you agree to come to the Reading Dragon Inn."

Jarlak nodded and spoke, "Fairly said then. What if we do not agree to come? What happens to clan Snowraven?"

I looked at him carefully, "I will do nothing to clan Snowraven unless their action draws my response. I will protect my own and honor my alliances, otherwise clan Snowraven is free to do as they decide. I can not make any promises for the elves of Letheron as I am not one of them or their representative."

Jarlak nodded again, "What will you do if we either refuse or agree to meet with the representatives of Letheron?"

I grinned at Jarlak, "You are wise to ask. If you refuse I will seek out another clan that proves they are wise and extend the same offer to them. They will reap any benefit gained instead of clan Snowraven, and they will also take the risk. If you agree then one benefit gained at least will be that we will continue to hinder the foolish clans, and provide more opportunities for clan Snowraven to prosper in the remains of their loss. We will also punish any adventurers who interfere with clan Snowraven in your territory if a treaty is made and kept between your people and the people of Letheron."

Jarlak looked across the orcs in the cavern who all returned his gaze solidly. They did not indicate if they agreed or disagreed with my offer, only that they would trust his decision. Jarlak thought a moment longer looking at his people. Then he turned to face me again.

Jarlak spoke, "This is not a decision which can be made by me alone. I will need to consult my people to find out their hearts. Please leave us and wait a ways off outside. We will send a messenger to you with our decision."

I nodded, "I can ask no more of clan Snowraven then. We shall wait until the evening star shows in the firmament. If your messenger does not arrive by that time, then I will consider that your answer."

I waited with Glorandel in a glade a mile away from the cavern entrance. Glorandel kept looking at the kobolds creating a perimeter of security around the clearing and the kobold shaman Mak sitting beside us with his spirit bear companion. It was only a little after midday so we sat down to a simple traveler's meal which had been prepared for our journey by Yuki's staff that morning.

Glorandel shook his head as he ate his pocket bread filled with spiced foul and fresh greens, "I don't know how to describe it. I have never seen an entire clan of orcs managed so effectively. Not one of them had to be touched, but they changed allegiance to their very own god at your behest. It was the most, well, dramatic bloodless social upheaval I have ever witnessed."

I sighed, "They lost their priest. I didn't intend that to happen."

Glorandel shrugged, "That could not be considered your fault. It was his own ability to adapt to the changing situation which failed him. The rest of the orcs made the change easily enough. I would say you've done better in that situation than I thought possible for anyone. I figured you would have to kill at least one tenth of them before they understood their danger."

I looked down, "I still consider it a loss to cost the life of even one of them."

Glorandel shook his head, "Then there was that demon you cast down. A herald of a god no less."

I shrugged, "It was just inconvenienced actually. It will simply have to wait one hundred years to manifest on the prime again. Such beings are rarely ever truly killed."

Glorandel laughed, "You underestimate the punishment it is likely to suffer at the hands of One Eye for its failure and One Eye's embarrassment. It was so quick to give that clan away because the knowledge you made it reveal tainted them. Through your acts the new clan Snowraven would never fully respect One Eye as their god again, and the demon was smart to cut his losses by offering them as a gift. Now they can at least be declared apostate liars to the other orcs by One Eye's priests. Given the fact that demon was quick on its toes to recover what it could of a bad situation; it will probably only be demoted to the assistant of that imp you frightened."

I shrugged, "Once more I don't think that matters at the moment. I am more concerned about how they will react to my offer. I have already put them through one dramatic change today. I don't know if they are ready to give up many generations of animosity with the elves, or even if the elves are willing to countenance a fair treatment of their position."

Glorandel shrugged in return, "You have given them the chance to form a peace for as long as it will last. They will still have to seize the opportunity before them."

Mak spoke to us, "Jarlak is a smart leader. He knows the opportunity as well as you both. The only obstacle he sees is presenting it in a way his clan will accept without division. He must convince them without seeming to force them. Otherwise they will fracture and break. Jarlak will always choose his clan first, and reject even a good offer if his clan will become divided over it. Give him time to work, you have already won him and the priestesses over."

Glorandel smiled, "Well spoken Mak. What is the decision of the kobolds?"

Mak smiled, "We are prepared to accept any alliance which gives us advantage over our competitors. The alliance of kobold tribes is allied with clan Snowraven. The alliance of kobold tribes is allied with kobold friend the Shinigami. There would not even be a current alliance of kobold tribes without the Shinigami. We are prospering, and more choices in females and more healthy pups are born. It is good times for our tribes. We would like an alliance with the elves so that they too stop killing the kobolds, we will respect their boundaries, and not enter their lands without permission as long as they seek the same from us. We will punish our transgressors as long as they punish theirs equally."

Glorandel looked thoughtful, "It is refreshing that you are willing to put aside your distrust enough to make this work."

Mak smiled, "All races look down on kobolds until the kobold friend the Shinigami comes to show us respect. Now we prosper, so we follow the lead of the Shinigami. We consider his advice, and have done well. There are no regrets in making the attempt here, even if there is no success at first. No promises have been made, and the allied tribes understand the chance of failure today. They will continue to try as long as there is a chance at an accord with the elves of Letheron."

A couple of hours later as mid afternoon approached two cloaked and deeply hooded figured approached our perimeter of kobold guards. The guards looked them over briefly and allowed them to pass. The cloaks bore the symbol of the Snowraven, and I could tell it was Jarlak and Munin that had come. Glorandel and I stood to greet them as they approached.

Jarlak spoke first, "This has been a difficult day for my clan. There is much uncertainty still among us. We do not know yet how this will change us, and whether we can survive the change. We have petitioned our new goddess for advice, and she has responded that we must respect the dead. That we must respect the Shinigami as the bringer of death, and one of the dead. My people are confused by this new approach, so I have come to you with questions they want answered."

I nodded at him, "I will attempt to answer as best I am able under the circumstances."

Jarlak spoke in return as he closely watched my face, "How can you be one of the dead, and still the bringer of death?"

I contemplated his question a moment, "It would be simplest to say that I died once in body, but that my spirit was not ready to surrender this life, and sought a way to return. This body is in truth just a shell for my eternal spirit. The same is true for your body, and even the bodies of the gods. It is only the spirit which holds immortality. The material must always eventually fade. That is simply the nature of existence. The shaman Mak there could have told you as much. The part about becoming the bringer of death is much more complex and hard to relate accurately in a short time. To put it as simply as possible, I made a series of mutually beneficial alliances against the expectations of many. All sides are benefiting and prospering as a result of this alliance."

Munin spoke, "The White Raven indicated something similar to us. She claimed you were no god and no servant, but an ally in a larger alliance."

Jarlak nodded, "Will you ally then with clan Snowraven as you have with the kobolds? Will you do so even if we do not reach an agreement with Letheron?"

I smiled at them, "I will be your ally as will those who work for me. I will respect your territory. I will protect those of your people I accept under my care. I may aid your purposes where mutual benefit is seen. I will not hinder your purposes where no harm comes to me or mine. Do you accept these terms, and agree to abide by the same conditions?"

Jarlak smiled, "Clan Snowraven agrees under the eyes of our goddess the White Raven. We are allied until such time as the alliance is mutually dissolved, or the conditions are considered violated by the actions of either side."

I shook his hand, and the hand of Munin before I spoke, "It is good that you have seen fit to trust me. Will you come to listen to what the envoy Eliasan has to say? I will accept you into my care until you are returned to this spot if you choose to do so."

Jarlak smirked, "That was the promise made to my clan. I was to only go listen to the elves if I could secure an alliance first with you. They trust you as you are not seen as an elf in their eyes, but as an ally of our new goddess. They still do not trust the elves. However, they are willing to listen to their words at your request. They also required your guarantee of your best attempt to protect our well being. It seems that responsibility is sometimes a troublesome thing for them. They sometimes still treat me as a human treats a treasured child."

Jarlak looked over at Glorandel standing at my side, "Do you work for the Shinigami Glorandel the Blue Flame?"

Glorandel nodded, "I am in his employ, and his partner as well in the inn business. I am known as Glorandel the Blue Sage these days as my days of killing other beings are two long centuries behind me."

Jarlak extended a hand, "Then to clan Snowraven you are no longer considered an orc foe. May there be peace between us."

Glorandel returned his handshake, "May there be peace between us. It is a worthy sentiment."

I spoke, "Shall we be going? There is an important meeting tomorrow, and I have some arrangements to verify. Follow us this way to our carriage. I hope you don t mind, but we're going to have to smuggle you into Letheron in a closed coach for this first meeting. If things go well, then that restriction should be lifted for any future visits."

Jarlak shrugged, "A closed coach sounds fine. It is much too bright outdoors at daytime."

I walked with the representatives at my side, and Glorandel a pace behind. The group of kobolds kept a perimeter around us, as their scouts went ahead to determine if the path remained clear. We eventually made it back to our carriage with our driver and Yastalus waiting nearby with a touch of anxiety.

Yastalus came forward, "You've taken longer than I expected. Are these the representatives?"

I nodded, "This is Chieftain Jarlak of clan Snowraven, Priestess Munin of clan Snowraven, and shaman Mak of tribe Kald. I have extended them my personal protection until they return to the safety of their people. Honored guests, this is Yastalus Leafbreeze who works for the customs agency of Letheron. He will briefly inspect your items to make certain nothing carrying a dangerous enchantment is brought to Letheron."

Yastalus spoke nervously, "It is just a formality. I will not confiscate anything, but may ask certain items to be left with your people or secured for everyone's safety."

Yastalus looked over their gear and declared nothing problematic for entry into Letheron. I entered the carriage with our guests and Glorandel, while Yastalus rode with the driver on the outside. Nothing unusual happened upon our return journey to Letheron. Yastalus cleared us through the checkpoint without the guards checking the carriage.

Jarlak commented after we passed the border, "It seems the elves have been enhancing this valley since my people last viewed it. There are more people here now, and not all of them are elves anymore. There are also greater defenses in place. Is this the heart of your lands The Shinigami?"

I smiled in response, "I own the inn here of course, but it has also brought many other businesses to take advantage of the growth which has come to this area. Also for convenience among the elves here I am known as Mica Lichan. The term the Shinigami is not known to them."

Jarlak's eyes narrowed a bit, "They don't know what you really are then?"

I shook my head, "Only a select few know the truth. It is only those in this carriage, a couple of key employees, and my wife of course."

Jarlak laughed, "You are a wolf among the sheep then."

I gave him a serious look, "Closer to a dragon among humans in that comparison. These people may look docile, but they can still fight."

Munin spoke with a slight smile, "It surprises me that a being like you would have a wife."

I shrugged, "I am not incapable of love. She loves me, and she accepts what I am as well as what I must do. I am a lucky person in that regard. We were married by a priestess of the White Raven. You should keep that in mind. The White Raven is not adverse to her followers finding love and marrying."

Munin leaned over to whisper in my ear, "Our chieftain is too young for me, but my youngest sister Jekla is drawn to him, and closest to his age. I will propose a match between them to our goddess. It will help secure our clan, and their future."

Jarlak looked at the two of us with suspicion, "Are you two plotting something I won't like?"

Munin leaned back, "I was asking him something regarding elf mating rituals."

Jarlak seemed embarrassed, "Leave me out of the discussion then."

I replied, "My wife is actually a human. However, we are still compatible for mating."

Munin looked over at Jarlak, "What do you think Chieftain Jarlak? Do you want an elf bride, or maybe a human one is more sensible?"

Jarlak flushed, "I'm not ready to go that far to secure an alliance. Let's change the topic already. Is that your inn on the hill?"

I nodded, "The Reading Dragon Inn has the most luxurious accommodations available in this part of Letheron."

Jarlak shrugged, "I don't know if I will be comfortable sleeping in a tree like you elves."

I smiled, "That issue has already been addressed. I have arranged a suite in the underground quarters for your use. We have no dwarf guests at the moment. So there are plenty of available rooms for your privacy and comfort."

Through the curtains of the carriage I could see Yuki step out from the back service entrance of the restaurant to wave at our return. We turned down the lane and went to the coach house at the back of the hill. We departed the carriage and traveled though the reception area to the lower reception desk. Will Crusher was at the desk to hand out the keys as well as room service menus to each of our guests.

I gave them a tour of the lower level guest facilities as well as their rooms. Chieftain Jarlak seemed impressed as did Priestess Munin. Shaman Mak seemed merely resigned to accept being kept indoors for the duration. I left them to their rooms after assigning them each a personal staff member to wait on their needs and act as their secretary as needed for the meetings scheduled tomorrow.

I took the underground service passage over to the restaurant for my dinner. A fair sized amount of people were at the restaurant. Yuki was waiting at my private table in the back office with my favorite dish ready to go. We ate together in relative silence just enjoying our company and the meal before us. After I finished eating she looked up at me.

Yuki spoke, "You took a while, but look no worse for wear. How did it go today?"

I smiled briefly, "Oh the usual day. Slew a demon, converted a clan to worship the goddess, and began a peace process. Really there was not much that happened today."

Yuki frowned, "I expect a full debrief when we get home tonight. It sounds like an eventful day, and I'm sorry I had to miss it."

I nodded, "I would have liked to have you at my side as well. We are almost done with this phase of the operation now. It is the most delicate part of our involvement. Then we enter our final phase soon. The rest after that will lie in Lirae's hands."

Yuki sighed, "It has been a good two years for us. It has almost been like we were normal people with normal lives for the most part. I'll feel a bit sorry to move on to our final stage of the operation."

I smiled, "We still have a few months left at least until everything is in place. This Reading Dragon Inn was always meant to be the first of many. We've already proven the concept to be a success with enough market research. So it will be time soon to move on to our next location."

Yuki smiled, "Back home to Ard next?"

I sighed, "I've been thinking about that more lately as this job reaches the next stage. I think I will visit Ard briefly when this is done, but not for the original reasons I thought I would three years ago."

Yuki looked concerned, "Isn't that what you wanted?"

I nodded as I looked her in the eyes, "It was at the time. I am very happy with what I have now though. I love you very much Yuki. I know our life can't ever be a perfectly normal life."

Yuki smiled at me, "I love you too Mica. I don't mind which way our life takes us. As long as we stay together through it I will make it work for us."

I lowered my head down, "I will miss you while I'm gone."

Yuki dropped her head, "When it is time don't be gone too long my husband. It would be like missing my heart."

I raised my head, "I will return. I shall always find a way back to you. It's time we both got back to work. We will talk in more detail tonight before bed, but there is a lot to arrange before then."

Yuki kissed me and returned to her kitchen to supervise the staff once more. I realized that although I seemingly had the harder task ahead of me, her role would eventually take a greater toll on her as a person. However, as Thomas had observed upon first seeing Yuki, she had a good core of steel which was both flexible and strong.

Three hours later in the library I saw Glorandel come in with a worried expression on his face. He had not looked worried through our entire encounter with the orcs, but it surprised me that he looked that way now.

Glorandel looked at me cautiously then came over to me, and whispered in my ear, "Let's talk in my room."

I followed him up to his room where he cast his privacy spell, and then surprisingly cast another unfamiliar spell around the space. He looked at me with a look of deep concern as he sat down in the chair beside me.

I looked at him calmly, "What has you so worried Glorandel?"

Glorandel sighed, "I made a mistake. I didn't think to fully examine the background of the retinue of the envoy Eliasan before they arrived. I just met them in the bar downstairs. One of their members is in the direct employ of a representative who openly supports Reminas."

I nodded, "I had got that information as well from Lirae just before they left Letheros. I'm sorry I forgot to relay it on to you. It was a necessary compromise the moderate representatives had to make when the faction backing Reminas' position caught on to their proposed talks tomorrow. As no authority beyond opening a dialog with the wild lands representatives has been granted, they really could not deny the moderate envoy. They could insist on having an observer present at the talks. The observer is not allowed to enter the discussions though, they are only to be the eyes and ears back to Reminas' faction."

Glorandel looked at me, "The faction backing Reminas' position is almost certain to interfere now. This peace process is too young to take a significant opposition to it at this stage."

I nodded, "I'm counting on their interference actually, and during my recent discussion with Lirae I am hoping to move up the timetable to make them feel obliged to step outside of legitimate channels to stop us. Then we shall need to be at the right place to catch them in the act."

Chapter 45 Betrayal

The next two months were productive ones for the Reading Dragon Inn. After the first successful discussion between the alliance of kobold tribes, the clan Snowraven, and the representatives of Letheron a growing movement in Letheron supported by Lirae's involvement generated more and more support for achieving stability and peace along the northern border of Letheron. Our observations of Reminas' faction's activities were that they were getting desperate as more moderates joined the peace faction.

As a result several moves were made against various parties within the government, and attacks began happening on the Reading Dragon Inn during the continuing treaty discussions we hosted. Our planning had provided a fairly secure facility which was not easy for outsiders to broach. Clan Snowraven chieftain Jarlak had been granted diplomatic status in Letheron and their clan began a campaign of conversion among the stray members from broken orc tribes. They were steadily growing and creating a stable region north of Letheros bordering on the size of a small city state.

Clan Snowraven had even integrated their territory structure to share their territories jointly with the allied kobold tribes. They were quickly moving along the path to being a small nation as other wild land races saw the advantages they were beginning to reap from stability.

In terms of our mission it was an even more productive two months. The number of elves sympathetic to Reminas' position had declined in membership among the more moderate minded elves. For the first time in fifteen years more elves were immigrating from the Fey Realm than into it from Letheron as the tension on the northern border eased. The representative members of the hard line isolationist position in the government began to argue back more bitterly, and in the process started alienating the other factions on their own without much help needed from Lirae.

In four more months the hard line political faction backed by Reminas had hunkered themselves into their political position, and prepared to weather the storm created by signing a new treaty with what had effectively become a stable nation of wild races north of Letheron. Reminas' organization itself had gone to ground. They obviously feared some kind of potential internal compromise, and had begun to purge formerly loyal members who were not considered committed enough to get the job done.

Our intelligence indicated extreme measures being adopted among the inner circle of Reminas' organization. They began covertly courting assassins to make attempts on key persons, both in the government, and more particularly directed against me. I made it a point to be very publicly vocal of my support of the shift in government. Among the local elves in my community I even became a leader as many of them had benefited by the business brought by the Reading Dragon Inn.

The first few attempts on my life were amateurish warrior bumpkins who were easily captured without significant harm, yet who ultimately could not be tied back to Reminas' organization other than by their basic philosophy. The next few attempts were hired professionals of a sort. They had been paid poorly, and were certainly not top tier assassins. These we roughed up and where necessary submitted to rudimentary interrogation until turning them over to the authorities. It was clear they really were not directly in Reminas' organization, or even aware who ultimately had hired them.

I lay in bed beside Yuki on a cold early morning in the winter months. It was nearly seven months since we had first opened discussions with clan Snowraven. I could see patterns of frost on the window beginning to glow with the light of the almost risen sun. Yuki lay in bed beside me warm and comfortable. I knew I loved her more than anything at that moment. I wanted that moment to last, but I knew it would not last forever.

I sat up in bed, and slid my gold and diamond ring from my right hand. I placed it on the ring finger of Yuki's right hand and it seemed to fit as if it had been made for her. She opened her eyes and looked at me with a touch of sadness.

I spoke, "Look after that ring for me. I think I will go for a run this morning."

Yuki gave me a faint smile, "I thought you had enough exercise last night."

I smiled back, "It was very good. However, something about a run on a cold frosty morning after a new snow makes me feel alive."

Yuki sat up herself, "I need to get ready too. I'll miss you while you're gone. I want you to be careful."

I looked at her with a touch of my old cocky assurance, "I think it's a good day to die actually."

Yuki replied back as I got dressed, "Don't get lost. I don't want to have to come looking for you."

I gave her a hug as she got out of bed, "I want you to be careful too my dear."

Yuki held up her wedding band before me. The emerald flashed brightly as she clasped my left hand with her left and kissed me. We held each other close, and kissed not as passionate lovers, but as two people who had long ago become as one.

I left out on my run. I did a bit of slope work as was my habit, and then I decided to run up the valley toward the border station. After I reached it I ran down through the growing village and could see the property of the Reading Dragon Inn ahead of me. I saw the delegates for the next peace conference heading from the inn to the restaurant. This time it was the first delegation from the human kingdom to the west of Letheron. Many of the representatives from Letheros were present for the event with the notable absence of any hard line isolationists.

It was then I noticed something out of place. I saw an elf wearing two short swords and carrying a short bow who was not on our guest list that day, and who certainly was not one of my staff. It looked like Phini Intos, the elf work boss we had used, but had not seen for almost two years now. He seemed to notice me coming and moved to block my view of him by going behind a building.

I only had my dagger at my side as I had left my saber at the chateau. I considered alerting the staff, and then knew it was best if I dealt with it myself. I hurried down on a projected intercept course, well aware that a number of dignitaries could become hurt if things got out of control. I rounded the building where I had lost sight of Phini Intos, but I could not see anything on the other side immediately.

I turned to look back just in time to catch the first arrow in my right lung. It had nicked my esophagus and would have struck my heart squarely if I had not turned at that moment. I ignored the pain and drew my dagger weaving to the side as the second arrow barely missed my artery as it hit and passed through my neck. Phini Intos had murder in his eye as he fired the third arrow at me while I closed on him.

I was struck in the head by the third arrow. It left a bloody furrow along the left side of my skull, but had not penetrated at that angle. I swung my dagger and made a loud scream as I struck at Phini Intos. Our fight had finally drawn the attention of several people outdoors, and they began either rushing closer or for cover depending on their level of panic or dispositions. Phini Intos turned my blade with his bow, but misunderstood that I wanted his bowstring more than him with that strike. I was at the disadvantage at a distance, and now had the fight in my optimal operating zone.

Phini Intos jumped back abandoning his bow, and drew his matched short swords with a precision, grace, and economy of motion which let me know he knew exactly how to use them. He came at me hard and fast with both short swords. I barely managed to deflect the one blow, and avoid the other. It was getting harder to breathe with the arrow in the top of my lung. I could tell I was starting to bleed into it pretty heavily. The blood also spattered the new snowfall.

I went on an aggressive offense, moving forward with some of my best knife work. However, Phini Intos knew I was only going to get weaker the longer the fight drew on this way. He went into a fully defensive mode blocking my attacks with seemingly little effort. I watched his pattern for a while and spotted two different kinds of openings. One was likely a feint designed to lure me into a poor position in desperation.

The other opening looked accidental, and much smaller. I made a feint at the obvious opening, and shifted my blow to smaller opening. Then I spotted the third real opening and once more moved from my second feint to the real attack. I took one of his swords down my left arm, numbing it, and possibly loosing the use of it for the rest of the fight. I managed to get my dagger in through his kidney and possibly up into his liver.

We jumped back away from each other and momentarily assessed our positions. I was bleeding heavily. I had a severed artery in my left arm bleeding profusely, and it was useless now. I might even lose it if a cleric didn't get to me soon enough. My right lung was practically useless, and blood was starting to come out of my mouth. My neck was slick with blood, and my head was feeling light. Surprisingly the pain was only a minor annoyance.

Phini Intos had a critical wound from my dagger into his kidney and liver, otherwise nothing was immediately fatal with his condition. That was when I noticed his blades were coated with poison.

Phini Intos grinned wickedly at me, "You realize you are a dead man walking now don't you. You stuck me good, but I'll live to fight another day. Goodbye Mica. Thomas the Poisoner sends his regards."

As I dropped to my knees I saw Yuki's magic pan crush the side of his face. A strange mask seemed to fall off, and a unfamiliar twiline elf was laying on the ground in front of me as I fell face forward into the blood covered snow below me.

Chapter 46 The Death of Mica Lichan

I felt an iciness begin to seep through my body. I was not bleeding out too fast anymore. This was mainly because there was not much blood left inside where it belonged. Of greater concern was the toxin mixing with what little blood was left in my veins. It was slowing my heart and causing minor convulsions as I lay face down in the blood soaked snow.

I felt a certain sense of familiarity, as if I was somehow heading home. I could no longer see, but I heard Yuki's voice shouting my name. My nerves were numb, and all the pain had gone. Then my heart stopped beating. I focused my will then, and stepped out of my body. I looked down upon it from above. I saw several elves clustered around with shocked looks on their faces. I saw Yuki crouched in the snow crying in grief, her knees soaked in my blood. Frankly speaking the body of Mica Lichan was an unrecoverable mess.

I felt a certain sadness. That body had been my home. I enjoyed it very much. I looked over at the body of the twiline and saw that it still lived. It's spirit was still attached, and it showed to my eyes now as being comprised of two colors, mostly orange, with a touch of violet. That was certainly a characteristic of Thomas' work. The elves around the twiline were binding it securely, stripping it of weapons, and any dangerous gear.

A couple of elves attempted to remove Yuki from where she crouched over the dead body of Mica Lichan. She fiercely held on and batted away any hands which attempted to touch her. I reached down with my spirit and stroked her head. A fresh set of tears started from her eyes as she knew I was dead. This was to be the hardest trial she would undergo in her life so far. Yuki did not fear death, but she still did grieve the loss of her loved one.

More bystanders came along gaping at the bloody mess the two of us had made. Eventually Glorandel came running down with an expression of shock in his eyes. A certain hardness remained in him for the moment. He was certainly no stranger to scenes such as this one in his life. Glorandel organized the staff to create a perimeter and to secure the twiline assassin inside the inn.

Glorandel then came over and crouched next to the body of Mica Lichan being clutched by Yuki. He ignored the red blood soaking his blue robes as he spoke to her gently. I couldn't hear the words, but I could read his lips.

Glorandel's lips kept saying to her, "Mica is gone Yuki. Mica is gone. You must let that body go. It is no longer who Mica is anymore."

Glorandel gently lifted Yuki away from my dead body. I saw the sobs rack her small form as several elves in my employ moved to position my body in a more seemly manner. Glorandel hugged her like a father comforting an injured child.

Yuki looked over his shoulder at me, and mouthed the words, "I love you Mica."

Without a physical form I was helpless to respond, but I mouthed the words anyway, "I love you Yuki."

I saw a faint smile cross her lips as she acknowledged my words. Then she allowed Glorandel to lead her inside the main inn structure. I looked back at my body one more time, and then moved inside as well.

I looked to find where they had taken the assassin. I followed the trail of blood and found that the twiline was securely fastened to a table in the winery portion of the sub levels. He was conscious again, and obviously in pain from his injuries. The right side of his face was a bloody ruin from where he had been struck by Yuki's pan. A simple bandage had been applied to the dagger wound I had given him, but that was a temporary measure at best. The wound was deep, and would likely prove fatal in a few days without proper aid.

There were four guards in the room. Two were closely watching the prisoner, and two were watching the door. They made certain only proper staff were allowed to enter. I moved over beside the golden chain leading from the ring on the twiline's right hand. It was a golden ring with a diamond which looked very familiar. I grabbed the golden chain with my spirit, and gave it a sharp tug. The chain dissipated, and the diamond on the ring cracked.

The twiline closed its one good left eye, and mouthed the words, "No escape."

An indeterminate amount of time later Glorandel entered the room. He cast a number of spells with no immediately obvious effect and then left again briefly. Then the lead Human and Elvish delegation members came into the room along with a couple members of their staff. They interrogated the twiline elf which was compelled by Glorandel's spells to answer and speak truthfully.

The twiline told a story of how it had first been hired to spy on the isle corporation's activities, and then subsequently been hired to assassinate Mica Lichan by a prominent representative of the isolationist faction. More importantly this representative was known to be a key member of Reminas' organization and had been strongly backed by them.

Of particular note was the look of shock among everyone in the room as the twiline revealed his name. I watched his lips carefully as he said, "Thomas the Poisoner."

A short while later Yuki entered the room still grieving and obviously maddened. None of the staff dared to intercept her as she approached the table. She removed her largest kitchen cleaver from under her winter cloak and in one hard stroke took the head off the twiline who had killed me as if he had been a slab of meat put out for butchering.

I watched the spirit depart the body, and I followed it to the plane of shadow. I looked over at the shortling Alvos standing there looking at me with a grin. I gave Alvos a bow as I moved over to it.

I spoke, "Nice performance. Do you think they were convinced?"

Alvos replied, "Don't doubt the quality of my work. It took you six months to figure out I was Phini Intos. Cogstone taught me pretty well actually. He said I die better than anyone in the business. I'm a professional after all."

I shook my head, "I never realized you were a twiline the whole time though."

Alvos smiled, "That's because I wasn't. Too many chances to get discovered that way. I used an elf body for most of the time when in Letheron, and only changed to a twiline body for the assassination. It took me two years of hard training with Hardtack to get good enough with that body to take you down too."

I smiled, "Don't get too cocky Alvos. I took it easy on you. I stuck with only my normal melee capabilities, and gave you the first three hits besides."

Alvos rubbed his neck, "Speaking of enhanced abilities, did Yuki have to put so much spirit force into that clever. It still smarts some even in the Shadow, that's a first really."

I shrugged my shoulders, "I'm sure she wanted to give you a clean cut is all. You were in plenty of pain already, so she wanted it to be quick."

Alvos laughed lightly, "I don't mind the pain really. It makes me feel alive after all. Its better than feeling nothing I guess. I was a bit worried when you broke Cogstone's ring though. I was afraid I might become lost trying to get back."

I smiled at him looking at the two Balinac which came running over the rise, "I figured you might appreciate a ride instead of a long walk this time."

Alvos nodded, "Thank you Mica. That's why I like you after all. You're so considerate of the needs of others."

I mounted on top of one of the two Balinac and Alvos mounted the other one. We rode together side by side. Alvos smiled at me later as we dismounted at the entrance to Thomas' tower.

Alvos asked, "Do you think Lirae can succeed?"

I nodded, "With your help Lirae now has the martyr and the villain she needs to win. She won't be able to fully implicate Reminas, but it is enough to destroy his chances for success with his goal and dreams. She will have also managed it without killing anyone who was not prepared to die for the sake of the mission. That is almost as important to her as the mission itself."

Alvos looked at me as we stepped inside the tower, "What's next for you then?"

I looked over at Alvos, "I think it is time to debrief with Thomas."

Alvos shook his head, "I mean in terms of your position here. You took a very long time working on the strategic setup of Lirae's mission. I can't remember any mission we've done which involved three years of ground work. You certainly look for a deeper approach than we normally use."

I smiled at Alvos, "Sometimes it is just too expedient to kill where another more involved solution may actually be the better course of action. As I explained to Lirae three years ago we could have just killed Reminas, and revenge would have been served. However, I think it is better to undo someone in that position, then others can see them for what they are. Lirae now has the perfect position to erode any remaining support for his cause until only a few bitter hard cases will be left with their broken dreams."

Alvos grinned, "So that's why you insisted I present myself to them when the time was right."

I nodded, "It was necessary to make it look like they were more willing to end up in collusion with the twiline queen Litha than to see reason about their cause. If there is anything that would turn elvish sentiment against them it would be cooperation with the twiline to eliminate a problem rival. There are too many reliable witnesses who put Phini Intos in contact with both us and their members. The public confession of the assassin under a truth spell before his execution in front of government witnesses only solidifies the case. However, none of those involved dare even seriously refute the claim because they can not hope to avoid a truth detection spell because of their involvement."

Alvos chuckled, "Still it takes a pretty solid pair to volunteer yourself to be assassinated. Until you came along I was the only specialist on the team for that task."

I smiled as we reached the door at the bottom of the stairs, "I never asked you why that is the case."

Alvos laughed, "Most of the others think dying is pretty horrible. I guess from their perspective it is. I find it is an incredible rush myself. I've accomplished more suicides and more "botched" attempts leading to my death than all the other members combined."

I nodded, "You've been the distraction or bait then."

Alvos smiled, "I don't mind. It was fun pulling off the master assassin role this time though. It was the first time I got to play someone other than a victim for a long time. I'm promoted to a senior now since Cogstone has entered semi-retirement and taken a ruby ring. Thomas even had me as lead on three assassination jobs as the twiline over the past two years to build up the credibility for the role."

I smiled, "Anyone of note?"

Alvos shrugged, "I killed a twiline priestess, a fire giant leader in the deep south, and a barbarian warlord in the wild lands of the north. It felt strange doing missions where I wasn't the decoy and was expected to get out in one piece without a trace. This mission felt like getting back to my roots a little. Though I must admit getting out in one piece has its challenges as well. My earlier approach didn't require much of an exit plan. It was mainly submit to torture, get eaten, get blown to pieces, get incinerated, or commit suicide."

I grinned, "The imminence of death does make you feel alive though does it not."

Alvos grinned along with me, "That it does brother."

Chapter 47 The Rebirth of Mikael Lidron

I awoke with the bright morning sun coming in through the window along with a fresh sea breeze. My body felt stiff, and somewhat strange to me. I could hear two people breathing in the room, one was deep and steady, and the other was light. I opened my eyes to see Yuki looking down at me, and Hardtack sitting in a chair by the window.

Yuki smiled, "You are back with us now Mica."

I nodded, "Yes, I am back. I'm surprised to see you beat me here."

Yuki gave a faintly strange look, "I only just arrived last week. Thomas was still preparing your new body. He said you should appreciate this one."

I gave a faint smile, "It's good to see you. How long have I been gone?"

Yuki looked over at Hardtack before answering, "It's been two months since your death my love. Don't you remember?"

I smiled, "I remember the fight, and I remember the journey to the Tower. I remember talking to Alvos after we arrived. After that my memory is dim."

Hardtack grinned a bit, "I've heard the others all mention that the process of rebirth is a bit disorienting. Some memories don't transition well from the land of shadow upon return, and time moves differently on the many planes. A return in two months is good time actually. We are still awaiting Alvos' return."

I noticed Yuki's frown as Alvos was mentioned, "You need not feel that way Yuki. Alvos was just doing his job."

Yuki sighed, "Alvos made such a mess of you though. I thought the plan was a single arrow quick kill."

I shrugged, "We had a change of plan. I thought it best if Mica Lichan at least went down fighting. It's better for the reputation that way."

Hardtack grunted, "More like two foolish boys breaking their very expensive toys."

I smiled, "Thomas gave us permission."

Hardtack shrugged, "Waste of my time as well. Why did I drill that silly shortling on your weak points for two years if Alvos is just going to wade in and try to melee with you?"

I grinned, "That was my fault. I spoiled Alvos' shots at me, and kind of forced the issue. Those bodies were bound to be killed anyway. I wanted to see what you could arrange if someone got off script. I didn't expect Alvos to be that good at improvising."

Hardtack grunted, "All of my students who pass are good at improvising. It's a requisite skill for any combat. What was Alvos thinking taking you in the middle of the day like that in plain sight?"

I shrugged, "The timing was up to Alvos. We only agreed upon the trigger conditions. It was always intended there would be reliable second hand witnesses present."

Hardtack shook his head, "Bloody fools. You've likely traumatized a lot of very sensitive elves."

I narrowed my eyes in his direction, "Is this a comment from the dwarf who carves up Captain Westly Robert's crew for amusement?"

Hardtack grinned at me, "Now that is for their benefit and education. They need to realize who their betters are."

I dropped my head back down on the pillow, "Hypocrite."

Hardtack laughed, "It's good to see dying hasn't dulled your sense of humor any. It seems your memory is still intact as well."

I looked at Yuki gazing down at me, "Well how do I look?"

Yuki seemed a touch surprised, "Very different, and not quite what I expected."

I asked, "Can you bring a looking glass over?"

I looked at myself in the glass and immediately recognized who I was. I was Mikael Lidron again. That is a Mikael Lidron as he might have been as a well muscled fit thirty-one year old if he had not died. I still bore the scars of my youth. In addition I bore an older scar along my temple on the right side of my head where Davel's boot had struck me in addition to the scars along my side and over my heart where his sword had struck me.

The surprise was the fact I had the relatively new scars of three arrow wounds, one over my right breast close to my sternum, one through my neck on the left side, and a long furrowing scar along the left side of my head above my ear. Finally there was a long jagged scar down my left biceps and forearm.

Hardtack noticed my temporary confusion, "I remember our discussion on the Mystic Dawn lad. About how the only scars you wanted to bear were the ones that had personal meaning. I made sure that they all made it back on this new body. Don't worry though, there is no underlying damage. That body is in top condition considering."

I felt a tear come to my eye, "Thank you Hardtack. What's wrong with my body though?"

Hardtack laughed, "I never realized what a relatively large man you were. You've got muscles to spare lad. I'm going to have to retrain you to fight with a technique which takes better advantage of it. I'm thinking that swapping a saber and dagger for a one handed long sword and short sword combination might be a more suitable mix for your base fighting style. It's probably also time you got to work on your bow skill so you are not so easy at a distance anymore."

Yuki commented with a smile, "There is plenty of dark wavy hair everywhere to spare as well. I never understood how hairy you used to be when you told me of your past."

I acted insulted, "Is there a problem with being hairy?"

Yuki raised an eyebrow, "The beard will have to go. I'm sure it must tickle. We'll discuss the rest later in private."

I nodded, "That we will. How about some breakfast? I haven't eaten in two months so I'm a bit hungry."

Hardtack got out of his chair, "It is mid morning already, but I think we can start up the lunch service early. Most of the others have been eager to welcome you back anyway. They haven't seen you for almost three years now."

As I walked out of the recuperation building I was surprised to see a small group of the Thomas' Isle residents had been waiting for me to awaken. I gave them an appraising look and then a smile. They nodded and smiled at me in return, and stood in an orderly receiving line waiting for our approach.

Cogstone greeted me first as he shook my hand, "I'm glad to see that you are back in action. That was quite a plan Mica. It was worthy of any senior member. I feel good having taken my retirement knowing that you're there to help the next batch of youngsters learn the business."

I replied, "It was only with a lot of help that we accomplished what we have so far. It is up to Lirae to finish the start we have put into place now. She's the new president of the Isle Corporation and the owner of The Reading Dragon Inn now."

Olivia stepped forward to give me a hug, "You've also done a good job of turning a profit against your operating costs by your first year of operation. In another ten to twelve years we should be fully out of the red and into the black with all of our initial investment money regained. After that it should be a steady money maker. At least until we start the next franchise location."

I noticed the emerald ring on Olivia's left ring finger as I replied, "I thought the concept was a solid one, and it was with your help that I was able to make it work. I notice you've got a ring like Yuki now."

Olivia reached over to put her right arm through Cogstone's elbow as she gave me a large smile, "It seems I owe you thanks. You're the one who talked Cogstone into finally settling down. I decided it was time to stop rejecting his offers. I wasn't prepared to settle down with a rambling man. I'm officially Mrs. Nimblehands now."

I smiled, "Congratulations to the both of you."

Yuki reached over to give her a hug, "You should have told me when I arrived."

Olivia blushed slightly, "We wanted to tell you both together."

I shook Cogstone's hand, "So you're finally an honest gnome now."

Cogstone laughed, "Well, seeing that wedding of yours got me to thinking I didn't have to put it off any longer. With my retiring to the island Olivia's objections to marrying me were not a problem anymore."

I gave Yuki a one armed hug, "You'll find it is a worthwhile choice I think."

Cogstone nodded, "We already have. As Olivia said already I give my thanks to you for getting me to think about my priorities."

I replied, "You're welcome.

I moved down to see Jack next in line, "It's good to see you again Jack."

Jack gave me a smile, "You've got to tell me what happened. I've only caught a little bit of it from Yuki, but I'm sorry I'd missed you fighting Alvos. He's a right tricky little shortling, and absolutely fearless about injuries or dying. I'll catch you later in the week to get the details. Hopefully Alvos will be back by then as well. I'd better stop talking before Hardtack decides to take my tongue out now."

I shook Jack's hand, "I'll catch up with you later in the week then."

I moved down the line to see Hiram standing there. He nodded in my direction, and I returned his nod. We gave each other a brief handshake and he gave me a smile before I moved on to the next person in line.

Puck was standing to greet me next, "It's good to see you back. I've kept your hut maintained in your absence, and I have several new items in stock you may want to look over later."

I clasped his forearm briefly, "Thank you for looking after our place. I'll come by in the afternoon after our lunch."

Quizak moved forward, "I want to let you know I've got a brace of sheep here now. There's enough for breeding stock and food purposes. I've heard that you're fond of mutton yet haven't had much the last couple of years."

I smiled as I shook his hand, "I'm glad to hear it Quizak, thank you. I have been missing mutton these last couple of years. It's hard to realize how much you miss something like that until it is not available anymore.

I moved down to see Talgash standing next to last in line, "It's good to see you Talgash. The alliance of kobold tribes north of Letheron is doing well. Your people are prospering and there are many children."

Talgash gave a wicked grin, "It is good the kobolds have found a friend in you Mica. Maybe I ask Master Thomas to bring female kobold here. I miss the young ones."

I shook his paw, "You should ask the next time you see him. I don't know if there is much for children to do here though. The island is not very large."

Talgash dropped his head briefly, "True. I need to think about needs of younglings. I will consider asking to make visits instead. Friend good for lunch soon?"

I smiled, "Friend is good for lunch."

I saw that at the end of the line stood tall lithe human woman with a dark smoky grey skin tone wearing a black leopard print dress. Her hair was black and shortly cropped. Her eyes were a striking jade green. She had a raised eyebrow and wore a slight smirk.

I hugged her warmly, "It has not been often enough Balinac. I like the new form, and it's good to see that you've been making friends here."

Balinac shrugged, "It was hard to keep my secret once the word got out. No one is afraid of me here anymore. It was just easier to join in the group than to stay apart."

I gave her a kiss on the cheek, "I'm glad to hear it. Let's go eat."

A week later I stood clean shaven with close cropped hair in the practice area facing off against Hardtack. I had begun my instruction in paired long sword and short sword. Instead of the traditional varieties used in the Kingdom of Ard I was instead using a matched katana and wakizashi set. I found that my background in saber and dagger was serving me pretty well to begin our training. I felt comfortable maneuvering both weapons in support of each other. It seemed that Hardtack had a different opinion about my technique.

Hardtack shook his head, "Mica, you have to stop treating those arms like plowshares. The idea isn't to hack your opponent into pieces. It is to put through a quick decisive strike to disable or kill your opponent without lodging your blade inside them. Keep focusing on the fact that you never want both blades dealing with the same opponent. The wakizashi is on defense, and only when needed on offense. When the katana is used on offense the wakizashi is on defense. If the katana is already occupied in offense, then the wakizashi shifts back and forth depending on the need. Your katana is never on defense. That is a waste of its abilities when using a paired style."

I nodded, "I understand what you are saying Hardtack. Just let me demonstrate something for you though. I've picked up a couple of new moves you probably don't know about."

Hardtack made a grunt, "It is likely nothing I have not seen before."

I gave him a wicked grin, "Are you certain?"

Hardtack grinned back, "Pick up those practice swords."

I nodded, "You want to do this then?"

Hardtack picked up his inexpensive yet sharpened metal katana, "I shouldn't even need a second blade to deal with you."

I smiled as I brought my weapons to ready position, "Defend yourself."

I came at Hardtack easy for the first couple of strokes. He deftly and almost casually blocked my strokes. I then sped up my next stroke and connected hard with his blade. Hardtack still blocked, but found the strength with which I connected greater than he had expected. I noticed him take a step back.

Hardtack nodded, "Your strength is better, and not at any cost to your speed. How is your precision though?"

I was pushed hard to defend myself with the wooden wakizashi from Hardtack's assault, but I blocked each attack he launched at me. I casually held my wooden katana in reserve. Then I launched a full power attack at his blade which he deftly deflected. I then released my aura through the wooden katana and struck at him with deadly intent.

Once more Hardtack properly intercepted my katana. Only this time he was momentarily surprised as my wooden practice katana cut through his blade like a reed before a scythe. He quickly moved out of the path of my blow, and held up a hand to halt.

Hardtack examined the clean shear on his broken katana, "Does this attack work equally well on flesh?"

I nodded, "It works equally well with any weapon I wield blunt or sharp against any material object."

Hardtack smiled, "What do you call it?"

I grinned, "I was thinking of naming it the unmaking."

Hardtack looked at me carefully, "Could it be taught to others?"

I nodded, "The possibility exists depending on their talent. Yuki knows the way of it now."

Hardtack grinned, "You'll find I'm a very talented student, master. It looks like I've got something new to learn. Your point is made. With an attack like that keep using your weapons like plowshares. There isn't much a conventional enemy will be able to do to stop your attack. Don't get lazy though. Improving your technique will help for those times you don't want to cut your enemy clean in half."

I looked back at him, "Aren't you going to ask if there was a counter?"

Hardtack shook his head, "I already know twenty counters to your attack, and they just all involve staying clear of your weapon and its abilities. Not an easy task I admit, but well within my abilities."

I stepped back into the shadow of a palm tree and shadow stepped behind Hardtack. I whispered, "Are you sure?"

Hardtack shadow stepped over to where I had originally been standing by the palm tree, "Yes I'm pretty certain. You're certainly not the only assassin who has learned that trick. Don't rely on it too heavily to get the job done."

I gave him a slight bow, "Yes master."

Hardtack laughed, "That's better. Just because you showed me something new don't go thinking you can best me yet. You have about three hundred more years of learning to go before that would happen, and by then old age will have done me in anyway."

I nodded, "Of course Hardtack that is only one new trick I've picked up. Thomas has taught me several of his in the last three years."

Hardtack's eyes narrowed, "It seems he failed to mention it to me. Well let's get this over with so I can evaluate your capabilities fully now. That will definitely let me know where to supplement your weaknesses. I suppose Thomas has also learned some things from you as well. That does seem to be the way he works. Let's start with the stuff that you think I might be able to replicate, and then you can move on to other abilities beyond my powers."

One month later I lay in bed in our hut between Yuki and Balinac watching out the window as the moon rose with a shimmer across the sea. I marveled at how Balinac seemed more human now, and I realized it was true the reverse had happened to me. I was perhaps less human now after spending all these years merged in spirit with Balinac, and in elfish form.

Yuki was my solid grounding point to the humanity of my spirit. I loved her deeply for it as well. No matter how quickly the changes were happening inside my being now as Balinac and I synchronised, I still felt that connection with Yuki keeping me balanced.

I knew that at some point in the far distant future Balinac and I would eventually become indistinguishable to others much like the Lucky Cricket was now primarily considered one being with twin aspects. For now it just felt right that a mutual balance was maintained with Yuki as our fulcrum.

I also thought back to the past month and my amazement at how Hardtack had easily learned the new martial abilities I had taught him. Now he was focusing on improving those abilities, and learning to counter their weaknesses. I had come to a conclusion that something wasn't right about him. Being unnatural myself I had come to the conclusion that there was something seriously unnatural about Hardtack as well.

Yuki looked over at me as if guessing my mind, "You can ask my dear."

I smiled, "What does Hardtack's aura look like?"

Yuki shrugged, "It's hard to explain. It is not a mortal's aura is the best way I could put it. The closest parallel I could make would be similar to the aura of the White Raven."

I looked at her with a touch of apprehension, "The aura of a god you mean."

Yuki had a slight grin, "Not as powerful as the White Raven of course, but a similar characteristic."

I looked at Balinac, "A fallen god then?"

Balinac nodded, "The once mortal avatar of a fallen god. The White Raven deemed it too dangerous to let roam freely, so she tasked Thomas with destroying it. Unfortunately this fallen god had completely abandoned its former planar abode to inhabit Harack. There was nothing Thomas could do to kill him at that point. No amount of injury was fatal. He simply healed leaving a scar. It was beyond the power of the White Raven to take the life of another god, even a fallen one."

I began to surmise the situation, "So Thomas calls upon his former mentor for advice. They strike a mutually beneficial deal to manage the problem. Hardtack is brought to the Lucky Cricket's realm where he can do no more harm. Thomas learns more about spirits and mortality, and begins to learn to create these shells. Thomas is also given more free reign by his goddess to operate independently."

Balinac nodded as she placed a hand on my head, "However, it is not that easy to calm down a rampaging berserker god. Not even a fallen one. I was called in as a favor to the Lucky Cricket to help manage his rampage. They figured the only being who could readily kill a god would intimidate it into behaving."

I nodded, "It didn't work did it?"

Balinac shook her head, "It did not work. The fallen god was too crafty and immediately recognized my limitations. I can not take the life of a god until their time was come. That was the agreement made by the numbers when existence was created for the gods. We would let the gods rule the material, and only guard against the corruption of the spirit."

I smiled, "So the elder gods?"

Balinac had a grim look, "I contained each one of them in the far reaches of the spirit realm as they became corrupted in spirit. It didn't leave me many friends among the gods. However, it was necessary. I agreed to serve that function, and so I shall eternally do so."

Yuki asked, "Why didn't you do so with the god possessing Hardtack?"

Balinac had a sad look, "I couldn't. That god had not become corrupt in spirit. Just slowly abandoned and forgotten as other newer more civilized gods came along. It is a pitiful thing to see a god abandoned so. The older ones become angered and hurt like a wild beast. This god somehow found an affinity for a barbarian dwarf, and they struck a pact to become vengeance incarnate as mortal and immortal in avatar form. Together they became Harack the Slayer, goblin slayer, orc doom, ogre bane, and slew a long bloody path together for many years."

Yuki asked, "How did you get him to settle down then?"

Balinac shrugged, "I failed. I could not intimidate that avatar. It challenged me to take its life and suffer the consequences for violating my purpose. I admitted defeat, and I was forced to call upon the Luck for assistance."

I chuckled, "Behave yourself."

Balinac nodded, "The Luck can be very persuasive when it is in a bad mood. Even the gods stay clear of its path when it is that way."

Yuki sighed, "I'm missing another long story again."

I reached over to kiss Yuki, "Sorry dear. Let me tell you a story Hardtack told me on the night you and I first met. It makes more sense in this new context now."

Chapter 48 The Drinking Dragon Inn

It was nearly four months later as I stepped away from the innkeeper's counter at the Drinking Dragon Inn in the capital of the Kingdom of Ard. I walked over to where Balinac and Yuki were drawing many puzzled looks from even the relatively jaded adventurers gathered inside. I was practicing my non-threatening manner learned in years of practice as Mica Lichan. So I only drew a few curious glances from people who likely wondered how I had ended up with these two exotic looking women.

I spoke to Yuki, "It seems our information was accurate. The rumors talk of a purge of the assassin's guild and their known members about two and a half years back during an unexpected attack by various undead. It was speculated they offended a highly placed necromancer somehow."

Balinac calmly spoke with a smug look, "I warned you about that letter back then. Now our trail may have gone cold. Was there any word about an assassin called Ulric?"

I nodded, "Our source reported that an assassin who used that alias was among those confirmed killed. They had no knowledge of anyone named Davel among the assassins though."

Yuki nodded, "He is likely the employer instead of a member then as you thought. Davel likely avoided the attack by the minions of Mortis since he wasn't a guild member."

I nodded, "The master's assets have not spotted any attempts on the Lidron family either in the last few years. They all remain healthy so far according to the reports."

Balinac spoke, "Shall I put a message through to Cricket?"

I shrugged, "I'm certain he knows we need his help already. Let's wait for the arrival of his support team here."

Yuki smiled, "I'll check out the kitchen if you don't mind. I think the food here could use some help. It doesn't look very appetizing."

I smiled back, "Have fun, but don't give away too many trade secrets. We'll need to keep our edge for when we open a branch here."

As Yuki moved to the kitchen Balinac and I sat down at a table. I thought back to my last conversation with Thomas before departing Thomas' Isle.

Thomas had looked at me with a fatherly smile as he said, "Hardtack has judged you ready to go."

I smiled back, "I feel ready to go. It has almost been seven years since I died now. "

Thomas nodded, "The anger and pull for vengeance?"

I shrugged, "Gone for many years as you well know."

Thomas smiled, "Then what remains?"

I thought a moment, "The need for justice remains. It has not faded one bit in seven years. Two innocent lives were taken, and an accounting remains to be paid."

Thomas gave me a subtle look, "Your life and the life of your love Firanda?"

I shook my head, "The life of the simple honest porter Larwick was taken that day, and the life of my half brother Davel was corrupted by his poor decision to become a fratricide, and the desire to move on to be a patricide. Thanks to you Firanda and I live on as you well know."

Thomas looked at me carefully, "So you know the truth of it then?"

I nodded, "I always knew in a way. In Davel I saw too much of the face of my father and my brothers, and yet no resemblance to our mother. He must be our father's bastard son."

Thomas nodded, "That is information you can use now. Remember what you've learned of such bonds. They can be hidden, but they can never go away. You are ready for your mission now. I have given you a body most suitable for the task. You have your old resemblance back, suitably aged and artfully detailed of course. I have made significant enhancements to the model as well. Senses as keen as an elf, resilient as a dwarf, strong as human, fast as a twiline, mind like a gnome, skilled like a shadowine, and as spiritually durable as any material mortal form can be. You may also find that Lirae has added her knowledge and considerable abilities to your new body as well. Frankly speaking I'm a tiny bit jealous. I am looking forward to learning how she managed that particular enhancement."

I bowed, "I thank you for all of your help."

Thomas smiled, "It was a part of our contract. You were a tough bargainer. It is almost as tough as making a deal with the Luck. So who do you want on your team this time?"

I nodded, "I've thought about it for a while. I think for my plan to work I'll need access to your information assets in the Kingdom of Ard. I would also like Yuki and Balinac to be my direct backup."

Thomas looked surprised, "You are of course welcome to choose your wife for your team as you both compliment each other well. However, it is beyond my ability to assign Balinac to assist you. You are also aware how her extended presence on the prime in multiple locations is a strain."

I smiled, "I have made arrangements already. Balinac is being relieved of her responsibilities on the prime portion of the Isle here. A suitable replacement has been found."

Thomas raised an eyebrow, "What arrangement is that?"

I gave him a grin, "Hardtack has been put on probation. He no longer requires Balinac nearby to contain his rage. On the next boat a female kobold shaman is coming to act as a watcher for the Lucky Cricket. Balinac has been reassigned to me."

Thomas shook his head, "The Lucky Cricket is sending a female kobold spirit shaman? That could prove eventually disastrous. Well, who am I to argue with the arrangements of the Luck then? It will free me up some to focus on learning how

Lirae accomplished those enhancements on you so I will not object. I take it you've learned what Hardtack is now?"

I nodded, "Does he understand what he is?"

Thomas had a sad look, "Unfortunately he still does. He is coming along well for a mere two hundred sixty years though. I have great hopes that he will look to ascend to a divine position again sometime in the future. There are already continually growing legends about him. They will hopefully allow him to become a more civilized barbarian god, perhaps even a future patron god of adventurers. The ebb and flow of divine fate perpetually fascinates to me."

I looked at Thomas, "What do you see for me in the future then?"

Thomas gave a sly smile, "Now that would be telling."

M y reverie was broken as a pair of young burly humans came over toward our table giving each other little nudges. Eventually they walked up ignoring me and looked at Balinac with an appraising eye. I noticed the general populous of the common room got quieter as they attempted to listen in on what would be said.

The yellow haired one spoke first, "Hey missy could you help my friend and me with a problem. We've been adventuring for quite a while now, and we've never seen a woman quite as strange as you."

The red haired one interrupted, "What my rude friend is trying to say young lady is that we were unfamiliar with your race, and we were hoping to learn from where you came, and if there are any more like you there."

Balinac gave them a sweet smile, "Isn't that cute Mica. The humans want to mate with me."

I shrugged, "Excuse me gentlemen, but it is considered poor manners to address the companion of a man without seeking his permission first."

The yellow haired one gave me a weak attempt at a mean look, "We were not talking to you. If you have problems go talk to someone who cares old man. Otherwise you can't start a fight with us here without getting pitched out on your ear. That's the rules here in the bucket dragon inns."

The red haired one started to step away from the table, "Lon don't start trouble again. Last time we got banned for a month. It is not worth it."

The one called Lon spoke, "If he has a problem he can take it outside if he dares."

I nodded to Balinac who replied, "The far realms."

Both of them stopped a moment and Lon asked, "What?"

Balinac stood up and gradually released her aura to subtly fill the room, "I come from the far realms. That is what you asked isn't it?"

I watched as the older more knowledgeable adventurers in the room turned pale and very quickly thought of better places to be. They started moving for the door as quickly as decorum would allow. The younger and brasher adventurers hung in a moment longer trying to figure out what they had missed.

Balinac opened a gateway to the plane of shadow behind her, "Would you like to see the rest of me? It is not what you humans generally consider pleasant. Most of them who have ever seen it have lost their sanity in the process."

The general panic set in then and the rest of the people in the common room cleared out of the building. The only exception was the innkeeper who raised an appraising eyebrow, and pointed his thumb at the sign behind the counter.

The innkeeper spoke, "No fighting in here."

I nodded, "It was just a discussion good sir. You would think none of these yokels had seen a gate to the plane of shadow before. They asked were she was from, so she showed them is all."

The innkeeper spoke again, "No disruptive spells either. I'm surprised you managed to get around our anti-magic barriers. I'll need to file a complaint with the wizard's guild about that. Now kindly close that gate, and please refrain from making my customers wet themselves."

Balinac sat down again with a pouting expression as the gate closed, "I get to wander around the prime for a while, and everyone spoils my fun."

I smiled, "It seems they don't make them like I remember in Ard anymore. I was always impressed with adventurers before. I seem to have overestimated them."

Balinac shrugged, "Ard is relatively civilized compared to Port Cirnore and the free lands after all. It is not that unusual that a lesser crowd of adventurers would be gathering here. It won't be long before someone official decides to come investigate. I do hope our contact gets here soon."

Yuki came out of the kitchen with a meal for us on a tray. She looked around the abandoned room and frowned in our direction.

Yuki scolded us as she set out our plates and food, "I leave for twenty minutes to make some tasty food, and you two go scaring off all the locals. This is supposed to be a quiet dinner not a splashy entrance."

I smiled at Yuki and replied, "We ran into some unwelcome company. Balinac simply convinced them to leave peacefully."

Yuki shook her head, "I could feel your aura pressing against me all the way over in the kitchen. You've made a big splash."

I nodded, "It should cause the Lucky Cricket's helper to hurry along some. If she is as sensitive as he indicated she could not have avoided feeling it. Let's eat already. Our clock has started, and it won't be long before some major forces come to look into the disruption here."

As we finished eating a waifish looking half elf maiden came into the common room from the doorway outside. She was poorly clothed, and it seemed like she was out of her element. It was clear that being in the city was a challenge to her. Her timid mannerisms suggested she had spent more of her life in a forested preserve than any towns.

As she looked over in our direction she seemed close to fainting. I realized that she had quite possibly become lost in the city, and had used her second sight to find us after feeling the aura of Balinac being released. I stood up and walked over to her in a friendly manner.

I ducked my head down to her eye level as I spoke, "Hello. My name is Mica. Are you the messenger from the Lucky Cricket?"

She hesitantly nodded, "Mayel knows the Shinigami on sight. It can not hide from her visions. So many threads tied to it. There are so many powers watching for it. Mayel sees them all, and can read them."

Yuki came over by my side, "Mayel please come join us. Our time here may be short."

Mayel looked at Yuki, "The handmaiden of the White Raven, reincarnation of her favored spirit made mortal yet another time in the great cycle. You are bound to the Shinigami, and a follower of the Lucky Cricket. Mayel knows you as well. Much is whispered about you in the places of power beyond. Many greater beings fear you nearly as much as the Shinigami himself."

Mayel looked over at the table where Balinac sat, "The abomination falsely hidden as flesh and blood, Balinac the guardian of the elder gods in their place of confinement. It is the horror that brought death upon all worlds. All except the White Raven and the numbers fear your true presence. All fear your place in the great cycle."

The innkeeper looked in our direction as he spoke with a quaver in his voice, "Look here. The isle put me in charge of this spot, and I'm supposed to give your members leeway here, but no one said anything about dealing with elder abominations and handmaidens of the White Raven as part of my job description."

Mayel continued, "What has the Lucky Cricket asked of me? How can I do this?"

I looked Mayel in the eye as I spoke calmly, "Mayel dear. Let's go somewhere more private. Perhaps out of the city would be more to your liking? I made a promise to Cricket to protect the spirt shamans. You will be safe with us."

Mayel nodded weakly, "None would dare harm me while your protection is extended. This city is too confusing. There are too many spirits closely packed here. Let us go to Mayel's home."

Balinac looked at me, "Mayel is what it known as a true prophetess. They have always been extremely rare among mortals. Much like the Lucky Cricket they can read the spirit connections beyond just seeing them in place as most spirit shamans. If Davel lives, she will be able to track him for you."

We stepped outside the inn as a group. I was leading with Yuki and Balinac gently flanking Mayel on either side. Mayel seemed very frail, but it appeared that it was less our presence causing distress than the unfamiliarity of the environment.

The crowd of curious onlookers outside the ring of the assembled guard and battle wizards probably was not helping the situation much. The innkeeper came to the door way and shut it behind us as we stood in the ring of authorities surrounding the courtyard of the building.

Thomas the Poisoner

Chapter 49 Confrontation

An elderly mage in deep purple robes covered in yellow symbolic shapes stepped ahead of the assembled guards. It seemed he was more perturbed than taking the situation seriously. He looked away from us at the assembled adventurers.

I could hear the tone of anger in his voice, "Are you all off your rockers this evening? I was called away from my dinner for a fighter and three women. I expected the inn to be destroyed or at least in flames from the report. Captain who reported this waste of my time? The regular guard can sort out this minor scuffle."

A soldier with a captain's plume on his helmet stepped forward, "It was Randalf there. He's one or your fellow mages sir, guild member in good standing and all. We would not have bothered you if his story did not seem credible."

The elderly mage looked over at us briefly, and then addressed the middle aged wizard standing just outside the ring of guards, "Weren't you one of my more promising students back in your academy days Randalf? Can't you tell a joke and a simple illusion from a serious spell anymore?"

Randalf spoke, "Master Argentine that was no illusion cast by the grey skinned female. She conjured a planar gate at will in spite of the barrier spells placed on the inn by the wizard's guild. I witnessed the renewal casting of that barrier just over two weeks ago Master Argentine. I know the difference between a real planar gate and a simple illusion of one. Check with the guild and you will find the barrier has been sundered."

Master Argentine shook his head, "I did check with the guild before coming over here. They only noticed a minor perturbation in the barrier, likely a failed casting of a minor spell is all."

A young mage student spoke up, "I'm sorry Master Argentine. I cast a minor detection spell inside the inn earlier when they arrived. I had forgotten about the barrier spell. However, what Randalf says is true. That woman there opened a gate of some kind. I had never seen the like before."

Master Argentine shook his head, "Fine, I will get to the bottom of this then. You there simple adventurer whose name is probably unremarkable and unimportant, tell me what happened. The brief version before my dinner gets too cold."

I smiled my friendliest smile, "I was waiting on dinner with my wife and companion while we awaited this guide we had hired. A couple of young men came by to ask where my companion was from, and she simply told them. When they didn't understand she showed them. There really was not anything more to it Master Argentine. No blows were struck, and no one was injured or harmed."

Master Argentine nodded, "I see. If that was the case then why was I summoned over something so minor?"

I gave a sly grin, "It seems some people took objection to the method my companion used in showing them where she was from. You'll have to forgive her as she is still a bit unused to the human customs of this region."

Master Argentine looked at Balinac closely with narrowed eyes, "She is not human you say? I presumed some kind of tribal paint. Of what race is she then?"

I gave a weak smile, "It really is much easier to show you than to explain the concept to simple wizards. Perhaps we could go somewhere more private. I would like to keep my personal business out of the public eye."

I heard the approach of a troop of armored men approaching the inn. A platoon of clerical troops approached the outer perimeter of the gathered crowd which parted to let them through. I noticed that Master Argentine wore an even more annoyed expression as he turned to look at the newest arrivals.

Master Argentine spoke to the cleric in the lead of the group, "Did some foolish adventurer raise a false alarm with you as well?"

The cleric looked at him with an incredulous manner, "Didn't your magic detect what happened? It set off every divine alarm in the temple. We sent a troop immediately to locate the source of the summoning. What kind of demon was it? How many did it kill?"

Master Argentine looked taken back for a moment and flustered, "Has everyone gone mad this evening? It is just a simple fighter and three women. One of them has some mystical talent apparently, but there was no demon summoned, no one hurt, and just a bunch of people standing around wasting their time."

The cleric looked at us and raised a clear gem before his eye. I watched as he paled and began to shake.

Yuki whispered to me, "We've been made; it's likely a true vision gem. You and Balinac are going to drive anyone looking at you that way insane. It's reportedly worse that using second sight for the unprepared."

Master Argentine took a look at the shaking cleric and seemed to get nervous himself for the first time, "What did you see? What's wrong?"

The cleric ignored Master Argentine and turned to yell at his troops, "Get these civilians clear of here immediately put the city on alert. This is not a drill. Move it!!"

Master Argentine looked at the cleric as if he had gone insane, "What is going on here? What did you see Werner?"

The cleric Werner turned to face Master Argentine, "Why couldn't it have been demons? Get help now you idiot. One of them is an alpha threat level; those other two are possibly omega level. It's hard to tell they are off the scale. They didn't break your theta class barrier; they went around it like it didn't exist."

Master Argentine looked at him with a touch of fear, "Alpha class is reserved for the highest level adventurer class threat. I've never heard of omega class."

Werner shouted back as he withdrew with the clerical troops, "Nation killer level threats you fool, the last known instance was Harack the Slayer three hundred years ago. They can destroy nations, and possibly even directly battle gods for all I know. They are off the scale I'm telling you."

Master Argentine turned back to look at me as the rest of the civilians disappeared from sight. The city guard and the battle mages looked like they would desperately like to join the civilians in full retreat as well. Master Argentine seemed to brace himself, and make a decision. He stepped forward from his contingent of troops and waited for a moment for our response.

I gave him a friendly smile, "I've got to do something about those magical devices. They keep getting me into trouble."

Master Argentine seemed to have a moment of hope, "Werner's crystal was interfered with by a magical device in your possession?"

I shook my head slowly, "I am afraid not. His was the device to which I was referring. Those blasted items keep seeing too much for their wielders own benefit."

I noticed that the wizard Randalf had remained behind as well when he spoke, "I forgot to mention that the grey one there said she was from the far realm. That was when I decided it best to get the guard."

Master Argentine dropped his forehead into the palm of his raised right hand, "Couldn't you have mentioned it earlier? Do you even have a clue what the far realm is?"

Randalf shrugged, "I never could keep track of all those planes, and I just figured it meant she was an outsider is all. You've dealt with outsiders before right?"

Master Argentine shook his head, "The far realm is where it is reputed the long gone elder gods are imprisoned. You don't just pop open a gate there you idiot. It is not a material realm at all. Other things supposedly dwell there; things which frighten the gods. Only the spirit shamans are foolish enough to even attempt casting their consciousness into that place, and it is well known the lot of them are crazy."

Master Argentine looked in our direction again, "If it is not a serious imposition on you mighty beings, may I inquire who or what you all are?"

I nodded, "Might I first present you with a logical condition. I'm certain you will appreciate my statement as it will hopefully rectify the situation somewhat. Are you willing to accept the supposition that a being is so dangerous it must be safe?"

I nodded to Balinac who locked every being which had seen us in the inn and afterward to the ground with their shadows. A look of brief panic set in Master Argentine's eyes for a second, and then Balinac released them all.

I spoke again, "If it was our intent to harm any being here, then any or all of those we intended to kill would be dead already. Their spirits would be irretrievable beyond even the power of the gods. I hope a more serious demonstration need not be arranged."

Master Argentine looked at me with fear in his eyes, "What did you do?"

I smiled, "I brushed your spirits from the plane of shadows. This is my wife Yuki handmaiden of the White Raven. This is Mayel prophetess of the Lucky

Cricket who is under our protection. This is Balinac also known as Number Two among the greater tailed beasts. I am Mica, also known as the Shinigami, or god slayer, although that last part is really a misnomer as I have never slain any intelligent being, let alone a deity."

Balinac made a coughing noise, "You forgot that one, with the orcs."

I shrugged, "Ah, I keep forgetting it. I did cast the spirit out of one of Mortis' demon heralds, but that doesn't really count. It did eventually make it back to Mortis after all."

Master Argentine's hands began to tremble, "You slew a herald of the dread god Mortis?"

I smiled, "It really wasn't all that much. I simply banished its spirit from its material form on the prime. I'm told it may be able to manifest here in a century or so, that is if Mortis did not punish it severely for annoying me. Technically speaking I didn't kill it."

Yuki tapped me on the shoulder, "It seems our time is getting close to done. They have mobilized their heavy resources. A petition has been issued on the divine circles asking for my peaceful departure before an incident occurs between the White Raven and Palnor."

I looked over at Master Argentine again, "You've heard my wife. The White Raven is requesting us to withdraw from the capital of Ard. I would hate to have yet another god annoyed at me this month, so we must depart now, unless you desire to ask any other questions of us?"

Master Argentine nodded, "I will inform my superiors of your decision to depart peacefully from the capital of Ard. Please don't think poorly of our treatment of you. We don't see beings of your kind very often in these parts."

I bowed, "Until the next time then."

I heard Master Argentine mutter, "Next time?"

Balinac shadow shifted us more than twenty miles away to a forested preserve. I looked over at Mayel who seemed to be on the verge of collapse.

I spoke to her gently as Yuki and Balinac lowered her to the soft grasses on the ground, "Are you feeling better now. I am sorry we have to seek your assistance. The Lucky Cricket says you are one of his best readers."

Mayel nodded her head faintly, "Mayel is one of his best. Mayel is much like he was as a youth I was told. Mayel is sometimes able to see too much to understand. The large groups make it hard to breathe. Out away from people is much better. Please allow Mayel a couple of hours, and then Mayel will be prepared to assist you."

I noticed Mayel drop into a light slumber on the grass. Yuki looked at her with a tender expression as Balinac moved off into the distance.

I looked down at Yuki, "Will she be fine when she wakes?"

Yuki shook her head, "This poor woman has probably never been fine, but she will endure what is required of her. There are many years in front of her yet, and she may learn to control her sight better in time. I think she must understand something of what Thomas feels, never being able to shut out the vision of the connections like he can never stop seeing the spirits of those which have passed. I feel sorry for her."

I looked down at the poorly dressed thin half elf and understood well what Yuki meant. I also felt sorry for her. Some are used harshly by fate. My destiny had brought us together. Perhaps my destiny could also help hers change.

Yuki looked over at me, "You're planning again dear. You know we can't help them all."

I nodded, "I know. However, I can ask for a favor for those who are called upon by us to provide a service. I will see my debt to her paid."

Balinac called over, "The Lucky Cricket will not take away her power."

I smiled my hard serious smile, "The Lucky Cricket will damn well let me give her a more comfortable place to live where she is not stressed so much by her power though."

Balinac shook her head, "Don't get too far in over your head. This service is costing enough already. You haven't even agreed on a payment already. That can never be a good sign when the Luck negotiates for future services rendered in payment for its help."

I nodded again with a softer look back at Mayel, "I think she is going to be worth the cost."

Balinac came over holding a crystalline sphere in her hand, "The Luck is on the crystal."

I saw the Luck grinning back at me, "I've already gotten the gist of your request. I'll accept your offer to care for Mayel as your payment for her services. Thank you for thinking of it for me. I was hard pressed to think of a means to charge you suitably. Once again you've outmaneuvered me. Best of luck there Shinigami. The Luck out."

Yuki shook her head, "Two steps ahead of you again my dear. You've got to start learning that."

I looked down at the frail Mayel lightly sleeping on the grass, "I think we got the better deal this time my dear."

Mayel awoke nearly four hours later. It seemed as she sat up that her time resting had helped. She appeared less worn than before her rest. Yuki handed her a cup with warm green tea. As Mayel sipped at the tea with a tenuous smile I sat down on the ground opposite her.

I gave her a gentle smile, "Once more we are sorry to ask this of you Mayel. I would like you to eat some food before we begin. My wife Yuki has prepared something to help restore your strength."

Yuki handed Mayel a fresh grilled fish wrapped in pocket bread. Mayel accepted the offer cautiously, and then began eating it rapidly almost as if she hadn't eaten anything in a month. Looking at her I suspected it was the most substantial thing she had eaten in that time.

Mayel spoke after she finished eating and drank the remaining green tea, "Mayel slept. Mayel dreamed. In Mayel's dream the Lucky Cricket came. He showed Mayel how to look for the right threads among the many in the Shinigami's life. Mayel can see them, the threads of the sons of the father: the thread of the eldest brother Gregoric, the thread of the second brother Stanis, the thread of the third brother Veldan, the thread fourth brother Kalach. Each of these threads are attached to the Shinigami their brother, and each are sons of Armand. Only Veldan does not share the mother Lisell with the others. Veldan's mother was Celnia, daughter of Archerand."

I nodded with a touch of uncertainty, "Duke Archerand Montoure is a highly placed advisor of his Majesty the King of Ard. What I don't understand is the fact that Duke Montoure has no daughters named Celnia."

Yuki had a slight smile, "I think your brother and I are not the only bastard children you know. Your brother was the bastard of your father and this Duke Montoure's by blow daughter."

I shook my head, "So my father slighted Duke Montoure's family honor by bedding his daughter, but Duke Montoure could not overtly accuse my father over the deed as it was with his own by blow. Thus he resorts to having his twice bastard grandson trained to take revenge behind the scenes."

Yuki nodded, "That seems the truth of it then. The only question which remains is why Davel, or Veldan actually, stopped seeking to finish the assignment set before him?"

I spoke with a serious look, "I plan to ask him when I find him. Mayel dear would you please show my wife Yuki which thread is connected to Veldan?"

I saw Mayel point into the empty air, "Mayel sees this thread lead to Veldan. It is faint as Veldan seeks to hide from all. Mayel's eyes are the ones from which he can not hide his thread. The terrible act of killing the Shinigami taints its color thus. Do you see it follower of the Lucky Cricket?"

Yuki answered sweetly, "Yes dear Mayel. I will never mistake it for another again. We give you many thanks for your help, and now we wish to help you as well."

Mayel looked at Yuki with wide eyes, "What do you mean?"

I spoke, "There is a special island in Shangri La created by the Lucky Cricket. Only a few dwell there. They will leave you in peace, and provide you food and shelter as you need. I would like you to accept my offer to join us there for as long as you desire."

Mayel smiled with tears streaming from her eyes, "Mayel has . . . I have seen glimpses of it in the dreams. I could only dare wish a vision of such a thing. Is your offer really true?"

I nodded with a smile, "I would be very disappointed if you decided to not come with us."

Mayel reached over to hug me and Yuki joined in as well as more tears streamed down her face, "I will join you there. Thank you, oh thank you. I never dared hope for such."

I helped her stand, "If you will prepare yourself, I'm going to try something new. This seems as appropriate a time as any. Just walk along with us."

Mayel reached out to hold my hand on her right, and Yuki's hand on her left. Balinac followed behind as we began walking forward. Gradually the character of the forested preserve around us changed. Subtle piece at a time we started seeing portions of a new forest which had never been known within Ard. After a couple of minute's worth of walking we were on a shimmering trail.

We rounded a bend in the trail and could see it before us. There stood a tree of impossible girth stretching miles into the unseen sky. Yuki looked at me with a slight bit of surprise. Balinac shook her head dolefully. Mayel looked at the sight of it with wide eyed wonder."

Mayel spoke with soft reverence, "It is so beautiful. Where are we? How did we come to be here?"

I smiled down at her, "We are in the Fey realm. Before us is the tree of life, the source of material life on all the planes. Our friend Lirae will watch after you here while we are gone. After our return we shall journey with you to Thomas' Isle in Shangri La."

Chapter 50 The Brothers Lidron

Balinac had a sour expression as we stepped out of the woods near the main road between my father's estates and the Capital of Ard. I looked over at her with a sympathetic grin.

Balinac gave me a hard look, "I should have been watching that unmentionable tree witch closer. I had not realized that she had gifted you with the ability to transition to the Fey Realm. Directly to her most guarded heartland as well. None among the Fey beings can do such."

I shrugged, "What can I say? You're the one who first told me that Lirae had more than a motherly interest in me."

Balinac groused, "I didn't realize just how much of an interest, or what form it would take. I just assumed her a silly smitten elf wench at the time. I didn't realize she was participating in Thomas' life experiments, or that you were to be the result of their combined efforts to distill their knowledge together."

Yuki laughed lightly, "Don't be so jealous. You've got the upper hand in that deal. Through Mica you can now enter the heart of the Fey Realm at will. She still has to seek assistance to enter the shadow plane. I imagine that multiple Fey deities will be rather nervous when they discover their sanctuary is no longer safe from your passage."

Balinac shrugged, "It really has never been a problem for me. There is a reason I can multitask so well. I have to be able to project into any plane for a necessary amount of time to retrieve a recalcitrant deity. It takes enormous effort to do so, but no magic, or hiding will ever help my intended target."

I looked at her, "Why is that Balinac?"

Balinac grinned, "I'm spirit locked to every deity in existence. It was one of the conditions put on the material beings by us Numbers. It is why I can read the state of their souls so well. The very nature of immortality for a physical form causes this link to occur. It is built into the structure of the very universe that way by our design. It is also a secret kept by us Numbers, so please don't let any other mortal or immortal beings know. It is more fun to catch them when they think they can get away with avoiding me."

I smiled, "Why did you tell us then?"

Balinac shrugged, "You would figure it out eventually anyway. Some of those deities think they are quite clever in avoiding their fate, but not one completely understands the mechanisms in place behind the root of existence like the Numbers."

Yuki asked, "Why is that?"

Balinac laughed, "Not one of them understands spiritual math. It is by its very nature counter intuitive to material beings. Thomas is of course the closest to stumbling onto some of the easier base principles. It is one of the reasons he is so closely watched by us and by them. For a material being Thomas is certainly gifted in many unexpected ways. Thomas is too dangerous to not watch him closely, and yet his capabilities are too valuable to not encourage him to pursue his interests. He is a very odd combination, almost as intriguing as you Mica."

I looked at Balinac, "Why do you say that?"

Balinac looked at Yuki and me, "Spirit in the Works."

I raised an eyebrow, "What do you mean by 'Spirit in the Works' Balinac?"

Balinac smiled, "You are much like your predecessor the Lucky Cricket that way, a mortal who at a very young age intuitively grasped some of the essential elements of spiritual mathematics. Thomas came close, but so far before you came along only the Lucky Cricket managed it as an infant. However, you took much the same approach as Thomas. You died and gained an insight."

Yuki asked, "What insight is that?"

Balinac smiled, "Death is just a small step in a much greater process. Most material beings are so stuck on holding onto their material forms that they lose sight of that point very quickly. Even the gods sitting further along the process can't seem to ultimately grasp this concept in regard to their own deaths."

I spoke, "I thought that the White Raven accepts her eventual demise."

Balinac nodded, "It is true she accepts it and thus does not fear me, it does not mean she understands it. Even Harack attempted to end his misery through a violent campaign designed to bring the other gods against him. Yet he did not understand the mechanism or the need."

Yuki asked, "What need?"

Balinac cryptically replied, "Spirit in the Works."

Yuki responded, "That answer is meaningless."

Balinac nodded, "Exactly so. That is the problem with explaining spiritual mathematics with material beings, even the gods. They can not derive meaning to understand it. They usually accept it without understanding, reject it without acceptance, or fail to even grasp it is there."

Yuki looked at me, "Yet Mica understands it?"

Balinac shook her head, "Of course he does not. Mica has grasped one of the elementary principals behind it, the same principle that Thomas is close to grasping himself. That is still a very long way from understanding."

Yuki stopped and looked carefully around, "Your brother's thread leads off this way, but the track seems to head in a different direction."

I nodded and whispered, "It is likely a diversion or ambush. I'm of a mind to fall into it. Let's see if the track pans out after a while. We can always switch back to following the thread directly if the track does not lead us where we want to go. Both of you keep sharp."

Balinac scoffed, "There isn't a mortal being made which can do lasting harm to me."

I smiled, "Remember he is to be intact and unharmed. I have the sapphire ring Cogstone gave us for transportation."

We walked along several miles of woodland. The three of us were alert and took our time advancing. There was no hurry since ultimately we could not lose our quarry anymore thanks to Yuki's second sight and Mayel's guidance. Balinac seemed particularly fierce in her concentration, or perhaps she was simply stalking using her cat like senses.

Yuki raised a hand. I stopped and nodded at her. I took the lead trusting Yuki to keep my rear guarded against unexpected attack while Balinac seemed to meld into the forest. I walked into a glade and saw an elderly seeming female half elf in simple clothes carrying a staff standing beside a huge fierce looking bear.

The female half elf had a fierce look in her eye as she spoke, "Who dares invade my wood?"

I gave her a casual glance, "I believe that if you check the record you will find that this wood is held in trust for his Majesty the King by Duke Archerand Montore. It has only been loaned for your use druid."

The female half elf gave me a hard look, "So you know of whose land it is then? Then you also know you do not have permission to tread here."

I looked at her, "The land you received from Duke Montore for laying down with him? I don't think the Duke has the right to disposition the King's land at his own discretion. It may be left to his rightful heirs to maintain, but never under law to his former mistresses to buy her silence."

The female half elf gave me a venomous look, "Silence you young cur! I don't have to listen to your impudent tongue."

I gave her a faint smile, "I will leave when I have what I came to get. Where is your grandson Veldan?"

The female half elf had a brief look of surprise quickly concealed, "I know of none with that name. So begone before I send Maldus to chase you off."

I opened my shirt to reveal the scar from the sword stroke over my heart, "I would ask my brother why he tried to kill me, and killed two others in the attempt."

The female half elf was briefly shocked and quietly uttered, "Not my grandson, not his own brother."

Yuki stepped out from behind me, "He is moving my dear. Veldan is circling our position even now, looking for a killing shot."

The female half elf looked at Yuki with real surprise, "From where did she come? Who are you?"

I called out loudly, "I am Mikael Lidron. You tried to kill me once Veldan. Are you too much of a coward to try again?"

A voice called out from the woods, "You're supposed to be dead. I watched you die. I watched Ulric drive his sword clear through your heart. Oh gods, I watched him do it, and I didn't stop him. Now he's dead in a bloody massacre, and I've been hunted and hounded everywhere I went ever since you died seven years ago. I buried you. I buried all of you. You can't be alive. The undead came for Ulric. Now you are here for me. Help me grandmother."

I saw a look of resigned regret enter the eyes of the elderly female half elf. She dropped her hand and the huge bear surged forward. Yuki stood her ground beside me. I looked deeply into the eyes of advancing bear and released a small portion of the force of my aura in its direction.

The bear dropped to the ground as if it had been poleaxed. A great cry of pain issued from it. It struggled back to its feet and started backing away as I stepped forward. I slowly released more of my aura, letting the pressure build. The bear backed up to the position of the elderly female half elf.

I dropped my aura on top of the bear like an extremely heavy blanket. It bent to the ground with a whimper, softly whining. The elderly half elf looked at me with fear in her eyes, but a unwavering determination as well. Her other hand dropped, and three arrows sped toward Yuki and I from the woods.

Yuki moved like a dancer in a blur. The three arrows were intercepted and shattered by her adamantine pan before they could hit us. Yuki grinned with her own fierce determination.

I raised a hand in a gesture of parley, "Are you certain this is what you want? Is it the deaths of everyone here? I can guarantee you will not survive, your grandson will not survive, and these allies of yours will not survive if you refuse to see reason. I will send you directly to the halls of the White Raven myself."

With that announcement Balinac opened a gateway to the entrance of the valley of death directly behind me. The bright light at the end of the dark tunnel shone behind me like a spectacular nimbus. I knew any mortal form would feel its call even across the intervening gateway.

The elderly female half elf looked at me with dread in her eyes, "What kind of unholy abomination are you?"

I looked at her sharply, "I am the Shinigami. I advise you to not stand between me and my intended target. Even if you are a god I will move you from my path by force if necessary."

A different voice called out from the woods, "Mistress Xan you can not have us stand against such a thing for your grandson. The council of druids will not allow it. It holds the gateway to the valley of death in its hands. What can mere mortals like us do to stop such a thing?"

Mistress Xan raised her head with fear and determination equal in her eyes, "I will stand in stead of my grandson. Take my life for his crimes and be satisfied."

I shook my head, "That is not a bargain you can make on his behalf. His spirit is the one tainted by his deeds. His spirit must stand to be judged for them, as must all moral spirits stand before the White Raven for judgement."

A figure rushed out of the woods from my right. Yuki stepped back as I automatically parried the blow with my wakizashi. I parried several more desperate strikes with ease as I slowly drew my katana. I gauged the amount of spirit power needed and sliced through Veldan's blade with my Katana ending my stroke just shy of his throat.

I saw that Veldan was a haunted looking figure. He was thinner and older than I remembered him, and there were dark circles under his eyes. A desperate desire to live still beat within his heart. I could see that he was also on the verge of madness from his seven years of regret.

I spoke, "Lock them all down Balinac. We have what we've come for now."

Balinac's shadow wrapped each of the figures in the woods for a two mile radius. The only figures not wholly enshrouded were Yuki, Mistress Xan, and Veldan. I withdrew my blades and sheathed them. I looked into the fearful face of Veldan.

I spoke to him without malice in my voice, "Hello Veldan. I'm sorry we won't get much chance to talk, but I really only have one question for you."

Veldan grunted then spoke, "What have you done to her?"

I shrugged, "Merely grabbed her spirit to hold her in place. There will be no harm done to her from it, and none to you either. Now please answer my question. Why did you stop trying to kill the rest of the Lidron family?"

Veldan dropped his head with an ill look, "I lost the stomach for it after Ulric killed you. I thought it was what I wanted. What my grandfather had trained me to do, but I couldn't follow through with it. Then they started watching for me. My description was being spread around. Do you have any idea what it is like to be hunted for four years?"

I shrugged again, "Do you have any idea what it is like to have the innocent woman you love killed before you eyes? Do you have any idea what a fatal blow feels like, knowing your life is seeping out of you? I think you may have had the easier path of the two of us brother. Now your time of reckoning is come."

I reached out to place an exquisitely made sapphire ring on Veldan's immobilized finger. His spirit became entrapped within the stone still linked to his body, yet isolated. Veldan's material form went limp. The shadow released his body as I moved it over my shoulder.

The shadows released each of the others and forming from the shadows was an enormous Balinac once more in her feline form. Yuki and I mounted her with Veldan still slung over my shoulder.

Mistress Xan dropped to her knees and implored me, "What will you do with the body of my grandson? Isn't it enough that you've slain him?"

I looked back down at her, "Your grandson is not dead, merely held for transportation. I will deliver him to the temple of Palnor in the capital of Ard, and the king shall mete out his justice accordingly under the eyes of the god Palnor. I am merely an agent in this matter. I don't take it upon myself to needlessly slay mortals. This time is only so that those lost at the time of my death can finally see justice served. My task is taking the lives of the gods when their times are come."

Mistress Xan looked at us with a new fear in her eyes, "You are the godslayer?"

I gave her a wary glance, "I prefer the Shinigami if you will. Remember that even the gods fear my presence. You did well to stand for your grandson against one such as me. However, there could never have been any other outcome."

Chapter 51 Temple of Palnor

Balinac changed the destination of the gate. We rode through to the parallel portion of the shadow plane. Balinac began running as hard as she could go which was quite considerable considering she was in her home element. As usual for us now, the ride was as smooth and easy as ever.

Yuki looked back at me from her position in front, "Are you certain this is what you want?"

I nodded, "I have almost finished my part."

Yuki had a little grin, "Your family's name will get brought out in any trial, along with the name of Duke Montore. All of their attempts at keeping personal matters secret all these years will come out if you turn Veldan over to the forces of Palnor."

I smiled, "Of course it is better that they all face the earthly judgment of Palnor now than allow their spirits to show before the White Raven without repentance. This is no longer about me or my family. It is about a kingdom filling with selfish cheating bastards pretending to rule in an honorable manner. This matter must be brought to light in order to end events like this which take innocent lives too soon."

Yuki rested her head against my chest, "It is time that personal honor match the appearance of honor then?"

I shrugged, "It is time that those responsible for ruling over others become responsible for their actions. I won't exempt my father from such, and in his own way he will understand. It was how he brought us up to believe after all."

Balinac looked back, "We are closing on the concordant position for the Temple of Palnor ahead. It will be best if we don't surprise them. It tends to make the gods nervous when I show up unannounced."

I nodded and spoke out loud, "The Luck could you please inform Palnor of our intent to deliver someone to his justice in the Capital of Ard location of his temple. Tell them we will be appearing relatively soon."

Yuki looked at me, "Do you think he got the message?"

Balinac nodded as she came to a stop, "The Luck got your message. Let's give him some time to process the request. Dismount here please."

Balinac transformed back into her grey skinned human female form. She drew a crystal sphere from a pocket of nothing and held it in her hand. After an uncertain amount of time the face of a tiger cub appeared in the crystal.

The tiger cub spoke in a female voice, "Thank you for using The Luck communications; putting you through to the Right Hand of Palnor now."

I could see the figure of miniature metallic dragon in the crystal as it spoke with a deceptively deep voice, "I am the Right Hand of Palnor. Who requests my attention?"

I spoke into the crystal, "I am the Shinigami. I have a mortal being I am delivering to the justice of the clerical forces of Palnor on the prime material at your temple location in the capital of the Kingdom of Ard."

The miniature dragon nodded, "Thank you for the courtesy of giving advance notice this time. You caused a large disruption the last time you appeared in Ard. It took us a week prime standard time to settle everyone down there. Is that Balinac with you?"

Balinac spoke, "I remember our last meeting Right Hand of Palnor. How is his divine health these days?"

The miniature dragon seemed a bit uncertain, "Everything seems fine. Is there something we should know about?"

Balinac shrugged, "I just have to check. Maybe I should pay a visit soon."

The miniature dragon hurried to change the subject, "Your advance notice has gone through, there will be a herald awaiting your arrival to prevent any mishaps among the mortals. Please do try not to frighten any of them to death."

I spoke into the crystal, "Thank you for your assistance Right Hand of Palnor."

The miniature dragon moved its sinuous neck up and down, "I am grateful for the advance notice. It makes us look pretty bad to our followers when we don't set up some prophesies, visions, or divine messengers before an event like this. No one likes to think their god is kept in the dark on important events. The Right Hand of Palnor signing off."

The face of the tiger cub appeared in the crystal again, "Thank you for using The Luck communications. Oh and Shinigami dear please do stop by and see me when you are finished in Ard."

I nodded, "Where do you want to meet?"

The tiger cub giggled, "The Cricket said something about a fish fry or clam bake on the beach. Bring the tables, chairs, and your friends. We'll bring the food."

I smiled, "Consider it done. Thomas' Isle it is then. I'll call when I arrive."

The tiger cub spoke, "The Luck out."

I looked at Balinac, "I think casual adventurer dress is a bit inappropriate for the occasion seeing as we are having divine guests."

Balinac motioned her hand and the three of us were dressed in elaborate dark grey silk robes embroidered with a black leopard spot pattern. Yuki looked at Balinac with a broad smile and I looked at how proper they both seemed in their formal attire.

Yuki spoke, "I've always wanted to wear an imperial Ran Li style kamishimo. I've only seen them in paintings. It is in your signature pattern as well, how appropriate."

I nodded, "Very appropriate Balinac. Thank you."

Balinac smiled, "A girl has to look good for these formal affairs. Stop smiling now. It's time to get serious."

Balinac opened the shadow gate to the prime. The three of us walked through with me carrying Veldan still over my shoulder. We stepped out into a the rear of a courtyard of the temple of Palnor. There were many ranks of robed clerics and armored paladins kneeling down on one knee in front of a nine foot tall herald of Palnor with a glowing nimbus around him. The clerics and paladins all seemed locked in place with a combination of divine awe and fear.

The assembled mass of attention turned to look at us where we had stepped through the gate. I kept a serious look on my face as I walked silently forward through the assembled clergy of Palnor flanked by Balinac on my left and Yuki on my right.

As we reached the front row of assembled forces I recognized my brother Kalach armored as a paladin with his head reverently bowed and undisturbed by our passing. I paused even with the front row parallel with my favored brother. The herald of Palnor looked in the direction of my gaze. It seemed to recognize the kinship between the two of us standing just a few feet apart.

The herald of Palnor spoke to the assembled group, "Worthy followers of the mighty Palnor. I am Archer his herald. I have come to you with a divine message from Palnor. Before you from the very plane of shadow stands Mica the Shinigami, along with Balinac the two tailed beast, and Yuki handmaiden of the White Raven. They come before us today with a request. Palnor would have you hear their words."

I stepped forward to stand before the base of the stairway below Archer. I slowly lowered my brother Veldan to the ground. I stepped over his body to stand on the first step, and turned to face the assembled crowd as Yuki and Balinac stood on either side of me. I looked them over noting that Kalach had raised his head and had a look of uncertain confusion on his face.

I pulled open my elaborate silken robe to reveal the scar from the sword strike over my heart. The newer wounds inflicted by Alvos could also be clearly seen. I had the full attention of the assembled mass.

I gave a hard look down at my half brother Veldan, and then raised my head again to speak, "I was born Mikael Lidron in Ard, fifth son of the Knight Armand Lidron, brother to Kalach Lidron who is one of the paladins here today who faithfully serves Palnor. I was slain seven years ago today by the plots of my half brother Veldan who lies before me now. His hand was guided by his grandfather the Duke Archerand Montore whose daughter Celnia bore my half brother."

A gasp went through the assembled crowd at the statement. My brother Kalach stood to look at me as a confused comprehension began dawning on his face. Kalach looked down at Veldan and could clearly see the semblance of our father just as I could.

I continued speaking, "Also slain at my side were Firanda Zarcha a student mage, and Larwick a member of the porter's guild who were victims of the unfortunate circumstance of being in my company. The blood of the innocent is on the hand of my brother Veldan. People in positions of responsibility and power attempted to hide these crimes by altering the record of events. I charge the followers of Palnor to validate the truth of my statements, and to seek justice for those innocents killed."

I looked down at the form of my brother Veldan, "I also ask that you have mercy as you see fit on my brother Veldan. While he perpetrated wrongs against the innocents I mentioned, he himself has also been wronged by our father and his grandfather. Our father ignored his responsibility to all of his family in the pursuit of position and the appearance of honor. Veldan's grandfather tried to turn him into a reluctant tool of vengeance against his own father. I believe Veldan regrets his actions, and a suitable penance could possibly be found for him with the assistance of Palnor's divine wisdom."

I bent down and removed the sapphire ring from Veldan's hand. He stirred and slowly sat up looking up at me.

Veldan had tears start flowing from his eyes as he spoke softly, "Why? Why do you speak on my behalf?"

I looked out at the assembled crowd with my answer, "I was Mikael Lidron. Mikael Lidron is dead. The dead have no need for vengeance. The dead will always have a need for justice. I am Mica the Shinigami, and I charge you followers of the mighty Palnor to assure that his justice is done."

I went silent as the crowd looked at us standing there. Kalach took a step forward and halted hesitantly as Archer spoke out loudly.

The voice of Archer rang clear through the courtyard, "What say you followers of the mighty Palnor? Will you investigate these charges and see that the justice of Palnor is done?"

A great roaring cheer rose from the assembled crowd. Kalach appeared stunned by the noise. I looked at him directly, and waved him forward to join us. Kalach hesitated a moment, and then seeing the nod from Archer hurried forward to stand before me with our half brother sitting on the ground between us.

Kalach looked at me carefully as he tried to put together a coherent sentence, "I don't . . . what happened? Where did you go? The rumors . . ."

I gave him a faint smile, "Focus Kalach. The Mikael your brother you knew has been dead these seven years. I am his eternal spirit in a seeming shell. I have moved on now, and forgiven our brother Veldan for his crimes against me. I ask you to do the same. I want you to become his advocate in this process. You are his family, and it is about time the Lidron name shows its quality in this matter, even if our father has failed it. Can you be strong and do this for me brother?"

Kalach nodded as tears came down his face, "I will try. I just don't understand what happened."

I looked at Kalach with a smile, "I've moved on to become something else. Something more than what I once was. Remember death is just another beginning. I needed this matter to be settled so I can finish moving on is all. The spirits of the innocent call out to me for justice. I have very little time to seek my own."

I looked away from Kalach for a moment to address Archer, "Make sure Kalach is given the resources he needs to be a proper advocate. I will not look kindly upon a halfhearted witch hunt in this matter. I expect a thorough investigation, and reasonable assignments of responsibility for what happened. Let Palnor know I will be watching the progress of his followers as my time allows."

Kalach and Veldan both spoke as I turned to face them again, "Thank you brother."

The two of them looked at each other in surprise. I thought I saw a glimmer of hope in both of their eyes. I turned to both Yuki and Balinac. They took me by either arm as we walked toward the rear of the courtyard.

I heard Kalach speak to Archer as we walked away, "I don't understand herald Archer. Why is my brother one of the White Raven's spirit hunters?"

Archer shook his head sadly, "You are mistaken Kalach Lidron. Mica is not a spirit hunter. It is The Shinigami; the godslayer that sits in judgment over the divine beings and takes their spirits if they become corrupted. All of the followers of mighty Palnor have been put on notice to diligently keep up our mandate. If we fail, then Palnor may become next on its list of gods to kill."

We walked out of the courtyard into the temple quarter of the capital of Ard. I looked at Balinac who grinned as she looked at me in return. Yuki looked over at me with a raised eyebrow.

I spoke, "I'm a bit tired of this drab and gloomy garb. The material is nice, but this color is too dull. How about it Balinac? Are you ready to use some of those new tricks we've learned?"

Balinac shifted our clothes to tiger striped Jade Green short yukata. A crowd of people stopped in the street to look at us. I saw that my brothers and the herald Archer along with the forces of Palnor had rushed over to watch as well. I also caught the surprised look from Master Argentine in the crowd staring at us. I reached over to give Yuki a long kiss.

I called out, "Let's pick up Mayel and then head home. Balinac please provide the transportation this time."

Balinac shifted form to a very large jade green furred lion with black stripes. I looked back at the three tails swinging from her rear as Yuki and I mounted.

Yuki rubbed Balinac's head behind her ears, "Three tails now? Lirae will be jealous."

Balinac gave a loud growling laugh, "She's the one that granted us access. We've come to an accord, so don't knock it."

We left a trail of spouting flowers behind us as we walked down the street leaving behind the amazed stares of the stunned people and a very worried looking herald of Palnor. Gradually we transitioned fully to the Fey Realm.

Chapter 52 Pantheon

uki and I watched from our towel on the beach at Thomas' Isle. Thomas was wearing his white shirt and shorts sitting in the shade of the porch of one of the beach huts. Lirae was splashing in the surf along with a gleeful Mayel. Jack was talking to Hardtack as they put the finishing touches on the beach side grill made of stacked stones.

Cogstone and Olivia sat on a nearby towel enjoying a quiet conversation together. Talgash, Rena, and their three new kobold pups looked as happy as any kobolds could be. Quizak and Puck were tossing a coconut back and forth to each other as they ran up and down the beach. Hiram sat under the shade of a nearby palm tree apparently dozing in the heat of the comfortably warm midday sun.

I watched Balinac wearing her bright jade green and black striped sarong. She brought Thomas a cool drink on the porch where he sat. They had a quiet conversation together. Reading their lips I saw her ask if he was certain about his plans, and I saw Thomas saying yes.

As Balinac walked away from the porch toward the shore I saw Alvos run up to her with a grin.

I nudged Yuki who covered her mouth as she laughed and muttered, "Idiot. Alvos really doesn't mind dying it seems."

I chuckled myself, "You've got to admire Alvos' openness to new experiences at least."

Yuki looked over at me, "So do you know anything about this surprise guest the Cricket said he was bringing over?"

I shrugged, "Your guess is as good as mine. He said it was a surprise, even Balinac doesn't know."

Balinac walked over to us as Alvos walked over by the grill temporarily dejected. I raised an eyebrow at her.

Balinac looked back at me, "What?"

Yuki laughed again, "Mica is being incorrigible again. He's a hopeless romantic you know."

Balinac looked at me, "The Numbers are not a mortal or material species. We do not reproduce. You know that already. So I fail to see what would be the point?"

I chuckled, "The adventure of it my dear Balinac is the point."

Balinac placed a hand on both Yuki and I, "The three of us have plenty of adventure together already."

Yuki raised an eyebrow, "Really?"

Balinac nodded, "Of course you are all that I need. Alvos is simply a buffoon besides. I've heard some of the tales Alvos tells Jack about aberrant adventures. Do you know Alvos claims to have performed unnatural acts with a dragon even?"

I laughed out loud, "From where could a shortling even attempt something like that?"

Yuki snorted, "Knowing Alvos from the inside of course. Just after being eaten whole and while waiting for the digestion to kill him off. That boy is just not right in the head."

I looked at Yuki with a laugh, "You don't know?"

Yuki looked back at me, "What?"

I chuckled, "Alvos is a girl. She is Thomas' favorite virgin sacrifice ploy."

Yuki chuckled, "I couldn't tell. The short hair, the pudgy shortling body, the cracking post pubescent voice, I just naturally assumed Alvos was a male."

I shook my head, "She's just the best actor in the group. She dies the best too."

Yuki looked serious, "You do a pretty convincing death too."

Balinac changed the topic, "The Lucky Cricket is arriving soon. Watch the waves."

Yuki laughed and pointed, "Our ribbons just shifted. He's out on that bearing."

I watched as a small boat with two people rowing came in toward the shore. One of them had a broad circular hat and peasant's clothing, while the other wore a smart looking blue shirt and navy shorts. Yuki smiled as they approached and the others on the beach all stood and watched. We approached the surf as the keel of Cricket's boat ground against the sand.

Thomas called out from his position on the porch of the hut, "All of you help unload the food. Hardtack and Jack get that grill started already. Cricket and Glorandel please come on over here in the shade while the others prepare our meal."

I nodded at Glorandel who seemed uncertain who I was as he walked up the shore, "Glad you could join us finally Glorandel. Hello there Cricket."

They nodded at me as the rest of the group moved to remove the baskets of fresh seafood from the boat. As Thomas was busy entertaining our guests I began organizing the others into individual tasks. Yuki supervised the food preparation as Hardtack and Jack became her cook and preparer. Lirae and Mayel watched the kobold pups along with their mother Rena. Puck and Hiram set up the tables and chairs as Alvos prepared the place settings. Cogstone and Olivia prepared the drinks. Quizak provided the cheese, and Talgash brought the fresh herbs for seasoning.

I pitched in wherever an extra hand was needed, and stayed clear where it was not. I noticed that Thomas and Cricket watched us from the porch as they genially conversed with Glorandel who seemed just slightly taken back by the whole situation. I saw Balinac bring them over some drinks. I walked to the grill preparation area and gave Yuki a kiss.

Yuki looked at me, "What is going on up there?"

I shrugged, "I haven't been watching the entire conversation. They are mostly inducting Glorandel at the moment, but I think some changes are coming with this visit."

Yuki raised an eyebrow, "Do you think there will be some new rules?"

I smiled, "I expect a change in management perhaps. I did tell them about Glorandel's information management skills already."

Yuki smiled, "Well worry about it later. Get the servers organized since the first course will be ready in five minutes."

I gave her another quick kiss and noticed that Glorandel had finally realized who I must be. I saw a sly smile came to his face as I nodded in his direction. This promised to be interesting.

Later that evening as the stars began showing in the darkening firmament I sat on the porch next to Thomas and across from Cricket. The others were sitting around the beach in chairs or on towels enjoying their genial conversation and bellies full of good food. Balinac sat in my lap with her arm around my neck.

Cricket spoke, "I've discussed this with Thomas, and we've agree to a change in his contract. There is to be a change in management here on the isle. Thomas will retain his lighthouse and its associated laboratories to continue his research. However, we have both agreed that a new manager would take over the task of dealing with matters on the Prime side of the business. Thomas has agreed to stay on in an advisory capacity for a minimum of another one hundred years."

Thomas spoke, "It is about time as well. Keeping on top of things in three planes is getting to be too much for me at my age. I'm looking forward to getting more focused into my research. What do you say Mica? I've put you forth as the best choice for the job."

I smiled as I rubbed Balinac's arm, "I think we will take it as long as Balinac agrees. I'm sure Yuki will be fine either way."

Balinac nodded, "I'm happy to let Mica take the lead in managing the material operations. As always I will continue to keep watch on the spiritual side of business."

I looked at Cricket, "We can finalize the details after you answer a question for me though. Is your eventual goal the creation of a new pantheon of gods?"

Cricket nodded, "Not a pantheon to replace the gods of the other worlds, but at pantheon to populate my world of Shangri La. Quite a few good possible choices have been brought together here through Thomas' recruiting efforts. Each of them has traits which are suitable for divine status. It takes a lot of real world experience to make a new god though. As evidenced by Harack even former gods can make mistakes and find it difficult to stay in the position. Most of the candidates here will likely not make the final cuts, and more good candidates remain to be trained and observed."

I looked at Thomas as I asked, "So have you made the cut then?"

Thomas shrugged, "I've made the first seven cuts, but I've been apprenticed under a very good example as well. The White Raven is very diligent in the pursuit of her duties. There are still plenty more cuts to go. However Hardtack and you have each made the first cut of this round."

Cricket spoke, "Both of you do well serving as leaders and examples to others, the Luck considers that a prerequisite divine trait to qualify as a god on Shangri La.

However, both of you also have an advantage over the other candidates. Hardtack has an advantage due to his former god status, and you do because of your hybrid blending with Balinac. It is likely that Lirae will also show an advantage over the others soon as a result of her direct connection to the Number Three of Life."

Thomas chuckled, "Two Number Threes; a Three of Life and a Three of Death. The other Numbers are going to be very annoyed when they learn of it."

Cricket shrugged, "The alliance we've formed outnumbers them for now. Even Number Thirteen will not be able to successfully stand against us since the rest of the unaligned numbers distrust it more than us at this point. Even now several other Numbers are considering taking the step to become connected with material avatars instead of relying solely on spiritual projections. More of them will have to form an alliance with either Number Seven or Number Thirteen to learn how to do so. The sides are being drawn, and two competing pantheons will likely be formed as a result."

Balinac and I both smiled and spoke as one, "We can't wait for the challenge."

Cricket nodded, "Good synchronization. You'll have to teach me how you do that some day."

Balinac and I both laughed and spoke, "Wouldn't you like to know Number Seven. The secret of that trick might just cost you."

Cricket shrugged, "You must drive Yuki to distraction with that trick."

I frowned, "Yuki doesn't think it's too funny really. I've promised to not use it on her."

Thomas smiled, "That is a good idea. Most beings find separate but linked consciousness to be disturbing."

I looked over at Thomas, "Speaking of that, how many distinct bodies are you running right now?"

Thomas grinned, "Only twenty-one at the moment. My limit seems to be about forty-two for now. I'm improving more over time though."

I looked at Cricket, "How many separate intelligences does the Luck operate on average?"

The Cricket smiled, "It only has one Prime material intelligence operating at a time, and it has several full intelligences on each of its other planes."

I nodded, "How many in the Far Realms, including sub-intelligences?"

The Cricket coughed lightly, "Approximately five million, since it has a sub-intelligence assigned to each spirit shaman for information processing you see."

I looked at Balinac, "We've got a long way to go to catch up to them."

Balinac nodded, "Yes we do Mica, but I think you're up for the task. I wouldn't have picked you otherwise."

I smiled, "Thank you."

 sat down on the towel next to Yuki, "Well that was interesting."
Yuki looked at me, "What did they want?"

I smiled at her, "I'm being promoted to managing the events here on the Prime material plane. Both Hardtack and I have passed the first hurdle for our application to godhood in Shangri La. As the leading candidate in the last round I've been assigned to work on helping you and the others to advance your applications next. Besides I wouldn't want to have eternity without you at my side."

Yuki giggled, "So am I to be the goddess of cooking or assassination?"

I kissed her and I answered, "What do you think about goddess of loyalty and honor instead?"

Yuki smiled, "It has a nice ring to it. What is your realm of influence then?"

I looked up at the lighthouse with its beacon shining in the night and illuminated by the glow of moonlight, "I've had my application for god of justice approved for processing."

Epilog

The aged weary seeming elf lifted his head to peer into the dark shadows of the room. He was certain he had heard a noise, and yet nothing was there to be seen.

He returned once more to his continuing contemplation of his failure. He had been so close. Everything had been going his way, and then that foolish idealistic innkeeper had come along. It was supposed to be just another insignificant obstacle which threatened his plans quickly and quietly handled like all the others. Suddenly with this one simple necessary death among all the others his allies and friends couldn't seem to abandon his great cause quickly enough.

He thought, what was it about that one simple life after so many secret removals of the foolish which supported the so called progressive faction. Could those imbeciles he had once called his allies not understand the necessity of sacrifice to build the great foundation for the preservation of elfish traditions.

A voice softly spoke behind him, "Reminas."

Reminas suddenly stood and turned to see a figure of an elf dressed in white robes standing behind him. He backed away from the figure until he bumped against his desk. The figure stood looking at him with a sad expression.

Reminas' voice quavered, "Who are you? How did you get into my private chambers? Where is my guard?"

The figure stood silent before his inquiries. Then it pointed at his desk behind him.

Reminas turned his head and saw an elaborate goblet filled with a mysterious liquid sitting on the desk where none had been a moment before. Reminas understood the contents must be poison. He looked back at the figure standing impassively looking at him.

Reminas trembled, "So you've come to kill me is that it?"

The figure spoke calmly, "I've come to offer you mercy. It is up to you whether you choose to take it."

Reminas spoke more firmly, "Who are you?"

The figure answered, "I am Thomas the Poisoner, the future god of death. I would suggest you accept my generous offer while it is still available. I promise it will be painless. This act of repentance and contrition for your crimes will look more favorable on your record when you meet the White Raven. As it stands now it is likely that only the twiline queen Litha will accept your spirit."

Thomas gradually faded into the shadows until Reminas stood alone in the room. Reminas turned to look at the goblet on his desk once more.

Afterword

Dear reader,

I hope you've enjoyed this work. It is the ambition of many writers to make a fortune from becoming the next best selling author. Not that I would be too proud to accept a fortune dropped into my lap as a result of my labors, but I don't have a reasonable expectation it will happen either.

The question then is, why write? Even more compelling, why publish your own work? In my case the answer is very simple. It wasn't done in an attempt to make a fortune. It was done in an exercise of both pursuing a childhood dream, and to put my money, frankly speaking, where I put my mouth several years ago.

You see I have a contentious nature, a family trait honestly earned among my father's side of the family. Several years ago I was reading several forums where "professional" writers were complaining about the bad deals they always got when signing over their copyrights for their work to get them produced by a faceless evil company (their chosen depiction).

I asked the question, "If you don't like the deal you're getting, and you think it is unfair, then why did you ever sign the contract?"

I was bombarded then with the response, "You're not one of us, so you don't know how it is in our business."

Now I'm an author who kept my own copyright, established my own publishing company, and didn't sign a deal with the metaphorical devil to get my work published. I don't have the money, fame, or adoration that many author's with major publishers get. However, I do have something more important to me.

I own my work. I'll make it or break it without selling my self respect to make money or obtain fame. My cover artist Lance Red owns his work as well. I have licensed it for my use with the full expectation he will keep capitalizing on the art as best he can in other ways as well.

My answer to all the others who complain about how the "industry" of writing is heartless and soul crushing. Don't take a bad deal. Not to get in the door, not to get your name in lights. If you don't think a deal is worth it, then keep negotiating, or walk away. What you shouldn't do is come complaining to the general public that you signed a bad deal, and now after they are making money with your work you feel bad about giving away your copyright to the evil corporation.

My question back to them. Why should I care that you did something that stupid?

Kelly R. Martin

Thomas the Poisoner

Tales from the
Reading Dragon Inn Series
Book I

The
Lucky
Cricket

Tales from the
Reading Dragon Inn
Book I

Kelly R. Martin

Tales from the
Reading Dragon Inn Series
Book 2

Tales from the
Reading Dragon Inn Series
Book 3